Also by
JENNIFER ROBERSON

THE SWORD-DANCER SAGA
SWORD-DANCER
SWORD-SINGER
SWORD-MAKER
SWORD-BREAKER
SWORD-BORN
SWORD-SWORN

CHRONICLES OF THE CHEYSULI
Omnibus Editions
SHAPECHANGER'S SONG
LEGACY OF THE WOLF
CHILDREN OF THE LION
THE LION THRONE

THE GOLDEN KEY
(with Melanie Rawn and Kate Elliott)

ANTHOLOGIES
(as editor)
RETURN TO AVALON
HIGHWAYMEN: ROBBERS AND ROGUES

And coming in hardcover in April 2006:
KARAVANS
A new series from Jennifer Roberson

JENNIFER ROBERSON

The Novels of Tiger and Del
Volume #3

DAW BOOKS, INC.

DONALD A. WOLLHEIM, FOUNDER

375 Hudson Street, New York, NY 10014

ELIZABETH R. WOLLHEIM

SHEILA E. GILBERT

PUBLISHERS

http://www.dawbooks.com

First Trade Paperback Printing, April 2006

2   3   4   5   6   7   8   9

 DAW TRADEMARK REGISTERED
U.S. PAT. OFF AND FOREIGN COUNTRIES
—MARCA REGISTRADA
HECHO EN U.S.A.

PRINTED IN THE U.S.A.

Sword-Born

*For Debby,
in memory of Pib.*

Acknowledgments

I would like to thank the excursion tour guides and ship's personnel affiliated with *Renaissance VIII* of Renaissance Cruise Lines, who helped make my visit to Greece and Turkey in the summer of 1996 not only immensely enjoyable, but also a true education for someone undertaking research for a new book. The back-burners of my brain are already sorting through ideas for novels yet to come.

Special thanks go to Pat Waldher, an old college buddy, who first proposed the trip, talked me into it when I waffled, taught me the first night on board how to play Blackjack, and who, like me, enjoys a good storm at sea; to Marta Grabien, Melanie Rawn, and Susan Shwartz, for suggestions regarding travel and historicity; and lastly to the cruise-tour participants who only occasionally—and very politely—murmured to one another as I clambered gracelessly over segments of Corinthian columns lying about like poker chips, ancient libraries, latrines, and bordellos, Crusader fortresses, akropoli, and Biblical amphitheaters: "Now why in the world is she taking a picture of *that?*"

"Even today the rocks . . . are no less than spiritual training grounds and arenas where faith is fashioned, sin is driven out and the personality is forged."

—THEOCHARIS M. PROVATAKIS
Meteora: History of the Monasteries and Monasticism

Prologue

Sword pierced flesh, broke bone. I felt it go in, felt the give, the tension in my wrists as steel cut into body. Heard my own hoarse shout as I denied again that this was what I wanted, what I meant—

—and awoke with an awkward upward lunge that smashed the back of my skull into wood.

One way to stop a dream, I guess: knock it clean out of your head.

Driven flat by the force of the collision, I lay belly-down on the threadbare blanket and scrunched my face against pain and shock, locking teeth together. I couldn't manage a word, just swore a lot in silence inside my rattled skull.

From above, warily, "Tiger?"

I didn't answer. I was too busy gripping the back of my abused skull, trying to keep it whole.

"Are you all right?"

No, I wasn't all right, thank you very much; I'd just come close to splattering my brains all over the tiny cabin we shared aboard a ship I'd learned to hate the day we sailed. But to *say* I wasn't all right?

I turned my head, carefully, into a slotted streak of brassy sunlight skulking fitfully through creaking boards bleeding dribbles of sticky pitch. "—fine." From between gritted teeth.

Movement overhead. A moment later a wealth of fair hair

barely visible in fog-tendriled morning light spilled over the side of the narrow bunk looming low above me, which was precisely what I'd cracked my head against. (The bunk, that is, not the hair.) Then the face appeared. Upside down.

Del is beautiful from any direction, in any position, wearing any expression. But just now I was in no shape to appreciate that beauty. "Was that your *head?*"

I unclamped my jaws a bit and removed my cheek from the lump of mildewed material that served inadequately as a pillow. It stank of salt and fish and, well, me. "I suppose I could point out that sleeping apart for months on end in bunks barely big enough for a dog makes it hard for a man to, um, *demonstrate his admiration and affection—*"

"Lust," she put in, stripping away euphemism neatly. "And it's only been two weeks. Besides, we had the floor." She paused, correcting her terminology. "The deck. Which we've used. Several times. Or have you forgotten already?"

Not to be thwarted by an annoying and convoluted interruption intended solely to sidetrack me into defensiveness, I continued with laborious dignity. "—and therefore I could claim it was something else entirely that smacked the underside of your bed with such force as to make the earth move—"

"Embroidering the legend of the jhihadi, are we?"

"—but considering that I'm always an honest messiah, er, man—"

"When it suits you."

"—I'll admit that, yes, that was my head." I moved my fingers gingerly through wiry hair. "I *think* it's still in one piece."

"Well, if it isn't, it matches the rest of you. Age does that to a man." And she withdrew her head—and the hair—so I had nothing to glare at.

"Your fault," I muttered.

She swung down from her bunk over mine. Short, narrow bunks, too small for either of us together or apart; Del is a tall woman. She landed lightly, bracing herself against the ship's uneasy wallowing with a hand on the salt-crusted, battered bunk frame. "My fault? That you're feeling your age? Really, Tiger—

you'd think it was always my idea that we, as you put it, 'demonstrate admiration and affection.' "

"Hoolies," I muttered, "but I'll be glad when we're on land again. Room to *move* on land."

Del sat down on the edge of my bunk. It wasn't a comfortable position because she had to lean forward and hunch over so she wouldn't bash *her* head against the underside of her bunk. I rearranged bent legs, allowing her as much room as I could; I wasn't about to sit up and risk my skull again. "Any blood?" she asked matter-of-factly, sounding more like man than woman preparing to blithely dismiss an injury as utterly insignificant unless a limb was chopped off.

Someone once asked me what it meant if Del was ever kind. I answered—seriously—that likely she was sick. Or worried about me, but that wouldn't do to say. For one, I hated fuss; for another, well, Del's kind of worrying doesn't make for comfort. A smack on the butt is more her style of encouragement, much like you'd slap a horse as you sent it out to pasture.

I inspected my skull again with tentative fingers, digging through salt-crusted hair. No blood. Just a knot coming up. And itching. But too far from my heart to kill me.

Then I dismissed head and irony altogether. I reached out and clasped her arm, closing the wrist bones inside my hand. Not a small woman, Del, in substance or height (or in skill and spirit); but then, neither am I a small man. The wrist fit nicely. "I dreamed about you," I said. "And the dance. On Staal-Ysta."

Del went very still. Then, eloquently, she took my hand and carried it to her ribs, where she opened it and flattened the palm against the thin leather of her tunic. "I'm whole," she said. "Alive."

I shivered. Felt older still than thirty-eight years. Or possibly thirty-nine. "You don't know what it was like. You were *dead*, bascha—"

"No. Nearly so. But *not* dead, Tiger. You stopped the blow in time. Remember?"

I hadn't stopped the blow in time. I managed only to slow it, to keep myself—barely—from shearing her into two pieces.

"I remember being helpless. I remember not wanting to dance

with you in the first place, and that cursed magicked sword making me fight you anyway. And I remember cutting you." Beneath my palm I felt the warmth of flesh, the steady beating of her heart. And the corroded crust of scar tissue mounded permanently in the skin beneath her left breast. "I remember leaving—no, *running*—because I thought you would die. I was sure of it . . . and I couldn't bear to see it, to watch it—" I levered myself up on one elbow, reached out, and slid my free hand to the back of her skull, urging her down with me. "Oh, bascha, you don't know what it felt like, that morning on the cliff as I rode away from the island. From you." But not from guilt and self-recrimination; I was sure she had only hours. While I'd have years to remember, to wish myself dead.

I shifted again as she settled; it was too small, too cramped, for anything more than the knotting of bodies one upon the other. "And then when you found me later, me with that thrice-cursed sword—"

"It's over," she said; and so it was, by nearly two years. "All of it is over. I'm alive and so are you. And neither of us has a sword that is anything *but* a sword." She paused. "Now."

Now. Boreal, Del's jivatma, she had broken to free me from ensorcellment. My own sword, the one I myself had forged, folded, blooded, and named on the icy island called Staal-Ysta, lay buried beneath tons of fallen rock. We were nothing but people again: the sword-singer from the North, and the sword-dancer from the South.

I flinched as she put her hand to the scar I bore in my own flesh, as gnarled and angry as hers over ribs now healed. She'd nearly killed me in that same circle. But it wasn't her touch that provoked the visceral response. The truth of it was, I wasn't even a sword-dancer any more, not a proper one. The Sandtiger was now *borjuni,* a "sword without a name." And no more proud—and proudly defended—title won in apprenticeship and mastery through the system that ruled the ritualized combat of the South, the oaths and honor codes of men who danced with swords within the circle and settled the wars of the tanzeers, princes of the Punja, the South's merciless desert.

Deserted at birth, then taken in as a slave; freed of that by oaths sworn to the man, the shodo, who taught me how to fight, to dance according to the codes; and now deserted by others who swore the same oaths and thus had to kill me, because I'd broken those codes.

Yet despite the price it had been easy to break them, because it was for Delilah. For *her* oaths and honor.

And so in the South, my homeland, I was prey to be hunted by any sword-dancer alive, to be killed without honor outside of the circle because I wasn't part of it any more. In the North, Del's homeland, I was a man who had turned his back on the glory of Staal-Ysta, the Place of Swords, and the sword-singers who danced in the circle with enchanted blades.

But here, now, with her, I was just me. Sometimes, that's enough.

Chapter 1

We left the North because Del agreed to go, if only because I forced her hand by winning a dance in the circle according to Northern rites. But I'd forced their hands, too, those blond and bitter people who'd sooner see Delilah dead even by deception because of broken oaths; once healed, once reunited, once free of Staal-Ysta and Dragon Mountain with its demon-made hounds of hoolies, we had eventually headed South—where within a year I'd broken the oaths I'd sworn to *my* people.

Now both of us were nameless, homeless, lacking songs and honor, abandoning our pasts in the search for a new present, but one linked uncannily to a past older than either of us knew: a baby's begetting, a boy's birth. The woman who had whelped me there on the Punja's crystal sands, and the man who had sired me far away in foreign lands.

Skandi. Or so we thought. So *Del* thought, and declared; I was less certain. She said it was only because I was a self-made man and didn't want to know the truth of my presence in the world, for fear I was lesser or greater than what I'd become.

Me, I said little enough about it. Mild curiosity and the dictates of the moment—the need to retreat, rethink, escape—had been diluted beneath the uncertainties of sailing, of odd, misplaced regrets, and something akin to confusion. Even homesickness. Except it was all very complicated, that. Because the South maybe wasn't my home at all. My birthplace, yes. That much I knew. Southron-born, Southron-reared. But not, we now believed, Southron-begotten. Which is one of the reasons we were *on* this thrice-cursed boat, sailing to a place where I could have been conceived.

Or not.

Someone might have told me, once. Sula. A woman of the tribes, of the Salset, who'd done more than any to make me a man in all the ways one can be. While the rest of the Salset ridiculed me as a chula, a slave, as an over-tall, long-limbed, big-boned boy awkward in body, in mind, wholly ignorant of grace, Sula had valued me. In her bed, to start with. Later, in her heart.

Mother. Sister. Lover. Wife. Yet neither bound by blood, rites, or ritual beyond the one we made at night, when I was allowed to sleep somewhere other than on a filthy, odorous goatskin flung down upon Punja sand. But Sula was dead of a demon in her breast, and there was no one to tell me now.

We left, too, because I was, well, a messiah. Or so some people believed. Others, of course, didn't buy any of it. People are funny that way. Some believe because of faith, needing no evidence; others have faith only *in* evidence—and I had not, apparently, offered any of worth.

At least, not the kind they believed in. After all, turning the sand to grass—or so the legendary prophecy went—was not the kind of imagery that really grabs a man, especially Southroners. It was a little too, I don't know, *pastoral* for them, who suckled sand with their mother's milk.

Whether I was the messiah, called jhihadi, and whether I had turned the sand to grass (or at least begun the process), was open to debate. Both were possible, I'd decided in a fit of self-aggrandizement fostered by too much aqivi and too little of, well, Del's admiration and affection one night beneath the moon, if one took the magic out of it and depended on a literal faith.

That's always a problem, dealing with religion. People take imagery literally. Or when the truth is presented as something unutterably tedious—such as digging canals and ditches to channel water from places with it to places without it—no one wants to listen. It's not flowery enough. Not *magical* enough.

Hoolies, but I hate magic. Even when I work it myself.

Having established once again that my bunk was not a particularly promising location for assignations of admiration and affection—I nearly smacked my head again, while Del cracked an elbow hard enough to provoke a string of hissed and dramatic invective (in uplander, which saved my tender ears)—we eventually wandered up onto the deck to greet the morning with something less than enthusiasm, and to placate discontented bellies with the sailor's bounty the crew called hardtack. Hard it was; anyone lacking teeth would starve to death. Fortunately neither Del nor I did, so we managed to gag it down with a few swallows of tepid water (Del) or a belly-burning liquor called rhuum (me). Then we stood at the rail and stared in morosely thoughtful silence at the wind-rumpled water, wondering when (or if) we'd ever see land again. It had been two days since we'd left behind a string of small islands where we'd stopped long enough to take on fresh water and fruit.

"Maybe it's not a real place," I observed, only half-serious, which, as usual with Del, provoked a literal response.

"What—Skandi? Of course it's a real place. Or they wouldn't have taken us on as passengers."

I slanted her a glance. Del couldn't possibly be any part of serious. "Are you any part of serious?"

"I didn't ask about Skandi in particular." She dismissed without rancor my unspoken suggestion that someone, somewhere, had done the impossible and taken advantage of Delilah. "I asked where the ships were going. Nothing more. So no, I did not play us into someone's greedy hands by planting the idea we'd go anywhere so long as we *thought* it was Skandi. They told me this one was going there, without prompting."

I vividly recalled the day she'd have scoured and scaled me with tongue and temper for even hinting someone had gotten the best of her. But the bascha had settled somewhat in the past three years, thanks to my benign influence. Now she *explained*.

Grinning, I settled once again against the rail. It creaked and gave. I moved off it again, promptly, scowling at damp, stained, salt-crusted wood. The ocean troughs were deepening, smacking unruly waves against the prow. So much water out there . . . and so little of anything else. Like—land. "You know, I just can't see how a pregnant woman would sail all the way to the South from a place so far away just to have a baby."

"Maybe she didn't."

"Didn't?"

"Well, maybe she didn't leave Skandi to have her baby in the South. Maybe she got pregnant *on* the voyage. Or maybe she got pregnant after she reached the South." Del eyed me assessively. "After all, half of you could be Southron. You look like a Borderer."

I'd heard that before, from others. I wasn't right for pure Southron blood, because the desert men were small, neat, and trim, dark-eyed, and swarthier than I. By the same token, I was too dark for a Northerner, who were routinely much fairer of hair than my bronze-brown. I was somewhere in the middle: tall and big-boned as Del's people, but much darker in skin and hair; too big, but not dark enough for a Southroner, and green-eyed to boot. Borderers, however, were halfbreeds, born primarily to folk who lived either side of the border between the North and the South. It made perfect sense that I was a Borderer. Which meant I wasn't Skandic at all, and this entire voyage of discovery was sheer folly.

But a man in Julah, where Del and I had stopped before going over-mountain to Haziz-by-the-ocean-sea, had thought I was of his people. Had spoken to me in his tongue. And he *was* Skandic. Or so he seemed, and so Del believed; she'd sworn he looked enough like me to be my brother. Which was possible—if I was Skandic, and *he* was—if not probable when considering the odds. Still, it was better odds than I'd been offered before beyond a dance in the cir-cle—which I couldn't do anymore, thanks to me breaking the oaths and codes of Alimat. And departing the South altogether. It was as good an excuse as any to leave a place where men who'd trained as I had, where men as good as I was, were hunting my head.

So. Here we were on a ship bound for Skandi. Where maybe I was from. Or not.

"Scared?" Del asked, following my thoughts.

Yes. "No."

She smiled slightly. Still following. "You are."

"Scared of what, bascha? I've fought I don't know how many men in the circle, killed a dozen or more fools outside of it, ridden to a standstill a stud-horse who kills *other* fools, fought off hounds of hoolies, an evil sorcerer who wanted to steal my body and my soul—or maybe just my body; we've argued enough about whether I *have* a soul—survived numerous deadly simooms bad enough to strip the flesh from my bones, withstood afreets and loki, sandtigers and cumfa, not to mention various tribes wanting to sacrifice me to some god or another; escaped murderous women and angry husbands . . . and I share your bed. Regularly." I paused. "What's to be scared *of*, after all that?"

"Knowing," she said. "Or—not."

Oh. That.

She waited, wind stripping unbound hair from her flawless face. Such blue eyes, had Delilah.

I spread legs, bent knees, set my balance to ride the lalloping sway of the boat and crossed arms against my chest. Tightly. Somehow, this mattered. "I suppose you *wouldn't* be. Scared. Of knowing. Or—not."

"I am scared of many things," she said simply, "and not the least of them is of losing you."

That shut me up in a hurry. After a moment I even managed to close my mouth.

Del, strangely satisfied, merely glanced sidelong at me, smiling, then looked across the bow again. "Ship," she said lightly.

So there was. With blue-painted sails. Behind us, above us, the crew of our own ship noticed the other also. Well, it wasn't land, but it was better than empty ocean. At least, until the crew swarmed like sandstingers over all the sails and ropes and timber. Next I knew, we were turning. Hard.

"Hey—" I grabbed the rail and latched on, not happy to hear it creak again ominously, but even less happy to feel the accompanying protests of the boards beneath my feet. Sandals slid, scraping on dampness and salt. The shift in wind filled my mouth with hair; I spat and stripped it out, then tucked it behind my ear, which did no good at all. Swearing inwardly, I resolved to have Del cut it as soon as possible. Or to hack it off myself.

Del also grabbed at the rail as we swung heavily through the choppy waves, grasping wood firmly. Even as she opened her mouth to make a comment or ask a question, a babble of shouting behind us pretty much answered it. I knew fear when I heard it. The whole crew suddenly stank of it.

"Trouble," I observed, wiping the slick of foamy spray off my face. Salt stung in my eyes.

The crewman nearest us looked away from the blue sails long enough to gesture urgently. "Below," he said. "Below. *Below.*"

"Trouble," Del agreed.

Of course, the last place I wanted to be was immured in a tiny cabin near the waterline as the ship wallowed and bucked. I hung onto the creaking rail, maintaining a now-precarious balance against the violent undulance, and scowled at the sailor.

"I'll go," she said.

Startled, I stared at her. "Wouldn't you rather stay on deck and see what we're facing?"

"And I'd rather have swords to face it *with*," she declared. "That's where they are. Below."

Ah. So they were. "Bring mine, bascha."

"I had planned on it."

The sailor saw her go, looked relieved, then noticed I remained at the bow. His eyes bulged as the ship continued its wallowing, graceless turn. "Below!"

No, *not* below, thank you . . . but as we swung around, the blue-sailed ship fell out of line of sight from my spot at the bow. I let the sailor believe I was following his suggestion; instead I made my way aft, moving so as to keep my eye on the other ship even as I clutched the rail, cursing in disgust as I caught a toe against a coil of prickly rope and nearly fell. This thrice-cursed boat, in rough seas, was harder to ride than the stud when he pitched a fit.

Still, I considered it curious that our captain would turn *around* rather than sailing on, especially as we were two days away from the last island, which meant there was no safe harbor within reach;

but we'd been heading into the wind, which slowed us down. Now we moved *with* it. The sails bellied, cracking against the sky as the crew worked rapidly. Wind shoved us along the way we had come, but more swiftly than before. The question now was whether the blue-sailed ship truly wanted us enough to chase us—and, if it did, was it faster?

Well, yes. The latter was obvious by the time Del came up beside me at the stern. She'd braided her hair back into a pale rope hanging down her spine. Naked now of everything save intent, her face and expression were clean and lethal as a new-honed blade. I took the hilt she offered, felt better for having a sword in my hand. "Our captain seems to place no faith in the fighting abilities of his crew."

"You've sailed with them for two weeks," she said, squinting against spray-laden wind. "Would you?"

They spent more time drinking, dicing, and swapping lies than anything else. Point taken. "Well, he might have faith in *us*." I paused. "You did tell him we hire out for this sort of thing, didn't you?"

"He's seen you smack your head or trip over ropes and nets about nine times a day, Tiger. Why should he have any faith in you?"

This sounded suspiciously as if our captain viewed me pretty much the way I viewed his crew. I was stung into a retort—especially as I had acquired any number of scrapes and bruises since coming aboard. "I'm taller than he is!"

"And clumsier, he seems to think. Although *I* don't believe it." She patted my arm briefly, absently, as if comforting a child—which of course was exactly how she wanted me to feel. "It's catching up."

She meant the pursuing ship. "I wasn't made for water," I said aggrievedly, "or boats. *Ships*," I amended, before she could correct me; the crew had been explicit. "I'm too big, or they're too small—"

"The world," she said gently, "is too small for you."

That stopped me cold. I eyed her, examined her expression closely, tried to figure out what in hoolies she was talking about.

Del burst out laughing. "Don't look so worried, Tiger! I only meant that you are large in all the ways so many men are small—"

"Thank you very much. *Many* men?"

"In all ways," she repeated, smiling peculiarly—and offering no answer. "Now, what were you saying?"

What *was* I saying—? "Well, look, bascha . . . I only mean I need land, something solid, something that stays put when I plant my feet—"

"Like the stud?"

Who was below, and not privy to this conversation. "Now that you mention it, I'd like to see what our esteemed captain, who thinks I'm so clumsy, would do on the stud . . ."

"Poor odds. *No* odds."

I scratched briefly at the salt-rimed scars in my face, four long clawmarks that scored me from cheekbone to jaw beneath a week's worth of stubble. "And anyway, the question now is not whether I'm clumsy on board a creaking hunk of flattened trees, but whether those fine folks would have come after us if we'd held our course—"

"The captain seems to think so."

"—or if we made ourselves look more attractive than we are *because* we turned tail and ran."

"The captain must have believed we had a chance at outrunning them."

"Or else he's just running scared."

"As well he might," Del observed as the blue sails swelled against the horizon. "We're losing the race."

I squinted across the narrowing gulf. "Maybe I should have a word with the captain about the benefits of standing your ground . . ."

"Unfortunately, as you've pointed out, there isn't any ground to stand *on*."

I spat hair out of my mouth again. "Well, *I'd* rather decide when there's to be a sword-dance than let the other man choose it," I reminded her. "There's merit to a good offense."

"Let me go," she suggested. "He's not much impressed by you. Me, he's impressed by; he comes up on deck to watch every morning when I loosen up."

"So do I, bascha—but watching you has nothing to do with

fighting!" Well, I suppose it did; but so far no one had challenged me. Even if I did crack my head on timber and trip over nets and ropes. "And maybe it's time I loosened up, too, out on deck where everyone can see me."

"Why?" Her voice was deceptively guileless. "Do you want men to watch you?"

I slanted her a sour glance. "I just meant it might be best if they don't assume I'm a pushover."

"A *fall*-over, maybe." Del smiled sunnily. "Well?"

I flapped a hand. "Go. Maybe you can find out who our friends are, and what they want."

Del left, was gone briefly, returned. She wore an odd expression. "They aren't friends."

"Well, no."

"They are, he says, renegadas."

"What the hoolies is that?"

"I believe he means borjuni. Of the sea."

That I understood. "What have we got that they want?"

"The captain did not trouble himself to tell me."

"Did you smile at him?" That earned me a scorching glance. "Well, no, I suppose not, not you—why smile at a man when a knife in his gut will work?—but did he at least trouble himself to say what we can expect once they get here?"

Matter-of-factly she explained, "They catch the ship, board it, steal everything on board. Or steal the ship itself."

"*Herself.* They call the ship 'she.' And what about the crew and the passengers?" All two of the latter; this ship generally carried goods, not people. We'd been lucky to claim some room. Although just at this moment, luck did not appear to be an applicable word.

Del shrugged. "They'll do what borjuni usually do."

I grunted. "Figures." Although not all borjuni and Border raiders killed their victims. Some of them were just after whatever they perceived as wealth, be it coin, trade goods, or livestock. (Or, in the occasional circumstance, people, such as Del and her brother.) Still, it was enough to make you skittish about leaving such things to chance.

Del frowned thoughtfully, marking how swiftly the other ship sailed. It didn't wallow like ours but sleeked across the water like a cat through shadows. "He wasn't much impressed when I said we could help them fight them. In fact, he said they wouldn't fight them at all."

"Did you offer to fight *for* him?" I asked. "For a fee, of course. Passage, at the very least."

"He says if they catch us, we'll all die anyway, so why should they bother to fight?"

"Did you explain *we* hadn't died yet?"

"At that point he told me he had no use for a woman except in bed," Del explained. "I decided I'd better come back here with you before I invited him into a circle."

"Well, we know there's no point in trying to change any man's mind about that," I agreed. "We're contrary beasts."

"Among other things." Del, with a sword in her hand and action in the offing, was uncannily content. "But I did manage to change *your* mind. Eventually."

I begged to differ. "I beg to differ," I said. "I just learned to shut up about it. I *still* think the best place for a woman is in bed." I paused. "Especially after a good, nasty, nose-smashing, lip-splitting, teeth-cracking fight in which she shows all the foolish men she's every bit as good as they are with a sword. Or any other weapon, for that matter—including her knee."

"Kind of you," she observed. "Generous, even."

"Merely honest, bascha."

She smiled into the wind. "Among other things."

"And now that we've settled the way of the world again as we know it, what do you propose we do when those—those—"

"Renegadas."

"—reach us?" I finished.

Del hitched a shoulder. "Not enough room to carve a circle in the deck. A dance wouldn't be particularly effective."

"Nope," I agreed. "Let's just kill 'em."

Chapter 2

*U*nfortunately we never got a chance to kill anyone. Because it became quite plain very early on that the renegadas in their blue-sailed ship weren't interested in engaging us. Working us, yes; they drove us like a dog on sheep. But they didn't come close enough to board, which certainly wasn't close enough for us to stick a sword in anyone.

At least, not immediately.

First they drove us, then fell back as if to contemplate further nefarious designs upon our ship. From a distance. They lurked out there smugly, having shown us they could easily catch us. And yet did nothing.

After all, why waste your efforts on forcibly stealing booty when the booty rather foolishly destroys itself?

Not being much accustomed to ships or oceans, I knew nothing about tides. Nothing about how a ship's draft mattered. Nothing about how *things* could be lurking beneath the water that could do the renegadas' work for them.

It didn't take long to figure it out. About the time the captain and his crew grasped the plan, it was too late. And I found out firsthand about tides and drafts and things lurking beneath the water.

I have to give him credit: the captain tried to rectify his error. Running for an island to escape the enemy is not a bad idea. Except he either didn't know about the reefs, which seems unlikely, or thought he knew the channels through the reefs well enough to use them. Because I found out what happens when an ocean-going vessel with a deep draft sails into a series of reefs that, at high tide, wouldn't matter in the least.

At low tide, they did.

Maybe he thought the renegada ship was as deep-drafted and would run aground. It wasn't, and it didn't. They just chased us onto the reefs, where, even as our captain frantically ordered his crew to come about, our boat promptly began to break up into hunks and chunks.

Trees float, yes. But they also do a good job of splintering, cracking, bashing, smashing, crushing, and otherwise impaling human flesh.

I did everything I could not to be bashed, smashed, crushed or otherwise impaled. This involved using both hands, which meant the sword had to go—even with renegadas lurking outside of the reefs. Del and I both took to ducking, rolling, leaping, sliding, cursing, scrambling and grabbing as we snatched at ropes and timbers. About the time Del reminded me that I couldn't swim, which I knew already, and announced she *could,* which I also knew already, I realized there was someone else in our party who was unlikely to be particularly entertained by having a ship break up beneath his feet. Even if he did have four of them.

Del was in the middle of shouting something about tying myself to a big hunk of timber when I turned away and began to make my way toward one of the big hatches. This resulted in her asking me, loudly and in a significant degree of alarm, what in hoolies was I doing, to which I replied with silence; my mouth was full of blood from a newly pierced cheek. I plucked out and tossed aside the big splinter as best I could, and reached to grab the hatch next to my feet.

"Tiger!"

I spat blood and bits of wood, dragged open the hatch. If I could get down to that first deck, I could unlatch the big hatch in the *side* of the ship, the one above the water-line which, when opened, dropped down onto land to form a ramp. Which is how we'd gotten the stud on board in the first place. Cloth over his head had made him a bit more amenable, and I'd managed to lead him up the ramp and into the ship's upper cargo hold. Ropes had formed a fragile "pen," layers of straw bedded him down. A cask of water was tied to a timber, and I personally doled out the stores of grass and grain. After two weeks he'd actually gotten pretty good about only kicking and biting occasionally.

"Don't go down!" Del shouted. "Tiger—you've got to get off this ship now, tie yourself to something—"

We weren't all that far from the island. Del likely could swim it, so long as she wasn't injured by the ship's breaking up. So could the stud—but not if he was tied. And I'd tied him well, too: a stiff new halter, a twist of thin knotted rope around his muzzle for behavior insurance, and two sturdy lengths of thick rope cross-tying him to two different timbers. He wasn't going anywhere . . . which had been the whole idea at first, but now wasn't quite the desired end. Or it *would* be his end.

I slipped and slithered my way down the ladder, uncomfortably aware that water was pouring in from every direction. I heard shouts, screams, and prayers as the sailors were trapped, crushed, impaled, or swept out through gaping holes. It was pretty amazing how quickly a ship can break itself to bits.

And a body, too, come to that.

"Tiger—"

I glanced back, shook wet hair out of my eyes; saw Del coming down the ladder. "Get out of here!" I shouted. "Go on—I'll bring the stud out . . ." I spat blood again. "You can swim . . . get out into the water—"

"You'll drown!" she shouted back. "Or else he'll kill you trying to break free!"

Water gushed against my knees. Over the screaming of the crew, the roar of the water, the dangerous death-song of a shattered ship, I heard the panicked beat of hooves against wet wood and the squealing of a frightened stallion. I slipped, was swept aside, caught something and pulled myself back up.

"Go!" I shouted at Del.

But she has her share of stubbornness and nothing I said could make her go where she didn't intend to go. For the moment it appeared she didn't intend to leave me. Fair enough. I wasn't about to leave the stud. He might yet die, but by any god you care to name he wasn't going to die tied up and helpless.

By now the ship was in pieces. There was no storm: blue sky and sunlight illuminated the remains uncompromisingly, so that I could see where our portion of the ship began and left off. Abruptly. A stiff wind shifted the wreckage against the reefs, pushing pieces of it toward the island, pieces of it out to sea. Larger portions remained hung up on the reefs. Ours was one. If it stayed steady long enough for me to reach the stud, to untie or cut the knots he'd undoubtedly jerked into iron—

I went down as the ship shifted, creaking and scraping against the reef. I heard Del's shout, the stud's scream. I clawed my way up again, spitting water, shaking soaked hair out of my eyes. Something bobbed against my knees, threatening balance again; I shoved the body away, cursing, and made my laborious way through rising water toward the thrashing stud.

He quivered as I got a hand on him, felt the heat of his flesh beneath the layer of lather. He was terrified. The knots, as expected, were impossible, and I had neither knife nor sword.

"Hold on," I muttered, "Give me a chance—"

The ship heeled over. What had been above the water-line now was not.

I came up coughing and hacking, one hand locked into the stud's floppy, upstanding mane; like me, he needed his hair cut. I hung on with that hand; with the other I reached over his muzzle and up between his ears, grabbing the headstall. "Don't fight me—"

But of course he did, which made it all the harder, and to this day I still don't know how I managed to jerk the halter over both ears. Once that was done, though, the rest came away easily. I peeled the knotted noseband off and tossed the halter, still cross-tied, aside. There was only one thing for it now.

Thigh-deep water makes it tough to swing up, so I didn't even try. I just grabbed bristly hanks of mane and scrambled up as best I could, flinging a leg across his spine. He quivered and trembled beneath me, fighting the rising water, the enclosure, the stink of fear and death.

"—out—" I gasped, pulling myself upright. I slammed heels into his ribs, felt him leap and scrabble against the pull of the water. I bent low over his neck as he fought for balance and freedom, trying to save my head a battering. *"—out"*—

But out wasn't easy. And as he crashed his way through the shattered timbers and boards, I prayed with everything I had that nothing would spear him from beneath. He was loose, now; all we had to do was get clear of the wreckage, get off the reef, and head toward the island.

Even as I lay against him, I looked back toward the ladder. Back where Del had been.

Had been.

Oh, bascha . . .

"Del—"

The stud swam his way free of his prison as it scraped off the reef and sank. He scrabbled against the reef, grunting with effort. I had images of his forelegs stripped of flesh, tendons sliced—

"Del—?"

Where in hoolies *was* she—?

The reef was treacherous. I felt the stud falter beneath me, slipping and sliding. Felt him go down, felt the fire bloom in my own leg. I came off sideways, but did not let go of mane even as I fought for footing in the pockets and gullies of the reef. Sandals were stripped off entirely.

"—up—" I urged, trying to suit words to action myself. If we could get free of the reef, back into open water—"Go—" I gasped. "Go on, you flea-bitten, lop-eared—" I spat out a mouthful of saltwater, sucked in air, "—jug-headed, thrice-cursed son of a Salset goat—" I used the reef, tried to launch and jerk myself up onto his back again. Made it partway . . . and then he lurched sideways, hooves slipping, scrabbling; something banged me in the head, graying out my vision. More flesh came off against reef. And then he was free at last, lunging off treacherous footing into water again, swimming unencumbered, save for me. But if I let go—

Never mind.

I kicked as best I could, trying to hold up my own weight even as he dragged me. He swam strongly, nose thrust up into the air. A hoof bashed my knee, scraped off skin. I got my head above water long enough to gulp breath.

"If I live through this," I told him. "I'm either never going on board a ship again"—hoolies, there went the *other* knee—"or else I'm going to learn how to swim—"

But for the moment, luckily, he swam for both of us.

I twisted, peering in snatches over my shoulder, looking for Delilah. My immediate horizon was transient at best: I saw a lot of slapping waves, the looming hulks of unidentifiable pieces of ship, floating casks, chunks of wood bound with rope. And a blue-sailed ship beyond, swooping in now like a desert hawk.

It crossed my mind, even as I hung on with all my strength to a panicked stud-horse, that the renegadas could not have meant the ship to break up so definitively. I could see the intent: to run us hard aground, then come in for the kill. But surely it was next to impossible to find any of the supposed goods they were after, now that the ship was in pieces.

Then again, maybe they hadn't intended the ship to break up quite so—dramatically. Or at all. Could be they meant to trap her, and were as startled as any of us by her quick demise.

I heard shouting. Couldn't say if it came from members of our ship's crew, or the renegadas. All I knew was I'd swallowed a gut-load of saltwater and had left a strip or two of skin on the reef. But I was alive, and so long as I didn't lose the stud I'd stay that way. So long as he made it to land, that is.

The next moment I wasn't so sure he would, or I would. His hooves struck something substantial, and he floundered. One hand slipped out of his short mane as he jerked and flung his head, seeking balance; my feet banged on something hard and rough. My turn to fight for balance. There was land under us, or reef, or something. Enough for the stud to plant all four hooves, and for me to slip and slide and eventually lose footing *and* handholds.

Before I could blurt out a word, before I could get my feet under me, the stud lurched off whatever we stood on. He was in the water again, swimming as strongly as before. Beyond him I saw a rim of land, a line of skinny, tall, spike-headed trees. He'd make it, I realized. He was but ten horselengths away. I, on the other hand, well . . .

I managed to stand up. It was reef, not land. Water slapped at my knees. Most of me was out of it now. I was in absolutely no danger of drowning—so long as I stayed on the reef.

A body floated by. My heart seized up as I saw the blond hair, then realized it was one of the sailors. I turned, trying to look beyond, trying to see *anything* that might be Del. Then a floating piece of wood banged into me and knocked me right off the reef.

Ah, hoolies—

Timber.

Floating.

I snatched at it, caught it, hung on with everything I had. Kicked my way closer, tried to pull myself up on it enough to get part of me out of the water. It rolled, bobbed; I got a mouthful of seawater for my trouble. Finally I just locked my hands into a strand of rope and hung on, floating belly-down. So long as I kept a death-grip on the timber, I wouldn't sink, wouldn't drown. Of course I had no idea where it *or* I might wind up. For all I knew it would float back out to sea . . . so, I applied myself to working out the magic it took to aim and steer the timber, which I thought might be part of the mast. If I kicked just so; if I pointed the wood in a specific way, and *then* kicked . . . hey. Maybe this is how you learn to swim—?

Not likely.

However, it did result in the mast and me ending up closer to land than to open sea, and I let out a long string of breathless invective as at last I felt sand beneath me, not reef.

Water sucked it out from under me almost as quickly as I found it. I staggered, caught my balance, lurched forward. The wind had stirred up the water enough to make footing and balance treacherous. I dragged myself out of it, feeling sand sliding beneath bare feet. Eventually I got free of waves and managed to escape the ocean altogether, staggering up onto the packed, wet sand of the beach.

I turned back, looked for Del, for the remains of our ship: saw a ship, all right, but not ours. And people clambering over the sides, dropping down into a smaller boat. Several gestured toward the broken-up remains. Toward land. Toward me.

Throw the dice, Tiger. Let them pick you up, put you on board a fast, sleek ship, give you food, rhuum; or run like hoolies.

I ran.

At some point, after I had stopped running, I fell asleep. Or passed out. Or something. I only woke up when a hand closed on my shoulder.

I lurched upright from the ground, then finished the movement by springing—creakily—to my feet. I had no weapon, but I could *be* one.

Except I didn't need to. "It's me," Del said.

So it was. Alive and in one piece. Which gave me latitude to be outraged. "Where in hoolies have you been?"

"Looking for you." She paused. "Apparently harder than you were looking for me."

"Now, wait a minute," I protested. "I didn't exactly *plan* to fall asleep. It was after I escaped those renegadas"—and threw up half an ocean, but I didn't tell her that—"and I figured I'd better lay low for a while, *then* go looking for you." I sat down again, wincing; actually, I'd been so exhausted by the fight to reach land I hadn't the strength to do anything *but* collapse. "Are you all right?—no. You're not." I frowned. "What did you do to yourself, bascha?"

She shifted her left arm away from me as I reached out. "It's just a scrape."

The scrape ran the length of her arm from shoulder to wrist. The elbow was particularly nasty, like a piece of offal left for scavenger birds. "Reef?"

"Reef," she confirmed. "I think we both left skin back there."

Now that she mentioned it, I was aware of the sting of salt in various cuts, scrapes, and scratches. I was stiff and sore and disinclined to move, and yet move was exactly what we needed to do. "Water," I said succinctly. "*Fresh* water. We need to clean off the salt, get a drink." My feet were a mess. I suspected hers were as well. "Have you seen any of the renegadas?"

"Not since I got back here in the trees and brush." Del's hair hung in salt-stiffened, drying ribbons. There was a shallow cut over one eyebrow, and her lower lip was swollen. "I don't think they ever saw me. They saw the stud, saw you . . . I made like a floater in the water, hoping they'd miss me. Once they headed off after you and the captain, I got ashore."

"The captain's alive?"

"He was when I saw him." Del shaded her eyes and peered back the way I'd come. Seaward. "We could wait until after sundown."

I gritted my teeth. "We could. Of course, I might go crazy from the salt by then."

"Or get so stiff neither of us can move," she agreed, then eyed me sidelong. "There is one cure for that, though. And now that there's *room*—"

I grinned. "Hoolies, bascha, you do pick the worst times to get cuddly!"

Del sniffed. "I am not 'cuddly.' I am too tall for 'cuddly.' "

I reached out and very gently touched the scrape on her arm. Del hissed and withdrew the arm sharply. "And too raw," I suggested. "Sand on top of salt? No thanks." I moved, wished I hadn't; got my legs under me. "Which way did the stud go?"

"That way." She jerked her head to my left. "He's not exactly a boat, Tiger. He can't very well swim us to Skandi."

"But he might take us *to* a boat." I stood up very slowly and couldn't bite back a blurt of pain. "Ouch."

"You're all sticky," she observed. "Is that blood? Tiger—"

"I got pretty intimate with the reef. With several of them." I worked my shoulders, waggled sore fingers. "Nothing but cuts and scrapes, bascha." I put out a hand. "Come on."

Del gripped it, used it. She set her jaw against any commentary on discomfort, but I saw it well enough in the extreme stillness of her face. Like me, she was sticky with oozing blood, fluids, salt, crusted with creamy sand.

I said it for her. "Ouch."

Del was looking at me. "Your poor face."

"My face? Why?" I put a hand to it. "What's wrong with my face?"

"First the sandtiger slices grooves in one cheek, and then you get a splinter through the other."

I'd forgotten that. No wonder my cheek and mouth were sore. I fingered the wound gingerly, tongued it from inside. "Well, it's just more for the legend," I said offhandedly. "The man who survives sandtiger attacks *and* shipwrecks."

Blandly, "But of course the jhihadi would."

I gifted her with a very black look.

Satisfied, Del smiled. "So, shall we hunt your misbegotten horse?"

"You mean the misbegotten horse who got me—nearly—to land, thereby saving my hide? That horse?"

"I'm only repeating what *you've* called him."

"I suspect he's called us much worse."

" 'Us'? I don't ride him."

"Me."

"Better." Del tucked a hank of sand-crusted hair behind an ear. "Water, or horse. Which one first?"

"Horse. He'll probably lead us *to* water." Rhetorically she asked, "But will he drink?" With much gritting of teeth but no verbal complaints, we moved slowly, quietly, carefully—and painfully— through the vegetation in the direction Del had seen the stud go.

Chapter 3

We found the stud. We found water. We found the wherewithal to clean off as best we could, stripping out of clothes to soak away salt from both fabric and skin, shivering and muttering and hissing and swearing vilely as we discovered various gooey scrapes, cuts, and gouges, and the promise of many bruises in places too numerous to mention. I put my leather dhoti back on, but nothing else was salvageable after introductions to the reef; I was barefoot and shirtless. Del's long ivory-colored leather tunic was scoured white in places, but remained serviceable. She wasn't as battered as I because she'd been able to swim *over* the reef—well, over most of it—but she had some nasty scrapes on her legs, and the one down her arm.

As expected, the soles of our feet were sliced up the worst because we'd both lost our sandals; Del scrunched her face in eloquent if mute commentary as she dangled sore feet in the water.

I was out of it now, checking the stud. His fetlocks were puffing, knees oozing, chunks were missing from shoeless hooves, and he stood with his weight on three legs, not four. "All right, old man—let me see . . ."

He didn't want me to. He told me so in horse language: pinned ears, swishing tail, bared teeth, an indifferent sideways snap in my general direction.

I popped him on the nose with the flat of my palm, insulting the injury, and as he stared at me, wide-eyed and aggrieved, I bent over the foreleg. "Give it here." I waited. "Give it *here*—"

He gave it to me eventually, if under protest.

"—hold still—" His head hung perilously near my own, but I ignored it and the quivering upper lip. "Let me just take a look . . . oh, hoolies, horse! Look what you've gone and done to yourself!" No wonder he was three-legged lame; he'd sliced open the tender, recessed interior vee of the hoof, called the frog.

"What is it?" Del was squeezing out hair darkened to wheat-gold by its weight of water.

"He's cut himself. Probably on the reef. It'll heal all right, but in the meantime he's no good for riding."

"We're on an island, Tiger. There's not much to ride *to*."

"Or from," I muttered, carefully looking for other signs of injury in the hoof. He was undoubtedly bruised as well. And every bit as sore and weary as we were. Plus there was a lot more of him to *be* sore. "It's going to take days for this to heal."

"I suspect we have days," Del observed gravely. "Probably even weeks, and possibly months—" She broke off. "What's the matter?"

I didn't say anything. Couldn't.

"Tiger?"

I was bent over the hoof. I don't know if that was it, or too much fresh water on top of seawater, or just reaction to nearly drowning. But my gut decided at that moment it was not happy with its contents. Very carefully I let the hoof back down, then slowly straightened up. Almost immediately I hunched over again, palms on knees.

"What's the matter?"

"Unnngffu," I managed. Unfortunately, my belly managed something else entirely.

Del had the good grace to wait until I was done retching and swearing. Then she said, politely, "Thank you for avoiding the water hole."

I scowled at her balefully, took the two paces to the water's edge. I huddled there miserably on aching, stinging, reef-scalped knees, rinsing my mouth out and my face off.

Hands were on my head, peeling hair aside so she might inspect the skull. "You smacked it on something," she said, fingering the swelling.

"I smacked it on several somethings." The ship, the stud, the reef. "I'm probably lumpy as a bad mattress—*ouch!*"

She patted wet hair back into place. "This reminds me of when the stud kicked you in the head in Iskandar. Before the sword-dance. That I ended up having to dance *for* you."

Well, yes. The stud had indeed kicked me. In the head. In Iskandar. I'd also ended up drinking too much aqivi on top of it, thanks to a well-meaning friend, and Del had indeed danced the dance for me against Abbu Bensir, before being interrupted. But there had been more to it than that. There'd been magic.

"You know—" But I stopped short. No one knew better than I what a bladetip set against the spine feels like. "Not worth it," I told her, feeling her tense beside me. And it wasn't. We were too stiff, too battered, too slow, in addition to being weaponless. They'd cut us down before we could even begin to turn.

Del muttered something succinct in uplander. The stud added a virulent, damply productive snort, then limped off a couple of paces.

Well, he was a horse, after all. Not a watchdog.

A big hand touched me, a rigid finger poked me—and with a garbled blurt of startlement I abruptly threw up again. Except there wasn't anything left *to* throw up, so all I did was heave.

Which served to amuse everyone but me. And maybe Del.

Someone cuffed me across the back of the skull, much as I cuffed the stud when he offended. "No sailor, this fool!" Amidst more laughter.

Well, no, so I wasn't. But then, I'd never claimed to be. I wobbled on my knees and one braced arm and thought very unkind and vulgar thoughts inside my abused head.

"Maybe you got stung by something," Del offered. "Something in the reef, maybe? Who knows what creatures could be lurking in those cracks and crannies. Or maybe something in the water itself."

I could think of many other things to talk about besides what was making me sick. I managed to cast her a pointed glance, then felt the meaty slap of a sword against my ribs. I winced as it connected with gnarled scar tissue. Lucky for me, it was the flat of the blade.

"Look." The same voice that had spoken earlier. "Look, fool!"

"I think you'd better," Del suggested after another blade-slap. "Look *at* them, I mean."

So I did, after a fashion. I sat back on my heels, let them see I was unarmed—which they probably knew already, but it never hurts to underscore such vital bits of information—then twisted my torso enough to look at them ranged behind us.

"Oh. Only six," I said, with carefully couched disdain.

"Four more than you," the closest man said, and thwapped me across the head with a broad-palmed hand as if I were an erring child.

"He's going to be sick again," Del warned as I clamped my jaws tightly. Which occasioned additional frivolity among the six renegadas.

"Maybe later," I said between gritted teeth, determined to impose self-control over an oddly recalcitrant stomach. "Hoolies, bascha—do you have to be so cursed helpful?"

"I just thought—" And then a sword lingered at her throat. Steel flashed, pale hair stirred—and a lock fell away. Nice warning, that. Sharp sword, that.

"No," someone said: a woman's voice, accented but comprehensible. "You will not distract us with foolish chatter." She paused. "Even if you are fools."

Oh, thanks.

"*We* are not fools," she went on. "You should sit very still, very quietly, and pray to whatever gods and goddesses you worship that we do not lose our patience. So that you do not lose your lives."

I eyed them, marking swords, knives, stances, expressions. Six. Five men, all fairly large, all quite fit, all poised and prepared to move instantaneously. One woman, not so big—in fact, she was rather small—but every bit as armed, every bit as fit, every bit as poised, every bit as prepared.

And there was absolutely no mistaking her for anything *but* a woman, either. Not in those clothes. Not with that body. I blinked, impressed.

"No," the man said, and cuffed me yet again.

Three times was more than I let anyone whack me, given a choice. So I ducked, rolled, came up with one of his ankles in my hands. Twisted, yanked the leg up, avoided the off-balanced sweep of his sword, cranked the ankle back on itself and dumped him on his butt.

Of course, they stopped all that pretty quickly. Someone threw Del facedown onto the sand and sat on her, one hand knotting up her hair in a powerful grip while the other oh so casually set the knifeblade across the side of her neck; three other men landed on top of me. By the time we'd sorted all of that out, I was scummed with sand once more, and grass, and my belly was turning back-flips. I discovered myself on my knees—*again*—while two of the larger men gripped my wrists one-handed and yanked my arms out from my sides, blade edges balanced lightly but eagerly on sand-dusted ribs, muscle, and scar tissue now standing up in rigid wash-board relief, since the renegadas had me all stretched out in the air as if I were a hide to be dried in the sun.

Del, sprawled face-down, managed to turn her head in my di-rection. Slowly. Carefully, so as not to invite repercussions. She spat out sand, a piece of grass. "Nice move," she commented briefly. "Forgive me if I don't thank you."

"He deserved it." I smiled benignly at the big, tanned man who sat on his rump in the sand, cursing, nursing a twisted ankle. Like the woman, he had an accent; none of the others had spoken. I no-ticed for the first time that he was bald, or shaved his head. Also that the head was tattooed. "And don't do it again."

He arched incredulous eyebrows. The woman burst out laugh-ing. Like the others, she carried a sword. Like the others, she was tanned and tattered by wind, salt, and sun. Her hair, trailing down her back in a tangled half-braided tail, was a flamboyant red. The eyes beneath matching brows were hazel. And every bit of visible skin on face, arms, and legs was thickly layered in freckles.

"Better not," she said to the tattooed man. "He is a dangerous fool, this fool."

"With a weak belly," he growled.

Well . . . yes.

Del, cheek pressed hard against the ground, asked, "Do jhihadis *have* weak bellies?"

"I'm glad everyone here is having such a good time at my expense," I complained. "And what in hoolies do you people want, anyway? As you can see by the state of what remains of our clothing, we aren't exactly weighed down with coin. Or jewels. Or even weapons." I glared at the woman. "And just how did you find us, anyway? We didn't leave any tracks." In fact, we'd been extremely careful about that, and neither Del nor I were precisely bad at being careful. We'd traded sand for grass as soon as possible, and moved with deliberation rather than carelessness.

The red-haired woman grinned, crinkling sun-weathered skin by pale eyes. Her teeth were crooked. "There is only one place with good water," she said simply. "We knew any other survivors would come here. So we sailed around the island, hopped overboard, and waited." She flicked an amused glance at Del. "And so you came, and here we are. Dancing this dance."

She didn't mean that kind of dance, although I'd just as soon she did. Because then I'd have a sword. But for the moment I focused on something she'd said. "*Other* survivors?"

She jerked her chin up affirmatively. "The man cursing us—and crying—about his lost ship."

"Ah. The captain." I indicated Del with a tilt of the head. "You can let her up, you know, before the fat man suffocates her." Most of the meaty bulk sitting atop Del's spine appeared to be muscle, not fat, but an insult is worth employing any time, regardless of the truth. "I don't think either of us is going anywhere."

"But you are," the woman said lightly. "You are coming aboard our ship."

"Thanks anyway, but I'd just as soon not. The last one I was on had an accident."

The man I'd dumped got up. He tested his sore ankle, shot me a malevolent green-eyed glance from under bronze-brown brows—which were neither shaved nor tattooed, but were, I noted with repulsed fascination, pierced with several silver rings—then scowled at the woman. "Well?"

She considered him. Considered me. "Yes. He is nearly as big as you. It will be less trouble."

"Good." The man took three strides across the sand and smashed a doubled fist into the side of my jaw. "Oh, dear," he cried in mock dismay, "I *have* done it again!"

Fool, I said inside my head, not definitively certain if I meant him or me—and then the world winked out.

I came to, aware we were on a ship again, because after two weeks I was accustomed to the wallowing. I lay there with my eyes shut and my mouth clamped tightly closed, tentatively asking my body for some assurances it was going to survive.

It was. Even my stomach. For a change.

This ship smelled different. Handled differently. Moved with a grace and economy that reminded me of Abbu Bensir, a sword-dancer of some repute who was smaller than I, and swift, and very, very skilled. A man whom I'd last seen in the circle at Aladar's palace, which had become Aladar's *daughter's* palace, when I had shattered every oath I'd sworn, broken every code of an Alimat-trained, seventh-level sword-dancer, and become something other than I'd been for a very long time.

We'd settled nothing, Abbu and I, after all. He still believed he was best. I believed I was. And now it would never be settled, that rivalry, because I could never dance against him *to* settle it. Not properly. Not where it counted. Because he would never profane his training, his sword, his honor, by accepting a challenge, nor would he extend one.

Of course, at this particular moment, none of that really mattered because my future might not last beyond the balance of the day.

"You there?" I croaked.

I heard movement, a breath caught sharply. Then, "Where else would I be?"

Ah. She was alive. I cracked an eyelid, opened the other. Rolled my skull against the decking so I could look at her. She sat across from where I was sprawled on my back on the deck of a tiny cabin, her spine set against the wall. There were no bunks, no hammocks. Not even a scrap of blanket. No wonder my bones ached.

"How long?"

"Not long. They lugged you on board, dumped you in here, pulled up the anchor, and off we sailed."

"The door bolted?"

"No."

"No?" I shot her a disbelieving scowl. "Then what in hoolies are you doing in here?"

Del smiled. "Waiting for you to wake up."

I put a hand to my jaw, worked it gingerly. I could still chew, if carefully—so long as they bothered to feed us. I undertook to sit up and managed it with muffled self-exhortations and comments to the effect that I was getting too old for any of this.

"Well, yes," Del agreed.

I jerked upright. "The stud!"

She poked a thumb in the air, hooking a gesture. "Back there."

I scratched at sand-caked stubble and scars. "How'd they get him on board? I figured he'd never go anywhere *near* a ship again—"

"They didn't. 'Back there' means—back there. The island."

"They *left* him there?!"

Del nodded solemnly.

"Oh, hoolies . . ." That image did not content me in the least. Poor old horse, poor old lame horse, poor old lame and battered horse left to fend for himself on an island—

"With fresh water," Del said, "and grass."

She never had liked him much. "Don't you dare tell me—"

"—he'll be fine," she finished. "All right. I won't. But he will be."

"We'll have to get back there and find him," I said gloomily. Then I frowned at her. "Are you all right? Did they hurt you?"

Del's expression was oddly amused, but she did not address the reasons. "I'm fine. No, they didn't."

"Did any of those men—"

"No, they didn't."

"Did any of the men waiting here on board ship—"

"No, they didn't." Del arched pale brows. "Basically they've pretty much just ignored us."

"Nobody ignores *you*, bascha." I tried to stretch some of the kinks out of my spine, winced as drying scrapes protested. And Del had her share, as well. "How's your arm?"

"Sore."

"How's the rest of you?"

"Sore."

"Too sore to use a sword?"

"Had I one, I could use it."

Had she one. Had *I* one. But we didn't. "Well, I guess now you can say that for the first time in your life a man took you seriously."

That set creases into her brow. "Why?"

"Because the minute I moved, that fat man sat on you. No one was about to let you try a move on anyone." I displayed teeth in a smug grin. "How's it feel to be treated like a man, instead of dismissed as no threat at all?"

"In this case," she began, "it feels annoying."

"Annoying?"

"Because if they'd ignored me, assuming I was incapable of defending you or myself because I am a woman, I might have been able to accomplish something." She rested her chin atop doubled knees. "I think it has to do with the fact their captain is a woman."

"She's their *captain?*"

"Southroner," she murmured disparagingly. "There you go again. And here I thought I'd trained you out of that."

Dangerous ground. I retreated at once. "Well, did they say anything about what they wanted us for?"

Del's eyes glinted. She knew how and why I'd come to change the topic so swiftly. "Not yet."

"Well, we're not tied up, and the door isn't bolted—what say we go find someone and ask?"

"Lead on, O Messiah."

This messiah led on. Slowly.

The red-haired woman was indeed the captain of the ship. She explained that fact briefly; explained at greater length, if succinctly, that despite what we might otherwise assume, it was perfectly permissible for either Del or I or even both of us to try to kill her, or her first mate—she indicated the shaven-headed, ring-browed, tattooed man standing a few paces away, smiling at me—or any of the other members of her crew because, she enumerated crisply: *first*, if we were good enough to kill any of them, they deserved to die; *second*, if we tried and failed, they'd simply heave us over the side; and *third*, if we somehow managed, against all odds and likelihoods, to succeed in killing every single one of them, where would we go once we *had?*

The first point annoyed me because it presupposed we weren't good enough to kill any of them. The second part did not appeal to a man who could not swim, and now had no horse to do it for him. The third point depressed that same man because she made perfect sense: Del and I couldn't sail this ship. And unless we killed every man aboard once we killed their captain, we wouldn't even get a chance to *try* to sail this ship.

An idea bloomed. I very carefully did not look at Del.

The woman saw me not looking, saw Del not looking back, and laughed. "That is why he is chained up," she said, grinning broadly, "in a locked cabin."

Del and I now exchanged looks, since it didn't matter. So much for the captain of our former ship, who likely could tell us how to sail our present one. If we killed everyone else first, starting with this captain and her colorful first mate.

"You can try to get him out, I suppose," the woman said musingly, "but we would immediately kill him, which would undoubtedly upset him, and then where would you be?"

"Where *are* we?" I asked, irritated. She wasn't taking any of this seriously.

"Oh, about five days' sail from Skandi," she answered, "and a lot more than that from wherever you came from." True. "Now, to business: Who in this world would pay coin to keep your hides whole?"

Promptly, Del and I pointed at one another.

"No, no," the woman declared crossly, "that is unacceptable. You cannot pay *her* ransom" —this was to me— "because you have nothing at all to pay with; and she cannot pay *your* ransom" —a glance at Del— "because she does not either." She arched coppery brows and indicated the ocean beyond the rail. "So, shall I have you heaved over the side?"

"How about not?" I countered, comprehending a distinct preference for staying put on deck.

"Why not?" The woman affected melodramatic puzzlement. "You have no coin, you have no one but one another to buy your hides, and you are no use to anyone at all as sailors." She paused. "What would *you* do with you?"

The tattooed sailor grunted. "Shall I tell you, captain?"

"How's your ankle?" I asked pointedly.

"How is your jaw?" he asked back.

"Boys," Del muttered in deep disgust, which elicited a delighted grin from the—female—captain.

"No, I want *them* to tell me." She rode the deck easily as the boat skimmed wind-ruffled waves, thick tail of hair whipping down across one delicate shoulder. "If they can."

"I'm sure I can think of something," I offered. "Eventually."

"Well, when you do, come back and see me." The woman flapped an eloquent hand. "Now, run along and play."

Chapter 4

I settled on fat coilings of heavy rope and looked at Del, who stood at the stern of the ship with her back to the rail. Wind whipped her hair into a shrouding tangle until she caught and braided it, then stuffed the plait beneath the neckline of her tunic.

We consulted quietly, but with precision. "So, what do we know, bascha?"

"There are eight men, and one woman."

All eight men and the woman were busy sailing the boat through roughening waters and a potential storm, judging by the look of the sky; we'd made certain before taking up our present positions no one was close enough to hear. "And three prisoners."

"One of whom could sail this ship, but is chained and locked into a cabin." She paused. "While the other two are seemingly without recourse."

"Seemingly, yes. For the moment." I considered the odds. "Eight men, one woman. Nine swords we know about, probably more; double the number of knives and assorted stickers, I'd bet."

"And any number of things with which to bash us over the head," Del added.

"Yes, but those items are just as available to us." I patted the top coil of rope, thinking of chains and hooks and lengths of wood. "We can improvise almost anything."

She crossed her arms, swaying elegantly with the motion of the ship. "An option," she agreed, though she did not sound convinced. "And?"

"And . . ." I tongued the inside of my cheek where the splinter had pierced it. "Men are frequently taken by you, my Northern bascha. If the captain were male—"

"She isn't."

"No, but—"

"She also isn't so stupid as to be taken in by false advances."

"How do you know?"

"A woman who captains her own ship—*and* a crew of eight males!—is likely immune to such blandishments as a man might devise, who hopes to win her favor merely to serve himself." Del caught her balance against the rail. "She is a killer, Tiger. She would not have survived to captain a ship—and this crew of eight males—if she lacked wisdom or ability."

"But she might be taken unawares," I countered, "with just the *right* man. Command gets lonely after awhile."

"She might," Del conceded eventually, "and you do have a full complement of what some women call charm—"

"*You* certainly seem to."

"—so it's likely worth a try."

I contemplated her expression. Inscrutable. "Well?"

Del's mouth twisted briefly. "I saw you looking at her. I think you would not be opposed to undertaking this option."

I opened my mouth, shut it. Began again. "If she were ugly, she wouldn't believe it."

"An attractive woman is more accustomed to such things, and therefore is prepared for unwanted advances. And defeats them."

I knew a little about that myself. "But if the woman carries a sword, knife, and whatever else she might have hidden on that body, a lot of men wouldn't consider making any advances at all." Not if he wanted to keep his gehetties.

"Which means it is left to the woman," Del said. "As it was left to me."

I jerked upright. "What?"

"It was."

Bruises, stiff muscles, and various scrapes protested my too-hasty motion. "Gods of valhail, woman, you were cold as a Northern lake when we met!"

"*When* we met, I wanted only a guide."

"That's what I mean. Ice cold. That was you."

"Arrogant," she said. "A braggart. A man who believed women belonged only in his bed."

I relaxed again, leaned against elbows propped on rope and stretched out reef-scoured legs. "All I ever claimed was to be the best sword-dancer in the South. Being honest isn't arrogant, and mentioning it from time to time serves a purpose in the right company. As for believing women belong only in my bed, well . . ." I cleared my throat. "I think it's fair to say there are indeed times when a woman in my bed is a worthwhile, um, goal." I waggled eyebrows at her suggestively. "Wouldn't you agree?"

"Which is why it was I who had to convince you to get into mine."

"You did *not*—"

"Oh, you put on a good show, all that bragging you did about being the infamous Sandtiger, feared by men and beloved by women—"

"Hey!"

"—but when it came right down to it, when it came to the *doing*, you were reluctant."

"Was not."

"Were so."

I considered mentioning ten or twenty names I could rattle off without stopping to think about it, just from the year before Del showed up, but decided even as I opened my mouth that names of women were not truly the issue, and if I named them, I might get myself in trouble. "*If* I was reluctant—and that's not an admission I was, mind you—it was because you'd been very clear about wanting only a guide." I sniffed. "For a woman who rarely explains anything, you were definitely clear on that point."

"That *is* my point," she said. "When I let you know there could be more between us, you ran the other way."

"Did not."

"Did so."

Impasse. Finally I asked, "What does any of this have to do with getting off this boat? In one piece?"

"Your plan seems to entail seduction."

"I said it was an option, yes. And it is. One of the oldest in whatever book you care to read." Which meant it might not work; then again, it had been used with success enough times to end up *in* the book.

Del's turn to sniff. "You were quick enough to volunteer *me* for the option—except the captain isn't a man, so that won't work."

"It was *you* who said I was looking at her!"

"You were."

"So were you."

"Tiger, I do have some acquaintance with the look in a man's eyes when he notes an attractive woman."

She would. "It doesn't hurt anything to look."

"Of course not."

That sounded suspiciously like she was pulling my leg—or else saw my point. Which raised another issue. "Do you look?"

"Of course I look."

"At other men?"

"A woman looks at other men the way a man looks at other women."

"She does?"

"Of course she does."

I had never considered that. It was new territory. Negotiating carefully, I said, "You mean women who aren't married."

"I mean any woman, Tiger. If she sees a man she considers attractive—or thinks he *might* be attractive, but needs additional study—she looks."

"Even if she's married." I paused. "Or sharing another man's bed. For three years."

Del smiled. "Yes," she said gently, "I look."

"How often?"

She was laughing at me. "Ask yourself the same question."

"*That* often?"

She crossed to the coil of rope, sat down beside me. Leaned her shoulder into mine. "You look. I look. Looking is not leaping."

"And is there any man here you might *look* at? Without leaping?"

"Oh, I might look at the first mate."

"Him? He's bald!"

"He shaves his head; I've seen the shadow. And the shape of his skull is good."

"He's got those blue tattoos all over it!"

"They are beautiful designs, too, so intricate and fluid."

"He has rings in his eyebrows!" And, for all I knew, elsewhere.

"That, I admit, is not so attractive. But—different." She shrugged. "He's interesting looking."

"Anything else?"

Del nodded, then tipped her head into mine. Softly she said, "He has your eyes."

"My *eyes?*"

"Green," she said. "And while one can see the competence in them, the confidence and willingness to risk himself, one can also see the laughter."

I digested that. "I don't see that there's much to laugh about, in our present situation."

"He does."

"He should!"

"Then it's up to us to find a way to stop the laughter in his eyes, and put it back in yours."

I twisted my mouth. "Which brings us around to the captain again."

"So it does."

"And if she's as smart as you believe she is, it might take a while. This—seduction."

"It might."

I scowled into sea spray. "You don't sound all that upset about it, bascha."

"Because I will have my own task to do."

"What's that?" I asked suspiciously.

"Seducing the first mate."

"*De-li-lah!*"

"Think with your head," she admonished, "not with—something else. If you should succeed in winning the captain's favors enough that it gains you a knife or sword so you may take her hostage against our safety, her crew will come for me."

So they would. I'd never believed otherwise.

"And so," she continued, "I should arm myself as well so they can't take me to force the issue, and then they will have no choice but to let us assume command. And have our captain freed, so *he* can sail this boat."

"Ship," I corrected. "And this is about the silliest plan I ever heard."

"Men who want something have seduced women throughout the centuries, Tiger. You yourself admitted it."

"I hope you're going to point out that women have used seduction to gain things, too."

"Of course they have. Men are ridiculously easy to manipulate from between the blankets."

I glared at her.

She shrugged. "You only think it's silly because we'll both be doing the same thing at the same time for the same reason."

"This is your revenge," I accused.

"You have no problem with me going into the circle, Tiger. Or killing to save our lives."

"Of course not." Now. Once I had, on both counts.

"And you were suggesting that I might seduce the captain, were he a man."

"I said it was an *option*—"

"But now that I'm so willing to seduce this first mate even as you are seducing the captain, the plan makes you uncomfortable." She paused. "Why is that?"

My head hurt. "I don't know!"

Del sighed. "Small steps," she murmured. "But enough of them lead to the same destination."

She was being cryptic again. I hate that. "What in hoolies are you talking about now?"

"I can fight enemies with you, kill with you, sleep with you. But not seduce someone else even as you are engaged in the same activity." She arched pale brows. "You do not—yet—care to share this thunder."

I hunched over on the coil of rope, elbows on knees, chin in hands. Aware of aches and abiding frustration. "I have a better idea."

"Yes?"

"Teach me to swim," I growled, "and then neither one of us has to seduce anyone!"

"Ah. Well, that, too, is an option. And then there is yet another."

I turned my head to glower at her. "I'm biting, bascha. See me biting?" I displayed teeth.

The Northern bascha was innocence personified. "You're the jhihadi," she said. "Why don't you just magick us up whatever weapons we need?"

I put the plan into action on captain's watch, just before dawn. It wasn't particularly difficult: I wasn't sleeping well, was stiff and sore, and desperately needed the exercise. So, taking my lead from Del on the other ship, I went up on deck and began to loosen up.

I'll admit it: there are times when a man postures and poses merely for effect. I'd seen it in the stud around mares. I'd seen it in male dogs as they gathered around a bitch in season. I'd certainly seen it in cantinas when a pretty wine-girl was the desired object in a room full of men just in off the desert. Sometimes one can't help it. Other times one—can. But chooses not to.

This was one of those times.

However, I had reconnoitered before undertaking the plan. Even as I had counted the crew, I assessed them as well. Eight men. All tall, all strong, all in condition. A small woman, no matter her personal skill and abilities, had surrounded herself with large men capable of using brute strength individually or jointly to protect their captain. I didn't question their loyalty; if they were not loyal, she'd be dead already. And if not dead, she certainly wouldn't be in command of a ship, leading renegadas bent on stealing from other ships equally full of men.

In the South, I am taller, heavier, stronger, and faster than other men, not to mention very good with a sword. It afforded me tremendous advantage in the circle, as well as in most other circumstances. But here, in these circumstances, I was enough like her sailors in height, weight, and bulk, not to mention coloring, to *be* one of them. Therefore I had to offer her someone other than what she knew.

Though Del was frequently rough on me with regard to physical aches and pains—not to mention opinions—I'd seen her with enough babies, children, and animals to know what got to her. She was without a doubt the toughest woman I'd ever known in strength of will, mind, and sheer physical gifts, but she was, after all, a woman. She had her soft spots.

The captain was also a woman, and I was certain she had soft spots, too. I just had to find one.

I stood on the deck in the open and commenced loosening up. I did not bite my tongue against grunts of effort, of oaths sworn against stiff, slow muscles, of the favoring of particularly sore areas. I hurt all over. It affected the way I walked, the way I stretched, the way I twisted this way and that. Even the way I stood: within minutes my feet were bleeding. Any other time I'd have shrugged it off, told Del or anyone else I was fine, no problem, nothing I couldn't handle. It's easy to let pride replace truth. Sometimes it's necessary. This time, I thought, it was not.

Understanding Del was the key to this woman, this red-haired, freckled woman who had acquired a ship and eight men, not to mention various weapons and booty. Del had called her a killer: she likely was, although I had yet to see her personally kill anyone. That she'd ordered her crew to run us up on the reef, I knew. Whether she could stick a sword into a man and cut his heart out, I didn't know. Del could. Del had. Del, too, was a killer.

That stopped me for a moment. In mid-stretch I halted, summoned up that thought, that image again. Del in the circle, circumscribed by ritual, by song. Del out of the circle, circumscribed by nothing but her will, her skill, her determination to remain alive.

Hoolies, she'd nearly killed *me*.

And while I recalled that, put fingers to the misshapen sculpture of scars along my ribs where her sword had cut into me, felt again the pain, the shock, the chilling flame of Boreal eating into flesh and muscle and viscera, the captain came up from behind.

"The reef was cruel," she said.

I glanced sidelong at her, saw red hair knotted back into a haphazard braid, the shine of glass beads and gold at earlobes and throat, the snug fit of the wide belt buckled around a waist I could span with my hands, and the freckled upswell of generous breasts at the droop of her neckline. A thin tunic, rippling in the wind. Baggy leggings tucked into low, heelless boots, but a curve of calf played hide-and-show in a rent. She *was* worth looking at. No question. And she was looking back.

So. The plan commenced.

"It wasn't the reef that drove us aground." I spread my feet again, bent to touch the deck with flattened palms. I let her see the effort not to show the effort, now that she looked. "Better to say you were cruel."

"So I am." She put a hand on my spine, into the small of my back above the dhoti, and pressed. "Does this hurt?"

I caught my breath, swearing inwardly. If she was *that* kind of woman . . . well, it made the plan problematical. To say the least. Maybe even impossible; I had not taken this quirk into consideration.

Queasy again, I straightened, felt the fingers walk up my spine. The hand, without warning, slipped around to the scar tissue, squeezed. "That hurt," she said. "Once."

Beneath that hand, beneath the dead tissue, the bones remembered. So did the softer insides. Indeed, it had hurt. Very much. And now I felt sicker than ever.

"Your feet are bleeding," she observed.

I swallowed tightly. "Forgive me for staining your deck." I waited for her to remove the hand. When she didn't, I removed it for her, lifting it off my ribs. She was close enough for me to consider making a grab for her sword or knife, but I was certain she wanted that. Therefore I decided not to do it. Not yet. Not yet.

"My deck will survive," she said. "Will you? Can you?"

"That depends on the alternative." I took a step away, then turned toward her. "A man will do many things to stay alive."

The skin by her eyes creased. "So will a woman."

"Does that include running other ships aground so they break apart?"

"You may blame your captain for that. His choice was to come about and allow us to take his ship, unharmed; instead, he misjudged and tried the reef."

"You knew he would."

"Other men have not made that mistake. I believed he would choose to let his ship and his crew live." She paused. "And his passengers."

"It makes no sense to lose the cargo, Captain."

"No sense," she agreed, "but that is my risk. I throw the dice—" A quick reflexive movement of her right hand. "—and occasionally I lose."

"This time."

"Perhaps. Perhaps not. There is no coin of it, that is true. But there are two men and a woman."

"And you already know there is no one to ransom two of us."

A negligent shrug of her left shoulder. "Probably no one will ransom the captain, either. I doubt he is worth much even if he has a wife."

"So much for booty, captain."

"Booty is many things. It shines, it sparkles, it chimes, it spends." She smiled. "It breathes."

This time I hid my reaction. It took everything I had. "Slavers?"

Her eyes, intently clear under sandy lashes tipped in sun-bleached gold, were patently amused. "A woman will do many things to stay alive."

I drew in a careful breath. "So will a man."

"Then do it," she suggested. "Do what is necessary."

I turned sharply to walk away from her, thinking it necessary as well as advisable—and nearly walked right into the first mate, whom I had not known was anywhere nearby. Which didn't please me in the least.

Behind me, as I stopped short, I heard the woman laugh softly, saying something in a language I didn't understand. In morning light, the rings piercing the man's eyebrows glinted. He answered her in the same language, but did not take his eyes off my face even as she departed.

I didn't doubt for a moment that had I tried for the woman's weapons at any time, he'd have killed me instantly. That was the point of surrounding yourself with men such as this.

"What are you?" he asked.

Not who. What. Interesting—

And then my belly cramped. Hoolies, but I was getting tired of this. Maybe Del was right. Maybe I *had* been stung by something in the reef. "I'm a messiah," I answered curtly, in no mood for verbal or physical games.

Teeth gleamed as his lips drew back in a genuine smile. "I thought so."

Of course, at the moment I didn't feel particularly messiah-ish. After Del's comment about me magicking weapons out of thin air, which of course I couldn't do, I hadn't been precisely cheerful. And now this blue-headed man was playing the same sort of game. With much less right.

He said something then. I didn't understand it; it sounded like the same language he and the captain shared. He watched me closely as he spoke, searching my eyes and face. I couldn't very well prepare to show or not show any kind of response, as I had no idea what he was saying. I just looked back, waiting.

He switched again to accented Southron. "Where were you bound, when we took you?"

"Skandi." I saw no harm in honesty.

Something glinted in his eyes. "*Io*Skandi."

"Skandi." I shrugged. "That's all I know. Never been there before."

Ring-weighted brows rose consideringly. "Never?"

"Southroner," I answered. "Deep desert. Punja. Bred and born."

"No."

"Yes."

"Skandic." He sounded certain.

"Maybe," I said clearly, curious now as well as irritated. "Depending on what you intend to do with us, we may never find out—"

Without warning he clamped a hand over my right wrist. I felt the strong fingers close like wire, shutting off the blood.

I moved then, used strength and leverage, was free with one quick twist. He did not appear surprised; in fact, he smiled. And nodded. *"Io."*

No help for it but to ask it straight out. "What is this about?"

He looked from me to the deck. He squatted then, put out a hand, fingered the blood left by my reef-cut feet. Rose again, rubbing his thumb against the fingers. Then he turned the hand toward me and displayed it palm-out, blood-smeared fingers spread, *"Io."*

"You sick son of a—"

"You are sick," he interrupted. "Look at your arm."

Part of me wanted not to. But part of me decided to play the game his way until I understood it better, or at least knew if there were any rules. So I looked at my arm.

Around the wrist, where he'd shut his hand, the skin was blotched with a fast-rising, virulent rash. Even as I watched, astonished, clusters of small pustules formed, broke. Wept.

"When you weary of emptying your belly," he said, "come to me."

I opened my mouth to reply, then turned and staggered to the rail. Where I promptly emptied my belly.

Chapter 5

Del came looking for me, found me: perched again upon the rope coiled back at the stem. She stopped, arching eyebrows. "Well?"

"Well what?"

"Any progress?"

"Progress at what?"

"With the captain."

"Oh. No. I mean—" With infinite care I examined a scrape across one kneecap. "—I'm not rushing it."

After a moment of silent perusal she squatted down so she could look into my face. "What's the matter?"

I hitched a shoulder. "She's not exactly what I expected."

"No—I mean, what's the matter with you?"

I eyed her warily. "What do you mean, what's the matter with me?"

"You've been ill again. I can tell. You get this greenish tinge around your mouth, and your nose turns red."

I fingered the nose, frowning, then sighed and gave up. "I'm sick of being sick. This is ridiculous!"

Her mouth twitched. "And no aqivi to blame it on, either."

I peered at her hesitantly. "Do I feel hot to you?"

She felt my forehead, slipping hands beneath flopping hair. "No. Cold." She moved out of the squat, sat down next to me on the rope. "I still say something stung you."

"Maybe so." I sat with both arms hooked over my thighs. The right wrist no longer wept fluids. The pustules were gone. The only trace of what had existed was a faint ring of reddened flesh, but it was fading rapidly. "Do you know what *io* means?"

Del shook her head.

I elaborated. "He said *io*Skandi."

"Who did?"

"The blue-head. First mate."

She shook her head again. "We know Skandi is a place, and Skand*ic* might indicate a person from Skandi, but *io?*" She shrugged. "Maybe a city in Skandi?"

I sighed, absently rubbing a wrist that felt and looked perfectly normal. "Could be. That makes as much sense as anything, I suppose." I slanted her a glance. "Well?"

"Well what?"

"Any progress on your end?"

She smiled. "I'm not rushing it."

I grinned briefly, but it died. Quickly. I stared steadily at the deck. This next part was going to be hard. "Del."

She closed her eyes against the wind. "Hmmm?"

"They took no coin, no jewels, no cargo, no ship. Only you, and me, and the captain." Now I inspected a cracked toenail. "They may intend to sell us."

Her eyes snapped opened. After a moment of tense silence, she said carefully, "That would make sense." And as I went rigid from head to toe, she put a hand upon my knee. "I know, Tiger."

"Del—" I bit into the pierced cheek, bringing fresh blood. "I can't do it again."

The hand tightened. "I know."

"We have to find a way off this ship. Before—" I shut my eyes, squeezed them, then opened them. "Before."

"We will."

I pushed myself to my feet then, took two long strides to the rail and gripped it. Sea spray dampened my face as wind stripped back my hair. It was harder than I'd thought.

"Are you sick again?"

I spat blood, then spoke steadily, without excess emotion. "I will drown myself before I let anyone sell me into slavery again."

"Oh, Tiger—" A half-hearted, desultory protest.

I swung to confront her, startling her with my vehemence. "And you had better not pull me out of the water. Promise me that."

Del stared at me, weighing words, tone, expression—and began to believe. The color drained until she was white-faced, horrified, sitting stiffly upon the rope. "I can't make such a—"

"Promise me."

She shook her head decisively. "There will be a way . . . we will find a way, make a way—"

"No," I said bitterly. "Not again."

"Tiger—"

"First the Salset for sixteen or seventeen years, then Aladar and the mines. I can't do it again. I *can't.*"

She attempted reason now, still not certain, but taking nothing for granted. "You freed yourself of the Salset. And you got free of the mines. There are opportunities that—"

"Enough." I cut her off curtly. "Don't ask it, don't wish it, don't expect it, Del. I can't."

Abruptly she thrust herself from the rope and stood there rigidly, trembling. She sought to speak, could not. Then turned to walk away with none of her usual grace.

"Del—"

She spun, furious. "Don't!"

I gestured futility. "I have to do—"

"No, you don't. You don't have to do any such thing."

I clamped my jaws shut. "I can't—"

"*I* can't do it! Do that? I can't! *I* can't!"

"Del—"

"No." In the coldest tone I had ever heard from her. "Are you so selfish, that you can ask this of me? Are you so blind, so arrogant?"

My voice rose. "Arrogant—!"

"What are you, to ask this of me? To expect me to watch you drown?"

"I didn't mean you had to *watch*—"

We were both shouting now. "You are a fool!" she cried, and then added something in uplander so vicious I knew better than to request a translation.

"It's not the first time," I reminded her sharply. "When Chosa Dei was in me, you agreed to kill me. This time I'm only asking you not to rescue me."

"And I couldn't do it!" she snapped. "Do you recall I had my jivatma at your throat?"

I did. Clearly.

"Do you recall how I promised then to make certain Chosa Dei would not be set free?"

I did.

"Do you recall how he very nearly took you as his own, as his body, so that he would have the means to destroy the land?"

Oh, yes. I recalled.

"I knew then I couldn't do it," Del said. "I *knew* it. I promised you then—and I couldn't do it."

"Del—"

"I will make no more such promises, Tiger. No more. Never." Tears stood in her eyes. Outrage, most likely. And maybe something else. "The only promise I shall make you is that I will die for you."

"Del, don't . . . you don't—"

"I do," she said. "Oh, I understand. I see. I *know*. And I refuse." She stepped close to me, very close, so that I felt her breath on my face. "In the name of my dead jivatma I swear this much: that I will do everything within my power to defend your life against any threat. Even one made by you." She was trembling with anger and, I thought, fear. "Don't ask anything more. Don't wish anything less. Expect *nothing*—but that I will die in your place to keep you from being a fool."

I caught her wrists, gripped them firmly. Opened my mouth to answer, to deny her this oath—and saw we had gathered a crowd of grinning onlookers. I swore, released her, and turned sharply back to the rail.

I stared blindly at the sea as I listened to her go.

Near dawn I awoke. I don't know if it was a sound, or the lack of. But I realized I was alone.

The emptiness was abysmal.

I stretched, twisted, and shook out parts of my anatomy until sweat sheened me. It was dawn, both breezy and cool, but I'd lost myself in the rituals I'd been taught at Alimat, in training to the shodo. He had explained that even a boy of seventeen should never assume his body was fit, and that as he aged fitness would become harder to achieve.

Of course, I didn't believe him. At seventeen (or sixteen, or eighteen; no one knew for certain), after nearly two decades of labor for the Salset, I was more than certain I was fit. After all, I'd survived slavery, had killed a sandtiger for my freedom, had been taken on as a student of Alimat. After I defeated Abbu Bensir, Alimat's best apprentice, I knew my conditioning was superb. Hadn't I nearly *killed* Abbu?

Well, yes; but accidentally. Killing him wasn't the object. Defeating him was, and that I'd accomplished. Quite unexpectedly.

However, the shodo himself, with unequivocal skill despite his advanced age, soon convinced me that despite the quickness and strength of my young body, and the potential for remarkable power and true talent, I was merely a boy. Not a man. Not a sword-dancer.

It had taken me years to understand the difference. By the time my body was honed the way the rituals of Alimat required, I was nothing like that boy who'd killed the sandtiger—and nearly killed Abbu. I was nothing like the man who moved quickly through the first four levels, followed by three more. I was a child of Alimat: conditioned to codes and rituals and the requirements of the circle.

And now I stood outside of all the circles, self-exiled. But the body remembered. The mind recalled. Reflexes roused, began to seep back despite scrapes and bruises and gouges. I was more than twice the age I'd been when Alimat had accepted me, and I knew intimately the weight of the shodo's wisdom: as a man ages, fitness becomes harder to achieve.

As years in the circle are measured, I was no longer young. I bore scars from all manner of battles and circumstances, owned a knee that complained occasionally, and had noticed of late that my distance vision took a bit longer to focus.

But I was a long way from being old, fat, or slow.

Fortunately for my plan, the captain noticed that.

She leaned her back against the rail, elbows hooked there idly—which, I could not help but notice, enhanced the jut of her impressive breasts. She rode the deck easily, graceful as cat, while wind whipped the red braid across one shoulder like a loop of twisted rope. Where the sun picked out highlights, strands of hair glowed gold as wire.

She smiled. "Do you know, I believe you might match Nihko."

"Who?"

"Nihko," she answered. "My first mate."

"Oh. Blue-head."

The woman laughed. "Is that what you call him? Well, he has a name for you, too."

"He does, does he?" I bent, flattened palms against the deck. "And what would that be?"

"Something vulgar."

I grunted. "Nothing new."

"I imagine not," she agreed. "And I expect your woman calls you something equally vulgar, now."

I straightened. "What 'my woman' calls me is none of your concern. And you of all people should know better than to describe her that way."

A red brow arched in delicate surprise. "What? Is she your woman no longer, now that you have argued?"

"She isn't 'my woman' *ever*."

"No?"

"No." I paused. "Not even before we argued."

"Do you not own her?"

I shook out my arms, flexed knees; I was cooling now in the

wind, and sweat dried on my flesh. "No one owns her. She isn't a slave."

"But she is bound to you, yes?"

"No."

"Then why would she stay with you?"

I scowled at her. "The reason any woman stays with a man she—admires."

"Admires!"

"Likes," I amended grudgingly.

"Even now, do you think? After you shouted at her?"

I stood at the rail. "She shouted back."

"And now she will leave you?"

"It's a little hard to leave me when we're both stuck on this boat."

"Leave you here." She touched one breast, indicating her heart.

"Ask her," I said grimly.

"Nihko says she refuses to let you die."

I didn't realize they'd overheard *quite* that much. "Del does what she pleases."

"And if she pleases to keep you alive?"

I shrugged. "A man can find ways to die."

She considered that. "And why should he wish to die?"

He doesn't. But. "There are choices a man makes about the way he lives."

"Ah." She smiled. "And now you have argued together and are in bad temper, like children, because she *likes* you enough to wish you to survive, even if you wish to die."

"No one should interfere with a personal choice."

"No?"

"No."

"And if *her* personal choice is to keep you from dying?"

I glowered at the water and offered no reply.

"Would you prevent her from dying?"

That one was easy. "I have."

"And she, you?"

I turned on her then. "What is this about?"

"So, you will not admit a woman may prevent a man from dying? Does it weaken your soul, to know a woman can?"

I set a hip against the rail and folded arms across my chest. "What's my prize, if I answer your questions correctly? And how would you know if I did?"

She laughed at me. "On this ship, there is truth among men and women."

"Truth?"

"I tell you a truth. There is no man of my crew who was born believing a woman could save his life. But they learned it was so, when I saved theirs."

"*You* saved theirs."

"Oh, yes. I bought them."

I stiffened. "*Bought* them—"

"Out of slavery," she answered. "All save Nihko. Nihko came to me."

"Why?" I asked sharply.

"Ask Nihko."

"No—I mean, why did you buy them out of slavery?"

"I required loyalty. And that cannot be bought, or beaten into a man."

"Loyalty for what?"

"My ship."

I began to understand. "You couldn't hire a crew."

"Coin does not buy loyalty."

"No men would hire on with you as captain. So you bought yourself a crew another way." I shrugged. "Slave labor."

"I bought them. I freed them. I gave them the choice. Eight of ten sailed with me."

"And the two who did not?"

She hitched a single shoulder. "Free men choose as they will. Those two chose to go elsewhere."

"Loyalty you couldn't buy."

In the sun, her eyes were pale. "They would have left me later. It was better to lose them then."

"And the others?"

"One is dead," she said. "The others are here."

"Still."

"Still." She tilted her head slightly. "The only man who would ask his woman to let him die rather than become a slave is a man who has *been* a slave."

Anyone who had seen my back knew that. I eyed her up and down. "You seem to have an intimate knowledge of slavery."

She lifted her chin in assent. "My father owned many."

I had been on the verge of assuming she had been one. Or a prostitute, which is, I'd been told by Delilah, a form of slavery. But this was nothing I had expected of the conversation. "And does your father know what his daughter does?"

"What she does. What she is." A strand of sun-coppered hair strayed across her face. She trapped it and pulled it back, tucking it behind a gold-weighted ear. "He is a merchant," she said, "of men. He sells, buys, trades."

"So," I said finally, "you bought these men from your father, freed them—and now you ask them to do to other men what was done to them."

She said matter-of-factly, "Booty is many things."

And the daughter of a slaver would have no trouble finding a market for me. Or Del.

I shook my head. "No."

Small teeth glinted white. Even the rim of her lips was freckled. "*She* believes you worth saving."

I shrugged. "No accounting for taste."

It startled a laugh from her. I watched her eye me up and down, assessing me; it was what I had hoped to provoke in her, an interest in imagining what might come of intimacy, but now I could not help but wonder if she assessed me as a man who might perform in her bed—or perform as a slave. The chill in my gut expanded.

"So," she said, "you are willing to die for your freedom, as you believe death is better than slavery. I ask you, then, will you live for your freedom? If you were offered the choice?"

"I saw the choice you offered our captain in the reefs."

"But there was a choice," she insisted quietly. "I did not require him to sail his ship aground. He could have surrendered to us and saved his ship, his cargo, and the lives of his men."

"Maybe *he* didn't want to become a slave either."

"But that is the final choice," she explained. "If you have the means to buy your safety, I do not insist upon selling anyone." She flicked a hand briefly and eloquently. "Find a way to buy your freedom, if you would not have me sell it. That is your choice."

I could ignore the opening, and risk not getting another. Or I could test the possibility while making no commitment. "And what," I asked steadily, "might you count as coin?"

The slaver's daughter smiled. A light came into her eyes. "There are seven intact men on board," she said, "and I doubt you may offer more than they have."

"Have offered?" I asked. "Or are forced to surrender out of loyalty?"

"You owe me no loyalty."

"No."

"You owe me escape," she said. "To prove you are better than we judge you. And that is what you plan even here and now, as we speak."

"Is it?"

She nodded once. "I do not rule my men. I *understand* them."

"And you believe you understand me."

"More than you understand me." She grinned. "I repeat: I doubt you may offer more than my crew have."

I shrugged casually. "There are men—and there are men."

She ignored that. "I have seen your hands."

"So?"

"So. I know what manner of work causes calluses such as those. Not slave labor, but skill. Practice. Dedication. Discipline."

"*I* repeat: So?"

"You seek a sword," she said calmly. "You believe that with a blade in your hand, it will prove no difficulty to overcome eight men and one woman."

"I do, do I?"

"It shouts from your eyes. From your body. In every movement you make here, returning your body to fitness." She was serious now. "There are two kinds of men in the world: fools, and those who are dangerous."

I spread my hands. "Me? Dangerous?"

"As Nihko is dangerous. You are two of a kind."

"I've got a bit more hair on my head."

"And testicles."

That startled me. "What?"

"Some men pay with more than simple coin."

I pondered that. I pondered the idea of a man surrendering himself so far as to lose that which makes him a man. But then, there was no certainty Nihko had *had* a choice.

I cleared my throat, trying to ignore the reflexive tightening of my own genitals. With effort I changed the subject—and the imagery. "And your price, captain?"

With no hesitation she answered, "The woman."

I bit down on my anger. "Why barter for what your men could take?" Del would account for a few, but in the end superior numbers would undoubtedly prevail.

"For my men?" Her smile was bittersweet as she shook her head. "Oh, but I want her for myself."

I stared at her, speechless.

"And now you know," she said, "why my father cast me out, and how I came to be a renegada."

Chapter 6

Del, in the tiny cabin we'd been "assigned," swung around as I shut the narrow door behind me. Her expression was pensive; that changed to studied patience as she recognized me.

I cleared my throat. "Well," I began, "it *seemed* like a good idea. I just didn't quite figure on this—minor complication."

Blue eyes narrowed; Del knows all my tones and euphemisms. "What minor complication?"

I spread a hand across my chest. "There is, after all, one woman in the world who is not overcome by my manly charms. *Only* one, mind you—but still. I am crushed. I am undone. I am destroyed. I will undoubtedly never recover."

"You made your move on her." She considered my expression. "I thought you said you weren't rushing anything."

"I didn't make any kind of move," I said. "Well—innuendo. But that's not really a *move*—"

"Depending on how such things are interpreted."

"—at least, not the sort of thing I really consider as an official move," I finished, ignoring her interruption. "There's an art to seduction, you know."

"Seduction requires subtlety," Del said. "You have none."

"None?"

"It is one of your charms," she observed, "that there is no guile in you. At least, not when it comes to such base instincts as copulation."

I affected horrified shock. "Hoolies, bascha, why don't you just take all the romance right out of it!"

"You say what you want, Tiger. I respect that."

I leered at her. "Respect this!"

Del sighed. "As I said, there is no subtlety in you."

"Well, there *was*," I answered. "At least, I *thought* I was being pretty subtle. But it's lost on that woman."

" 'That woman?' " Del eyed me curiously. "My, this sounds serious."

I began again. "She wounded me. She cut me to the quick. She utterly shattered my spirit—"

"Which will recover," Delilah put in, arid as the Punja, "with liberal applications of *my* affection and attentions, I assume."

I dropped the pose, took a step forward, hooked an arm around her neck and pulled her close against my chest. Into her hair I said, "Forgive me, bascha."

Her breath was warm on my neck. "For failing to seduce the captain?"

"No. For picking a fight with you. But I couldn't think of any other way."

Del, chin resting on the top of my shoulder, held her silence.

"You did know," I said, aware of her stiffness. "You realized, didn't you, what I was doing? Out there on the deck, in front of all the crew?"

After a moment she inhaled. "A man is often the most convincing in what he says when he *means* what he says."

"Del—"

"That was no lie, Tiger, what you said. That was not for effect. You may have intended to mislead them, but you did not mislead me. I will say it again: you have no subtlety in you. You are honest in all things, even when you lie." She set the flat of her hand against my chest and stepped away so that she could look me in the eye. "You have an honest heart. And that is what you spoke from."

This was not exactly heading in the expected direction. I tried again. "Del—"

"You meant this as much as you meant it when you repudiated all the honor codes of Alimat." Her voice was oddly flat, as if it were hard for her to speak. "When you stepped out of the circle that day before Sabra, before Abbu Bensir and all the other sword-dancers, renouncing—"

"I know what I did," I said sharply, cutting her off.

"You meant that," Del declared, "and you meant this."

I exhaled noisily, expelling all the air from my lungs, then scrubbed the heel of one hand across my forehead. "Yes, well, we all do things we have to. Even if we don't want to."

Her tone now was almost gentle. "You used me, Tiger."

I didn't shirk it. "To make them believe. Yes."

Del nodded. "As I used you to buy my way back onto Staal-Ysta."

I blinked. This was an *entirely* different topic.

"I used you, manipulated you," she said. "Offered you to them, like meat on a platter. I bought my way into a place I could no longer go, because of oaths and codes I once honored."

"To see your daughter." Whom I had not at the time known existed.

"I felt it worth the price," Del agreed. "The—risk. But I was wrong. I never should have used you so poorly."

I shrugged, discomfited as much by her emotions as by such painful recollections. "That's in the past, bascha."

"You might have left me at any time. No doubt some people would have counseled you to. Some would have named you mad, to stay with me in such circumstances. What I did was—unconscionable. Unforgivable."

I tried to be offhand. "Well, there's no accounting for a man's folly when a woman is involved."

Del's bittersweet smile was of brief duration. "Or a woman's, when a child is involved."

"So," I said after a moment, "we're even."

"Are we?"

"We've done things to—and *for*—one another." I hitched my shoulders briefly. "And will, I assume."

"Do things to and for one another?"

"Well, yes. It seems to be our habit."

Del nodded. "And knowing that," she said, "you will perhaps forgive me."

Oh, hoolies . . . "*Now* what have you done?"

"I have undertaken my own seduction."

The first mate? But the captain had said the man lacked testicles!

Del read my expression. "No," she said, "not like that. Why do you assume the obvious?" Then she answered herself immediately and matter-of-factly. "Because you are male." She went on before I could raise a protest beyond opening my mouth. "There is the seduction of the mind as well as of the body. It requires subtlety. It requires duplicity." She pressed both hands against her breast. "And both of those live here."

"Now, bascha, I don't think that's an accurate summation of—"

"Take pride in that you were convincing," she said. "I believed you. That's what you wanted—*needed*—so the others would believe as well. And so I do believe, and now so do they."

"But it was only to make the captain think we were fighting. So that it might seem more likely I'd look to her, to make you jealous."

"That would be a logical assumption, yes," Del agreed, "but I have said she is not a stupid woman. She will not be taken in by ordinary means."

"You calling me ordinary?"

"Surely the gods would curse me if I said such of a jhihadi." She doesn't miss anything, this woman. "So of course I will never do so. Ordinary you are not." Her mouth tensed into a flat, thin line as she thought of something, then relaxed. "And I have taken pains to make certain the first mate knows it."

Alarmed now, I blurted it. "What have you done, Del?"

"Undertaken to tell him the truth of you."

"The—truth?"

"So far as we know it." Pale brows arched. "We have established that truth is much more convincing."

"*What* truth?"

"That you may be Skandic. That we believe you are. That a man appeared to believe you were, when he saw you. That we are—were—sailing to Skandi to investigate."

None of it sounded terribly fascinating. "Why would the first mate care about any of this?"

"Because he said so."

I thought that over, weighing scenarios. "In what way?"

"In the way of a man who desires coin."

"Now wait a minute, bascha. Apart from making some coin off me in the slave markets—and you'd probably bring more—there're not many options."

"He came to me, Tiger. He asked questions about you. Because I was angry, I answered them."

"Angry." One should always be careful when Del admits to anger. "In what *way* were you angry, what questions did he ask, and how did you answer them?" Better to string the whole thing together, or this might take all day. "And what did he say once you had answered them?"

"He was—unsurprised."

That made me uneasy. "Unsurprised about what? Me? You?" I raised a silencing hand. "Never mind that. Let's go back to the questions before that one. The ones about you being angry, what he asked, and what you said."

"I was angry in just the way you intended me to be, when you made that scene on the deck," she said simply. "He asked who you were, where you were from, who your parents were—"

I interrupted sharply. "And did you tell him I don't know?"

"I told him the truth, Tiger. As I had decided—but also because I had no choice."

"What do you mean, no choice?"

"It was the only way I could think of to keep you alive."

I growled frustration. "What in hoolies—"

She continued steadily. "He says there is no doubt you are indeed Skandic—*io*Skandic, he called you—and that he will speak to his captain about taking you there."

This sounded suspicious. "Just like that?"

"Well, no," she confessed. "They are renegadas, after all."

"Ah." It made more sense now. "For a price."

"But you do not have to pay it."

"Well, that's a relief! Seeing as how I have nothing to pay it with!" I scowled at her. "Spill it, bascha. What in hoolies is going on?"

Del hitched her shoulders. "He said they would make a plan, he and his captain, and then they would tell us."

"Oh, *that* sounds promising!" I caught the string of sandtiger claws tied around my neck and yanked it straight; one of the curved claws had caught in my hair. "Did he tell you her father is a slaver?"

"This has nothing to do with slavery," Del said gently. "It has to do with a boychild born in the Southron desert of parents he never knew, who grew to become a man who grew to become a jhihadi— and who apparently looks enough like a man *from* Skandi that others speak to him in that language."

"But we don't *know* that I—"

"He says you are. And I believe him."

"Why? What has he done to earn your trust?"

"I don't trust him," she explained coolly. "I said I *believed* him. And it is for what he is, rather than what he says." Del smiled a little, studying me. "You see a bald man with rings in his eyebrows and blue tattoos on his head."

"That pretty much sums him up, I'd say."

"But *I* see a man who is of the same bone, the same body, even the same eyes. With hair, Tiger, he could be you." She paused. "Though he is older than you, and the hair might show more silver."

"Oh, thanks." I glared at her, thinking about the silvering strands she'd begun finding in mine. "You think we're long-lost brothers, or something?"

She made a dismissive gesture. "No, no, of course not. That would be too much like a tale told around the fire-cairn."

"No kidding!"

She looked straight at me. "I said there was no telling who you might be related to. Kings even. Or queens."

"What, no godlings? I'm a messiah, after all."

Del smiled blandly.

"In the name of—" But I broke off as the door opened. Del looked over my shoulder. I swung in place, badly wishing I had my sword. I felt naked without it.

Blue-headed Nihko stood in the doorway. With him was the captain. "Come out," she said. "We have decided what it is we shall do with you."

"Feeding me would be nice."

"Oh, no." The red-haired woman smiled, glanced pointedly at my waist. "Best you lose the extra flesh."

I swore as Del—thank you, bascha—smothered a laugh.

"Come out," the captain repeated. "Or shall I have Nihko *fetch* you out?"

Nihko and I eyed one another. We had history now. I'd up-ended him on the island, he'd laid hands on me. We were, as Del and the captain had noted, similar in size, in bone, in strength. It would undoubtedly be a vicious—and very long—fight.

Or else a very short one, equally devastating.

We reached the same conclusion at the same time. And offered one another faint smiles of acknowledgment as well as unspoken promise.

The captain shot an amused glance at Del. "I might pay to see it. Would you?"

"No," Del answered promptly. "But I would collect the coin—and a portion of the wagers—for allowing others to."

"Nah," I retorted. "It would be over before anyone could pay."

Nihko smiled blandly. "Likely so. You would be too busy losing the contents of your belly to offer a decent fight."

I scowled at him blackly, mostly because I *was* feeling a trifle queasy. Again.

"Out," the captain said crisply. "Up on deck. Now."

Up on deck, now, in the clean, salt-laden air, I could breathe again. A stiff breeze whipped hair into my eyes. I crossed my arms and leaned my spine against the rail, affecting a nonchalance I didn't really feel, especially with the deck heaving beneath us and the rail creaking a protest under my weight. But such poses are necessary; and either they believe you, or they know exactly what you're about.

Nihko and his captain knew exactly what I was about. But they let me have the moment regardless. "So?" I began. "What is it you plan to do with us?"

The woman's pale eyes glinted. "I told you to find a way to buy your freedom."

"You did."

She glanced briefly at Del, as if seeking an indication I'd told her what the captain had said about being interested in my companion rather than in me. Del, who didn't know any such thing—we hadn't gotten that far, and I wasn't certain I'd have told her anyway—merely looked back. Waiting. Which she does very well.

After a moment the captain smiled a little and met my eyes. "And so this woman has done it for you."

I didn't know if that was for my benefit, or the truth. She knew *I* knew what she meant, even if Del didn't; if Del did, well, it made for an interesting little tangle.

I refused to play. Besides, as far as she knew, Del and I weren't on friendly terms. "Whatever the woman offered was without my knowledge."

"Men do precisely that for women often enough." But the captain indicated the first mate with a tilt of her head. "Nihko says you are Skandic."

"I might be. But Nihko doesn't *know* that I am. No one does, including me."

"That does not matter. Explain it, Nihko."

Blue-head explained it.

By the time he finished, I was shaking my head. "It'll never work. It *couldn't* work. Not possible."

"Everything is possible." The captain was unperturbed by my refusal. "Certainly this is. Because it might be true." She smiled, eyes bright with laughter. "A man with no past could be anything at all."

"Or nothing." I shook my head again. "I'm not a mummer. I could never pull this off."

She captured whipping hair, pulled it forward over a shoulder and began to braid it into control. "There is no mummery involved. We are not asking you to be—or to behave as—something you are not."

"That's *exactly* what you're asking."

"You present yourself as what you are." The captain paused in her braiding to meet my eyes. "Or, rather, *we* present you as what you are."

"Your captive?"

Unprovoked, she went back to braiding hair. "I am known in the city."

I made it into an insult. "Undoubtedly."

She continued serenely. "I am known for precisely what I am. It would be accepted by all the families as truth: Prima Rhannet seeks to spit in her father's eye by parading herself, her crew, and her lifestyle throughout the city: an ungrateful, unnatural, outcast daughter who ignores custom to present herself to one of the finest families *of* the city."

"That's you," I said. "What about me?"

"Who presents herself to one of the finest families of the city in order to reap a reward of such incredible value that in one undertaking the ungrateful unnatural outcast daughter outdoes her father." She did something with the end of the braid to keep it intact—how women do that is beyond me—and waited for me to respond.

I nodded, understanding. "This is personal."

"It is many things," she—Prima—said. "It is a means to make coin; the reward would be incalculable. It is a means to spit in my father's eye; because no matter that I was so crassly rewarded, I would still be acknowledged as the woman who returned to the Stessa family something of great value: the means to continue the line."

"A line near extinction, as you have explained it." I shook my head. "It will never work." I glanced at Del. "Tell her."

"But it might," Del said mildly.

So much for help from *that* quarter.

"Nothing need 'work,' " Prima elucidated. "It need only be believed."

"For how long?"

"Long enough for us to receive the reward, accept the public gratitude of the Stessa metri, to hear of my father's resentment, to resupply the ship . . ." She made a graceful gesture with one hand. ". . . and sail away again."

"Leaving me behind?"

"Leaving you behind with a dying old woman—a dying old *rich and powerful* woman—whose only goal now is to find a legitimate way to continue the family line. If you see no advantage in that, you are truly a fool."

I shook my head definitively. "Never work. I won't do it."

Prima Rhannet arched sun-gilded brows. "No?"

"No."

Nihko promptly hooked my feet out from under me and heaved me over the rail.

Water is hard. It felt like a sheet of hardpacked dirt when I landed, smashing into it flat on my back. For a moment nothing in my brain or body worked. I was so shocked I didn't even breathe—and then I realized I couldn't.

Water is *hard*. And when you land in—or *on*—it the way I did, taken completely unaware and utterly inexperienced with such things as flying followed by swimming, you get the air knocked right out of your lungs.

Then, of course, I sank.

Chapter 7

After I had swallowed enough saltwater to founder a dozen ships, I felt hands touching me. Pinching me. But I'd already exhausted strength with remarkably dramatic and equally ineffective struggles, and had reached the point where it seemed much easier simply to let go. Because the lungs weren't working at all anymore, and pretty much everything had grayed to black.

Something seized my hair. It yanked. Then something else pinched my chest again, and *it* yanked.

Not breathing didn't bother me in the least—until I was hauled by rope up the side of the ship, banging dangling limbs; jerked painfully over the rail; dumped unceremoniously on the deck. Whereupon someone set about pummeling my abdomen and ribs until I felt certain the cook was simply tenderizing my hide before chopping it up and tossing it into the pot.

About this time my lungs decided they wanted to work again, and in the middle of whooping for air, my belly expelled the ocean.

This time several hands shoved me over onto my side, so I wouldn't choke. Supposedly. I'd already gagged and coughed and choked enough to die three times over. But eventually the spasms passed, air made its way back into abused lungs, and I lay there in a tangle of knotted rope, sprawled facedown on the deck with absolutely no part of me beyond those lungs capable of moving.

Someone bent over me. I felt forearms slide beneath my armpits, then elbows hooked. I was heaved up from the deck like so much refuse and set upright on my feet with belly pressed against the rail and held firmly in place, where I was permitted to view what had very nearly been my grave. It didn't look any better from above than it had from inside.

"The ocean is large," Prima Rhannet said lightly, "and between here and Skandi there is much of it. Shall we begin again?"

I was so muddled with the aftermath of confusion, shock, and near-drowning that I could barely remember my name, let alone what we were talking about. Standing upright seemed a fair achievement. Speaking was beyond me.

"Is he always this stubborn?" she asked.

Del said, "Yes."

That raised a croak of protest from me. Where in hoolies was *she* as they heaved me into the ocean?

"Perhaps you might suggest to him that he had best do what we ask," Captain Rhannet said. "This was your idea, after all."

I realized it was Nihko who pinned me against the rail. Or held me up, depending on your point of view. I was wet. So was he. One big hand was knotted into my hair, holding my skull still. Wobbly as I was, it wouldn't take much to dump me overboard. Again.

"Stubborn," he said, "or stupid."

"Well," Prima observed, "the same has been said of you."

The first mate laughed. "But none of them has lived to repeat the calumny."

Calumny. A new word. I'd have to ask Del what it meant.

"So," the captain began, talking to me this time, "shall you count the fish for us again?"

I spat over the side. *That* for counting fish.

Of course, it was much less intended as an insult than the clearing of a throat burning from seawater and the belch that had brought it up. I did the best I could with the voice I had left. "Being rich," I managed, "has its rewards."

Nihko grunted and turned me loose. I promptly slid to the deck and collapsed into a pile of strengthless limbs and coils of prickly rope.

After a moment, Del squatted down beside me. "They're gone, Tiger."

Here. Gone. What did it matter?

"You can get up now."

I wanted to laugh. Eventually I managed to roll from belly to back. The sun was overhead; I shut my eyes and draped an arm across my face. "I think I'll just . . . lie here for a while. Dry out."

"I expected them to beat you up," she explained, "not throw you over the side."

Ah. Vast difference, that.

"But now they'll take us to Skandi, which is where we meant to go in the first place, and we can get on about our business. I think it is easier than seducing people who may not be seduceable, and trying to steal weapons from large men who wish to keep them."

I lifted my arm slightly and squinted into the face peering down from the sky. Against the sun, she was an indeterminate blob. "This was your idea of keeping me alive?"

She appeared to find no irony in the question. "Yes." A pause. "Well, not precisely *this*."

"Was that you who pulled me out of the water?"

"Nihko did."

"He was the one who flung me into it."

"Well," Del said, "I suppose it was rather like watching a bag of gold sinking out of reach."

"And where in hoolies were *you* while this was going on?"

"Watching."

"Thank you."

"You're welcome." She put her hand on my shoulder and patted it. "It takes longer than you think to drown, Tiger."

Well, *that* made all the difference in the world.

"So," I said rustily, "we scam a dying old woman who happens to be very rich, and very powerful, with no living heirs but the grandson of a distant cousin from an offshoot branch of the family she detests—and then Prima Rhannet and her Blue-Headed Boy will turn us loose."

"That is the plan," Del affirmed.

"Nothing to it," I croaked, and dropped the arm over my eyes again.

Several days later, at dawn, I stood at the bow of the ship as we sailed into Skandi's harbor. There were, I'd learned, *two* Skandis. One was the island. One was the city. To keep them straight, most people referred to the city as the City. This had moved me to ask if there was only one city on the island, because if there were more, calling one city City among several other cities struck me as unnecessarily confusing, but Nihko Blue-head and Prima Rhannet simply looked at me as if everyone in the world knew Skandi was Skandi and Skandi was City and all the other cities were cities. Period.

I then reminded them that if I were to portray myself as a long-lost relative of some old *Skandic* lady, in line to inherit all her *Skandic* wealth and holdings, it might be best if I, supposedly Skandic myself, knew a little something about Skandi and Skandi.

Whereupon Prima merely said that it would be best if I remained ignorant, because knowing a little might be more confusing than knowing nothing. Whereupon the first mate suggested I was admirably suited for the role just as I was.

So now I stood at the bow of the blue-sailed ship that had driven us into the reefs (thereby destroying our ship, our belongings, and very nearly ourselves); abducted us from an island (and from my horse!); and now planned various nefarious undertakings with some poor little old lady who wasn't long for the world. A world that was, to me, markedly alien, if only to look at. I suppose one harbor is very like another. But this one struck me as— creative.

Skandi itself was an island. But it wasn't shaped like a proper island, supposing there is such a thing; it was in fact very much a *ruin* of an island, the leavings of something once greater, rounder. This island was not like any other I'd seen on the way, because most of the island was missing.

Imagine a large round clay platter dropped on the floor. The entire center shatters into dust. Oddly, all that remains whole is the *rim* of the platter, but it's bitten through at one point. And yet Skandi's platter rim isn't flat. It juts straight up from the ocean as a curved collection of cliffs, layer upon layer of time- and wind-carved rock and soil, afloat, anchored by some unseen force far beneath the surface. And the platter, viewed from above, might better resemble a large cookpot, a massive iron cauldron, with the ocean its stew. We, a ship in the harbor, were one of the chunks of meat.

Del came up beside me. She gazed across the harbor that more closely resembled a cauldron, eyes moving swiftly as she took in the encroachment of island that opened its arms to us in a promised embrace. Our little chunk of meat floated now in the center of the giant cauldron, and I had the odd sensation that the invisible giant looming over our heads might spear us with his knife as a delicacy.

"It's a crown," Del mused. "A crown of stone, encircling a woman's head, and the water is her hair."

That sounded a lot more picturesque than my stewpot. "Not a very *attractive* crown."

"No gold? No precious stones?" Del smiled briefly. "But there is the City, Tiger. Is it not jewel-like?"

Well, no. Unless Del's giantess with her crown of stone was clumsy, because it looked to me as if she'd dropped her box of pretty rocks and spilled them over the edge of her skull.

Skandi was stewpot, crown, broken platter. From the water the remains of land reared upward into the sky, ridged and humped and folded with all its bones showing. The interior of the island itself was broken, cruelly gouged away, so that the viscera of the body gleamed nakedly in the sun.

The jewels Del spoke of were clusters of dome-roofed buildings. A parade of them thronged the ragged edge of the island's summit, then tumbled over the side, clinging haphazardly to shelves and hummocks all the way down to the water's edge. There were doors in the rock walls themselves, wooden doors painted brilliant blue; there were blue doors, too, in lime-washed buildings growing out of the gouged cliff face. Against the rich and ruddy hues of soil and stone, the blue-and-white dwellings glowed.

"The vault of the heavens," Prima said, coming up on my other side. "The domes and doors are painted blue to honor the sky, where the gods live."

"I thought I wasn't supposed to know anything about Skandi."

She smiled, looking beyond me to the face of the island. "A man seeking his home may ask his captain about it."

"Ah." I nodded sagely. "And can this captain tell me what comes next?"

"Harbor fees," she said crisply. "Port fees. Inspection fees. Docking fees."

"Lot of fees, that."

Prima Rhannet's eyes laughed at me. "Nothing in this life is free. Even for renegadas."

"And after all these fees," I said, "what happens next?"

"Say what you mean," the captain admonished. "What happens to *you*."

"Us," I corrected.

Prima's brows arched. "You and me?"

"No, not you and me . . ." I jabbed a thumb in Del's direction. "Me and *her*."

The captain affected amazement. "But I thought you were having nothing to do with one another!"

"There are times," Del put in, "when we don't. Then there are times when we shouldn't, but we do."

"And times when you do because you think you should." Prima nodded, slanting a glance at me. "I thought as much. But did you really believe it would work, that performance?"

"Stupid people fall for a variety of things," I mentioned.

"Is that to be taken as flattery?"

I cleared my throat, aware of increasing frustration and a faintly unsettled belly. "Returning to the point at hand . . ."

"Oh, yes." She nodded, bright hair aglow in the sun. "What happens to you."

"Us," Del amended.

Hazel eyes were laughing at us. "But there will be no 'us.' "

I drew myself up in what many consider a quietly menacing posture.

This time the captain laughed aloud. "Do you believe I would permit you both to go ashore? Together?" She paused. "Do you believe that *I* do not believe you would not try to escape?"

"I don't believe I care what you believe," I retorted. "The simple fact of the matter is, if Del doesn't come ashore with me, *I* don't go ashore with me. Or, for that matter, with you." I smiled at the petite woman. "And I don't think you're strong enough to throw me overboard."

As she shrugged, her blue-headed first mate appeared.

I promptly turned and latched onto the rail with both hands in the firmest grip I commanded. "If you have him try to toss me overboard again, I'll take a piece of your ship with me!"

Prima Rhannet looked worried. "No," she murmured, "we could not have that."

Whereupon Nihko closed thick arms around Del and tossed *her* overboard.

I heard the blurted cry of shock, followed by the splash. I still hung onto the rail, but not because I feared to follow her. Because, shocked, I couldn't let go. This I hadn't expected any more than she had.

I saw her head break the surface, then pale arms. She slicked hair back from her face and squinted up at me. Whereupon I grinned in immense relief, then turned upon the captain my sunniest smile. "Del, on the other hand, can swim. And *now* we're not all that far from the shore."

That stripped the smirk from Prima's face. She glanced sharply at her first mate. "Nihko, go."

I spun in place, blocked his way, jammed a rigid elbow deeply into his abdomen just below the short ribs. As he began to bend over in helpless response, I brought the heel of my right hand up hard against the underside of his chin. Teeth clicked together, eyes glazed over, and he staggered backward.

It was beginning as much as ending. Prima was a small woman, no match for a man as big as me, but she knew it. Which is why she did not attempt to threaten me with her knife. She simply stabbed me with it, cutting into the back of my thigh.

I yelped, swore, started to swing on her—but by this time

Nihko was upright again. He caught me before I could so much as see Prima's expression. I was slammed hard into the rail and bent backward over it. One broad, long-fingered hand was on my throat.

He did not squeeze. He did not crush. He did not in any way attempt to strike or overpower me. He simply put his hand on the flesh of my throat, and it began to burn.

I heard Prima say something about throwing a rope down. I heard her shout to Del, something about rejoining us if she knew what was good for me. Briefly I thought Del should just swim for it, but I doubted she would; and anyway, I had more on my mind than whether Prima would fish Del out of the water or if Del would condescend to *be* fished. My teeth were melting.

I thought my head might burst. Not from lack of air, because I had plenty of it. But from heat, and a pressure on the inside of my skull that made me sweat with it, gasping at the pain. It was if someone had set a red-hot metal collar around my neck.

Nihko murmured something. I didn't have the first idea what he said, because it was a language I didn't speak. Something muttered, something chanted. Something *said*.

Then he took his hand away, the heat died out of my head, and I fell down upon my knees.

"Io," he said.

I put one trembling, tentative hand to my neck, expecting to feel blood, fluids, charring, and curled, crusted flesh. But all I felt were the sandtiger claws upon their leather thong, and healthy flesh beneath.

"Io," he repeated, in satisfaction commingled with anticipation.

"Go to hoolies," I responded, though the voice was hoarse and tight.

"You go," Nihko suggested.

I recalled the rash around my wrist, triggered by his touch. And now the heat in my head, the blazing of my flesh. "What are you?"

The rings in his eyebrows glinted. "IoSkandic."

"And what precisely does that mean?"

He displayed white teeth. "Secret."

I got my legs under me and wobbled to my feet. "The word means secret, or it *is* a secret?"

"Nihko," Prima said, and he turned from me.

A rope hung over the side, taut against the rail. The captain glanced at me, then at Nihko; he leaned over, grasped the rope, pulled it up even as Del herself clambered over the rail. Fair hair was slick against her skull, trailing down her back in a soaked sheet. The ivory-colored leather tunic, equally soaked, stuck to her body and emphasized every muscle, every curve.

Prima Rhannet stared. Nihko Blue-head did not. That more than anything convinced me the captain had not lied: the first mate was not, as men are measured, a man anymore. And the *woman* was more than a little attracted to the woman who slept with me.

I had seen it in men before. With someone who looks like Delilah, it's a daily event. But I had never seen the reaction in a woman before. Generally the women of the South are shocked and appalled by Del's sword, her freedom of manner and dress, her predilection for saying what she thinks no matter how it sounds. Some of the younger women were vastly fascinated, even if they had to be subtle about it lest they alert or alarm their men. Or they are intensely jealous. But no woman I'd ever seen had looked at Del the way a man looks at Del.

Until now.

And I hadn't the faintest idea how to feel about it.

There were jokes about it, of course. Crude, vulgar, male jokes, men painting lurid pictures with words, suggesting activities for women *with* women designed to titillate. And of course there were men who preferred men, or boys, who also prompted jokes. But *seeing* a woman react to a woman the way a man reacts to a woman was—odd.

Should I be jealous? Angry? Insulted? Upset? Should I say something? Do something?

Did *Del* recognize it?

Maybe. Maybe not. I couldn't tell. She was wearing her blandest expression, even sheened with water. And *would* a woman be aware of another's interest? Did Del even know such things existed?

For that matter, did Del have any idea what kind of reaction she provoked in men? I mean, she knew they reacted; how could she not? Most men aren't very subtle about it when everything in them—and on them—seizes up at the sight of a beautiful woman of immense physical appeal. There'd been enough comments made about and to Del that she couldn't be oblivious. On the whole she ignored it, which didn't hurt my reputation any: the gorgeous Northern bascha was so well-serviced by the Sandtiger that she neither noticed nor looked at another man.

But then, for a long time I hadn't known she'd even notice or look at *me*.

The way Prima Rhannet was looking at her.

"Well," I said brightly, trying to sound casual, "just what did you have in mind, then? You and I are to go ashore and go visit this old lady?"

Prima blinked, then looked at me. "No. I will stay here, aboard ship. It is best that Nihko goes as my representative. Him the metri will see. And once she understands what I have to offer, she will see me as well."

"And why will this—metri?—see him, but not you?"

Prima smiled faintly. "I have told you what I am. The ungrateful, unnatural, outcast daughter of a slaver. I am not of the proper family for the Stessa metri."

"But she'll see him?" I jerked a thumb at Nihko. "He's an ugly son of a goat with rings in his eyebrows and a hairless head painted blue. *That's* not unnatural?"

Nihko bared his teeth in an insincere smile. The captain looked amused. "She will see him because of what he is."

I prodded. "Which is?"

The first mate grinned in genuine amusement. "Secret."

I turned on my heel and stalked away, though it was somewhat ruined by the limp; the wound in the back of my thigh *hurt*. I couldn't go very far—we were on a ship, after all—but it made my point nonetheless.

Prima raised her voice. "Get dressed."

"In what?" I flung back over a shoulder. "All I've got in this whole gods-forsaken world is what I'm wearing!" Which wasn't much, being merely a leather dhoti and the string of claws. And blood trickling down my leg.

The captain shrugged elaborate dismissal. "Nihko will have something."

Nihko wasn't wearing a whole lot more than I was at the moment. But I shut my teeth together and followed him below, wanting very much to warn Del against—whatever.

Chapter 8

"Wait, wait," Del said crossly. "Let me look first."

Accordingly, I waited, swaths of lurid crimson silk and linen clutched in one hand. Having shed the dhoti, I wore absolutely nothing. Except my string of claws.

I arched brows and tilted my head in elaborate invitation. "You have something in mind?"

She flapped a hand at me. "Turn around."

"You prefer the back view?" I paused. "Or perhaps I should say, the *backside* view?"

Del whacked me across the portion of my anatomy under discussion. "Stop being uncouth. I'm trying to see that stab wound."

"Well, *that's* not any fun." I winced. "It'll do a lot better if you keep your fingers out of it."

"I've seen worse," she said after close inspection, "but it needs bandaging. Or you'll bleed all over your clothes."

"Not my clothes. *Nihko's* clothes. Do you really think I'd be caught dead in these things?"

"You are caught," she observed, commencing to tear spare linen, "but at least you're still alive. For the time being. And anyway, I've seen you in red before. It suits you."

I had once owned a crimson burnous, it was true, for meetings with tanzeers considering hiring me, or feasting me after a victory. It had even boasted gold borders and tassels. But I had never heard Del mention anything about me being suited before. "Does it?"

"Hold still." She began wrapping my thigh.

"Ummmm . . . maybe I'd better do that."

"Why?"

"If you don't know, just wait a minute. It'll be obvious—*ouch!*"

"Not anymore," she said crisply, knotting the bandage tightly. "Now, get dressed so you can accompany Nihko to this household. The sooner you are accepted as the long-lost heir, the sooner we'll be free of the renegadas."

"You act like you think I *will* be accepted as the long-lost heir," I accused, "and you know as well as I it's a load of—"

"—potential," Del put in. "Possibility and potential. Which need have nothing to do with this dying old woman—this metri?— but rather with the opportunity to get free of the renegadas once you are accepted by this metri."

"Leaving you in Prima Rhannet's clutches? Not a chance!"

Del, noting my vehemence, looked at me curiously. "It's no worse a danger to me than any other I've been in."

I had no reasonable explanation at hand (or at tongue), and began to hastily don clothing. Eventually I rather lamely settled on: "I'd hate to have any actions on my part jeopardize your life."

"After three years, you should know better. Any actions on your part *always* jeopardize my life."

"Yes, but . . ." I jerked the sash tightly around my waist and knotted the rich silk; Nihko apparently liked to wear good cloth while running ships aground. "I'm older, and wiser, and less fond of danger than I used to be. For me or for you."

"We don't have much choice," she pointed out. "They are going to take you to the Stessa metri, whatever that is, and keep me here as insurance against your escape. But that is precisely what you must do as soon as you have a chance. And meanwhile I will contrive a way to escape as well."

"You make it sound so easy!"

Del shrugged. "It's merely a matter of seeing the opportunity, and taking it. Or making it."

Considering I had planned to do precisely that by seducing the captain, I couldn't very well get specific with objections. Especially since I could think of no reasonable way to explain.

"I will find a way," Del said.

Having no answer to that and equally no explanation for why her presence aboard ship with its captain unsettled me, I glumly went out of the cubbyhole masquerading as cabin and took myself up on deck.

From up close, Skandi was even more impressive. Sharp-faced cliffs appeared as if some giant's hand had broken off huge chunks of raw land, leaving behind rough folds of visible horizontal layers, bands of multihued rock, soil, and mineral. And up that cliff, zigzagging back and forth in blade-sharp angles, was a track of some kind. Even from the deck I could see colored blobs moving on the track. Some ascended, some descended. People on foot, and smaller versions of what we call danjacs in the South, long-eared horselike animals used to carry loads. I suspected horses might make a better job of it by hauling carts up and down, but one glance at the narrowness of the track, the sharpness of its turns, and the steepness of the cliff convinced me the last thing I'd want to do was attempt to ride the stud up that trail. Maybe it was better to trust smaller loads to animals less minded to state dissenting opinions.

About halfway up the track, pocking the cliff face like a disease, were blue-doored holes dug out of the porous stone. No trees and little vegetation clung to the sides; the soil seemed disinclined to pack itself tightly around root systems, so that nothing got a foothold strong enough to encourage vast growth. What was there was pretty scrubby, and twisted back upon itself to huddle against the cliff as if afraid of heights.

"Homes," Prima said, coming up beside me.

I glanced at her, then stared back at the track. "Why would anyone choose to live in a hole?" Let alone put doors over the holes and paint them blue. "Why not build homes like those?" A gesture indicated the squat, white-painted dwellings with their hump-backed roofs.

"This island was born of smoke," she said simply, "and when

the gods decreed a place for Man was required, they made the smoke solid. But there were pockets in the smoke that became as holes in the rock. When the gods placed Man here, he was poor. He settled in the rudest shelter available." She smiled. "I was born in one of those caves."

"And did yours have a door on it?"

"Of course. We are civilized, Southroner."

"Ah. And should I assume that only the wealthy live in those?" This time I indicated the houses tumbling over the edge of the cliff like oracle bones.

"Only the wealthy live in those," she confirmed, "or those who aspire to wealth and behave as if the aspirations are already fulfilled."

"Your father?"

"My father aspired for a very long time. Eventually those aspirations *were* fulfilled."

"But not, I take it, in a line of work openly approved by the truly wealthy."

She grinned. "Oh, the truly wealthy detest my father and others like him. But they require slaves to work in the vineyards, on the ships, in the kilns. There are not enough of us who are freeborn."

"Or enough of you who wish to dirty your hands with hard work."

Prima held up both hands and displayed callused palms. "My hands are very dirty," she pronounced solemnly.

"And bloody," I said gently, "even when washed clean."

The humor faded from her eyes, but not the determination. "And how often do you wash the blood from yours?"

"I dance," I retorted. "Rarely do I kill."

"I steal," she said. "Rarely do I kill."

Impasse. I sighed and jerked my head toward the cliff. "Which one of those are we bound for, captain?"

"None of those," she answered. "The Stessa household is on top of the island, in the midst of the vineyards."

"Well," I said resignedly, "at least they'll have something to drink."

The captain laughed. "Do you take nothing seriously in this world?"

"I take you *very* seriously."

She eyed me sidelong. "No, I do not believe so. In fact, you have no idea at all what to think of me."

"You ran our ship aground and plucked us off the island like so much ripe fruit," I remonstrated, "which is not precisely easy to do, plus you had me heaved me over the side of this ship—which also is not easy to do—and nearly drowned me. Not to mention the hole you poked in the back of my leg. Why shouldn't I take you seriously?"

"Because you are a Southroner."

"Ah-hah!" I stabbed the air with a forefinger. "But I'm really Skandic, am I not?—or we would not be undertaking this deception of a dying old woman designed to gain you coin. And anyway, what do *you* know about Southroners?"

"You very probably are Skandic," she agreed, "in blood and bone, if not in mind, which is definitively Southron. As for what I know about men like you, you forget I am the daughter of a slaver. As heir, I was trained in the business from childhood."

I very nearly asked if her father had sired no sons—and checked abruptly as I realized that kind of question would back up her argument. Which was not a particularly comfortable realization on my part. I scowled.

"I saw many Southroners brought beneath my father's roof," Prima continued. "Not a man among them respected women."

As annoyed with myself as with her, I challenged sharply. "You don't even *know* me, captain. I submit that you are in no position to evaluate my mind."

"I was taught to evaluate men's minds as much as their bodies," she said serenely.

"As the daughter of a slaver," I shot back, "which somewhat limits your capacity to make a legitimate evaluation. Having been captured and made over into a slave when one was freeborn is not designed to bring out the best attitude in a man, you know?"

"*You* know," she answered. "You may be a sword-dancer now, and very likely freeborn—but sword blades do not leave the kind of scars your back bears."

"Which renders me somewhat more familiar with the experience than you. No slaver ever knows a slave's mind."

"And is that how you escaped? Because your owner did not know your mind?"

"I didn't escape. I *earned* my freedom." And bore other scars to show for it as well as a name; the sandtiger I'd killed had been devouring children of the tribe who had made me a slave.

"As my crew earned theirs," Prima said quietly. "But there is more inflexibility to a Southron man's mind than what slavery may cause. And if you are truly as free in thought as you suggest, you will admit it."

"Now *that's* a double-edged sword if I ever saw one. Cursed if I do, cursed if I don't."

She grinned. "Then you may as well answer."

I glowered at her. "You're as inflexible, captain."

"Why?"

"You said you prefer women. Isn't that inflexible?"

"*You* prefer women."

"Of course I do!"

"Then you are against men."

"I *am* a man—" I began.

"As your lovers," she clarified.

"Hoolies, yes," I said fervently.

"Then we are the same, are we not?"

"How can we be the same? You're a woman. You're supposed to sleep with men, not with other women!"

"Why?"

"Because that's how it's supposed to be!"

"Is it?"

"*Yes!*"

"Why?"

In frustration, I set fingers into my hairline and scratched vigorously. "Because that's just the way it is."

"For you."

"For *most* people!"

"What about the woman?"

"Which woman?"

"The one you sleep with." She paused. "The one you *currently* sleep with."

"Three years' worth," I snapped. "Don't assume I take our relationship lightly."

"But of course you do. Did you not intend to seduce me?"

I scowled. Cursed if I did, cursed if I didn't.

Her expression was impish. "And would you have pursued it had the captain been a man?"

"Hoolies, no!"

"Therefore because I was a woman I was judged fair game, and you assumed I would succumb to your charms the way so many other women have." She nodded. "An inflexible—and purely Southron—way of thinking."

She was tying me up in verbal knots. "Now, wait a minute—"

"Of course, were I a woman who desired men in her bed, I might well have allowed myself to be seduced. Because you *do* have a certain amount of charm—" Startled, I shut my mouth on an interruption. "—and you did approach the campaign with more integrity than another man might."

That made no sense. "Integrity? I thought you were accusing me of having no respect for women."

"Integrity. Because you were at pains to pick a fight with your woman so there was *reason* to look to me as an alternate bedmate, and because you did not approach me directly. It was, as I said, a campaign. And I respect that. It requires imagination and forethought."

"You yourself just said I picked a fight with Del. If you value truth, how can you respect that?"

Her eyes were steady. "You *would* rather drown than be made a slave again. A man may lie for effect, to manipulate, and while the truth served you, it was indeed truth."

"You know that, do you?"

"I am a very good judge of slaves—"

"I'm not—"

"—and you are no longer one in mind or body," she finished. "There is no need for you to lie."

It was time to take control of this discussion. "Then if you respect truth, let me offer you this." I paused, marking her calm expression and determining to alter it. "If you attempt to seduce Del, I'll take you apart. Woman or no."

Calmness indeed vanished, but was replaced by an open amusement I hadn't expected. "Male," she said, and "Southron. *So* male, and so Southron!"

"I mean it, captain."

"I know you do. Honesty, if couched as a threat. Save I wonder which frightens you more: that I will attempt to seduce her—or that she might accept."

I shook my head. "She won't."

"And so I offer to you my own truth, Southroner: I will let the woman decide what she will and will not do. It should be *her* decision, yes? Because anything else is a slavery as soul-destroying as that which you experienced."

The Southroner in me hated to admit she was right. The man who had accompanied Del for the last three years, thereby learning truths he'd never imagined, did admit it—if privately—and could muster no additional argument that contained validity.

"Well," I said finally, "at least you've got to give me credit for threatening you the same as I would a *man*."

Prima Rhannet's generous mouth twitched, but she had the good grace not to laugh aloud.

It was midmorning as Del stood at the rail by the plank, waiting silently. I saw the stillness of her body, the posture of readiness despite that stillness, and knew she, as I, missed her sword badly.

Or even *a* sword. We'd both of us lost our true swords: I three years before, when Singlestroke had been broken; Del to the maelstrom of angry sorcerers who considered themselves gods. She had broken that sword, the jivatma named Boreal, to save my life, and nearly extinguished her own. Meanwhile, I had also lost the sword I'd made in Staal-Ysta. It was, in fact, buried in the rubble that covered Del's broken jivatma. We had purchased new swords, of course—only a fool goes weaponless—but neither of them had suited us beyond fulfilling a need. And now we had none at all, thanks to the renegadas.

Two of those renegadas waited just behind Del, as ready as she to move if necessary. I knew by the expression in her eyes that she would not make it necessary. Not yet. Not until after I was off the ship and on firm ground again, where no one could toss me into the water. She would permit me to risk myself in a true fight, but not to drowning.

Nihko came up behind me; behind him, his red-haired captain, with gold glinting in her ears and around her throat. I grimaced, thinking of the plan, our circumstances; shook my head slightly, then stepped forward to bend my head to Del's.

Instantly four renegadas surrounded both of us. Hands were on Del, hands were on me. I was shoved down the plank toward the dock and nearly tripped, catching my balance awkwardly before I could tumble headfirst into the sea. By the time that was avoided I was halfway down the plank, and when I turned to look at Del they had taken her away.

So much for good bye, good luck, or even a murmured "Kill 'em when you get the chance."

Nihko prodded me into motion as the plank bowed under our weight. I moved, not liking the instability over so much water. He escorted me off the ship, off the dock, onto the quay, and to the bottom of the track slicing its way up the cliff. From here I could look straight up and see the cliffside dwellings looming over my head like white-painted, blue-doored doom. The back of my neck prickled; the haphazard manner of construction made it appear as though everything rimming the cliff might fall down upon my head at any given moment.

"One good shake," I muttered.

Nihko glanced at me. "And so there was."

"What?"

"The histories says once Skandi was whole, and round, not this crescent left behind."

I gazed at the cliff face of the crescent uneasily. "What happened to it?"

"This was a place built of smoke," Nihko began.

Having no patience with stories about gods, I interrupted rudely. "I know all about that. Your captain already gave me the speech."

"Then you should understand that what the gods do, they can also undo." He gestured. "What was smoke became smoke again."

Hoolies, but I hate cryptic commentary! With exaggerated patience I inquired, "And?"

He turned, gesturing into the harbor behind us. "Do you see that smoke? The small islands?"

I had marked them, yes. Two crumpled, blackened chunks of land that appeared uninhabitable, in the middle of the cauldron. Rather like burned-down coals after a light rain, exuding faint drifts of smoke into the morning air.

Nihko nodded. "They are the children of the Heart of the World."

"The—what?"

"Heart of the World. It lies now beneath the sea. But the children have risen to see whether this place is worthy of their presence once again."

I gazed at him steadily. "You do realize none of this makes any sense at all."

He grinned cheerfully, unoffended. "It will."

"Meanwhile?"

"Meanwhile, the island was turned into smoke again. The land bled. Burned. Became ash. The island shook and was split asunder. You see what remains."

Not much, if what he said was true. But it seemed unlikely that such a calamity could really happen. I mean, land bleeding? Turning to ash and smoke? Shaking itself apart? More than unlikely: impossible.

Of course, I'd said a lot of things were impossible—and then witnessed them myself.

"We have maps," he said quietly, seeing my skepticism. "Old maps, and charts, and drawings. Histories. This island was once far more than it is."

Rather like Nihko himself, if what Prima had said of his castration was true. I stared at the cliff again. "I suppose we're going up that poor excuse for a trail?"

"But on four feet," he replied.

"You want me to ride one of *those?*" "Those" being the danjac-like beasties that rather resembled something crossed with a small horse and a very large dog.

"It will save time," the first mate explained, "and keep our feet clean. Otherwise we will slip and slide in molah muck all the way up, like the lesser folk." A tilt of his shaven head indicated men and women on foot toiling up and down the cliff.

"Molah muck?"

"They are molahs." He waved at a string of the creatures waiting patiently at the bottom of the track. "And they can carry four times their weight without complaint."

"I'd just as soon carry my own weight, thanks. I'm kind of used to it."

"Molah," he said gently, and I thought again about how his grip had made my wrist weep, and my throat flesh burn. "And if you are presenting yourself to the wealthiest metri on the island as a man who may be her heir, you shall ride."

"Fine," I said glumly, surveying the drooping animals tied to a rope beside the trail, "we ride. But it looks to me like we'll be dragging our feet in the muck anyhow, all the way up."

Chapter 9

We did not actually drag our feet in molah muck all the way up, though it was a close call. Initially I yearned for stirrups, since dangling long legs athwart a narrow, bony back only barely padded by a thin blanket was not particularly comfortable, but I realized soon enough that stirrups would have made it worse. Riding with legs doubled up beneath my chin isn't a favored position for a man with recalcitrant knees.

For a sailor, Nihko Blue-head rode his molah with a grace I didn't expect; but I reflected that balancing atop the beastie wasn't so much different from maintaining balance aboard a wallowing ship, and therefore he had an advantage. I was more accustomed than he to riding an animal, perhaps, but horses and molahs have vastly different ways of going. Horses basically stride, planting large hooves squarely on the ground. Molahs—mince. On something that feels disturbingly like tiptoes. Very rapidly, so that one ascends at a pace that can only be called a jiggle.

I reflected that perhaps Nihko had no testicles because he'd ridden a molah up this cliff once too often.

As we climbed, tippytoeing our way around people on foot, I cast glances back the way we'd come. From increasing height it became very clear just how round the island had once been. Despite all of this silly talk about gods and smoke turning into stone (and back again), there was no question that once there had been more to the island. And it struck me as oddly familiar to Southron-raised eyes: what Nihko and I climbed was the vertical rim of a circle. The interior below, a brilliant greenish blue, was where two men would meet in the center for a sword-dance.

If they could walk on water.

Me, I couldn't, any more than I could magic weapons out of the air. What I *could* do was change the sand to grass.

Or so the legend went that others in the South viewed as prophecy. Of course, *I* put no stock in such nonsense. Even when a handful of deep Desert dwellers, led by a holy man who claimed he could see the future, claimed I was the jhihadi of the prophecy, the man meant to save the South from the devouring sands.

Horse piss, if you ask me.

And that's precisely what gave me the idea to dig channels in the desert and bring water from where it was to places it was not. Horse piss. Thanks to the stud.

Who would have been a *lot* more comfortable to ride up this gods-cursed track than a stumpy-legged, bony-backed, mincing little molah.

Hoolies, I wouldn't even mind getting bucked off if I only had the stud!

Then I shot a quick glance down the cliff. Well, maybe not.

It struck me then, as we climbed, that this was what I had come for. To see Skandi, this place I might be from, if indirectly; I'd been born in the South, but bred of bones shaped in a different land. Here? Possibly. As Del had remarked, as Prima Rhannet, as even *I* had noticed, Nihko and I were indeed similar in the ways our bodies were built, even in coloring, which seemed typical for Skandi.

And yet not everyone toiling up and down the track had green eyes and bronze-brown hair—or shaven heads decorated by blue tattoos, come to that. It was obvious, in fact, that not everyone walking the track was even Skandic, if Nihko and I were the prevailing body type; many were shorter, slighter, or tall and quite thin, with a wide variety in hair color and flesh tones. I'd grown accustomed to certain physical similarities in the South, where folk are predominantly shorter, slighter, darker, and in the North, where folk are as predictably taller, bigger, fairer. But here upon the cliff face walked a rainbow of living flesh.

And then I recalled that Skandi's economy depended on slave labor, from the sound of it, and I realized why the variety in size and coloring was so immense.

A chill tickled my spine. Here I'd come to a place that could well have bred my parents, and yet it was peopled as well by those unfortunates who had no choice but to service others who had the wealth, the power, the willingness to own men and women.

I'd been owned twice already. Once for all of my childhood and youth among the Salset, then again in the mines of the tanzeer Aladar, whom Del had killed to free me.

The South is a harsh and frequently cruel land. But it was what I *knew.* Skandi was nothing but a name to me—and now a rim of rock afloat in the ocean—and I realized with startling and unsettling clarity that I had, with indisputably childish hope, dreamed of a place that was perfection in all things. So that I would be born of a land and people far better to its children than the South had been to me.

A sobering realization, once I got beyond the initial pinch of self-castigation for succumbing to such morbid recollection. I knew better. Dreams never come true.

I shut my eyes at that. *My* dream had come true. The one I'd harbored in my soul for as long as I could recall: to be a free man. And I had won that freedom at last, had dreamed it out of despair and desperation into truth, at the cost of Salset children.

Guilt stirred, and unease. And then I thought again what I might have been had I remained with the Salset, and what I had become since earning my freedom.

As for what I was *now*—well, who knows? Sword-dancer, once. Now borjuni to some people. And, others would say; others *had* said: messiah.

Who was, just at this moment, captive to a man wearing a vast complement of rings in his eyebrows.

Eventually we reached the top of the cliff. Gratefully I began to hoist a leg across the molah's round little rump, but Nihko fixed me with a quelling look and told me to wait.

If he thought I was preparing to leap off the molah and sprint for freedom, he was wrong. I just wanted to stand on my own two feet again—and to be certain I hadn't permanently squashed my gehetties on the way up. I contemplated dismounting anyway—it was a breath-taking drop of three whole inches—but took a look around and decided I'd better not. I was barefoot, after all, and we had just arrived in a clifftop area full of molahs (and their muck), throngs of people, yelping dogs (and their muck), a handful of chickens, and a dozen or so curly-coated goats. And their muck.

All of whom saw Nihko aboard his molah and abruptly melted away.

Well, the *people* did; the chickens, goats, and dogs remained pretty much as they were. They were also a lot louder, now that every person within earshot had fallen utterly silent.

I saw widened eyes, surprise-slackened mouths, and a flurry of hand gestures. About the time I opened my mouth to ask Nihko what in hoolies was going on, he spoke. A single word only, very crisp and clipped, in a language I didn't know; I assumed it was Skandic. When a stirring ran through the crowd, he repeated it, then followed up the word with a brief sentence. Quick, furtive glances were exchanged, different hand gestures were now made close to the body so they weren't as obvious. But no one spoke. That is, except for one hoarse shout issued by someone I couldn't see.

A path was instantly cleared through the crowd. A man in a thin-woven, sun-bleached tunic came toward us. He carried a stamped metal basin in both hands. Lengths of embroidered cloth were draped across his arms, and strung over his shoulders was a wax-plugged, rope-netted clay bottle glazed blue around the lip. Puzzled, I watched as he knelt there in the dirt and muck and care- fully set down the basin. He unhooked the bottle, unstoppered it, poured water into the basin, murmured something that sounded like an invocation, then dipped the cloth in, meticulously careful that no portion of the fabric slipped over the side of the basin into the dirt.

All very strange—and it got stranger. He came to Nihko, bobbed his head briefly, deftly removed Nihko's shoes, and began to wash his feet.

Astounded, I stared. When finished, the man slipped the shoes back on Nihko's feet, rinsed the cloth in the basin, set it aside into a rolled-up, draining ball, then approached me with yet another embroidered length.

"Uh—" I began.

"You will allow it," Nihko said curtly.

I considered drawing my feet away, if only to spite the first mate. I considered sliding off the molah. I considered telling the basin-man with tone if not in a language he knew that I was fine with dirty feet; he didn't need to wash them for me; I'd take care of it myself when I found a public bath.

But I was in a strange place, ignorant of customs and their potential repercussions, and self-preservation prevailed. I clamped my mouth shut and let the man wash my feet.

He said something very quietly as he worked; remarking, I thought, over the healing cuts and scrapes. His hands were unexpectedly gentle, diffident. When I didn't answer, he glanced up at me briefly, waiting expectantly; when I shook my head once, he looked away immediately and completed his task without further speech. It became clear he was perplexed by my lack of shoes.

Nihko said something to him. The man blanched, collected the balled-up, soiled cloths, basin, and clay bottle, and hastily lost himself in the crowd.

I wiggled my clean toes, shot a glance at the first mate. "Wouldn't it make more sense to wash our feet *after* we get where we're going?"

Nihko smiled, but there was nothing of humor in it. "If you touch the ground with cleansed feet, you will seal yourself as one of them."

Them. "And I take it that is not a good thing?"

"Not if you wish to be sealed as heir to the Stessa metri."

I sighed. "What, are these Stessas too good to walk the streets like everyone else?" I looked pointedly at his feet. "Are you?"

"Oh, but *I* am not expected to walk anywhere," he said casually. "I am ioSkandic, and I am expected to fly."

I blinked. "Well, that would certainly save you the ride up the cliff."

One corner of his mouth quirked, but he offered no comment. I scowled. "You're serious."

"Am I?" His expression was privately amused. "And do you know me so well that you may judge such things?"

Ah, hoolies, it wasn't worth the breath to debate. "When exactly are we supposed to go to this infamous household?" I paused. "And do we walk, ride, or fly?"

His mouth twitched again. "Even in ignorance, you ridicule possibilities."

"No, I ridicule *you*. There's a difference."

"Ah. I am remiss in my comprehension." Without glancing around to see if anyone noticed, Nihko made a slight gesture. The crowd, which had begun to speak quietly among themselves, noticed. It fell silent once again. Once again, people flowed out of the way. This time it wasn't the man with basin and embroidered cloths who came to us, but an entirely different man, a wiry man on foot leading two dust-colored molahs hitched to a kind of bench-chair on wheels.

"What in hoolies is that contraption?"

"Transportation," Nihko answered.

"And here I thought you could fly."

"But you can't. Good manners require me to travel as you travel."

"Good manners? Or because I'm your prisoner?"

"Ah, but you are my prisoner only because you have not learned the ways to avoid such things." He gestured again. The man with the molah-cart came up to us, stopped his animals, then set about collecting a rolled mat from the underside of the cart, which he unrolled and spread upon the ground. "As my companion, you may go first." Nikho paused. "And do not soil your feet."

It was clear to me that after the ritual washing, followed by the laying out of the mat, it was vital I do as Nihko said. Despite the seeming meekness of the crowd, for all I knew any transgression would earn me a quick journey over the edge of the cliff, whereupon I would descend in a faster and more painful way than on molah-back, which was bad enough. So I got off the stumpy little beastie, making certain I ended up in the center of the woven mat, and moved toward the cart. Which, from up close, looked more like a bench-chair than ever. It was woven of twisted vine limbs, bound with thin, braided rope. The bench was padded with embroidered cushions, while the back was made of knotted limbs that once must have been green and flexible, but now were dried and tough.

The ground beneath me swayed. I reached out and caught hold of the bench, gripping tightly. I didn't feel sick, but my balance was definitely off. And yet no one around me seemed to notice that the ground beneath them was moving.

Nihko swung off his molah onto the mat with the ease of familiarity. He strode past me and stepped into the cart without hesitation, beckoning me to join him.

I clung a moment longer, still unsettled by poor balance. I saw Nihko's ring-weighted brows rise, and then he smiled. "The sea has stolen your legs," he said briefly, "but she will give them back."

Ah. Neither magic nor sickness. With an inward shrug I climbed into the cart. Good thing the molahs could carry four times their weight; Nihko and I together likely weighed close to five hundred pounds.

"Akritara," he said only, and I heard the murmuring of the crowd.

The molah-man rolled up his mat, slid it into a narrow shelf beneath the bench, and went to his animals. With a jerk and a sway the molahs began to move, and I wrapped fingers around twisted limbs. Two wheels did not make for stability; the balance was maintained by the rope-and-wood single-tree suspended between molah harness and the bench itself.

"So," I began as we jounced along, "just why *is* it we're not supposed to walk anywhere?"

"Oh, we will walk. But only on surfaces that have been blessed."

"Blessed?"

"By the priests."

"You have priests who bless your floors?"

"Priests who weave the carpets in the patterns of the heavens." He glanced skyward briefly.

I made a sound of disgust. "Let me guess: they're blue."

Nihko smiled. "Only their heads."

Of course I'd meant the rugs, but that no longer mattered in view of his comment. And his head. "Don't tell me *you're* a priest!"

His expression was serene. "If you can be a messiah, surely I can be a priest."

That shut me up. But only for a moment. "So, your Order makes a nice living supplying men to destroy ships, steal booty, and kill passengers?" I arched brows elaborately. "A rather violent priesthood, wouldn't you say?"

That earned me a baleful glance. And silence.

"So, what becomes of the mats at the end of the day? Doesn't the blessing wear out? Or does this poor man have to scrub the mat each night, before picking up passengers tomorrow?"

"He will scrub it, yes. And each first-day he will take it to the nearest priest to have the blessing renewed."

"Once a week."

"So I said."

"For a price, I assume."

"Do you know of anything in this life that bears no cost?"

"You're sidestepping," I accused, "like someone in the circle who doesn't want to start the dance. So, this man pays to have his mat blessed each week so that blue-headed folk like you don't have to walk in the dirt." I nodded. "Sounds like a racket to me."

Nihko scowled blackly. "You would name faith and service to the gods a *racket?*"

"Sure I would. Because it is."

His expression was outraged. "You blaspheme."

"But only if there *are* gods. And only if they care about such things." I shrugged. "I'm not certain they give a sandrat's patootie about anything we do. If they exist."

"You are disrespectful, Southroner."

"I am many things, Blue-head. So far the gods haven't bothered to complain."

"You are a fool."

"That, too."

With a mutter of disdain, he subsided into silence. I sighed and twisted to look back the way we'd come. Already the edge of the cliff receded. Beyond it I could see nothing but a blindingly blue sky, and wisps of steam rising from the smoking islands in the middle of the cauldron of blue-green sea.

Oh, bascha, I wish you were here. As much to share Skandi with me as to be free of Prima Rhannet.

After wending through the twists and turns of narrow, packed cart- and walkways, we left Skandi-the-City behind entirely. In its place was a rumpled land of worn, rocky hillocks made of dark, thin soil and heaps of pocked, crumbly stone. The top of the island swelled from the cliff toward the sunrise, crowned with a bulbous but smooth-flanked rise that could not possibly qualify as a mountain, and yet was paramount nonetheless. Between the city and the soft-browed peak stretched acres of land that had broken out in a plague of rounded, basketlike heaps of greenery. A rash of wreaths, set out in amazingly symmetrical rows. As we passed the field near-est the road, I leaned somewhat precariously over the edge of the cart to get a closer look.

Baskets. Big baskets. Big *living* baskets; the vine limbs had liter-ally been woven into a circle and groomed to grow that way per-manently. I realized the cart-bench itself was made of the same vine.

I had seen many strange plants in my life, having been North *and* South, but never vines coiled upon the ground into gigantic wooden pots. "What in hoolies are those?"

Nihko spared the edge of the track a glance. "Grapes."

"Grapes?" It astonished me. Every vineyard I'd ever seen boasted upright vines trained to grow along the horizontal, like a man standing with arms outstretched.

"Skandi is a land of winds," Nihko answered absently. "The vines here are too tender to be grown as other vines are, lest the wind strip them away. So they are cultivated low upon the ground."

There wasn't so much wind right now as to risk the vines. A breeze blew steadily, but it wasn't hearty enough to shred vegeta-tion. The baskets of woven grape vines, crouched upon the ground, barely stirred.

"So," I said, "just why is it we can't walk on the ground? Unless it's blessed, that is. Didn't you and I walk off the ship and across the quay to the bottom of the cliff?"

"The wind and saltwater rots the mats," Nihko explained, "or we would not be required to tolerate that soiling. Thus the custom of cleansing at the top of the cliff."

"But why would we be *soiled* just by walking?"

He glanced at me sidelong. "In your land, do your priests or kings set bare flesh to muck-laden ground?"

"We don't have kings," I said absently, "and all of the holy men I ever saw were willing to walk anywhere."

Nihko made a soft sound of disgust. "But they are foreign priests. I should not be surprised."

"You walk on the boat, priest. Or have you somehow had *it* blessed?"

"Ship," he corrected automatically. "And that is not Skandi. Nowhere is Skandi but Skandi."

"Ah. Doesn't count, then, what you do elsewhere, only what you do here." I nodded sagely. "Very convenient."

He hissed briefly. "Convenience has nothing to do with it!"

I laughed at him. "Here you are refusing to soil yourself by setting foot to ground that hasn't been properly blessed, and yet you carve open the bellies of men and spill out their innards, or lop their heads off. Isn't *that* just a little messy?"

Nihko sealed up his mouth again into a thin, retentive seam. He opened it only to say something curtly to the molah-man, whose head was turned slightly in our direction as if he listened closely. The man's head snapped back around in response to Nihko's tone. I saw him make a hand gesture, and then he tugged at the molahs to encourage a faster pace.

Something to be learned of Nihko Blue-head, it seemed. And if I got lucky, maybe it was something I could use against him.

Smiling, I relaxed against the woven-limb back and let the sun beat on my face.

Chapter 10

I'd thought this place called Akritara was a village, or settlement. Instead I discovered it was a collection of rooms all interconnected like a bulbous hive, sprouting multiple mounds of arching roofs and rounded domes on half-levels, like a pile of tumbled river stones. The arched roofs were painted white, the domes blue. Perched atop a hillock and surrounded by miles of ground-level wreaths of grapevine, Akritara looked precisely what it was: the preeminent household of Skandi.

So, Prima Rhannet and Nihko Blue-head didn't just intend to pass me off as a descendant of a wealthy house, but heir to *the* house.

"Never work," I murmured.

Nihko said nothing to me, though he spoke to the molah-man, directing him in a clipped, authoritative tone. On board the ship, as first mate, he'd been at ease with second-command, accepted by the crew as one of them and yet the captain's most trusted man. But ever since we'd set foot on Skandi, Nihko had behaved differently. I sensed a coiled power within him, an unspoken emotion, something akin to hostility. The people at the clifftop had clearly been afraid of him, making gestures against him—or perhaps against what he represented, with his shaven, tattooed head and silver brow rings. By admission he was a Skandic priest, and certainly he was treated as something other, something more, than merely a man. But there is a vast difference between being respected for your power, and feared.

"What did that mean?" I asked abruptly. "You said if I ever got tired of feeling sick, I should come to you."

He glanced at me briefly, then returned his attention to the drive before us. "Do you feel sick?"

Startled, I realized I didn't, and hadn't for some time. "Not any more."

"Then there is no need for me to answer."

"Sure there is. There's simple curiosity—"

"Enough," he said curtly, cutting me off. "There are other concerns facing you now than the condition of your belly."

Piecing bits together, I ignored that. "There's only one thing that has ever exerted that kind of—of manifestation, had that kind of effect," I continued thoughtfully. "Except for the occasional bouts with too much aqivi, or getting kicked in the head. But all of those had cause." Which had happened with more frequency than I preferred.

Steadfastly he ignored me.

I did not ignore him. "And now you say you're a priest."

No answer.

"But priests can be many things. Men of conviction. Fools. And men of magic."

Sunlight glinted off the silver in his eyebrows.

"Are you a fool, Nihko?"

That got him. He studied me a long moment, measuring my own conviction. Then his mouth hooked down briefly. "Some would say so."

"Magic," I said, "has always disagreed with me. I have some acquaintance with it. It and I don't get along, much."

"Magic is a harsh and unforgiving master."

"And here I've always thought men desired to be *its* master."

"Fools," he said tightly. "Fools desire such things." And then he called out to the molah-man, and we passed through open gates into a sunny courtyard made less blinding than the white-painted arches by the profusion of vegetation.

Everything everywhere was blooming. There was no subtlety,

no careful ritual in arrangement. Things simply—grew. Many-branched, silver-gray trees; taller trees with cloudlike crowns boasting clusters of lavender draperies; long-leaved bushes bedecked by sprays of pinks and whites and reds; a strange, twisting vinelike plant that crawled up and over walls to display its bounty of leaves that, changing from green, were part red and part purple and all incandescence. The white-painted walls, the intensity of the sun, the brilliance of the skies, all combined with the gardens to make a palette of rich color and fragrance almost dizzying to behold.

The molah-man scurried about, pulling his mat from the shelf beneath the cart. He spread it carefully across swept bricks, and even as he did so two men hastened forward from the shadows of the courtyard to unroll a narrow runner of carpet extending from the entry way. We would not soil our feet on the bricks of the courtyard or the stone of the steps, but be separated from the earth by one poor mat and an exquisitely woven carpet of creamy wool.

Nihko exited the cart-bench, then gestured for me to follow. He led me to the shadowed, deep-set entryway, spoke briefly to the carpet-men, then gestured me to wait. One of the men went inside. When he appeared again, he made way for a second man. A tall, thin, older man, gray of eyes and hair, adorned in sheer linen kilt and a necklet of glass and gold hanging against his bare chest. He was too well-trained to stare at Nihko, but his quiet scrutiny was nonetheless obvious.

Nihko spoke at length. His tone was courteous, but not in the least deferential. The older man listened gravely, never once glancing in my direction. When Nihko was done making his explanations, whatever they might be—not knowing the language placed me at a distinct disadvantage—the man said one soft word, then turned neatly on his heel and led us into the house.

I paused theatrically at the threshold. "What about the floors? Do we dare—?"

Something glinted in Nihko's eye that was not humor. He turned from me and followed the older man. Laughing inwardly, I did the same.

We were led into a small, low-ceilinged room through which

we could see another much larger room with a high arched roof. The kilted man gestured briefly to shelves set against the wall; Nihko removed his shoes and placed them there. I noted there were several other pairs of shoes as well. I wiggled bare toes again, and succeeded at last in drawing the older man's attention. He watched me gravely, measuring me in his own quiet way. That I came barefoot to the house meant something, but I had no idea of what; surely Nihko had told him I'd been properly cleansed despite being shoeless. I sensed neither disdain nor fear. He simply looked at me, expressionless.

The ground swayed again, or seemed to. I put out a hand to steady myself against the wall. With the kilted man's scrutiny so fixed, I was abruptly aware of everything about that hand: its calluses, nicks and scrapes and scars, discolorations, cracked nails, the broad palm-back ridged with tendons that flexed and rolled beneath sun-bronzed skin, the long, limber fingers that felt far more at home gripping a sword hilt than a smooth, flat, cool wall in a house called Akritara on an island named Skandi.

I thought abruptly of Del, being held on a ship as surety of my behavior.

I took my hand from the wall and stood straight with effort, trusting years of training to replace sea-stolen balance. This was a land of tall men, strong men, and nothing about me, physically, indicated I was anything unlike anyone else, save a brief, quickly hidden flicker in the older man's gray eyes. Not judgment. Curiosity. A need to *know*.

He gestured then, ushered us into the much larger room beyond. Murals adorned the walls, elaborate and brilliantly colored scenes of boys with strings of fish, of ships asail, flowers, and beasts with horned heads. The ceiling flowed overhead in a high, elegant symmetry pleasing to the eye. I followed the line up, over, and down, marking the spare, simple angles of ceiling, wall, floor, hollows like windows cut into thick walls to display adornments, the wide doors leading into other arched and domed places. Everything about the room fit, as Singlestroke had once fit my hands. Cleanly, without excess. A perfection of purity and purpose. Like a circle, and the dance.

My breath stilled in my throat. Home. I was *home*. And all of me knew it.

The back of my neck tingled. I hitched shoulders, rubbed my neck in irritation; felt again the kilted man's attention. There was a single chair in the large, airy room; neither of us was directed to sit in it. Instead, we were gestured toward large cushions on the floor. Nihko seated himself. I did not. Not even when he told me to.

"Look," I said irritably, "you brought me here. You can tell them I'm a demon or a god, and I can't protest because I don't speak the language. Right now your plan is to present me as the heir to this house, and here I am. You'll have that chance. But you can't dictate if I stand or sit." Especially since he carried neither knife nor sword, and we neither of us had established who was the stronger.

Nihko opened his mouth to answer with some heat, but shut it again as he glanced briefly at the older man. He was clearly displeased, but could say nothing now. Instead he sat stolidly on his cushion, shaven head bowed slightly, and prepared himself to wait.

Once upon a time I was good at that. An impatient man makes mistakes in the circle, dangerous and occasionally deadly mistakes. I knew very well it was best to conserve strength and energy by remaining quiet, by steadying the rhythm of my breathing, by letting my body rest. But circumstances precluded that. I was a prisoner to this man, to his captain. As much as I was a prisoner of uncertainty and self-doubt.

This moment was what I had come to Skandi for. And I was frightened of it.

Oh, bascha, lend me your strength.

But Del, as much as I, was a prisoner to people who planned unknown outcomes for equally unknown actions.

Not my choice, to be in or of this moment. But I was helpless to alter it.

The kilted man glided quietly from the room. I expected Nihko to speak to me now, but he didn't. He simply sat there, head bowed, eyes closed. Praying? Maybe. But I wasn't certain I wanted to know anything about his gods or his priesthood, or the content of his convictions.

I walked. I paced the length of the rectangular room with its arching, airy ceiling and counted my steps. Back again to the other end of the room, where the low doorway led into the entry chamber containing no more than shelves and shoes.

Beneath my bare feet lay stone, cool stone composed of tiny square tiles of similar but subtly different hues. My soles were callused from years of fighting barefoot in the Southron sand, so my flesh wasn't sensitive enough to mark pits and seams and hollows. Merely stone to me: tiles carefully cut, shaped, and laid with precise attention, grouted and fitted together into quiet, soothing patterns. The walls and ceilings, the doors and the floors formed a subtle variety of shape, and shadow, and structure. My body knew this place, knew the appeal of purity, answered seductive symmetry. It knew without knowing; there was no way it *could* know, any more than my mind could embrace the comforting familiarity of a place I had never been.

I walked. I paced. I stopped only, and at last, when the woman came into the room.

Nihko rose at once. He caught her eye briefly, then instantly fixed his gaze on the patterned floor. I, on the other hand, merely waited. I folded my arms, set a shoulder against the wall, hooked one ankle casually over the other as I leaned, and waited.

Now I could be patient. Now it mattered.

Nihko said a single word. The one I knew. Not precisely what it meant, not the infinite possibilities of semantic subtleties, but I knew as much as I needed to know.

"Metri," he said.

This, then, was the Stessa metri, the woman who would be so desperately grateful for the return of the long-lost heir that she would grant Nihko Blue-head and his impulsive, slaver-reared female captain the welcome, the status, the wealth both desired.

I looked at the woman. I marked her stature, her posture, the cool and calm smoky gray-green eyes, darker than my own, and I realized what a fool Nihko was, and Prima Rhannet, and even Del, who had told them enough of me to make them plan this plan.

She wore sheer, sleeveless linen that fell to the floor, bleached nearly white. It made her skin seem darker than the warm copper-bronze it was. Around her waist was doubled a bright green sash, and over it a soft-worked leather belt chiming with golden circlets and brilliant blue beads. Larger circlets rang softly against both arms, depended from her ears, encircled her throat. Her hair, swept back from her face and fastened into a thick tail by a series of gold-and-enamel clasps, was darker than mine. There was silver and white in it just as there were threadings of age in her face, her throat, her hands, but nothing about this woman suggested she was old. Not in body, not in bearing, nor in the clarity of expression.

"Metri," he said again.

She seated herself in the single chair. The kilted man glided silently into the room and set down upon the small table beside her a delicate crockery jar and one cup. He poured, he lifted, he offered; she accepted. And all the while she looked only at Nihko. There was no indication she was aware of me at all.

So much for desperation. So much for a dying, weak old woman badly in need of an heir. I doubted the Stessa metri would allow anything so insignificant as death to defeat her will and purpose.

The woman set down the cup, then flicked a finger in Nihko's direction. He began speaking quietly and steadily, putting little emphasis in his words. I knew nothing of what he said, what lies or truths he told, but his tone did not suggest coercion or contrived charm. Perhaps he was, after all, as aware of her strength as I.

When he was done at last, the woman retrieved the cup and drank again. Still she did not look at me. Her expression was unmoved. I've been in the circle with men less suited to hiding their thoughts. Serenity was not her gift, but she knew how to be quiet. She knew how to still her mind so her judgments were sound—and absolutely unpredictable until she declared them.

Eventually, the woman looked at me. She spoke a single accented word, and this one I knew. "Undress."

I blinked. Then bestowed upon her my most charming smile. "You first."

Nihko was on his feet instantly. Even as I came off the wall onto the balls of my feet, he struck, spewing anger and invective in a tone thick with shock. It was a blow with the flat of his hand designed to catch me across the face, the way a man strikes a slave, but I moved quickly enough to avoid the power of it. I clamped one hand around his wrist and held it.

Before I could do anything more than stop him, before I could even phrase a response, the woman rose from her chair. In three long strides she reached Nihko, and her blow, unexpected and powerful, rocked him on his feet. Shocked, he staggered back, one hand to his face. I released his wrist, wondering warily if I might be her next target.

But I was not. It was Nihko.

With timed, meticulous blows, using the flat of her rigid hand, she drove him to the ground. He knelt there, shoulders rounded in submission, tattooed head bowed before her as she spoke with quiet, vicious emphasis. When she stopped speaking, stopped striking him, when he raised his head at last, I saw the blood. The tears.

The palm of her hand was reddened from the blows. She turned to me again, and again said, "Undress."

I stared back at her, matching determination, then grinned slowly. "Hoolies, woman, all you had to do was *ask.*"

She waited.

I untied the sash, dropped it; stripped off the tunic, dropped it; undid the drawstring and let the baggy trousers fall. I stepped out of them, kicked them aside, offered a cheery smile. "I detest red anyway."

From a distance of two paces, she studied me. I've been examined before: by slavers, by sword-dancers, by enemies, by sorcerers, even by friends. Certainly by women. But her perusal of my nudity was uncannily different. There was no sense of ownership or impending purchase; no sexual hunger, no arousal, no predatory promise; no assessment to weigh my worth as a man or a sword-dancer hired to do a task. She simply looked, so intent as to be unaware of surroundings, the way an artist might study the line of bone and shadow, the play of light on flesh, the fit and function of form. To see how the body was made, how it worked, in order to recreate it—or to recognize it.

I expected her to gesture me to turn, or to demand it with a curt command. She did neither. She walked beyond me with smooth, measured strides and stood at my back.

Nihko remained on the floor. He was watching her, not me, making no effort to wipe the blood from his split lip, to erase the drying tears. He knelt there, knees doubled up beneath him, green eyes transfixed by the woman's actions.

"Getting an eyeful?" I asked lightly.

She caught a handful of hair and lifted it briefly from the back of my neck. Then let it fall as she moved from behind me. She returned to the chair and seated herself quietly. "What have you been," she asked in a cool, accented voice, "to deserve such punishment?"

"What have I been?" I hitched a shoulder, wondering what Nihko had told her. What he expected me to tell her. What *she* expected me to tell her.

I gave her the truth. Briefly, explicitly, without embellishment. Naming off the names of the tasks I had done, the dances I had won, the enemies defeated. All the truths of my past, despite the ugliness, the brutality that had driven a terrified boychild into tenacious manhood.

Her voice was uninflected. "How many years have you?"

I shook my head. "No idea." Still the truth.

Her eyes narrowed slightly. "Guess."

I laughed then, genuinely amused. "Better to throw the oracle bones. The odds are better."

She flicked a glance at Nihko, then returned it to me. "Has he told you, this man, this renegada, this *ikepra*, what you would gain if I accepted you?"

"Yes," I answered bluntly. "My freedom, and the freedom of the woman who travels with me."

"No more than that?"

"That's enough."

"So you say."

"So I mean."

She nodded. "Then go. This ikepra cannot prevent you. I give you your freedom. Go."

I shook my head. "Can't do that."

"Because of the woman?"

"Yes."

"There are other women."

I laughed softly. "There is no other woman like this one," I said simply, "any more than there is anyone else like you."

She studied me again. "Well," she said finally, with exquisite matter-of-factness, "of course that alters everything." A hand flicked in Nihko's direction. "Rise."

He rose.

"Do you know why I beat him?" she asked me.

I shrugged. "You don't like him?"

A spark of amusement leaped briefly in her eyes, was extinguished. "He insulted my house."

"I assumed something of the sort."

"He insulted you."

"Me?" I blinked. "Why in hoolies would anything he said of a foreigner matter to you?" Enough that she would strike him blow after blow with her own hand.

"Do you know what he is?"

I thought of any number of explicitly vulgar things I could say Nihko was, but restrained the impulse. She probably knew anyway, judging by her contempt. "Not as you mean it, no."

"Ikepra."

I shook my head. "You've said that before. I don't speak or understand the language. I have no idea what you're talking about."

"Profanation," Nihko said, hushed but not hesitant.

Startled, I looked at him. His eyes glittered, but the tears were gone. He was—ashamed. In that moment, before this woman, he detested himself.

"Well," I said, "there are a lot of things I could call you, but that's not one of them." I paused. "Why? Who are you? What did you do?" Another pause. "Besides sailing away with a slaver's daughter to rob and capture harmless Southroners like me, that is."

"Harmless?" Nihko's smile was ghastly. "A blind man sees neither power, promise, nor danger."

"And this blind man isn't hearing much either," I retorted. "Fine. You brought me here, told this woman I'm her long-lost heir. We're done. You can turn Del loose now, and we'll get on about our business."

"Nihkolara will not do so," the woman said, "until he has been rewarded. That is why he came."

"Not for me," he said sharply. A wave of color suffused his face, then faded; had he insulted the house again? "I serve Prima Rhannet."

"Oh, yes." Smoky eyes glittered coldly. "You would have me receive her. Here."

"She would have it. Yes."

"Is there a problem with that?" I asked cautiously, wondering what in hoolies I'd do if this woman refused to cooperate and Prima Rhannet decided to keep Del.

The metri was displeased. "That would seal her acceptable to the Eleven Families."

"That doesn't mean you have to *like* her, does it?"

She ignored me and spoke to Nihko, whom she'd called Nihkolara. He had never named himself in any of the words he'd said to her, or to the kilted servant. But she knew who he was. "There must be proofs."

"Name them, metri."

I frowned. The balance of control had shifted. He was ikepra, whatever that meant, self-proclaimed profanation, but the tension in the room was all hers now. He knew what he was, knew his place, and for the moment he ruled it.

She shook her head. "He is scarred all over. Had the *keraka* ever existed, it is banished now."

The—what?

"There are things from within the body," the first mate offered, "far more convincing than marks upon the flesh."

She shook her head again. Gold chimed faintly. "There are others in this world who appear to be Skandic, even those with real or falsified keraka. And many of them have been presented to me as you have presented him. Pretenders, all of them." She smiled. "I am old. I am dying. I need an heir of the house. Were I a malleable woman, I would have ten times ten the number of men standing in this room, this moment, vowing with utter conviction that they are my one true heir."

"Look," I said, exasperated, "I don't even care if I'm Skandic, let alone your long-lost heir. I mean, yes, I suspect I *am* Skandic—it's why we set out in the first place, to see—but I'm not vowing to be your heir or anything else supposedly special. I don't care about your wealth, your influence, your legacy, whatever it is that all these other men want, what Prima Rhannet wants. *I* just want my freedom." I looked at Nihko pointedly. "And Del's."

She remained unconvinced. "A clever man will deny a birthright in order to win it."

"A clever woman, an old, dying, desperate woman"—I made it an irony between us—"would discern the attempt and discount it."

"Metri," Nihko said, and then added more in Skandic.

When he was done, her face was taut and pale. She looked at me, hard, and was old abruptly, older than her age.

"What did you say?" I asked sharply. "What did you tell her?"

"About sickness," he said. "About the weeping of your wrist"—he touched his throat—"and the burning of your flesh."

She gestured then, cutting us off. I saw the minute trembling in her hand as she stretched it toward the kilted man and spoke a single word.

He placed a small knife in her palm.

I stiffened. "Wait a moment—"

"You will see," Nihko said quietly, "and so shall she."

The woman rose. Her steps now were not so steady, though there was no less purpose in them. She walked to me, touched me briefly on the wrist as if in supplication—or apology—then raised both hands to my neck. She was a tall woman, nearly as tall as Del. I felt her touch, the coolness of her fingers, the trembling in her hands. There was no pain, only a deft cut in something I thought was hair, until she lowered her hands and I saw a strip of braided twine with a single ornament attached, a thin silver ring worked into the weave.

"What—?" I put my hand to my throat, curling fingers around the leather thong with its weight of sandtiger claws. "Where did that come from?"

"Here." Nihko brushed a finger against his left eyebrow. "When you lay on the deck after I dragged you out of the water, vomiting up the ocean, I attached it to your necklet."

"What in hoolies *for?*"

A single long step and he put a hand on my chest. "This," he answered gently.

I didn't get sick. I didn't vomit up the ocean, or the contents of my belly. I simply lost control of every working part in my body: of the eyes, the ears, the voice, the movements of my limbs, the in- and exhalation of my lungs, the beating of my heart.

And died.

Chapter 11

I jerked bolt upright, sucking air into starving lungs in one long, loud, spasming gasp. Once I had it, I held the air so as not to let it out again, to know the horrific helplessness of simply *stopping*. I clutched both hands over my heart, blind to the world until I felt the steady, if pounding, beat, and then I became aware that I was no longer in the big, arch-roofed reception room, but in a smaller, round room with a dome huddled atop it.

And in a bed. With people around it.

I let my breath out and fixed the blue-headed first mate with a baleful glare. *"What in hoolies did you do to me?"*

Casually he replied, "Killed you."

I thought that over, reassuring myself that my heart yet beat and my lungs yet worked. "Then why am I alive now?"

"I resurrected you."

"Can you do that?"

"You are breathing, are you not?"

"*How* did you do it?"

His lip was swollen from where the woman had struck and split it. "I am ikepra," he said simply, "but there remain those things of the Order of which I do not speak."

I noticed then that the Stessa metri sat in a chair beside the bed, hands folded in her linen-swathed lap. Beyond her, leaning casually against the wall, was Prima Rhannet.

The first shock had worn off. And I knew . . . I whipped my head to the right and saw her there, waiting "Bascha!"

She was unsmiling, but the relief in her eyes was profound. There were many things I wished to say to her, but I offered none of them now. Not until we were alone again. But she understood. We both of us understood. It's handy when you know someone well enough, intimately enough, that many things pass between you with no need for actual words.

Relief brought with it an outward rush of released tension. Feeling wobbly, I scooched back in the bed and leaned against the headboard. A quick automatic self-inventory within a moment of waking had told me I was still unclothed, but modesty was served by a linen coverlet, which I yanked up over my lap as I noted Prima Rhannet's crooked smile and laughing eyes. And why was *she* looking, anyway? I scowled at her; was rewarded with a wide, mocking grin.

The Stessa metri sat very still in her chair. I looked at her, weighed the extreme degree of self-containment evident in her posture and expression, and sighed. "I take it you paid them."

Her gaze was steady. "Nihkolara proved beyond a doubt you are Skandic," she said. "Whether you are my grandson is as yet unknown, but I dared not take the chance."

I blinked. "Grandson?"

"It is possible," she said calmly.

"Grandson," I repeated, astonished by the complexity of emotions that single word—and its context—roused. "But—" But. There was nothing to say. I just looked at her, stunned, and shook my head.

One dark eyebrow rose a fraction. "No?"

No. Yes. Maybe. I don't know. Ask me later.

Hoolies.

I focused on something else. "You paid them, so why are they still here?" I flicked a glance beyond her to the red-haired woman in the corner. "You didn't seem too enamored of the idea of receiving a slaver's daughter in your home."

I was rewarded by the slow bloom of color in the freckled face. Prima glowered at me, all trace of mocking amusement wiped away.

"And so I am not," the metri replied. "But there is more involved in this enterprise than coin."

I glanced at Del. "Get your feet washed?"

That baffled her utterly. "My feet—?"

Prima Rhannet laughed harshly. "We were denied the honor," she said in a clipped tone, "but be certain the floors shall be cleansed when we have gone, and the carpets reblessed."

"But . . ." I looked now at Nihko. "I don't get it."

"I am ikepra," he answered steadily, "and all know it. But they had rather take no chances."

"Any more than I," the metri put in quietly.

I cleared my throat. "So. Here we are." I glanced around, marking faces one by one until I came to hers again. "What happens next?"

"You shall be accorded the hospitality of my house, you and your woman."

"And your new friends," Prima said pointedly, a certain amount of malicious glee underscoring her tone.

The metri didn't miss the point. "As well as your companions."

"Now, wait," I said. "They aren't my companions. They are my *captors*. There's a difference."

"But of course there is not," replied the woman who might— or might not—be my grandmother. "Because if it is true you are my heir, then of course your companions must be treated with honor, received as my guests before the Eleven Families of Skandi."

"Kind of a rock and a hard place, isn't it?"

The spark flickered in her eye, was gone. "Such bruises heal."

I grinned. "So they do."

"As for now . . ." She rose. "I will have your companions conducted to rooms worthy of their status, while you and your woman reassure yourselves that you are indeed both whole."

Even Nihko and his captain capitulated and followed her out of the room. With their departure I felt the last bit of tension drain from my body. My skull thumped against the wall. "Gods, I'm tired." I stretched out my hand; Del took it. Tightly. "Was I really dead?"

She hitched a hip onto the bed and perched beside me. When

I tugged insistently at her hand, she moved closer, finally matching her length to mine as she settled shoulders against the headboard. "You weren't breathing when I came here, nor was your heart beating. If both of those symptoms constitute death, then yes, you were dead."

I felt at the flesh of my chest, seeking answers. The heart continued to beat, and I was aware of steady breathing. Not dead, then. Now. "I don't understand. How did Nihko do such a thing?"

"Let us be more concerned with the fact he *undid* it," Del suggested. "It took him two days."

"Two days?" I stiffened. "You're not saying I was dead for two whole days!"

"I am."

"No."

She shrugged.

"This is impossible, bascha!"

"Be grateful it's not," she replied, "or you would likely be buried somewhere on this rock."

"Oh, no. If I'm buried anywhere, it'll be in the South."

She slanted me a sidelong glance. "You might be somewhat rank by the time we got you there."

"Too bad," I retorted. "At least *I* don't have to smell me!"

"Of course, I could have you burned," Del said consideringly, "and take you back in an urn. That would be more convenient."

"Oh? And what kind of urn would be appropriate for a man who is also messiah?"

Her expression was guileless as she looked at me. "Likely an empty aqivi jug."

"Empty!" I glared at her aggrievedly. "Hoolies, bascha, if you're going to drag my remains around in an aqivi jug, at least let it be a *full* one!"

She broke then, laughing, and turned hard against me, setting her head down into the hollow of my shoulder. I hooked an arm around her and contemplated the immensity of being alive after one has been dead. And the simple, unadorned joy of having this woman here beside me, as glad of it as I was.

"Del—"

She breathed it into my neck. "I know."

"Del—"

She put fingers across my lips. "If you say anything, you will regret it."

I extruded my tongue and licked her fingers purposefully. She removed them hastily. I grinned. "Why will I regret it?"

"Because I've seen you when you've had too much to drink. You get sad. Sappy."

"Sappy!"

"And the next day you've forgotten it entirely, which is no more flattering than you wishing you hadn't said it."

"I never wish I hadn't said what I've said to you." I reconsidered. "Well, maybe sometimes. When we have disagreements, though those are extremely rare." I was rewarded by the crimped mouth I expected to see. "But hoolies, bascha, I just came back from the dead! Doesn't that allow me some latitude to say what I want?"

"But then the Sandtiger will have divulged a portion of himself he wants no one ever to see."

"His sappiness?"

Del laughed. "You have survived by letting them think you are not soft."

I grunted. "Softness doesn't survive in the circle."

"So I have said." A strand of silken hair trapped itself against stubble and claw scars. "But I know what you are. You needn't say it where anyone else might hear."

"At the moment what I'm feeling has nothing to do with, er, softness."

Del patted my lap. "I know."

I couldn't help the startled reflexive twitch of every muscle in my body. I caught her hand, gripped it, fixed her with a forbidding scowl. "Gently, bascha!"

"No," she said. "*Fiercely.* So I know, and you know, you're very much alive."

Oh. Well, yes. I could manage that. Being brought back from the dead does give a man the motivation to make certain all the parts still work.

* * *

Some hours later, the silent, kilted servant led me out of the house to a small, private terrace tucked into one of the niches between domed room and arched. Akritara appeared to be full of such places, cobbled together over the years from a set of chambers into a sprawling assemblage of them. And here I found an array of potted plants, all blooming so that the air was rich with fragrance. I was startled to see that a rising breeze blew the hedges along the low wall into tattered fragments; this must be the wind Nihko had mentioned, forcing the people of Skandi to train their grapevines into baskets.

I squinted against the dust, then turned back toward the house as the servants touched my arm. And there was the Stessa metri, seated in a chair. The linen of her belted tunic rippled slightly, but her chair had been set back into a niche that the wind only barely reached.

Her eyes appraised me coolly. "Do you feel better?"

I ran a hand down the front of my tunic. "A bath, fresh clothing, a meal—what more could a man ask?"

"I referred to none of those things."

I blinked, then felt my face warm. Which in itself annoyed me; I haven't blushed in, well, so many years I couldn't count them.

"Well?"

"Well what?"

"Do you feel better?"

"I'm just glad I'm alive to feel anything."

Her gaze yet probed me. "Did you not release your seed in her?"

I looked around for a chair. Didn't find one. Looked around for the servant in hopes he might bring one, but he was gone. So I sat down on the nearest portion of knee-high wall, in the wind, and smiled sweetly at her. "Aren't you a little blunt for a woman of your, um, maturity? Or are you just trying to shock me?"

One brow rose slightly. "Do you shock?"

"Not often."

"I thought not." She smoothed a fold in the sheer linen of her tunic skirts with a deft hand. "Did you?"

"Did I what?"

"Release your seed in her."

I considered her. "Do you *want* me to believe you're a woman who takes pleasure in hearing bedroom tales of others?"

"Tell me," she said only.

I stood up then, left the wall, took three strides to her. Leaned down, looming, so that my face was but a thumb's length from hers. "Yes," I said. "Anything else you want to know? How many times, who was on top, how long I lasted?"

She did not recoil from my closeness, or my tone. "My heir," she said quietly, "must be capable of bedding a woman. Of what use is an heir if he can sire no children?"

I straightened, startled. "This is about children?"

Her gray-green eyes were smoky. "Do you *wish* to believe I'm a woman who finds pleasure in hearing bedroom tales of others?"

I opened my mouth, shut it. Could find no response.

"Give me your hands."

"My hands?"

"I want to examine them."

"Didn't you get a good enough look at me before?"

Her eyes locked with my own. "Who was your mother, that she taught you no manners?"

Unaccountably, it stung. "Your daughter?" I challenged.

From that, she flinched. Color moved in her face, fading. Abruptly I regretted what I had said—exactly as Del had suggested a matter of hours before. It was true this woman had taken me completely off-guard with her questions, but that didn't mean she deserved rudeness in return.

Unless she expected it. Wanted it. To make it easier for her to dismiss me as yet another pretender.

I walked away from the woman then, returning to my perch upon the low wall. I spread my legs, felt the underside of my thighs clench to grip. Tapped sandaled toes faintly against the stone beneath my feet even as the breeze whipped my hair flat against one side of my head. "What happened?"

She told me. Calmly, quietly, with no obvious pain or sorrow, but it was there in her eyes. When she was done, I watched her watching me, weighing her story even as she had weighed mine three days before.

I rose, went to her. This time I didn't loom. I knelt down and offered my hands.

She took them, held them. Turned them. Felt the sword-born calluses, the scars, two knuckles that were enlarged, a little finger left slightly crooked in the healing after a break. I could not read what was in her face, but I thought I knew. This flesh could be hers, and the blood that ran beneath it. As much as perhaps it wasn't.

She released me. "I must *know*."

Still kneeling, I shook my head. "There are no easy answers."

"Even difficult answers are answers."

"Maybe," I said. "Maybe not."

Her eyes were shocked. "You would rather not know what became of her?"

"Either way offers no comfort. If she died, knowing won't bring her back. If she gave me away voluntarily—"

"My daughter would never have done so!"

"Then maybe she wasn't your daughter. Maybe I'm not your grandson. Maybe I'm just a Southron/Skandic half-breed, or a full-blooded Skandic lost to the desert of a foreign land." I shrugged. "Or maybe I'm just the unwanted result of some man releasing his seed, and so the girl—released me." Into the Punja, where a new-born infant would die in a matter of hours, offering no proof of one night's pleasure. Or rouse the memory of rape.

"That, too, is possible."

"In which case I'll thank you for your hospitality, collect Del, and go."

"Wait." She gestured briefly as I rose, then dropped the hand to her lap. "Does it mean nothing to you that I might be your grandmother? A wealthy, powerful, dying old woman who was bred of the oldest and most respected family of the island?"

I had at some point shattered her demeanor. She was still proud, still strong, but a sere bitterness chilled her tone. I thought then of all the men who had come before her, claiming to be the grandson of a wealthy, powerful old woman bred of the oldest and most respected family of the island.

She had undoubtedly heard countless lies. I gave her none. Only honesty. "It would mean more," I told her, "just to have a grandmother. No matter who or what she is."

I left her then, as she wept.

Chapter 12

As guests, we had been given the run of the place. Servants tended the household assiduously, all kilted, all quiet, all perfectly courteous. I didn't know where Nihko and his captain were, but I did know where to find Del. She intended, she'd said when I left her to see the metri, to drown herself.

She meant in a *bath*, of course. So I went to the chamber housing the tub.

It was far more than a tub, actually. The builders had dug a large, shallow, square hole in the ground, plastered it, laid out tiny tiles on the sides and bottom in an elegantly precise pattern of waves and clouds, blue on blue of every shade. Overhead arched the ceiling, very dark blue with a spray of silver and gold stars painted to mimic the night skies. Squares and slots were cut into the deep walls through to the exterior, then covered against wind-born dust and debris by membranes, opaque but scraped thin enough to let in the light. The shelf around the pool itself was stone as well, pale, worked slabs fitted together into an almost seamless array. Through some builder's trick with pipes the water was warmed and let in and out from beneath the surface. I had enjoyed myself immensely earlier, forgoing a shared bath only because if Del and I *had* shared, I'd never have answered the metri's request to attend her.

Now I was finished with that, and Del was still in the pool. Alone.

Perfect.

For the second time in three days I stripped down for a woman, leaving borrowed clothing heaped upon the floor, although I confess this time the experience was much more pleasurable. Del, floating easily, challenged me to dive in, which she knew very well I couldn't and wouldn't do. Instead, the best I could manage was to bend down, catch my balance one-handed against the stone shelf, and slip over the edge.

The water came to mid-chest even in the center of the pool; I was in no danger of drowning. Unless Del had some nefarious plan to rid herself of me.

The closest she came to it was to hook a hand into the thong holding the claws and tug gently, urging me closer. "Well?"

"Well what?"

"What did the metri say?"

The metri. I sighed, dipped down to wet myself to my chin, stood up again. Soaked hair straggled down well onto my shoulders; I *really* needed to cut it. Del's was slicked back against her skull, baring all of her face. The Southron sun had not been kind to her Northern skin, incising a faint fan of lines at the corners of her eyes, but with a sheen of moisture over her face and the dissipation of habitual readiness, she also shed years. She looked maybe eighteen. At the most.

I felt a stab of some unnamed emotion: more than ten, possibly as many as fifteen years separated us. Before me there had been only Ajani, the Northern borjuni who had, with his men, slaughtered her family, save Del and her brother, and burned the caravan. Who had utterly altered her life, making a sword-singer out of the girl who would have been wife and mother, instead of living vengeance.

Before Ajani, she had been fifteen. And innocent of men.

Those days, those years were past now. She had slain her demons, the living as well as the dead. She was as much at peace as I had ever seen her. And young again. So young.

"Well?" she prodded.

The metri. "She wants to be certain."

"That's understandable."

"And she doesn't know how."

Del was silent a moment. "No," she said finally. "There is no way to be certain. It must be taken on faith."

I shook my head. "I'm not the man for it."

"To be her grandson?"

"To be trusted. To be taken on faith."

She stood before me, facing me: a tall, strong woman of immense will and purpose. Unsmiling, she put a hand on either side of my head and stripped my hair back, combing it behind my ears. "You are the most trustworthy man I have ever met."

"Not for this. This is—important." I recalled the metri's expression as she examined my hands. "This may be more important than anything in my life, because it's *her* life."

Del stared hard into my eyes. "And do you see why, now, I say you are the most trustworthy man I have ever met?"

"It's only the truth, bascha. Nothing more."

"And nothing less."

I turned my face into her hand, kissed it. "I don't know why, bascha. I think she *wants* me to be the one, but she's afraid."

"Why would she be afraid? Surely she has prayed to have her grandson returned to her."

"Returned for how long?"

Del frowned. "What do you mean?"

I shook my head. "I can't stay here. Even if I *am* this grandson. This isn't my place."

"You could make it your place."

I recalled how comfortable I was in Akritara, how very much at home I *did* feel, despite never having been here before. I had never in my life felt so at ease in an unknown place. Skandi fit me. Somehow, some way, it fit me.

"Why not?" Del asked.

I turned and pushed my way through the water. At the side I hooked arms over the edge, spreading elbows along the stone, and settled chin on wrists layered one atop the other. Frowning even as Del came up next to me and mimicked my posture, one elbow lightly touching mine.

"It . . . I'm—" I sighed, ducking my head to scrub forehead

against hands. "I don't know. I guess I'm still just a Southroner at heart."

"No. Not since I taught you wiser ways."

It raised a smile, as she meant it to, but I couldn't hold it. "I think I will *always* be a Southroner. Even if I meant not to be. Too much of it is in my blood."

"And if your blood is Skandic?"

"It's more than blood that makes you of a place," I told her. "More than blood, or bone, or flesh. It's as much spirit, and heart, as anything else." I turned my head to look at her, even as I leaned my temple into my hand. "You are a Northerner, born and bred of its customs, its people. The rituals." She nodded slightly. "And no matter if you never return there for the balance of your life, it's what you will always be."

Del's expression was sober now, almost severe as she considered. I had stripped away the youth with my words. Now the woman was back, the tough-minded woman who stepped into the circle and danced.

Or killed.

"But I am who I am no matter where I am," she said at last. "As you would be."

"Bascha, I don't know—don't understand . . ." I shook my head again. "I have never *belonged* to anyone. Never been *of* anyone. Owned, yes, by the Salset. Trained, yes, at Alimat. And that was the closest thing I had to a family, those men at Alimat who learned as I learned the rituals of the dance, but there was always competition. Never friendship; we all knew one day we might meet one another in the circle. And now . . ." I set my forehead against my wrists, spoke into the stone. "Now there's—this."

"Yes," Del said quietly. And as quietly, "Would it be so bad if you became what you would have become anyway?"

I turned my head. "What do you mean?"

"If you are this woman's grandson, then what she offers is what you would have had."

"If."

"Toss the oracle bones ten times," Del said, "and you will win, and you will lose. That is the only certainty in the game."

"In other words, the odds are about as good *for* me being her grandson as against." I reached out and cupped the back of her skull in my palm. "Or is it just that *you* want to benefit from the wealth?"

"Of course," she agreed. "I am selfish."

I ruffled slick hair, disarranging it. "I wouldn't have had it, Del."

"What do you mean?"

"The metri's daughter fell in love with an unsuitable man. He was not of the Eleven Families, not even remotely acceptable. He was a molah-man, responsible for carting the Stessas around the island, making certain they never soiled themselves by touching unblessed ground." I smiled sadly at her perplexity. "The metri's daughter asked that he be adopted, raised up by the metri herself, so he would become acceptable. And her mother refused."

"They left," Del said, seeing it now. "They left Skandi together, and sailed away to a place where they could be man and wife with no concerns for such things."

"She was pregnant," I told her. "Due to give birth in a month. The metri intended to give the child away."

Del's eyes closed. I knew she remembered *her* daughter, Ajani's daughter, the child of rape. The child she gave into others' keeping, because she had a task. A vow. An obsession. And no time, no room, for a baby in her life.

I continued. "But the only daughter—and only heir—of the Stessa metri left Skandi with the molah-man, and neither were seen again."

Her eyes opened. The clear blue, strangely, had been swallowed by black pupils. "Such a woman would never expose an infant in the desert," she said. "A woman who gave up a life of privilege, leaving her mother, her people, her land, her legacy." She looked at me. "Such a woman would not have left you there, in the sand. Not by choice."

I closed my hand around the thick tail of soaked hair adhering to her spine. Squeezed. "There is no way we can ever know, bascha. None."

"You could *choose*—"

"—to believe that was my mother? That she loved a man

enough to leave her homeland so near to term, and travel into the Punja? Yes, I could choose to believe it. I could also choose to believe otherwise."

Her gaze was steady. "And if it's true?"

I shook my head. "It changes nothing. Not who I am, what I am, or what I will be."

Del opened her mouth to answer, but it was someone else's voice I heard. A man's. Saying something in a language I didn't know, but the tone was clear enough.

We turned sharply as one, pushing off the side of the pool. A young man stood there on the far side, legs spread aggressively, arms loose at his sides. He was not kilted as the servants, but wore a thin-woven sleeveless linen tunic that displayed muscled, tanned arms. A copper-studded leather belt was wrapped around a slim, sashed waist.

He stared down upon us, green eyes fixed and fierce in a dark face. Brown hair sun-bleached bronze on top, not yet combed tame from the wind, tumbled carelessly around wide shoulders. His eyes narrowed a moment, and then he switched to a language we could understand despite the accent. "Are you the *renegadas*, who presume upon the *metri's* courtesy?"

He was young, big, angry, and of unmistakable presence. He was a man you couldn't ignore, especially when he stared at you. When he grew into himself, knew his body and its power as much as I knew mine, he would be formidable.

"Gods," Del breathed.

I glanced at her sidelong, saw the startled expression commingled with something else I didn't like much. She had told me once before that indeed she looked at other men, even as I looked at other women. Now I witnessed it.

I was naked, he was not. But not much was shielded by the thin linen. "Answer me!" he snapped.

I couldn't help myself: I smiled winsomely. "Guest," I declared, "presuming upon nothing we haven't been given by the *metri* herself."

Dark brows arched up beneath a lock of thick hair fallen across his unlined brow. "Then you must be the latest pretender."

So much for being winsome. I was none too pleased to be caught weaponless and naked in the water, arguing with a boy. "What I am is none of your concern."

He stepped to the edge of the pool. "It is," he said with surprising equanamity, "when I am the metri's only living—and acknowledged—relative." He smiled as he saw us exchange disbelieving glances. "Ask," he suggested gently, eyes alight with triumph, then turned on his heel and walked away. It was then I marked the sheath at the small of his back, and the knife riding lightly in it.

"*Now* I'm confused," I muttered as he disappeared. "And I don't like being confused. Not when I don't have a sword." Being without a blade set the fine hairs on the back of my neck to rising, now that I was challenged.

I pushed my way through water to the edge of the pool, grasped stone, and pulled myself up. Dripping, I bent down to reach for Del's hand. "Either he's a pretender, or I am, or the metri herself is conducting some kind of competition—" I broke off. "Are you getting out?"

As if it were afterthought, Del finally reached up so we could clasp wrists. I braced and pulled; she came up from the pool in one fluid motion, all ivory-silver and bleached gold as the water sheeted off her. Her expression was a combination of perplexity, disbelief, and startled comprehension.

I picked up the drying cloths left by a servant. Flung one at her even as I started rubbing myself down with the other. "All right," I said crossly, "you've proved that women look, too. But he's gone, Del . . . you can stop now."

"What?" Coming belatedly out of her reverie, she bent and began to dry off.

"The young godling here a minute ago." I tossed down my cloth, grabbed up the baggy trousers and began dragging them on one leg at a time. "*I* don't think he's that impressive, but you certainly seem to."

Del blinked at me. "Tiger—"

"He's a kid, bascha . . . barely formed. Not much character there yet—other than arrogance, of course, which he obviously has in full measure." I hitched the waist over my hips, tied off the drawstring, snatched up the tunic and tugged it on over my head. "But I suppose he's pretty enough to look at." I scowled. "So long as that's all you do."

"Yes, he's pretty enough to look at," Del declared. "He looks like *you*."

That stopped me cold. "What?"

"Without the years. Without the scars." She pulled a long linen shift over her head, yanked folds free of hips and buttocks so that the hem settled around her ankles. "But very much *with* your ill temper." She bent over, swept her hair into some kind of complicated turban, all wrapped up in the cloth.

"My what?"

"And arrogance." She straightened, balanced the turban, snugged the woven belt around her waist with sharp jerks, stalked off.

I watched her back. It was very stiff.

"Looks like me?" I turned back to study the place where the young man had stood, recollecting my first impressions of him. "Him? Nah."

Surely not.

Scowling, I went off to find the metri and learn for myself what in hoolies was going on.

Chapter 13

By the time I found the metri, the others already had. The kid, for one—although I confess he didn't look like much of a kid from the back. With Del's observation still foremost in my mind, I studied him with new eyes. He was broad enough, tall enough, and the coloring was the same. Aside from that, though, I didn't think there was so much resemblance.

He wasn't the only one with the metri. Prima Rhannet and her first mate were there as well. Everyone except the metri was talking loudly, trying to raise voices over one another until the room rang hollow with shouting. Dumbfounded, I stopped short in the doorway and stared. Didn't even blink as Del joined me there, wet hair combed out, saying something cross about enough noise to wake the dead.

The metri sat in a chair, hands folded into her lap. She wore the mask I associated with her so long as we were not discussing her daughter or the man her daughter had married: calmly self-contained and utterly unmoved by anything anyone said.

There was much gesticulation and tones of hissing hostility. Del's godling rounded on Prima and Nihko, seemingly accusing them of something they didn't much like, as they answered in kind. I was not surprised to see the red-haired captain so animated, because it was like her; but Nihko Blue-head only rarely showed so much emotion. As for Del's godling, well, I didn't know him at all, but he seemed extremely comfortable with shouting, so I assumed he had lots of experience.

This looked and sounded like nothing so much as a family quarrel. I began to suspect there was a lot more to the story than a renegada captain and her tattooed first mate, and a kid who looked enough like Nihko to be his son. And since Nihko himself resembled *me*, this made it a very tight-knit family indeed.

And I couldn't understand a word of what anyone was saying.

Out of patience, I drew a very large breath deep into my lungs and let loose a roar that overrode them all. *"Hey!"*

Even Del jumped.

Now that I had everyone's attention, I smiled my friendliest smile. "Hello," I said with cheerful courtesy. "Would you care to repeat all that in a language I can understand?"

"We," Del murmured.

"We," I amended. When no one said anything at all, I glanced at them one by one.

Prima Rhannet's hand was at her waist where her knife generally resided tied to her belt, but she wasn't wearing the knife, or even that particular belt. Like Del, she wore an ankle-length sleeveless tunic gathered at the waist into a woven sash. Nihko never was so blatant about his weapons, which he didn't have at the moment, either; he just stood with his head turned slightly toward me, eyes glittering. But the godling, as youth so often does, had turned to face me squarely, to challenge the unexpected, every powerful part of him poised for movement.

Hoolies, Del was right. He *could* be me. If you stripped away fifteen years and all the scars from me.

Or added them to him.

It was eerie. You don't usually recognize yourself in others. For that matter, you don't usually recognize yourself in a silver mirror or a pool of water unless you *know* it's you, and only then you know it's you because logic argues it must be: if you're peering into a mirror or water, the image staring back very likely is your own. I knew my hands best of all because I was so accustomed to using them, to watching them as I did things with them, even without thinking about them. But unless one studies oneself from head to toe every day, one isn't even aware of certain aspects of one's appearance.

But he was me. Or I was him. Del had already noted it, and now the renegadas and the metri did as well. The kid and I stood there staring at one another in startled recognition and unspoken, unsubtle territorial challenge, while Prima Rhannet began to laugh, and Nihko . . . well, Nihko grinned widely in a highly superior and annoying fashion, brow-rings glinting.

They had tossed the bones, the captain and her mate. And won.

I touched the thong of sandtiger claws around my throat. The metri had given me back the brow ring she'd cut from the necklet, saying that so long as Nihko was present I'd do better to wear it lest I lose most of my meals. Since I had yet to learn a way of maintaining any measure of decorum while spewing up the contents of my belly, I accepted the ring, knotting it back into the thong. One of these days I was going to find out just *why* Nihko made me sick.

Other than for the usual reasons, of course.

The kid said something under his breath. The metri responded with a single word that flooded his face with the dusky color of embarrassment, or anger. As he glared at me I began to appreciate, in a very bizarre and detached sort of way, just why so many people gave way to me when I employed the most ferocious of my stares.

There was no subtlety about Del's godling, but he might learn it one day. If he lived.

"Family argument?" I asked lightly.

"They soil this household," the kid hissed, switching languages easily. "As do you."

"Herakleio," the metri said only.

His hands were fists. "They do," he insisted. "All of them. Prima is a disgrace to her father, her heritage—and Nihkolara is ikepra! *This* man"—he meant me, of course—"is a pretender." He shifted his furious glance to Del, all fired up to make other accusations, and realized rather abruptly he knew absolutely nothing about her.

Except that she was beautiful. And, I didn't doubt, that he had seen her in the pool. Without clothing.

I watched the change in him. The anger, the touchy pride remained, but slid quietly beneath the surface as something else rose up. Color moved in his face again. He drew a breath, expelled it sharply through his nostrils, then consciously relaxed the fists into hands again.

I gave him marks for honesty: he did not try to charm the woman who had just seen his childish display of temper. He accepted that she had, was ashamed of it, but did not deny it.

The metri moved slightly forward in her chair, immediately commanding the attention of everyone in the room. She was smiling in triumphant delight, rather like a cat, as she looked first at the boy who claimed he was her kin, then at me who claimed I was not.

The woman laughed. Slowly, as if tasting something unexpected and quite delicious. "I should have both of you sheathed in plaster," she said calmly, "and placed on either side of my gate. Surely everyone in the islands would come to marvel at my new statuary."

"Naked?" Prima inquired.

Rather surprisingly, the metri did not take offense. "Oh, I believe so. Unclothed, and ambitiously male."

The kid—Herakleio?—was stunned. He turned jerkily toward her, jaw slackening. "Metri?"

"Come now, Herakleio," she said. "Admit the truth. He is you."

"He's old!" the kid announced.

Nihko grinned. Prima gulped a laugh. Del put fingers across her mouth as if to hide a treacherous response, expression elaborately bland.

I smiled, vastly unoffended. "Older than you," I agreed, "which serves me just fine, as the first one born inherits soonest."

A glint in the metri's eyes told me she understood and appreciated the provocation. Especially as it worked.

"First born!" Herakleio shouted, furious all over again. "First born of what whore?"

"*Stop.*" This time it was the metri, all amusement wiped away. "You soil this household with such shouting, all of you."

Herakleio shot a venomous glance at Prima Rhannet. "And why do *you* care if we are naked? Men are nothing to you."

"Oh, men are a great deal to me," she replied, unperturbed. "I have no complaint of them, in general. I merely choose not to sleep with them."

He colored up again. "You slept with *me.*"

Ah. More and more interesting.

Prima grinned. "It passed an otherwise long night."

"But—"

"And it served to show me my preferences were other."

I blinked. She said it so blandly, without pointed offense, and yet no man could help *but* take it as an offense.

Herakleio did, of course, and responded by hissing something of great emotion, though he said it in Skandic so I couldn't understand. Prima merely laughed at him. Nihko, perhaps wisely, kept his mouth shut.

I frowned at him. "What is your stake in this?" I asked. "Do you fit?"

It instantly diverted Herakleio. "Oh, *he* fits. Has he not told you what he was, and is?"

"I've heard a word," I said clearly. "I've even heard sort of a definition. But I haven't the slightest idea what any of it means."

"Ikepra," Herakleio sneered, glowering at Nihko. "Tell him, Nihkolara."

"Tell him yourself."

Always an impressive response. I sighed and exchanged a speaking glance with Del. She was as much at sea as I.

"Ikepra," Herakleio declared curtly, as if I should discern from tone and posture all the complexities of definition. "He should have been thrown from the cliff."

"But then I would have flown," Nihko countered mildly.

"You sailed," Herakleio gibed. "You sailed with *her.*" A finger punched air in Prima's direction.

"And have not regretted it."

This time it was Del who cut off the conversation. She looked at the metri, who was watching both Nihko and Herakleio with an unfathomable expression, and asked what undoubtedly should have been asked at the very beginning. "What do you mean to do with us?"

The woman arched one eloquent brow. "Decide."

"Decide?" Herakleio asked suspiciously, who knew this woman better than any of us.

"I have two heirs, now," she answered. "Only one may inherit."

"Two?" Herakleio exploded. "How is this possible? He is a pretender—"

"Is he?"

"Am I?" I fixed the metri with a scowl. "Is he kin to you?"

"This boy?" She smiled. "Oh, yes. He is my brother's wife's brother's grandson."

I gave up trying to work that one out. "Then you don't need me or anyone else. You've got your heir."

"Male," Herakleio pronounced darkly.

I raised my brows at him. "Is there some doubt as to that?"

"He means he descends from the male line," Prima supplied.

I shook my head. "So?"

"The *male* line," Herakleio gritted between clamped teeth.

I sighed. "In case you've forgotten, I'm not from around here."

"We are counted from the female line," Nihko explained.

Prima nodded. "And from the gods."

I stared at her. "You think you're descended from *gods?*" So much for my self-description of Herakleio as a godling being effective sarcasm; irony doesn't work if you believe it's the truth. "This is ridiculous. You're people just like everyone else!"

Prima slid a veiled glance at Nihko from beneath lowered lids. "Some of us are—more."

"Were more," Herakleio corrected pointedly with intense scorn.

After a moment I just shook my head in disbelief and looked again at the metri. "I think it's time I left. I've got no stake in any of this, and no time to sort it out. I'm not your grandson, and I'm certainly not a godling!"

"Jhihadi," Del murmured.

As quietly I retorted, "You're not helping."

"But you may be," the metri said quietly, "and I cannot afford to lose you if it be true."

"You can't very well *keep* me," I shot back. "You bought my freedom from renegadas—"

"Precisely," the metri confirmed. "There is a debt between us now."

"Debt?" I was incredulous. "How in hoolies do you expect me to pay you back?"

Unsmiling, she looked at Herakleio. "Take this boy and make of him a man."

In the ensuing hubbub—Prima was laughing while Herakleio sputtered furious protest—I turned on my heel and walked out.

Del followed me right out into the courtyard entry. There she stopped, as if surprised I hadn't. "Where are you going?"

I swung at the gated entrance, stiff with frustration. "Away."

"Away *where?*"

"Just away. I don't belong here. I don't belong with these people. I don't want to have anything to *do* with these people!"

"Not even if they are your kin?"

"I disown them," I answered instantly.

Del examined my expression. "I think the person with no coin or property can't disown anyone."

"Then I repudiate them."

She nodded. "You can do that."

"Good. I do. I have. Let's go."

She was by all appearances stuck on one question. "Where?"

"Out of here. I've had enough of Skandi, metris, blue-headed priests, women ship captains, women ship captains who sleep with other women, and wife's brother's grandsons."

"Have you coin?"

"No. Where would I get coin?"

"Where indeed?"

I glowered at her. "Are you suggesting we *stay?*"

Del assumed her most innocent expression. "The metri did pay for your release . . . but I merely suggest we devise a plan before we go anywhere."

I opened my mouth to answer, shut it as I saw Nihko come out behind her, stepping from shadow into sunlight. "Plans are useful," he observed. "Have you one?"

I switched my scowl from Del to him. "I have done very well

making a living in this world without any plans. This situation is no different."

"But it is," Nihko disagreed politely. "You don't even speak the language."

"You speak mine," I said. "So does Prima, so does the metri, so does Heraklitus."

"Herakleio," Del corrected, and I shot her a ferocious glare.

"We speak it," Nihko said, "because we have been made to. My captain and I sail to foreign ports. The metri deals with merchants and traders of other lands, and to be certain dealings are honest one must speak the language. Herakleio has learned because the metri required it of her heir."

"Then he *is* her heir."

"He is her kin," Nihko elaborated. "But male-descended. It matters."

"Why does it matter?"

"This is Skandi. Things are—as they are."

"And you?" I asked curtly, angry enough to offend on purpose. "What exactly are you, ikepra?"

Nihko did not provoke. He wasn't Herakleio. "Ikepra," he answered. "Profanation. Abomination."

"Why?" Del asked.

He did not flinch from it. "Because I failed."

"Failed what?" I asked.

"The gods," he said, "and myself."

I stared at him a long moment, matching stare to stare, then shook my head. "Let's go, bascha."

"Tiger—"

Nihko's brow rings glinted in the sunlight. "You would abuse the metri's hospitality?"

"Look, I don't want to abuse anyone's hospitality. But you certainly didn't offer us any when you destroyed our ship, and you didn't improve matters by attempting to sell me to the metri—"

"*Did* sell," he put in.

"—and she's not exactly being hospitable by ordering me to make a man of her brother's wife's brother's brother's grandson," I finished.

"That's one 'brother's' too many," Del pointed out helpfully.

"Do you not believe he needs it?" Nihko inquired.

I glared at him again, eyes narrowed. "Just where do you fit, Nihkolara? Aside from being profanation and abomination, that is. What are you to these people? What are they to you?"

"My past," he said only.

Another figure moved out of shadow into light. The boy whom the metri wanted to be a man. "Tell him, Nihkolara," Herakleio challenged, lounging against the white-painted stonework of the entry way. "Tell him the whole of it."

Nihko made a gesture. "Herak . . . let it be."

"Herakleio. Ikepra are not permitted familiarity."

Color stained the first mate's face, then flowed away so he was alabaster-pale. There was tension throughout his body; Herakleio had reached inside him somewhere, touched a private place.

Herakleio displayed white teeth in a sun-coppered face. "Tell the pretender how you *fit*, Nihkolara."

And Nihkolara told me, while the heat beat on our heads.

Chapter 14

I flopped flat on the bed and stared up at the low ceiling. "This is all too complicated. And getting worse."

Del, sitting as she so often chose to sit—on the floor against the opposite wall—shrugged. "What is complicated? There were eleven women placed upon the island by the gods, and each bore eleven daughters *of* those gods. Then the gods sent those daughters sons of other women, and so the Eleven Families took root and flowered here."

"How poetic," I observed sourly. "And of course you'd find it easy: it's all about *women*."

"I suspect it is simpler even for gods to get babies on women."

I rolled my head and looked at her. "You're finding entirely too much amusement in this, bascha."

"Am I amused?"

"Inside. Where I can't see."

Her mouth twitched. "And from those eleven daughters came sons and daughters of the sons sent to lie with them, and so the people of first couplings may name themselves gods-descended."

"But not everyone on Skandi is gods-descended." I realized what I'd said and amended it immediately. "Not everyone *believes* they are gods-descended. I mean, they aren't gods-descended, of course, because no one is, but if they think it's possible, they might believe they aren't. Even if others are. *Believe* they are, that is." I dropped my forearm across my face and issued a strangled groan. "I *said* this was too complicated!"

Del seemed to grasp it well enough. "They believe they aren't gods-descended because certain sons came to Skandi from other islands, not from gods, and married the daughters of those first divine couplings."

From under my arm I added, "And so those who can count the generations back to those specific eleven women consider themselves superior to everyone else."

"Well," Del said judiciously, "I suspect that if I were descended of gods, and the others weren't, I might count myself superior."

I removed my arm and hiked myself up on one elbow. "*You* would? And here I thought you considered yourself no better than even the lowliest slave, bascha."

"I said 'might,' " she clarified. "And it doesn't matter, here. Here I am a woman."

"You are a woman anywhere. And I know for a fact a lot of men are convinced you *are* gods-descended."

"Thank you."

"Of course, they don't know you as well as I do." I flopped down again, pondering the information. "It seems obvious enough to me: these eleven women found themselves in the family way, and, thus disgraced, were exiled here." I shrugged against the mattress. "It's a pretty story they all made up to excuse their wanton behavior, and the eleven little outcomes of it."

"But it might be true."

"Oh, come on, bascha—gods impregnating women?"

"It would be an explanation for why there's magic in the world."

"Magic? Hah. Maybe superstition. Stories. Meant to entertain—"

"—or enlighten."

"—or to pass the night—"

"—or to keep a history alive."

"—or to simply waste time." I thrust an arm beneath my head and changed the subject. Sort of. "So Nihko and the metri are related through the now-infamous Eleven Families—"

"And Herakleio."

"—which explains why so many Skandics look alike."

"Which explains why you look like so many Skandics. You are."

"But not necessarily related to the metri, or Nihko, or your boy Herakleio."

"He's not my boy," Del declared. "He's older than I am."

"By what, one or two years?"

"That's still older, Tiger."

"While I'm just *old*."

"You should take a nap," Del advised after a moment.

"Why? Because I'm old?"

"No. Because you're cross-grained."

"Cross-grained?"

"Out of sorts."

"I know what it means, bascha. And if I am, it's because I'm tired—"

"I said you should take a nap."

"—of all these convoluted explanations," I finished with emphasis. "Hoolies, this is ludicrous! Women impregnated by gods, and men sent to marry their daughters—"

"Most history *is* a collection of stories," Del said. "It is so in the North."

"And I got my name because I killed a sandtiger I magicked up out of my dreams," I blurted in disgust. "Hoolies, do you think I really believe that? I was a kid. Younger even than Herakleio. Or you."

"You have done things," she said finally, "that are not explainable."

"There's an explanation for everything."

"And your sandtiger?"

I shut my eyes. "Coincidence. Hoolies, I just wanted a way out of slavery. I took advantage of something that happens once or twice a year. It was just the Salset's turn to be meat for a beast."

"And changing the sand to grass?"

"The sand *isn't* grass, Del. It's sand. And besides, all I did was suggest they bring the water to where it wasn't."

"Which can change the sand to grass."

I grunted. "In time, I suppose."

"Magic, Tiger, wears many guises."

"Like Nihko?"

Del was silent.

I turned my head against my arm. "Well?"

"I don't know."

"Maybe *you* should take the nap."

"I am neither tired nor cross-grained. I am, after all, younger than you." She smiled sunnily even as I scowled. "Besides . . ."

"Besides what?"

"You were dead only yesterday."

"But alive today—and lacking a sword." I swore. "I *hate* to be without a sword. I get into trouble when I don't have a sword."

"You get into trouble when you *have* a sword."

"But I can also get myself out of it. If I have a sword."

Del observed me. "You are on edge."

"Aren't you?"

"They haven't offered to harm us."

"But they haven't told us what they intend to do with us either. I don't find that comfortable."

"Especially when you lack a sword."

"If I had one, we'd be gone from here already."

"There's more to it than that."

I sighed, conceding it. "Something doesn't feel right."

Del was silent.

I glanced at her. "Well? Don't you feel it?"

She nodded.

"There. See?" I smiled triumphantly.

"All we can do," she said, "is wait. Watch. Be ready."

"I'd rather be ready with a sword in my hands."

"Well, yes." Del's smile was crooked. "But we have none, either of us, and until we can get them I think we'd best do what we can to preserve our energy." She paused. "As I said, you were dead only yesterday."

Rather than debate it any further—I *was* on edge, and tired—I took a nap.

* * *

Upon awakening alone, I went off in search of Nihkolara to clear up a few matters. It took me a while to track him down, but I found him at last seated upon one of the low perimeter walls surrounding Akritara, staring off into the distance. Beyond him, the setting sun leached the blue of the sky and transmuted it to dusty purple, streaked with ribbons of orange and gold.

As if a friendly companion, I sat down upon the wall next to him and swung both legs over, perching comfortably even as the evening breeze stripped hair out of my face. (Which was one thing the shaven-headed first mate didn't have to contend with.) "So, how did you do it?"

He made no sign he was aware of my presence, though obviously he was. I figured Nihkolara was only rarely taken by surprise.

I kept my tone light. "It's not every man who can make another appear to be dead—"

"You were."

"Dead?" I expelled air through my nose in sharp commentary. "I don't think so. But I'll admit it's an effective trick."

He continued staring into the sunset. "Believe as you will. You are an apostate."

"I?" I slapped a hand against my chest with a meaty thwack. "But I am a messiah. How can *I* be an apostate?"

He shook his head slightly. "You treat it all as a huge jest, Southron. Because you are afraid."

"Afraid of what? You? That kid?"

"Afraid of the truth." He glanced at me briefly, then looked back into the fading day. "What you do not understand, you ridicule. Because you know there is something in the heart of it that may be dangerous."

"I understand danger well enough." I swung my feet briefly, thumping heels against plastered brick. "But you're avoiding my question."

"You appeared to be dead because you were."

I sighed. "Fine. For the sake of argument, let's say I was dead. How, then, did you bring me back?"

Nihko grinned into the air. "Trickery."

"More secrets, I take it?"

The grin faded. He looked at me now, gaze intense. "Because I am ikepra does not mean I lack belief," he said, "and it is belief which rouses power. It means only that I failed in the maintenance of my oaths, in the convictions of my heart." Something moved in his face, briefly impassioned, then was diluted beneath a careful mask. "The body was weak."

"Strong enough," I commented. "We've wrestled a little, you and I."

"Flesh," he said dismissively. "I speak of the heart, the soul. But the body is a base vessel of vast impurities, and if one cannot cleanse himself of such, the vessel is soiled."

"Ikepra?"

"Broken oaths," he said, "provide a weak man with weaker underpinnings. Eventually they crumble—and so does he."

I had intended to comment, but the words died in my mouth. We were more alike than I wanted to admit, Nihkolara and I. Possibly related, though I didn't see how that would ever be settled. But certainly linked in the heart by knowledge of broken vows and shattered honor, and lives warped because of it.

"So you found Prima Rhannet, because the kind of oath she wanted was one you could serve."

"Without doubt," he confirmed. "Without hesitation. It is far easier to kill other men than to kill one's soul."

"Killing other men *does* kill the soul."

He stared at me as if weighing my intent. Brow rings glinted. In clear light I could see the hint of a scab in his left eyebrow where he had cut from his flesh the ring I wore on my necklet. "If one's soul is not already dead."

I meant to answer, to dredge up some kind of witty remark that would diffuse the tension. But Nihkolara stood up and stepped over the wall onto the cobbles of the courtyard. I smelled the perfume of the blossoms, the acrid tang of dust lifted by wind. And the sweat of fear.

"I think," he said, "you have a stronger heart than I."

"I have *what*—?" But he turned from me before I could complete the question and walked away with purposeful strides.

Realizing he had deflected my questions away without divulging answers beyond glib, unspecific replies and personal challenges, I stared scowling into the sunset, disgusted that I'd let him get away with it.

From here you couldn't see the actual edge of the cliff, or know that the world currently was little more than a crescent of wracked remains, but the heart sensed something. It knew the island was paramount upon the waters, and yet subject to them. I felt at once isolated, apart, humbled, despite the awareness that the earth stretched far beneath me as if I were a god.

God. Hoolies. Nihko and everyone else had me thinking like they did.

I shifted my weight then, an infinitesimal amount. A slight redistribution forward, leg muscles bunching, so that it would require very little effort on my part to spring up and turn, balanced for defense *or* offense. Because I knew he was there.

"You fool no one," Herakleio announced belligerently.

I smiled into the sunset. "Not anyone? Oh, I am irredeemably devastated."

"You believe you are clever, claiming to want no part of us, when it's obvious you mean only to mislead us, to convince the metri that you are the son of her daughter."

Still smiling, I said, "You are a gloriously self-indulgent, self-centered fool, Herakleio. What makes you think I *should* want any part of you?"

"Because of what we are," he shot back. "The Stessoi are gods-descended, one of the Eleven Families . . . we are wealthy and powerful beyond any man's dreams, pretender, and certainly beyond yours. You come here thinking to fool the metri—"

"I was brought here," I interrupted crisply, "against my own will. But I came because the choice was simple."

"To be poor, or rich."

"To be free, or enslaved. And there was the small matter of my companion being held onboard ship, to insure my cooperation." I shrugged. "Some choices are easy. Especially when they concern others."

"But you are free now. The metri has paid the renegadas. Your companion is here, not there. You may go."

"But the metri has reminded me of a thing called a debt." I sighed. "Unlikely as it may sound, I don't like owing anyone. I prefer to pay such debts."

"*I* will pay it!"

I turned then, swinging legs back over the wall so I might face him. "And then the debt would be yours."

He was prepared for that. "You would pay it by leaving."

I examined him, marking the look in his eyes. "Are you so very afraid that I am who the metri wants me to be?"

He denied it, of course, but his eyes told the truth. "There has been a parade of pretenders presenting themselves to the metri. You are no different."

"But I am," I replied. "And now that I have seen you, I understand why." I grinned. "Like it or not, boy, we are seeds from the same plant."

"Every islander born bears some resemblance to us," he countered quickly. "Do you think there are so many of us on Skandi that we would never intermarry?"

"But only those from the Eleven Families are permitted to intermarry," I said. "The gods-descended, naturally, wouldn't dream of marrying anyone else. Which means that descendants of those families are bound to closely resemble *one another*, but not necessarily anyone else." I raised inquisitive brows. "Do you know if any of the other metris is missing a relative?"

He hissed something at me in Skandic, stiff as an affronted cat.

I grinned at him. "Relax," I said. "There's a way out of this."

"I could kill you."

That language I understood very well. "Well, yes, that's one way, though I confess it's not the way *I* would prefer. And since the metri is not a stupid woman, she'd likely know it was you right off." I shrugged. "I don't know what the customs are like in Skandi—maybe murderers are still allowed to inherit."

Something in his expression suggested they were not. "What is your way, then? And why would you tell me it?"

"Because I suspect the metri wants you to inherit," I answered calmly.

It perplexed him. He *was* young.

"First," I said, "it's not as easy to kill another man as you might expect. And I'm not talking about the physical ability to take a life, but the will." Before he could protest, I continued. "Anyone can kill in self-defense, or to protect their kin. But to purposefully track a man and challenge him requires an entirely different part of the mind." I tapped my head. "And to carry through without getting killed yourself . . . well, it doesn't always work out the way you'd like."

"*You* are alive."

"How old are you? Twenty-three?"

The question took him aback. "Twenty-four."

I nodded contemplatively. "For every year you have been alive, I've killed a man. Or maybe two. Possibly three. I'm alive not because I wanted it more than the others, but because I learned how to find the *ways* to survive. And the ways to kill. In here—" I touched my forehead,"—as much as in here." This time my heart.

He frowned. "Why are you saying such things? Do you mean to frighten me?"

"You're twenty-four. Nothing frightens you."

It stung. He glared at me, lips tight.

"Good," I said. "It shut you up. Maybe if you listen, you'll learn something."

He stopped listening. "This is not your place. This is not your world. This is not your legacy."

"It's yours," I agreed. "But if you want it, you're going to have to learn how to deserve it."

"*Deserve* it—!"

I stood up, wiped my palms together to brush away dust, then took one long stride that put me right up against Herakleio. Before he could step away or protest, I poked fingers into his breastbone. "You're soft," I said gently. He made to move; I caught a wrist, clamped, and held him in place. "Big, broad, strong, and likely very quick, but soft. Soft up here—" I placed one forefinger against his brow and nudged. "—and soft down here." I dug stiffened fingers into his belly.

Outraged, he opened his mouth to shout but I raised my voice and overrode him.

"I suspect you spend most of your time drinking in cantinas—or whatever you call them here—hanging out with your friends—likely young men of the other ten supposedly gods-descended families about your age—and entertaining women. You repeatedly ignore the metri's requests that you learn how to do the accounting because figures are boring, and you haven't the faintest idea how the vineyards are run because you'd rather drink the results than make them." I released his wrist. "In short, you are a perfectly normal twenty-four-year-old male of a wealthy, powerful family who believes his ancestors were sired by gods."

He sputtered the beginnings of an incoherent response. I cut him off.

"She's dying," I said. "She needs you to be prepared. She needs to know everything her family has worked for will be secure in your hands."

He managed a response finally, sharp and aggressive. *"Not in yours?"*

"There is no proof I am the son of her daughter. There never can be. She may want to believe it, but she doesn't *know* it. And it matters."

"She's the metri. She can simply declare you heir."

"But she didn't," I told him. "She asked me to make a man of the boy who is."

"As if you could!"

I shrugged. "Try me."

His lip curled. "Southroner. I know what you are, you sword-dancers. Kill-for-hires. All these games about honor codes and oaths—I *know* what you are. Men of no family, no prospects. Honorless men who worship a sword, who worship death, because there is nothing in your lives otherwise, no heritage, no pride, no place with the gods when you die." He leaned into me, challenging with his body. "And *you* speak of making me a man."

He definitely had mastered scorn. Fortunately, I had mastered patience.

Well, sometimes.

I crossed my arms and grinned. "Heard of us, have you?"

"You are as bad as ikepra, you and men like you. And you dare to come here into this house, into the *metri's* house, and profane her dwelling."

"I'm sure she's capable of hiring some priest to come cleanse and re-bless it once I'm gone."

"Go now," he hissed, spittle dampening my face. "Go *now*, sword-dancer."

I did not wipe my face. Softly, I said, "Make me."

He was, no doubt, accustomed to striking slaves, because he drew his right arm across his chest as if to backhand me. I, meanwhile, jammed a fist deep into his belly, and when he bent over it, I hooked an ankle around his. A quick leveraged jerk to upend him, and he was all flailing arms and awkward body.

He landed hard, as I meant him to, sprawled flat on the stone of the terrace. Taken completely unaware, he drove elbows into stone, smacked the back of his skull, scraped his forearms, all before his legs and butt landed. When they did, he bit his tongue, which bled all over his chin and fine linen tunic as he wheezed and coughed.

I stood over him, but not within range even if he'd had the wherewithal to attempt anything. "Insults don't accomplish much," I told him, "unless you're better than the other man." I flicked a spot of dust off my tunic. "And then you don't need 'em."

Spittle mixed with blood came flying out of his mouth. He missed.

"I pay my debts," I told him. "If you don't like it, take your complaints to the metri."

Rage contorted his features. Even if he had been quick enough, skilled enough, he was so angry now any attack would have been ineffective. Breathlessly he loosed a string of teeth-gritted invective that undoubtedly would have scorched my ears had I understood the language.

Then again, maybe not. I've been sworn at by the best. And she was far preferable as company than the metri's brother's wife's brother's grandson.

I waved farewell at him. "Come see me in the morning."

Chapter 15

It was conveyed to us by the kilted servant that the metri would have us all in to dinner. I got the impression this was a rare occurence; not that guests weren't hosted properly, but that two of those guests were renegadas.

Ah well. After my discussion with Herakleio, I was primed for a more interesting atmosphere.

Which is exactly what I got. Del and I were escorted into a large, airy dining chamber already peopled by Prima Rhannet, her first mate, Herakleio, and the metri herself. Who, standing quietly beside the door, greeted me courteously, then smashed the flat of her hand into the side of my face.

The shock of it drove me back a step. Instinct took over instantly, and I trapped her wrist in one hand before she could strike again, though she did not appear to intend it.

I rubbed the knuckles of my other hand against my stinging cheek. "What in hoolies was *that* for?"

"Punishment," she said crisply, "for striking Herakleio."

"Now, wait just a moment—"

"It was required. I am the metri. Discipline is dictated by me."

"And what about Herakleio trying to strike a guest in the metri's household?"

"Herakleio has been punished as well."

I glanced beyond her to the table. Herakleio glared back at me. Yes, his left cheek bore a ruddy spot high on the bone.

I released her wrist. "If you intend me to make a man of him, it's going to require more than sweet words and soft caresses."

She inclined her head. "I give you leave to do what is required."

"At the risk of getting smacked around by you?" I shook my head. "That's not in the contract."

"We have no contract," she answered at once. "This is a debt, which you intend to discharge." Her eyes glinted. "However, the point has been made and need not be repeated. Now, seat yourselves at my table and enjoy the bounty of the house."

I turned as she moved through the door *away* from the table. "What about you?"

She paused. "There are things to be settled among you. It were better done without my presence, so you may speak freely."

And then she was gone, leaving Del and me staring in bemusement at the others.

Prima snorted, poured herself wine from a jar. "Neatly done," she said. "Why soil herself by eating in the same room as renegadas?"

"What about me?" Herakleio shot back. "*I* am left to eat in the same room as renegadas."

"But you are already hopelessly soiled," Prima retorted. "You slept with a renegada."

"You weren't one then!"

"No," she agreed. "I was the daughter of a slaver. Likely the metri believes that every bit as bad." She gulped wine, smiled through glistening droplets painting her wide mouth. "Herak, you are such a child sometimes. But pretty, I will admit."

He recoiled. "Pretty!"

She waved a hand in my direction as Del and I took our seats at the table. "All you Stessoi are pretty. Even the women."

"*You* would know," he sneered. "Though no Stessa would ever demean herself and dishonor her family by—" A pause. "—cohabiting with such as you."

"Such as I," Prima said silkily, "come from the best families."

"Not yours."

"Oh, mine is a family of slavers. But what of the original Eleven Families? Can you swear there is no other woman such as I, nor a man who might prefer another man in his bed?" She smiled sweetly. "One such as you, perhaps."

Beneath his tan, Herakleio turned pale as bleached linen, then reddened nearly to purple. He was so shocked and outraged he couldn't summon a voice to speak with.

Prima laughed at him. "No, Herak, I do not suggest your taste runs in that direction. Be at ease. I only meant that certain men may desire you even as women do."

Clearly he had never considered that. But then, neither had I. I knew of such men, such interests, of course, but had never really contemplated how I'd feel were I the object of another man's interest.

Prima Rhannet, having plunged both Herakleio and me into mutual black scowls and deep thoughts, grinned at Del. "Men are such fools, sometimes. They think they *are* that which dangles between their legs." She lifted her cup as if in salute. "While we women know the only truly important part of the body resides within our skulls."

"Perhaps," Del agreed, dipping a chunk of bread into olive oil, "but that need not mean we are better than they."

"Women *are* better than men."

"Some women are better than some men," Del countered quietly, and filled her mouth with bread.

I had poured myself some wine. Now I stopped the cup halfway to my mouth. "That isn't what you claimed when we first met!"

Del arched brows at me and continued to chew.

"It isn't," I repeated. "You told me men were nothing but beasts driven by lust and violence."

She hitched a shoulder. "The men I knew were. I had gone South, remember?"

"What about me?"

She didn't answer, which was answer in itself.

I set the cup down with a thump. "If I'm that bad—"

"You were," Del said. "But you aren't anymore. I have leavened you—" She grinned. "—like bread."

"Thank you for that, bascha!"

"You inspire me." Prima took off a chunk of bread from the loaf in the center of the table and sopped it in olive oil. "The truth is, all men are born fools," she declared, "and if you forget, they remind you."

Nihko was being conspicuously silent. I fixed him with a hard eye. "What have you to say?"

He had bypassed the bread and was serving himself a large fish from the platter. "I? Nothing. I know better."

"He has heard it before," Prima said.

Herakleio's color was high. "And he has little to say for men, anyway. He is missing a significant portion of those parts Prima repudiates so eloquently."

It was purposely cruel. It was also a killing offense, though Nihko simply began stripping meat from the fish.

Prima wasn't smiling or laughing anymore. "He will not provoke," she said. "But I will, Herak."

Herakleio feigned fear, then looked at me. "Did Nihkolara explain why he is—without? How he came to lose that which he most adored, and wielded most assiduously?"

"Enough," Prima said.

"How he alone seemingly intended to people several islands with his byblows," Herakleio continued, "and might well have accomplished it had he kept himself to whores and unmarried women. But he did not. There was the Palomedi metri's daughter, you see—when the metri herself believed he was faithful to *her.*"

"Recall what he is!" Prima said sharply.

Herakleio filled it with scorn. "Ikepra."

I poured more wine. It was very good. Maybe it wouldn't be so difficult to remain here for a while. "This is what I enjoy most in life," I said lightly, "good food, good wine, good friends."

Del's expression was guileless. "Pity Abbu Bensir isn't present." Before I could say yea or nay, she served me with something from a common dish.

"Who?" Herakleio asked crossly, even as I scowled at Del.

I peered at the food, frowning. It looked like leaves all rolled up into miniature sleeping bundles.

"Abbu Bensir is a sword-dancer," Del answered. "A very good sword-dancer. In fact, he claims to be the best in the South."

"Ah." Prima shot a grin at me. "Surely there are those who disagree."

"Surely there are," Del confirmed demurely.

"What is this?" I poked the rolled plant with a wary finger.

Prima leaned, plucked one bundle from my plate, paused long enough to say "stuffed grape leaves" and bit it in half.

"Stuffed with what?"

"Kill-for-hires," Herakleio said dismissively.

For one bizarre moment I thought he meant that's what was rolled up inside the grape leaves. But no.

Del turned at once to me. "Is that true? That all sword-dancers are hired murderers?"

She could answer as well as I. For some reason she didn't want to. I bestowed upon her a look that promised we'd discuss this later, then glanced at Herakleio.

"I have killed," I said. "But then most men have, in the Punja, because there is often no choice. But that has little to do with being a sword-dancer."

"How not?" Prima asked, having survived the leaf-bundle.

Herakleio snorted disdain, helping himself to the common bowl.

"I dance," I pointed out. "I am hired by tanzeers—our desert princes—to settle disputes in the circle so that men need not die." I shrugged. "Skirmishes, battles, and wars waste men in a hostile land that kills too many by itself. It's simply good sense to save lives by settling disputes in the circle."

"But you say you've killed!"

I picked up one of the leaf-bundles Del had bestowed upon me. "Bandits," I answered. "Borjuni. Slavers. Tanzeers." I bit into the bundle, contemplated its flavor, swallowed. "Sorcerers."

That shocked Herakleio. "Sorcerers!"

"Have you none here?" Del asked.

"IoSkandi," Prima said, avoiding Nihko's look.

"Who?" I asked. "What *are* they, anyway? I've heard the term before." I shot a glance at Nihko. "Though it seems to be a secret."

He smiled enigmatically. "And so it shall remain."

Herakleio turned the topic back upon itself. "This Abbu Bensir," he said. "*Is* he better than you?"

I opened my mouth to answer, shut it. Was aware of Del's attention though she hid it, and the scrutiny of the others. In the South I might have immediately confirmed my status with dramatic bravado, but I was not in the South. And for some reason, here and now, I felt like telling the truth. "I don't know."

"Have you ever danced against him?"

"Many times."

"Then you should know who is better. Or are you afraid to admit he is?"

"We were trained together, Abbu and I. We sparred many times then, and have since, to test skills and conditioning. But we have met only one time in a circle that would have determined who truly was better."

"And the result?"

I shook my head. "There was none. The dance was never finished."

"Ah." Herakleio smiled as if he knew why. "And so the true answer must wait for another time, another circle, and another dance."

"No," I said.

"What, then? Is he dead?"

"He was very much alive the last time we saw him."

"Then why will you never settle things?" Herakleio demanded. "Are you afraid?"

The food was suddenly tasteless in my mouth. "There are rituals. Honor codes, oaths, things that bind those of us who are trained by swordmasters such as I was, and Abbu. In the circle dishonor is not tolerated, nor broken oaths. Not among true sworddancers; there are men who fancy themselves sword-dancers, who attempt to act the part, but they aren't. They just want the glory without the years, the work."

"Or the oaths," Del said softly.

I shrugged. "Abbu and I might meet again someday, but it

won't be to settle who is better. It will be a death-dance, to punish a man who broke all the codes and honor of Alimat."

"Why?" Herakleio demanded.

"Elaii-ali-ma," I answered. Then phrased it in a word they'd understand, as I looked at Nihkolara. "I'm ikepra, too."

The muscles of his face stilled. His hands stopped moving. Even his eyes, fixed on me, were hard as stone.

Among dangerous men there are two kinds of quietude of the body: when he is at ease, and when he wishes to attack. The latter is not the same as being prepared to fight or to defend, though it can be mistaken as such by the inexperienced. The latter is neither bluster nor challenge, but the willingness and the wish to tear into pieces the offending party.

And not doing it.

Beside me, Del, too, stilled. Prima Rhannet had stopped breathing. Only Herakleio, blind to the tensions, was relaxed. And smiling, as if pleased by my answer. I had, after all, confessed my unworthiness in terms he understood.

Nihkolara rose. His hands at his side trembled minutely, as if he could not bear the demands of his body. He had not reacted when Herakleio disdained his manhood, but for some inexplicable reason, my casting myself into his place stirred in him some deep response.

"Nihko," Prima said softly.

He did not look at her, but only at me. With effort he moved his jaws. "A man living in darkness," he said, "has not known the light and thus may not repudiate it, nor hold common cause with one who has."

With immense self-control and no little dignity, he walked from the chamber.

Prima was unsmiling as she looked at me. "That was ill done."

"Was it?" Del inquired with a softness I recognized. "Tiger is what he is, and may confess it freely to anyone he wishes."

Prima, who did not recognize such softness, began with some heat. "Nihko is what *he* is—"

"And has the freedom to be so," Del interrupted. "So do we all: man, woman, renegada, sword-dancer. Skandic or Southron."

"But *is* he a man?" Herakleio, of course, was focused on insults. "Nihko no longer claims the part of—"

"Stop," I said, so coldly that he obeyed me. "There is more to manhood, as Captain Rhannet put it so eloquently, than that which dangles between our legs."

Herakleio laughed. "The willingness to use it?"

Prima ignored the comment, ignored Herakleio, and stared searchingly at me a long moment. Her expression was unfathomable. Then her mouth twisted, and she looked at Del. "You do have him trained."

Del neither smiled nor replied. This time, Prima recognized the softness in the Northern woman that had nothing to do with weakness of will, and everything to do with strength of purpose. And her eyes shied away.

"The metri," I said as I picked up my wine, "is a very wise woman."

"For avoiding this?" Herakleio suggested.

"For allowing it," Del answered.

Prima didn't much like what that implied. Her eyes narrowed thoughtfully as she contemplated the idea. She shook her head slightly, then downed her wine as if to gulp it might wash away her suspicion.

I looked at Herakleio. "Among the powerful," I said, "there are reasons for everything. And results wrung from those reasons."

Clearly puzzled and irritated by it, Herakleio made a curt, dismissive gesture. "That makes no sense."

"The metri knows it does," I said. "And for some inexplicable reason, she seems to think I can teach you to understand."

Herakleio favored me with a withering glance. "A waste of time."

I grinned at him. "Yours? Or mine?"

Prima laughed. "It might be worth watching."

Herakleio glared at her. "Do you think to *live* here?"

"My ship is my home," Prima replied. "But the metri has said she will receive me here before the other families." She paused. "Formally."

At that Herakleio stood up, stiffly affronted. "You soil this household," he announced, and took himself out of the chamber with definitive eloquence.

The captain grinned a slow, malicious grin, then cut her eyes at me as she poured her cup full once again.

"Good food, good wine . . . good friends."

I smiled back in kind. "Or interesting enemies."

Chapter 16

After dinner I paid a visit to the kilted servant, whose name I learned was Simonides, and put my request before him. He agreed it could be fulfilled, and would be by morning. I thanked him and departed, wanting very much to ask him how he'd become a slave, how he bore it, and if he hoped for freedom one day. But I did not ask him those questions, because I knew that a hard-won tolerance of certain circumstances, the kind of toleration that allows you to survive when you might otherwise give up, was fragile and easily destroyed. It was not my place to destroy his.

From Simonides I went in search of Prima Rhannet, whom I found alone in the chamber she shared with Nihkolara. The metri's hospitality had not, apparently, extended to *two* rooms for such people as renegadas.

Or else she believed the captain and her first mate were lovers.

"What?" Prima asked crossly as I grinned at the thought.

"Never mind." I didn't enter, just lounged against the door-frame. "Where's Nihko?"

She was drinking more of the red Stessa wine, sitting on the bed against the wall with her legs drawn up beneath her skirts, tenting linen over her knees. A glazed winejar was nested in the mattress beside her hip. "He has gone back to the ship."

"Upset with the dinner conversation?"

"It is his task," she said lugubriously, "to be certain all is well with my crew and vessel."

"Oh, of course."

Her tone was level. "What have you come here for?"

"Explanation. Introduction. Education."

She frowned. "About what?"

"Herakleio," I answered. "You share a past. I want to know about it."

Coppery brows leaped upward on her forehead. "You want to hear *gossip?*"

"Truth," I said. "It seems you know it."

She studied me, assessing my expression. After a moment she hooked a hand over the lip of the winejar and suspended it in midair. "I have only the one cup," she said, "but you may have the jar."

I remained where I was. "Is it so difficult for you to be in this household that you seek courage in liquor?"

Her chin came up sharply even as she lowered the jar. "Who are you to say such a thing?"

I moved then, entered the room, did as Del so often did and took a seat upon the floor, spine set into plaster. I stretched out long legs, crossed them at the ankles, folded arms against my ribs. "Someone who knows as well as you how to read others."

She smiled at that, although it was shaped of irony and was of brief duration. "So."

"The daughter of a slaver hosted in the house of the Stessa metri, *the* metri of Skandi—and a woman who once shared a bed with the heir. You must admit it has implications."

Bright hair glowed in lamplight. "Herakleio," she said dryly, "has slept with any woman willing to share his bed."

"And you were willing."

"I was."

"Even—" But I let it go, uncertain of how to phrase it.

She knew. "Even. But you see, it was many years ago. Before I understood what was in me. And I fancied myself in love with him."

"What about him," I asked, "is even remotely loveable?"

Prima laughed. "Oh, you have seen him at his worst. You inspire it in him. But Herak is more than merely a spoiled pet of a boy. There is stone in him, and sunlight as well."

"And so you slept with him."

She got up then, climbed out of the bed and came across to me, winecup in one hand and winejar in the other. She sat down next to me, set her spine against the wall even as I had, and handed me the jar. "Have you never done a thing that took you at the moment as a good thing, a thing that needed doing, only to regret it in the morning?"

"I never slept with another man." I lifted the pottery jar, set lip against mine, drank. "Nor ever want to."

"Oh no, that is not in you." She said it so casually. "But what of women? Surely there have been women you regretted in the morning."

"There have been *mornings* I regretted in the morning."

She laughed deep in her throat: she understood. "But it is true, is it not, that we too often do what we wish we had not?"

"You regret sleeping with Herakleio."

"Yes. And no."

"Oh?"

She drank her cup dry, then stared blindly at the opposite wall. In the ocher-gilt wash of lamplight, her many freckles merged. "He was my first man," she said, "and my last." She saw my frown of incomprehension. "Oh, there were other men in between. But I realized they offered nothing I wanted, not in my heart. It was women . . ." She let it go, shrugging. "But I was afraid of myself, of the truth, and so I sought out Herak again to prove to myself that I was like other women."

"And instead—?"

"He was drunk, was Herak. He did not even know me. I was merely a woman, and likely his second of the night. He slept hard when we were done, and did not awaken even as I withdrew." She swirled the lees in her cup. "By morning I understood the truth of what I was, what I wanted; what I was not, and did not want. So Herak twice had the awakening of me."

"*You* are drunk, captain."

Prima smiled, blurry eyes alight. "Of course I am."

"Why?"

"Because I am here. Because Herak is. Because Nihko is not." She recaptured the jar from me and poured her cup full. "Because I want your woman, and she will not have me."

It startled me because I had not been thinking of Del, or of Del in those terms. And then it lit a warmth deep in my belly that had nothing to do with lust.

Prima Rhannet turned her head to stare hard at me. "And that is what you *truly* came to me for."

"It is?"

She was drunk, but for the moment a smoldering anger burned away the liquor. "You wanted to know if I bedded your woman while I kept her on my ship."

"That isn't why I came."

"Why else?"

"To ask about Herakleio."

"Hah." She drank deeply, wiped her upper lip with the back of her hand, then tipped her skull against the wall. "It must be in your mind. A woman who sleeps with women. Others find it perverse. Disgusting. Frightening. Impossible. Unbelievable. Or at the very least, awkward."

"Well," I said consideringly, "you must admit it's a bit out of the ordinary when compared to most people."

"As is being a woman who captains her own ship when compared to most women."

"So instead of limiting yourself to only *one* extraordinary achievement, you accomplish two."

After a moment she said, "I had not thought of it that way."

"Which means you're doubly blessed—"

"—or doubly cursed."

"Depending on who you talk to." I gestured. "Then again, you're also a renegada. A *woman* renegada."

"Thrice cursed!" She sighed dramatically, then glanced sidelong at me. "I enjoy being—unpredictable."

"I figured you did."

"But that is not why I do what I do, or am what I am."

"I figured it wasn't."

She contemplated me further. "She told me you were, once, everything she detests in a man."

I drank deeply of my cup, then hitched a shoulder. "Depending on who you talk to."

"I talked to her."

"Then I was. If she says so. To her."

"She no longer detests you."

I grunted. "That is something of a relief."

"She told me you still have some rough edges, but she is rubbing them off."

I grinned into the winejar as I tipped it toward my face. "I enjoy having Del rub me off."

"That is disgusting!" Prima Rhannet jabbed a sharp elbow in my short ribs, which succeeded in startling me into a recoil and coughing spasm that slopped wine down my chin and the front of my tunic. "But amusing," she conceded.

I caught my breath, wiped my chin, plucked the wet tunic away from my skin. I reeked of rich red wine.

The captain hiccoughed. Or so I thought initially. Then I realized it was laughter she attempted to suppress. I scowled at her sidelong. "What's so funny?"

"You want to know how, and why," she said. "Every man does, except those who understand what it is to desire in a way others declare is wrong. They wish to know about mechanics, and motivation."

I opened my mouth to respond, shut it. Converted images in my head, and realized with abrupt and unsettling clarity that she was no different than I. I had been, after all, a slave, someone vilified, excoriated, for something I could not help. For being what I was, had no choice in being.

And I recalled so many nights when I cried myself to sleep, or when I hadn't slept at all because the beaten body had hurt so much. And how I had longed for, had dreamed of a world in which I had value beyond doing what others told me. What others *expected* of me, and punished to enforce it.

"I think," I said slowly, "that it shouldn't matter what others think."

"But it does."

"It does," I agreed bleakly. "But maybe it shouldn't. Maybe . . . maybe what's important is how we feel about ourselves."

I, of course, had believed I deserved slavery. Because I had been told so. Because I knew nothing else. Thus even the wishes, the dreams, had worsened the guilt.

"And if she thought of you now as she thought of you originally?" Prima asked. "Your Northern bascha?"

I stared into the darkness of the winejar, unable to find an answer. Not one that made any sense, nor *could* make sense to her.

"It matters," she said. "One can justify that it does not, that the opinions of others are without validity, but if the one person you care for more than yourself believes you are beneath contempt, then your life has no worth."

I stirred then. "I disagree."

"Why?"

"Because true freedom is when the only person whose opinion matters is your own. When you know your own worth."

Prima smiled. "But so often it is difficult to be comfortable in your own skin."

"Well, mine's a little battered," I said, "but on the whole I'm pretty comfortable in it."

Now.

"While hers no longer fits the way it used to."

I looked at Prima sharply. "What do you mean? And how in hoolies do you know anything about it?"

"We spoke," she answered, "as one woman to another. Women who have made a life among men no matter how difficult the task, no matter how vilified we were—and are—for it. As sisters of the soul."

"And?"

"And," the captain echoed, "she admitted to me that she has lost herself."

"*Del?*"

"Her song is finished," Prima said. "So she told me. She found her brother. Found the man who destroyed her family, her past, the future she expected to have. And she killed that man." Her eyes were smoky in the light. "Her song is finished, and now she hears yours."

It startled me. "Mine?"

"Of course. She came here with you, did she not?"

"You made certain of that, captain."

Prima laughed. "But you were bound here regardless of my actions."

I conceded that yes, we had been.

"But Skandi had nothing to do with her life," she continued. "It played no role."

"I don't know that Skandi plays much of a role in anyone's life," I pointed out, "except to people who live here."

"You are avoiding the truth."

I sighed. "All right. Fine. Yes, Del came with me to Skandi. In fact, it was Del who suggested it." I brightened. "Which means it does *too* have something to do with her life!"

The captain laughed and lifted her cup in salute. "But my point is that her song now is yours, not her own."

"And are you suggesting she'd be wiser to hear *your* song?"

The smile fled Prima Rhannet's mouth. "I might wish it," she said softly, "but no. She is a woman for men. For *a* man," she amended, "since no other man but you has taken her without force."

I was not comfortable with this line of conversation. I knew well enough of Del's past, but saw no need to discuss it with anyone other than Del. Who never did.

At least, with me. Seems she had with the renegada.

Prima saw my expression, interpreted it accurately. "I only mean you to realize what it is to have a woman such as she with you," she said. "A woman who *chooses* to be with you, because it is what she wants. There is honor in making such a choice, if that choice agrees with your soul. It is no diminishment for a woman to be with a man, to *want* to be with a man—but neither is it diminishment for a woman to want to be with a woman."

Put that way, well, I guess not. It was the other side of the mirror, the reflection reversed. So long as both sides of the couple were happy, with needs met, honor respected, no one forced or harmed, did it matter if the couple was comprised of two women, or two men?

Maybe not. Probably not. But it was hard to think of it in those terms. It made me uncomfortable. It was too new, too *different.*

More questions occurred. Should a woman be with a man because she was expected to? Because she was made to? Was it not akin to slavery to be forced to do and be what others insisted you do and be?

I had been what the Salset had made me. Prima Rhannet had apparently tried to be what she was expected to be, and found it slavery of the soul. For Del, raped repeatedly by a man who murdered her family, it might be simpler to avoid men altogether. She hadn't. She'd sought and found me, because she needed my help. But that time was long past, that life concluded.

The captain was right: Del had *chosen* to be with me. Such choices, freely made, were framed on personal integrity, not on expectations. That satisfaction of the soul was paramount.

With quiet fierceness Prima went on. "Men do not believe women have honor. They are threatened by such things in us, because they fear our strength. Better to discount it, to ridicule it, to diminish it, before we recognize and acknowledge our worth. Because then their lives would change. They would no longer be comfortable in their own hearts, and skins."

I knew that in the South, what she said was true. "And yet here in Skandi, *women* rule the households, the family business ventures." I paused. "Even the lines of inheritance."

"But such things are expected of women," Prima countered. "I speak of the things women are not believed capable of doing."

I couldn't help it: I was relieved to be back on ground made familiar by discussions with Del. Many discussions with Del. "Such as captaining a ship?"

"Women," she said, "should be permitted to do anything. And accorded honor for it."

I smiled. "Even if they choose to remain in the household doing those very things *expected* of women."

Prima opened her mouth to argue. Shut it. Glared into her cup.

I provoked intentionally. "Women should be accorded the same choices, no?"

She was crisp and concise. "Yes."

"But not every woman wishes to captain a ship."

"No."

"And if she chooses not to do so, women who choose *to* do so should not discount it, ridicule them for it, or diminish it."

She continued to glare, mouth hard and taut.

"The blade cuts two ways, captain."

"Yes," she said finally. "But there should be a choice. Too often there is not." Then, challenging me, "And would you have argued that before you met your Delilah?"

I smiled. "It's Del who put the other edge on that blade, captain. Before then I would have vowed no blade had more than one."

"So."

"So."

"You are a better man because of her."

"I am a better man because of her."

She nodded. "So."

"So."

Prima drank long and deeply, stared broodingly at the wall, then abruptly changed topics. "Herak," she said, "has ambitions to exceed Nihko's legend."

"*Nihko's?*" In the sudden switch, all I could think of was what he now lacked.

She waved a hand. "Not because of that. Because of what he was. Before." Prima drank. "Nihko was the son of the Lasos metri's sister. And women wanted him."

"I take it he wanted them back."

"Oh, indeed. And got them."

"And paid the price."

"Oh, indeed. He paid it." Prima sounded tired. "Herak, at least, keeps himself from married women, and metris, and metris' daughters."

I shifted my legs a little, cleared my throat, tried to wipe out of my mind the vivid imagery. The ultimate punishment for a man who loved women too much, as well as the wrong ones.

"Why do you care?" she asked. "Why ask me about Herak?"

I smiled. "A dance is undertaken inside the head as much as with the body."

It mystified her.

"Tomorrow I invite Herakleio into his first circle. I like to know a man's vices before I use them against him."

Prima Rhannet pondered that. Then she smiled in delight. "You think like a woman."

"Flattery," I said comfortably, and grabbed the winejar back.

Del awoke in the darkness as I slipped into bed beside her. She didn't turn to me even as I fit my body to hers, snugging one arm over and around her waist. "Wine," she said disapprovingly.

It was, I thought, self-evident. I buried my face in her hair, inhaling the clean scent.

"Who with?" she asked. Then, thinking she knew, "Did you drink the boy insensible?"

I bestirred myself to answer. "Not the boy. The captain."

Del went stiff.

"What's wrong, bascha?"

"Why her?"

"She had the wine."

"Why *her?*"

"I had questions."

Del did not relax. "And curiosity?"

Yawning, I offered, "Curiosity is generally the father of questions."

"Did she answer them?"

"Those she could. And raised some others." I tightened my arm at her waist, settled closer. "Go back to sleep, bascha."

"Why?" she asked. "Are you sated?"

My eyes sprang open. I lifted my face from her hair. "Am I *what?*"

"In curiosity. In body."

"Hoolies, Del, you think I slept with her?"

For a moment there was silence. "I think you might want to."

"What in hoolies *for?* She doesn't like men, remember?"

"To prove to her she's wrong."

I was so muddled by then I couldn't even dredge up a comment.

"To change her mind."

I snorted. "As if I could!"

"But wouldn't you wish to try?" Del's tone went dry. "Surely you could rise to the challenge, Tiger."

I laughed then, letting the wine overrule my better judgment. My breath stirred her hair.

In the voice of confession, she said, "I don't understand men."

I was fading. "Oh, I think you understand men all too well, bascha." I yawned again. "Beasts driven by lust and violence."

"I was driven," she said, "by lust *for* violence."

I wanted to understand, to tell her I understood, but I was too sleepy. "I'd rather you were driven by lust for me."

She relaxed then, utterly. The tension drained out of her on a resigned sigh. I knew better than to believe she'd never come back to the topic, but at least for tonight I was to be allowed respite.

Maybe I was getting old. (Well, old*er*.) But at that moment I was content merely to hold her, to share the warmth of this woman in my bed, and slide gently over the edge of sleep undisturbed by self-doubts or complex questions.

Chapter 17

I stood there on the summit, poised to fall. Except I wouldn't, couldn't fall, because I could fly. Was expected to fly.

Needed to fly.

The wind beat at me. It whipped moisture from my eyes and sucked them dry. Stripped hair back from my face. Threatened the breath in my nostrils and thus the breath in my lungs. Plucked at my clothes like a woman desiring intimacy, until the fabric tore, shredded; was ripped from my body. And I stood naked upon the precipice, bound to fly. Or die.

Toes curled into stone. Calluses opened and bled. I lifted my arms, stretched out my arms, extended them as wings, fingers spread and rigid. Wind buffeted palms, curled into armpits. I swayed against it, fragile upon the mountain. Poised atop the pillar of the gods.

"I can," I said. "I will."

Wind wailed around me. Caressed me. Caught me.

"I can. I must. I will."

Wind filled me, broke through my lips and came into my mouth, into my throat, into my body. It was no gentle lover, no kind and thoughtful woman, but a force that threatened, that promised release and relief like none other known to man.

Arms spread, I leaned. And then the wind abated. Died away, departed the mountain, left me free to choose.

I leaned, seeking the wind. Waiting for it to lift me.

Soared.

Plummeted—

—and crashed into the ground.

"Tiger?" Del sat up, leaned over the side of the bed. "Are you all right?"

I lay in a heap on the stone floor. Groggily I asked, "What happened?"

"You fell out of bed."

Groaning, I sat up. Felt elbows, knees. Peered through the darkness. "Did you push me?"

"No, I did not push you! You woke me up trying to shout something, then lunged over the edge."

"Lunged."

"Lunged," she repeated firmly.

I felt at my forehead, aware of a sore spot. Likely a lump would sprout by morning. "Why would I *lunge* over the side of my bed?"

"I don't know," Del said. "I have no idea what makes you do anything. Including drinking too much."

Back to that, were we? I stood up, tugged tunic straight, twisted one way, then the other to pop my spine. The noise was loud in the darkness.

"A dream?" she asked.

I thought about it. "I don't remember one. I don't remember dreaming at all." I rubbed briefly at stubbled jaw. "Probably because I feel so helpless without a sword. Kind of—itchy."

"Itchy?"

"Like something bad is going to happen."

Del made a sound of dismissal. "Too much wine." And lay back down again.

"Here," I said, "at least let me get between you and the wall. That way if I lunge out of bed again, I'll have you to land on."

Del moved over. *To* the wall. Leaving me the open edge, and below it the stone floor.

"Thanks, bascha."

"You're welcome."

I climbed back into bed, examined the side with a careful hand, found nothing to suggest a structural weakness. Likely I'd rolled too far, overbalanced, and just tipped over the edge. No matter what Del said about lunging.

Since she wouldn't cooperate and give me the wall side, I compensated by wrapping both arms around her. If I went, *she* went.

Smiling my revenge, I fell into sleep again.

In the morning I had indeed sprouted a lump, though not a bad one. Del caught me fingering it, pulled hair aside to look, then made a waving gesture. "You smell like a winery."

I grinned. "Not inappropriate, since we're *living* in one at the moment."

"Look at you." In tones of accusation.

I didn't have to. I knew what she referred to. A tunic stained red with spilled wine the color of old blood. I grasped the hem cross-armed and yanked the tunic off over my head. "There," I said. "All gone."

She eyed me askance, sorting out the spill of fair hair. She was rumpled, creased, and sleepy-eyed in a sleeveless, short-cut tunic that displayed nearly all of her exceptionally long and lovely limbs, incontestably magnificent despite her morning mood. I leered and made as if to swoop down upon her.

Del ducked away. "Not until after you've had a bath!"

"That'll have to wait," I said. "And so will you, if you think you can stand it."

She frowned, finger-combing her hair. "What are you talking about?"

"Today I begin transforming Herakleio into a man. It's dirty, sweaty business, that. The bath will come later."

Warily she asked, "How are you intending to transform him into a man? By outdrinking him?"

"Oh, I have no doubt I can outdrink him. I expect I can outdo him in most things, frankly." I recalled Prima Rhannet's comment about Herakleio's appetite for women. "Though I have learned some self-restraint over the years."

"*Have* you?"

"At knife- and sword-point, maybe, but self-restraint all the same." I stretched long and hard, waiting for the bones to settle themselves back into place. Some mornings they were slower to do so than others.

"You," she said dubiously. "You, transforming him into a man."

I twisted my torso in one direction, then back again. "You think I can't?"

Del considered her answer. "I think there are indeed things you can teach anyone," she said finally. "But—you know nothing about Skandi."

"I know a little something about being a man."

She contemplated my expression, made the decision not to allow me any more rope lest I take it and hang her with it. "Can I watch?"

I bent over to touch my toes, gripped them. "Later," I said tightly. "There's something I need you to do, first."

"Me?"

"Go see Simonides, the metri's servant. He's got a few things for you."

"For me."

"Well, for me and Herakleio, actually, but we'll be busy first thing. When you see what Simonides has assembled, you'll know."

"Will *he* know I know?"

I clasped palms behind my skull and pushed it forward, twisting, letting the knots in my neck pop loose. "Probably not."

"You're being obscure, Tiger."

"No, I'm not." I shook out my arms, let my hands flop like fish fresh off the hook. "I'm being *entertaining*."

In a severe tone, she said, "You're not going out like that."

"I'm not?" I wore lightweight, baggy trousers held up by the drawstring pulled tight across my hipbones. No shirt, no shoes; I was free of encumbrances, which is the way I preferred it. "Why not?"

"You'll frighten the poor boy half to death."

The "poor boy" was one year older than Del. "Good." I displayed my teeth in a ferocious grin. "Now, come here."

"Why?" Warily.

"Don't trust me, bascha?"

"Sometimes."

"Come here." I paused. "Please?"

Somewhat mollified, Del got up and approached.

"Here." I grasped her arms, lifted them, urged them around me. "Tight."

"Tiger—you *stink* of wine!"

"Would you, please?"

She sighed and wrapped her arms around me.

"Squeeze," I directed. "Tight."

She squeezed.

"Tighter."

"Tighter than this?"

We were plastered together. "Tight as you can, bascha."

She squeezed, and several of my spinal bones decided to pop back into place. Noisily.

"Gods," she said, and let go in shock.

"Better," I sighed, then grinned at her. "Now *you* smell of wine."

"Which was likely your intent all along."

"Oh, no. At least, not my *sole* intent." I leaned forward, smacked her a kiss that landed half on her mouth, half on her chin, and headed out the door. "Don't forget to go see Simonides."

"After my bath," she muttered.

Herakleio was spoiled. Soft. I opened the door to his room and walked in, with nary a blink from him. Probably because his eyes were sealed shut in a sleep so heavy as to verge on unconsciousness.

He was sprawled all over the bed, limbs tangled in linen. Apparently he had gone out on the town after dinner; I smelled wine and harsher liquors as well as a tracery of smoke. It wasn't huva weed—I doubted that grew in Skandi—but something similar, very rank even in a small amount when mixed with the traditional *perfume of cantina,* as Del had once described it.

The first test: failed.

"Up," I said quietly.

Not a flicker of response. Second test: failed.

The nearest foot stuck out from the side of the bed. I clamped hands around the ankle and headed toward the door, dragging the slack body out of bed entirely so that he flopped to the floor.

That woke him up.

Most of the bedclothes had accompanied him, so that he remained tangled even on the floor. In a flurry of linen and curses, Herakleio finally dug himself out from under and recognized me.

"You!"

"Me."

"What do you *want?*"

"You."

"Me?"

It was quickly becoming a repetitive conversation. "You."

"Why?"

Well, at least it was a change. "Orders."

"Orders? Orders? Whose?"

Maybe after a night out all he could think in were single words of single syllables. "The metri's," I answered. "Remember? I'm supposed to make a man of you."

He sat rigidly upright in a tangle of bedclothes and naked brown skin. "*This* is supposed to make me a man? Dragging me out of bed and dumping me on the floor?"

"It's a start. Not much of one, I'll admit, but a start."

He was beginning to wake up. He blinked outrage from his eyes and focused properly, brows lancing down to knit over his nose. He looked at me, and then the expression changed. "Gods," he murmured, staring fixedly at my abdomen.

Ah. The infamous scar.

"Up," I said, waggling fingers at him.

"Who did that to you?"

"A woman. Now, get up."

He didn't move. "A *woman* did that to you?"

"She did have a sword," I clarified. "Up, Herakleio."

"A *woman* cut you? With a sword?"

"A woman. With a sword."

"Gods," he said again.

"I'm just full of little mementos," I told him. "Nihko wears tattoos, I've got scars." I bent down to grab a wrist, but he scrabbled back. "Then get *up*," I said. "You can't learn much sitting on the floor."

"Much about what?" he asked warily.

"Anything. Look, this wasn't my idea, remember? I owe the metri a debt, and this is how she wants me to repay it."

He stood up then, letting the bedclothes drop entirely. He wore nothing but a sullen, smoldering resentment. "And just what is it *you* are supposed to teach me about being a man?"

"Come along and find out."

"Come along where?"

"Out."

"Out where?"

"Hoolies, Herakleio, is there anything in your mouth besides questions? Why don't you come along and see for yourself?"

"Breakfast," he challenged.

"After. If you've still got the belly for it."

That stung. "I've got the belly for it now."

"Maybe so, but we're not going to put anything in it now. Now we are going to introduce you to the dance."

"The what?"

"The dance."

"With *you*?"

"Not that kind of dance."

"I don't want an introduction to *any* kind of dance with you." He paused, then in tones of discovery, "You mean a sword-dance."

"Yes, I mean a sword-dance." I gestured. "Come on."

More outrage. "I have no clothes on!"

"Not willing to risk the valuable parts to a sword blade?" I grinned. "Why not, Herakleio? Too slow after last night?"

He glared. "I know nothing about using a sword, or dancing with men."

"That's right—you prefer to dance with women. So I've heard." I indicated the door. "Put some pants on, then, if it makes you feel better."

He swatted tangled hair out of his eyes. "Going back to bed would make me feel better."

"Undoubtedly, after all that you drank—and smoked?—last night. But you've mastered that already. Now it's time to master something else."

"A sword?" Asked with contempt.

"Among other things." I picked up a soiled tunic from a bench beside the door. "This ought to be enough."

He caught it as I flung it, curled his lip at me.

"Be a good little heir," I suggested. "Do as the metri wants."

It was reminder enough that another potential heir was in the metri's household. He shook out the tunic and tugged it on over his head. With grand scorn, he said, "Can I take a piss first?"

"You'd better," I suggested, "or otherwise you'll have soiled yourself before the morning is over."

Then I told him where to meet me and left him to his nightjar.

The house itself was built upon a lumpy pile of rumpled, porous, windblasted stone. It wasn't *much* of a rise—except for the cliff face, none of the crescent-shaped island was sharply cut or dramatically taller than the rest—but it was somewhat higher than the land surrounding it. Akritara was encircled by outgrowth pockets of stone-tiled courtyards and terraces delineated by low, slick-blocked walls painted white. Imagine a series of spreading puddles joining up here and there with one interlocking series of rooms plopped down in the middle, on different half-levels interconnected by sloping stone staircases, and you have an idea. Despite the hand-smoothed, rounded exterior corners of the rooms, the house was in no way strictly curved, in no way cleanly defined by a square room here, a square room there. It was a whole bunch of rooms clumped and mortared together, somehow forming a whole.

Having grown up in the hyorts of the Salset, individual roundish tents set in a series of ranked circles around the headman's larger hyort, I decided Akritara wasn't all that different than a tribal village. But it was made of stone because, I'd been told, there was no wood on the island except what was brought in from other lands, and none of the domed, arched rooflines followed the rules of precedence or symmetry.

But one low-walled, stone-tiled terrace on the side of the house was larger than the rest, and overlooked the part of the island that led to the city, and then to the rim of the caldera. It was here I went, here I groomed the tiles free of larger pebbles, grit, of shrubbery deadfall blown inside the wall. Barefoot, I walked the stone, feeling with the soles of my feet how the tiles were fit together, how the mortar joined them into permanence. I walked the terrace slowly, carefully, letting my feet come to know the place. I searched the surface with eyes as well, and fingertips. Some of the tiles were chipped at the corners, pitted by time and water. Hairline cracks ran through many of the squares, formed larger seams in others. But it was good stone well fit together. There were no significantly loose tiles, no broken or shattered pieces, nothing that could cause a foot to catch and falter, to betray the balance.

In Alimat, shodo-trained, we learned to dance on all surfaces. The Punja, the deep desert, was composed mostly of sand, but the South was also made of other blood and bone. The shodo had samplings of these other surfaces brought in from the borders of the South, and circles were made of each. Sand, pebbles, gravel, hard-pan, cracked and sunbaked mudflats, the crumbly border soil, the shell-seasoned sand of the coast near Haziz, hand-smoothed slabs of mud brick slick in the coating of water poured across it to simulate rain. On all these surfaces, in all these circles, we learned to stand, to wait, to move, to *dance*—long before a sword was ever put into our hands.

There was a faint tracery of windblown powdered grit across the tiles. I would ask Simonides about having the surface washed daily, to strip the face of the tiles of obstruction that could cause a bootsole, sandal, or callused foot to slide, but for now there was nothing to do for it but bear it. And we wouldn't be moving all that much. Not at first.

When Herakleio came at last, he found me walking the wall. It was perhaps knee-high, two handspans wide. I followed its curving spine surrounding the terrace, from the corner of one room to the corner of another, and all the distance between.

Bemused, he watched me. His posture was impatient, stiff, all hard bone and angles. There was no grace in him as he stood there, no interior balance. There is harmony in the body required by the dance. For the moment he had none.

He had, I was certain, gotten his height early. I suspected his hands and feet had seemed larger than life; he tripped over things, dropped things. Elbows were knocked against lintels, thighs scored by table corners, shins mottled by bruises. He'd outgrown that at last and now was in control of hands and feet, comfortable in the way his bones fit together, the angles of the joints, the smooth flow of tendon and sinew beneath the brown skin, the distribution of his weight. But there is spirit in bones and flesh that has nothing to do with how a man is made, only in how he thinks.

I walked the wall. Heel to toe and back again, then stood sideways across it and marked my way by instep one pace at a time. Eventually he grew bored, irritable, not even remotely curious.

As he opened his mouth to speak I stepped down off the wall. "Hop up, Herakleio."

"Up," he echoed in disbelief. Then, condescendingly, "I think not. I can conceive of better ways to waste my time."

I jerked a thumb. "Up."

"I am no longer a child, pretender, to play at such things."

"Well, the metri seems to think you are." I shrugged. "Indulge her by indulging me."

A parade of emotions flowed across his face. Resentment, realization, annoyance, impatience. But he moved. He stepped up onto the wall in one easy movement, muscles flexing smoothly beneath the flesh of his thighs below the hem of his tunic, and stood there.

"Well?" he inquired with elaborate contempt.

I pushed him off.

He didn't fall. Didn't wobble. Didn't flail with arms. Overbalanced, he simply stepped off. Now the wall lay between us.

"What—?" he began hotly.

"Get back up," I said, gesturing. "This time, stay up there."

He glared at me. "You're only going to try to knock me off again."

"Yes," I agreed. "And you're going to try *not* to be knocked off."

"This is a waste of time!"

"I thought so, at first." I shrugged. "I learned."

"Learned?"

"Many things," I told him. "Among them how to fall . . . and how not to fall."

"But this is—"

I stepped across the low wall, placed the flat of my hand against his spine, and shoved.

Herakleio, as expected, as intended, took one long pace in an attempt to reclaim his balance, smashed his toes into the wall, and saved himself from a nasty fall only by jerking a leg up and over, planting the foot. He barked his shin on the way, straddled the wall with a rather ungainly posture once he'd caught himself, but didn't fall.

"There," I said. "Not so hard, is it?"

He had three choices. He could pull one leg up and over on the far side of the wall, moving away from me; he could pull the other leg up and over, moving toward me; or he could stay exactly where he was, one leg on either side of the wall.

Herakleio stayed put.

"Good," I commented. "Keep both feet on the ground whenever possible."

He was furious. He told me so using clipped, hissing words in a language I assumed was Skandic.

"Hop up," I said. "Walk the wall, Herak. Imagine you'll die if you step down on either side." I paused. "That is, if you have any imagination."

"What, with you waiting to push me off?"

Mildly I suggested, "So don't let me."

He sucked in wind enough to blister me with all manner of vulgar commentary, but just then Del came around the corner into view and he shut his teeth with a click.

She carried two four-foot sticks in her hands—Simonides had donated precious broom handles—plus a couple of shorter, narrower pieces of wood, leather strips, a fruit knife, cloth, and a waterskin. She wore, as she had since arriving at Akritara, a long sleeveless linen tunic, very sheer, bound at the waist by a sash of crimson cloth. Flat rings of hammered brass were stitched into the fabric. They glinted in the sunlight.

She took in the sight of Herakleio straddling the wall, me waiting at ease very nearby, and chose to perch upon the wall at some distance from us both. She laid out the makings and without saying a word set about her task.

"Walk the wall," I said.

Herakleio shot me a glance of smoldering fury. But Del was within earshot. Del could see what he did or did not do. Del was a woman; Del was a beautiful woman; Del was the kind of woman for whom a man would fall down and eat dirt until he choked if she so much as indicated an interest in seeing him do so.

He stepped up onto the wall and began to walk it.

Chapter 18

*E*ventually I let Herakleio off the wall to stand on the ground again. He was hot, dusty, sweaty, and immensely frustrated. From time to time he'd muttered to himself, but it was quietly done, and only when he had made certain Del's attention was focused on her work. When she did glance our way, he stood very straight, shoulders level, arms loose at his sides, head put up with a proud lift.

Oh, he was a good-looking young buck, no question. A veritable godling, as I'd noted before. He was gifted with the tools that could make an expert sword-dancer: the balance, the reach, the grace, the power, the explosive quickness. His body was not built for elegance, for litheness, but it nonetheless understood how to compensate. And it wanted badly to win. The reason it didn't win was because *my* body knew how to defeat it.

Looking at Herakleio, understanding completely the needs of a young and vital body hungry for activity and proper focus, I understood at last why the shodo of Alimat, petitioned weekly by anxious boys, had unaccountably accepted as student a former slave in the year he refused to accept anyone else.

Fifteen years, give or take, and the desire to learn. That was what lay between us, the metri's heir and me. A thin line, I thought, albeit built of tension.

I looked beyond him to Del, raising eyebrows in a silent question. In answer, she came to us and presented me with two practice swords cobbled together from broomsticks, vine wood, and leather. One I handed to Herakleio.

"Now's your chance," I said. "Have at it."

He stared blankly at the sword, then looked at me. "What?"

"Hit me," I invited. "Beat the hoolies out of me."

"I would *like* to," he said with cold viciousness, "but—" And broke it off abruptly.

"But?" I prompted.

He slid a glance at Del, firmed his chin, glared back at me. "I am not a fool. I know what you are. I know what you will do."

"And what am I?—besides all the vulgar things you are no doubt calling me inside your head."

"Sword-dancer," he said bitterly.

"Ah." I smiled. "Is that an admission that I might know what I'm doing?"

"That you know how to kill people, yes."

"But killing people, as I explained at dinner, is not what the dance is about."

He sneered. "What *else* might it be?"

Gently I shook my head. "Some questions are better answered by the student, when he has learned them."

He wanted very badly to throw down the wooden sword. He probably wanted worse to smash it across my face. But Del was with us—and his eyes told me he knew I would win the argument, be it verbal or physical.

"Try," I suggested. "You might get lucky."

He tried for a long time.

He did not get lucky.

Later, much, much later, I soaked the sweat and grit and soreness—and the residual taint of wine—out of a filthy body. I'd excused Herakleio around midday, watched him consider breaking the broomstick "sword" over his knee, watched him eventually decide to simply stomp away. But he took the sword, as I'd told him to.

Now, with Del sitting beside the pool resetting the leather wrappings on my wooden weapon, I dawdled in the water. It was warm, relaxing, and I felt the muscles ease themselves out of knots and stiffness.

Del, hearing my noisy sigh of satisfaction, glanced up from her work. "Tired?"

"He's strong."

"He never touched you."

"*Keeping* him from touching me took some effort." I sloshed arms through the water. "And I'm out of shape. Out of practice."

Del was startled. "You admit it?"

"Hoolies, I'll admit a lot of things, bascha. You just have to make sure I'm either drunk, or wrung out like I am now."

"I will remember that." She paused. "Why did you let him try you so early?"

"Everyone who ever wants to learn a skill wants to learn it yesterday," I explained. "They're not interested in what comes before. I remember how frustrated I was that I wasn't even allowed to *hold* a sword for so many weeks, while I learned footwork. Not even a practice sword."

"So?"

"So I let him hold it. Let him try it, and me. Let him see it's not so easy as he might think."

"I doubt he thinks it's easy."

"Kids his age always think it's easy."

Del averted her gaze. "Sometimes, it is."

"Sometimes. For some people. For specific reasons." I knew what she meant. She'd been an apt pupil of the sword, surpassing most if not all of the *ishtoya* on Staal-Ysta who had begun before she had. Because she was gifted with the body to be so, but also because she had needed to be better so very badly, to achieve her goal—and to be considered good enough. "Now he understands the fundamentals are imperative. You'd better know how to *avoid* a blade before you try to use one."

"Defense is much more difficult to learn than offense," Del agreed. "And far more vital in the circle."

I ducked beneath the surface of the water, came up with my head tilted back. Water ran down from my hair. "So, bascha, who do you think is better? Me, or Abbu Bensir?"

She blinked in surprise. "That is not something I can answer."

"Why not? You know what I'm capable of. You've sparred *and* danced with Abbu. And you saw us dance in Sabra's circle."

She shook her head. "I can make no answer, Tiger. I think only a dance could settle this."

"But there won't ever be a dance. Not a proper one." I worked at a tight shoulder, schooling my voice into a bland matter-of-factness I didn't feel. "No proper dances ever with anyone, only excuses for killing."

She set the sword beside her and turned all her attention to me. "It's what the metri expects of you, isn't it? Having to train Herakleio has put you in this mood."

"He could be good."

"But he won't be."

"He doesn't want it. Doesn't *need* it. But then that's not the metri's point."

"No," Del agreed.

"Discipline," I said crisply, lending to my words the tone and enunciation of lecture. "Adherence to the requirements of responsibility. A mature understanding of how mind and body is bent to the will of the task. I am to teach him what she can't, so he will be what she needs. What the family needs." I grinned at Del. "Isn't that about the stupidest thing you ever heard? *Me* teaching this kid about responsibility?"

Del didn't smile. "I think it's very wise."

"Come now, bascha. You've spent three years chiding me about things I've said and done, my refusal to accept responsibility . . . my affection for aqivi."

She tilted her head in acquiescence. "If I felt explanation was appropriate, so you might better understand how such ideas can offend, or when I felt you should accept responsibility. Yes. I've chided."

Clutching a ball of soap, I lathered my chest vigorously. "I'm always offending someone."

"Sometimes intentionally. But it is those times when it is not intentional, when it is merely a reflection of ignorance—"

"Like believing women are mostly suited for bedding?"

"That," Del confirmed. "And other things."

"Like believing a woman can't handle a sword the way a man can?"

"And other things."

"Like believing—"

"Tiger, if it has taken three years to train you out of such things, it will surely take three *additional* years to declare them!"

I grinned. "This seems a good place to spend three years."

She went very still. "Do you want that? To stay?"

"Don't you mean do I want to knock Herakleio out of the running and let the metri name me heir?" I scratched at the skin beneath chest hair. "It's an idea."

Del clearly did not know how to answer.

"But then there's you," I said.

"Me?"

"What do you want to do?"

"Me," she said again.

I waited.

"I don't know," she answered eventually.

"Stay?" I asked. "Go?"

"I don't know."

"But you have that choice, Del."

"Yes," she said, frowning.

"You don't have to stay if you don't want to."

"I know that."

"Which means you could go down to the dock and take ship today, if you wanted to."

"I have no coin."

"Oh, let's not be *practical*," I said severely. "We're discussing the heart, here, not the head."

"We are?"

"And the heart is never practical."

"It isn't."

"The heart, in fact, is a rather perverse part of the body, when you think about it. A heart wants to do all manner of things the head doesn't want any part of."

"It does."

"My heart, just now, isn't sure what it wants. It's in conflict."

"It is?"

"In fact, it's very curious as to what *your* heart wants."

"My heart," she said faintly.

I very nearly laughed at the expression on her face. "Del, what do you want to do?"

"Until we know—"

"Not 'we,' " I interrupted. "You."

She was getting exasperated. "What do you want me to say?"

"No, no." I waved a finger at her. "That's not it, bascha. This is about what you want. This is not about what I want, or what I want you to say—which, for the sake of argument, is to decide for yourself."

Del's brows locked together. "Who have you been talking to?"

"Are you suggesting I can't come up with such questions on my own?"

"The captain," she said suspiciously. "You drank wine together, and discussed—me?"

"We discussed all manner of things, the captain and I. Men, women, you, me, Nihko, Herakleio." I gestured. "She mentioned you were sisters of the soul."

"In some things, yes. We believe in freedom of choice, regardless of whether we are male or female. The freedom to follow our hearts."

"Yes!" I nodded vigorously. "That's what *I'm* talking about. And I want to know what your choice is. What your heart wants."

Del eyed me closely. "Did Herakleio hit you in the head when I wasn't looking?"

"Can't you just answer the question?"

She opened her mouth. Shut it. Scowled at me and mutinously held her silence.

"Del," I said gently, "you're different now."

The flesh of her face startled into hardness. "What do you mean?"

"You're not the same woman I met three years ago."

"Nor are you the same man."

"But we're not talking about me."

She thought about not responding. But did it anyway. "I do feel—different. But what do *you* mean by it?"

"Not as driven." I raised my hand. "I don't mean you've gotten soft, bascha. The edge is there when you need it, when you summon it . . . I only mean that you seem less—" I hesitated, said it anyway. "—obsessed. Than you were even two months ago."

Del looked into the depths of the water. "My song is done."

So the captain had said. "All of it?"

"Oh, there is more song yet to be sung. The undiscovered song, made as we move. But—what I *was*, the song I sang all those years I honed my body and mind and swordskill, is finished."

"And?"

"And," she said, "I am learning what it is I am to be. Who I am to be."

"You are you, Delilah. Always."

"More," she said. "And less. Depending on the day."

"Today?"

"Today," she said tartly, "I am somewhat confused by your mood."

I grinned. Then asked, "Why is it that you can admit to Prima Rhannet how you feel and what you want, but you can't admit it to me?"

Color crept into her face. When she is angry or embarrassed, her fair skin often betrays her, despite her best efforts to lock away her feelings so no one else can read them.

Eventually Del said, "Sisters of the soul."

"Is that different from being bedmates?"

"Oh, yes," she answered at once, so easily that I knew it was the unadorned truth. "Women can—talk."

"And men and women can't? Isn't that a bit unfair, telling things to women you won't tell to men?"

"Don't men tell men things they won't tell women?"

"Almost never, bascha. But that's because men don't generally talk much to one another about anything serious."

Now she was perplexed. "Why?"

"Men just don't."

"But they could."

"Sure they could. They don't." I shrugged. "Usually."

"Sometimes?"

"Maybe a little. But not very much. Not very often."

"But—you talk to me, Tiger."

This time it was my truth, and as unadorned. "You make me want to."

Del understood that truth, the emotion that prompted it. I saw the quick-springing sheen of tears in her eyes, though they were hastily blinked away. "It should be so," she said firmly. "Between men and women. Always the truth. Always the wanting to say what is in the heart."

I stood now at the side of the pool, hands gripping the lip of stone. "Then let me tell you what's in mine."

"Wait—" she blurted, as if abruptly afraid to hear such honesty.

"I want you with me," I said simply, "wherever I go. But not if the cost is the loss of your freedom."

"Tiger—"

"Do what you wish to do. Go where you wish to go. Be what you wish to be."

"With you," she said quietly. "With you, *of* you. As much as I have ever wanted anything."

It was more than I expected to hear from her. Ever. It shocked me. Shook me.

"That," I said lightly, unable to show her how profound the relief, "doesn't sound very practical to me."

"Practicality has nothing to do with the heart," she countered loftily, taking up the wooden sword. Del's eyes were bright as she smacked me lightly atop the skull. "And now you will tell me what prompted such serious talk."

"Herakleio."

"Herakleio?"

"And vanity. Age." I shrugged as she rested the blade on my shoulder. "I look at him and see what I was. What I can never be again."

"Tiger, you are hardly old!"

"Older," I said. "In horse parlance, I've been ridden hard and put away wet."

Del stared searchingly at my face, into my eyes. Then in one smooth motion she flipped the wooden sword aside and stretched out upon the stone, fingers curled over the edge. I could feel her breath upon my face. "*I'll* ride you hard," she declared, and pulled herself off the stone into my arms.

Air-billowed linen skirts floated to the surface and proved to be no impediment.

When Herakleio came into the bathing chamber, Del—fortunately—had gone. I was out of the pool but not yet dry, dripping onto pale stone. I slicked hair back out of my eyes and over my skull, paused to note the intensity of his interest in my body. After talking with Prima Rhannet about such things, I couldn't help the question. "Is there something you'd like to tell me?"

He put his chin up, eyes glittering. "She said you have no keraka."

It took me a moment to sort out the who and the what: the metri and her examination of me the first night of my arrival. "No, no keraka. Whatever this keraka is."

"We have it, each of us." He paused pointedly. "Those who are Stessoi, and thus gods-descended. From the gods'—" he paused, translating. "—*caress,* bestowed upon us before birth."

I sighed. "Herak, I don't even know what this mark is supposed to look like—"

"A stain in the flesh," he answered. "As of old blood, or very old wine. But it never washes away."

I grinned. "Well, my flesh has been stained plenty of times with blood *and* wine, but it always washes away." I bent to grab a towel.

"Wait." His tone was a snap of sound, so evocative of the Salset that I did as he commanded. Before I could banish the response, he was beside me. "This," he said, and displayed the back of his left elbow.

It did indeed resemble a stain, of wine or old blood. Ruddy as a new bruise, and the size of a thumbnail. A keraka, "caress"—which I supposed was as good a description as any.

I shook my head. "Nope."

"It need not be where mine is, nor shaped like this."

"Nope. Nothing. Not anywhere."

Triumph lighted his eyes. "*All* Stessoi have it."

"Then I guess I'm not a Stessa." I caught up the towel.

"Wait," he said again.

"I'm done waiting, Herak."

"She said—she said it could be that a scar has removed the ker-aka."

I said nothing, simply began toweling myself off. I'm not modest; nudity doesn't bother me. Though I confess I wasn't much on close scrutiny such as this: front, back, and sideways. I considered inviting him to inspect that portion of my anatomy men value above all others, but restrained myself. No matter what Prima said about his taste for women, I didn't know Herakleio. He might do it.

Abruptly Herakleio turned and strode away. Then stopped and swung back awkwardly. I was dry. Had donned the baggy trousers. Half of me was covered. Half of me was not. He was looking again at the big fist-sized pile of scar tissue that surrounded the hollowed flesh below the ribs on the left side of my chest.

"Why didn't you die?" he asked.

That I hadn't expected. After a moment I hitched a shoulder. "Too far from my heart to kill me."

"The others—the whip weals, the blade cuts . . ." He shook his head. "None of them is enough to kill a man. But that one . . . that one was. It should have."

"Why does it matter to you?"

Though he didn't avoid my eyes, his odd manner was lacking in belligerence or confrontation. "Because of Nihko. What he said."

"What did Nihko say?"

Now his eyes slid away. "IoSkandic."

I grunted. "Nihko says that a lot." I flung the damp towel over my shoulder and proceeded past Herak.

The belligerence was back. His raised voice echoed in the chamber. "What did you do to the woman?"

It brought me up short. I turned. "What?"

"You said a woman did that."

"One did."

"What did you do to her? To make her take up a sword against you? To make her do *that?*"

"Danced," I told him simply, and walked out of the chamber.

Chapter 19

Sunset was glorious. Even as I prepared to go through the conditioning rituals, I paused to look. From deep in the caldera rose the plume of smoke issued of living islands, the faintest of drifting veils. Wind lifted, bore it, dissipated it with the dying of the day. I felt the sighing against my face, the prickle of it in the hair of my forearms and naked torso. Only the scar from Del's blooding-blade was unaware of its touch.

Born and bred of the South, of the desert and its sands, of relentless heat and merciless sun . . . and yet something in me answered to this place. To the wind of the afternoon, dying now into night. To the lushness of vegetation fed by ocean moisture, not sucked dry into dessication. To the smell of the soil, the sea, the blossoms; the blinding white of painted dwellings and the brilliance of blue domes, the endless clean horizons that stretched beyond the island to places unknown to me.

I smiled into the sunset, watching the colors change, then bent my mind and focus upon the slow, graceful, meticulous positioning of flesh and bone and muscle, answering with a contentment verging on bliss the blessed familiarity of ritualized movements I'd learned so many years before from the shodo of Alimat, who understood the needs of the soul as well as of the body.

*　　*　　*

The metri's servant found me there some while later. Sweat sheened me, but did not run my flesh; the breath moved freely in my lungs and did not catch; the protest of muscles left too long to ships and happenstance was fading. It would require dedicated daily practice before true fitness returned, but I was already looser than I had been since we'd left the South.

Simonides waited until I broke the pattern of the ritual. Diffidently he took up the cloth I'd draped over the courtyard wall and handed it to me. I patted myself dry even as he spoke. "The metri sends to say Herakleio has gone into the city."

It was the longest sentence I'd heard from him. His words were heavily accented, but decipherable. Still, the topic baffled me. "And?" I prompted.

"The metri sends to say this is your responsibility."

"Is it?"

"The metri sends to say you will find him in a wine-house with other young men of his age, consorting with women."

"Ah." Of course.

"The metri sends to say this is your responsibility."

"That he drinks and consorts with women?"

"The metri sends to say—"

I cut him off with a gesture. "And what do *you* say?"

It startled him. He blinked. "I?"

"You."

"I say?"

"You say."

He opened his mouth. Shut it. Thought thoughts. Eventually opened his mouth again. "I say the metri expects you to bring him home."

"That's obvious, Simonides. What I'm wondering is, why?"

"Your debt."

"My debt doesn't include playing nursemaid."

For the briefest of moments a hint of amusement seasoned the quiet courtesy of his eyes. "The metri sends to say it does."

"How can the metri send to say something in answer to a statement she hasn't heard me make?"

"The metri sends to say I am, in her absence, her eyes and ears."

"And what do *you* say, O Eyes and Ears?"

Simonides folded his hands together primly at the belt atop his kilt. "I, who as the eyes and ears of the Stessoi have seen and heard this before, say he will make a drunken fool of himself at the winehouses, provoke battles of wit and words and, eventually, provoke battles of the body as well, which other men will answer. Many songs will be sung. Much damage will be done. Much coin will be spent to set the winehouse to rights."

I grinned. "The metri's coin."

"Herakleio has only what the metri gives him."

That explained a lot. "She treats him like a child, yet expects me to make him a man?"

"Here in Skandi," he said, "the mother raises the child. When the child is of age, the father raises him. The infant becomes a man. But Herakleio has only the metri, who is not his mother."

"And I'm not his father, Simonides. Send to say to the metri that *I* say that."

"But kinsman," he rebuked gently.

I looked at him sharply. His expression was guileless, arranged in the bland mask of trusted servants. There was no fear, only acceptance. This was his place. He would do it no harm, nor his people. "You truly believe that?"

His gaze was level. "I have seen all of the pretenders come before the metri. And I have seen you."

"I didn't come," I countered. "I was brought. And I had no choice."

"I have seen all of the pretenders come before the metri. And I have seen you."

I understood him then. He made a clear delineation between pretenders, and me. For some inexplicable reason, it sent an icy prickle down my spine. As if such belief were a harbinger of—something. Something dangerous.

To be someone's heir.

I sat down abruptly upon the wall. Simonides smiled.

"How old are you?" I asked.

"I have sixty-two years."

"How long have you served the Stessas?"

"Sixty-two years."

"Since *birth?*"

He had the grace to gesture acknowledgment of my incredulity. "It is true I did not begin to serve until I had five years. But I was born into this household."

Five years. And every year since in service to the Stessas— Stess*oi*—to the metri. I said, "You know what I was."

He inclined his head slightly; a slave always knows another.

"And that I am free now, and have been."

Another slight nod.

"And yet you believe I am not a pretender hoping to gain wealth?"

"What you pretend," he replied simply, "is that you can be nothing others expect of you."

After a lengthy moment I managed an answer. "That is about the most convoluted piece of nonsense I've ever heard."

With utmost sincerity he demurred. "Surely you have heard better."

I eyed the metri's servant. Simonides had a sense of humor after all. "You're being obscure. On purpose."

His expression betrayed no inkling of his thoughts. "The expectations of others," he said quietly, "can cause the bravest men to tremble."

I assessed his overly bland expression. "And what do *you* expect of me?"

Simonides smiled. "To go and fetch Herakleio home before he embarrasses the metri's name—and the metri's purse."

"I'm trembling," I said dryly.

Simonides bowed.

I looked down at myself. Baggy trousers, barefoot. "It would probably be better if I had a shirt, then, yes? And shoes?"

Simonides bowed again, then took himself away.

Well, hoolies. I wasn't ready for bed yet anyway.

Del was more than a little surprised when I stopped by our room to tell her where I was bound. "You?"

"Me."

"Tiger . . ." She sat up from an ungainly sprawl across the bed. "Sending you to retrieve Herakleio from a wine-house is not unlike asking the hawk to ward the rabbit."

"But hawks know all the secret ways into the hutch." I now wore a tunic over my trousers, and sandals. "Want to come along?"

She frowned. "You don't know these people, Tiger . . . what if it's a trap?"

My eyebrows shot up. "Why would it be a trap?"

"Why wouldn't it be?"

I eyed her narrowly. "What are you suggesting?"

"I don't know." Del sounded as frustrated as I. "Maybe it's only because we're stuck here in this house, bound by its rules without knowing what they are. It makes me uneasy."

"So does not having a sword."

A muscle jumped briefly in her jaw. "Yes."

"I know, bascha. Trust me, I know." I sighed. If *both* of us suspected the metri's motivations, or intentions . . . I shook it off. "Meanwhile, you coming?"

She considered. Then stood up. "But only to be certain the hawk does not overset the hutch."

"Of course." I bared teeth. "Little rabbit."

Del tugged at the rucked up folds of her long tunic, sorting out her clothing. "This little rabbit feels somewhat naked without a sword to hand."

"This little rabbit has teeth," I reminded her.

"And the hawk?"

"The hawk has talons. But yes, he isn't pleased to be without a sword either."

"We should remedy that."

"We should. Maybe tomorrow." I stopped in the doorway, turning back. "Do you suppose they even *have* swords on Skandi?"

Del thought about it. "I haven't seen anyone with one."

"Me neither." I scowled. "What's a self-respecting man to do for a weapon?"

Del slid past me. "Use his teeth and talons."

*   *   *

We did not, of course, have any idea which winehouse Herakleio habituated. We didn't even know how many there were in Skandi, *on* Skandi, nor even what they looked like. Simonides, however, met us at the front door.

He arched a single eyebrow as he saw Del.

"She's the rabbit," I explained. "Also known as bait."

His face cleared even as Del glowered at me. "The molah-man will take you both into the city. As he has taken Herakleio into the city on many similar occasions, he knows which winehouses to try."

"Winehous*es*," I stressed—winehous*eoi*?—getting a better idea of the task. "Ah. And just how many are we to root around in?"

"Why, as many as are required to find him."

"And how many might that be?"

"We are an island," he answered. "The first in a chain of islands. We import goods and export goods."

"He means," Del translated, "that many ships come here with many men aboard them and likely every other building in the city *is* a winehouse."

"Even so." Simonides didn't smile, but I detected a faint glint of amusement in his eyes before he turned them to the ground.

I nodded. "And might this molah-man be the same molah-man who took Herakleio into the city tonight?"

"The metri employs many."

Del sighed. "Is Herakleio in the habit of sending his molah-man home before he's done drinking?"

"Sometimes. Sometimes not." He flicked a glance at me. "Sometimes he does not return home at all."

We were men. We both knew what that meant.

So did Del. "And is there a favorite woman?"

Simonides cleared his throat faintly. "Herakleio consorts with many."

"In other words, this could take us all night."

The servant inclined his head. "And even part of the day."

I glanced at Del. "Care to change your mind about coming along?"

Her expression was elaborately incredulous. "And permit the

hawk to overset *all* the hutches?" She went on before I could answer. "If I stay, I won't be able to sleep until you're back. So I'll come."

"Why won't you be able to sleep?"

"Because I can't when you're gone. Not well." She shrugged. "I'll wake up every time I turn over, wondering how near dawn it is and if your dead body is lying in some rank alley somewhere in the middle of a puddle of horse piss."

The imagery was vivid. "Gods of valhail, why?"

"Because," she said matter-of-factly, "it's what women do."

"Imagine men dead and lying in horse piss?" I shook my head. "It's foolish to paint such pictures, bascha. A waste of time."

"Undoubtedly," she agreed dryly. "But it is our nature."

"To worry."

"To wonder."

"To imagine things that aren't true and won't come true?" I shook my head again, more definitively. "I always said an imagination could get women into trouble."

"But occasionally these things *are* true and they *do* come true, and dead bodies *are* found lying in rank alleys in the middle of puddles of horse piss." She paused. "Which is why women the world over began worrying in the first place."

"But it's never come true with me."

Her expression was as bland as only Del could manage. "Yet."

I scoffed. "I could also live to be an old man and die in bed with no teeth left in my head."

"You could also die in a puddle of horse piss with no teeth left in your head." She paused. "Tonight."

"And you'd rather *see* it happen than simply imagine it."

"Yes."

"Why?"

"Because perhaps I could stop it." She shrugged. "Or, if not, I could at least go home to bed *knowing* you were lying dead in a puddle of horse piss, and not merely imagine it."

Simonides, apparently recognizing where this discussion might lead—and how long it would take to get there—cleared his throat again. "The molah-man awaits."

So he did. So did Herakleio. Somewhere on an island that was full of winehouses and puddles of horse piss.

If they *had* horses on Skandi. Which I don't think they did.

The moon was nearly full. Feeling virtuous—and oddly relieved—because I'd taken the first serious steps toward regaining fitness, I relaxed against the back of the molah-cart, one arm slung around Del's shoulders as we drew closer to the city on the rim of the caldera. Now that I had my land-legs back, I didn't mind the joggle of the cart. It was soothing in a way. "Too bad we have to waste the night on finding Herakleio."

Del doesn't cuddle in public, but she did lean. With pale hair and in paler linen, she was aglow in the moonlight. "We could perhaps find him immediately," she said, "or find him very, very late."

I laughed and set my chin atop her tilted head. "You don't think *he's* lying dead somewhere in a puddle of horse piss, then?"

"He would not be so foolish as to put himself in the position to end up so."

"Why not? And why would I?"

"Because he is the heir of the Stessa metri. Heirs of wealthy, powerful people only rarely go into rank alleys with puddles of horse piss in them so that they can be killed."

"But I would? And I'm not?"

"You have. And I think even if you are the metri's grandson, she prefers Herakleio in the role."

"Thank you very much."

"You're the jhihadi, Tiger; isn't that enough? Or must you be wealthy, too?"

"Isn't it a rule that the jhidadi should be rich? I mean, what's good about being a messiah if you can't afford to enjoy it?" I patted her head. "Not that you believe I *am* the jhihadi, mind you."

"Well," she said thoughtfully, "I doubt very many jhihadis end up dead in puddles of horse piss."

"Lo, I am saved." Something occurred to me then. "Um."

Del, having heard that opening before, lifted her head and looked at me warily. "Yes?"

"We don't exactly speak the language of the locals."

"Not exactly, no. Not even *in*exactly."

"Then how are we supposed to tell the molah-man where to go?"

"Tiger," she chided, "you've never had any trouble telling people where to go."

"Hah," I said dutifully. "You don't suppose he's just going to stop at every one, do you?"

"Well, that would be a way of making sure we found the proper winehouse."

I eyed her sidelong. "You surprise me, bascha. I never thought I'd hear you describe any cantina—or wine-house—as 'proper.' "

Her turn to say "hah," which she did. Then, "We could split up."

That jerked my head around. "You expect me to let you go into a slew of winehouses in a strange land *by yourself?*"

Del arched pale brows eloquently. "And just what do you think I did when I first began looking for the sword-dancer known as the Sandtiger?"

Since Del had in fact eventually *found* me in a cantina, I couldn't exactly come up with a good retort. So I scowled ferociously.

"Besides," she went on ominously, "I don't expect you to 'let' me do anything."

"Well, no . . ." I knew better than to argue that point. "But think about it, bascha. You don't even speak the language."

"The language of the sword is known in all lands—" she began. And stopped. "Oh."

"Oh," I agreed; neither of us had one. "Look, I know the 'little rabbit' can bite—"

" 'Little,' " she muttered derisively; because, of course, she isn't.

"—but it's not exactly wise for the rabbit to walk right into the mews when the hawks are very hungry. There's only so much teeth can do against talons."

"But Skandi is not the South. It may well be that Skandic hawks would treat a Northern rabbit with honor and decorum."

"Male hawks full of liquor, and a lone female rabbit?"

"Why, Tiger . . ." Blue eyes were stretched very wide. "Are you suggesting men full of liquor might behave toward a woman in ways less than kind?"

I sniffed audibly. "Kinder than a gaggle of women gathering together after the men have left."

Del batted her eyes. "But we're only rabbits, Tiger. What can rabbits do?"

"Precisely my point," I declared firmly. "Which I guess means we aren't splitting up to look for Herakleio."

Del, who doesn't lose as often—or as well—as she wins, subsided into glowering silence the rest of the way to town.

Chapter 20

Winehouses the world over, whatever they may be called, bear a striking resemblance to one another. There are almost never any windows, no source of natural light; illumination is left to lamps, lanterns, candles fueled by bad oil, worse tallow, and cheap wicks. Each winehouse smells the same, too: of whatever liquor is served, of oil, smoke, grease, the tang of unwashed bodies, cheap perfume, and bad food, be it on the table, in the body, or issuing from either end.

As Del had predicted, this portion of the city was indeed pretty much comprised of winehouses every other building. The molah-man deposited us at the end of a beaten, stony pathway that wound its way through the moon-washed buildings, possibly even leading into alleys full of horse piss. From there we walked.

"Pick a place, any place," I muttered.

Del obliged. "This one."

In we went. And to a man—and even to the women—everyone stared.

In the South, in the Desert, it would have been me they stared at. But here in Skandi I looked very much like everyone else. It was Del they stared at.

But then, everyone stares at Del every chance they get.

"Hawks," I muttered, "weighing out the flesh."

I felt Del's amusement. "Enough flesh on *this* rabbit."

"But tough," I said disparagingly.

She grinned. "Do you see him?"

"No. But let's ask around." I eyed the crowd and raised my voice. I knew next to nothing of Skandic, save three important words. "Herakleio," I announced. "Stessa. Metri."

Nothing. Except for stares. Only eventually did the discussions began, low-voiced, curious and suspicious. But none of them was addressed to us, and no answers were forthcoming.

"Next?" Del murmured.

Next indeed. And the next after that, and the next after that.

"Why," I complained as we headed to Winehouse Number Five, "did we not bring Simonides with us? He speaks the lingo."

"Or the captain."

"Or even the metri."

Del laughed. "I doubt she would have come!"

"Maybe what she needs is a night out on the town."

"You're talking about the woman who may well be your grand-mother, Tiger."

"Well, who says she wouldn't enjoy it? Especially if she's *my* grandmother."

"Here." She gestured to another deep-set door. "Shall we ask—"

Del never got to finish her question because a body came fly-ing out of the winehouse.

"This could be the place," I murmured, as the body picked itself up off the ground. Since it was right there, convenient to queries, I took advantage of the moment. "Herakleio," I said, "Stessa metri."

The body staggered, stared at me blearily, wobbled its way back into the winehouse. Sounds of renewed fighting issued from the place.

"Could be," I muttered, and stepped up close to the open door-way.

Del cleverly used me as a shield against anything else the door-way might disgorge. "Do you see him?"

"Not yet. He could be in the middle of it, or else not here at all."

"Do you want to go in?"

"Not until the bodies and furniture stop flying around."

* * *

They did, and it did, and eventually I poked my head in warily.

"Well?" Del asked.

"Not that I can tell. Just the usual mess." I withdrew my head. "I don't know that he'd be here in the dregs of the town, anyway."

"The molah-man was told to bring us to the places Herakleio habituates."

"Well, it could be that he likes to rub rump and shoulders with the scum of the world—" I stepped back quickly as someone punctuated the end of the fight by hurling a broken piece of chair in my direction. Or possibly part of a table. "—or not," I finished hastily, picking splinters out of my hair. "Let's move on. I don't see him in here."

A little later as we walked the circuitous tracks throughout the city, poking our heads inside various winehouse doors, Del made the observation that perhaps I was not feeling myself. After assuring her I did indeed feel very much myself, I inquired as to what prompted that observation.

"Because you're not drinking in any of these wine-houses."

"Possibly because I don't know enough of the language to ask for a drink."

"Oh, surely not," Del retorted. "No man I ever knew needed to speak the language to ask for liquor."

"And how many men is that?"

"No man I ever *saw*," she amended.

"It takes less time to look and ask if I don't drink."

"That is true—but truth never stopped you before." She picked her way around a pile of broken pottery. "Could it be that you're taking your task seriously?"

"Which task is that?"

"To teach Herakleio."

I ruminated over that a moment. "I don't really care about Herakleio. But the metri . . . well, I do owe her a debt."

"Especially if she is your grandmother."

"Of course I could argue that *you* owe her the coin."

"Why?"

"It was you her coin bought free."

"I thought it was *you* her coin bought free."

"She could have refused to pay Captain Rhannet and her first mate anything. I'd have still been a guest in the household—or perhaps a despicable interloper sent swiftly on my way—but you would have remained a prisoner on the boat."

"Ship. And since the captain asked me to join her crew, I'm not so certain I'd have continued being a prisoner."

"You? A pirate?"

"Certain of my skills appear to be better suited for such a role than, say, a wife."

"Stealing from innocent people?"

"They stole from us," Del observed. "Coin, swords, the wherewithal to earn and buy more. There are those in this world who would claim we lost our innocence many years ago."

I would not debate that. "But you don't steal, Del."

"There are those in this world who would claim I steal lives from others."

"You don't steal anything but men's peace of mind."

"I refuse to accept responsibility for what you say I do to men's minds," she declared testily. "And if men thought with their minds more often than that—"

"—which dangles between our legs," I finished for her. "But I'm not talking about that. I'm talking about how you challenge entrenched customs, ways of thinking. I was perfectly content to go on about my business as a Southron man before you came along."

"And now?"

"Now I can't help but think about how unfair a lot of Southron men are where women are concerned."

"Oh, truly you are ruined," she mourned dolefully.

"Surely the men of the South will exile you from the ranks of manhood for thinking fair and decent thoughts about women."

"Surely they will," I agreed gloomily. "It's hard to be good when everyone else is bad."

"Good is relative," she returned. "But you are *better*."

"And what about you?"

"What about me?"

"You don't often have anything good to say about men in general, or me specifically."

"There could be a reason for that."

"See? That's what I'm talking about."

She considered it. "You may be right," she said at last, if grudgingly. "It's very easy to say things about men."

"Unfair things," I specified. "And you do."

"I suppose that yes, it could be said I am occasionally unfair. Occasionally."

"Does that make unfairness fair?"

"When the tally-sticks are counted, it's obvious who wins the unfairness competition. By a very *large* margin."

"Does that make it right?"

Del cast me a sidelong scowl, mouth sealed shut.

"Point made," I announced cheerfully; another notch in my favor for the tally-stick. Then, "Would you really consider being a renegada?"

"When one has no coin, and no obvious means to make any, one considers many opportunities."

"Ah-hah!" I stopped so short Del had to step back to avoid running into me. "That's the first sign of sense you've shown, bascha."

"It is?"

"You always were so hoolies-bent on doing things your way *no matter what* that you never stopped to consider the reason a lot of people do things in this world is because they have no other choice."

"What are you talking about, Tiger?"

"I'm talking about how often you suggest my plans and ideas are not the best alternatives to the plans and ideas *you* believe are best."

"Because mine are."

"Sometimes."

"Usually."

"Occasionally."

"Frequently."

"You are a mere child," I explained with pronounced precision, "when it comes to judging opportunities and alternatives."

"I am?"

"You are."

"Why is that?"

"You're twenty-two, bascha—"

"Twenty-three."

"—and for most of those *twenty-three* years you never had to think even once about how best to win a sword-dance, or beat off a Punja beast, survive simooms, droughts, assassins—"

"Kill a man?"

"—kill a man, and so forth." I shrugged. "Whereas I, on the other hand, have pretty much done everything in this world there is to do."

"But that's not because you're better, Tiger."

"No?"

"It's because you're old."

Even as I turned to face her, to explain in eloquent terms that being *older* was not necessarily old, a body came flying out of the nearest winehouse door. It collided with me, carried me into the track, flattened me there. With effort I heaved the sprawled body off me and sat up, spitting grit from my mouth even as I became aware that most of my clothes were now soaked. Even my face was damp; I wiped it off, grimacing, then caught a good whiff of the offending substance.

"Horse piss?" Del inquired, noting my expression.

No. Molah. I got up from the puddle, grabbed hold of the body that had knocked me into it, preceded to introduce *his* face to the puddle.

Of course, he wasn't conscious, so he didn't notice.

"Oh, hello," Del said brightly. "We were looking for you."

I turned then, straightened, saw him standing there in the doorway, looking big, young, strong, insufferably arrogant, and only the tiniest bit wrinkled.

"Ah," I said. "About time. Come along home, Herakleio, like a good little boy."

The good little boy displayed an impressive array of teeth. "Make me," he invited.

"Uh-oh," Del murmured, and moved.

"Feeble," I retorted.

Herakleio raised eyebrows. "Yes. You are."

"Oh, my." Del again.

"No," I said. "Your attempt at banter. And unoriginal to boot."

"Unoriginal?"

"It's my line."

"Well? Are you even going to try?"

"I never try, Herakleio."

"No?"

"I only *do*."

He laughed. "Then let's see you *do* it."

So I waded into the middle of him.

Oh, yes: big, young, strong. But completely unversed in the ultimate truth of a street fight.

Survival. No matter the means.

He expected to punch. He *did* punch. One or two blows even landed—I think—but after that it was all me swarming him, using the tricks I knew. I caught him in the doorway, trapped him, lifted him, upended him over a shoulder using all the leverage I had, and dumped him on top of the body in the puddle.

The body meanwhile was attempting to get up and wasn't completely prepared for the addition of two hundred pounds-plus. Both of them went sprawling.

"Well," Del commented as, fight over, I nursed a strained thumb.

Herakleio was not unconscious, though I wasn't sure the same could be said of the body beneath him. He was, however, now somewhat more wrinkled—and furious.

"Shall we go?" I asked. "The molah-man awaits."

He stopped swearing. The sound issuing from his mouth went from growl to roar. He lunged to his feet and hurled himself at me. All two hundred pounds-plus of him.

I expected to collide with the wall even as he smashed into me. But either Herakleio was a smarter fighter than I'd given him credit for, or he was lucky. Whatever the answer, I missed the wall entirely, which would have provided some measure of support, and flew backward into the deep-set doorway.

The door was open. Thus unimpeded, Herakleio carried me on through and into the winehouse. Somewhere along the line we made close acquaintanceship with a table, which collapsed beneath our combined weights, and landed on beaten earth hard as stone.

From there it devolved into mass confusion, as cantina battles usually do. I was no longer concerned with making Herakleio accompany us back to Akritara and the metri, but with keeping breath in my lungs, teeth in my mouth, eyes in their sockets, brains in my skull, and dinner in my belly.

Out in the street it had been just me and Herakleio. Inside the winehouse it was me and Herakleio—and all of Herakleio's friends.

Like I said, smarter than I'd given him credit for.

From inside a fight, it's difficult to describe it. I can sing songs of ritualized sword-dances—or would, if I had the taste for such things *and* could carry a tune—but explaining the physical responsibilities and responses of a body in the midst of a winehouse altercation is impossible. The best you can do is say it hurt. Which it did.

I was vaguely aware of the usual sorts of bodily insults—fists bashing, fingers gouging, feet kicking, knees thrusting, teeth biting, heads banging—and the additional less circumspect tactics, such as tables being upended, and chairs, stools, and winejars being pitched in my direction. Some of them made contact. Some of them did not.

The same could be said of *my* tactics, come to think of it.

From time to time Herakleio and I actually got near one another, though usually something interfered, be it a bench, bottle, or body. By now I was not the sole target: a good cantina fight requires multiple participants, or it's downright boring. I doubt many of the men even realized I was Herakleio's target. They just started swinging. Whoever was closest got hit. Some of them went down. Others of them did not and returned the favor.

At some point, however, a pocket of Herakleio's friends did put together a united front, and I realized it was only a matter of time before I lost the fight. I'm big, quick, strong, well-versed in street tactics, but I *am* only one man. And here in Skandi pretty much everyone is my size and weight, give or take a couple of inches and ten or twenty pounds.

It was about this time, I was given to understand later, that Del decided to end it. Or rescue me, whichever method worked. All I saw, in between hostilities, was a pale smear of woman-shaped linen coming in through the doorway—head, shoulders, and breasts shrouded with fair hair.

My subconscious registered that it must be Del, but the forefront of my brain, occupied with survival, remarked with some amazement that walking into the midst of a winehouse fight was a pretty stupid move for a woman.

Then, of course, that woman, after observing the activities, took up a guttering lamp from an incised window beside the door, selected her target, blew out the dancing flame, and smashed said lamp over said target's head.

The target snarled something in response, no doubt thinking it was yet another tactic undertaken by an enemy. But he did glance back, smearing hair out of his face, and stopped what he was doing to stare in astonishment.

Del picked up a second lamp, its flame strong and bright, and simply held it out at the end of her arm.

The target, soaked in lamp oil, lunged away from her with a shriek. The move took the legs out from under another man, who fell over and atop him.

Now two men were soaked with lamp oil. And two men were less than enamored of the idea of seeing the woman toss a lighted lamp into the middle of the wine-house.

Fights don't end at once. But when enough men—those who are still among the conscious—realize everyone else has frozen into utter stillness lest even a breath cause the woman with the flame to lose control, fights die a natural death.

As this one did.

Being intimately acquainted with Del's control, I sat up. It required me to kick a shattered bench out of the way and jerk a miraculously unbroken winecup from under my butt, but I managed. And sat there, knees bent, arms draped over them. Watching the woman.

"Herakleio," she said in her cool Northern voice.

Curious, I looked around. I had no idea where Herakleio might be. The body closest to me, groaning piteously into the floor, was not his.

Someone obligingly found him for Del. He was in a corner trying to get up from the floor. I didn't think I'd done the damage; I hadn't seen him for quite a while. At some point the man with friends had simply become another target of opportunity.

Herakleio sat up at last, slumping against the wall. One side of his face was marred by a streak of blood; wine-soaked hair adhered stickily to the other cheek. He peeled it off gingerly, as if afraid skin might accompany it. His eyes found me, glowered angrily. I acknowledged him with a friendly wave. He spat blood from a cut lip, then managed to notice Del standing inside the winehouse door with the lamp in her hand.

That got him off the floor. He rose, stood against the wall, stared at her uncomprehendingly.

He must have missed her entrance. And the smashing of the first lamp over the man's head. Now he saw her standing straight and tall in the midst of chaos, pure and pristine against the backdrop of unlighted night. Lamp-glow feasted on her hair, the bleached linen tunic, pale arms, glinted off brass rings adorning the sash that belted her waist. It painted her face into the hard and splendid serenity of a woman unafraid to walk the edge of the blade, to step inside the fire.

Ah, well, she has that effect on me, too.

"Herakleio," she said again.

He seemed oddly dazed. "Yes?"

"You are to come home."

There was no man alive in that winehouse who would not have answered that cool command, could he understand it; nor any who blamed Herakleio for answering. They were silent as he picked his way across the debris, paused before her briefly, then walked out of the wine-house. I had no doubt we would find him waiting in the molah-cart once we got there.

I stood up, shook out my clothing, brushed off my hands, followed Herakleio outside. What Del did with the lamp I couldn't say, but when she came out the light remained behind.

Except for the wash of it still caught in silken hair.

Chapter 21

*S*imonides, who had not spent most of the night seeking, finding, and fighting Herakleio, rousted me from bed at dawn. I expected a murmured protest from Del, for her to burrow back under the light covers, until I realized I was alone. Which made me even grumpier.

I sat up and bestowed upon Simonides my most disgruntled scowl. "What?"

"The metri sends to say you are to attend her at once."

"Of course she does," I muttered. "She got a full night's sleep."

"At once," Simonides repeated.

I reflected there likely were two meanings for "at once" in the world: the metri's, and mine. Rich, powerful people concerned with appearances generally believe the rest of us are as concerned and will thus take time to take appropriate actions—which means their version of "at once" is different from everyone else's. But since I wasn't rich or powerful, I didn't feel bound to abide by her expectations. Which meant she'd see me as I was.

"Fine," I said, and climbed out from under the covers.

Simonides opened his mouth to say more—probably something to do with my general dishevelment in mood and person—but I brushed by him and stomped into the corridor.

The metri received me in the domed hall. I found my senses marveling again, albeit distractedly, at the fit of stone to stone, tile to tile, the flow of arches and angles, the splendid murals. Then I fastened my attention on the woman who was, or was not, my grandmother. And realized that she as much as the house was made of stone and arches and angles, and the mortar of self-control.

If she was offended by my appearance—wrinkled, stained, slept-in trousers; the string of claws around my neck; nothing else but uncombed hair, bruises, and stubble—she offered no reaction. She merely sat quietly in the single chair with her hands folded in her lap.

"There has been an accounting," she said.

As I'm sure she knew, there are many types of accountings in this world. I waited for her to explain which one this was.

"The winehouse sent it up this morning."

Ah. *That* kind of accounting. The owner was fast with his figures. Then again, he'd probably started tallying costs the minute the first winejar was flung.

I waited longer, anticipating a discussion of Herakleio's continued fairings and her expectations of my plans to correct them as soon as humanly possible.

Instead she said, "I shall be extending your term of service."

There are times I can be as cool and calm as Del. Or the metri. This was not one of them.

Alarm bells went off. Noisily.

I hate alarm bells. And so I told her explicitly that I was under no "term of service," nor had any intention of being held accountable for the damage done to the wine-house by her relative, nor would pay a single whatever-the-lowest-coin-of-the-island-was when I had been on her business in the first place bringing her errant heir home. At her request.

"I shall be extending your term of service," she repeated, "to cover the cost of the damages for which you are responsible—"

"How in hoolies am *I* responsible?"

"—and to further educate Herakleio in the proper ways of manhood." She fixed me with a cold stare. "That was neither proper manhood nor acceptable behavior."

"Well, then I guess I'm not the man for the job," I shot back. "We might as well just call it off right now. And you can find someone else."

She arched expressive brows. "And how then shall you discharge your debt to me?"

"In the South," I began with careful precision, "such things are often settled in the circle. If you would care to hire a sword-dancer to contest this debt, I will be more than happy to meet him in the circle."

"Her," she said.

"What?"

"Her," she repeated.

"*Who* her—?" And then I understood.

I don't know how much of what I said the metri understood—likely none of it, since it was a polyglot of languages and none of it polite—but the tone was clear enough.

Finally I ran out of breath. "No," I said simply.

"She has already agreed."

"*Del* agreed to this?"

"She explained that sword-dancers dance for coin and debt dischargement as well as for honor."

"Doesn't matter," I said crisply, refusing to acknowledge her accuracy. "I'm not going into the circle against Del."

Not ever again. Never.

"She has agreed."

"I don't care."

"You yourself suggested I hire a sword-dancer to contest the debt. So I have done. And now your part is to meet her." She smiled faintly. "Happily, I believe you said."

"I won't do it."

"Then you have no choice but to agree to my extension of the term of your service."

"I have every choice," I retorted. "I refute your reasoning, to begin with—I did not personally, as far as I know, break a single table, or even a lamp; fingers, maybe, and a jaw or two, but the winehouse owner can't exactly charge me for that, now, can he?"

"Discharge the debt in coin, or accept additional service with me." She gestured regret and helplessness. "What I ask is not unfair. It does not approach usury."

"Maybe slavery."

She disapproved. "Hardly that."

I shook my head. "I could walk out of here today, right this minute, and get the hoolies off this gods-cursed island." Which was beginning to sound like the only possible course of action.

"And have you learned to swim?"

I frowned. "What has swimming to do with it?"

"How do you propose to get off this gods-cursed island if you cannot swim?"

"Little matter of boats," I answered. "You know—things that float."

"But none of them will float for you."

"Unless you have somehow contrived to sink all of them, I suspect I'll find one that'll float for me."

"You have no coin."

"I'll work for my passage."

"For whom? No captain will hire you on."

"No?"

The metri smoothed a nonexistent crease from her tunic skirts. "Have you not yet come to realize that the very reason people *desire* power is so they may use it?"

"And?"

"And," she continued, "I have sent to have your description carried to the owners of every ship, every boat, every raft on the island. You are an easy man to describe; one need only tell about the scars on your face."

There were things a man might do to disguise himself, but peeling the skin of my face off was not one of them. "And?"

The metri smiled. "I have power."

It took effort to remain calm, with the ice of apprehension spilling down my spine again. "The Stessoi are one of eleven of the so-called gods-descended families," I said. "Of those ten others, I have no doubt one among them will be pleased to put me on a ship. Because when you have power, you also have enemies."

Her smile was gone. "They will not aid you."

"No?"

"I own every grapevine on the island," she said simply.

"So?"

"Would you have them denied wine—or the income from its trade—because of so little a thing?"

We locked glances for a long moment, weighing the quality of mutual determination. Neither of us so much as blinked.

"So," she said eventually, "you have found me out."

"And you me."

"And I you." She relaxed in her chair, loosening only slightly the rigidity of her spine. "I should be grateful that you are as willing as I to stand your ground simply for the sheer ability to do so, no matter the consequences, because such men are occasionally valuable, but . . ."

It wasn't like her to not finish a sentence. "But?"

"But it makes our situation more difficult."

"In what way?"

The metri's cool glance appraised me. "In the matter of honor, a man may choose to be manipulated. Through custom, if nothing else; or perhaps he has no temperament for finding the way to win if it entails hardship in his house."

"A woman is indeed capable of causing hardship in a house," I said dryly.

"But a man who makes a rock of himself, a mountain of himself to stand against the wishes of the wind for the sake of honor *or* intransigence can only be moved when the gods decree it. As they decreed Skandi should break itself apart so many years ago."

"I rather like the idea of being a mountain."

"You promise to make a substantial one," she agreed with irony. "But you forget one important thing."

"And what's that?"

"I am gods-descended," she said with startling matter-of-factness, "and I can break apart even the largest of mountains into so much powder and ash."

"You," I said finally, "are one tough old woman."

"So old?"

I displayed teeth. "Older than the rocks."

It did not displease her. She was beyond the flatteries of youth and the needs of middle age. "So old," she agreed serenely. "It is well you recognize it."

"Herakleio doesn't stand much of a chance."

"Herakleio stands *no* chance," she corrected. "No more than you."

"Ah, but I'm the mountain."

"Mountains fall."

I smiled back. "And become rocks."

"But I am the island," she said, "and the island shall always prevail, even in catastrophe."

"Is Herakleio a catastrophe?"

"He has it in him to become one," she said, amused, "but I think he will not. He claims the stubborn fickleness of a child trying to make a path where no one has gone before, but lacks the werewithal to *insist*. He will turn back."

"Then you don't need me at all."

"I need you," she told me, "for things you cannot imagine."

I went very still. "And is that supposed to make me feel better?"

"What it isn't," she said, "is to make you afraid." She smiled faintly. "Do you think I intend to draw you into deadly and dangerous plots?"

"I think," I said, "you would. If you felt it would benefit you. Now, as for me—"

"I need you," she repeated, "for things that will strengthen this household."

"What *I* need," I said, "is to get off this island."

"What?" It was false amazement, dry as dust. "And not take your place as heir to Akritara?"

I scoffed. "I am no more your grandson than you are gods-descended."

Her eyes gleamed. "Truth means nothing," she said. "Perception is all."

"And since you *are* accepted as gods-descended . . ."

"If you would be accepted as my heir," she said quietly, "you might consider behaving as one worthy of the place. I have requested you teach Herakleio the responsibilities of a man, not to encourage him to behave as a boy by behaving as one yourself."

"For what it's worth," I declared, "I didn't start the fight."

"Perhaps not. But neither did you end it."

No. That had been Del.

"Maybe you should hire *her*," I muttered between my teeth.

For the first time since I'd met her, the metri laughed. "But I have. Should you not go meet her now? She is waiting in the circle."

I found Del on the terrace where I'd begun teaching Herakleio. As requested of Simonides, the stones were swept and scrubbed clean. My bare feet, trained to such things, appreciated the surface. I was callused from years of dancing on all sorts of footing, but nonetheless my body responded. It felt *right*.

She sat upon the low wall encircling the terrace. Wind rippled linen, set hair to streaming. Her face was bared, unobscured by stray locks or scowls, or even the mask she wears when uncertain of surroundings; she was at ease, and her expression reflected it. She was lovely in the sunlight, laughing at something her companion was saying.

He, unlike me, had taken time to set himself to rights. Freshly bathed, clothed, shaved, and showing few signs of the fight the night before, save for one modest bruise beginning to darken a cheekbone and a slightly swollen lip.

Hoolies, maybe I *should* have taken the time to clean myself up. "Excuse—"

But Herakleio was up and taking his leave of Del before I could finish the sentence, thereby depriving me of the opportunity to *send* him on his way. I stared after him sourly as he strode smoothly away. Then recalled why I was here, and why Del was here.

I rounded on her. "What in hoolies do you mean by hiring on with the metri?"

"Work," she replied matter-of-factly, unperturbed by my thunderous expression. But then, she's seen it before.

"But a sword-dance? With me?" I paused. "*Against* me? Why? Why would you? What do you hope to gain, Del—some bizarre form of reparation for something I've done that I've forgotten I've done? Or something you expect me to do, today or ten years from now?" I glared down at her, locking fists onto my hips. "If you think for one moment I intend to step into a circle with you, you've

gone loki. You *know* I won't. You know why. You know why I *can't.*
I refuse. I told the metri I refuse. You *knew* I'd refuse; so, what?—
is this a plot hatched by you and the metri, women both, to manipulate me into staying here longer? Some kind of wager? An idle
whim? A trick to *make* me step into a circle with you?" I sucked in
a noisy breath. "Just what is it you hope to gain?"

"Swords," she replied.

"Of course, swords," I said testily. "That's why it's called a
sword-dance. Swords are required. It's not a knife-dance, or a *fist-*
dance, now, is it? It's a sword-dance. Which I've vowed never to
undertake against you. Again. Ever."

"Well," she said musingly, "I thought this might be the easiest
way to *get* swords. On an island where there don't appear to be
any."

"Which makes a whole lot of sense! It's a little difficult to undertake a sword-dance when there are no swords."

"Exactly," Del said.

"Then we can't dance."

"That's true."

"Which means nothing can be settled."

"That's also true."

"So why did you accept when the metri offered the dance?"

"She didn't offer the dance. I suggested it to her as a means of
settling the question of extended service."

"You suggested it? Why?"

Del smiled a little. "Swords."

"Yes, but we don't *have* any . . ." And then I ran out of fuel altogether. My face got warm all at once and, I didn't doubt, red as a
Southron sunset. I said something self-castigatory in succinct and
vulgar Desert, the tongue of my youth, and plopped myself down
on the wall. After a moment I cleared my throat. "Was there any
particular reason you allowed me to make such a fool of myself?"

"You were having such a grand time getting all hot and bothered that I didn't dare stop you." She paused. "Besides, you do it so
well."

"And did you find it amusing?"

Del grinned. "Yes."

I sighed, shuffled callused feet against grit-free stone. "So."

"So."

"So the metri will find us swords."

"So the metri will."

"Thereby saving us coin we don't have."

"And time, and effort."

I squinted into the morning sun. "I knew there was a reason for keeping you around."

Del made an exceptionally noncommittal noise.

"So," I said again, "now that we've figured out how we're to get ourselves swords—" As expected, she cast me a pointed sidelong glance. "—there's something else we have to do."

"What is that?"

I caught her hand, pulled her up from the wall. "Go see a man about a horse. Or, in this case, a woman about a ship."

"Why?"

"To test a theory."

"What theory?"

"The one that says the metri can't sink every ship." I tugged. "Come on."

Del resisted. "What are you talking about? Why would she sink every ship? Why would she sink *any* ship?"

"It's a figure of speech," I said. "Will you come?"

"I've already been aboard one ship that sank out from under me," Del said darkly, arm tensed against my grasp. "I'm not interested in repeating the experience."

"Our ship is fine. It's Herakleio's that's sinking. Bascha—will you *come on?*"

Reluctantly she allowed me to pull her up and toward the nearest narrow stairway leading into the house. "Tiger, whenever you get cryptic, it means there's trouble on the horizon."

"Not this time. I just want to see if there's a *ship* on the horizon."

"And if there is?"

"See what it would cost to sail on it."

"Last time it cost us everything we had."

"She owes me," I explained, "for that and other things. It's her fault I'm in this mess."

"*That* won't convince her to do anything."

"Oh, I'll think of something."

Whatever Del said by way of observation was declared in idiomatic Northern, and I didn't understand a word. Which was probably for the best, being as how the bascha has as great a gift for malediction and vilification as I do.

Chapter 22

When it became clear Prima Rhannet was not in the household, I dug up Simonides and asked where she was. He responded by asking what I wanted her for; possibly he could help me instead.

Since I knew very well he could not and *would* not give me any kind of answer that might permit Del and me to hire the renegada captain to sail us away from Skandi—and by default away from the metri and her spoiled godling—I simply said I needed to ask Prima Rhannet a question.

Whereupon Simonides, with unctuous courtesy, said perhaps I might ask him the question, as perhaps he might know the answer.

Impasse. We exchanged a long, speaking look, measuring one another's determination not to say what each of us wanted to say, and our respective experiences with outwaiting others in identical situations. Whereupon Del sighed dramatically and inquired as to how old we were to be before the verbal dance was settled. Which reminded me all over again that the metri expected Del and me to dance with *swords* to settle the question of my "term of service," which in turn made me anxious to be going.

"Never mind," I said. "We can walk."

Simonides' expression transformed itself from confident servitude to startlement, followed rapidly by mounting alarm. "Walk?"

"One step after another all strung together until you get somewhere else," I clarified. Then added, "Somewhere you *want* to be."

"You cannot walk," he said severely.

I smiled cheerfully. "Actually, I learned a long time ago."

He waved a hand dismissively, familiarly; clearly he had accepted me as someone who required his very special attention and personal guidence. His version of Herakleio, maybe. "You cannot walk," he repeated. "That is what molah-men are for."

"Fine. Can we borrow one?"

His expression was infinitely bland. "In order for me to summon a molah-man and his cart, I must know where you are going."

"Nice try," I said dryly. "But all you *really* have to do is summon him. You don't have to tell him a thing. Which means you don't have to know where we're going, and I don't have to tell you."

Simonides inclined his head the tiniest degree. "You do not speak Skandic." Clearly he believed he'd won.

"I speak enough," I said, dashing his hopes. "All I have to do is say 'Skandi.' I think he'll catch my drift."

"*Where* in Skandi?" Simonides inquired diffidently.

"We could be there and back by now," Del observed.

Simonides switched his attention to her. "Be where and back again?"

Exasperated, I permitted my voice to rise. "What does it *matter,* Simonides? We're not prisoners here—" I paused with great elaboration, letting the implication hang itself upon the air in glowing letters of fire. "—are we?"

I had succeeded in horrifying him. He said something quickly and breathlessly in Skandic, which eluded both of us, then clasped both hands over his heart in a gesture of supplication. His breathing came fast and noisy, as if he were overcome.

"I'll take that as a 'no,' " I said dryly. "Now can we have our cart?"

His facial muscles twitched out of horror into subtle triumph. "The metri sends to say you must tutor Herakleio."

"What, the metri sends to say *right now* that I am to tutor Herakleio?"

"Indeed."

I raised a skeptical brow. "And when exactly, at what precise moment, did she send to say this? Just now, while we're standing here? If so, I didn't see her. And surely not *before* I found you to ask about a cart. Because surely you would have told me then the metri had sent to say I was to tutor Herakleio—except she hadn't sent to say anything, because *I* found *you*, you didn't come find me."

"Tiger," Del said, "I'm getting gray hair."

"Trust me, I have a lot more than you do, bascha . . ." I smiled in a kindly manner at Simonides. "Well?"

He drew himself up. "I am the eyes and ears of the metri."

"So, I'm assuming one of your tasks is to *guess* what she might or might not like, and thus control the issue?"

"I do not guess," he said with some asperity, "I *anticipate*." Then, lowering head, eyes, and shoulders, he said, with a shift to dolorous dignity, "I am the metri's slave. There is so little choice in my life—"

"*Oh*, no." I cut him off abruptly. "You're not using that line—or that expression!—on me. I know you, Simonides: you're a master manipulator. You'd have to be to serve the metri so devotedly for all these years." I gifted him with an overfriendly smile. "Now, where were we?"

"Walking," Del said.

Whereupon Herakleio wandered into the room and, through a mouthful of some kind of sticky confection, which also filled his hand, asked what we were talking about.

"Going into Skandi," Del answered.

He blinked. "Is this a difficulty?"

"We seem to be having a difficulty convincing Simonides, here, that we need a molah-man and his cart," I explained.

Herakleio shrugged. "Walk," he suggested, and wandered out again.

I bent a brief but sulfurous glare on Simonides, who was looking rather deflated, then turned on my heel. And walked.

It was a long walk, and hot, but the breeze cut much of the heat and made it bearable. Then again, I'm so accustomed to the sun and the dryness of the desert that I found Skandi a gentle country, though with more moisture in the air. I think had there not been the breeze I might have been less enthralled; better the dry if searing heat than the wet thickness of moist air. People could choke in that.

Del and I, from habit, matched paces—not many men can do that with me, and no other women—and fell into a companionable, long-striding rhythm. The air was laden with the scent of grapevines, a tracery of cooksmoke, the taste of the sea. I realized it felt incontestably good simply to be out from under roofs, with the sun shining on my head. Which made me smile; *May the sun shine on your head* is one of the ritual blessings of the South.

"What are you grinning about?" Del asked.

I shrugged. "I don't know. Just glad to be alive, I guess." And free, for the moment, of the nagging apprehension.

"And glad to be alive to *be* glad you're alive." She nodded vigorously. "I feel it, too. We are free of—encumbrances."

I glanced at her as we walked. "Encumbrances?"

She thought about how best to explain. "We have chased," she said finally, "and have *been* chased without true respite for too long."

"What have we chased, bascha?"

"My brother," she replied somberly. "Poor lost Jamail, who, by the time we found him, wasn't truly my brother anymore, nor—" She broke it off abruptly as tears filled her eyes.

"Nor?" I prompted gently, though I had an idea where she was headed.

She blinked furiously; Del hates to cry. "Nor had any wish to be."

I couldn't adequately comprehend the loss, the sense of failure and guilt that had driven her so mercilessly and now seemed merely futile. I had no brother, no sister, nor ever had. But one thing that had come clear to me in three years with Del was that family, kinship, was part of the heart of the North.

"But you couldn't have known that," I said. "There is no way you might have predicted he would be so drastically changed by his experiences that he could bear no part of his past."

"He wasn't—normal, anymore," she said with difficulty. "I don't mean because of what they did to him physically, but in his mind. He wasn't my brother anymore."

Jamail had, I felt, fallen off the edge of the known world even as his sister shaped a new one. Made mute by the loss of his tongue, rendered castrate by the slavers, it did not in the least surprise me that he had sought relief as best he could, even if it meant surrendering sanity as we knew it. I had come close myself in the mines of Aladar.

"He could never be what he was, Del. But he found respect among the Vashni, and a measure of affection after the hoolies he inhabited. In like circumstances, I don't know that I'd have left them either."

She shook her head. "You have been changed by your experiences, yet you do not turn your back on your past. You've let it shape you into a stronger man instead of . . . instead of what Jamail became."

"Maybe. But I was older than Jamail. For me it wasn't a question of having had stolen the means to return to my past, because my past was nothing any sane person would want. I understood that much, at least, and why I had to use the past to shape my future, and that I had to learn *how* to do it. That wouldn't come naturally." I shook my head. "You can't compare him to me, bascha. It isn't fair to Jamail."

"But you became stronger because of what happened."

"Not for a long time." I scuffed through the cart-track, head bent as I watched dust fly. "When I was free of the Salset at last, I didn't know what I wanted to do. Just—be free. But no part of life *is* free; it costs. Always. And I had to find a way to pay for it."

"Sword-dancing."

"Eventually. Once I'd seen a few matches in the circle, realized what a man alone in the world might accomplish. It seemed far more fair than anything I'd encountered with the Salset. So I found out what I could, and pursued it. But . . ."

"But?"

"But it was the shodo at Alimat who took the former slave—the angry, ignorant, terrified former slave—and made him truly free."

She nodded. "Because you were good."

"No. Because I might *become* good. Might. If I worked very hard at it."

"You are the single most physically gifted man I have ever seen," she argued vehemently, who had trained as rigorously on Staal-Ysta. "You are completely at ease in your body, and *with* your body; I think there is nothing you could not accomplish if you wished to."

"Sheer physical ability is one thing," I said, then tapped my skull. "There is the dance up here as well."

"That is what Alimat and the shodo taught you," Del said. "You had the body: quickness, stamina, size, power—"

"But no discipline. No patience. No comprehension of what the rituals meant, and were meant to instill. What I wanted most was to prove I was free, was no man's chula, no matter what was said, or implied, or rumored, or believed about me . . ." I let it go with a hitch of one shoulder. "Let's just say I wasn't the most popular student."

"You bested Abbu Bensir." She touched her throat. "You gave him the broken voice he has even to this day."

"I got lucky."

"He underestimated you."

"That's what I mean: I got lucky."

She smiled. "But did you believe so then?"

"Of course not. I felt it was my due; how could I *not* best a man older, smaller, and slower than I?"

"And now it is your due."

"But look how many years it took me to get here."

"And here we are," Del said quietly. "On Skandi, without encumbrances. No brother to find, no sword-dancers to defeat, no sorcerers after our swords or our bodies. No prophecies to fulfill."

"I'm pretty sick of prophecies, myself. They come in handy now and again, I suppose, to keep things from getting too boring, but mostly they just stir up trouble."

Her smile was hooked down, ironic. "But you are the jhihadi."

"Maybe." I knew she didn't believe it. Me, a messiah? The deliverer of the desert? Right. As for me, well, I'd decided it depended on interpretation; I *had* come up with an idea that could eventually change the sand to grass, albeit it had nothing to do with magic, and thus lent an infinitely banal culmination to a mysterious and mythic prophecy. Which many found disappointing for its utter lack of drama; but then, real life is comprised of such banalities. "Or maybe I just got lucky. Whatever the answer, I think this jhihadi's job is done."

"Leaving him with the balance of his life to live."

"With and without encumbrances."

"What encumbrances do you have now? The metri? Herakleio?"

"Oh, I was thinking more along the lines of you."

"Me!"

"What am I to do with you?"

"*Do* with me? What do you mean, *do* with me? What is there *to* do with me?"

I couldn't help myself: I had to laugh out loud. Which resulted in Del swinging around in front of me and stopping dead in her tracks, which also were mine, so I stopped, too. As she intended.

She poked me hard in the breastbone. "Tell me."

"Oh, bascha, here you say you've changed me over the past three years, but what you don't realize is I've changed you every bit as much."

"*You* have! Me?" Her chin went up. "What do you mean?"

"You argue like me, now."

"Like you? In what way? *How* do I argue with you?"

"You slather a poor soul with questions. The kind of questions that are phrased as challenges."

She opened her mouth, shut it. Then opened it again. "In what way," she began with deceptive quietude, "do I do this?"

"That's better," I soothed. "That's more like the old Delilah."

"And that is?"

"You as you are just now. Cool and calm." I dropped into a dramatic whisper. "Dangerous."

She thought about it.

"It's not the end of the world if you lose a little of that icy demeanor and loosen up, you know," I consoled. "I was just making an observation, is all."

She thought about it more, frowning fiercely. "But you're right."

"It's not necessarily a bad thing, Del." I paused. "Loosening up, I mean, not me being right. Though that isn't a bad thing either."

"By acquiring some of your mannerisms, your sayings?" She twisted her mouth. "Perhaps not; I suppose that is bound to happen. But . . ."

"But?"

"But I am not pleased to be told my self-control has frayed so much."

"What self-control? Self-control in that you sound like me? Self-control in that I don't have any? Is that what you mean?"

Del abruptly shed the icy demeanor and grinned triumphantly. "Got you."

"You did not."

"I did."

"You can't *'get'* somebody if they know what you're doing."

"You're saying you knew?"

"I did know. That's why I answered the way I did."

"Slathering a poor soul—in this case, me—with questions? The kind of questions phrased as challenges?"

"Now you're doing it again."

"Tiger—"

I caught her arm in mine, swung her around. "Let's just go," I suggested. "We can continue this argument as we walk. Otherwise we'll never reach the harbor by sundown."

"I don't think I'm anything like you."

"I believe there are a whole lot of men who would agree, and be joyously thankful for it unto whatever gods they worship."

"You were such a *pig* when I met you!"

Our strides matched again as we moved smoothly down the cart-road leading to the city. "Why, because I thought you were attractive? Desirable? All woman? And let you know about it?"

"You let the whole world know about it, Tiger."

"Nobody disagreed, did they?"

"But it was the *way* you did it."

"Where I come from, leering at a woman suggests the man finds her attractive. Is that bad?"

"That's the point," she said. "Where you come from . . . every male in the South leers at women."

"Not all women."

"Some women," she amended. "Which really isn't fair either, Tiger; if you're going to be rude to women, you ought to be rude to *all* women, not just the ones you'd like in your bed. Or the ones you *think* you'd like in your bed. Or the ones you think would *like* to be in your bed."

"Leer indiscriminately?"

"If you're going to, yes."

"This may come as a surprise, bascha, but I don't want to sleep with all women."

"We're not discussing sleeping with. We're discussing leering at."

"What, and have every woman alive mad at me?"

"But there are less vulgar ways of indicating interest and appreciation."

"Of course there are."

She blinked. "You *agree* with me?"

"Sure I agree with you. I'm not arguing that point. I'm trying to explain the code of men, here."

That startled as well as made her suspicious. "Code of men?"

"When a man leers at a woman, or whistles, or shouts—"

"Or invites her into his bed?"

"—or invites her into his bed—"

"—with very vulgar language?"

"—with or without very vulgar language—"

"*Insulting* and vulgar language!"

"—it's because of two things," I finished at last.

"What two things?"

"One, it lets all the other men know you've got first dibs—"

"First dibs!"

"—which is what I meant about the code of men; first dibs and rite—and right—of ownership—"

"What?"

"Well, so to speak."

"It shouldn't be part of what anyone speaks."

"Look, I've already told you about the code of men, which is never to be divulged—"

"And do you believe in this code?"

I hesitated.

"Well?"

"I can't tell you that."

"Why not?"

I chewed at my lip. "The code."

"The code won't let you tell me about the code?"

"That's about it."

"Then why did you?"

"Because I tell you everything. That's a code, too."

"It is? What's this one called?"

"The code of survival."

Del shot me a look that said she'd punish me for all of this one day. "Getting back to this 'because of two things' issue . . ."

"What two things?"

"First was first dibs. You know, the reason men leer and say vulgar things to women."

"Oh." I took it up again. "—and two, it certainly saves time."

"Saves time?"

"Well, yes. I mean, what if the woman's interested?"

"What if the woman isn't?"

"Then she lets you know. But if she is, you sure get to bed a lot faster if you don't waste time on boring preliminaries."

Del stopped short and treated me to several minutes of precise and cogent commentary.

When she was done, I waved a forefinger in her face. "Vulgar language, bascha. *Insulting* and vulgar language."

She bared her teeth in a smile reminiscent of my own. "And I suppose you want to go to bed with me now. Right here in the middle of the road where anyone might come along."

I brightened. "Would you?"

Del raked me up and down with her most glacial stare. Then

she put up her chin and arched brows suggestively. "Not until after we waste a lot of time on boring preliminaries."

"Oh, well, all right." Whereupon I caught her to me, arranged my arms and hers, and proceeded to dance her down the road toward the distant city.

Chapter 23

"Oh, hoolies," I said with feeling.

We stood at the top of the cliff face, overlooking the switchback trail leading down to the cauldron of water. Steam rose gently from the living islands in the center.

"What?" Del asked, as the breeze took possession of her hair.

I pointed. "The ships are all down there."

"Yes, Tiger. That's where the water is."

"It means we have to ride those molahs down."

She shrugged. "Or walk."

Uneasily I eyed the individuals who were on foot. Obviously they were laborers, or slaves, or people not of the Eleven Families. "Maybe this wasn't such a good idea. Maybe what we've already done—walking to and through town—is unconscionable, or something. Maybe that's why Simonides was upset—and why, come to think of it, Herakleio would suggest we walk, if only to get my goat."

Del was perplexed. "Why?"

I chewed at my lip, marking the commerce at the trailhead. The place thronged with people and animals, not to mention the small-time merchants who laid out their wares on tattered cloths spread along the walls. There were cheap necklaces, bracelets, earrings; sash belts, leather belts, single blue pottery beads hung on leather thongs or multicolored cord—maybe some kind of charm; sunbaked pots, painted bowls, multitudinous other items. Del and I were in the middle of it all, bumping shoulders with people and trying not to be run into by loose goats and dogs, not to mention chickens. I occasioned little more than incurious glances, but Del, as usual, reaped the benefit of her height and coloring.

I sighed. "When Nihko brought me up, he made it clear I was not to, as he put it, *soil* myself by standing on the ground."

Del's irony was delicate. "Were you supposed to hover?"

"Mats," I explained. "First we had our feet washed, and then we stood on mats."

She shrugged, catching and separating her hair into three sections preparatory to braiding. "When Prima Rhannet brought me up, nothing was said of that. We rode up, then she rented a cart to take us to the metri's home."

"Nihko was pretty plain about it all." I glanced around. "But no one seems to be taking much notice."

Del began to braid the sections of hair, something I've always enjoyed watching for the deftness of her hands. "We walked while touring the winehouses looking for Herakleio."

"But we went right to the bathing pool, remember?" I leaned forward a little, enough to see a few more of the hard angles of the cliff track as I peered over the low wall. "Well, I suspect it's too late even if there is something to all this foot-washing. Guess we may as well head down."

Finished with the single plait, she did something with a strand that captured and held the braid, tucking and looping it into itself. "Walking, or riding?"

Neither appealed to me. Walking meant dodging molahs and their muck. Riding meant sitting atop a jouncing beast heading downward at a rate of speed I considered breakneck, when you took into account the pitch of the track.

Resolution presented itself. I looked around at the ground, saw a stone, scooped it up. "Stone wins," I said, and stealthily passed it from hand to hand several times. Eventually I held both fists out, knuckles up. "Choose."

"Stone, we walk." Del flipped the braid behind her back and tapped one of my fists.

I opened it, displayed the empty palm. "Wrong choice, bascha." And tipped the stone from the other hand, dropping it back to earth.

"Well," she said with limp cheeriness, "it's a pretty day for a ride."

"Can't say as it'll be pretty by the time I get to the bottom," I declared sourly. "It's not *your* gehetties at risk!"

"That's why I've never understood why men are almost uniformly considered superior," Del opined seriously. "The easiest way to put a man out of action is to plant a knee in his gehetties, or threaten them with a knife, or—"

"All right, bascha, you've made your point," I said hastily, cutting her off before she got more detailed about threatened gehetties. "Let's find us a couple of molahs."

Del pointed. "There."

"There" constituted a congregation of molah-men hanging about the trailhead. Their molahs were tied some distance away, dozing in the sun, but the men themselves competed enthusiastically for space and custom, calling out imploringly to each passerby something I assumed was an advertisement of their services—although how one molah might be considered particularly better than another was beyond me; they weren't horses, after all. As Del and I approached, it was no different: we were accosted, surrounded, swarmed by all the men as they competed for our coin.

"Might be a problem," I muttered to Del.

"What's that?"

"Coin to pay them with."

"Ah." It had occured to neither of us; we're used to having coin of some sort, and since our arrival such things as transport and comestibles had been provided. "I have nothing. Maybe we should walk after all."

From close up, the trail was a mass of puddles and droppings mashed by feet into a slimy, odoriferous layer of something approaching mud, or heaped cairns of fresh, as yet unmashed muck. Slaves and laborers stolidly stomped their way up and down the track, feet and ankles smeared, as they followed the beasts. No wonder Nihko had been so picky about us getting washed.

"Nah, let's ride," I said.

"What about coin?"

"Maybe this . . ." I untied the knot in my necklet, pulled it free of my neck.

"Tiger! You wouldn't!"

"Not the claws . . ." I worked at thread, finally slid the silver ring free of thong. "Nihko's little gift." I held it up so the molah-men could see it clearly in the sunlight, then pointed over the wall. "Down," I said, though I doubted any of them understood the word. Shouldn't need to; it seemed pretty obvious what we wanted.

Some of the men shrugged, shook their heads, stepped back, indicating they worked for coin, not barter. A few others stepped forward to inspect the ring more closely—and then surged as one backward into the others, crying out something I couldn't understand. Hands flashed up and made the warding away gestures I'd seen before with the first mate. Gazes were averted, heads lowered, palms put up into the air in unmistakable intent: we were not to come any closer.

Such an innocuous little thing glinting in my fingers. And yet it appeared to mean so much. "Are you sure?" I asked. "It's good silver."

More gestures, more whispered, hissing comments made to one another, and the cluster of molah-men melted away to their animals until Del and I stood in the open with no one near us at all but a single ignorant chicken, pecking in the dirt.

I let the ring slide down out of my fingers into my cupped palm. A small, plain ring about as big around as my forefinger. It wasn't whole, but cut at one point so the filed ends could pierce and be fastened into flesh. No different from what a woman might wear through her ear-lobes, though Nihko wore his—and many more of them—in his eyebrows.

And then I recalled that he'd put it on my necklet to keep me, he'd said, immune to his magic. Or whatever you wanted to call whatever it was about him that made me feel ill.

IoSkandi. I'd heard—and still heard—that word said by the men who now stood away from us. I'd heard it used by Nihko, Prima, Herakleio, the metri.

Silently I hooked the brow ring back onto my thong, looped leather around my neck again and knotted it. "Let's go," I said curtly to Del. "We're burning daylight."

"Wait." She caught my wrist and halted my forward momentum. "What is it?"

I stopped short. "What's what?"

"Something's made you angry."

"I'm not angry. I'm *irritated*."

"Fine." She had immense patience, did the Northern bascha. "Why are you irritated?"

"Let's just say I don't like mysteries."

"And you want to know why they won't take the ring."

"I know why they won't take the ring. At least, I have an idea."

"And?"

"Nihko." I made the sound of it a curse. "I want to know what all this ioSkandi nonsense is, and what this ring is *really* supposed to do and mean."

"Perhaps we should ask him."

"I intend to—if I can ever get down to the boat."

She removed her hand from my wrist with alacrity. "By all means, go."

I sighed. "All right . . . look, bascha, I'm sorry. It's not your fault. But I've had it up to here—" I indicated my eyebrows. "—with all this magical mythical mystery stuff. I don't speak the language, so I haven't got the faintest idea what these people are saying about us; an arrogant old woman who may or may not be my grandmother is pretty much keeping me a prisoner in her house; and a young buck who may or may not be my kinsman, albeit removed umpteen hundred times, is trying to move in on my woman." I paused, rephrased immediately. "In on *a* woman. Whom I happen to care about a great deal."

"Thank you," she said gravely. "But why do you think Herakleio is, as you put it, trying to move in on me?"

"I just know," I said darkly.

Del is accustomed to my moods. Sometimes she ignores them, other times she provokes them. This was one of the times she wanted an explanation. "How is it that you know?"

I shook my head. "I just do."

"Is it something to do with the code of men?"

"No, it isn't something to do with the code of men. It's something to do with him being young, and you being young, and me being—well, older."

"I could make a joke of this—" she began.

"You could."

"—but I won't," she finished. "I think this is something you must sort out for yourself."

Startled, I watched as she strode the last few paces to the head of the trail and took the first step downward. "Sort out for myself? What do you mean, sort out for myself?" I went after her. "Can't you at least tell me you don't think I'm old, and that I'm being a fool? Couldn't you even *lie*, just to make me feel better?"

She slanted me a sidelong glance as she strode down the track. "Would it be a lie if I said you were being a fool?"

"Oh, Del, come on. Humor me."

"You're going to believe whatever you decide to believe, no matter what I say."

"Well, that may be true," I conceded, "but you could say it anyway."

"I'm saving my breath."

"For what?"

"Getting to the bottom."

"He *is* young."

"Yes."

"He *is* good looking."

"A veritable godling."

"And I suppose some women might even find his attitude appealing."

"Some would."

"He's even rich—or he will be."

"So he is, and so he shall be."

"So why would you remain with me if you had a chance to be with him?"

"Possibly because you've never given me an actionable reason to leave you."

This was a new phrase. " 'Actionable reason'?"

"You give me reasons to leave all the time. None of them has been of such magnitude that I acted on it."

"Oh." We walked quickly, steadily downcliff, leaving the trail-head behind. "So, reasons, but no 'actionable' reasons."

"Until now," she said with bland clarity.

"Oh, come on. Do you blame me?" I dodged a molah and rider making their jouncing way up the track. "Hoolies, I'm not exactly what I was at seventeen, or even what he is at twenty-four."

"More."

"More? More what?"

"More than you were at seventeen. More than he is at twenty-four."

"In what way?"

"For one thing," she said, "he doesn't doubt himself."

"That's one way of putting it!"

"And I doubt he questions his appeal to women."

"I'll go that."

"And I don't doubt he *thinks* he could have me if he wanted me."

"No kidding!"

"But it really doesn't matter what he thinks, Tiger. About me or anything else."

"No?"

"What matters is what *I* think."

"Well, of course it does—" I stopped short to avoid a laborer whose load was tipping precariously, made my way carefully around him.

Del marched on. "And if I were attracted to him to the degree that you seem to think I could be, or should be, enough that I'd rather be with him than with you, I would make it plain to you."

I caught up. "You would."

She stopped and turned to me, which necessitated *me* stopping. Again. "I promise," Del said. "I vow to you here and now, on this filthy trail with muck nearly to my knees, that if I decide to leave you, if the day comes when I feel I must leave you, for another man or simply to go, you will be the first to know."

Transfixed, I stared back at her. "Is that in the code of women?"

Del's mouth twitched. "I can't tell you."

"Oh, well, all right. I understand about codes." I looked down at my muck-splashed legs. "This is disgusting."

"Yes," she agreed, "it is. And the sooner we get to the bottom, the sooner we can wash everything off."

"Race you," I offered.

But Del was not sufficiently intrigued by that suggestion to agree, so we proceeded to traverse the balance of the track at a much more decorous pace.

Which meant we were even more disgusting by the time we reached the bottom.

As might be expected, Del and I headed straight toward the harbor once we hit the docks, intending to dunk ourselves up to the knees in seawater. I was thinking about finding a good stout rope to hang onto since too deep a dunk might result in me drowning, and was thus more than a little startled when a cluster of shouting men came running up to us. Not for the one hundredth time I wished I had a sword; by Del's posture, so did she. But we had no weapons, not even a knife between us. Which reminded me all over again that Del's suggestion to the metri that she hire her to dance with me in the circle was done for a purpose, not to upset me.

Meanwhile, we found ourselves as surrounded by men vying for our attention and custom as we had been at the trailhead. Except this time what they wanted us to buy was water from pottery bottles hung over their shoulders on rope, and their washing services. Rainwater, I was assuming, gathered in the many rooftop cisterns, tubs, and bowls, since Skandi, I'd been told, had no springs, lakes, or rivers. And even the rain was scarce, and thus hoarded, and thus worth selling to people who wanted to wash molah muck off legs and feet.

I glanced around. None of the laborers and slaves and others afoot were cleaning themselves off in the harbor. In fact, none of them were cleaning themselves off at all. Apparently they figured they'd just get filthy again walking back up the track, so they didn't bother. I guess Del and I looked like strangers. Soft touches.

They weren't wrong, either. I *would* have paid for the rainwater and the drying cloths draped over their arms, had I any coin.

Inspiration mingled with curiosity. I untied the thong, pinched the silver ring between precise fingers, and held it toward the nearest man.

He looked, examined, then backed off jerkily. I saw the now-familiar gesture, heard the now-familiar hissing and whispering commingled with blurted invocations against—something. To a man they stumbled over one another to distance themselves from us.

I knotted the claw-weighted thong around my neck again. "Let's find us a ship with a blue-headed first mate, shall we?"

This time was different. Instead of wobbling my way down the plank from ship to shore, I marched *up* the plank and planted my feet at the top of it. Yes, it was a precarious position; all anyone had to do to knock me off into the water was to tip me over the edge, but I was angry enough that I didn't care.

Besides, Del was there to make sure that if I got knocked in, she'd fish me out again.

A familiar face—and the body to go with it—met me there. Not the first mate, but one of the crew. He was mildly startled to see us. But his expression smoothed into cool assessment when I said a single word: "Nihkolara."

Nihko was fetched. His expression also reflected surprise, though it was replaced a moment later by a mask of blandness. He folded his arms against his chest and neither invited us aboard, nor told us to leave.

"All right," I said, "I give up. You said something to me once about when I got tired of heaving my belly up, I was to come see you. Well, I haven't heaved my belly up ever since you put this ring on my necklet, and I want to know why."

Nihko Blue-head smiled.

"I also want to know why it is that every time I try to use this ring as payment, they all break out in a rash of warding signs, babbling to one another words I can only assume are prayers, or curses; or, for all I know, proposals of marriage."

Nihko Blue-head stopped smiling. "You used the ring as *coin?*"

"Attempted to," I clarified. "We've got nothing else. It's good silver; where I come from, silver in any shape is worth something."

"Oh, that brow ring is worth a lot more than *something*," he retorted. "No one on this island will accept it in payment, or as promise of payment, or anything at all other than what it is."

"And what *is* that, Nihkolara?"

"Mine," he said crisply.

"Cut the mystery," I snapped. "We're sick of it. Give me some straight answers."

"You have your answer, be it straight, crooked, or tied in knots. That is not coin. It buys nothing any man or woman on Skandi will give you. It buys only a degree of peace for you, in your body and your mind."

I jerked the ring from the thong and held it up. It glinted in the sunlight. "And if I gave it back?"

"You are certainly free to do so," Nihko answered evenly.

"And?"

He was guileless. "Your luck will turn bad."

I flicked it in a flashing arc toward the water. "Really?"

Nihko flung out a hand and snatched the ring from the air—"Fool!"—then mimicked my flicking gesture with deft fingers.

Something slammed into my breastbone. I folded, empty of breath, of sense, and tumbled backward into Del. She yelped once as I came down on a foot, grabbed for air, caught me, and then somehow the plank was no longer beneath either of us.

Not *again* . . . I twisted in midair, grabbed for the edge, caught. Clutched wood, digging fingers in so deep the pads of my fingertips flattened until nails cracked to the quick. I hung a moment, dangling over water; heard the splash as Del went in. Then I jerked myself up even as Nihko set foot on the plank to check his handiwork.

Breath screamed in my lungs. It wasn't fear of drowning; I had no time for that. It was pain, it was burning, it was absence of self-control over that most primitive function: the ability to breathe without conscious effort.

My chin was even with the plank. I caught movement from the

corner of my eye. Nihko realized now I hadn't gone in with Del. His hand came up; would a second gesture peel my fingers from the edge?

Not this time, you bastard.

I swung under, released, twisted and caught plank again, this time on the other side. Shoulder tensed briefly, then I thrust myself upward even as I swung a leg up and over. Toes caught, then the ball of my foot. I used the momentum. Came up, reached, grabbed the closest ankle, and jerked as hard as I could.

Nihko fell. He landed hard on the planking, rolled from his back to his side, then scrabbled wildly as he overbalanced. I thought briefly what might happen if he ended up dangling from his side of the plank while I dangled opposite him. Decided I didn't like that much.

So as he swung down, I dropped from the edge again and kicked him in the gut. His entire body spasmed as his lungs expelled air, and his hands released the plank. The impact of his body flat upon the water soaked me thoroughly. But it was the best bath I'd ever had.

I hung there a moment, enjoying the view of Nihko floundering his way to the surface, then became aware of Del's sea-slick head not so far away. "You all right?" I called.

She waved an assenting hand, treading water.

Relief. I clenched my teeth, hoisted myself up to the edge of the plank again, and hooked the foot on wood. A kick with my free leg gave me a little added momentum, and I thrust myself up the rest of the way. It was an ungainly maneuver that left me sprawled facedown on the trembling plank, but at least I was above the water instead of in it.

Then I saw the foot all of inches from my nose. And the glinting tip of a swordblade gesturing me to rise.

I looked up. Saw the wide smile in the freckled face, the wind-tangled swath of red hair, the gold and glass in her ears and wrapped around her throat.

"Someday," Prima Rhannet said, "you will have to learn how to swim. It might save you some little trouble."

Since she seemed to want it, I climbed to my feet. "Maybe."

The sword was lifted. I saw the flash of light on the blade, the tip brought up to skewer, knew what she meant to do. I would leap back, of course, to preserve my skin, and by doing it I'd take myself off the plank and into the water.

Not this time, you bitch.

I smashed the blade down with a forearm, stepped into her, tossed her over the edge, caught the sword as it flew from her grasp.

About damn *time* I had one of these suckers in my hands again.

Chapter 24

hey came for me, of course, the members of Prima's crew.
But I was ready for them. I waited at the head of the plank
where it was lashed to the ship. It was steadier here, not so vulnerable to the motion of the ocean or the weight of men upon the
wood. I'd chosen my ground, and now I stood it.

It felt gloriously invigorating to hold a sword in my hands
again. "Come on," I invited, laughing for the sheer joy of empow-
erment and the promise of engagement. "Come ahead."

They did.

Maybe some day they'll write about it, how a lone man took on
seven others. The advantage, it might be argued, was theirs; they
knew the ship, knew one another, understood better the mechanics of planks between ships and docks. But they were none of them
sword-dancers, none of them trained by the shodo of Alimat, none
of them born to the sword.

I hope they do write about it, because from inside the engagement I couldn't see what happened. I knew only that I took them
on one at a time, trapping guards, smashing blades, cutting into
flesh that wandered too near my sword. It was Prima Rhannet's
blade and thus the balance, for me, was decidedly off, but that's
purely technical; the weapon was more than adequate to the purpose, to my needs of the moment.

By the time I'd disarmed three of them, the others drew back to reconsider options.

I laughed at them, still poised at the brink. "Come on!" I exulted, inexpressibly relieved to be rid of the prickle of apprehension engendered by our presence at Akritara, and focus strictly on the physical fight. I'd needed this. "I'm one man, right? I can't swim, this isn't my sword, I'm not really in proper condition—what's stopping you? *Come ahead!*"

It was enough to lure one of them in. Three of his crewmates bled upon the deck, though none of them would die of it. Within a matter of moments he had joined them, nursing a wounded wrist. His sword, like the others, had been slung by my own over the rail into the water.

"It's only me." I was grinning like a sandsick fool. "Of course, this is what I do for a living . . . in fact, what I've been doing for a living for nearly twenty years. Probably I'm a *little* better at it than you. Maybe. You think?" I gestured expansively. "Why not find out? Three against one? Surely that's enough to take me. Isn't it?" I waggled fingers, inviting them closer. "You're all strong men . . . you're enough, aren't you? Dreaded renegadas, cutting throats with the best—or worst!—of 'em. What's to stop you? What's to keep you from taking me?" Another came in, came close. "There, now, *that's* better!"

The remaining two fanned out, approached obliquely from the sides. I had hoped to entice them to rush me. Three against one can be a little tricky, but I did have the advantage. They could undoubtedly sail a ship far better than I, but there are not many, if any, better with a sword.

We danced. Oh, it wasn't a proper dance; there was no circle, no ritual, no comprehension of the beauty of the patterns, the movements, but the intent was the same: to defeat the opponent. In this case they had one and I had three, but the desired end was identical.

They came on. I took them one at a time, cutting, nicking, piercing, slashing, driving each of them back. They stumbled over themselves, one another, over their brethren already sprawled on the deck, discovering that a man born to the sword understands it implicitly, how it demands to be employed. A sword is not just a weapon, not just a means of killing a man, but has a soul and needs of its own. It isn't made to be looked at, nor to be used by incompetents. A sword is dead in the hands of an inferior wielder, it will hurt him as often as it will aid. But it comes alive in the hands of a man who understands it, who shares its desires.

I felt the plank thump and tremble beneath my feet. I'd expected it for a while; Nihko and his captain had had more than enough time to pull themselves from the water. So I completed my chore with alacrity, adding three more bleeding men to the pile upon the deck even as I disposed of their swords, and spun, poised and ready. Prima Rhannet stopped short, lurched backward out of range. She stood there, furious, two long paces away.

"He will kill her," she promised.

I looked beyond her, as she intended. Nihkolara stood on the dock at the end of the plank. His left hand rested on the back of Del's neck. Pretty much as I'd expected; I'd known I could take the crew—well, *believed* I could—but was not foolish enough to assume victory would be all-encompassing. Not when Del was at risk. But it takes small things as well as large to win, outside the circle as much as within.

Del's clothing, soaked and dripping, was wrapped closely around her body, more like shroud than tunic. Fair hair, now unbraided, was slicked severely back from her face, baring the bones of her skull, the bitter acknowledgment that she was surety of my behavior once again. I thought of what his touch had done to me: set a weeping rash around my wrist, burned the flesh of my throat, stopped the heart in my chest. Thought of what else—and to whom—that touch might do.

I grounded the swordtip in the wood of the plank. "All I wanted," I told Prima truthfully, "was an explanation."

Sopping hair, stripped of coils and curls and darkened to the color of old blood, streamed over her shoulders. The thin fabric of her clothing, plastered against flesh, underscored how lush her compact body was. "About what?"

"IoSkandi, ioSkand*ic*," I said. "What it is, what it means—and why the touch of his hand upon a person can do things to him." Or to her.

Prima's lips peeled back from her teeth. With great disdain, she said, "Have you never heard of magic?"

I arched brows. "Your implication being that Nihko has it."

"Nihko *is* it," she hissed between clamped jaws.

"I thought Nihko is—or was—a priest."

"IoSkandic," she said. "Priests. Mages."

"Both?"

Prima Rhannet laughed. "He'll pray for you," she promised, "even as he kills you."

"How economical. Priest *and* mage for the price of one." Smiling, I tossed the blade aside before she could demand its return; steel flashed on its way to the water. As expected, the action enraged her. "Now, captain. Suppose you and I discuss how it is we can all of us get new swords."

Back aboard a ship I'd hoped never to see again, let alone revisit, Prima and her first mate were coldly angry that I had accomplished so much in so little time, even if they'd regained the upper hand eventually. I'd cost them the pride and self-confidence of their crew, which had survived the encounter even if the decks were now stained with their blood; had cost them every blade they had on board; and had proven the only way they could truly defeat me was to use coercion or magic. Not a pleasant realization or prospect for people who believed they were naturally superior at everything.

I leaned against the rail, arms folded, more relaxed than I'd been in weeks. There are people in the world who want to win at any cost, who will use any means to win. But Prima Rhannet and Nihkolara were not so ruthless as they might prefer me to believe. She'd said more than once they only killed people if there were no other way. Now I knew, and they knew, and they knew *I* knew that *they* knew I was not so easily dealt with as they'd believed—and that unless they truly did mean to kill me they'd better not dismiss me quite so easily.

Prima scowled at me as she paced the deck. She was damp, but drying, and her wiry hair, wind-tossed, had begun to curl again.

"So," I said cheerfully, "what comes next?"

She stopped pacing. "You go back to Akritara."

"Won't you even consider giving us passage elsewhere?"

"I will not."

"*Why* not?"

"Business," she said coolly, "with the metri."

"Still?"

"Still."

I swore briefly, which amused Prima and her first mate.

"Back," the captain said, "to Akritara."

I feigned shock. "May we do that? After all, we walked all the way down here—"

Nihkolara made a sound of disgust. "And after what you were told about soiling, and cleansing—"

"And having no coin, I attempted to barter with that ring you've got in your hand," I continued with blithe disregard for his comment. "But no one would permit us to go near them, let alone take us down on molah-back, or wash our feet at the bottom."

Nihko inhaled a long, hissing breath of intense displeasure.

"Fool," his captain said coldly. "You may have ruined everything."

"How is that, exactly?" I inquired. "Just what is it you and the priest-mage are after?"

"Swords," she said sharply. "Thanks to you."

"Ah. Well, then, speaking of swords—"

Prima cut me off. "The metri has sent to say she will hire me to supply a sword to you, and to her." The direction of her eyes flicked to Del. "But this will cost the metri far more, now, than before, because she must make good our losses—due to your folly—and you will then owe her even *more* of your time." Her blazing smile was unexpected and maliciously sweet. "Is that what you hoped for?"

Cheerfulness dissipated. I glared.

It pleased her; her mood shifted to crisp competence tinged with victory. "You will be escorted back to Akritara, where the metri will be told of your behavior. Punishment lies within her purview—"

"Wait," I interrupted sharply. "Punishment is not part of the plan."

"What *is* the plan?" Prima asked with poisonous clarity. "Have you one? Or are you hoping merely to take advantage of a dying old woman who so desperately wants a proper heir?"

"*You're* the ones who took advantage of *us!*" I shot back.

"Yes," the captain agreed with elaborate precision. "We are pirates. That is what we do."

When I could not immediately come up with a properly devastating retort, Prima turned away. To Nihko, she said, "Is he soiled beyond redemption?"

He looked at Del briefly, then at me. For a long time. "No," he said finally. "But it will prove costly to have him cleansed appropriately so he may walk among the Houses again. The metri will not be pleased."

"Will the priests do it?"

He shrugged. "She is the Stessa metri, and they will accept her petition—"

"And coin?" I inquired sweetly.

"—with the proper rituals invoked and completed." Nihko's gaze flicked to me. "Provided he does no more damage to her Name and House than has already been done."

"Look," I said, "I'm getting pretty tired of—" And was slammed to my knees, though no one touched me.

"Enough," Nihkolara hissed, so stiff he trembled with it. "If you will not hold your silence when it serves us, I will seal your mouth permanently."

My knees, mashed against hard wood, were most unhappy. But I didn't have the time or inclination to listen to their complaints. I cleared my throat experimentally, making sure nothing had been permanently sealed quite yet. "You can do that, huh?"

"What I can do," he said, "you cannot begin to comprehend."

"*That's* encouraging."

He flipped something at me. Wary now of what he next planned, I ducked, squeezing my eyes closed. Whatever it was struck my forehead, bounced off, rolled briefly against the deck. I opened my eyes and saw it then, clearly: the discarded brow ring, glinting in sunlight.

"Priests in general have a facility for mercy," Nihko observed coolly. "But be wary of mine."

"You know," I said conversationally, "I'm right here with you, and I don't feel sick at all."

"That may be remedied," he suggested. "Shall I have you spew your guts here and now?"

"Magic," Del said intently, and put up a hand to forestall question or comment. "Magic, Tiger. It has always affected you."

I arched brows. "Magic affects a lot of people. That's sort of the point."

"No. I mean *how* it affects you, much of it. You have said many times it makes you feel odd, as if your bones itch." She paused delicately. "And we know how it affects your belly."

I scowled at her briefly, then shrugged. "I notice it, one way or another."

"It means nothing," Nihko said lightly.

Del looked at him. "No?"

"Magic simply *is*," he declared. "Some people are sensitive to its existence."

"How is that?" I asked.

"The way some are made ill by certain foods," he explained matter-of-factly. "Or those poor souls who cannot ride the ocean without emptying their bellies."

"Or keep cats," Prima Rhannet contributed with an ingenuous glance at Del; her expression suggested a subtext I decided not to pursue.

"It's different with Tiger," Del said. "Magic puts him seriously out of sorts. As if it argues with him."

Nihko shook his head. "There is no significance in that."

"Indeed," the captain said, "no more than in a man claiming a woman is out of sorts once a month because she *is* a woman."

I knew better than to get into that. "And I'm supposed to believe you?"

"I am a priest-mage," Nihkolara said with devastating modesty. "I have a measure of experience with such things."

"And we have a measure of experience with *you*," I pointed out. "Why should we believe anything you say?"

"Because of the alternative," Prima replied.

"What, you'll kill us?"

"No," she said seriously, "because in Skandi, being a priest-mage means you are mad—"

I gaped inelegantly. *"What—?"*

"—and madness is not tolerated in Skandi." Her gaze was steady; she avoided looking at her first mate. "Such people are too feared to be killed outright, so they are sent away. Just as Nihko was."

"And here I thought he got in trouble over bedding the wrong woman." Nihko was not amused by my amusement at his expense. "Sent away where?" I asked, enjoying his expression.

"IoSkandi," the first mate answered with a vast contempt for ignorance.

"IoSkandi is a lazaret," Prima Rhannet explained gently to my incomprehension, as if taking pity on a child. "It's where madmen are sent to live until they cease to do so."

I looked at Nihko. "For someone who's supposed to be mad or dead, you're very calm about all of this."

Del spoke before he could answer. "Why?" she asked him intently. "Why didn't you die?"

Nihkolara said only: "I am ikepra."

"I thought you said that meant you were abomination," I put in sharply. "Profanation."

"Those with power are known to be so because they go mad," he said, "and are sent to ioSkandi. There they survive to purposely rouse the power, if it may be done, so they may control it for the needs of their own salvation; if they cannot, they die of it. Those who survive learn what the true nature of magic is, and how to cohabit with it."

"And?"

"Those who reject it, those who leave ioSkandi and the priest brothers, are abominations."

"Yet you left."

"And thus I am adjudged apostate by my priest-brothers, the mages. As I am adjudged *io*—mad—by the people of the island."

"And feared even more because you are not in your proper place." Del nodded. "You do not fit. You live *outside*, without rules, without rituals." She glanced at me briefly, using the Southron word. "Borjuni."

He shrugged. "Ikepra."

But borjuni were simply men without morals. None of them had any magic, any priestly trappings. In Skandi, where eleven specific families were considered gods-descended, what Nihko represented as a member of one of those families—as madman, priest-mage, *and* ikepra—was far more fearsome than mere Southron bandits.

I understood now the intent of the warding gestures, the whispered comments, the rejection and outright abhorrence of the concept of the brow ring as barter. And yet the solution seemed obvious. "You could leave, you know. Avoid all kinds of unpleasantness."

Nihkolara hitched a shoulder. "And so I do leave. Every time my captain's ship sails."

"But you come back. I meant leave *permanently*," I clarified. "Only a fool would remain."

"A fool." Nihko smiled. "Or a madman."

I shook my head. "So, you'd have us believe you still have this power, even though you're exiled from the brotherhood." Even as I was exiled from the oaths and rituals of the sword-dance.

"He has power," Prima said sharply. "You have experienced it. Exile need not strip one of one's gift."

Any more than being denied the circle stripped me of *my* gift.

"But he rejected it," I maintained, which was entirely different; I'd never reject my sword-skill. Then I looked piercingly at Nihko. "Or did it reject you?"

Something flared briefly in his eyes, some deep and abiding emotion so complex I could not begin to define the elements that comprised it.

"Tell him," Del commanded the first mate, as if she had acquired the pieces of an invisible puzzle and put them together even as we stood here. "You have used this magic on him more than once, and have provided him the means to control his sensitivity to it when in your presence." She nodded at the brow ring glinting on the deck. "If you are—or were—a priest in service to the gods, whatever gods they may be, it is your duty to inform those who are at risk what it *is* they risk."

Prima Rhannet inhaled a quiet, but hissing breath. "You see too much."

"Well, I'm blind," I said curtly. "Why not explain it to me?"

Nihkolara did. "The power, once understood, once acknowledged, once invoked, will never reject its vessel. But that vessel may reject *it*."

"And?"

"Tie a string around your finger as tightly as you may, and leave it so," he said, "without respite. What is the result?"

Del said, "It withers."

Prima said, "It dies."

I looked at Nihko. "And you're not dead."

"Nor ever will be," he agreed, "until such a time as the gods decree I have lived out my allotment."

"So, if I broke your neck even as we stand here, you wouldn't die?"

The contempt was back in his eyes. "I am not immortal," he said. "But I will not intentionally tie a string around my finger so that it may wither and die." He paused. "And you would not be permitted close enough to break my neck."

"Really?" I grinned toothily at him. "Is that why I've dumped you on your rump more than once?" I made a show of examining his soaked but drying person. "And knocked you into the water?"

Del's posture was suddenly such that we all became aware of the sheer power of her presence simultaneously. It was a subtle magic she had in good measure, and a power I understood and admired.

To Nihkolara she said, "You have relied on magic to defeat this man, always. What are you without it?"

Prima's sun-coppered brows slid up in startlement. "My, my," she murmured with elegant implication. "So the tiger's mate defends her male. He *has* trained you well."

"Oh, stop," Del said coldly. "You invoke such imagery to provoke, and without cause. You would do precisely the same for Nihkolara, with nothing in it of men and women beyond coincidence of gender. You don't sleep with him. He *can't* sleep with you. Do you then count the binding between captain and first mate, friend and friend, as the lesser because bedding is not involved?"

Color flared in Prima Rhannet's face, filling in the spaces between freckles, then ebbed away so thoroughly all one could see *were* freckles, the angry glitter of her eyes. And yet she offered no answer because there was none that gained the victory.

Oh, yes. She would defend Nihkolara with her life, and he her with his.

Nihko recognized challenge no matter the gender. "But I *have* the magic," he said coolly in answer to Del's original question, "and only a fool refuses to use an advantage."

"A fool," I said, "or a madman."

Nihko turned on his heel and marched away.

Prima was rigid with surpressed rage. "Perhaps it is time I had you both declawed."

I spread my hands. "In case you've forgotten, captain: *None* of us has blades with which such a thing might be done."

Which brought us around all over again to where we'd begun.

Prima's chin rose. It jutted the air. "You will have swords," she said, "as the metri has suggested. But if you press Nihko, you may well discover that a blade is no weapon at all." She stared hard at us both. "Now get off my ship."

We got off her ship. But not before I retrieved the brow ring from the deck. Only a fool refuses to use an advantage.

And I'm not a madman, either.

Chapter 25

efore Del and I had even reached the gate of the front courtyard entrance—the one where the metri had suggested Herakleio and I, wearing plaster and nothing else, should stand on display—Simonides met us. His expression was stern as stone as he put up a hand in a gesture that could be interpreted no other way save *stop*.

We stopped.

Whereupon men arrived from all corners of the courtyard, swarming into industry. A mat was laid down first, then a fine-loomed carpet was unrolled atop it. As men labored to do that, others came to Del and me with amphora, soaps, oil, and linen cloths. Another man, shaven-headed but bearing no tattoos or rings in his flesh—thus not mad, I assumed, only holy; though in my opinion a certain emphatic degree of holiness bears its own weight of madness—waited in the shade of a tree. Other men brought stools upon which Del and I were directed to sit.

We sat.

As Simonides looked on in meticulous supervision; as the priest beneath the tree murmured softly to himself; as Del and I stared at one another in baffled astonishment, we were scrubbed nearly raw from the knees down, with particular attention given to the soles of our feet. A harsh soap first, followed by scented; followed by clean rinse water; followed by oil that was, I assumed, blessed, as the oil-men first glanced to the murmuring priest for a nod of permission before pouring.

It wasn't entirely unpleasant, having rich oil worked into my flesh, except as the man's hands rose toward my knees I stiffened a little. A sidelong glance at Del showed me a bemused expression, but she did not appear entirely discontent with the direction of her oil-man's hands.

Perhaps it was time I bought my *own* bottle of oil.

Once that ritual was completed, we were gestured to rise and stand upon the carpet that was layered over the mat. Simonides escorted us with grave deliberation toward the recessed doorway. I glanced over my shoulder as we stepped out of sunlight into shade, saw the carpet-and mat-men rolling everything away; and then the priest came out from beneath the tree to begin *his* ritual.

"So," I said to Simonides, "this is why you didn't want us to walk."

Simonides said nothing, simply opened the door and stepped away, gesturing for us to enter.

"Well, look," I told him as I passed into the household, "at least we gave everyone something to do with their afternoon."

Del produced an elegant little snicker of amusement. Simonides bestowed upon me an almost mournful expression. "The metri sends to say you are to attend her in her bedroom."

That stopped me. "Her bedroom?"

"She is abed."

"That's a little redundant," I told the servant. "Why is she abed, and why am I expected to attend her *while* she's abed?"

"She has sent to say to me she wishes me to send to say to you—"

Exasperated by the circuitous manner of speech, I cut him off rudely. "Save your breath, Simonides—just point me in the right direction."

Quietly, he said, "She wishes to see her grandson."

The simplicity of the statement rocked me. Even Del marked the implications, glancing to me immediately. I nodded, offering neither commentary nor expression. Simonides led me into the depths of the household even as Del murmured tactfully of a desire to nap, and eventually I was given entry into the metri's private quarters.

She was indeed abed, propped into a sitting position by a generous arrangement of embroidered cushions. Silvering hair had been taken from its multiple plaits and loops, freed of decorative baubles, so that it streamed down across the cushions, her shoulders, and the coverlet. It softened the severity of her features. For the first time I saw beyond the metri, beyond the self-proclaimed gods-descended woman born of and into the Eleven Families who ruled in its entirety the wine trade of Skandi, and who needed so desperately to keep every facet of her empire under control, even an individual who merely *might* be her relative. She was in this moment simply an aging woman who walked the road toward death, and knew the distance left her was shorter than for others.

"Am I so cruel," she asked, "that you feel you *must* leave?"

Not the beginning I expected. In bed with her hair loose, with her body swathed in a coverlet and linens, I had expected to hear a voice to match the impression of weakness. But her voice was the same, her tone identical to the one she used habitually: firm, clear, meticulous in its delicacy of emphasis.

She was not unlike many of the tanzeers who'd hired me to dance for them. Stern, hard, proud, possessive, but also realistic; what was undertaken was from necessity, not whim. But she was as unlike them as could be: a woman, and possibly my mother's mother. She was a stranger to me in spirit, in the large and small aspects of the heart, but potentially a woman whose bone was my bone, whose blood was my blood.

This woman had had no shaping of me, not in the smallest degree, but she could very well be *in* me. If so, I was as much of her as I was of the Salset. And without the shaping the tribe had given me, I would not stand here today to have this woman speak to me of needs and expectations.

If I left her, if I left *here*, I left myself as well.

Without accusation, I said, "You have no intention of naming me your heir."

One eyebrow twitched. "Have I not?"

"I am a tool. An adze to shape the boy you *will* name your heir."

She smiled faintly. "Or perhaps a lance point, to jab him where he is most soft."

"You admit it?"

"I admit nothing," the metri said, "beyond a promise that I will do what I have always done: whatever I perceive is required for the task."

"And Herakleio is my task."

"Herakleio is the task I have selected for you, as you have selected none for yourself."

That stung, as no doubt she intended it to. "Excuse me?"

"What are you but a man whose home is what he builds of a circle drawn in the sand? No mortar, no bricks, only air. And dreams."

"And skill."

"Oh, yes, there is skill; and I believe it not so different from the skill I employ each day for the betterment of my Name."

"Well, then we share a goal," I threw back at her. "I have a name of my own."

"Chula," she said gently.

Had I not already been standing, I'd have leaped to my feet. As it was, all I could do was contain the shame, the shock and outrage her tone and the word engendered by standing excruciatingly still. Because if I moved, if I spoke, if I so much as blinked . . .

She gave me no time to respond with anything other than quivering silence. "You are indeed skilled," the metri declared with a quietude that in no way diminished the power of personality, "and it is a skill few men have, the ability to build walls merely of the air and to abide within them, defending those walls against every enemy." One hand moved slightly on the coverlet; fingers spasmed, clenched briefly. "I asked you what you were. I have *said* what you are, and I will say this as well: you have not been given, nor have you taken, responsibility beyond what is required to keep yourself—and your woman—alive."

I gifted her with a ghastly grin. "Good enough for me!"

"But that you have taken no more does not mean you cannot

accept more. And so I give you Herakleio, that both of you learn the requirements of responsibility. Because recognizing, acknowledging, and accepting responsibility is the hallmark of adulthood."

I wanted to smirk, but didn't; she was deadly serious, and I owed her that much. "Is it?"

"And because the boy I have given over to you as your task may well be your kinsman."

I studied her expression very closely. "You admit I am a tool—and seemingly an irresponsible one at that—yet insist I may still be a Stessa? Why? What do you gain?"

"Leverage," she answered simply.

Well, *that* was truth. "Herakleio doesn't believe any more than you do that I'm your grandson."

"It doesn't matter what he believes. All that matters is what I do."

"But naming a stranger, a foreigner, as heir to the Stessa fortune is not a possibility."

She shook her head. "You still do not understand."

"Explain it to me, then."

"You may indeed not be my grandson. You *are* a stranger, a foreigner in everything save, perhaps, blood. But neither precludes you from inheriting."

I blinked. "You're right. I don't understand."

Her eyes were fixed on mine. "I am required only to name an heir. The heir is heir. It is the naming that matters."

I shook my head slowly. "We know very well what I am, you and I. A Southron barbarian who makes a living in the circle with a sword . . . a man who builds a home with walls of air. That makes me fit to dance for you, but not to run your household, the vineyards, or the economics of the Stessas—Stess*oi*—which affect the economics of Skandi."

The metri smiled. "A man who understands the mechanics of ambition is fit to do whatever he wishes to do. He finds ways to deal with such things as he does not know, and learns from those who do."

"And?"

"And," she continued pleasantly, "so I am moved to ask you if

I am so cruel that you feel you *must* leave a place in my household, a position for which you are as fit as any man I know, who will learn because it is in him to learn, and who wishes to pay his debts."

I put a finger into the air. "You're forgetting: I was just down at the docks checking on the possibility of convincing Prima Rhannet to sail us away from here. Since you so kindly explained how it is no one else on the island will."

"There is nothing you may offer Prima Rhannet that will convince her of such an undertaking, when I can convince her against it." Her eyes were very calm. "Unless it is your woman."

"Del is not an issue in this!"

"Coin is minted in many shapes," she said, "not the least of which is knowledge of what another will accept. You owe me a debt; I have said you may discharge it by teaching Herakleio what it is to be a man. But you have nothing in the world Prima Rhannet will accept, *except* the companionship of your woman."

I shook my head again, shoving down the anger so I could be very plain. "Del is not coin. Del is not barter. Del is not in any way an object, nor available for trade."

The metri's smile did not reach her eyes. "Whatever it is someone else wants very badly is indeed coin, barter, and object. Availability is the only factor remaining open to negotiation, and subsequent arrangement."

"I don't accept that."

"You may reject the truth as it pleases you to do so. But it alters no part of it."

I backed away, displaying both palms in a gesture of abject refusal. "This conversation is over."

She waited until I reached the door. "And so is this test."

I froze, then swung back sharply even as I released the latch. "This was a *test?*"

"All things are tests," the metri said obliquely. "Each day as I rise, offering thanks to the gods *for* the day, I understand that the hours left to me before I retire again are tests of themselves, of my strength, of my loyalty and devotion, of my will to make certain the Stessa name survives as it was meant to survive: a piece of the gods themselves, made flesh. For they placed here upon the island a woman who was delivered of a child who in turn bore her own, and in turn another was born of that woman, until the day came that I was born to do my mother's work. It is heritage. It is legacy. It is *responsibility:* to see that one small piece of the gods, made flesh, remains whole in the world, and alive, lest that world become a lesser place for its loss." She leaned forward then, toward me, away from the cushions. Intently she asked, "Who is to say that if a single candle is blown out, the remainder of the world does not go dark as well?"

"But . . ." But. It was a debate in which I was ill-equipped to participate. And yet the argument existed of itself because it *could* exist.

No one knew.

Each time I shut my eyes on the verge of sleep, I gave myself over to trust that I'd awaken again. Because I *had* awakened each and every day.

But who was to say I would tomorrow?

Could you put coin on it?

No. Only belief *in* it. Only trust.

Only faith.

She leaned back again, abruptly ashen. One hand was pressed to her chest as she labored to breathe. Her lips and nails were blue-tinged. This was not a woman feigning illness or weakness to gain my sympathy. I had seen that look before in men with weak hearts.

"I'll call Simonides," I said sharply, and made a hasty departure.

Herakleio found me out on the terrace, moving through ritual movements designed to condition both body and mind. I had anticipated his arrival, and the accusations. I let him make them without a word spoken to stop him, because he needed to make them. And I, in his place, might well make them, too.

When he ran out of breath and I was cooling down, I finally addressed him directly. "You've said she isn't in immediate danger."

"Yes, I said that." He nearly spat the sibilants. "And no, she is not in *immediate* danger, so the physician says; she should live for another year or more. But she is clearly ill, and weakening."

"Which is why you've come to me now: you view me as a threat. And now a more *immediate* threat."

He glared. "And so you are."

"Unless she has already declared me her heir, I am no threat at all." I was loose, relaxed, sweat drying as the wind snapped against my flesh. "Has she?"

He remained hostile, if somewhat mollified. "She has not."

I took up the cloth draped over the low wall and scrubbed at my face, speaking through it. "Then you're safe. Akritara, the vineyards, the power and wealth . . . all of it is still meant to be yours."

He looked away from me then, staring hard across the land that fell away against the horizon, rushing toward the cliff face miles away. "I want it," he said tightly, "but I want her alive, more."

Prima Rhannet had said it one night in her cups: there was sunlight in him, and stone. She had not said there were tears.

I flipped the cloth over one shoulder and sat down on the wall. "Truth, Herakleio, in the name of an old woman we both of us respect: my coming here had nothing to do with hoping to replace you as heir. I knew nothing about Skandi at all, let alone that there were Stessoi, or metris, or even vineyards and wealth to inherit."

He didn't look at me, nor did he pull wind-tossed hair from his face because such a gesture would remove the shield. "Then why did you come?"

"To find out . . ." I let it go, thought it through, began again. "To find out if there was a home in my life where the walls were built of brick and mortar instead of air."

Herakleio turned sharply into the wind to look at me. "I have heard *her* say that!"

I nodded. "She said it to me earlier today, before she became ill."

He flung out an encompassing hand. "And so you came and found that these walls were made of more than brick and mortar, but also coin and power!"

"But I didn't necessarily find my home," I said. "I found *a* home. Her home. Your home."

He shook his head vigorously. "But you want it. Now that you know it, you want it."

I drew in a deep breath, let it fill my chest, then pushed it out again in a noisy sigh of surrender. "There is a part of me that wishes to be *of* it. Yes."

"You see!"

"But being of something is not the same as being that thing," I pointed out. "There is a difference, Herakleio. You are of the Stessoi, and you *are* a Stessa. You *are* these walls; your bones are made of them. It's your home."

He was clearly perplexed.

"*I* am my home," I said. "Where I go, that is my home. My walls are built of air. There is no substance—no brick, no mortar—except the substance I give them, and that is air. A circle drawn in the sand." I hitched a shoulder. "A man born in and of a house doesn't truly comprehend what it is to *be* a house. Because there is no need."

"But," he said, "you have that woman in it."

That woman. Not *a* woman. That one. Specifically.

Herakleio understood semantics better than I'd believed.

"Because she chooses to be in it," I said finally; and that in itself was so different from what I would have said three years before, when every part of me knew a woman was in a man's house because he *put* her there.

"Does she build them of air as well, those walls?"

"The walls of my home?" I shook my head. "Del is my brick. My mortar."

His intensity went up a notch. "And if she left your house, would those walls collapse?"

This time it was my turn to stare hard across the horizon. "I don't know."

For him, for that question, the answer was enough.

Chapter 26

A spire of stone tore a hole in the sky, punching upward like a fist in challenge to the gods. I poised upon the foremost knuckle of that fist, aware of the breath of those gods caressing naked flesh.

Caress. Keraka. The living embodiment of the gods-descended, sealed by spell or wish into the infant's flesh before it even knew the world, was yet safe in its mother's womb. All the colors of wine, all the shapes of the mind, staining the fragile shell before the sun so much as could warm it.

But there was none on my body. I was free of the blemish also called caress; was nothing more within or of myself than stranger, than foreigner, lacking the knowledge of gods-descended, the gifts of the Stessoi, the birthright of the Eleven.

What was I but a man born of a womb unknown to any save the woman and the man who together made a child, but who could or would not nurture that child; so that he was raised a slave in the hyorts of the Salset?

The spire beneath me shook. Bare feet grasped at stone. Wind beat into my eyes, blinded me with tears.

Skandi, they said, had been smoke made solid, then broken apart again.

If I was not to lose the spire, if I was not to let it shake me off its fist, I would have to sacrifice my own. Not to die, but to survive; not to destroy flesh, but to preserve it.

There was wind enough to do it, if I let it carry me.

There was power enough to fly, if I let myself try.

I stretched, leaned, felt the wind against my palms. Closed my eyes so I could see.

Was lifted—

"Tiger?" A hand came down on bunched, sweat-sheened shoulder. "Tiger—wake up."

The spire fell away, crumbled to dust beneath me, took me down with it—

"Tiger."

—and all the bones shattered, all the flesh split into pulp—

"Tiger—wake up!"

I lurched, twisted, sat up as the fingers closed tightly into muscle taut as wire. I stared into darkness, aware of the noise of my breathing, the protests of my heart.

The metri's heart was ailing. And I might be her grandson.

"What is it?" Del asked.

All around me on the ground the stone of the spire was broken.

She got up then, crawled over me, got out of bed, fumbled around in the darkness, hissed a brief oath as she fumbled again. But I heard the metallic strike-and-scratch, smelled the tang, saw the first flare of spark as she used flint and steel to light the candle in its pottery cup.

She held the cup up high so the light spilled over me. "Gods," she whispered, "what's *wrong* with you?"

I blinked then, and squinted, then shook my head to banish the visions. "Bad dream."

"You look scared out of your wits," Del said dubiously. "Rather like the stud when he's really spooked: all white of eye, and stiff enough to shatter his bones."

Shattered bones.

"Don't," I said simply, then swung my legs over the edge of the bed so my feet were flat on the floor. I hunched there, elbows set into thighs, the heels of my hands scouring out my eyes. "Just—a bad dream."

Del set the candle-cup down on the linens chest, then came to sit beside me. "What was it?"

I shook my head. "I don't know." I looked up then, still squinting against the flame. "I've had rather a lot to think about, lately."

"Magic," she said grimly.

I began to object—magic was not something I gave much thought to—then refrained. Magic *was* part of it; Nihkolara was more than priest, and he had proved it. Time and time again, simply by putting his hand on me. Time and time again my body had warned me *before* he touched me, and I had refused to listen.

Some people, the priest-mage had said, were more sensitive to magic. It made them ill, he said, like certain foods or herbs.

"Magic," I muttered, and closed my hand around the necklet with its weight of sandtiger claws, and one silver ring.

Del was silent a long moment. Then, very quietly, "Do you believe he's right?"

I knew whom she meant. "No."

"In your heart."

The pounding, spasming heart. "No."

"All right—in your soul."

I laughed a little. "Just how many pieces of my anatomy do you want me to consult before you get the answer you want?"

"How about in your earlobe?"

I grinned, leaned into her with a shoulder even as she leaned back. "He has rings in his earlobes, our blue-headed first mate."

She nodded. "You always swear you don't believe in magic—"

"I said I don't *like* it. There's a difference."

"So, you mean you don't believe in *this* magic. This specific magic."

"I don't necessarily believe I have it, no."

"But—"

"But," I said, overriding her, "if what Nihko says is true, it doesn't mean I have it. It means I'm sensitive to it."

"But he has called you ioSkandic."

"I suspect Nihko has called me a lot of things."

"Besides all that. You have a history of personal experience with magic. Shall I name all the incidents?"

"Let's not," I suggested; likely it would fill six volumes to do so. "But reacting to magic doesn't mean I have any magic myself."

"Even after hosting Chosa Dei?"

"Hosting a sorcerer does not make the body of itself powerful.

Only powerful by proxy." I looked at my fingernails, which had often indicated the state of my body while infested with the sorcerer who considered himself a god. They were whole, normal, not black or curling, or missing. "I can't work any kind of spells, Del. You know that."

"You sang your jivatma to life."

"So did you sing yours to life," I reminded her. "Does that make you a sorceress; or is the *tool*—in this case, the sword—the embodiment of magic?"

"No," Del said decisively. "I am not a sorceress."

"There you are, bascha. You don't like the idea any more than I do."

"But what if it *were* true? That you have magic?"

"Then I guess I'd be a sorcerer."

"You say that so lightly."

Because I had to, or admit how much the prospect frightened me. "Do you want me to say it in a hushed whisper? Shall I go out onto the terrace, thrust my right fist and sword into the air and shout 'I have the power!'? like some melodramatic fool?"

"Well," she said, "I suppose being melodramatic is better than being mad."

"Which is the problem," I pointed out. "Here in Skandi, anyone with magic is considered mad, and sent away to this lazaret place."

"Is *that* what you're afraid of?"

"What, being mad? Oh, hoolies, some people would swear I am even without benefit of Skandic blood—*if* I have any—"

"Oh, Tiger, of course you're Skandic!"

"—simply because I have the gehetties to suggest I am the messiah who is to change the sand to grass," I finished. "Remember Mehmet? And the old hustapha? That deep-desert tribe more than willing to believe I am the one they worship?"

"And my brother," she said glumly. "Who was, according to Southron belief, the Oracle."

"Meant to announce the coming of the jhihadi." I nodded. "And so he announced me. And look at what it got him. They murdered him."

Del sighed deeply. "Likely they'd murder you, too."

"If we went back South? Oh, absolutely. If the religious zealots didn't get me, if the borjuni didn't kill me for whatever reward there must be on my head, surely the sword-dancers would track me down."

"Abbu Bensir?"

"I have dishonored the codes of Alimat, not to mention betrayed the faith and trust of our shodo," I said. "Abbu would call me out in the blink of an eye, except there'd be no circle drawn, no dance, no rituals of honor. He'd just do his best to execute me as quickly as possible."

"And if he failed?"

I shrugged. "Someone else would step forward."

Her voice was very quiet. "But if you *had* magic, no one could defeat you."

"I have magic," I declared firmly. "Sword magic. Just give me a blade, and I'll wield it."

"Then why," Del began, "are you so afraid?"

"Am I?"

"You didn't see your face just now when I lighted the candle."

"Bad dreams bring out the worst in anyone, bascha. Remember who it is I sleep with? I could tell you all the times *she's* had bad dreams. I never suggested she was afraid of anything . . . likely because she'd have knifed me in the gullet."

Del scoffed. "I'd have done no such thing." She thought it over. "Maybe planted an elbow."

"At the very least. Anyway, the point is I don't believe I have any magic, be it Skandic magic, Southron magic, or even Northern magic—which is buried with my jivatma anyway, back beneath those heaps of rocks in the middle of the Punja."

"You could always dig it up."

"I don't *want* to dig it up. I don't *want* any magic. I don't *want* to be a messiah, or mad, or anything other than what I am, which is a—" And I stopped.

"Sword-dancer," Del finished softly, with something akin to sorrow. Because she understood what it meant, to know myself other than what I *had* been after laboring so long to become more than a chula. "In Skandi," she said, "you may be a grandson, and heir to wealth, power, position. No magic is necessary, any more than a sword-dance."

"You're telling me to stay. To let the metri name me her heir."

"I'm pointing out potentials."

"Herakleio may have something to say about that."

"Herakleio is a boy."

"Herakleio is—" The door opened abruptly, and there he was. "—*here*," I finished. Then, "Knocking would be nice."

"Knocking wastes time," he replied. "Come out onto the terrace. Simonides has set the torches out for us."

"That must be very charming," I said, "but why am I to go out to the terrace, and why has he set torches out there for us?"

"The better to see by," he retorted, "while we dance." The wooden practice blade was in his strong young hand. Green eyes glinted hazel in candlelight. "Come out, Sandtiger. The metri wishes you to make me a man. Perhaps it is time I permitted you to try."

" 'Try'?" I asked dryly. "Are you suggesting you may fail in the attempt?"

He displayed good teeth. "I may already be a man. Shall we go and discover it?"

"It takes more than one dance, you know."

"Of course," he agreed, "as it takes more than one man in her bed for a woman to fully understand what it is to *be* a woman."

I felt Del stiffen beside me into utter immobility. That kind of comment had gotten me into plenty of trouble during the early days of our relationship. But then she had been the one who hired me, and had the right to disabuse me of such notions as she saw fit; now she was a guest in the metri's house and would not abuse the hospitality by insulting the woman's kin.

There are more ways than verbal of insulting another. I stood up, grabbed my practice blade from where it was propped against the wall. "Fine," I said. "Let's dance."

Imagine a sheet of ice, pearlescent in moonglow. Imagine a rim of rock made over into a wall surrounding the sheet of ice. Imagine a necklet of flames spaced evenly apart like gemstones on a chain, whipped into flaring brilliance by the breeze coming out of the night. Imagine the humped and hollowed angles of domes and arches and angles, demarcations blurred by wind-whipped torches into impression, not substance. Imagine the solidified wave of the world running outward beyond the wall as if upon a shore, then pouring off the invisible edge into the cauldron of the gods.

It was glory. It was beauty. And I walked upon it with a sword in my hand, albeit made of wood instead of beloved steel. But it didn't matter. A blade is a blade. The truth of its power lies in the hand that employs it.

Simonides, either as directed by Herakleio, or intuitively understanding the requirements of the moment, had taken care to set the torches properly. The stakes had been driven into a series of potted plants, so they were anchored against the breeze. The pots themselves had been set at equidistant points atop the curving wall, or tucked into niches formed by the architecture of the dwelling itself. Herakleio and I Inhabited the terrace proper, swept clean of sand and grit and other windblown debris. White tile glowed, showing no blemish, no seams.

It was not a dance. Nor was it sparring. Herakleio didn't yet know enough to be capable of either. What he desired was contact, a way of exorcising the demon residing in him, given life by his fear that the metri might die, leaving him alone and perhaps unnamed; leaving him to deal with the only man on the island who might comprise a threat.

I gave him that contact until he was gasping, flooded with sweat even as the wind dried it; until he bent over in a vain attempt to regain a full complement of air within his lungs. Eventually he let the blade fall and stood there, bent, panting, hands grasping thighs to hold himself upright.

At last he looked at me. "Water," he rasped. "There." A flopping hand indicated a jar set atop the wall next to one of the potted torches.

Too weary to walk, was he? Or simply accustomed to giving orders?

Or, possibly, offering it to me because I was sweating as well.

Before I could decide which it might be, someone else took up the jar. I knew those hands; knew the woman who settled the jar against one hip as she stepped over the wall.

Herakleio, looking up at last, saw her and knew her, too.

She had put off the long linen tunic and wore for the first time since leaving the ship the garb I knew best of all: pale leather tunic embroidered with blue-dyed leather laces at the hemline, neckline, and short, capped sleeves. The sheer linen tunics of Skandi left little to imagine, but somehow this tunic, even made of heavier leather, gave the impression of nakedness far more than Skandic garb suggested. For one, the hem hit Del at the midline of her thighs. That left a lot of leg showing, long limbs that were, for all their femininity, sculpted of muscle refined by the circle, by the requirements of a life built upon survival in the harshest dance of all. And though the arms had been bared before by the Skandic tunics, now it was clear they matched the legs. The context had altered.

Del is not elegant, not as it might commonly be described. She is too strong for it, too determined in her movements, which are framed on athleticism and ability, not on how such movements might be perceived by a man and thus refined as a tool to draw the eyes. Del didn't *need* elegance, nor a tool; she drew the eyes because of the honesty of her body, the purity of a spirit honed by obsession: the brutal need to be better, lest being lesser kill her.

She had braided back her hair into the plait most often worn when she stepped into the circle. The shadows upon her face were made stark in relief by flame and the movement of the light, the contours and angles of strong bone beneath her flesh sharpened beauty into steel. Herakleio, who believed he had seen Del that night in the winehouse, discovered all at once he had never seen her at all.

She took the jar off her hip and handed it to me, eyes locked onto Herakleio. It was a message, though he didn't comprehend it. I smiled, raised the jar to my mouth, took several swallows of cool, sweet water. Then lowered it and looked across at Herakleio, who now stood upright with his shoulders set back, forcibly easing his breathing into something approaching calmness. Beneath Del's cool gaze, being male, there was nothing else he could do.

I drank again, then held out the jar in Herakleio's direction. He would have to come get it. "Here. And I think I'll sit this one out, if you don't mind. The old man needs a rest."

Herakleio, who had taken the steps necessary to reach the jar, looked at me hard as he took it. It was clear to anyone's eyes that I was not in need of a rest; the daily rituals on Prima Rhannet's ship and here on the terrace had restored much of my fitness. "But if you sit this one out, there is no dance."

"This isn't a dance," I explained. "This is an exercise. In futility, perhaps." I grinned, offering the sword. "Del will take my place."

She accepted the blade, looked expectantly at Herakleio. Who still hadn't drunk.

"Her?" he asked.

"Me," she confirmed quietly.

"But—"

"Drink," she said, "or don't. But *move*. Waste no more time, lest you begin to stiffen. Because then you will be easy to beat, and I prefer a challenge. Nothing is gained otherwise; time is merely lost."

Herakleio's response was to stuff the jar into my arms, to turn on his heel, to stalk out to the center of the terrace.

"Fool," Del murmured, and followed.

Me, I sat down on the wall and drank some more, enjoying the prospect of seeing the Northern bascha beat the hoolies out of a big, strong young Skandic buck who was also an idiot.

Wondering, as I settled, if I had *ever* been so obnoxious as Herakleio Stessa.

Chapter 27

el, in short order, took him to the edge and pushed him over. It was not difficult for her; Herakleio was not a weak man, nor without promise, but he didn't know what she knew, including how to *use* his body. He had the potential, but he'd never realize or utilize it. He was meant to be a wealthy landowner, one of the Eleven Families, and such things did not require the learning of the sword.

She did not overpower him. She did not tease him. She did not lure him into traps. She simply used the alchemy of ability, talent, training, and a splendid economy of movement. She is peculiarly neat in her battles, is Delilah, even in her kills.

Herakleio was neither a battle nor a kill, but he undoubtedly felt as though he'd lost *and* died by the time she finished with him.

As with me, he finally pulled up, shook his head so that sweat-soaked strands of hair flew, then flopped over at the waist.

Del took one step into him, slid a rigid hand between his arms, and jabbed him in the short ribs. "Stand up," she commanded. "If you want to win back your wind, give your lungs room."

Thus accosted, no one doesn't stand up. He jerked upright, scowled at her, then walked away to circle with his hands on his hips, head tilted back, sucking air.

Del turned to me, took three strides, picked up the water jar, walked back to Herakleio. "Next time, drink when water is offered. Only a fool passes by an oasis even when his botas are full."

I smiled to hear my own words quoted. Herakleio was less amused. He snatched the jar from her, took it to his mouth, tipped his head back to drink. Then he raised the jar higher, held it in both hands, and proceeded to pour what was left over his face and head. It splashed in a silvery steam upon the clean white tiles that had hosted and honed scraping bare feet.

Del watched, apparently unmoved. She was sweat-sheened and undoubtedly thirsty as well, but she pushed for nothing. She waited.

When Herakleio handed the empty jar back, there was challenge in his eyes. "Only a fool allows the enemy to drink when she herself has not."

"I am not your enemy, nor are you mine," Del responded, clearly unwinded. "This was not a dance, nor was it war or skirmish."

"What was it, then?"

"Lesson," she said simply. "What did you learn from it?"

He flicked a glance at me, then looked back at her. "Never underestimate a woman with a sword in her hand."

"Then you have learned nothing." Del turned abruptly and strode away from him. In one step she was over the wall, and disappeared around the corner of the house.

Herakleio was baffled. Eventually he looked at me. "Isn't that what she *meant* me to learn?"

"That's a bonus," I said. "But the point was for you to learn something from the engagement. One maneuver, perhaps; even one that didn't work so you *know* it won't work." I shrugged. "Did you?"

His expression was peculiar. "No."

"Then she's right. You learned nothing." I stood up, stretched briefly, gifted him with a lopsided smile. "What woman did you *think* I meant when you asked about my scar?"

He looked at that scar immediately, and had the grace to color. "Oh."

" 'Oh,' " I echoed. "Ah, well, now you know. And it's not like you're the first to dismiss her out of hand."

He ran an arm over wet hair plastered to his scalp. "Has she ever killed a man?"

"Men," I clarified. "And I never kept count."

He nodded absently, gone away somewhere inside his head. I watched him a moment, then smiled again and turned to step over the wall.

"Wait," he said. When I turned back, his expression was calm. "Tomorrow morning?"

"Tomorrow morning is likely *today.*" It was a not so subtle reminder that he'd dragged me out of bed in the middle of the night. "Get a few hours' sleep, then we'll begin again. And this time, I suspect, you'll pay attention."

He nodded, looked down at his wooden blade, nodded again.

I left him there debating his abilities, and took myself off to bed.

Life continued in that manner for the next tenday, as they reckon time on Skandi. I worked Herakleio to a standstill, pointed out his failures, guided him into small gains. Without years of study he could never match me, but he was a quick learner and not unwilling, once he decided *to* learn. His temper flared now and again and he was not beyond hurling curses at me when impatience led him into folly that I quite naturally took advantage of, but for the most part he kept his mouth shut and did what he was told.

Del, too, took part, though he shied like a wary dog the first couple of times she went at him with the sword. Me he accepted as a true challenge because I, in addition to being male, was on other levels a threat, but Del, despite his acceptance of her expertise with the blade, was yet a *woman*, and though Skandic men were not raised to believe women were lesser beings, neither were they raised to learn the sword from one.

Herakleio's natural tendency with Del was to take his punishment instead of fending it off, which occasionally led to some measure of hilarity on my part, playing spectator; a certain focused and relentless determination on Del's; and utter frustration on his. I recalled how Nihkolara had made no sound nor attempted to escape the blows rained upon him by the metri that first day. It seemed on Skandi that women in authority were permitted complete autonomy in a given situation. And while ordinarily that might be the kind of thing Del appreciated, it didn't much aid her when her express desire was for Herakleio to fight back.

The rhythm of hours, of days, of sessions settled into a comforting discipline. Herakleio and I warmed up together, performed ritual exercises designed to train the body's reflexes and control, sparred briefly; then I set about showing him techniques and maneuvers; then Del came in to test his comprehension of what I'd explained and demonstrated while I stood apart to make suggestions and comments. We trained during the day, but also at night with the torches lighted, so the eye would not be prepared only for daylight.

Occasionally I'd step back in and correct Herakleio's grip on the leather-wrapped hilt, or show him a maneuver that might offset whatever it was Del had just done to disarm him, but most of the time I simply watched and critiqued as the young Northern woman and the young Skandic man moved closer to the dance.

Then, of course, I made the mistake of shouting out for Del to correct one of *her* maneuvers.

It was growing late in the evening and the torches fluttered in the breeze. She shot me such an outraged and venomous glance that I was moved to immediate defense. "Well, hey," I said, "there's no sense in letting you make mistakes either."

Herakleio, having learned one thing, held his stance and made no assumptions as to whether this incident was unplanned, or specifically designed to catch him off guard.

"Was it a mistake?" Del asked coolly. "Or merely a maneuver different from the one you might favor?"

As she lowered her sword to look at me, Herakleio realized it was a true disengagement. He stepped away warily, out of her reach, but did not relax completely.

"I favor whatever might help you win," I shot back. "You'd have *lost* with that maneuver. You left yourself wide open."

"To whom? You?"

"To anyone with wit enough to see the opening."

"Then come test me, Tiger."

"No."

"Come on, Tiger. Show me. *Test* me."

"No."

Herakleio asked, "Are you afraid?"

"Stay out of this," I said grimly, "or you'll end up with more bruises than you already have."

"But if she's right—if her maneuver is correct for her and merely different from one *you* might use . . ."

I glared at him. "Ten days have made you an expert, I see."

He didn't flinch; but then, he wouldn't. "Ten days have taught me that each opponent may have his—or her—own individual style, and one had better learn to adjust one's own style to it at any given moment."

Well, I couldn't argue with that. But I sure wanted to.

"Tiger," Del said with admirable self-restraint. "I'm not saying you were wrong. Only that I did it intentionally. With specific purpose."

"That's all very well and good," I returned, "but you'd have ended up dead. Unintentionally dead, perhaps, but dead. And without specific purpose."

"Then come show me."

I glared at Del, then included Herakleio in it. "I don't want to spar with you. Even with wooden swords."

"Tiger, we have sparred *many* times! Even after the dance on Staal-Ysta, where we nearly killed one another."

Herakleio, leaping head-first into stupidity again, said, "I'd like to hear about that."

I set my teeth and ignored him, speaking only to Del. "The last time we danced was in the big rockpile in the Punja, when you wanted to lure Chosa Dei out of my sword."

"Which I did."

"Del . . ." I shook my head. "We have danced two times with intent beyond conditioning one another. Once in the North on Staal-Ysta, because the voca tricked us into it—and both of us nearly died, as you pointed out. Then again a matter of two months ago, out in the desert, when Chosa Dei nearly ate me alive from the inside out."

"Yes," Del said.

"In both circumstances, it was far too dangerous for either of us. We're lucky we didn't die on Staal-Ysta—"

"Yes."

"—and lucky you weren't swallowed by Chosa Dei when he left my sword for yours—"

"Yes."

"—and each time the threat came to life *only* when we faced one another with blades."

"Yes," she said again.

I stared at her. "Well?"

Del smiled. "It means in each case that our skills have proved equal to luck."

"I would like to see it," Herakleio said seriously.

I rounded on him then, blistering him with every foul curse I could think of on the instant. I only stopped when I became aware of applause, and noticed both Del and Herakleio had turned away from me.

I shut up. There on the other side of the wall was the metri, being seated in a chair with Simonides' aid, and beside her two people: Prima Rhannet and her blue-headed first mate. The captain was applauding.

"*Foul* tongue," she said, grinning. "One might suggest it be cut out of your head."

"Care to try?" I asked sweetly.

"Oh, no," she returned, unperturbed. "I think not. But you *will* be tried, and by the woman Herakleio is so intent upon seeing dance against you. Which means he must believe she is better." Smiling, she gestured briefly at Nihko, who bent and lifted something from the ground at his feet.

Swords.

He set them lengthwise precisely atop the wall, then took a single step away as if to repudiate any link to them. The message was clear: these were the swords the metri had hired them to find, so Del and I could enter the circle to settle my term of employment.

I looked at the metri. There was little resemblance to the ill woman I had seen in bed. Her hair was pulled off her face and gathered into a variety of plaits and loops, secured with enamel-and-gold pins. She wore a tunic and heavy beaded necklace; also a loose robe that billowed in the breeze. She sat quietly in the chair, arms folded neatly across her lap, but her expression was severe.

"Now," the metri said, "let it be settled, this argument of service."

"Here and now," I said skeptically.

"Indeed."

I looked from her to her servant. "How is she?"

He seemed to understand I asked him because she would not give me the truth, even if she answered. "Well enough," he said.

"Much improved," the metri snapped, clearly annoyed. "Now, be about it. If you win, you may be excused from service beyond our original agreement. If she wins, you will stay on an additional length of time to be decided by me."

I shook my head.

The metri looked at Nihko. "Make him."

Nihko looked at me. "I can."

Del threw down her wooden blade. "I want no part of this. I agreed to dance with Tiger, but I will not do so if he is forced. It abrogates the honor codes and oaths."

"*What* 'honor codes and oaths'?" Prima asked scathingly. "He's his own kind of ikepra. He has no such thing."

"We make our own," Del declared, stung. "He and I, between us."

Herakleio hooked a foot beneath her wooden sword and scooped it into the air, where he caught it easily. "Then do so," he suggested. "The metri has hired you. You accepted. Is that not honor? And dishonor if you refuse?"

Prima's tone was sly. "You renounced your honor, Sandtiger; she has not. Do you expect her to break all of her oaths simply to be with you? Or has she none left *because* she is with you?"

The terrace was round, but we were cornered anyway. Del and I did not even bother to look at one another. They had found the holes in our individual defenses and exploited them perfectly.

I took up the blades from the wall and handed one to Del. Her eyes searched mine, asking the question.

In answer, I walked to the center point of the terrace. It wasn't a proper circle, but our minds would make it one. I leaned, set down the weapon with a faint metallic scrape, turned my back on it and paced to the wall farthest from the spectators. Torchlight filled my eyes; I half-lidded them against it.

Prima's tone was startled. "Don't you want to practice first? To test the blades?"

Del walked deliberately to the center, bent, set her sword alongside mine. Rising, she asked, "Why? If they are meant to break, they will. But I doubt that's what you want."

"Indeed not," the metri said testily. "This is to be an honorable engagement."

Herakleio grinned widely. "Then perhaps you would do better to excuse the Sandtiger. He has none."

"Enough," Del said sharply, taking position across from me.

I didn't look at Herakleio, but he knew whom I meant. "Say it."

But it wasn't Herakleio. Nihko said, "Dance."

Feet pounded, gripped, slid against tile; bodies bent; hands snatched, closed; blades came up from the ground. They met, rang, clashed, scraped apart, clashed again as we engaged. The blows were measured, but not so restrained that no damage would be done if one of us broke through. There is no sense in pulling back when one intends to win, or if one intends to learn. To do so alters the dance into travesty, with nothing learned and thus nothing gained even in victory.

We tested one another carefully. Last time we'd met it hadn't been sparring, hadn't been a contest to settle a complaint, but a dance against the magic that had infested my sword, that had wanted me as well. I had lost that dance, but in the losing I won. Del lured Chosa Dei out of my blade into hers, then purposefully broke her jivatma. We had not since then set foot in any kind of circle, being more concerned with surviving a journey by ship.

Now here we were, off that ship at last and on the soil of what I'd begun to believe actually was my homeland, dancing for real at the behest of a woman who had no idea what it meant to be what we were.

Or else she knew very well and used this dance to prove it.

The night was loud with sound, the clangor and screech of steel. As always, with Del and me, there was another element to the object, an aspect of the dance that elevated it above the common. We were that good together. In the circle. In bed.

—step—thrust—spin—

—catch blades—catch again—

—slide—step—thrust—

—parry—again—slash—

It was a long dance, one that leached from us all thoughts of the metri, her intentions, of Prima and her first mate, of Herakleio and his attitude. As always, everything else in the world became as water against oilcloth: shed off to pool elsewhere, while inside the circle, our dwelling, we stayed dry, and warm, and so focused as to be deaf and blind. But we were neither of us deaf *or* blind; we marked movement, responses, the slight flexing of muscle beneath taut flesh; heard the symphony of the steel, the rhythm of our breathing, the subtle sibilance of bare soles moving against stone.

—slash—catch—scrape—

—the shriek of steel on steel—

Walls of air, the metri had called it. My home was built of walls I fashioned in the circle, because only here could I define myself, could I find my worth in the world. *Only* here had I become a man. Not in the use of my genitals, a use once copious and indiscriminatory; nor in the language of my mouth, sometimes vulgar, always ready, but inside the heart, the soul. Inside the circle I was whatever I wished to be, and no one at all could alter that.

Except me.

And I had.

One day at Aladar's palace, when I had broken all the oaths.

"No—" Del said.

I grinned.

"Tiger—"

I laughed.

With an expression of determination, Del tried the move I'd chastised her for.

"Oh, Del—" Disgust. I couldn't help it. Because now I had no choice. I broke her guard, went in, tore the hilt from her hand.

"What did I *tell* you?" I roared. "Did you think I was joking? That kind of move could get you killed!"

Furious, she bent and retrieved the sword. "Again."

"Del—"

"*Again,* curse you!"

Again. As she insisted.

I stepped back, renewed the assault. Saw Del begin the maneuver again. I moved to block it, break it, destroy it—and this time something entirely different happened. This time it was *my* sword that went crashing to the tile. And I was left nursing a wrenched thumb.

"What in hoolies was that?" I asked.

"The reason I created that maneuver."

"But I defeated it the first time."

"Not the second."

"You'd have been *dead* the first time. There wouldn't have been a second."

"Maybe," Del said, "maybe not. Not everyone fights like you."

"No one fights like me," I corrected with laborious dignity, then shook out my thumb.

"Shall I kiss it?" The irony was heavy.

I bared my teeth at her. "Not in front of witnesses."

"Stop," the metri said.

I turned toward her, startled by the hostility in her tone.

"You must begin again," she declared.

"Why?" I asked.

"One of you must win. Decisively."

"I did win," I explained. "I disarmed her."

"Then she disarmed *you.*"

I shook my head. "That doesn't count."

"Why not?" Del asked.

I shot her a disbelieving glance. "Because I'd have killed you. I broke your pattern. You'd be dead."

"But I broke *your* pattern the second time."

"Finish it," the metri commanded. "One of you must win decisively."

I displayed my thumb. "I have a slight disadvantage."

"Poor baby," Prima cooed.

The metri was relentless. "Is it not true that such impasses are settled in the circle?"

"Yes, but—"

"Then settle it. Now."

I glanced at Nihko. "I suppose you'll *make me* if I don't agree." A thought. "Or will your little ring protect me from your power, and therefore this threat is nothing but a bluff?"

But Nihko made no response. He wasn't even looking at me. He looked beyond me, beyond the wall, beyond the torchlight that bathed the terrace in gilt flickering swaths of ocher and ivory and bronze. I saw the whites of his eyes, the pallor of his face; saw with disbelief as he began to tremble.

"*Sahdri,*" he whispered, as if the word took all his breath.

The metri stood up abruptly from her chair. "You are not to be here! You and your kind are not to be here!"

I spun then, even as Del did, and we saw beyond the torches, walking softly upon the wall, a barefoot man in night-black linen.

And then I realized his feet were not touching the stone.

Chapter 28

"You are not to be here!" the metri cried. "This ground is mine; you profane it! You soil it! You are not to be here!"

The man atop the wall—no, the man *floating above* the wall—paused, smiled, lifted a hand as if in benediction. Rings glinted on fingers, in brows, in ears, depended from his nostrils, pierced the flesh of his lower lip. In guttering torchlight, his shaven head writhed with blue tattoos.

Ah. One of *those*.

His tone was immensely conversational, lacking insult, offering no confrontation beyond the fact of his presence. "But I *am* here, because I choose to be here. And your tame ikepra can wield no power against me, even if I permitted." His dark eyes were rimmed in light borrowed from the flame. "Nihkolara Andros, you have been gone much too long. We have missed you. You must come back to us." For all the world like a doting relative.

A shudder wracked the first mate from head to toe. And then he dropped to his knees, bent at the waist, set his brow upon the ground. In clear tones, he said, "I cannot. I am ikepra."

The multitude of rings glinted in torchlight. "Forgiveness is possible."

Nihko shuddered again, hands digging into the soil. "I am ikepra."

"Forgiveness is possible," the man—Sahdri—repeated. His language was accented, but comprehensible. "You need only come with me now and begin the Rituals of Unsoiling."

"Come with you where?" I asked, since no one else seemed willing to.

The light-rimmed eyes turned their gaze on me. I wasn't sure if the illumination came from the torches, or from the eyes themselves. "IoSkandi," he answered. "Where people such as the great and gracious metrioi of the gods-descended Eleven send us all to die."

I glanced at Prima Rhannet. I expected her to speak, but she offered nothing. She stood there, locked in silence, staring at the priest-mage as her first mate knelt to him in abject obeisance.

"Well," I said finally, "it doesn't look like *you* died."

"That hour will arrive. Just as it shall arrive for Nihkolara Andros." He inclined his head toward the kneeling man. "He has returned, you see, and now is ours again. Or shall be, when he understands what lies before him, and what he is to do."

The metri too was trembling, but not from fear. "Go," she said thickly. "This man has guest-right."

The irony in his tone was delicate. "*This* man? Here?"

"This is business of the Stessoi," she said with a curt-ness I had never heard in her. "You are not of this family, nor do I grant you guest-right. Unless you and the others have forsworn all rites of courtesy in the Stone Forest, you know what you must do."

"Depart," he said with evident regret. "I had hoped for a cup of fine Stessa wine."

If possible, she stood a little straighter. "Save you steal grapes from the vines themselves, no wine of my vineyards shall pass your lips."

"I am desolate." But his gaze had shifted again to Nihko, who still knelt in the dirt. "You have a fine ship, Nihkolara," he said gently. "Surely you can find your way home again."

At last, Prima's voice. It scraped out of her constricted throat. "He *is* home."

Rings glinted as he lifted an illustrative finger. "His home is ioSkandi. It has been so since the day he understood what he was; was *made* to understand by such as the metrioi and the Eleven, who will not tolerate such as he, such as me. He has no place here. He came willingly to ioSkandi and embraced the service of the gods."

"He left," she said. "He *left* you."

"And so became ikepra, and abomination." His tone was matter of fact. "He was tolerated when he lived on your ship upon the seas, but he spends more time now on the earth. And so, according to the laws of the Eleven, he must be sent to live with us." He spread his hands gently. "Is this not so?"

"He has guest-right," the metri repeated tightly.

"For how long?" the priest-mage countered. "Shall you have him live among you as a Stessa? But no. Shall he go to the Palomedi metri, whom he insulted by bedding her daughter while he also bedded her? But no. Shall he go to his own folk, the Androsoi?"

From his position in the dirt, Nihko cried, "No!"

"There." The man nodded. "He knows his place."

"He's mine," Prima declared hoarsely.

Sahdri looked at her and smiled. "But he was mine first."

"Look," I said, "I'm not exactly sure what's going on here, but the metri has asked you to leave. Just when do you plan to do it?"

And he was *there*, before me, his breath warm against my face. I hadn't seen him move from the wall to the terrace. Hadn't seen any indication he would.

"Who are you?" the priest-mage asked.

I opened my mouth, shut it. This was magic, living, breathing magic in the body of a man, encompassed by no more than fragile flesh. He *stank* of power. By rights I should be spewing my dinner across the terrace, but Nihko's brow ring, still attached to my necklet, was doing its task.

Sahdri saw it. Saw me. Smiled. "Are you vermin, that I should squash you?"

The metri's voice rang out. "He is my grandson."

Every head, including mine, whipped about. I heard Herakleio's inarticulate cry of outrage, Prima Rhannet's hissing indrawn breath; saw the smoothing of Simonides' face as he donned his servant's mask.

And for some strange reason, the metri's announcement frightened me.

Nihko still knelt against the ground. Not even for such an un-expected declaration would he raise his head in Sahdri's company.

The priest-mage himself bowed in my direction. *"Kallha nahkte,"* he murmured, and the torches blew out.

I blinked into the sudden darkness, aware of the man's absence. "What did he say? What was that spell he spoke?"

Darkness was replaced with the pale, soft luminance of moon and stars, a glow from lamps inside the household. Nihko lifted his dust-powdered face from the dirt. "He said 'good night.'"

Only Del was detached enough from the emotions of the moment to find that amusing. I heard the expulsion of breath in brief, smothered laughter, glanced at her; saw how she immediately set her face into bland innocence. She met my scowl with a guileless smile.

I shook my head, drew in a deep breath, looked at the metri. "Nice timing," I said. "Do you think it worked?"

Her face wore its customary mask. "The truth often is of great effect."

Herakleio, who had been gripping the two wooden practice blades, hurled them down. They clattered against the tile. Even in muted illumination I could see how high the color stood in his face. "Truth," he snarled. "Truth, is it? *Why?*"

The metri answered steadily, "Truth is truth."

His cry was anguished. "You would put him in my place?"

She was unmoved. "No more than I would put you in his. The place is the place. The proper man shall be put in it when I am certain of his worth."

Oh, she *was* the stone, as she had told me less than a month before. Hard, sharp, brilliant, and scintillatingly shrewd.

"Let's start over," I suggested. "I take it our unexpected visitor is someone with connections to our friendly first mate?"

Nihko had risen. Having recovered much of his equanimity now that the priest-mage had departed, he glared at me. "One holds one's tongue when in ignorance, lest one lose it."

I saluted him with the sword, letting moonlight like liquid run down the blade. "Any time you like."

"Stop," the metri said. "We are done with this tonight."

"Done?" Herakleio's chopped-off bark of laughter contained no humor. "I should say we have *begun* this tonight!"

Prima Rhannet seemed to have no interest in Herakleio's concerns. Her attention was fixed on Nihko. "What can Sahdri do? Take you? Against your will?"

Grimly he said, "IoSkandics have no will. IoSkandics set no foot upon the soil of this island once one *is* of ioSkandi. We live in the Stone Forest."

"But you did set foot," she said. "This time. You've always stayed aboard ship before. But you never said *why*—"

He cut her off. "It does not matter."

"But it does, Nihko—"

"No. A brief amount of time is tolerated. More is—not." He looked at his hostess, lowered his eyes, inclined his head. "Metri, I thank you for the guest-right."

"We have unfinished business," she stated crisply. "Until it is finished, the guest-right shall apply. And then you will remove yourself from my home and my land *immediately*."

The flinch was minute, but present. Nihko kept his head bowed and murmured an answer in Skandic that apparently suited the metri, for she simply turned away with a gesture at Simonides for his aid.

"Wait," I said, and she paused. "What happens now?"

Her mask was in place. "I have now claimed you my grandson in front of witnesses as well as a priest. He may be ioSkandic, not of the proper Order, but he serves the same gods. It has been said, and so it is."

"And—?"

Her brow creased slightly. "And you will continue to do what I have bidden you do. Teach Herakleio to be a man."

That worthy's breath hissed between clenched teeth. *"Metri—"*

She looked at him. "And you will do whatever I say you shall, without question, without hesitation, no matter what it may be. That is the term of *your* service."

All the tendons stood up beneath his flesh as he fought not to shout denials and curses at her. When he spoke, each word was squeezed out with such immense precision that I expected his head to explode. "If it is to be sword-work, then I will have the woman train me." His gaze shifted to me. "Because she is better."

Prima gulped a laugh. Nihko arched an eyebrow. I merely blinked.

It was Del who answered the intended insult. "Sometimes," she said. "Some days, some moments, some particular movements. Other times, not."

I nodded consideringly. "That about sums it up."

So, we had robbed him of that small revenge. Stiffly, Herakleio bowed to the metri, then took himself off.

"Well," Prima said when his shape was swallowed by darkness, "I would not wish to share *his* winehouse tonight."

I smiled across at her. "Or his bed?"

The captain met the gambit. "Oh, it might be worth it. Herakleio in a temper . . . indeed, it might be worth it." She fixed me with a bright, challenging eye. "*You* might even enjoy it."

"Go to bed," the metri commanded; and then, surprising us all, added: "Anyone's bed," and gestured for Simonides to escort her into the house.

"Well," I said after a moment of startlement shared equally by the others, "at least my grandmother isn't a prude."

Prima smiled sweetly. "That must mean the blood runs true."

I scoffed. "Blood? I think not. She used the tool she had at hand: information designed to throw off that other blue-headed priestling for the moment." I looked hard at her first mate. "Who in hoolies *is* he? And what's he to you?"

Without a hint of irony Nihko said, "Secret."

I clamped my jaws tightly even as Del asked, "Need we be concerned?"

Prima shrugged. "Why should you?"

"Because we are here," Del answered steadily. "Because priests and mages often take an interest in people and topics seemingly unrelated, with dramatic effect. Because he looked at the brow ring hooked onto Tiger's necklet, and recognized it. It was then and only then that he offered a threat to Tiger. Therefore I ask, need we be concerned?"

"No," Nihko said coldly, even as his captain's expression stilled to a feral blankness for a brief, stark moment before settling once again into its normal expressive mobility. "All that concerns you now is how soon the metri will announce her heir before the priests—the *proper* priests"—he made it a derisive label—"and the assembled metrioi."

"Yes?" I invited.

"If it's you," Prima drawled, "you will inherit all the wealth and power of the Stessoi. Centuries of wealth and power." Her smile was arch. "And all the dreams you ever dreamed will come true."

"And what about *your* dream?" I countered. "Aren't you done here yet?"

"We have guest-right," Nihko snapped.

"And just what does that entail?"

Prima's smile shifted into unadulterated triumph. "It means every metri in the city must pay me respect *to my face*. It means I will gain a reputation that surpasses my father's."

"I thought you'd already accomplished that part," I retorted. "You steal men, their coin, their ships; he sells them."

Her smile vanished. But before she could answer, Del cut her off. "We're not on board your ship anymore. You can't tell us to leave the household of the woman who has now announced before witnesses she is his grandmother."

"That's right," I said brightly. "I guess I'm the one who can tell *you* to leave."

"It is not your household yet," Prima shot back.

Nihko's voice was cool. "And who says you will survive to inherit?"

With one deft move, Del tossed her sword to the first mate. Steel flashed, arced; he caught it without thought, hissed startlement, then stared at her. "Settle it," she suggested. "Man to man, here and now. In this circle."

Oh, thanks is what I wanted to say; my wrenched thumb ached dully. But I knew better. I just waited for Nihko's answer.

"I will not dishonor the metri," he said. "But, of course, I merely referred to the illness of her heart. Who is to say her grandson has not inherited its weakness?"

Double-edged blade, that. And we all of us knew it.

Prima took the sword from him, shoved its hilt toward Del. "The metri bought it for you. I suggest none of us dishonor her."

"Ah," I said sagely, "there must be some form of terrible punishment if you kill the heir of a metri."

"Sometimes," Nihko said gently, "one need not be killed to suffer the worst punishment."

Ikepra. Borjuni. We both knew the truth in his statement.

For the second time in the space of one evening, I saluted him with my sword.

Prima made a sound of disgust. "Men," she said, her sidelong glance aimed at Del. "Why is it they can fight, and then immediately be friends again? They waste a perfectly good grudge that way."

Del's eyes glinted even as her mouth twitched, and I knew none of us was going to kill one another.

Tonight.

Chapter 29

rom beside me in bed, Del spoke quietly into the darkness.
"You're awake."

"So are you."

"But I *was* asleep. I don't think you've slept since we came to bed."

"Long night."

"Full night," she emphasized dryly. Then, "*Is* this what you dreamed of?"

From my back, I stared hard at the ceiling I could not see. "I dreamed of no such thing in the hyorts, or even when I slept beneath the stars after a beating."

"A sandtiger," she said softly. "And freedom."

"Never beyond that. Never beyond the moment *of* freedom, when I could walk away and know myself able to make my own choices about my life."

"And now?"

"Now I'm no more free . . . no, it's not the same and I don't mean it to be, but she said something, something about responsibility, and the acceptance of it marking adulthood."

For a moment Del was silent. Then, softly, "The metri is a strong woman."

"But is she right?"

"About responsibility and adulthood?" Del sighed, shifted onto her back so that we lay side by side and flat, shoulders touching. "Taken of itself, I believe she is. Children live for their freedom, for the moment their tasks are done—if they have any—so that they may make choices about their lives. Of course, those 'lives' comprise the next-few moments, little more . . . but the impulse is the same. *To* be finished, so they may be free."

When she fell silent, I prompted her. "And?"

"Adults understand that freedom must be earned, not given by someone else."

"No?"

"No. We set ourselves the tasks, we execute them, and we are free then to accept other tasks."

"What has this to do with the metri?"

"The metri decides *for others* what she believes are the tasks that must be completed. For the benefit of her house."

"In other words, she doesn't permit anyone of her household— or in her family—to seek out their own tasks. And thus no one of the—Stessoi?—is truly free."

Del tilted her head toward me. "I think the metri believes no one is strong enough to hold her place unless he be as she is."

"Ruthless. Cold. Hard."

"Is she?"

"Ruthless? Yes. Hard? Absolutely. Cold?" I fell silent. Then, "I can't say so. Because passion drives her. Her ruthlessness and hardness is framed on a passion for her household and the future of the Stessoi."

"Does Herakleio have it?"

"From the sound of it, Herakleio has enough to illuminate the island!"

"That's lust," Del countered. "Youthful passions, yes; he has never been permitted to grow beyond them. But the passion requiring coldness and ruthlessness?"

"Not yet," I answered slowly.

"You?"

We both knew the answer to that. "You're saying if I employed it now, she would hand me the household and the future of the Stessoi."

"She would expect you to *take* them."

"And Herakleio?"

Del lay very still beside me. "The first ten times you and he spar with live steel, be very careful."

"And the eleventh?"

"By the eleventh, either he will have acknowledged that you will always defeat him . . ."

"Or?"

"Or you will be dead."

In a matter of ten days, Herakleio had learned he had the body, the reflexes, the power, to be what I was. In a matter of moments, in the face of the metri's announcement that I was her grandson, he had learned he needed the mind and determination as well as the body. Because he believed now the metri favored me, and the only way he might regain that favor was not to replace me, but to *become* me.

The implications of this conviction astonished me. Not the motivation—the metri played us all like counters on a board; not the impetus—she had moved him to precisely this position on that board. But that he understood and acknowledged what it was she wanted *of* the game, and that she justified her approach because she believed it required.

And it astonished me also that he accepted it instead of railing against it as a spoiled godling might.

Herakleio may not have believed in her certainty for himself. But clearly he had done more than merely exist in the metri's household; he had learned her mind. Until now, apparently, he had never attempted to invoke and employ that knowledge. Until now, apparently, he had never felt the need.

Beyond the mechanics of technique, a sword-dancer is not required to know why an opponent moves the way he moves. Only *that he does* move, only *when he will* move, so he may anticipate and counter that move, or remove the potential for it before the idea of the move exists within the opponent's mind.

Herakleio asked for Del. He did it with premeditation, and with a deliberate shrewdness I hadn't anticipated. My opponent had won the initial pass; my first move was countered before it occurred to me I might need to make it.

He asked for Del not because he believed it would hurt me if he believed she was better—he was, surprisingly, less petty than he was clever—but because Del of anyone in the world knew best how to fight me. Knew best how to defeat me.

This move made him better than clever, and therefore dangerous.

I'd made the mistake of not judging Herakleio shrewd enough to see the option. I did not make the mistake of assuming he'd offer no contest if it came to a dance with the Stessa legacy on the line, nor did I make the assumption he could not win. Because on any day, in any circle, any man might win.

Or woman.

Abbu Bensir, on our first day in the training circle beneath the implacable eye of the shodo of Alimat, had made such assumptions about a boy with fewer than twenty years to his twenty-five; with weeks at Alimat when Abbu boasted years; with a wooden blade in a hand that had not yet wielded steel.

Abbu Bensir had lost that dance and nearly his life.

While I, in disbelief as the man lay choking from a partially crushed throat, asked what manner of magic had stood in my place, because surely there was no other way I might have defeated Abbu.

The shodo, an immensely patient and practical man, had upon the instant lost all patience and told me in no uncertain terms the only magic any man needed was that of his mind and heart; that no other existed, lest he weaken that mind and heart by setting crutches beneath them.

From that day forward the only magic in my life had been pure skill, determination, and the technique to employ both using the context I understood: I was born to and of the sword, and no other power would ever control me beyond my ability to *use* the sword.

I didn't believe Herakleio could defeat me. But neither had Abbu believed I could defeat him.

And so I won the second pass, because I accepted as truth what another might, in disbelief, name falsehood. I would not be defeated by an accident of misassumption, but by carefully constructed design, correct execution—and luck.

Technique, timing, talent. Two could be taught, refined. One could only be born. But talent without focus, without determination, without obsessive need, is wild, unchanneled, and therefore diluted. Easier to be defeated. Easier to succumb to the ravages of emotion, of excess passion, instead of controlling and using the power that could fuel technique and timing.

Del, who had more insight about people than anyone I knew, was training Herakleio. Del, who had an even greater insight into the workings of my technique, timing, and talent, was teaching Herakleio how to comprehend and counter all three.

And unlike anyone else, he had the physical tools to do it.

Unlike anyone else save Del. Who *had* done it once in a circle on Staal-Ysta, even as I had done it to her in the self-same circle.

We were a long time removed from that circle and the circumstances that put us into it. But the bones remembered. The flesh recalled. The mind retreated from the brutal honesty of that dance, because in its unyielding purity it had nearly killed us both.

And each day, as Herakleio learned from Del, he also learned from me. It was a task set before me by the woman who was, she said, my grandmother; who wanted to put into her place the man best suited to it; who believed the acceptance and execution of the task marked a boy's passage into manhood. Herakleio and I, nearly two decades apart in age, were nonetheless children in the eyes of the woman who was agelessness incarnate. And in the completion of the task, we each of us would have embraced her convictions if for differing reasons: Herakleio to prove he was worthy of her place; and *me* to prove he was worthy of her place.

It wasn't me she wanted. It wasn't me she needed. Herakleio was and always would be both. And therefore Del taught him, and therefore I taught him, so that on the day we met in the circle it would be a proper dance according to the honor codes that lived in our own souls.

I knew of men who would swear I was mad to teach my opponent. But if I didn't, if I merely watched him learn, I learned *his* abilities without offering him the same opportunity in return. That was dishonest. If I taught him with intent to sabotage his efforts, that was dishonest. Because I was already better. And the shodo had taught me to be honest in all things to do with the dance.

I knew of men who would blister Del with oaths and suggest she depart at once. But I didn't do either, because that, too, was dishonest. Del made her own decisions. Her honor was unassailable; it was one of the things I most admired and respected about her. And my honor—as *elaii-ali-ma*, as borjuni, as a Southron ikepra—was nonexistent.

In the circle, the sword-dancer with the mind that sees and creates potentials, that manufactures opportunity, is the one who wins. Anyone may kill another by stealth, by deception. But only one who invokes the honesty of the circle may call himself a sword-dancer. Because it was the circle and its inherent codes that bound our souls. No one who stepped inside could deny that, because the circle was the arbiter of our survival.

The dance Herakleio and I undertook would be honest in the extreme, because though I had the advantage of years of training and experience, he had the advantage of a peculiarly dangerous truth.

If Herakleio won, he won. If Herakleio lost, he won.

If I lost, I died.

Because I wouldn't kill Herakleio, but I believed he would kill me. And so my next move was obvious.

I stood up from the terrace wall and asked Del to halt their current exercise. It was afternoon, we were slick with sweat. Del had bound her hair back into its habitual braid, and Herakleio had tied a length of leather around his brow so wind-blown locks would not obscure his vision.

I nodded at Del, smiling, and offered a blade to Herakleio. A *steel* blade.

Once he'd have shut his hand on the hilt immediately. Now he waited. "Why?" he asked warily.

I hitched a shoulder lazily. "Only so much you can learn with wood. After a while you get complacent. Bruises sting, but they don't kill."

He nodded his head at Del. "Then *she* will show me."

I shoved the pommel of the sword into his flat belly. "Take it, boy."

It stung, as I meant it to. Color stained his face. Anger brightened his eyes as he took it as I intended: with simmering contempt. "So, you will skulk around for table scraps and wait for the metri to die no matter how long it takes."

I shrugged again. "Not like I'm a total stranger. I *am* her grandson."

"Herakleio," Del said sharply. "Be aware of what he's doing."

I shot her a glance that told her to back off. Del scowled back, telling me she refused. Herakleio, for his part, stared at me angrily, then shut his hand around the hilt. He settled the matter for us by turning to set the blade onto the tile in the center of the terrace.

"Stop it," Del hissed at me. "This is too soon."

"*He* can stop it if he wants."

"You're making it impossible!"

"All it requires is a little self-control." I saluted her with my blade. "Care to step out of the way?"

"Tiger—"

"Go," Herakleio told her. Then, belatedly, "Please?"

It was the first polite word I'd heard out of the boy. Del was no more happy for his request than she was with my suggestion, but she got out of the way.

Herakleio stood a pace from the sword he'd set upon the tile. "Well?"

I stepped to his blade, then on it. And set the tip of mine against his throat. "First mistake," I said. "You assumed this was a dance."

He lifted his chin, stretching flesh away from the steel. I let the tip drift idly up to follow. "This is how it begins," he declared. "I watched you and the woman!"

"That was a dance," I told him. "This is not. This is a lesson."

"*Lesson*—" he began furiously.

I hooked a foot beneath his sword, scooped it upward, caught and deflected it directly at Herakleio. He was quick enough to catch it, but in the doing of it he incurred a scratched throat from my blade. Blood trickled in a thin ribbon of crimson.

I smiled, stepped away a single pace. "Now," I said gently, and set to with my sword.

It took very little time. Very little effort. He had a firm enough grasp not to lose the sword at once, but there was no grace in his movements, no technique in answer to mine, merely desperate self-preservation. I chased him across the terrace, against the wall, *over* the wall and a good ten paces beyond before I finally took pity on him and ended it with a trap that broke his guard, caught the sword, snatched it out of his hands. I stood there before the panting young man with a hilt in each of my hands, both tips coyly resting on his shoulders. On either side of his neck.

"Lesson," I said. "Two swords are better than one. And if you can't keep yours, be certain the other man will take it."

Without waiting for his response I lifted the blades from his shoulders and turned to go; stopped briefly as I saw the woman on the terrace but a pace or two away. I heard Herakleio's hiss of humiliation; he knew she had seen the ease of his defeat.

I met the woman's eyes steadily. "Your move, metri."

She understood. She knew now that *I* knew. And it altered the strategy.

"Go," she bade me. "Herakleio and I have something to discuss."

I'll just bet they did. I raised eyebrows at Del, who turned and preceded me into the house as the metri and her kinsman discussed the repercussions of abject defeat.

Chapter 30

el had the grace to wait until we were on the threshold of our room. "He is good, isn't he?"

"*Oh*, yes." I smeared a forearm against my forehead beneath a shock of too-long hair. "And getting better in a hurry. Why else do you think I did it?"

She nodded. "Scare tactics."

"A little intimidation is good for the soul. It makes you cautious before complacency can set in." I set the swords atop the linens chest, then took up the waterjar set on a small tiled table and unstoppered it.

Del waited until I was halfway through a swallow. "And sets back his training so you have more time to hone your edge."

I choked, turned away lest I lose control of the spray and soak her with it. Once I'd completed the swallow, I managed, "That obvious, am I?"

"Not to him; he doesn't know you well enough." She shook her head. "I didn't expect this of him, this attention to detail. Not yet." She paused. "If ever."

I handed her the jar. "And here we are so nicely helping him along."

She drank, handed it back. Her eyes were guileless. "You are not Abbu, Tiger, so full of complacency you forget to be cautious. And Herakleio is not you. He won't take you by surprise."

"You just never know what anyone . . ." But I let it go as the echoing sound of voices intruded. Vigorous, unhappy voices just this side of anger and full of throttled consonants and hissing sibilants, trying not to shout.

"Prima Rhannet," Del said.

"And Nihko Blue-head." I turned toward the open door to listen more closely; not that it mattered, since I couldn't understand them anyway. The voices grew louder briefly, then fell away as if the captain and her first mate had moved from the hallway to another room.

"Discord," Del said, "And unsubtle."

"Subtle enough even if audible," I retorted. "Neither of us speaks Skandic."

"Others here do."

I shrugged. "Then I guess everyone but you and I knows what the quarrel is all about."

Del sat down on the edge of the bed. "But there was one word I did understand. A name."

"Sahdri." I nodded. "Wouldn't you like to be a mouse in the floorboards?"

Del said dryly, "Only if I was a mouse who spoke Skandic."

I smiled. "I know a mouse who speaks Skandic. A mouse who also speaks a language I can understand. I think maybe it's time I paid a visit to the person who is truly in charge of the household."

Del frowned. "You think the metri will tell you?"

I paused on the threshold. "Not the metri. She only gives the orders. Someone else entirely makes things *work*."

I tracked down Simonides in a tiny suite of rooms, numbering two. A petite sitting room, a room beyond holding a bed. It was a spare, unadorned chamber of little exuberance but much meticulous tidiness, like the man himself.

If he was startled to find me on his doorstep, he made no indication. But a family servant knows how to express no emotions at all unless he is bidden to do so, and I was not the metri to bid him to do anything.

I had come full of questions, full of demands for explanations.

But now that I was here, I hesitated. Even as Simonides gestured invitation and stepped aside to allow me entry, I could not cross the threshhold.

A slave's privacy is hard-won. I had claimed none of my own among the Salset, except for inside my head. This man had a place within the household, and rooms within the rooms. I robbed him of that privacy with my presence.

He read my face, as a good slave will do. One learns to survive by recognizing what even a blink portends, the slight tilting of the head or the tension in the mouth. He knew what I was thinking. And for that reason, his second welcome was warm.

This time I stepped across. This time I was more than a guest in the house, or even the metri's heir.

He set out a bowl of fruit, a small jar of wine, two shallow dishes. Poured them full, then motioned me to drink. I raised my dish in tribute to his courtesy, then sipped the vintage grown on the metri's lands. It was very good wine.

I told him then what I had come for, what had provoked my curiosity. He listened in silence, making no attempt to answer before he understood precisely what I wished to know, and why. And when I was done giving him all my reasons, he told me what he could.

It wasn't enough. But it was a beginning.

It took a while to hunt her up, but eventually I found Del in the bathing pool. I couldn't remember a time when either of us had spent so many consecutive days in the water—especially considering I couldn't swim!—but I'd discovered it was a pleasant way to pass the time. Being clean was nothing to scoff at, but hanging about in warm water was far more relaxing than I'd ever contemplated.

Too bad the South didn't have enough water to build bathing pools like this.

Then again, wasn't my idea for channeling water from places it was to places it wasn't the means to afford us such luxury?

Hmm. Worth considering, that.

I added my clothing to Del's heap of same and slipped over the edge, trying not to splash too much. My skin contracted at the first touch of warm water, then relaxed. It felt good.

It felt *wonderful*.

Maybe I needed to learn how to swim.

Del, who had elbows hooked over the side and her chin resting atop flattened palms, turned her head to speak over her shoulder. "Well?"

I leaned back in the water, wishing I could float the way she could. But that required the ability to lift one's foot off the bottom without immediately sinking. "IoSkandi is an island a half-day's sail from here. The only people who live there are the priest-mages, like Sahdri."

"And Nihko."

"The 'Stone Forest' is what people call Meteiera, a place on the island full of great stone spires. The priest-mages live in and on the spires, in caves and nooks and crannies, or in dwellings built on top."

"On top?"

"On top."

"How do they get up there?"

"I don't know."

"What do they do there?"

"That I know: worship and serve the gods," I answered, "and grow crops and raise livestock, and—"

"On top of the spires?"

"The worship-and-serve part takes place on top of the spires. The growing-crops and raising-livestock part takes place down below, in the valley."

She shrugged. "Sounds peaceful enough."

I went on with my unfinished line of discussion. "—and otherwise examine, learn, refine, and implement the magic that makes them mad."

"Oh," Del said.

"It kills them eventually, according to Simonides. The madness—and magic—manifests at a particular age, and while they *can* learn to control both, it's only for a while. Maybe ten years. Eventually the madness wins, and they die."

"Just—die?" Del was intrigued. "How?"

"They hurl themselves off the top of the spires."

Intrigue was replaced by shocked horror. *"Why?"*

"To merge with the sky."

"What for?"

"That's where the gods live. The best way to truly join the gods is to give oneself to them. Literally."

"But . . ." Her expression was perplexed.

"But," I agreed. "No surprise, is it, that everyone thinks they're mad."

"How do they explain the bodies smashed to pulp all over the ground?"

"Don't know that they bother."

"But if the bodies are smashed, they haven't merged with the gods."

I grinned. "I think it's considered merging in the strictly spiritual sense."

"Ah."

"Ah." I sank down so the water lapped at my chin. "No one really knows all the details of what goes on in Meteiera," I explained. "Simonides says it's a combination of rumor, speculation, and winehouse tales. The metrioi—I found out the 'oi' is the plural, by the way—don't talk about it at all because it's considered terribly dishonorable if anyone in the Eleven Families manifests this magic."

"But if they are gods-descended themselves, doesn't this mean a few of them might be considered more so?"

"That's one interpretation," I agreed. "Except the metrioi don't much like it. They consider madness a flaw of a rather extreme sort."

"So they send away to ioSkandi anyone who manifests this magic."

"And promptly delete from the family histories—and the histories of Skandi—any mention of these people."

"Unfair."

"Being utterly removed from existence and any memory thereof? I would say so."

"But what has any of this to do with Nihko setting foot on the earth?" She paused. "I think that's what the priest-mage said."

"It is. Simonides tells me that because the ioSkandics are themselves cast out of 'polite society,' if you will, they compensate by making up even *stronger* rules governing the behavior of anyone living in the Stone Forest."

Del nodded. "When excluded, become even more exclusive."

"Exactly. So if a man who has already been deleted from his family then leaves ioSkandi, he is considered abomination—ikepra—for turning his back on his fellow priest-mages and the gods."

"In other words, live with us and die in a few years, or leave us and die *now.*"

"More or less."

"So Nihko left ioSkandi and became ikepra, but so long as he didn't set foot on the earth of Skandi itself, the ioSkandic priests didn't care."

"They cared. There just wasn't anything they could do about it."

"But there *is* something they can do about one of their own coming back here to Skandi?"

"The people of Skandi don't want to have anything to do with their mad relatives. But they won't kill them; they consider themselves a civilized society." I grinned derisively. "They have no problem with priest-mages coming back to the island briefly, so long as it's only to gather up the occasional lost chick now and again."

"So they can take that chick back to the henhouse of other mad chicks."

"And feed it to the fox."

"Dead is dead," Del said.

"Exactly. As long as the mad little chicks are *gone*, the civilized Skandics don't care what becomes of them, whether they die voluntarily merging with the gods, or are hurled off the spires after the Ritual of Unsoiling. Which of course means that even if the chicks don't want to merge with the gods quite yet, they can forcibly *be* merged. After the proper ceremonies."

"The choice therefore lies not in deciding to die, but in deciding the time and manner."

"Hurl yourself, or be hurled," I agreed. "Of course, it's not 'dying,' bascha. It's 'merging.' "

"Semantics," she said disparagingly. "Tiger—this is barbaric. It makes no sense. There is no logic in it."

"Only if you're mad."

"So this Sahdri has come here to gather up Nihko."

"And take him back to ioSkandi so they can clean him up and dump him off one of the spires."

"No wonder he doesn't want to go."

"No wonder he lives on board a ship." I blew a ripple into the surface of water. "If you don't set foot on Skandi, you're safe from Skandic repercussions and *io*Skandic retribution."

Del contemplated this. Eventually she said, "Not a comfortable way to live."

"And a less comfortable way to die."

"But so long as Nihko has guest-right, Sahdri can't take him."

"You'll recall Prima asked that very thing: could Sahdri *take* Nihko."

"Who dismissed the possibility."

I shrugged. "Nihko seems not to want to talk about any of this."

"Well," Del said, "he's been tossed out of his family, and then tossed *himself* out of this fellowship of men who think they can toss him into the sky. I don't know that I'd want to talk about it either."

"And the metri has made it clear as soon as her business with him is finished, the guest-right is revoked."

"What *is* her business with him?"

"I'm assuming it's connected to this whole discovery-and-recovery-of-the-missing-heir issue," I said. "We don't know what kind of bargain Nihko drove on his captain's behalf before presenting me as the long-lost grandson."

"Which you are."

"Which I *maybe* am—but am as likely not."

"Maybe."

"Maybe." I tilted my head back, let the surface of the water creep up to surround the edges of my face. "I don't think it really matters."

"You can't be certain of that, Tiger."

I sighed. "No. I can't read the woman."

"So she may well *mean* you to inherit."

"Maybe."

"Maybe."

"And then there's Herakleio," I said, "who stands to lose more than any of us."

"Who's 'us'?"

"You, because of me. Me because of me. Prima Rhannet. Nihkolara."

"Why do you include them?"

"Because the connection is there. It's like a wheel, bascha—the metri is the hub, and everyone else is a spoke. But the spokes fall apart if there is no hub, and then the wheel isn't a wheel anymore. Just a pile of useless wood."

"So you believe there is more to it than a simple reward for finding the long-lost heir."

"I have a theory." I smiled, staring at the arch of the dome high overhead. "And I don't believe 'simple' is a word the metri knows."

"What is your *complicated* theory?"

I had sorted the pieces out some while back. Now I presented them to Del. "That I am a threat to all of them for very different reasons."

Del, understanding, began naming them off. "The metri."

"Either I am or am not her grandson; either way, it doesn't matter. It's Herakleio she wants. If I remain, I'm a threat to him."

"Herakleio."

"Obvious. I repeat: if I remain, I'm a threat to him."

"Prima Rhannet."

"If I'm *not* the metri's long-lost heir, Prima loses out on whatever reward it is she demanded."

"And Nihkolara?"

"The same applies to him as to his captain, but there's more . . ."

She waited, then prompted me. "Well?"

"I just don't know what it is."

"If his captain lost the reward, he'd lose his share."

"That's the most obvious factor, yes. But I think there's more." I shrugged. "Like I said, I just don't know what it is."

"Maybe," Del said dryly, "it has to do with his chances of being flung off the spire. So long as you're accepted as the metri's grandson, he's got guest-right. He's safe from Sahdri and his fellow priest-mages who'd like to forcibly merge him."

"Maybe that's it," I agreed. "But I still believe there's a piece missing."

"And once it's found and all the pieces are put together?"

I stood up in the water, let it sheet off my shoulders. The name for the unflagging unease was obvious now.

Expendability.

"Once it's found, they'll kill me."

Chapter 31

Though clad again in the leather tunic, Del dripped all the way to the room we shared. She hadn't done much in the way of drying off, and her hair was sopping. "We *will discuss* this," she declared, following. "You can't announce they'll kill you, then let the subject drop."

I was considerably dryer than Del and less inclined to drip, which I had no doubt Simonides and the household staff would appreciate. "I'm not expendable *yet*," I told her, striding along through room after room and doorway after doorway. "At least, I don't think so. But I'm just not sure there is more to say right now."

"Tiger, *stop*."

I recognized that voice. Accordingly I stopped just across the threshold of our room, turned to her, and waited.

Rivulets of hair dribbled water down the leather. Her eyes were fierce as she came into the room behind me. "We have to come up with a plan."

"I'm listening."

She gestured. "Leave?"

"We discussed that before. No one will hire on to sail us off the island, even if we had the coin *to* hire them."

"Give up your claim?"

"I never made a claim. The metri made it for me; everyone else just *assumed* I wanted to be heir."

"Give it up anyway," she said urgently. "Reject the metri outright. Say you aren't her grandson and you want to leave."

"Yes, well, there's a little matter of this 'term of service,' remember? The metri is likely our only way off the island, and she's not about to arrange it for us until she's accomplished whatever it is she wishes to accomplish, or I've accomplished for her whatever it is she wants me to accomplish for her."

"Herakleio?" she suggested. "Wouldn't he help? If you said you'd voluntarily give up any claim on the metri, would he help us get a ship?"

"Can he?" I shrugged. "He has no coin of his own, remember."

Del answered promptly. "He can borrow against his inheritance."

"But could he do that, and would the metri allow him to inherit if he did?"

She glared at me. "Do *you* have any ideas?"

"Play the game out."

Del was annoyed. "What game?"

"The metri's game. Give her what she wants until I see an opening."

A movement in the hallway. Del and I turned to see Prima Rhannet coming to a halt at the threshold. "I am your opening," she announced.

I looked her up and down, purposefully assessing her. "And just how is that?"

There was neither amusement nor irony in her expression. Only determination. "I need your help."

"How precisely is that *our* opening?" Del asked icily.

Prima shot her an angry, impatient glance, then looked back at me. Her expression was, oddly, guilty. "I have drugged Nihko."

That was pretty much the last thing I'd ever thought to hear exit her mouth. "You've drugged your first mate?"

She glanced over her shoulder furtively, then stepped into the room and shut the door with a decisive thud. Ruddy hair spilled like blood over her shoulders. No doubt about it; she *was* feeling guilty. Through taut lips, she said, "I gave it to him in his wine at dinner, while you took your ease in the bathing pool."

The imagery was amusing. "And is he therefore unconscious with his face in the plate?"

Prima, who was not amused, set her teeth so hard jaw muscles flexed. "He is unconscious in bed in our room," she said with precise enunciation, then let it spill out of her mouth in a jumble of words as if to say it fast diluted some of the guilt. "I want to get him back aboard ship as soon as possible, and I need your help for that."

"Why can't he just *walk* aboard ship?—that is, if you hadn't drugged his wine," I added dryly. "Isn't it his home?"

Her expression was bitter. "So long as the metri has extended guest-right, he will not leave. He honors her for her courtesy." Something glinted in her eyes that wasn't laughter. It was, I thought, a desperate pride. "You know nothing about him. You have no idea what manner of man he is—or what they will do to him."

Oh, yes, I did. "Throw him off the spire," I said quietly.

It shocked her that I knew. For a moment she stood very rigidly, staring at us both; then she set her spine against the wood of the door and slowly slid down it until she sat loose-limbed on the floor, staring blankly at the wall. I recalled the evening we'd sat so companionably upon the floor, the wall propping us up, as we shared a winejar.

"I will not lose Nihko," Prima said finally, voice stripped raw of all but her fear. "I could not bear it."

It wasn't love, not of the sort that bound many men and women. But it was a binding in its own way: friendship, companionship, loyalty, respect, admiration, dependence on one another for the large and small things, even the dependence to *not* depend, but to share in the freedom to do what they would do and be what they were. The slaver's daughter and the castrated ikepra had filled the empty spaces in one another's souls.

"A bargain," I said.

The captain looked up at me. "What do you want?"

"A way off the island."

She nodded at once. "Done."

Del scoffed. "And sacrifice what you came here for? What you brought Tiger here for?"

Pale eyes glittered with a sudden sheen of angry tears. "My father kept me fed by selling men. I would rather starve than sell Nihko."

I sat myself down on the floor and leaned against the bedframe. "Have you a suggestion as to how this might be managed?"

Her tone was steady. "You must ask the slave to get us a molah."

She meant Simonides. "And you believe he would do that."

"For you, he will. You were as he is: a slave. He has accepted his fate; you defeated yours. He will do this thing if you ask it."

I drew in a tight breath, expelled it carefully. "You seem to think you know us very well, the metri's servant and me."

Her smile was wintry. "I know slaves. And men who were."

"All right." Del sat down on the edge of the bed. "Let's say Tiger gets a molah. What then?"

Prima, seeing we were not entirely dismissing the idea, spoke rapidly and forcefully. "We put Nihko on the molah and take him down to the harbor. Once on board ship, we will sail. All of us." She spread her hands. "And you will be free of the metri, and Nihko free of Sahdri."

I considered it. "Might work," I agreed at last. "There's just one thing. One minor little detail."

Prima frowned impatiently, clearly eager to implement the plan.

I reached beneath the bed and slid out two swords, handing one up to Del. "It's a trap," I said gently.

The mouth came open slightly in astonishment, then sealed itself closed. As color drained from the taut flesh of her face, the freckles stood out in rusty relief. Something more than anger glinted in her eyes; there was also comprehension, and a bitter desperation.

"It is not," she declared, and pressed a hand flat against the floor as if to lever herself to her feet.

She did not rise after all, because Del and I were across the room with blade tips kissing her throat.

"A trap," Del said.

Prima Rhannet did not move again, not even to shake her head.

"Well?" I prompted.

"It is not," she repeated.

"Prove it."

Her eyes were cold as a Northern winter. "Go to my room. You will find Nihko there—"

"—lying in wait for me?" I grinned, shook my head. "Do better, captain."

Her words were clipped off between shut teeth. "Then we will *all* go to my room, and find Nihko there unconscious in the bed."

Del read the slight shift of my weight. We moved a step away, and I gestured Prima to her feet. A second gesture indicated she was to turn around, which she did. I pulled from her sash at the small of her back the meat-knife she carried—she wore no sword— and tossed it back onto our bed, then nodded. Del sank her left hand deep into the captain's red hair and wound a hank of it around her wrist.

"Don't want to be running off quite yet," I said lightly, and opened the door with my sword at the ready.

The corridor was empty. We proceeded down it, me in the lead and Del bringing up the rear with Prima just before her linked by hair, certainly close enough that a blade could slice through her spine or into her neck with little effort expended. It was not a comfortable position for the captain to be in, head cranked back on her neck, but she made no complaint. She merely indicated the proper door once we reached it.

I nodded at Del, who stepped against the far wall with Prima in tow. Then I stood to the side and quietly pushed the door open.

Sure enough, Nihko lay facedown on the bed, limp and unmoving.

"Just so you know," I said conversationally, "Del is prepared to cut your captain's spine in two the moment you move."

He didn't move. I approached slowly, blade poised. I could smell the wine, and a faint, sour tang of something I didn't recognize.

I thought about his magic, and how I'd reacted. Thought about the brow ring hooked to my necklet. Bent and clamped one hand around his wrist. He was alive; I felt the beat of the pulse against my hand. But he did not move.

I set the flat of the blade against the back of a thigh, bared by the short tunic. "And I'll cut *your* spine in two the moment you move."

No answer. No movement.

I carefully insinuated the edge of the blade between thumbnail and flesh. Sliced.

From the corridor, Prima Rhannet hissed her objection. But Nihkolara Andros did not so much as flinch. All he did was bleed.

I straightened, stepped away, glanced briefly at Del. "Take her back to the room. Keep her there. I'll go have a discussion with Simonides."

Prima's face lighted. "You will help?"

"I think it's likely this may be our only opportunity to get off this island." I jerked my head at Del. "I'll be back when I've made arrangements."

It was quite late when we met Simonides in the courtyard. Nihko, bowed across my back and shoulders like a side of meat, was slack and very heavy, and I thought I stood a good chance of rupturing myself before the night was through. But the molah waited for us in the deeper shadows, safe from prying moonlight, and with relief I heaved the body onto the beastie. The first mate sprawled belly-down, hands and feet dangling; I'd been hauled around the countryside in similar fashion a time or two myself and knew very well what he'd feel like when he roused: rubbed raw across the belly, hands and feet swollen, and head pounding from the throb of so much blood pooling inside the skull. And no telling what the drug would do to him.

Which didn't bother me in the slightest, in view of how often I'd surrendered the contents of my belly merely for being in his presence.

Prima complained that Del should release her. "Not yet," I answered, making sure Nihko was tied firmly onto the molah. I didn't relish the thought of picking him up from the ground if he tumbled off. "First things first."

Simonides himself stood at the molah's head, insuring the animal's cooperation and silence. Once Nihko was trussed to the beast, I stepped back and nodded. Del released Prima, who went immediately to check that he still breathed.

I looked at the servant, slim and silent in the darkness. "You're sure you won't be punished."

"The household is my responsibility," he answered. "The metri does not keep count of her molahs, or how often one goes out or comes in. Herakleio took a cart to the city earlier this evening to drink in winehouses; this will not be remarked. She will believe you simply left Akritara."

"Walking," I said dryly.

Simonides' expression did not change. "You are all of you uncivilized barbarians. I shall have to have the priests in to cleanse the household. It will be very costly."

Prima, satisfied Nihko would survive his uncomfortable journey, went to the molah's head and took its halter rope. "No more talk," she said, and tugged the animal. It stretched its neck, testing her determination, then grudgingly stepped out. She turned it to the front gate.

Del, at my nod, moved quickly to cut Prima off.

"You stay," I told her softly. "*I* will take Nihko to the ship."

She was outraged. "I will not—" But she shut up when Del's sword drifted close to her throat.

"You stay," I repeated. "You and Del will be Simonides' guests in his rooms until word is brought by one of your sailors that Nihko and I are safely on board, and I'm certain the trap isn't waiting for me down there. Then and only then will Del permit you to leave. Simonides will escort you both out of the house, and then you'll join us on the ship." I grinned at her toothily. "Call it insurance."

Prima was furious. "This is not a trap!"

"Prove it," I challenged. "Do this my way."

She stared at Nihko's slack body, then jerked her head in angry assent once and stepped out of the way. I traded glances with Del, promising renewed acquaintance later, then took the molah's halter and led it out of the gate.

Behind me, very quietly, Del ordered Prima to *move*.

Aside from a certain residue of tension, it was quiet and not unpeaceful as I led the little molah along the track from Akritara to the city. Simonides had offered me the use of a second molah, but I'd decided borrowing one was enough; the metri's servant was already risking himself. Besides, I'd found it more comfortable to stretch my legs and stride than to be jounced atop one of the little beasts, even if it was faster to ride.

Around me stretched baskets of grapevines huddled like worried chicks against the soil. Illumination was provided by the full moon and wreaths of stars. The breeze tasted of saltwater, smoke, and soil, but also of molah, wine, sweat, and the bitter tang of the drug the captain had used on her first mate. Nihko had not yet so much as snored, nor stirred atop the molah.

I wondered what Prima would have done had we refused to help. She was a small woman; and I'm not certain even Del, much taller and stronger, could have managed him this slack and heavy. Likely the captain had believed she stood a better chance of gaining our aid if the first mate was already unconscious, but it was amusing to paint a mental picture of Nihko in the morning, in very poor temper, confronting Prima Rhannet after awakening in the metri's guest bed, attempted abduction in vain. I suspected the confrontation aboard the ship would be no friendlier, but at least Prima would have the consolation of knowing she'd gotten Nihko away. Otherwise he'd still be in the metri's household and subject to Sahdri's claim once the guest-right was rescinded.

It crossed my mind also to imagine the metri's reaction when she learned we were gone. I didn't for a moment believe I was truly her grandson; she was enough of an accomplished opportunist to use the tools at hand, and I was one she could employ for multiple reasons in as many circumstances. I had no doubt anymore that I was Skandic; that seemed certain, in view of how closely Herakleio and I resembled one another, or Nihko and I, or even Nihko and

Herakleio. But the Eleven Families did not have the monopoly on bastardy; they'd simply managed very cleverly to transform it into some kind of family honor instead of insult. Some Skandic man—possibly even a renegada—had sailed to the South and there impregnated a woman; I was the result. Wanted or unwanted, exposed or stolen, it simply didn't matter. It made more sense that I wasn't the metri's gods-descended grandson; especially since I knew very well I wouldn't live long enough to inherit. Herakleio was her boy.

And *he* wouldn't weep when he learned we were gone.

Ahead of me the land fell away. I saw clusters of lamplight glowing across the horizon, crowning the edge of the caldera. The molah and I plodded our way into the outskirts of Skandi-the-City, winding through narrow roads running like dusty rivulets across the top of the cliff. The winehouse district was ablaze with candles and lantern light. In one of them—or possibly in some alley awash in molah muck—was Herakleio, oblivious to the fact his legacy was safe.

I shook my head, then turned as I heard a thick-throated groan from Nihko. A brief inspection convinced me he was not likely to recover full consciousness any time soon, but neither was he as drug-sodden as before. His body didn't like where and how it was even if his mind was unaware of the offense.

I led the molah out of the streets to the track along the cliff face near the steep trailhead. Far below lay the waters of the harbor, all but one of the ships denied to Del and me by the metri herself, who wasn't, for whatever reason, finished with us yet. All it wanted was for me to lead the molah down the precarious trail to the blue-sailed renegada ship, deliver him, send someone after Prima, then wait for Del and the captain to appear. Which gave me the rest of the night and likely part of the day to somehow survive.

Nihko groaned again, stirred again atop the molah. The weight abruptly shifted; the molah, protesting, stopped short. I turned back to check on the bonds holding the first mate on the beastie, saw the half-slitted green eyes staring hazily at me in the moonlight, the shine of brow-rings.

"Go back to sleep," I suggested cheerfully, setting a shoulder under his and heaving him over an inch or three. "You don't want to see this next part."

He mumbled something completely unintelligible and appeared to do what I said. The eyes sealed themselves. Smiling, I turned back to take up the molah's headstall again—

—and there was a man in front of me.

Three men. Five.

A whole swarm of men.

Ah, hoo—

Something slammed into the small of my back and then into my ankles, driving me to my knees against the molah even as I reached for the sword hooked to my sash. Hands were on me, imprisoning me, digging into shoulders, throat, hair, wrists, dragging me away from the little animal with its load of Nihkolara; a knife threatened the back of my neck as I was forced to kneel there, head held by dint of a handful of hair snugged up tight, much as Del had imprisoned Prima Rhannet. But they didn't kill me immediately. They just *held* me.

Then they began to strip me of my clothing.

"Now, wait—" I managed, before an elbow was slammed into my mouth. The next thing that came out of it was blood.

It is somewhat disconcerting to be thrown down in the dirt as men strip the clothes off your body. It is even more unsettling when they also inspect all of your parts, as if to make certain you're truly a man. At the first touch of a hand where only my own or Del's ever went, I heaved myself up with an outraged shout expelled forcefully from my mouth, and made a real fight of it.

Something caught at my throat. My necklet. I saw the gleam of a blade in the moonlight, gritted teeth against the anticipated stab or slice even as I heaved again, roaring, attempting to break loose of the swarm. The necklet of claws pulled briefly taut, then, released, slapped down against my throat. And then abruptly everything in my body seized up as if turned to stone, and I fell facedown into the dirt.

"Throw him over," a familiar voice said in a language I understood.

I wanted to tense against the hands that would grasp, lift,

heave. But nothing worked. Nothing at all—except my belly. Which relieved itself with vivid abruptness of the meal I'd eaten earlier.

Ah, hoolies, not *this* again.

"Throw him over," the voice repeated, and I heard a muttered complaint from Nihko.

From the dregs of darkness, from the misery of my belly and the helplessness of my body lying sprawled in muck left by molahs, goats, chickens—and me—and through a haze of blood, inhaling that and dust, I dimly saw the naked body on the ground grasped, rifted, heaved over the cliff. It fell slackly out of sight before I could even blink.

Thoughts fragmented as I saw the body go. The first thing through my mind: *Prima was right*—

Or else it was as much a trap for Nihko as for me.

Herakleio—?

But why would he have *Nihko* killed?

Then someone touched cool fingers to the back of my neck and I went down into darkness wondering if Nihko was conscious as he fell, and if I would wake up before I hit the bottom.

Chapter 32

*T*he shadow passed across the cliff, flitted down the sheer face with its convoluted track folding back upon itself from harbor to clifftop. A bird.

The shadow soared, circled, returned, drifted closer. The body was a body, but broken. The skull was pulped, the face smashed beyond recognition, limbs twisted into positions no limb was supposed to go; nowhere was it whole.

The shadow fled across the body, turned back.

It had been heaved over the edge near the track, but not on it; and so the body was not immediately visible from any angle. Bereft of clothing, the brown skin blended with the soil, the rocks, the small plots of vegetation trying valiantly to cling to the cliff's face. No human eyes beheld it, but animal nose smelled it. It was too soon for rot to set in, but the odor of death was something every animal recognized, and avoided. Unless it was a carrion-eater.

Molahs were not. And so when a string of molahs being led down the track rebelled, their molah-man called out to another man to search lest a body be found, some drink-sodden fool fallen from the cliff after stumbling out of a winehouse; it had happened before. And so men looked, and the body was found. It was remarked upon for its nakedness, for the scars on its body, for the ruin of its face and skull, but it was not recognized. It might be one of them. It might not. But it was indisputably dead.

The bird, deprived of its meal, soared east away from the caldera, *crossed the ocean, crossed the valley, found other prey atop a stone spire piercing the sky, and there the bird drifted again, judging its meal.*

And then of a sudden the bird stopped. Dropped. Hurtled out of the skies with no attempt to halt its plummet, and crashed into the body that lay sprawled atop the spire, naked of clothing, naked of consciousness; a shell of flesh and bone empty of awareness or comprehension.

The body opened, accepted the bird, closed again.

I awoke abruptly, startled out of senselessness into the awareness that I lived after all. I sat up, poised to press myself upright, saw the sky spin out from under me. I was conscious of a vast gulf of air, of a blue so brilliant as to be overwhelming, and the physical aware-ness of *nothingness*. The body understood the precariousness of its place even if the mind did not.

I rolled, flopped down upon my belly, realized an arm-span away the surface beneath me fell away utterly into sky.

Stone bit into the flesh of my face. Naked, I was not comfort-able. Genitals protested until I eased them with a shift of position, though I did little more than alter the angle of one hip. I breathed heavily, puffing dust from beneath my face. I tasted it. And blood.

Beyond one outstretched hand lay the edge of the world, such as what I knew. In that moment what I knew was what I felt be-neath me, what I saw. Sky and sky. Nothing more.

I lifted my head with immense care. Rotated it so that my chin touched the stone. Saw the edge of the world stretching before me, its horizon distant.

Another rotation of the skull, to the left. Again, sky; but this time land as well: stone, and soil, and the scouring of the wind.

Even now it touched me, teased at my flesh, insinuated itself beneath the hollows of my body at ankles, knees, hips; the pockets under arms. It caught my hair, blew it into my eyes, altered vision. I saw hair and stone dust and sky.

My belly cramped. There was nothing to expel, but that wasn't the intent. From deep inside, rising from genitals, something *squeezed*.

I wondered briefly if it was fear.

As swiftly as it seized me, the cramp released me. Surely fear would last longer?

A tremor wracked me from skull to toes, grinding flesh into stone.

I shut my eyes, let my head drop. I lay there very still, save for in- and exhalations; was relieved to manage that much.

I knew where I was. I just didn't know why.

Meteiera.

Stone Forest.

IoSkandi.

Where madmen were sent to die, while they made an acquaintanceship with magic.

Not me.

Surely not me.

Wind crept beneath my body, insistent. It shifted the stone dust, drove it into the sweat-slicked creases of my flesh. I itched.

The tremor wracked me again.

I painted a portrait: me atop the spire. I lay at the edge; to my right, the world fell away. To my left, it stretched itself like an indolent cat, the bones beneath lean flesh hard and humped as stone.

It *was* stone.

This cat was neither indolent, nor stone. This cat was flesh, and afraid.

I painted a portrait. I knew where I was. Comprehended the risks, and where the dangers lay. To my right, an arm-span away. To my left, much farther.

The body gathered itself, rose onto naked buttocks, moved away from the edge of the world. It stopped when it sensed stone encompassing it: an island in the center of the sky. It sat there, arms wrapped around gathered knees, and made itself small.

Wind buffeted.

I shut my eyes against it. Hair was stripped from my face. Sweat evaporated as the wind wicked it away. Buttocks and the soles of my feet clutched at the stone.

All around me was sky, and sky, and sky.

And, according to io- and Skandic alike, gods.

It occurred to me, finally, to wonder why.

Why this?

Why not simply heave me over the edge of the caldera cliff, as they had Nihko?

Why *this?*
And then, belatedly, wondered how.
If there was a way up, there was also a way down.
I smiled then, into the face of the wind.

The spire's crown was not so small as I had initially believed. It was, in fact, approximately the surface area of two full circles, a good thirty paces across. This afforded me the latitude to move without fearing I'd fall off the edge: I'd spent half my life—or possibly longer—learning how to stay inside a circle, and *two* of them was a surfeit.

Eventually I stood up against the wind. I let it curl around me, buffet me, try to drive me down or off the edge. But I understood my place now, and how to deny the wind purchase. I used weight and awareness, and comprehension. I learned what to expect of it, to respect it, to use it. By the time I paced out the crown of stone I was no longer afraid of the wind, that it might blow me off into the sky.

By the time I had inspected every edge of the spire's crown, I knew no ropes existed.

As the sun went down, I sat atop the tower of stone and made note of the valley below, the distant glow of lanternlight, of cookfires. My spire was not the only one. I counted as many as I could see, clustered throughout the valley, suspecting there might be more beyond. No two spires were alike: some were thick, knobbed with protuberances, shelves, cave-pocked. In the dying of the day I saw light sprout atop other spires; saw the arches and angles of dwellings built there; the wooden terraces clinging to shelves and cave-mouths. As the light faded, plunging the valley into darkness, I lost definition and saw only the wavery glimmers of lanterns, the dark blocky bulwarks of stone against moon and stars.

There was no lamplight for me, no lantern, no cookfire. Only what I took for myself out of the luminance of the skies. Doubtless a priest-mage would say the moon and stars were a gift of the gods.

Before he merged with them.

I shivered. The sun took warmth with it, and I had no clothes to cut the wind. I was hungry, thirsty, and confused.

If there was a way up, there was also a way down.

Wasn't there?

Eventually I lay down atop the stone.

Eventually I slept.

In my dream Del found me. She sailed to ioSkandi, walked into the Stone Forest, came to the proper spire, found a way up and climbed over the edge to rise and stand beside me. We linked hands, stood together against the wind, and knew ourselves inviolable.

The touch of her flesh against mine granted me all the peace I knew, all the impetus for survival and triumph a man might know, were he to trust a woman the way I trusted Del. Together we stood at the edge of the crown of stone, arms outstretched, and let the wind have us. Let it tip us, take us, carry us down and down, where we walked again upon the earth as we were meant to do.

I turned to her, to embrace her, to kiss her, and felt stone against my mouth.

I sat up into wind, into light, and watched the day replace night. Dew bathed the spire, and me. Sweat joined it, welling up beneath hair to bathe my skull, my face; to sheen the fragile flesh stretched over brittle bone.

No food, no water, no way down.

Why *this?*

Why not a clean kill, a body tossed off the cliff?

I don't believe in gods.

I don't believe in magic.

I don't believe in the power of a man to float above a wall, to move without indication of it.

Yet I had witnessed the latter.

I had witnessed magic.

I had *worked* magic.

I don't believe in gods.

I believe in myself.

I put my hand upon the necklet of sandtiger claws, counted them out. None was missing. Only the silver brow ring Nihko had attached, and I had reattached when it came clear to me that no matter how much I wished to disbelieve in its efficacy against magic, it made every difference.

They had cut it from the necklet the night before.

No, the night before that.

Or the night before *that?*

How many days had I been here?

Two.

That I knew about.

Two, in which I was conscious.

Before that?

Before *that?*

I was hungry. Thirsty. Weakening.

More days than two.

How many?

Did it matter.

If I were to find a way down, it mattered.

If there were a way down.

How had I come up? How had they brought me up?

Sahdri. Sahdri, who could float above a wall, who could move across a terrace with no indication of it.

Sahdri's voice, bidding them toss the body over.

What would Prima say, to learn her first mate was dead?

What would Del say, to learn I was missing?

To learn I was dead?

More days than two.

How many?

How many left?

How long?

How many days before she accepted I was gone?

And unlikely to come back.

We had never, not once, discussed it. Because we knew, both of us, what was necessary. What I had done before, believing she would die; believing she was dead despite the breath left in her body.

I could not now recollect what emotions had led to that decision, had permitted me to leave her. Certainty that she was dead; certainty that to see that death would destroy me. But the emotions *of the moment* were long banished, and unsummonable. I recalled that I had felt them, but not how they felt beyond the memory of anguish, guilt, grief, and indescribable pain.

I had stood upon the cliff overlooking Staal-Kithra, lumpy with barrows, dolmens, and passage graves, and beyond it Staal-Ysta, the island in the glass-black lake flanked white-on-white in winter, stark peaks against bleak sky. I had bidden her good-bye; had apologized in my own fashion. Had thrust the sword's blade into turf, into soil, into the heart of the North.

I had named the sword to her, spoken that name aloud, so she would know it: *Samiel.* Now that Northern sword lay buried beneath Southron rock, drained at last of the sorcerer that had infested it. I was free of sorcerer, free of sword.

Free to die alone on ioSkandi, abandoned atop a towering spire punching a hole into the sky.

Piercing, one might hope with forgivable bitterness, the liver of the gods whom others worshiped by leaping off the spires.

That instant, with startling clarity, I knew. Understood what was expected.

I was *to merge.*

I wondered, with no little cynicism, who it was that collected all the bones found at the bottom, shattered into bits. Or were they simply left there, ignored, ground into ivory powder beneath the feet of priest-mages come to rejoice in the merging?

I tipped my head back and back, gazing up into the sky. For the first time since awakening atop the rock, I spoke.

"You're not mine!" I shouted. "You are *not my gods!*"

Because I had none. Worshiped none. Believed in none.

"Not!"

The wind whispered, *No?*

No.

No and no.

Had none, worshiped none, believed in none.

Gods, and magic.

Magic.

Had none, worked none, believed in none.

Liar, the wind whispered.

Gods, but I was thirsty.

And then I laughed. Because even a man who believes in no gods believes in the *concept* of them, believes that others believe. Or he would not rely upon a language that embraces the presence of gods.

Habit. Nothing more. One grows accustomed to others saying it, praying it, believing it. One need not believe it himself. One need not pray himself.

Would praying get me off the top of this rock?

The wind curled around me. *Hypocrite.*

Would magic get me off the top of this rock?

The wind asserted itself, but offered no answer.

Sahdri, who could float above a wall. Who could move with no indication of it. Who could require that Nihkolara Andros hurl himself off a spire to merge with the gods he had repudiated . . . but there had been no Ritual of Unsoiling, and thus Nihkolara Andros had *been* hurled. Not from the spire, not from ioSkandi where priest-mages served, worshiped, and went mad, but from the caldera clifftop.

Ikepra. Abomination.

What then was I?

I laughed again. "Fool."

The wind engulfed, embraced, tugged. I went with it; let it take me to the edge. I knelt there, supplicant to the sky. And refused.

A shadow drifted over me, across the spire. Unfurled wings. I looked up. Saw the bird. Felt something inside myself respond. My belly cramped. Genitals clenched. I bent at the waist, folding upon myself. Something within me stirred.

Grew.

Unfolded.

Felt *imminent.*

I shook upon the rock, knees ground into stone. Flesh stood up on my bones; the hair stood up on my flesh. Against my will my arms snapped out, palms flattened, fingers spread. Breath was noisy in my throat. Was expelled from my mouth, and sucked in again. Loudly. And as loudly expelled.

Sweat ran from me. I felt it roll down flesh; saw it splash

against the stone. Every inch of that flesh itched. I knelt there, shuddering, aware of the rattling of my bones, the quailing of my spirit.

So easy to let go.

So easy to lean forward.

So easy to tip myself off the rim of the world.

So easy to fall.

So easy to *end.*

"Del!" I shouted. Louder, again, *"Dellllllllll!"*

She was my walls. My house.

Did Herakleio want her so badly?

So easy.

To let go.

To fall.

To end.

Night found me there. Kneeling. Denying the gods. Repudiating magic.

Putting my faith in Del.

Find me.

Find me.

Find me.

Bascha. Please.

Find me?

I lay atop the spire, spine pressed into stone. I was heavy. All of me, heavy. And yet it seemed impossible that I should be so, because there was no food, no water. Only wind. Only sun. Only endless skies, and endless days, and nights that fed me on stars.

In the South, I would have died days before. Here, with moisture in the air, with morning dew, with the breath of seawater against my flesh, death was tardy. But it came. The carrion bird above me, inside me, assured me of that.

Del hadn't come.

Couldn't.

Did not know where, or how.

Or even *if* I lived.

Had anyone else died atop the spire? Did the carrion bird feast upon the body, scattering the bones? Did the wind blow them off?

Could the wind lift a body?

Carry it?

Could the bird rift a body?

Carry it?

Could I rise and try the skies?

Flesh itched. Bones burned.

Emptiness abounded, save for the imminence.

I was glass, and I would break.

Lift me, carry me, drop me, and I would shatter.

Better *I* lift me. Better *I* carry me.

Better I shatter myself.

Hollowness.

Spirit honed to an edge no one could see, but it would cut; oh, yes, it would cut through the flesh before anyone knew.

And kill.

Cut. Slice. Pierce.

Like a sword.

I was a sword.

I *was* the sword.

The sword.

Conceived in the skies, of the metal made into steel; given birth above the earth.

Falling.

Falling.

Found later, and smelted. Folded. Hammered. Heated. Cooled in the waters, and blessed. And honed.

Wielded.

Jhihadi. Messiah. Slave. Sword-dancer.

Wielded.

Broken?

And heated again. Folded again.

Hammered.

Honed.

Wielded.

My eyes snapped open. I stared up into the skies, aware of but not blinded by the sun. A shadow passed across it, across me. Wings unfurled.

The noise I made sounded not unlike the cry of a carrion-eater.

I rose from the stone and stood upon it for the first time in days. Gazed upon the doubled circle and the world beyond it, the endless skies filled with wind, and gods.

And a bird.

Conceived in the skies, found later, and smelted. So that the essence of *me* was retained, worked, heated and hammered and honed.

There was nothing left of me but steel.

Sword-dancer.

Dancer.

Sword.

Imminence was a *presence*.

Wings unfurled.

Shadow passed, darkening my eyes.

Heal me.

Anneal me.

Wings within unfurled.

Anneal me.

I stood on the edge of the spire and unfurled arms, palms, fingers. Felt the wind upon my flesh. Felt it enwrap, enfold, engulf.

Anneal me.

Heels lifted from the stone. Toes gripped. Clung. Balanced.

Anneal me.

Skull tipped back. Sun warmed my face; wind kissed it. Seduced, I let the lids drop closed; saw the red brilliance behind them, filling my head with light.

Comprehension.

Acknowledgement.

I poised there, a man at the edge of a stone circle, the only sword available the one I made of myself.

Shadow winged over me.

"Anneeeeeeaallllll meeeeeeeeeeeeeee!"

No gods.

Only me.

Only me.

The shadow within unfurled.

The wind came again. I felt it in my eyes, my nostrils, my mouth; felt it enter throat and lungs and belly. Felt it bind my bones, so brittle, so hollow, so light.

And imminence *arrived*.

And power.

Comprehension.

Acknowledgment.

I whelped it there upon the rock; gave birth to the child I had carried for more than three decades, now labored in pain to bear upon the spire in the skies. The child I might have been had I been born in Skandi. The child thrown away in the sands of the Southron desert. The child I was never permitted to be; the child I never permitted myself to be. To conceive. To bear.

I whelped it there upon the rock and screamed out the pain and rage: that the choice was taken from me. Decades after the vessel had been shaped of a man and a woman, the child was born at last. The vessel was annealed. The flesh was strong enough at last to contain the child.

Oh, it wanted freedom!

I spun then and ran.

Ran.

To the edge of the circle.

The edge of the spire.

The edge of the world.

And beyond.

No gods.

Only me.

Leaping into the day.

The shadow passed across the spire, flitted down the sheer sides. A bird.

The shadow soared, circled, returned, drifted closer. The body was a body, unbroken. The skull was whole, the face recognizable, the limbs untwisted.

The shadow fled across the body, turned back.

It had leaped near the edge, and so the body was not immediately vis-

ible from any angle. Bereft of clothing, the brown skin blended with the soil, the rocks, the small plots of vegetation trying valiantly to cling to the spire's footing. No human eyes beheld it, but animal nose smelled it. The odor of impending death was something every animal recognized, and avoided. Unless it was a carrion-eater.

Molahs were not. And so when the molah pulling the cart rebelled, its molah-man looked, and the body was found. It was recognized for its nakedness, for the scars on its body, for the shape of its face and skull. It might be one of them. It might not. But it was indisputably alive.

Chapter 33

*S*ound. The wind, rustling vegetation. Lifting sand and dirt. The scratch of grit, rolling. The tickle of air in the hairs on arms, and legs, and head. I could hear it. *Hear* the hairs rising.

Could feel it.

Feel.

In a single spasmodic inhalation my lungs filled, expanded my chest; I was afraid to let it go again, lest it never be repeated.

My head was filled with light.

Breath whooshed out again. Came back, like a dog, when I called it.

I breathed.

Sound. The clink of stone on stone, the dig of hoof into soil, the whuffing snort of an animal.

And a person, walking.

Eyelids cracked. Daylight filled my eyes; I lay on my back. I saw the animal: molah. Saw the shape: male. Black against the sun.

The molah was stopped. The man tied its lead-rope to a scrubby tree, then came to me. Knelt down beside me. Inspected me, though he put no hands upon me.

"For forty years," he said, "you have been dead. Only now are you born. Only now are you whole."

Forty?

Had I so many years?

No one had known. No one had told me. All of it a guess.
Forty.

"Only now are you whole," he repeated.

I realized then he was speaking Skandic.

And that I understood it.

His smile was ironic. "I know," he said. "But now you comprehend what a newborn baby encounters. So much of a new world. So much to overwhelm it."

I opened my eyes fully. Saw the shaven, tattooed head; green eyes in sun-bronzed skin; the glint of rings in his brows.

"Dead," I said.

"You were," he agreed.

"You."

"Ah." The ironic smile deepened. "No."

"Saw it."

"You saw *a body*. It was dark, you were in some distress—and the magic was in your body, once they took this from your neck-let." A finger indicated the healed cut where the ring had once resided; had been sliced out. "A body," he said. "Nothing more. A dead man, and convenient: your height, your weight, your coloring; we are all of us similar."

"You?"

"Me they pulled from the molah; I was in no position to argue."

No. He had been drugged to insensibility by his captain.

"Why?" I asked. "Why present a body?"

"Because of your woman," he answered.

Del?

"If she believed you lived, she would search for you. They wish her gone."

"Who?"

And how many?

"Sahdri, lest she come looking. The metri, lest she become what Herakleio desires. Prima, because—because she hopes in grief Del might turn to her."

"Who did this?"

"Any one of them."

"You."

"No."

Certainty. "Del will come."

"But she believes you are dead. Your body was found."

"Not mine."

"They believe it is yours."

"They?"

"The metri. Herakleio. Prima."

Disbelief was manifest. *"Prima?"*

He did not smile. "She believes you are dead. She is meant to believe it, as are the others."

"But she knows you're alive."

"No."

"No?"

"I disappeared."

"How convenient."

"They assume I am dead. They know you are."

"Not Del."

"And Del."

"No."

"They are priests," he said gently, *"and* mages. Do you believe a body would be found that did not resemble yours even in certain details?" For the first time he touched me. It was brief, impersonal, without intent beyond indication. "Here." The travesty of an abdomen reshaped by Del's jivatma. "And here." The claw marks graven deeply into my cheek. "Not much skull left, nor face, but enough for the scars."

"I don't believe it. Neither will anyone else." Certainly not Del. "Even a smashed body bears specific blemishes."

"They are mages," he said with infinite precision. "This is not beyond them. They simply lifted the scars from you and set them into another man's flesh."

It robbed me of breath. "Lifted—?"

"No scars," he said, "beyond those they left you. A dead man bears them. And so *you* are dead."

I wanted desperately to move, to lift a hand to my cheek, but the body betrayed me.

"Dead," he repeated. "To everyone who knew you."

"*You* know me."

Nihko smiled sadly. "But I am a priest, and I am a mage, and I am a madman."

"Ikepra."

"Not any more."

"*How?*"

"Payment," he said, "for this."

"For—?"

"This."

"This?"

"The first steps," he said, "following birth. You have ten years. Possibly twelve. You are a candle now, burning brighter and hotter than any other. You will consume yourself with the heat of your spirit, with the power in your bones. You have no time to crawl, but must be made to walk."

I lay sprawled against the ground, unable to move. "Am I— whole?"

"Better than whole," he answered. "Now you are *complete.*"

I knew what I was. "Sword-dancer."

Nihko said, "Not any more."

"I danced atop the spire."

"You had no sword."

"I *am* the sword."

"No."

"You can't take that from me."

"I will not. They will."

"No one can."

"You are a child," he said kindly. "The magic is wild. These are men who have learned its nature and how to control it. Trust me in this: you will do as they say, become what they decree."

"You didn't."

"And they would kill me for it."

"You're alive."

"Payment," he said. "For this."

I laughed then; was shocked that I could. "I'm dead. *Really* dead. This is not real. You're dead, and I'm dead, and this is not real."

"Well," he said philosophically, "I said much the same myself."

"And did you leap off a spire?"

Nihko's face was serene. "We all of us leap," he said. "It is how we know."

"Know what?"

"That the magic has manifested."

"To me," I said, "leaping off a spire suggests *madness* has manifested!"

"Yes," he agreed. "Any man may do so, and die of it. But those of us who survive are something more than simply mad."

"Magic," I said in disgust.

"Mages," he clarified. "Men who are made of it, and who learn how to wield it."

I stirred for the first time. The body—did not cooperate.

"Be still," Nihko said. "The body has used itself up."

"Used up—?"

"It was a circle," Nihko said, "for you. But in truth it is what each man makes of it. He learns himself up there, learns what and who he is. He must recognize it, acknowledge it, comprehend it, and employ it. Rely upon it. Use it up."

"Then if it's used up—"

"Gone," he said. "Extinguished."

"Then I *am* dead."

"The man you were. The slave. The messiah. The sword-dancer."

"No."

"You surrendered it in the circle. You *left* the circle. You flung yourself out of it."

"Elaii-ali-ma," I whispered.

"You are not what you were. You are what you will be. You are not *who* you were. You are who you shall be."

"Sword-dancer."

"Mage."

I laughed; it tore my throat. "Would you have me be a priest? Me?"

"You gave yourself to the gods."

"They aren't my gods."

"You gave yourself to gods, be they mine or yours."

"Semantics," I muttered.

"You survived," Nihko said. "You are what you are."

"Mad?"

"Indisputably."

"I don't feel mad."

"You don't feel anything. Yet. Come morning, you will."

"And what will I be in the morning?"

Nihko said, "Mage. And aware of it."

I shut my eyes. I did not echo him. I named myself inside where no one else could see.

"Mage," he repeated.

Sword-dancer, I said.

In, or out of the circle.

In the morning I wasn't a mage. I was merely a man sick unto death. Fever burned my bones, wasted my flesh, turned my eyes to soup in their sockets. Lips cracked and bled. A layer of skin sloughed off. My belly, bowels, and bladder expelled what was left; after uncounted days atop the spire without nourishment, little enough *was* left. I was weak and wracked, joints ablaze. What moisture remained spilled out of my eyes. My tongue swelled and filled my mouth, then cracked and bled like the lips. I drank blood, until Nihko gave me water.

He bandaged my eyes, because I could not close them.

He splinted fingers and toes, because I could not open them.

He restrained the skull that risked itself in frenzy against the ground.

He did what was necessary to bring me across the threshold, and when that much was accomplished he did even more.

He made me rise.

I stood upright again for the first time in days. Felt the earth beneath bare feet, felt the wind in my hair. Saw—everything.

Nihko heard the ragged gasp that was expelled from my mouth. "Clarity," he said.

It was too bright. Everything, too bright. Too rich. Too *brilliant.* I thought it might well blind me. My skin burned from the sun.

Ached over the bones. Everything hurt. Everything was *too much*. I quivered like a child, trying to sort out things I could not comprehend. Things I had comprehended for most of my life, such as taste, touch, odor, sound, light.

All of it: too much.

"What do you hear?" he asked.

It thrummed inside my head. The whisper was a shout. I recoiled. "Too much," I said, then hissed. Then winced.

"All the senses," he said, "Everything is *more*."

More was too much. I stood for the first time in days and was blinded by the world, deafened by the world, filled with the scent of the world, tasted all of its courses, felt it impinge so much upon me that the flesh ached from it.

Everything was *more*.

I sought escape inside. But *more* existed there. I beat against the cage that was my own skull, attempted to withdraw, escape. And knew defeat.

"You cannot," Nihko told me. "It *is* you, now."

I barely spoke. "What is?"

"Everything."

I stood there and trembled, while the man's hand steadied me.

And then I knelt. Sought solace in the soil. Its scent was overwhelming. "I can't," I mouthed.

"You can."

"I *can't*."

"You will.

I bent, pressed my hands into the earth. Put my brow upon it, so that the sun beat on my spine. It made its way through flesh into muscle, into viscera. Into my very soul. It illuminated me, betrayed my frailties.

"You can," Nihko told me.

The world was too large. And everything in it too bright, too loud, too *much*.

To the earth, I said, "I want . . ."

Nihko waited.

"I want," I said with difficulty, "to go back."

"You are dead."

"I'm *alive*." I rolled back onto my haunches then, rose to my feet. Confronted him. "I'm too alive to be dead. I feel it in me. *Taste* it in me. I can hear my blood!"

"Yes."

I clamped palms across my eyes. "I want to go back. To be what I was."

"You are what you were."

My hands fell away so I could see his face. "You said I wasn't!"

"You were unborn," he explained. "For forty years, the vessel was shaped as it was shaped. The magic was dormant. But it began to rouse two or three years ago. The seeds of it were in you. As you approached the threshold, the seeds began to sprout. Atop that spire, you celebrated your birth forty years before. And the magic manifested."

I remembered unfolding. Unfurling. Within me, and without. The imminence that burst into being as I whelped it on the rock.

"You knew," I said abruptly. "That day on the ship, when you first took us aboard. You *knew*."

"As you will know it in another. Others will come. And you will serve them as I have served you: lift them up, nourish them, help them across the threshold."

"I want to go back."

"There is no 'back.' "

"I'm not you, Nihko!"

It echoed against the spire. I recoiled and slapped hands over my ears.

Nihko smiled. "Quietly," he said. "Control is necessary."

"Like yours?" I threw at him; but very quietly.

"My control is negligible," he said with irony. "It is why I deserted my brothers."

"And now you're back?"

"Am I not here?"

"Helping me," I said bitterly, "across the threshold."

He extended his arm. "Take my hand," he suggested, "and cross."

"Haven't I already?"

"A step or two."

I laughed at him, though there was no humor in it. "The first step I took off the spire was a killer."

"Yes," he agreed. "For many men, it is."

"Then if they have no magic, why are they up there?"

"They have magic," he answered, "and it manifests. But some vessels are not strong enough. They do not survive the annealing."

"Gods," I said, remembering. Recalling how I begged.

Anneal me.

Nihko smiled. "Precisely."

"No," I blurted. "No, not that . . ." But to speak of what happened wasn't possible. It was too new. Too—large. "How did I get up there?"

"Sahdri."

"He took me up there?"

"Took you. Left you."

"How?"

Nihko's brow rings glinted. "He is a mage, is he not?"

"I want to know how. How *exactly?*"

His tone was devoid of compassion. "And how *exactly* did you come down from the spire?"

"How did I—?"

"Come down," he repeated. "Should you not have broken to pieces here upon the ground?"

I inspected a hand. "Didn't I?"

"How did you come down?"

"I leaped." I grimaced. "Like a madman."

"Should you not be dead?"

"Aren't I?"

"Be in no haste," he said grimly. "You have ten years left to you."

"You told me twelve."

"*Possibly* twelve."

I looked into his eyes. "How many have you?"

"Two," he said. "Possibly."

"How do you know?"

"I know."

"How can you tell?"

"I can."

"This is ridiculous," I snapped. "You feed me this nonsense of scars being lifted and put onto another man; of Sahdri using magic to set me atop this rock; of me *being born*, as if once wasn't enough; of me surviving this leap that only a madman would make—"

"A madman did."

"—and then you expect me to believe this nonsense?"

"This nonsense will convince you."

"I don't think so."

"Look at yourself," he commanded. "Look at your flesh."

I scowled. "So?"

"He *lifted the scars from you.*"

I looked at myself. Peered down at my abdomen, where the Northern blade had sculpted flesh and muscle into an architecture I hadn't been born with.

The flesh was whole. Unblemished.

I clapped a hand to my face. The cheek was whole. Unblemished.

I looked then at my hands, seeking the cuts, the divots, the over-large knuckle where a finger had been broken, the nails themselves left ridged from hard usage. All of me was whole. All of me was new.

I stared hard at Nihko. "*You* have scars."

"You begin anew," he answered. "What damage you do to yourself from this day forward will be manifested in your flesh—it can even kill you—but you were reborn on the spire. A child comes into the world without blemish."

I knew better. "Not all children!"

He conceded that. "But not all children are ioSkandic."

"And the ones who are?"

"Are mages. Are mad."

I laughed harshly. "You tell me I have power, now; that I'm a mage, now. And also that I'm mad? What advantage is that?"

"None."

"Then?"

"We are transient," he said. "We burn too brightly. We burn ourselves out."

I stabbed a finger at him. "This is not helping."

He grinned toothily at me. "I live to serve."

"Clothes," I said, focusing on nakedness; on what I could understand.

"In the cart."

"Good. Get them."

"Ah. I am to serve."

"You said that's what you were here for."

"For the moment." But he went to the cart, found a bundle of linen and tossed it at me.

I caught and shook it out. "What is this?"

"Robes," he answered, untying the molah's lead-rope. "But you need not concern yourself with how they suit you."

Slipping into the linen, I eyed him irritably. "Why not?"

"Because you will not be wearing them for very long."

The hem of the robe ended just above my ankles. "Why not?"

"Because," he said, "Sahdri will have you stripped."

I froze. "Why?"

"Rituals," he said briefly, leading the molah over. Cartwheels grated on stone.

"*What* rituals?" I asked suspiciously. "No more leaping off of spires!"

"That is done." He gestured. "Get in."

"Little chance of that," I retorted. "There's only one thing that will convince me I should."

"Yes?"

"That this cart is going to a ship that can take me back to Skandi."

"No," he answered.

"Then I guess I'm going nowhere. Not to Sahdri. Not *with* you."

Nihko sighed. "Do you believe I cannot make you?"

"If I'm a mage," I said promptly, "you can't make me do anything."

"But I can," he said, and touched me.

I tumbled into darkness.

And into the cart.

Chapter 34

Sense returned with a rush. Ropes cut into me, rubbed wounds into newly sensitive flesh; I felt everything as if it were hot as wire. The pounding of my heart filled my skull, reverberated in my chest. I heard the hiss of blood running back and forth in its vessels, as if my skin were too thin.

I flailed, felt ropes give; realized it was net. I was cradled, captured. Bundled up within the ropes fashioned into nets. And I was suspended.

From a spire.

I flailed again, spasming. Felt the net, harsh as wire. Felt the sway of the rope used to haul me up.

I depended from the spire. Depended *on* the spire.

Movement. I was being hauled up, winched up; I heard the creak of wood, the rubbing of the rope. Was this how Sahdri had taken me up the other spire?

There had been no rope. And nothing to which rope might be attached. There had only been stone. And spire. And me.

This was different.

I was meat in a net, hauled up. If my flesh wasn't eaten, my spirit would be.

Sahdri. Who had known the moment he saw me. Saw the brow ring hooked in my necklet.

I snatched at necklet. Found it. Caught it. Closed my hand

upon it. Ten curving claws, strung upon a thong. I had cut them from the paws. Pierced them. Strung them. Wore them as a badge: see what I have become? I am the boy that killed the sandtiger; that saved the children; that saved the tribe; that freed himself.

Twenty-four years I had worn the necklet.

I knew that, now. I was forty years old. Nihko had told me. The magic had manifested. Sixteen when I killed the sandtiger; sixteen when I conjured it. And thirty-seven when I met Del.

Not thirty-six. Not thirty-eight.

I had a name. An age. One I gave myself. The other was given to me.

Sandtiger.

Sandtiger.

They would not take it from me.

"There is no magic," I said aloud, "and I am no mage."

Wood creaked. Rope rubbed as it was wound.

"There are no gods," I said, "and I am no priest."

Sandtiger.

Sword-dancer.

No less.

No more.

This spire was taller than the one I had roused upon, danced atop, leaped from. This spire was wider, thicker, shaped of twists and columns and shelves and pockets and caves cut into the stone by wind, by rain. Trapped in my net I stared at the stone. Saw *through* the stone. Saw deep into its heart where the minerals lay, wound within and around the bones.

I blinked. The stone was stone again.

Wood creaked. Rope rubbed.

Higher by the moment.

I swung in the net. Spun in the net. Saw the sky encompass stone, stone overtake sky. I shut my eyes: saw it. Opened them: the same.

I lifted a hand. Studied it. Saw no blemishes. Saw only flesh that had existed for forty years. Not young. Not old. Somewhere in the middle, were I to survive to be as old again as I was now.

I turned the hand. The palm was lined, callused. It was a hand, not a construct. Rebirth had renewed the flesh, but not leached away the time.

The flesh of a sudden went white. Stark white, like snow. I blinked. In shock, I watched flesh thin to transparency. Saw the vessels pulsing beneath, the blood running in them; the sinew, the meat, the bone.

"Gods," I blurted, and clamped my eyes closed.

When I opened them, the hand was a hand again. Whole. Normal. The bones were decently clad in human flesh once more.

My own.

I touched my face. Felt the cheek that had borne the scars for so long. Rubbed fingers across it. Stubble had sprouted; I was not so much a child newly born that I couldn't grow a beard. I needed to shave. I needed a haircut. I needed to eat, to drink, to empty bladder and bowels—though nothing was in them—so I knew I lived again as a man is meant to live.

And I needed Del. To know I lived again as a man is meant to live.

Gods, bascha. I want you.

No scars met seeking fingers. I dug them in, scraped fingers across the stubble. No marks of the sandtiger.

I sealed my eyes with lids. Clamped a hand around the necklet. Let the claws bite into palm.

Bleed, I said. Bleed.

There was no blood.

Nihko had said I could manifest such wounds as a man might, were he given to injury.

Bleed, I said, and shut my hand the tighter.

When two mage-priests hooked me into the winch-house, undid the net, pulled me free of rope, I at last un-clamped my hand and displayed the palm to Sahdri, who waited.

"Bleeding," I said.

His eyes were dark. They were not rimmed with light. It had been a trick that night. "Then you must have wanted it so."

"I'm a *man*," I said. "I bleed. I can die."

"Is that what you wish?"

Blood ran down my hand. It dripped to the floor of the winch-house. I followed the droplets, saw them strike the stone. Saw them swallowed by the stone. Saw them go down and down through stone until they reached its heart, where they were consumed. Changed to mineral.

Transfixed, I knelt upon the stone and tried to reach through it, to recapture the blood. It was mine.

"You are very young," Sahdri said gently, "and very new. But give me time—give _yourself_ time—and you will understand what it is to be one of us."

I looked up at him. "I saw through it," I said. "This hand."

He smiled. "It takes some people so." He gestured briefly, indicating two shaven-headed, tattooed men with him. "This is Erastu." The man on the left. "And this is Natha." The man on the right. "They are acolytes here, as you shall become shortly. They shall assist you."

I stood. I ignored Erastu and Natha. I looked into Sahdri's face. "I can see through _you_."

And I could. I saw the rings in his flesh melt, saw the flesh of his face peel away, saw the bones of the skull beneath tattooed flesh glisten in a bed of raw meat. Beneath the meat, the bone, I saw the brain. And the light of his madness, pulsing as if it lived.

The shudder took me. Shook me. I fell. Pressed a bleeding palm against the stone; felt blood and substance drawn away, pulled deep.

"Lift him," Sahdri said to his acolytes. "He is far gone, farther than I expected. But he is not to merge yet. There is too much for him to learn; he is as yet soiled with too many things of the earth, and the gods would repudiate him."

Merge. Not me.

Only madmen did such things.

"No," I managed.

"No." Sahdri's voice was gentle as the hands of Erastu and Natha were placed upon me. "Not yet. I promise you that."

I looked into his face. It _was_ a face again. "I'm not mad."

"Of course you are," he said. "We all of us are mad. How else could we survive? How else would we be worthy?"

"Worthy?"

"To merge." He gestured to the acolytes. "Bring him to the hermitage. We shall leave him food and water and let the sickness settle."

"Sick," I murmured. I could not walk on my own. The body refused. Natha and Erastu held me up. Natha and Erastu carried me.

Sahdri said, comfortingly, "It takes us all this way."

They took me deep into stone, beyond a door. Gave me food. Water. And left me there.

I drank. Ate. Slept.

Dreamed of Del.

And freedom.

The boy crept out of the hyort. It was near dawn; he was expected to tend the goats. But he did not go to the goats. He risked a beating for it—but no, it was no risk; he would be beaten for it. Because if he failed—but no, he would not fail. He had only dreamed of triumph.

He took with him the spear shaped painstakingly out of the remains of a hyort pole. It was too short, the spear, but better than bare hands; and they permitted him nothing else save the crook to tend the goats. A crook for goats was not meant for sandtigers; even he knew that much.

Even he who had conjured the beast.

In the hyort, Sula slept on. Mother. Sister. Lover. Wife. She had made a man of him before the others could, and had kept him so that others would not use him. He was a likely boy, she told him, and others would use him. Given the opportunity. He was fortunate they had not already begun. But she was a respectable widow, and the husband, alive, had also been respected. The old shukar muttered over his magic and made comments to the others that she was foolish for taking to bed a chula when she might have a man; but Sula, laughing, had said that meant the old shukar wanted her for himself. And would not have her. The chula pleased her.

Son. Brother. Lover. Husband. He had been all of those things to her.

And now he would be a man. Now he would be free.

He had only to kill the beast.

I woke up with a start. Dimness pervaded; the only illumination was the sunlight through the slotted holes cut out of stone into sky.

I flung myself to my feet and stumbled to the stone, hung my hands into the slots, peered out upon the world.

Sky met my eyes.

None of it a dream.

All of it: real.

I turned then, slumped against the stone. In the wall opposite was a low wooden door, painted blue.

Blue as Nihko's head. Blue as Sahdri's head. Blue as the sails of Prima Rhannet's ship.

Prima. The metri. Herakleio.

Del.

All of whom thought me dead. Had seen the body bearing my scars: the handiwork of Del's jivatma; the visible reminders that the beast conjured of dreams had been real enough to mark me. To nearly kill me.

Sula had saved me. When the sandtiger's poison took hold, she made certain the chula would live.

As the chula made certain the beast would die.

Its death had bought my freedom.

What beast need I kill to buy my freedom now?

I shut my hand upon the claws strung around my throat, and squeezed. Until the tips pierced. Until the blood ran.

When Sahdri came for me, flanked by his acolytes, I showed him my palm.

"Ah," he said, and gestured the two to take me. Natha and Erastu.

I shook myself free of their hands. "No."

His tattooed brow creased. "What language is that?"

I bared teeth at him, as I had seen the sandtiger do. "The language of '*No.*'"

The brow creased more deeply. Rings glinted in slotted sunlight. "What language is that?"

"Don't you speak it?" I asked. "Don't you understand? I can understand you."

"Tongues," he said, sounding startled, even as Natha and Erastu murmured to one another. "Well, it will undoubtedly be helpful. You can read the books for us."

I stared. "Books?" This time in words he knew: Skandic. That I had not known the day before.

He gestured. "We speak many languages. But not all. There are books we cannot translate." His eyes were hungry. "What language did you speak a moment ago?"

"I don't know," I answered, because I didn't. I merely spoke. What came out, came out. I understood it all. "What do you want with books?"

"We trade for them," he said. "We are priests, not fools. Mages, not simpletons. We were born on Skandi and raised in the ways of trade. We value books, and we trade for them." Dark eyes glowed. "You can read them to us, those we cannot decipher."

I laughed at him. "I can't decipher anything. I never learned to read."

He, as were his acolytes, was astonished. "Never?"

"Maps," I conceded. Any man in the South who wishes to survive learns to read a map.

"But you have the gift of tongues," Sahdri said. "It has manifested. Undoubtedly you can read." He paused. "Now."

A new thought. It stunned me.

Rings glinted as the flesh of his face altered into a smile of immense compassion. "Did you believe it would be terrible, our magic? That all of it should be painful?"

With difficulty I said, "I saw the bones of your skull break open. I saw what lay beneath."

"Control," Sahdri soothed. "A matter of control. The gift is beautiful. The power is—transcendent."

"I don't want it." The truth.

Ring-weighted brows arched delicately. "Surely once in your life you wished for magic. For a power that would give you the aid you required. Everyone does."

Testily—because he was so cursed right—I asked, "And does everyone get what they wish for?"

"Only some of us." He gestured. Natha and Erasru laid hands upon me. "There is much for you to learn. We had best begin now."

I struggled, but could not move the hands. "Just what is it I'm supposed to be learning?"

"Who you were. Who you are." He stepped aside so the young men might escort me out of the chamber he'd called the hermitage. "Did the ikepra not tell you?"

"He told me he's not ikepra anymore."

"Ah. But he is ikepra. He will always be ikepra. He turned his back on the gods."

"Maybe," I said tightly, "he didn't want to merge."

"Then he will only die. Alone. Quite mad." He shook his head; rings glinted. "All men must die, but only we are permitted to merge. It is the only way we know ourselves worthy, and welcomed among the gods."

"That was his payment," I said. "Freedom. Wasn't it? For bringing me to you."

Sahdri offered no answer.

"He's free now, isn't he? No longer subject to your beliefs, your rules."

The priest-mage's tone was severe. "He does not believe in the necessity."

"Neither do I!"

"Most of us do not," he agreed, "when first we come here. But disbelief passes—"

"It didn't for Nihko."

"—and most of us learn to serve properly, until we merge."

Abruptly I recoiled, even restrained by strong hands. My lips drew back into a rictus. "You stink of it," I said. "It fills me up."

Sahdri studied me intently. "What do you smell?"

"Magic." The word was hurled from my mouth. "It's—alive."

"Yes," he agreed. "It lives. It grows. It dies."

"Dies?"

He reconsidered. "Wanes. Waxes anew. But we none of us may predict it. The magic is wild. It manifests differently in every man. We are made over into mages, but until the moment arrives we cannot say what we are, or what we may do."

"At all?"

His expression was kind. He glanced at the acolytes. "Natha, do you know what each moment holds?"

"I know nothing beyond the moment," the man answered.

"Erastu, do you know what faces you the next day?"

"Never," Erastu said. "Each day is born anew, and unknown."

I shook my head. "No one knows what each moment or day holds."

"This is the same."

"But magic gives you power!"

"Magic *is* power," he corrected gently. "But it is wholly unpredictable."

"Nihko can change flesh. Nihko can halt a heart."

"As can I," Sahdri said. "It takes some of us that way. It may take you that way."

"You don't know?"

"I know what I may do today, this moment," he answered. "But not what I may be able to do tomorrow."

" 'It grows,' " I quoted.

"As the infant grows," the priest-mage said gently. "On the day the child is born, no one knows what may come of it. Not its mother, who bore it. Not its father, who sired it. Certainly not the child. It simply lives every hour, every day, every year, and *becomes*."

"You're saying I'm one thing now, this moment, here before you—but may be something else tomorrow?"

"Or even before moonrise."

"And I'll never know?"

"Not from one moment to the next."

"That's madness!" I cried. "How can a man be one thing one moment, and something else the next? How can he survive? How can he live his life?"

"Here," Sahdri said, "where such things belong to the gods. Where what he is this moment, this instant, here and now, need not reflect on his next, or shape it. Where a day is not a day, a night is not a night, and a man lives his life to merge with the gods."

"I don't want to merge with anyone!"

"But you will," he told me. "You have leaped from the spire once, with no one there to suggest it, to force it, to shape your mind into the desire. Do you really think there will fail to come another day when you wish to leap again?"

"*Nihko* has no desire to leap."

"He will leap," the priest-mage said. "One day it will come upon him, and he will leap. As it will come to Natha and Erastu."

They inclined tattooed heads in silent assent. Rings in their flesh glinted.

"Then why does it matter?" I asked. "Why does it matter *where* a man lives?"

The dark eyes were steady. "A man such as we may love his child one moment, and kill it the next. It is better such a man lives here, where he may serve the gods as he learns to control his power. Where he may harm no one."

It was inconceivable. "I don't believe that. What about Nihko? Why did you let him go if you believe he will harm someone?"

"He keeps himself aboard ship. He sets no foot upon the earth of Skandi. He may harm himself, or his captain, or his crewmates— but mostly he harms the people he robs." His tone made it an insult: "He is a *renegada*."

"You're saying anyone with this magic is capable of doing anything, even something he finds abhorrent?"

Unexpectedly, tears welled in Sahdri's eyes. "Why do you think we come here?" he asked. "Why do you think we desert our families—our wives, our mothers, our children? Why do you think we never go back?"

I scowled at him. "Except to gather up a lost chick."

"That lost chick," Sahdri said plainly, "may murder the flock. May bring down such calamity as you cannot imagine." His expression was peculiar. "Because if you *do* imagine it, it will come to be."

"You're saying you come here willingly, but only after you've been driven out by the people on Skandi."

"We do not at first understand what is happening. When the magic manifests. It is others who recognize it. A wife. Perhaps a child." He gestured. "It is unpredictable, as I have said. We know only that symptoms begin occurring with greater frequency as we approach our fortieth year."

"What symptoms?"

He shrugged beneath dark robes. "Any behavior that is not customary. Visions. Acute awareness. A talent that increases for no apparent reason. Or one may imagine such things as no one has imagined before."

Such as turning the sand to grass.

Such as conjuring a living sandtiger out of dreams.

Such as knowing magic was present and so overwhelming as to make the belly rebel.

Sensitivity, Nihko had called it. When the body manifested a reaction to something it registered as too loud, too bright, too rich. *Too powerful.*

My voice rasped. "And once here, you make a decision never to go back. To stay forever. Willingly."

"Would you kiss a woman," he asked, "if you knew she would die of it?"

"But—"

"If you *knew she would die of it?*"

I stared at Sahdri, weighing his convictions. He was serious. Deadly serious.

I would not kiss a woman if I knew she would die of it. Not if I knew. How could I? How could any man?

"Know this," Sahdri said clearly. "We are sane enough to comprehend we are mad. And mad enough to welcome that comprehension—"

"*Why?*"

"Because it keeps us apart from those we may otherwise harm."

Desperation boiled over. "I'm not a priest! I don't believe in gods! I'm not of your faith!"

Sahdri said, "Faith is all that preserves us," and gestured to the acolytes.

Too much, all at once. Too bright, too loud, too painful. I ached from awareness. Trembled from comprehension.

Not to know what one might do one moment to the next.

Not to know what one was *capable* of doing.

Not to know if one could kill for wishing it, in that moment of madness.

Understood fear: Imagination made real.

It ran in my bones, the power. I felt it there. Felt it invading, infesting, infecting.

How much would I remember?

How much would I forget?

How many years did I have before I leaped from the spire?

"You will find peace," Sahdri said. "I promise you that. Only serve the gods as they deserve, and the day will come when you will be at rest."

Erastu and Natha put hands upon me. This time I let them.

Chapter 35

*T*he winch-house was built into a cave in the side of the spire, whose mouth opened to the skies. The hermitage was also a cave, but lacking a mouth: it was a stone bubble pierced on one side with slotted holes to let the light in, and closed away by a door. From these places Sahdri took me up to the top of the spire, into and through a proper dwelling built of brick and mortar and tile. So closely did the dwelling resemble the spire itself that it seemed to grow out of it, a series of angled, high-beamed rooms that perched atop the surface like a clutch of chicks, interconnected as the metri's household was.

Men filled it. Men with shaven, tattooed heads, faces aglint with rings. All seemed to be my age, or older, but none appeared to be *old*. They attended prayers, or had the ordering of the household. Some worked below in the valley, going down each day by rope net, or crude ladders, to work in the gardens, the fields, to conduct the trade that came in from foreign lands.

The crown of this spire was much wider than the one I had leaped from. There was room for the dwelling. Room for a terrace. Room for a man to walk upon the stone without fearing he might fall off.

Room for a man, standing atop it, to realize how very small he is. How utterly insignificant.

I walked to the edge and stood there with the wind in my face, stripping hair from my eyes and tangling the robes around my

body. I gazed across the lush, undulant valley with its multitude of
spires springing up from the ground like mushrooms. The valley itself was rumpled, cloaked in greenery; we were far from the sere
heat of the South, the icy snows of the North. Here there was wind,
and moisture, the tang of earth and seasalt, the brilliance of endless skies. A forest of stone, like half-made statuary stripped of intended images.

"Beauty," Sahdri said from behind. "But outside."

Distracted, I managed. "What else is there?"

"*In*side," he said. "The beauty of the spirit, when it works to
serve the gods."

I looked at the clustered spires, the inverted oubliettes. "Are
there people in all of them?"

"In and on many of them, yes. This is the *iaka*, the First House,
the dwelling of those who must learn what they are, what they are
to be. How to control the magic. How to serve the gods."

"And if one doesn't?"

"One does."

"Nihko," I said, denying it.

"Ikepra."

I sighed. "Fine. Let's say I'm ikepra, too—"

He came up beside me and shut his hand upon my wrist. "Say
nothing of the sort!"

"But I might be," I said mildly, trying with annoyance to detach
my arm, and failing. "I may make that choice."

"Do you think you are the only one who has pleaded with the
gods?" As if aware of my discomfort, he released my arm. "Those
who go home die of it."

"Die of what?"

"Of going home."

I turned to look into his face. "But Nihko is free. Alive."

Sahdri's expression was still. "The ikepra will die. He has two
years, perhaps three. But he will not stay on Skandi, and so he does
not risk harm to his people."

Because it mattered, I said, "Skandi isn't *my* home. I would go
there only so long as it took to collect Del, and leave. What risk is
there in that?"

"She believes you are dead."

I grinned. "Faced with the flesh, she might be convinced otherwise."

From stillness, Sahdri turned upon me a face of unfettered desperation. "You would risk their lives? All the folk of Skandi?"

It burst from me, was torn upon the wind. "How do you *know* I would? How can you *swear* I am a danger to them?"

His expression was anguished. Unevenly he said, "There has been tragedy of it before."

I blinked. "From ioSkandics who went back?"

Sahdri nodded, too overcome to speak.

"What happened?"

He drew in a harsh breath. "I have told you: the magic is random, the madness unpredictable. When you marry the two . . ." He gestured futility, helplessness. "And I have told you why we remain here."

I stared out across the vista with the wind in my hair, mentally making a map of the spires thrusting from valley floor to the sky. Marking their shapes, their placements. An alien land, alien people. Alien gods.

Desolation was abrupt. "I want to go *home*."

With great compassion Sahdri said, "We all of us wish to go home. The welfare of our people lies in not doing it."

Even as I shook my head I felt myself trembling. "This is not where I belong."

"You can belong nowhere else. Not now."

I swung on him. "I'm not one of you! I wasn't born here, wasn't raised here . . . I know nothing of Skandi beyond what I have learned since I came. There is nothing of Skandi *in* me—"

"Your blood," he said. "Your bone. You were bred of this place, even if you were not born here. Skandi is in you; how not? How can you believe otherwise? *You leaped from the spire, and survived.*"

"And I don't even remember why, let alone how!" I shouted it. Heard the echoes amid the spires.

Gently he said, "You will."

I turned away again, to stare fixedly at the Stone Forest. "There is only one life that matters, and I would never harm her."

"You may believe so. But you are wrong. Others have been wrong before."

"I would never hurt Del—" And then I stopped short. I *had* hurt Del. Had nearly killed Del.

"Trust me," Sahdri said, seeing my expression. "I entreat you to remain here, and I pray you will be brought to wisdom—"

I shook my head.

"Afterward," he said earnestly, "after you understand what you truly are—"

I interrupted. "Sword-dancer. There is nothing else in the world I am or wish to be."

He closed his eyes. I marveled again at the trappings of his order: ornate blue patterns tattooed into shaven skull, ring after ring piercing lips and ears, brows and nose. He glittered in the sunlight, features aglow with a haze of silver. He was not an old man, but neither was he young. Lines of character and strength of will shaped his features.

When he opened his eyes again, the darkness was rimmed with fire.

I fell back a step. Stared at him, transfixed by the expression of his face, the transcendent power in his eyes.

"Who are you?" he asked.

I swallowed. "Sword-dancer."

"Who are you?"

"Sandtiger."

"Io," he said. "Io. Who are you?"

"Sandtiger. Sword-dancer."

"Io."

"No," I said. "Not mad. Not *io*."

"Kneel."

"I'm not kneel—" And I did. Without volition. One moment I was standing, but the next I knelt. I could not connect the moments, could find no bridge between them.

Sahdri stood over me and put his hands upon me. Settled them into my hair, captured the skull with his grip. Tipped the skull up so I had no choice but to look into his face. "Who are you?"

I opened my mouth to answer: *the Sandtiger.* But the world was ripped away.

The bird drifted. Below it stretched the endless sands, the Southron desert known as Punja, alive and sentient. It moved by whim of wind, swallowing settlements, caravans, tribes. It left in its wake bones scoured free of flesh, and tumbled. Buried later, unburied later yet. Scattered scraps of bone, eaten of flesh; stripped by sand, by wind; clean of any taint of life.

No meal here; others had feasted before it. The bird flew on, winged shadow fleeing across the sands. And then it came to an oasis, a cluster of trees around a well framed in stone. Men were there, gathering. A circle was drawn in the sand. Blades were placed in the center, while two men stood at the inner rim, facing one another.

A man said "Dance," and so they did. Ran, took up swords, began the ritual so pure in its intent, so splendid in execution, that even the death was beautiful.

One man died. The other did not. He was a tall man, a big man, with dark hair bleached to bronze from the sun, skin baked to copper. His strength and quickness were legendary; he had come to be reckoned by many the best. There was another, but he was older. And they had never met to settle it since one bout within a training circle, beneath the eyes of the shodo. This man wondered which of them might win, were they to meet again.

With meticulous care, he cleaned his blade. Accepted the accolades of those who watched. As one they turned their backs on him and walked to their horses, to depart. He expected no more. He had killed one of their own.

One man threw down a leather pouch: it spilled a handful of coin into the sand. The victor did not immediately take it up but tended his sword instead, wiping it clean of blood. Or the leavings of the dance.

Not always to the death, the sword-dance. Infrequently so; ritual was often enough, and the yielding. But this dance had been declared a death-dance.

He survived. He cleaned his blade, put it back in its scabbard, slid arms into harness straps. He wore only a leather dhoti, leather harness. From the ground he took the coin, took the burnous, took the reins of his horse.

He had won. Again.

The bird circled. Winged on. Watched the man, watched the dances, watched him win. So many dances. Nothing else lived in the man but the willingness to risk himself within the confines of the circle. He was the dance.

The bird circled. Winged on. North, to mountains, to water, to winter. To a circle in the lake: the island named Staal-Ysta; to the circle on the island, drawn by Northern hands. The man in the circle, dancing. The woman who danced with him.

Pain there, and grief. Desperate regret. The wish to leave the circle . . . the capacity to stay, because it was required. Because honor demanded it.

The man and the woman danced, hating the dance, loving one another. Each of them wounded. Each of them bleeding. Each of them reeling to fall upon the ground. Each of them believing there was no better way to die than in the circle, honoring its rituals. Honoring one another.

The circle. The sword. The dance. And the man within the circle, dancing with a sword.

Dancing against the beast. Dancing for the beast.

The sandtiger he had conjured to also conjure freedom.

The bird circled. Swung back. South to the desert, southeast to the ocean, east to the island. To the Stone Forest, and the spires of the gods.

It knew. It understood. It acknowledged.

I roused to the rattle of claws, the tautness of leather thong against my throat. I meant to set my hand to the necklet, to preserve it and my throat, but I knelt upon the stone with legs and hands made part of it, encased, and I could do nothing.

A hoarse sound escaped me. Sahdri said, "Be still." And so I was.

He took the necklet from my throat. Leather rotted to dust in his hands, was carried away by wind. All that remained were claws.

One by one he tossed them into the air. Into the skies, and down.

With each he said, *"The beast is dead."*

They fell, one by one.

Were gone.

He knelt before me. Set hands into my hair, imprisoned the skull. *"The beast is dead."*

Unlocked from stone, I stood as he raised me. I was hollow, empty. A husk.

"Come inside," Sahdri said. "There are rituals to be done, and the gods await."

The bird perched upon the chair. It watched as the hair was shorn, then shaved. The flesh of the skull was paler than the body, for the Southron sun had only tantalized it, never reached it. When that flesh was smooth and clean, men gathered with dye, with needles. The patterns were elaborate, and lovely. Blood and fluid welled, was blotted away. The canvas on which they painted made no sound of complaint, of comment, of question. The pupils had grown small; the eyes saw elsewhere. The house of bone and flesh was quiescent as the spirit turned away from the world and in upon itself, to consider what it was now that the beast was dead.

When the patterns were complete, rings were set into his flesh. The lobe of each ear was pierced three times and silver rings hooked through. Three rings also were put through each eyebrow. Then the man was taken out upon the spire, was shown the wind, the world. He was made to kneel again; was blessed there by the others. Was made to lie facedown upon the stone. The arms were pulled away from his sides and placed outstretched upon the stone, palms down.

He lay in silence, rapt. Seeking the beast perhaps; but the beast was dead.

Shadow winged across the man's back. His head was blue, and bloody.

The bird circled. It watched as the fingers of the hands were spread with deft precision. Saw how the thumbs and first three fingers were sealed into stone; how the small finger on each hand was left as flesh, and free.

Two knives were brought. Two men, Natha and Erastu, priests and mages, knelt beside the man who lay upon the stone.

At Sahdri's brief nod, they cut off the smallest finger of each hand.

At Sahdri's brief nod, they lifted the severed fingers and gave them into his keeping.

He turned to the rim of the world, to the wind, invoked the blessing of the gods, and threw the fingers away.

One by one they fell.

Were gone.

The man upon the stone made no sound until Sahdri knelt beside him, put a hand upon his neck, and let it be known what had been done to him.

The man upon the stone, rousing into awareness, into comprehension, began to cry out curses upon them all.

"Be at peace," Sahdri said kindly. "The beast is dead, and you are now a living celebration of the gods."

The man upon the stone—shaven, tattooed, flesh pierced and amputated—continued to cry out curses. To scream them at Sahdri, at the brothers, at the gods.

The bird winged higher, to catch and ride the wind.

I roused into fever, into pain. And when the fever was gone, I lived with pain. The stumps were sealed, so there was no blood, but pain remained. As much was of knowledge as of physical offense.

For days I lay upon the floor of the hermitage. I was given food and water; wanted neither. But eventually I drank, though I spurned the food. And when I drank, cup held in shaking hands now lacking a finger each, I tasted blood and bitter gall.

Sahdri said they had killed the beast. The sandtiger. The animal that freed me, that gave me identity and purpose, a name. The animal I *was* in the stories of the South: the Sandtiger, shodo-trained seventh-level sword-dancer from legendary Alimat; the man who lost no dances; who had, as a boy, defeated Abbu Bensir.

I was all of those things, and none of them. I understood what was done, and why: rob a man of his past, of the ability to live in it, to continue it through present into future, and he has no choice. He becomes something else. Other.

But understanding came fitfully. There were other times it deserted me. Times when *I* deserted me, left the abused body and went into the stone, plunged my spirit into the blood and bone of it, seeking escape. It was not difficult to do. I detached from the body, and left it.

And while the spirit was housed in stone one day, men came and took up the body.

It walked with them. The flesh of the skull had healed, no longer wept blood and fluid. The scabs of the brow piercings had fallen away, so the rings shone clean and bright; the earlobes were no longer swollen. The hands still trembled, still curled themselves, still pressed themselves high against the chest, crossed as if in ward because the stumps were yet tender, but the flesh there healed as well. The body went with them out onto the spire and saw how they restrained one brother. How he fought to be free; how he cried to be released.

When all of them gathered there upon the spire beneath the vault of heaven, the brother was released. Sobbing his joy, Erastu thrust both arms up into the skies in tribute to the gods, and ran.

And leaped.

And fell.

The priest-mages of the iaka, the First House, of the Stone Forest of Meteiera on ioSkandi, sang blessings unto the gods, begging their acceptance of the newly merged spirit.

The body knelt. Was still. And the others left it there as they left the spire, went back into the dwelling still singing blessings. To gather together and worship. To conduct rites and rituals.

The body, alone atop the world, remained. And when I let the spirit flow back out of the stone and into the flesh, *I* knelt there alone atop the world.

For the first time I looked at my hands. They were—unbalanced. Out of true, lacking symmetry. Four fingers were three, and no counterbalance to the thumbs.

I had no sword. No broom handle. Not even a stick, here atop the spire. But I had two wrists.

I stretched out my left arm. Placed my right palm against it, from underneath. Both hands trembled; the spirit quailed from anticipated pain. But I closed the thumb and three fingers of my right hand around my wrist.

Imagining a hilt.

Imagining grip, and balance.

Imagining a sword.

Imagining a dance.

"You will forget," Sahdri said.

Startled, I stiffened. Gripped the wrist, and hissed against the pain.

"You will forget."

"I can't."

"The beast is dead."

"No."

"The memory survives, for now. But that, too, will die."

"No."

"You have a very strong will," Sahdri said. "Stronger than I expected. To be stripped of the beast . . . to be stripped of the means to *be* the beast within the circle—"

I snapped my head around to look at him. "You're saying *I* am the beast?"

"The sandtiger," he said, "And so you were, since the day you conjured and killed it. But it is dead, that beast. And the man who killed it, who became it, will forget what he was. He will be what he *is*."

"And what *am* I?"

"Mage," Sahdri answered.

"What?" I arched eyebrows; felt the alien weight of rings depending from flesh. "Not priest?"

"Not yet. But that will come."

"When I'm willing to 'merge' as Erastu did?"

"Oh, long before. You will understand why it is necessary, and you will accept it. Willingly."

"I will, will I? Willingly?"

"Within a year."

"So certain of me, are you?"

"Certain of the magic. The madness." Sahdri's robes whipped in the wind. "Surely you understand the need for discipline."

"Discipline!"

"The beast," Sahdri said, "learned of rules, and codes, and rituals and rites. Was circumscribed by such things, even as it was circumscribed by the circle. As it was taught by its shodo."

I stared at him as I knelt upon the stone.

"It understood that without the rules, the codes, lacking rituals and rites, it had no discipline. And without discipline, it was merely a beast. A boy." He paused. "A chula."

I flinched.

"Discipline," Sahdri said, "is necessary. Tasks, to fill the hands. Prayers, to fill the mind. Rituals and rites. All of the things we do here, how we fill our days, our nights, our minds." His eyes gazed beyond me. "To keep the madness at bay."

I sat back on my heels. *"That's* why—"

"With discipline," he said before I could finish my comment, "we may last a decade. Possibly even fifteen years, as I have. But without it . . ." He looked once more beyond me, stared into wind and sky. "Without it, we have only power without control, without purpose, and the madness that will loose it."

"Wild magic," I murmured, thinking of seeing through flesh, through bone; of seeing the heart of the stone from the inside.

"If you let it," Sahdri said, "it will consume you. Burn you up. And in the doing, you may well harm others. Magic and madness, married, is calamity, given form. It is catastrophe. But here upon the spires, with rituals and rites, *with discipline*, we keep it contained. Lest there be tragedy of it."

"Erastu killed himself."

"Erastu merged with his gods."

"But died doing it."

"A man without faith may choose to believe so."

"You're saying it would have happened anyway. Someday."

"Better it should happen here."

"But if he would have gone mad no matter where he was—"

"Here, he filled his hands with tasks. His mind with prayers, rites, rituals. He was a *disciplined* man—and thus he harmed no one."

"But himself."

"He went to his gods."

"And killed no one doing it."

Sahdri inclined his head.

In disbelief, incomprehension, I clung to one thing. "You let Nihko go. For me. In payment for me. You let *him* go."

Sahdri smiled. "Did we?"

Chapter 36

Discipline.
I learned the prayers.
Said the prayers.
Discipline.
I learned the rites.
Performed the rites.
Discipline.
I learned the rituals.
Performed the rituals.
Discipline.
I believed in no prayers, no rites, no rituals.
I acknowledged and invoked one god.
Whose name was *Discipline.*

When stubble bristled, they shaved it. Face and head. There were no claw marks now to make it difficult, lest the scarred flesh be cut. And when Sahdri saw I had learned the prayers, and said them; learned the rites, and performed them; learned the rituals, performed them, he had more holes pierced, more silver shaped, more rings set into my flesh. Two more for each brow. Two more for each ear.

Discipline.
I said nothing.

Did nothing.

Beyond what was expected.

And I forgot nothing. Beyond what was expected.

Magic, Sahdri said, was bred in my bones, knitted into flesh. Was as much a part of me as the heart that beat in my chest. No man, he said, considered the heart's task until it failed; the heart simply was. And magic was the same.

I believed in none of it. I acknowledged none of it. To do so gave power to those who wished to use it. I believed in myself. And I fell asleep each night invoking no gods, only myself. The essence of who I was, and what. Sword-dancer. Sandtiger. No more. No less.

Each night.

Discipline.

No more.

No less.

I stood atop the spire. Wind blew in my face, but it moved no hair; there was no hair to move. I waited. Feeling it. Knowing it. Hearing it in the stone.

She came. She climbed over the edge of the spire, rose, and stepped into the circle. Set both swords into the center.

Pale hair glowed in the sun. Blue eyes were ruthless.

"Dance," she commanded, in a voice of winter water.

I moved then.

Ran then.

Took up the sword.

Danced—

—and nearly died, when her blade sheared into ribs.

My eyes snapped open. I lay in my hermitage, arms and hands as always—now—tucked up against my chest. With effort I let go the tension, let the body settle. Felt the stone beneath my cheek.

The memory of steel. Of a man in the circle. Of the woman, the sword, the song.

I lay very still upon the stone, not even breathing. Tentatively I slid one hand beneath the fabric of the robe and felt the flesh of my abdomen, recalling the pain, the icy fire, the horrific weakness engendered by the wound. Touched scar tissue.

Breath rasped as I expelled it in a rush. Scar tissue, where none had been after Sahdri lifted it from me. Knurled, resculpted flesh, a rim around the crater left by the jivatma. My abdomen burned with remembered pain.

Sweat ran from me. Relief was tangible.

Magic. Power. Conjuring reality from dreams. Using it without volition even as Sahdri had warned.

But for this? Was this so bad, to find a piece of myself once taken away and make it whole again, even though this wholeness was a travesty of the flesh?

Yes. For this. For myself.

I shut my eyes. *Thank you, bascha.*

From the winch-house I took a length of wood, carried it to my hermitage. From the wall I took a piece of stone. Made it over into the shape of an adze. Then dropped it as I fell, as I curled upon the stone, and trembled terribly in the aftermath of a terrible magic.

Discipline.

When I could, I sat up and took the stone adze, took the wood, and began to work it. To shape a point of the narrowest end.

Discipline.

When the spear was made, I lay down upon the stone and gripped it, willing myself to sleep. Willing myself to dream.

—sandtiger—

At dawn the boy crept out of the hyort. He was to tend the goats, but he did not go there. He carried a spear made out of a broken hyort pole, painstakingly worked with a stone, and went instead to the tumbled pile of rocks near the oasis that had shaped itself, in falling, into a modest cave.

A lair.

He knelt there before the mouth and prayed to the gods, that they might aid him. That they might give him strength, and power, and the will to do what was necessary.

Kill the beast.

Save the tribe.

Win his freedom.

He received no answer from the gods; but gods and their power, their magic, were often random, wholly unpredictable. No man might know what or when they might speak. But he put his faith in them, put his faith in the magic of his imagination, and crept into the lair.

The sandtiger had fed only the afternoon before. It was sated, sleeping. The boy moved very carefully into the cave that was also lair, and found the beast there in the shadows, its belly full of girl-child.

He placed the tip of his spear into the throat, and thrust.

And thrust.

Bore the fury, the outrage. Withstood even the claws, envenomed and precise. One knee. One cheek. But he did not let go of the spear.

When the beast was dead, he vomited. The poison was in him. Retching, he backed his way out of the lair that reeked now of the death of the beast, its effluvia, of his own vomit.

He stood up, trembling, and made his way very carefully back to the cluster of hyorts. To the old shukar, maker of magic. And claimed he had killed the beast.

No one believed him.

But when he fell ill of the poison, Sula took him in. Sula made them go. And when they came back with the dead beast and the clawed, tooth-shattered spear she bade them cure the pelt even as she cured the chula.

When he was healed, when he could speak again despite the pain in his cheek, he asked for the sandtiger. It was brought to him. With great care, with Sula's knife, he cut each claw out of the paws, pierced them, and strung them on a thong.

It was argued that he was chula, and thus claimed no rights for killing the beast. But Sula insisted; how many men, now many women, how many children now would survive because of the chula?

Wearing nothing but the necklet, he stood before the tribe and was told to go.

Sula gave him clothing. Sula gave him food. Sula gave him water.

Sula gave him leave to go, to become a man.

I fell back in the dimness, gasping, cheek ablaze with pain. Blood dripped; I set the back of my hand against it, felt the sting of raw and weeping flesh. Then fingers, to seek. Examine.

I counted the fresh furrows. Four. Welcomed the pain, the tangible proof that I was I again. With or without magic.

I looked then at the sandtiger in its lair, where I had tracked it. Where I had killed it, so I might win my freedom.

Sahdri, in a rictus of astonishment, lay dead of a spear through the throat.

Sahdri, who had served his gods with absolute dedication, so absolute as to amputate fingers, pierce my flesh, tattoo my scalp.

To see nothing wrong in robbing a man of his past, his freedom, so his future would be built on the architecture of magic, and madness.

The shudder wracked me. I bent, cradled hands against me. Felt the heat running down my face to drip upon the stone. To trickle into my mouth.

I straightened slowly. Licked my lip and tasted blood. Tangible blood.

I welcomed the pain. And I gave myself leave to go, to become a man. Again.

Sword-dancer.

Sandtiger.

Again.

Still.

In the winch-house I weighted the net and sent it plunging downward. When it reached the bottom, I tied the winch-drum into place and took hold of the rope that spilled over the lip of stone.

I had leaped from a spire. I could surely climb down a rope.

At the bottom I released the rope. Walked four paces. Saw the world reverse before me: everything light was dark, everything dark became light. Black was white, white was black. With nothing in between.

I knelt down, shut my eyes, prayed for the fit to pass.

When I could stand again, walk again, I sought and found seven of ten claws. Gathered them up. Tied them into the hem of my robe. And walked through the Stone Forest to the edge of the island.

At the ocean I looked for boats, for ships, and found none. That they came to ioSkandi, I knew; Sahdri had said there was trade of a sort. But none was present now.

Wind beat on the waves. Weary, I knelt upon the shore, let sea spray cool my burning face. Gripped the claws through linen, counting seven of ten.

I sat down then in the sand. Waves lapped, soaked me. I didn't care. I took the claws from the hem, pulled thread from the fabric, and began to string a necklet.

When I was done, when the necklet was knotted around my throat, I sat in sand, soaked by wave and wind, and gripped the curving claws. Pain flared anew in the stumps of the missing fingers. It set me to sweating.

Abdomen. Cheek. Claws. Bit by bit, I would fit the pieces of me back together again.

Magic or no.

Madness or no.

Discipline.

Sahdri and the others made of it a religion, a new and alien zealotry I could not embrace. So I embraced what I already knew, renewed in myself *that* zealotry: the rituals and rites of Alimat. Lost myself in the patterns of the dance, the techniques of the sword. Stepped into the circle of the mind, and won.

Discipline.

I took seawrack, driftwood, a tattered piece of linen, and after four days of desperation, futility, and multitudinous curses, vows, and promises made to nonexistent gods, I finally conjured a ship.

Discipline.

A half-day and blinding headache later it sailed me into the caldera, where I saw no blue-sailed ships. No redheaded women captains. No fair-haired Northern baschas.

They believed I was dead. All of them.

Except the one who had set the trap.

I left behind seawrack, driftwood, and tattered linen. The basin-men, the molah-men, spying the shaven, tattooed head, the rings in ears and brow, fell away from me without offering their services even at exorbitant prices. Instead they shouted, called out curses, made ward-signs against magic, madness, and the ikepra.

Discipline.

I climbed the treacherous track to the top of the cliff, where basin-men, molah-men, women, wives, children, and merchants made ward-signs against the ikepra.

The ikepra, who by now was exhausted enough to want nothing better than to tumble into bedding and sleep for two tendays, ignored it all and walked.

In truth, the ikepra did more wobbling than walking, but the end result was the same: I reached Akritara. By sundown.

Simonides came out of the house to tell the ikepra to leave. Then blanched white as he truly *saw* the ikepra. "Alive!"

I wasted no time. "Where's Del?"

He swallowed, closed his eyes, stared at me again. Said, in Skandic, "Praise all the gods of the sky!"

"Where's Del?"

He set a trembling hand to the wall, as if he might fall without the support. "Gone. Both of them. They sailed."

I had expected it. Had prepared for it. But the despair was profound.

The ikepra showed none of it. Only cold control. "When?"

Simonides took his hand from the wall and gathered himself. "A threeday ago."

"At whose behest?"

His face was strained. "Mine."

He meant the metri's. "I was dead, so why extend the guest-right to unnecessary people?"

"There was no place . . ." He attempted to regain self-control, began again. "There was no place here for the renegada woman."

"Del?"

"She said—she said this was not her home. Nor yours." His expression was anguished. "She would not stay in the place that had killed you."

"Well," I said, "that's settled for the moment. Time I saw the metri."

"Wait!" His hand extended to stop me, fell away limply. "She is unwell. The shock . . ."

I offered neither diplomacy nor compassion. "Too bad."

His eyes sought my face, examined the ring-pierced brows, the tattooed patterns on my skull. Had the grace to comprehend some small measure of the shock *I* had been subjected to.

"Of course," he murmured, turning to escort me into her presence.

The metri stood in the center of an arch-roofed room, surrounded by pools of rich fabric—tunics—draped over the bed, the chair, the chest, puddled on the floor; a scattering of jewelry glinting of gold and glass in the lamplight; a handful of old flowers, dulled by years into brittle, pale, dusty semblances of what once had been bright and lively, and fresh.

As I came into the room she looked up from the flowers. Saw me. And the blooms were crumbled into dust and ash by the spasming of her fingers closing into trembling fists.

Even her lips were white. *"Alive."*

"Despite every effort to insure otherwise," I said, "and somewhat more and certainly less than I was"—I held out my hands, palms up—"but incontestably *alive*."

She was transfixed by my hands, by the evidence of mutilation. The stumps had healed, but were pink-and-purple against the tanned flesh. I have big hands, wide palms, long fingers; anyone, looking at my hands, would see at once something was missing.

Her pupils swelled to black as she stared into my face.

"A man born to the sword," I said, "is somewhat hampered by an—*injury*—such as this." I watched the flinching in her eyes. "Is this what you intended?"

She exhaled it. "I?"

In some distant, detached way, I appreciated the delicacy of her tone, the reaction honed to just the right degree of shock and denial. "Your boy," I said, "was feeling threatened. Your boy was truly afraid you might name me in his place. Your boy was on the verge of stepping outside your control. So you removed a piece from the board. A piece that had served a very important, if temporary, function, and was now viewed as unnecessary. Possibly even dangerous to the overall intent of the game." I paused. "Could you not have told him the truth from the beginning?"

The metri said, "He would not have played his part properly."

"Ah." I nodded. "And when will you teach him the rules?"

"There are none. Only an object: to win."

"Whose body was it that came in so handy?"

The tilt of her head shifted minutely. "*I* believed it was yours."

I laughed sharply, a brief blurt of sound. And in pure, unaccented, formal Skandic, the kind spoken only among the Eleven Families, I told her she was a liar.

The Stessa metri began to tremble.

"What did you think would happen?" I asked. "Did you think I would *merge*, thus removing all possibility I might return to complicate your life? Did you think I would forget everything I knew of my life before I was put atop the spire? Did you think I would be *unchanged*, and therefore not even due a momentary memory of my presence in your world?" I shook my head slowly. "I am as I always was. A sword-dancer. The Sandtiger. But with a little extra thrown into the pot. A pinch more seasoning than I had before."

Simonides, behind me, said very quietly, "Mage."

The metri met my eyes. "Mad."

"If I am either, or if I am both," I said, smiling, "perhaps you should be afraid."

The metri gazed down at her hands, still doubled into fists. Slowly she opened them, saw the crushed remains of ancient flowers. After a moment she turned her hands palm down and began to shed those remains. Dust, and bits of stem and petal. Drifting to the floor.

Tears shone in her eyes as she looked at me. "This was my daughter's room."

Tunics, jewelry, the keepsakes of a woman's life. Surrounding the woman who had borne her.

Who had banished her.

"My daughter," she said, "has been dead for forty-two years."

And I was forty.

"Go," the metri commanded.

The ikepra went.

I stepped out of the house into the courtyard, bathed in moon- and starlight, and the sword arced out of the darkness.

I caught the hilt one-handed. Hissed as pain kindled into a bonfire in that hand.

"Alive?" Herakleio stepped from shadows into moonlight. "Well then, perhaps we should remedy that." And brought his own blade up.

I thought of laughing at him. I thought of saying no. I thought of pleading fatigue. Pain. Inability to even grip the sword properly.

But all of that was what Herakleio wished to hear.

He came at me then, as I had gone at him the evening Sahdri arrived in our midst, floating atop the wall. This was no circle, no dance, no sparring, but engagement with intent. No rules, no codes, no vows, no honor.

I had meant to intimidate, because I knew the difference. Herakleio meant to take all of his anger and frustration out on me. To punish me. Put me in my place. Render me defeated.

Kill me? No. Unless he got lucky.

Of course, I had two fingers fewer than before, and all wagers were off.

I heard Simonides' blurt of shocked denial from the doorway. But Herakleio was on me, and I had no time for servants, metris, or magic. All I had was myself.

A sword.

And the dance of the mind, contained within its circle.

Discipline.

When I was done, Herakleio lay sprawled upon the courtyard tiles. He bled from a dozen cuts. His blade had been flung well out of reach against a wall, hidden by shadow; he had only himself now, winded, wounded, humiliated, and that was not enough.

Not for me. Not for himself. Possibly not for the metri.

But she had no one else.

I tossed my sword aside, so he would not see me shaking.

"We're done," I said. "I bequeath to you all of the things you believed I had taken from you, or would. I want none of them. None of you, none of her, none of this place. I am due nothing as a son or a grandson; I am neither. I am a seventh-level sword-dancer, trained by the shodo of Alimat and sworn to the rites and rituals of the circle. That is all. And that is more than ever I dreamed of."

Because all I had ever dreamed of was freedom.

And, one night, a sandtiger.

I turned from him then, and walked. Out of the courtyard. Away from the household. Down the track toward the city, the cliff, the caldera.

Simonides found me. I had collapsed at the side of the track, overtaken by pain so intense it bathed my body in sweat and set tears in my eyes; by reaction so profound I could not even manage to sit. I lay curled on my side, arms tucked in against my chest in vain attempt to ward my hands from further offense. I rocked against the soil, smelling saltwater, grapes, and blood from a bitten lip.

The hand touched my shoulder. "I have water," he said in a rusty voice.

Eventually I sat up. Let him give me water, since I dared not even hold the jar, or the cup. A rivulet ran down my chin and dripped onto the dusty linen of my robe.

"I have food," he said, "and clothing. And coin."

"Sword?" I rasped.

"No."

Ah, well. I had come without one. Why expect to leave *with* one?

"They sailed a threeday ago," he said. "The metri owns swift ships. I will pay your passage and inform the captain he is to take you wherever you wish to go. But there is only one renegada ship boasting blue sails. He will know it."

"Is this at the metri's behest?"

"It is at my behest."

In the moonlight, the slave's face was both worried and compassionate. "You're risking yourself again, Simonides."

"This is no risk."

"Or is it you think it's owed me, slave to slave?"

"Slaves," he said, and stopped. Then began again, with difficulty. "Slaves do what they must to survive. To make a life, and to find the freedom within. But there need not be dishonor in it, if there are ways to find a measure of dignity and integrity."

Dishonor lay in what one thought of himself. Not in what others believed.

I nodded. "Will this captain take orders from you?"

Solemnly he said, "I am the eyes and ears of the metri."

I drank again, nodded thanks for the aid. Stood up with effort, but got there. "So, what kind of clothing did you bring?"

The smile was slight. "What you arrived in."

In mock horror I cried, "Not the *red* clothes!"

"Well," he said, "red does suit you."

Del had said that once. Maybe she would approve of the garb when I caught up to her.

Or maybe she wouldn't notice at all.

Or maybe she'd notice, but I wouldn't be wearing them long enough to matter.

I grinned into moonlight.

I'm coming, bascha.

Chapter 37

Wearing Nihko's dreadfully red tunic and baggy trousers—and a necklet of seven sandtiger claws newly strung on leather—I hiked through waves, wet sand, dry sand, and vegetation. My head itched abominably, but I had hair again. About half the length of an eyelash.

And here I'd been complaining about needing to cut it only a matter of weeks before.

The metri's ship lay anchored behind me. The lookout had spotted a blue-sailed ship two hours before and the captain laid in a course to follow it. Prima Rhannet's vessel now was anchored on the other side of the island, near the only fresh water available; as I did not want to risk the metri's ship being taken by renegadas— not because it was hers, but because we needed it—I requested the captain to stay clear. And anyway, this was for me to do.

Although I had an idea what *Del* was trying to do.

I grinned. Shook my head. "Never work, bascha. You and the stud have worked too hard at cultivating a mutual dislike."

Of course when I finally broke through the vegetation and found them near the spring, the stud was standing with his head shoved against Del's shoulder, rubbing hard, resembling for all the world a very large brown dog. Del was attempting to stop him from rubbing, apparently in a vain effort to hug that big jug-head.

Silly bascha.

Prima Rhannet and her first mate stood very near Del.

All of them had their backs to me, except the stud. Who stopped rubbing against Del's shoulder when he noticed me, stuck his head high in the air, and snorted his alarm. Loudly, and with typically emphatic dampness.

Too bad he hadn't done that the first time Prima and her blue-headed companion mate showed up. The warning might have been useful.

"So," I called, "I guess they didn't see fit to merge you after all."

Nihko spun, even as Prima and Del. The stud snorted again, this time in disgust, and wandered off, as he was wont to do; everyone else just stood there. Gaping.

I didn't look at Del. My first hard glance as she turned had surmised she was fine, if white and wobbly with shock. But there was time for a proper reunion later. Now that I knew she was safe, and she knew I was alive—at least, I *think* she knew it was me—other business came first.

I looked at Prima and Nihko. "Surprise."

The captain's hand was plastered to her left breast where, if she had a heart, it lay beneath flesh and bone. Pounding hard enough, I hoped, fit to burst her chest.

In Skandic, Nihko told her, "There is nothing he can do to us."

In Skandic, I retorted, "Care to wager on that?"

He had the grace to color. His eyes flickered a moment, then stilled again into implacability.

"What I would like to do," I told him, "is forget all about this magic and beat you to a pulp. But maybe later." I held up my hands. "For now it'll have to wait."

I heard Del's blurt of shocked anguish. Wanted to say something, to console her, but my attention was on Nihkolara Andros.

"Did you think," I began, "that I couldn't follow the same road you did? That I would not repudiate the magic, the madness, and leave Sahdri and the others atop their rocks? *Oh*—" I paused with deliberate drama. "—and by the way, Sahdri's dead. He had a sore throat. Little matter of a spear stuck into it."

Nihko blanched to a sickly grayish pallor.

"Was he the one?" I asked with acid solicitude. "The one who found you at the foot of the spire, after you had leaped? The one who lifted you up, nourished you, led you across the threshold?" Pointedly I added, "The one who named you ikepra?"

"And you." His grin was a ghastly echo of what I had seen before. "Ikepra."

"But I've been that," I told him. "In the South, we call it borjuni. In the circle, we call it *elaii-ali-ma,* for an oath-bound man cast out of the circle forever." I shook my head, affecting pity. "Did you *really* believe a man such as that would shrink from adding one more bad name to his collection?"

"But you," he said with a brittle honesty so edged it cut, "are yet a man."

I opened my mouth to answer yes, I was, because I had seen fit not to sleep with the daughter of the Palomedi metri while I also slept with the Palomidi metri—and then I understood.

Sahdri and his brothers had cut only fingers from me.

"Stop." It was Prima Rhannet, very white of face. "Stop."

I looked at her, saw the fear in her. For Nihko.

"He did not do it," she said. "It was not Nihko's plan."

"Nor yours," I told her.

It startled her that I believed her. "The metri," she declared firmly. "The metrioi of the Eleven are capable of anything."

"No, not the metri. Not even Herakleio, though I don't doubt he wished for it."

Del spoke for the first time. Her tone was ice and steel. *"Who is left?"*

For a moment I looked over her head into the sky beyond, unable to meet her eyes. Then I did, swallowing painfully. "Simonides."

They none of them believed that answer.

" 'Slaves,' " I said, quoting him, " 'do what they must to survive. To make a life, and to find the freedom within. But there need not be dishonor in it, if there are ways to find a measure of dignity and integrity.' "

Dishonor lay in what one thought of himself. Not in what others believed.

I sighed. "He did it for her. Because he saw no other way to be true to his household. I think after sixty-odd years beneath her roof, he really perceived no choice."

"How can you say that?" Del cried. "We believed you were dead! And he let us!"

"But I'm not." I smiled crookedly. "I'm a bit more *colorful* than I was"—I brushed a hand over my tattooed, stubble-fuzzed skull—"but I'm also not dead. And he was genuinely glad of that. I think he felt there was a chance I'd survive."

Del's eyes were full of tears. *"Your fingers . . ."*

It hurt to see her anguish. Softly I said, "Let it go, bascha."

She did. Because I asked it.

I looked at Prima and her first mate. "Go. We have our own ship. We won't be needing yours."

Her chin shot up. "And are you giving the orders now?"

"Ask Nihko if I can." I let him see my eyes. "Ask."

Prima, being Prima, remained unconvinced. "Perhaps we should simply *steal* your ship, like we did before."

"You broke it, you didn't steal it." I grinned. "And certainly you may try."

Nihko put one big hand on the small woman's neck and aimed her toward the blue-sailed ship. "Go."

She was outraged. "Nihko—"

"Go."

When she had gone, he inclined his head briefly. "Young," he said, "and strong. You would have killed Sahdri anyway, eventually. The iaka would have been yours."

"I never wanted the First House," I said. "I never wanted Meteiera, Akritara, the vineyards, the ships, the slaves. All I ever wanted was to know who my people were."

"And so you know.'

I shook my head. "I'm not of Stessa blood. Skandic, undoubtedly—and *io*Skandic, so it seems—but not the metri's grandson. Her daughter was dead two years before I was born."

"The metri," he said calmly, "lies."

I smiled. "So do we all, ikepra. When it suits us."

The shift of his body was minute. He was prepared. "Shall it be now?"

I arched ring-weighted brows. "You really want to merge that badly?"

"I do not wish to merge at all."

"Then don't. You have two, possibly three years left. Go and live them." I paused. "Although it might be suggested for the sake of innocents that you find other employment."

Nihko displayed his teeth. "I am what I am, what I have made of myself. It is what I wish to be."

"Ah." I bared mine back at him in a ferocious grin. "Then that makes two of us."

He inclined his head again in brief salute, one ikepra to another, and turned to go.

"Wait."

He paused, looked back.

"How do you do it?" I asked. "How do you control it? Suppress it?"

He flicked a glance at Del briefly, then met my eyes. "With discipline," he said, "and the aid of the gods."

I laughed harshly. "And does it work?"

Nihko said, "Sometimes."

When he was gone, Del came to me. Took each hand into hers, kissed the palms with infinite care.

"There is not," I said, "that I know of, any medicinal value in that."

"Gods." She wound her arms around my neck, pressed herself against me. "Gods, Tiger—you're shaking."

"So are you, bascha."

She turned her face into my neck and began to cry.

I was a little damp myself as I carefully locked both arms around her, sealing myself against her.

After a moment, I said, "I hate these clothes."

She laughed, pressed herself harder against me. "Red suits you."

"I kind of thought you might prefer me without them. You know. *Out* of them."

Her breath was warm against my throat. "You are being terribly unsubtle."

"Subtlety has never been one of my great gifts, bascha. As you have said yourself."

Del slid to her knees. Untied the drawstring of the baggy trousers. Tugged them away. They fell into a heap at my feet.

"So," she said, "is this to be just for you?"

"I wanted you to see I still had all of my working parts." I paused, turning my palms into the light. "Well. Most of them."

And then I bent down, knelt, and took her into my arms.

Epilogue

*L*ater, as we lay in warm sand beside the rock-rimmed pool, Del amused herself by tracing the tattoos on my head. At first it tickled. Then I decided it felt rather good.

Idly she asked, "Will you keep your head shaved?"

I grunted drowsily, sprawled belly-down in blissful abandon with eyes closed. "Not likely."

"It isn't *un*attractive."

She had said something similar about Nihko, months before. Sternly I said, "It also isn't me."

Her fingers stroked. "It is now. Unless you think you can take them off, these tattoos."

I thought of Sahdri, lifting the scars from my body. "No," I said, suppressing a shiver. "I think I'll just let the hair grow back."

"Are you sure you want me to cut those rings out of your eyebrows?"

"I am."

"It will hurt."

I grunted again.

"Maybe you could leave the ones in your ears."

I opened my eyes, frowned thoughtfully, rolled over onto my back. "Are you saying you *like* me like this?"

Del, looking down on me, smiled winsomely. "I like you any way I can get you."

I thought about it. "All right," I said finally. "We'll leave one ring each in my ears—"

"Two."

I scowled. "Two. Just for you." I fixed her with a firm stare. "And that's *all*."

She nodded, tracing patterns on my head again. "Such a pretty blue," she said. "Except for here." Her hand stopped just behind my left ear.

"Why? What's different about there?"

"You have a little smeary bubble here"—she tapped it—"like spilled wine."

I sat bolt upright.

Del blinked at me. "It's only a birthmark, Tiger. And once your hair grows back out, it will be hidden. I never saw it before."

I swore. Lay back down. Thought about it.

"Tiger—?"

Then I began to laugh.

"Tiger, what is it?"

I hooked an elbow over my eyes to blot out the sun. "Nihko said it."

"Nihko said what?"

"That the metri lies."

"Yes," Del agreed emphatically. "She said you were dead."

I was thinking of other things. Of caresses called keraka, formed of any size or shape. Found anywhere on the body. A Stessa-born body. "Well, I'm not dead."

Not yet.

Her hand moved down my abdomen. Closed. "I can tell."

I tried not to flinch. "Be careful with that."

"I rather think—not."

I thought about the implications of *that* a moment. "All right." I sat up, hooked an arm around her, pulled her down on top of me.

Afterward, Del asked, "What do you want to do?"

"Go home."

A delicate pause. "Where is home?"

"Where it's always been. The South."

"But—you said if you ever went back there—"

I interrupted. "I know what I said. I don't care. It's home. And it doesn't matter if there's a price on my head, or if borjuni and sword-dancers come hunting me—"

Her turn to interrupt. "Abbu Bensir?"

I hitched a shoulder. "Him, too. Let 'em all come."

After a moment she asked, "Why?"

We lay on our sides. I scooped an arm beneath Del and dragged her closer, fitting my body to hers, ankles entwined. I set my lips against cornsilk hair. "Because," I said, "it's time I built my home of something more than walls of air. I want brick, stone, wood, tile. I want *substance*."

"What kind of substance?"

"Alimat."

Del stiffened. "I thought you said Alimat was destroyed years ago in a monstrous sandstorm."

"So it was, most of it. But the bones are there. I'll rebuild it."

"Will they let you?"

"Who?"

"Abbu. The others."

"That will be settled in the circle. And once I'm done settling things, the students will come."

Astonishment was profound. *"Students?"*

"I taught Herakleio, didn't I?"

"Yes, but—you?"

"Why not?"

"You've always been so . . . independent."

"Well, maybe it's time I accepted responsibility." I pondered that a moment. "*Some* responsibility."

Del snickered politely. "And how long do you think this will last?"

"Ten years," I said evenly. "Maybe twelve. Fifteen if I'm lucky."

She poked me with an elbow. "Be serious, Tiger. You?"

I wanted to smile, but didn't. "Trust me, bascha, I have never been more serious in my life."

She closed a hand over one of mine, carefully avoiding the sensitive stump. Her voice was rusty. "Can you?"

"Oh, yes. It will take time—I have to learn new grips, new balance, new techniques and maneuvers; strengthen my wrists and remaining fingers—but yes. I can." I smiled. "It's called discipline."

"And until then?"

I knew she was thinking of Abbu. "Until then," I whispered into her ear, "you'll just have to protect me."

The stud, grazing contentedly on a patch of nearby grass, snorted.

I glanced across at him. "She can, you know. She's better than I am."

This time it was Del's turn to snort, albeit with more delicacy.

"Well," I conceded, "sometimes. Some days, some moments, some particular movements. Other times, not."

Del laughed softly. "That about sums it up."

"And speaking of particular movements . . ."

In mock disbelief, she asked, "What—*again?*"

I grinned. Then the grin fell away. I pulled her very tightly against me, held her there. Set my face into her hair. Told her I loved her.

In uplander, downlander, Northern, Southron, Desert, and every tongue in between. All the tongues of the world.

It took a long time.

But Del did not complain.

Geography

*T*he model for "Skandi" is a Greek island called Santorini (from "Saint Irene.") Originally named Thera, Santorini was a large round island until approximately 1500 BC, when catastrophe struck in the form of a massive volcanic eruption. (It is believed Thera and its destruction may be the historical foundation for the stories of Atlantis.) Though the residents of Thera had enough warning to flee, thereby not becoming memorialized in lava and ash the way the victims of Vesuvius were, most of the island exploded. Chunks of what had been arable land collapsed and sank to the bottom of the ocean, leaving only the rim of the island above the waterline. Akrotiri, one of the settlements buried by the eruption, was discovered in 1967 by Greek archeologist Spyros Marinates. Excavations continue to this day, peeling back the layers of an advanced civilization that may have been a direct offshoot of Minoan culture. The "living islands" described briefly in the novel are still-steaming portions of the volcanic cone visible in the center of the water-filled crater.

Geographically speaking, Santorini and its primary city, Fira (perched atop and built into the cliff), is as I have described it, even to the switchback donkey rides up and down the face of the caldera (which is especially interesting when one is lugging along a case of Boutari wine) and the grapevine "wreaths" grown against the ground. However, it should be noted that I have freely adapted elements to suit my story, and if anyone visits Santorini subsequent to reading this novel it should be noted that the most significant threat to them lies not in wading through molah muck, winehouses, dark alleys, or being tossed off the cliff to merge with the gods, but in surviving winding streets full of jewelry shops catering to tourists.

The model for Meteiera, the "Stone Forest," is an extended cluster of startlingly dramatic rock formations in Thessaly. Collectively called Meteora ("in the air"), the massive spires form a complex of monasteries, retreats, and cells built atop the crowns, and the home of traditional Orthodox monasticism founded in the eleventh century. (It is also the birthplace and home of Asclepius, classical antiquity's first and finest physician.) The crowns of the spires were originally accessed by rope and wooden ladders, scaffolding, and nets attached to winches; today the monasteries, with drivable roads to several of them, continue to function as retreats for contemplation and worship.

Sword-Sworn

In 1998, I finished a historical novel just at the end of the year. My next task was to begin this one. I took a couple of months off to recharge the batteries and planned to get started in early '99.

But that March, my mother was diagnosed with cancer. As the only child of a long-divorced woman, I became primary caregiver; within ten days of the diagnosis, I became executor.

Some authors work through their grief. But I found myself caught in the midst of a tremendous sea-change: my mother, dead; plus the responsibilities of packing up, closing down, and preparing for market the house I grew up in, while also doing the same with my own home as I prepared to move to another locale along with ten dogs and three cats. Frankly, writing a book became incidental.

Life has settled down now. I have returned to writing full time. But I must pay tribute to my mother, who was the classic "guiding force" behind my love of books; who read to me nightly as I fell asleep; who critiqued my early attempts at fiction; who never once failed to support my efforts; who took such joy in my publication. From the time I was fourteen and writing my first novel until a few days before she died, she encouraged me always to chase my dreams.

Mom, you never got to read the most recent of my works.
But I know you are a part of those books,
as you will be a part of everything I write.
God speed.

Prologue

The sand was very fine and very pale, like Del's hair. As her skin had been once; but first the Southron sun, followed by that of the sea voyage and its salt-laden wind—and our visit to the isle of Skandi—had collaborated insidiously to gild her to a delicate creamy peach. She was still too fair, too Northern, to withstand the concerted glare of this sun for any length of time without burning bright red, but definitely not as fair as she'd been when we first met.

Oh. That's right. I was talking about the sand.

Anyway, it was very fine, and very pale, and I had worked carefully to smooth it with a good-sized peeling of the skinny, tall, frond- and beard-bedecked palm tree overlooking the beach, the ocean beyond, the ship I'd hired in Skandi—and then I had ruined all that meticulous smoothness by drawing in it.

A circle.

A *circle*.

I had thought never to enter one again.

But I smoothed the sand, and I drew the circle, and then I stepped across the line into the center. The center *precisely*.

Thunder did not crash. Rain did not fall. Lightning did not split the sky asunder. The gods, if any truly existed, either didn't care that I had once again entered a circle, or else they were off gallivanting around someone else's patch of the world.

"Hah," I muttered, indulging myself with a smirk.

"Hah, what?" she asked, from somewhere behind me.

I didn't turn. "I have done the undoable."

"Ah."

"And nothing has smited me."

"Smitten."

"Nothing has *smitten* me."

"Yet."

Now I did turn. She stood hipshot in the sand, with legs reaching all the way up to her neck. They were mostly bare, those legs; she habitually wore, when circumstances did not prohibit, a sleeveless, high-necked leather tunic that hit her about mid-thigh. In the South she also wore a loose burnous over the leather tunic, so as to shield her flesh from the bite of the sun, but we were not in the South. We were on an island cooled by balmy ocean breezes, and she had left off most of such mundane accoutrements as clothing that covered her body.

I did say she had legs up to her neck. Don't let that suggest there wasn't a body in between. Oh, yes. There was.

"Lo, I am smitten," I announced in tones of vast masculine appreciation.

Once she might have hit me, or come up with a devastating reprimand. But she knew I was joking. Well, not entirely—I *do* appreciate every supple, sinuous inch of her—but that appreciation has been tempered by her, well, *temper,* out of unmitigated lust into mere gentlemanly admiration.

Mostly.

Del arched one pale brow. "Are you practicing languages and their tenses?"

"What?"

"Smite, smote, smitten."

I grinned at her. "I don't need to practice. I speak them all now."

The arch in the brow flattened. Del still wasn't sure how to take jokes about my new status. Hoolies, joking about it was all I *could* do, since I didn't understand much about the new status myself.

Del decided to ignore it. "So. A circle."

I felt that was entirely self-evident and thus regarded her in fulsomely patient silence.

Her expression was carefully blanked. "And you're *in* it."

I nodded gravely. "So is my sword."

Now she was startled. "Sword?"

I hefted it illustatively.

"That's a *stick*, Tiger."

I clicked my tongue against the roof of my mouth. "And here you've been telling me for years I have no imagination." I pointed with said stick. "Go get yourself one. I put a few over there, by that pile of rocks."

Both brows shot up toward her hairline. "You want to spar?"

"I do."

"I thought—" But she broke it off sharply. Then had the grace to blush.

Delilah blushing is not anything approaching ordinary. I was delighted, even though the reason for it was not particularly complimentary. "What, you thought I was lying to you, or giving in to wishful thinking? Maybe fooling myself altogether about developing new skills and moves?"

She did not look away—Del avoids no truths, even the hard ones—but neither did the blush recede.

I shook my head. "I thought you understood what all the weeks of physical training have been about."

"Recovery," she said. "Getting fit."

"I have recovered, and I am fit."

She did not demur; it was true. "But you did all that without a circle."

So I had. And then some. Though I had yet to sort out how I had managed it. A man entering his fourth decade cannot begin to compete with the man in his second. But even my knees of late had given up complaining.

Maybe it was the ocean air.

Or not.

It was the *"or not"* that made me nervous.

Clearing my throat, I declared, "I will dance my own dances, Del."

"But—" Again she silenced herself.

But. A very heavy word, that "but," freighted with all manner of innuendo and implication.

But.

But, she wanted to ask, how does a man properly grip a sword when he's missing the little fingers on both hands? *But,* how does he keep that grip if a blade strikes his? *But,* how can he hope to overcome an opponent in the circle? How can he win the dance? How can he, who carries a price on his head, win back his life in the ritualized combat of the South, when he has been cast out of it by his own volition? When the loss of the fingers precludes all former skill?

But.

I saw the assumption in her eyes, the slight flicker of concern.

"I have every intention of dancing," I said quietly, "and none at all of dying." For as long as possible.

"*Can* you?" she asked, frank at last.

"Dance? Yes. Win? Well, we've never properly settled that question, have we? Some days you'll win, other days I will." I shrugged. How many of those days I had left was open to interpretation. "As for the others I'll dance with . . . well, we'll just have to wait and see."

"Tiger—"

In the distance, the stud neighed ringingly. I blessed him for his timing, though he wouldn't have much luck finding the mare he wanted. "Get the 'sword,' Del."

She held her ground. "If I win this dance, will you stop?"

"If you win this dance, I'll just have to practice harder."

"Then you still mean to go back to the South."

"I told you that. Yes." I studied her. "What, did you think I meant to live out my life here on this benighted island?" Which had, nonetheless, saved our lives in more ways than one.

"I don't know." Her tone was a mixture of frustration, annoyance, and helplessness. "I have no inkling as to what you will or will not do, Tiger. You're not predictable anymore."

Anymore. Which implied that once I had been.

I bared my teeth at her. "Well, good. Then I'm not boring."

Once again I waved my stick. "The sooner we get to it, the sooner we'll know."

Her expression suggested she already knew. Or thought she did.

"Not predictable," I reminded her. "Your own words, too."

Del turned on her heel and stalked over to the tree limbs I'd groomed into smooth shafts. There was no point, no edge, no crosspiece, no grip, no proper pommel. They were not swords. They were sticks. But whichever one she chose would do.

"Hurry up," I said. "We're burning daylight, bascha."

The world, through glass, is magnified. Small made large. Unseen made visible. Dreams, bound by ungovernable temperaments and unpredictabilities, may do the same, altering one's vision. One's comprehension. The known made unknowable.

Grains of sand, slightly displaced. Gently jostled one against another. Gathered. Tumbled. Herded.

I blink. The world draws back. Large is made small; immense becomes insignificant. And I see what moves the sand.

Not water. Not wind.

Blood.

First, they rape her. Then slash open her throat. Twice, possibly thrice. The bones of her spine, left naked to the day in the ruin of her flesh, gleam whitely in the sun.

Blood flows. Gathers sand. Makes mud of malnourished dust. Is transformed by the sun into nothingness.

Even blood, in the desert, cannot withstand the ceaseless heat.

It will take longer for the body, for flesh and bone are not so easily consumed. But the desert will win. Its victories are boundless.

They might have left her alive, to die of thirst. It was their mercy to kill her swiftly. Their laughter was her dirge. Their jest was to leave a sword within reach, but she lacked the strength to use it against herself.

As the sun sucks her dry, withering flesh on bone, she turns her head upon the sand and looks at me out of eyes I recognize.

"Take up the sword," she says.

I jerk, gasping out of sleep into trembling wakefulness, tasting sand in my mouth. Salt. And blood.

"It's time," she says.

Her breath, her death, is mine.

"Find me," she says, "and take up the sword."

Del felt me spasm into actual wakefulness. She turned toward me and sleepily inquired, "What is it?"

I offered no answer. I couldn't.

"Tiger?" She propped herself up on an elbow. "What is it?"

I stared up at the dark skies. Something was in me, something demanding I answer. I felt very distant. I felt very small. "It's time." Echoing the dream.

"Time?"

The words left my mouth without conscious volition. "To go home." *To go home. To take up the sword.*

After a moment she asked, "Are you all right? You don't sound like yourself."

I didn't *feel* like myself.

She placed a hand upon my chest, feeling my heart beat. "Tiger?"

"I just—I know. It's time." No more than that. It seemed sufficient.

Find me.

"Are you sure?"

Take up the sword.

"I'm sure."

"All right." She lay down again. "Then we'll go."

I could feel her tension. She didn't think it was a good idea. But that didn't matter. What mattered is that it was time.

Chapter 1

Having sailed at last from the island, we now were bound for Haziz, the South's port city. We had departed it months before, heading for Skandi; but that voyage was finished. Now we embarked on an even more dangerous journey: returning to the South, where I carried a death sentence on my head.

Meanwhile, Del and I passed the time by sparring. She didn't win the matches. Neither did I. The point wasn't to win, but to retrain my body and mind. Tension was in me, tension to do better, do more, *be* better.

"You're holding back," I accused, accustomed now—again—to the creak of wood and rigging, the crack of canvas.

Del opened her mouth to refute that; holding back in the circle was a thing she never did. But she shut her mouth and contemplated me, though her expression suggested she was weighing herself every bit as much.

"Well?" I challenged, planting bare feet more firmly against wood planking.

"Maybe," she said at length.

"If you truly believe I'm incapable—"

"I didn't say that!"

"—then you should simply knock me out of the circle." We didn't really have a proper circle, because the captain had vociferously objected to me carving one into his deck, but our minds knew where the boundaries lay.

Del, who had set one end of the stick against the deck, now made it into a cane and leaned upon it idly with the free hand perched on her hip and elbow outthrust. "I don't think anyone could knock you out of the circle even if you were missing two *hands*."

Not a pretty picture. "Thanks." I grimaced. "I think."

Blue eyes opened wide. "That's a compliment!"

I supposed it was.

Now those eyes narrowed. "You *are* using a different grip."

"I said I would." I'd also said I'd have to. Circumstances demanded it.

She unbent and put out the arm. Her tone was brusque, commanding. "Close on my wrist."

I clamped one big hand around her wrist, feeling the knob of bone on the left side, the pronounced tendons on the underside. A strong woman, was Delilah.

Her pale brows knit. "There is a difference in the pressure."

"Of course there is." I was not altogether unhappy to be holding her wrist. "I have *three* fingers and a thumb, not four."

"Your grip will be weaker, here." She touched the outside edge of my palm. Nothing was wrong with that part of my hand. There simply wasn't a little finger extending from it any more. "If the sword grip turns in your hand, or is forced back at an angle toward the side of your hand . . ."

"I'll lose leverage. Control. Yes, I know that."

She was frowning now. She let her own stick fall to the deck. She studied my hand in earnest, taking it into both of hers. She had seen it before, of course; seen them both, and the knurled pinkish scar tissue covering the nub of severed bone. Del was not squeamish; she had patched me up numerous times, as well as herself. She regretted the loss of those fingers—hoolies, so did I!—but she did not quail from their lack. This time, in a methodical and matter-of-fact examination that did not lend itself to innuendo or implication, she studied every inch of my hand. She felt flesh, tendon, the narrow bones beneath both. I have big hands, wide hands, and the heels of them are callused hard with horn.

"What?" I asked finally, when she continued to frown.

"The scars," she said. "They're gone."

I have four deep grooves carved in my cheek, and a crater in the flesh over the ribs of my left side. I raised dubious brows.

"On your *hands,*" Del clarified. "All the nicks are gone. And this knuckle here—" She tapped it. "—used to be knobbier than the others. It's not anymore."

I suppose I might have made some vulgar comment about Del's intimate knowledge of my body, but didn't. There was more at stake just now than verbal foreplay.

I had all manner of nicks and seams and divots in my body. We both did. Mine were from a childhood of slavery, an enforced visit to the mines of a Southron tanzeer by the name of Aladar, and the natural progression of lengthy—and dangerous—sword-dancer training and equally dangerous dances for real. The latter had marred Del in certain characteristic ways, too; she bore her own significant scar on her abdomen as a reminder of a dance years ago in the North, when we both nearly died, as well as various other blade-born blemishes.

I had spent weeks getting used to the stubs of the two missing fingers, though there were times I could have sworn I retained a full complement. Beyond that, I had paid no attention to either hand other than working very hard to strengthen them, as well as my wrists and forearms. It was the interior that mattered, not the exterior. The muscles, the strength, that controlled the hands and thus the grip. Not the exterior scars.

But Del was right. The knuckle, once permanently enlarged, looked of a size with the others again. And the nicks and blemishes I'd earned in forty years were gone. Even the discolored pits from working Aladar's mine had disappeared.

Wholly focused on retraining myself, I had not even noticed. I pulled the hand away, scowling blackly.

"It's not a *bad* thing," Del observed, though a trifle warily.

"Skandi," I muttered. "Meteiera." I looked harder at my hands. "Did they work some magic on you?"

I transferred the scowl from hand to woman. "No, they didn't work any magic on me. They cut my fingers off!" Not to mention shaving and tattooing my skull and piercing my ears and eyebrows with silver rings. Most of the rings were gone now, thanks to Del's careful removal, though at her behest I had retained two in each earlobe. Don't ask me why. Del said she liked them.

"You do look younger." Her tone was carefully measured.

Ironic, to look younger when one's lifespan has been shortened.

"Of course, maybe it's the hair," Del suggested. "You look very different with it so short."

"Longer than it was." I rubbed a hand over my head; and so it was, all of possibly two inches now, temporarily lying close against my skull, though I expected the annoying wave to start showing up any day. Del had said the blue tattoos were invisible, save for a slight rim along the hairline. But that would be hidden, too, once my hair grew out all the way.

"I don't mean you look like a *boy*," she clarified. "You look like you. Just—less used."

Hoolies, *that* sounded good. "Define for me 'less used.' "

"By the sun." She shrugged. "By life."

"That wouldn't be wishful thinking, would it?"

Del blinked. "What?"

"There are fifteen-plus years between us, after all. Maybe if I didn't look so much older—"

"Oh, Tiger, don't be ridiculous! I've told you I don't care about that."

I dropped into a squat. The knees didn't pop. I bounced up again. Still no complaints.

Del frowned. "What was that about?"

"Feeling younger." I grinned crookedly. "Or maybe it's just *my* wishful thinking."

Del bent and picked up her stick. "Then let's go again."

"What, you want to try and wear down the old man? Make him yield on the basis of sheer exhaustion?"

"You never yield to exhaustion," she pointed out, "in anything you do."

"I yielded to your point of view about women having worth in other areas besides bed."

"Because I was *right*."

As usual, with us, the banter covered more intense emotions. I didn't really blame Del for being concerned. Here we were on our way back to the South, where I had been born and lost; where I had been raised a slave; where I had eventually found my calling as a sword-dancer, hired to fight battles for other men as a means of settling disputes—but also where I had eventually voluntarily cut myself off from all the rites, rituals, and honor of the Alimat-trained sword-dancer's closely prescribed system.

I had done it in a way some might describe as cowardly, but at the time it was the right choice. The only choice. I'd made it without thinking twice about it, because I didn't have to; I knew very well what the cost would be. I was an outcast now, a blade without a name. I had declared *elaii-ali-ma*, rejecting my status as a seventh-level sword-dancer, which meant I was fair game to any honor-bound sword-dancer who wanted to challenge me.

Of course, that challenge wouldn't necessarily come in a circle, where victory is not achieved by killing your opponent—well, usually; there are always exceptions—but by simply winning. By being better.

For years I had been better than everyone else in the South, though a few held out for Abbu Bensir (including Abbu Bensir), but I couldn't claim that any longer. I wasn't a sword-dancer. I was just a man a lot of other men wanted to kill.

And Del figured it would be a whole lot easier to kill me now than before.

She was probably right, too.

So here I was aboard a ship bound for the South, going home, accompanied by a stubborn stud-horse and an equally stubborn woman, sailing toward what more romantic types, privy to my dream, might describe as my destiny. Me, I just knew it was time, dream or no dream. We'd gone off chasing some cockamamie idea of me being Skandic, a child of an island two week's sail from the South, but that was done now. I *was*, by all appearances—literally as well as figuratively—Skandic, a child of that island, but things hadn't worked out. Sure, it was the stuff of fantasy to discover I was the long-lost grandson of the island's wealthiest, most powerful matriarch, but this fantasy didn't have a happy ending. It had cost me two fingers, for starters. And nearly erased altogether the man known as the Sandtiger without even killing him.

Meteiera. The Stone Forest. Where Skandic men with a surfeit of magics so vast that much was mostly undiscovered, cloistered themselves upon tall stone spires ostensibly to serve the gods but also, they claimed, to protect their loved ones by turning away from them. Because the magic that made them powerful also made them mad.

Now, anyone who knows me will say I don't—or didn't—think much of magic. In fact, I don't—didn't—really believe in it. But I'll admit *some*thing strange was going on in Meteiera, because I had cause to know. I can't swear the priest-mages worked magic on me, as Del suggested, but once there I wasn't precisely me anymore. And I witnessed too many strange things.

Hoolies, I *did* strange things.

I shied away from that like a spooked horse. But the knowledge, the awareness, crept back. Despite all the outward physical changes, there were plenty of interior ones as well. A comprehension of power, something like the first faint pang of hunger, or the initial itch of desire. In fact, it was *very* like desire—because that power wanted desperately to be wielded.

I shivered. If Del had asked what the problem was, I'd have told her it was a bit chill in the morning, and after all I was wearing only a leather dhoti for ease of movement as I went through the repetitive rituals that honed the body and mind. But it wasn't the chill of morning that kindled the response. It was the awareness again of the battle I faced. Or, more accurately, battles.

And none of them had anything to do with sword-dancing, or even sword fighting. Only with refusing to become what I'd been told, on Meteiera, I must become: a mage.

Actually, they'd said I was to become a *priest*-mage, but I'm even less inclined to put faith in, well, *faith*, than in the existence of magic.

And, of course, it was becoming harder to deny the existence of magic since I had managed to work some. And even harder to deny my own willingness to work it; I had *tried* to work it. Purposely. I had a vague recollection that those first days after escaping the Stone Forest were filled with desperation, and a desperate man undertakes many strange things to achieve certain goals. My goal had been vital: to get back to Skandi and find Del, and to settle things permanently with the metri, my grandmother.

I got back to Skandi by boat, which is certainly not a remarkable thing when attempting to reach an island. Except the boat hadn't existed before I made it exist, conjured of seawrack and something more I'd learned on Meteiera.

Discipline.

Magic is merely the tool. Discipline is the power.

Now I stood at the rail staring across the ocean, knowing that everything I'd ever been in my life was turned inside out. Upside down. Every which way you can think of.

Take up the sword.

I lived with and for the sword. I didn't understand why I needed to be told. No; commanded.

"You're still you," Del said, with such explicit firmness that I realized she was worried that *I* was worried, not knowing my thoughts had gone elsewhere.

I smiled out at the seaspray.

"You are." She came up beside me. She had washed her hair in the small amount of fresh water the captain allowed for such ablutions, and now the breeze dried it. The mix of salt, spray, and sun had bleached her blonder. Strands were lifted away from her face, streaming back across her shoulders.

I have been less in my life, dependent on circumstances. But now, indisputably, I was more.

I was, I had been told, messiah. Now mage. I had believed neither, claiming—and knowing—I was merely a man. It was enough. It was all I had wanted to be, in the years of slavery when I was chula, not boy. Slave, not human.

I glanced at Del, still smiling. "Keep saying that, bascha."

"You *are*."

"No," I said, "I'm not. And you know it as well as I do."

Her face went blank.

"Nice try," I told her, "but I read you too well, now."

Del look straight at me, shirking nothing. "And I, now, can read nothing at all of you."

There. It was said. Admitted aloud, one to the other.

"Still me," I said, "but different."

Del was never coquettish or coy. Nor was she now. She put her hand on my arm. "Then come below," she said simply, "and show me *how* different."

Ah, yes. That was still the same.

Grinning, I went.

When we finally disembarked in Haziz, I did not kiss the ground. That would have entailed my kneeling down in the midst of a typically busy day on the choked docks, risking being flattened by a dray-cart, wagon, or someone hauling bales and none too happy to find a large, kneeling man in his way, and coming into somewhat intimate contact with the liquid, lumpy, squishy, and aromatic effluvia of a complement of species and varieties of animals so vast I did not care to count.

Suffice it to say I was relieved to once more plant both sandaled feet upon the Southron ground, even though that ground felt more like ship than earth. The adjustment from flirtatious deck to solidity always took me a day or two.

Just as it would take me time to sort out the commingled aromas I found so disconcertingly evident after months away. Whew!

"They don't need to challenge you," Del observed from beside me with delicate distaste. "They could just leave you here and let the *stench* kill you."

With haughty asperity, I said, "You are speaking about my homeland."

"And now that we are back here among people who would as soon kill you as give you greeting," she continued. "What is our next move?"

It was considerably warmer here than on Skandi, though it lacked the searing heat of high summer. I glanced briefly at the sun, sliding downward from its zenith. "The essentials," I replied. "A drink. Food. A place to stay the night. A horse for you." The stud would be off-loaded and taken to a livery I trusted, where he could get his earth-legs back. I'd paid well for the service, though the sailhand likely wouldn't think it enough once the stud tried to kick his head off. Another reason to let the first temper tantrum involve someone other than me. "Swords—"

"Good," Del said firmly.

"And tomorrow we'll head out for Julah."

"Julah? Why? That's where Sabra nearly had the killing of us both." Unspoken was the knowledge that not far from Julah, at the palace inherited from her father, Sabra had forced me to declare myself an outcast from my trade. To reject the honor codes of an Alimat-trained seventh-level sword-dancer.

"Because," I explained. "I'd like to have a brief discussion with my old friend Fouad."

" 'Discussion,' " she echoed, and I knew it was a question.

"With words, not blades."

"Fouad's the one who betrayed you to Sabra and nearly got you killed."

"Which calls for at least a few friendly words, don't you think?"

Del had attempted to fall in beside me as I wended my way through narrow, dust-floured streets clogged with vendors hawking cheap wares to new arrivals and washing hung out to dry from the upper storeys of close-built, mud-brick dwellings stacked one upon the other in slumping disarray, boasting sun-faded, once-brilliant awnings; but as she didn't know Haziz at all, it was difficult for her to stay there when I followed a route unfamiliar to her. She settled for being one step behind my left shoulder, trying to anticipate my direction. "Words? That's all?"

"It's a starting point." I scooped up a melon from the top of a piled display. The melon-seller's aggrieved shout followed us. I grinned, hearing familiar Southron oaths—from a mouth other than my own—for the first time in months.

Del picked her way over a prodigious pile of danjac manure, lightly seasoned with urine. "Are you going to pay for that?"

Around the first juicy, delicious mouthful I shaped, "Welcome-home present." And tried not to dribble down the front of my Skandic silks. Still noticeably crimson, unfortunately.

"And I've been thinking . . ."

Hoolies, I'd been *dreaming*.

And I regretted bringing it up.

"Yes?" she prompted.

"Maybe . . ."

"Yes?"

The words came into my mouth, surprising me as well as her. "Maybe we'll go get my true sword."

"True sword?"

I twisted adroitly as a gang of shrieking children ran by, raising a dun-tinted wake of acrid dust. "You know. Out there. In the desert. Under a pile of rocks."

Del stopped dead. "*That* sword? You mean to go get *that* sword?"

I turned, paused, and gravely offered her the remains of the melon, creamy green in the dying sun. I could not think of a way to explain about the dream. "It seems—appropriate."

She was not interested in the melon. " 'Appropriate'?" Del shook her head. "Only you would want to go dig up a sword buried under tons of rock, when there are undoubtedly plenty of them here in this city. *Un*buried."

Again the answer was in my mouth. "But I didn't make those swords."

Which conjured between us the memories of the North, and Staal-Ysta, and the dance that had nearly killed us. Not to mention a small matter of Del breaking, in my name, for my life, the sword that *she* had made while singing songs of vengeance. Boreal was dead, in the way of broken *jivatmas* and their ended songs. Samiel was not.

And something in me wanted him. Needed him.

Del said nothing. Nothing at all. But she didn't have to. In her stunned silence was a multitude of words.

I tossed the melon toward a wall. It splatted, dappled outer skin breaking, then slid down to crown a malodorous trash heap tumbling halfway into the street. "We'll stay the night, buy some serviceable swords and harness, then go to Julah, to Fouad's." I said quietly. "A small matter of a debt between friends."

And the much larger matter of survival.

Chapter 2

el was a little leery about the two of us striding around Haziz, instantly recognizable to any sword-dancers who'd seen us before. I tried explaining that Haziz wasn't all that popular with sword-dancers, who generally kept themselves to the interior, and that I didn't precisely look the way I used to, thanks to my sojurn at Meteiera, but Del observed that even with short hair, earrings, the tracery of tattoos at my hairline, and no sandtiger necklet, I was still a good head taller than most Southron men, decidedly bigger and heavier, still had the clawmarks in my face—and who else traveled with a Northern sword-singer? A *female* Northern sword-singer?

Whereupon I pointed out we could split up while in Haziz.

Del, tying on her high-laced sandals as she perched on the edge of the bed—we'd spent the night in a somewhat squalid dockside inn, albeit in the largest room—lifted dubious brows. "And who then would protect you?"

"Protect me against what?"

"Sword-dancers."

"I already told you there's not likely to be any here."

"*We're* here."

"Well, yes, but—"

"And you already admitted you needed my protection."

I was astounded. "When was *that?*"

"On the island." Now she slipped on the other sandal. "Don't you remember? You were talking about starting a new school at Alimat. I was talking about Abbu."

Come to think if it, I did vaguely recall some casual comment. "Oh. That."

"Yes. That." She laced on the sandal, tied it off, stood. "Well?"

"That was pillow talk, bascha."

"We didn't have any pillows. We had sand."

"I'm fitter than I've been in months. Leaner. Quicker. You've sparred with me. You know."

Del cocked her head assessingly, pointedly not observing that I also lacked two fingers. "Yes."

"So, you don't need to protect me."

"Are you prepared to meet Abbu Bensir?"

"Here? Now?"

"What if he *is* here? Now?"

I gifted her with my finest, fiercest sandtiger's glare. "So, you want me to hide up here in this pisshole while you go hunting a swordsmith in a town you don't know?"

She was not impressed by the glare. "You don't know it much better. And I can ask directions."

"A lone woman? In the South? Looking for a swordsmith?"

Del opened her mouth, then closed it.

"Yes," I said. "We're in the *South* again." Which was very different from the North, where women had more freedom, and very much different from Skandi, where women ran things altogether.

"I could," she said, but there wasn't much challenge in it. Del was stubborn, but she understood reality. Even when it wasn't fair. (Once upon a time she ignored reality, but time—and, dare I admit it, my influence—had changed her.)

"Tell you what, bascha. I'll compromise."

With excess drama, *"You?"*

I ignored that. "We'll send a boy out to the best swordsmith in Haziz and have him come here."

Del considered. "Fair enough."

"And after that," I said, wincing, "I'll have to pay a visit to the stud."

"Ah, yes," she agreed, nodding. "Maybe he'll save the sword-dancers some trouble and kill you himself."

"Well, since you're so all-fired ready to protect me, why don't you ride him first?"

Del scowled. Grinning, I exited the room to scare up a likely boy to run the message summoning a swordsmith.

The swordsmith's two servants delivered several bulky wrapped bundles to our room as well as a selection of harnesses, swordbelts, and sheaths. Then they bowed themselves out to permit their employer to conduct business. That employer was an older man in black robes and turban, gray of hair and beard but hardly frail because of it. Anyone who spends years pounding metal to fold it multitudinous times trains his body into fitness. A different kind from mine, perhaps, because of different needs, but age had not weakened him. Nor his assessment of customers.

After formal pleasantries that included small cups of astringent tea, he had me stand before him, then looked at me and saw everything Del had described earlier, cataloging details. All of them mattered in such things as selecting a weapon. Most tall men had long legs but short to medium torsos; shorter men gained what height they had in a long torso. I, on the other hand, was balanced. My height came from neither, but from both. I had discovered that in Skandi mine was the normal build. Here in the South, it was not. Southroners were shorter, more slender but wiry, very quick, and markedly agile.

Fortunately, I had been gifted with speed despite my size, and superior strength. Both had served me well.

Now the old man examined me to see what kind of sword would serve me well.

After a moment he smiled. He lacked two teeth. Without a word he turned, knelt, and set aside four of the bundles. He pulled out a fifth bundle I hadn't noticed, much narrower than the others and more tightly wrapped, and began to undo knots.

Del, seated on the bed, exchanged a glance with me, eyebrows raised. I shrugged, as baffled.

The swordsmith glanced up, saw it as he began to unwrap the

bundle. A spark of amusement leaped in dark eyes. In a Southron dialect I hadn't heard in well over a year, he said, "It is a waste of time to display my best to undiscerning customers. Then, I begin with the lesser weapons."

"And I'm a discerning one?"

Tufted brows jerked upward into the shadow of the turban. "With a body so carved and cut by blades? Yet still breathing?" He grinned again. "Oh, yes." He opened wrappings reverently, folding back the fabric with great care. Steel glinted like ivory ice in meager, sallow sunlight slanting through narrow windows chopped into mudbrick. He rose and gestured. "Do me the favor of showing me your hands."

Mutely, I put them out. Saw the abrupt widening of his eyes, the startled glance into my face. That he wanted to speak of such things as missing fingers was obvious; that to do so would offend a discerning customer was equally obvious and went against his training as tradesman as well as artisan. After a moment he took my hands into his and began to inspect them, measuring breadth of palm, length of fingers, feeling calluses. He took great care not to so much as brush the stubs.

Then, quietly, he bent, took up a sword, set it into my hands, bowed. And stepped away even as Del moved back on the narrow bed, giving me room to move, to lend life to the sword as I tested its quality.

It took me no longer to judge the blade than it took the swordsmith to judge me. He had selected the one he believed was most appropriate. And indeed it was, in every important way. It was more than adequate—for a temporary weapon.

But then, that was all I required, until I found Samiel.

The swordsmith's expression was a curious blend of surprise and reconsideration. Though he had correctly surmised I knew how to handle a blade—or had, at one time—it was clear he had been dubious because of the missing fingers. The stumps were still pinkish; anyone familiar with wounds, particularly amputation, would recognize that the loss of the fingers was relatively recent. He paid me tribute by displaying his best to me, but he clearly expected less of me in the handling of the weapon.

Unfortunately, testing a blade and going against another sword-dancer were two very different things.

"It will do," I said, after complimenting him on his art. "What is your price? I will need a sheath and harness as well."

He named an outrageous amount. I praised his skill, the product, but politely refused and offered less. He praised my obvious expertise, my experience, but politely declined my counter. So went the bargaining until both of us were satisfied.

His eyes glinted briefly. He knelt again and began to rewrap the bundle of his best.

"Wait." When he glanced up, I indicated Del.

At first he did not understand.

"A sword," I explained, "for the lady."

It was fortunate he spoke a dialect Del did not, or she very likely would have tested one of the blades on him. As it was she knew by his tone, his expression, by the stiffness in his body, what he said. She was a woman. Women did not use swords.

"This one does." I said. And then, grateful Del didn't understand, "Indulge me."

That, he would accept: that a man might be foolish enough, or lust-bound enough, to woo a woman by seemingly giving into her fantasies, however ludicrous they might be. It lessened me in his eyes, but so long as it resulted in the desired end, I didn't care. For this insult to his person, his skill, his Southron sensibilities, he would vastly overcharge, and I would vastly overpay, but Del would have her blade.

She rose from the bed and stood before him in creamy pale leather tunic, legs and arms bare, a plaited rope of fair hair fallen forward over one breast. He shut his eyes a moment, muttered a prayer, and asked to see her hands. As he touched them, his own shook.

Del shot me a look over his bent head. "Since you're the jhihadi," she said pointedly, "why don't you start changing the Southron male's perception of Southron women as inferior beings?"

I grinned. "I suspect some things are impossible even for the jhihadi."

"Changing sand to grass is very dramatic," Del observed, "especially for a desert climate, but changing women to humans in Southron eyes—*male* Southron eyes—would be far more proof of this jhihadi's omnipotence."

This jhihadi knew better than to travel that road. He smiled blandly and did not reply.

"Coward," she muttered.

Finished with his assessment, the swordsmith dropped Del's hands with alacrity and turned away from her. With skilled economy he selected a sword, rose with it, then gazed upon it with obvious regret. His beautiful handiwork, intended for a man, would belong to a worthless woman merely playing at men's games.

We needed the sword. Carefully avoiding Del's eyes, I told the swordsmith, in his dialect, "When she's done playing with it in a week or so, I'll sell it back to you. At a reduced price, of course, because of its taint."

That seemed satisfactory. He placed the sword in Del's hands, then moved back to the farthest corner of the room, pressing himself into it. Knowing what she would do to test the weight, balance, response, I moved only so far as I had to. The swordsmith stared at me out of astonished eyes.

I grinned. "Indulge me."

Del danced. It was a brief but beautiful ritual, the dance against an invisible opponent, intended only to allow one to establish a rapport with one's weapon, to let the hands come to an understanding of the fit of the hilt, how the pommel affected balance, how the blade cut the air. It lasted moments only, but enough time for him to realize what he was witnessing.

Impossibility.

Del stopped moving. Flipped the braid behind her shoulder. Nodded.

The swordsmith drew in a rasping breath. He named a price. Knowing there was no room for bargaining under the circumstances, I accepted. Paid. Saw him to the door.

Del's voice rose behind us. In clear Southron, albeit not his dialect, she said, "I will not dishonor your art."

His eyes flickered. Then his face closed up. With his back to us both, he said fiercely, "Tell no one that sword is mine."

I shut the door behind him, then turned to look at Del. She had sheathed the sword and buckled on the harness, testing the fit. It would require adjustment, but wasn't bad. "Happy now?"

She smiled languorously. "With a sword in my hand again, I can indulge even pigs like him."

"Then indulge *me*, won't you? Let's visit the stud together." I grabbed up my own new harness, slid the sword home. "I may need you to pick up the pieces."

The stud was, predictably, full of piss and vinegar. I sighed as the horse-boy led him out of the livery, recognizing the look in the one rolling eye I could see. The pinning of ears, the hard swish of tail, a peculiar stiff readiness in body indicated the stud had an opinion and was prepared to express it.

I didn't really blame him. He'd been cooped up on a ship, nearly drowned in a shipwreck, deserted on an island, refound, then stuck aboard a ship again. Someone had to pay.

I sighed. "Not here in the street," I told the boy. "Someplace where no innocent bystanders might be injured."

He bobbed his black-haired head and led the way through a narrow alley between the livery and another building to a modest stableyard. The earth had been beaten into a fine dust, and the muckers had already shoveled and swept the yard. At least when I came off, I wouldn't land in manure.

Del, following, raised her voice over the thunking of the stud's hooves. "Shall I send boys out to invite wagering?"

The tone was innocent. The intent was not. Del and I had indeed managed to make some money here and there with wagers on who would win the battle—but that was when the stud was well ridden, and I was more likely to stick. Del knew as well as I that this battle would be worse than usual.

"The only wager here is how soon I come off," I said glumly as the boy slipped the reins over the stud's dark-brown neck. Ordinarily his mane was clipped close to his neck, but time on the island had allowed it to grow out. Now it stood straight up in a black hedge the length of my palm. I ran a hand through my own hedge. "I have a sneaking suspicion this is going to be painful."

In deference to the Southron sun if not Southron proprieties, Del had donned a striped gauze burnous before exiting the inn. Now she arranged herself against a whitewashed adobe wall, arms crossed, one leg crooked up so the toe of the sandal was hooked into a rough spot. The thin, hand-smeared slick coating was crumbling away to display the rough, hand-formed block of grass-and-mud brick beneath.

She smiled sunnily. "It won't be painful if you stay on."

Despite my desire to discuss things with the stud in private, an audience was already beginning to straggle in. Horse-boys, muckers, even a couple of bowlegged, whip-thin men I suspected were horse-breakers. All watched with rapt attention, murmuring to one another in anticipation. It felt rather like a sword-dance, except no circle was in sight. Merely an open-air square, surrounded on three sides by stable blocks and on the fourth by the solid wall of an adjoining building. With a horse as my opponent.

"Don't embarrass me," Del said. "I still need to buy myself a mount, remember?"

"I'll sell you this one cheap."

Her smile was mild. "You're burning daylight, Tiger."

Muttering curses, I stripped out of harness and sword, left them sitting on a bench near Del, and strode across to the stud.

Groundwork was called for, a chance to settle him to some degree before I even mounted by circling him around me at the end of a long rein, by handling head and mouth, by singing his praises in a soothing tone of voice. Actually, it's the tone of voice that counts; I often called him every vulgar name I could think of, but he was never offended because I did it sweetly.

However, I'd had the stud long enough to know groundwork was ineffective. It never seemed to change his mind when he was in the mood for dramatics. Certainly not on the island, when I'd mounted him after months away. *That* had been a battle.

And now another loomed.

There isn't much to a Southron saddle to begin with, and this one was borrowed from the livery since all of my tack had been lost when the ship sank under me on the way to Skandi. Supremely simple, it was merely an abbreviated platform of leather with the swelling humps of pommel and cantle front and back atop a couple of blankets, a cinch around the horse's barrel to hold the saddle on, stirrup leathers no wider than a man's belt, and roundish stirrups carved out of wood.

Almost simultaneously I took the woven cotton reins from the boy, grabbed handfuls of overgrown mane, and swung up into the saddle with a burst of nervous agility that put me right where I needed to be, even without benefit of stirrups. I'd done that purposely. It was a shortcut into the saddle and gave me an extra instant to set myself before the stud realized I'd beaten him to the punch.

I wore soft Skandic boots instead of sandals, the latter not being particularly helpful atop a recalcitrant horse, and the crimson silks bestowed weeks before on the island. Waiting back at the room was more appropriate Southron garb, but I'd opted to try the stud in clothing I could afford to have ruined. In the whitewashed stable yard, beneath the Southron sun, I must have glowed like a blood-slicked lantern as I eased boots into the stirrups.

Then the stud blew up, and I didn't have time for imagery.

Unless he falls over backward—on purpose or not—riding a rearing horse is not particularly difficult. It's a matter of reflexes and balance. Which is not to say a rearing horse can't do damage even if you survive the dramatics; if you're caught unaware, there is the very real possibility that the horse's head or neck will collide with your face. Trust me, the nose and teeth lose when this happens. And I'm not talking about the horse's.

A bucking horse is tougher to ride, because unless the horse gets into a predictable rhythm, which then becomes a matter of timing to ride out, a jolting, jouncing, twisting and repetitive rear elevation can not only hurl you over the horse's head and eventually into the ground, but can also shorten your spine by a good three inches. And turn your neck into a noodle.

Then, of course, there are the horses that can contort themselves into a posture known as "breaking in two," where they suddenly become hinged in the middle of their spines, drop head and butt so that the body forms an inverted V, and proceed to levitate across the ground in abrupt, stiff-legged, impressively vertical bounds.

Naturally, *my* horse was supremely talented. He could rear, buck, and break in two practically simultaneously.

The stud is not a particularly tall horse. Southron mounts aren't, for the most part. But he was all tight-knit, compact, rock-hard muscle, which is usually tougher to ride than a big, rawboned animal, and, being a stallion, he packed on extra heft. He was broad in the butt, round in the barrel, wide in the chest, and had the typically heavy stallion neck, crest, and jaw. It made it much more difficult for me to get any leverage with his mouth and head.

Which he delighted in demonstrating.

After I dragged myself out of the dirt for the fourth time, I noted a subtle change in the stud's posture. The tail no longer swished hard enough to lash eyeballs out of a skull. Ears no longer pinned back swiveled freely in all directions. He swung his head to peer at me quizzically through dangling forelock, examined me (maybe looking for blood?), then shook very hard from head to toe as if to say he was done with his morning warmup, and nosed again at the dirt in idle unconcern.

I slapped dust out of silks. Pulled the tunic into such order as was possible when seams are torn. Made certain the drawstring of my baggy Skandic trousers was still knotted. Managed to stand up straight and stride across to the stud. He stood quietly enough. I mounted, settled myself in the saddle, walked him out enough to know he was done with the battle.

Applause, whistles, and cheering rang out. Coin changed hands as wagers were paid off. But I knew better than to count it a victory, no matter what the crowd believed. The stud had merely gotten bored.

I dismounted and walked back over to Del with said stud in tow, supressing a limp. Her expression was sublimely noncommital.

In a pinched voice, I said, "Remember how just the other day I said I felt younger?"

Del raised brows.

"Add about two hundred years to the total."

One of the horse-boys came up, offering to strip down the stud and walk him. It was a warm day and all the excitement and exertion had resulted in sweat and lather. He needed cooling. *I* needed cooling. I wanted water, ale, and a bath. In that particular order.

Oh, and a new spine.

But of course under the eyes of the audience, many of whom had wandered in from the street when they heard the commotion, I stood straight and tall, saluted them, and strolled casually toward the alleyway leading to the street, pausing only to ask Del if she were coming, since she showed no signs of it.

"And stop laughing," I admonished.

"I'm not laughing. I'm smiling."

"You're laughing *inside*."

"My insides are mine," she observed, "to do with as I please."

"Are you coming?"

"I'll stay here and buy a horse, I think. And tack for both mounts. I'll meet you back at the inn."

I opened my mouth to oppose Del's foray into shopping without my presence, then thought better of it. She was a woman, and it was the South, but Del had proved many times over that only the rare man got the better of her.

That rare man being me, of course.

I gathered up harness and sword and took myself off to the inn. And ale. And a hot bath.

Chapter 3

*F**lesh has turned to leather beneath the merciless sun. Eye sockets*
are scoured clean. Teeth shine in an ivory rictus. Wind, sand, and
time have stripped away the clothing. She wears bone, now, little more,
scrubbed to match the Punja's crystalline pallor. Modesty lies in rills of sand
blown in drifts across her torso—

I woke up with a start as Del came into the room, creaking the
door. Completely disoriented from the dream fragment, I stared at
her blankly, slowly piecing back awareness, the recognition that I
was still in the half-cask I'd ordered brought up and filled with hot
water. That the water had cooled. That there was a real possibility
I might never move again.

Del's expression was quizzical as she shut the door. Her arms
were full of bundles. "I can think of more comfortable places to
sleep—and positions to sleep *in.*"

With care I pulled myself upright, spine scraping against rough
wood. In an hour or so I might manage to stand. Scowling, I asked
if she'd spent every last coin we claimed.

Del was piling bundles on the bed. "Supplies," she replied
crisply. "I assume we're leaving tomorrow, yes?"

I rearranged stiff legs with effort and hauled myself dripping
out of the cask, swearing under my breath. "Yes."

Del tossed me the length of thin fabric doubling as a towel, examined my expression and movements, then frowned. "Your hands are hurting."

"Yes." I wrapped the cloth around my waist.

"Tiger—"

"Leave it, Del. I just banged them around on the stud, that's all." I bent, carefully grasped the jar of ale I'd set on the floor beside the cask, and upended the remaining contents into my mouth.

She clearly wanted to say more, but did not. Instead she turned back to the bed and began sorting through bundles. "Food," she announced, "suitable for travel. New botas; we can fill them in the morning. Medicaments. Blankets for bedding. A griddle. Flint and steel." There was more, but she left off anouncing everything.

"What about a mount for you, and tack?"

"Arranged. We can collect the stud and my horse first thing tomorrow morning."

"Do we have any money left?"

"Not much," she admitted. "Refitting is costly."

I could not get the memory of the dream fragment out of my mind. I turned away from Del and dropped the towel, rooting around in my belongings for fresh dhoti and burnous. I was done with Skandic clothing. I was in the South again. Home.

Where the dead woman was.

Del held out a small leathern flask. "Liniment," she said. "One of the horse-breakers gave it to me. He said it would help."

I tied the thongs on my dhoti. "I think the stud got the better end of the deal. I'm not sure he needs any help."

"He didn't mean it for the stud."

Ah. Trust a horse-breaker to know. And Delilah.

Sighing, I surrendered pride and annoyance and limped to the bed. "Be gentle, bascha. The old man is sore."

"It will be worse tomorrow."

I closed my eyes as she began to work aromatic liquid into my shoulders. "Thank you for that helpful reminder."

"There's a bota of aqivi in the supplies. For the road."

My eyes flew open. "You packed aqivi?"

"Only for medicinal purposes, of course."

I smiled and let my eyes drift shut again. Del herself was the best medicine a man could know.

She lifts an arm. Beckons. Demands my attention. When I give it, understanding, acceding to that demand, I see that the fragile bones of her hands have begun to fall away. A thumb and three fingers remain. The fourth, the smallest, is missing.

The jaw opens then. A feathering of sand pours between dentition. Shadowed sockets beseech me.

"Come home," she says.

"I am home," I say. "I have come home."

But it is not, apparently, what the woman wants. The hand ceases its gesture. The bones drop away, collapsing into fragments. Are scattered on the sand.

"Take up the sword," her voice says, before the wind subborns it as well.

I opened my eyes. Square-cut window invited moonlight. Illumination formed a tangible bar of light slicing diagonally across the bed. Del's hair glowed with the sheen of pearls. Her breathing was even, uninterrupted; though neither of us slept deeply in strange places, we had grown accustomed to one another's movements and departures.

Were the dreams my heritage from Meteiera? Would I spend my life viewing the remains of a dead woman in my sleep? Was I doomed to hear her voice issuing nightly from a broken mouth?

Or was there something I was to do, some task to undertake that I didn't yet understand?

I was too restless, too disturbed to sleep. Carefully I peeled back the threadbare blanket, warding tender stumps from rough cloth, and slipped from the bed, trying not to permit the ropes to creak. Trying not to groan about the stiffness of my body. The liniment had helped, but time and movement were the only true cures.

I halted three steps away from the bed, brought up short by a sense of—*something*. Something in the room. Something in the darkness. Something in the moonlight.

Something in me?

I lifted my face. Closed my eyes. Saliva ran into my mouth. Flesh prickled on my bones. Thumbs and six fingers splayed.

Something was *here*. Begging for recognition.

It sang in my body. The mantra of the mages.

Discipline.

Nihkolara, blue-headed mage of Meteiera—and apparent relative—had told me denying the magic was impossible. That to do so was to invite the madness, to commit self-murder.

I had no inclination to do either.

They had tried to steal my name, the priest-mages, and my knowledge of self, there atop the stony spires. Very nearly had succeeded. But something in me, something more insistent than burgeoning power, despite its insidious seduction, had given me the strength to throw off the infection. At least, enough that I retained my name, rediscovered knowledge of self.

I am Sandtiger.

I am sword-dancer.

More than enough, for me. I needed nothing more.

Even if I had it.

Sweat filmed my body. Soreness remained, bruises had bloomed. But such petty things as discomfort are bearable when weighed against the greater needs of the world.

Or the dictates of magic.

I took up the new sword. In the midst of the moonlight, with eloquent precision, I began yet again to dance, to hone the flesh that sheathed the bones. And the mind that controlled them.

So that I could control *it*.

I was, as expected, still stiff in the morning, though the midnight dance had helped. Del and I dressed respectively in tunic and dhoti, donned sandals, gauze burnouses, and buckled on harnesses over the clothing. Once we'd merely split the left shoulder seams to allow sword hilts freedom, but that was when challenges were to dance, not to die. Now we didn't have that luxury. We packed up the balance of our belongings and headed out to the livery to collect and tack out our mounts, grabbing something to eat from a vendor along the way.

The stud, when led out into the stableyard square in the kindling sun of early morning, gifted me with a sublimely serene expression suggesting he was nothing but a big, sleepy pussycat. Though one of the horse-boys offered, I saddled him myself to give my body the chance to get used to movement. I took my time examining the fit of new tack, including bridle, bit, long cotton reins knotted at each end, and of course the saddle. Satisfied, I loaded my share of the supplies, checked the weight distribution, tossed a colorful woven blanket over the new saddle, and turned to see what progress Del was making.

"What is *that?*" I blurted.

She glanced up from assessing stirrup length. "I think he's reminiscent of you after a particularly drunken cantina fight." She paused. "A little pale, with two black eyes."

A little pale? He was *white*. And she didn't mean his actual eyes were black, because they weren't, but the two circles painted around them. The actual eyes were blue, and looked even lighter peering out from black patches.

"Why in hoolies did you pick *him?*"

"Beggars," she declared succinctly, "cannot be choosers."

Well, no. But . . . "A white, blue-eyed horse in the desert?" Actually, he was a *pink*-and-white, blue-eyed horse, because he lacked pigmentation. His nostrils and lips were a fine, pale pink.

"That is why I've put grease around his eyes," she explained. "It will cut down on the sun's glare reflecting off his face. And I slathered alla paste on his nose and lips."

"Del, this is a *horse*, not a woman painting her face."

"Yes," she agreed equably, continuing to tack out the gelding.

"Do you know what you're doing?"

"Yes."

"Are you *sure?* We've got the Punja to get through."

"I had a white dog when I was a child," Del remarked casually after a moment. "He had blue eyes and no pigmentation. My father wanted to put him down, but I insisted he be mine. I was told that with the sun reflecting off the snow, he might in time go blind. So I mixed up grease with charcoal, and painted around his eyes. He lived to be an old, old dog. And he never went blind."

"Is that why you bought this horse? Because he reminds you of your dog?"

"I bought him because he was the only gelding." She glanced up. "Would you want to risk another stallion anywhere near yours?"

"There are mares."

"I tried that before. Your horse, as I recall, spent most of his time trying to breed her. Sometimes when I was on her."

I recalled that, too. "There are other liveries in town, I suspect. With other geldings."

"But not with one we can afford. I did look." Del reached up and tied something onto the left side of the gelding's headstall, then ran it beneath his forelock to the other side.

My mouth dropped open. *"Tassels?"*

"Fringe," she corrected.

"You're putting fringe on a *horse?*"

"It will help shade his eyes."

First she painted black patches around his eyes, now she hung fringe across his brow. Gold fringe, no less.

I shook my head in disbelief. "Where in hoolies did you find that?"

"I bought it from a wine-girl in one of the cantinas. I don't know what it once was. I was afraid to ask."

"You went into a cantina by yourself?"

"Yes."

"Kind of risky, bascha. Dangerous, even."

"Tiger, I was in a cantina by myself when I met you."

"Well, I *said* it could be dangerous."

Del slipped a foot into the left stirrup and swung up, settling herself into the blanketed saddle with ease. "Now, do you want to spend all morning arguing about horses, or shall we actually ride them?"

It was ridiculous. We were bound for the Punja and all its merciless miseries, including unceasing sun. Del herself certainly knew the risks; she had once been so sunburned I was afraid she'd never recover. A blue-eyed, white horse lacking pigmentation was a burden we couldn't afford.

But Del was right: neither could we afford something better. I suspected we had only a few coins left from Del's shopping expedition. If we didn't take the gelding, we asked the stud to carry two across the searing Punja, or we'd have to take turns riding and walking, which was slower going yet. Besides, if the gelding dropped dead on us from sunstroke, we could always eat him.

On that cheerful note, I mounted the uncommonly cooperative stud, winced at the creaking of my body, and began the careful process of relaxing complaining muscles fiber by fiber. Eventually my body remembered how it was supposed to sit a horse, and some of the soreness bled away. The stumps of my missing fingers were still a trifle tender, but once the stud hit his pace and settled, it wouldn't take more than index and middle fingers to grasp the soft cotton reins.

Del, mounted atop her white folly, leaned down to hand the horse-boy a few copper coins. Likely our last. I sighed, turned the stud, and aimed him out of the stableyard into the narrow alley between livery and adjoining building. He sucked himself up into stiff condescension as the gelding came up beside him, snorting pointed disdain. Then he caught a glimpse of one sad blue eye peering at him out of a circle of black greasepaint coupled with dangling gold fringe and shied sideways toward the nearest wall.

I planted a heel into his ribs, driving him off the wall before my foot could collide with adobe brick. "Let's not."

The stud took my hint and kept off the wall. Now he turned sideways, head bent back around so he could keep both worried eyes on Del's gelding. Ears stabbed toward the white horse like daggers. The accompanying snort was loud enough to drown out the sound of hooves.

Del began to laugh.

"What?" I asked irritably, trying to point the stud back into a straight line as we exchanged alley for street.

"I think he's afraid of him!"

"A lot of horses are afraid of the stud—"

"No! I mean the stud's afraid of *my* horse!"

"Now, bascha, do you really think—" But I broke off because the stud, now freed of the confines of the narrow alley, took three lunging steps sideways into the center of the street and stopped dead, stiff-legged, snorting wetly and loudly through widened nostrils. Fortunately it was early enough that the street was not yet crowded, and no one was in his way.

Del was still laughing.

"Maybe you should have gotten a mare after all," I muttered. "Look, bascha, just go ahead. I'll bring up the rear."

Grinning, she took my advice. The stud eased after a moment, ears flicking forward as Del departed. "What, you like the view from behind better?" I asked him. "Fine. Can we go now?"

And indeed we might have gone beyond the first two strides, except someone stopped dead in front of us. On foot. It was either ride over the top of him, or halt yet again.

I reined in sharply, swearing, and looked down upon the interruption. A young man in an russet-gold burnous, a Southroner, with smooth dark skin, longish dark hair, strong but striking features, and the kind of liquid, thick-lashed, honey-brown eyes that can melt a woman's heart. It might have been happenstance that he stepped in front of the stud, impeding my way, except that one hand was on a rein, holding the stud in place—and the other held a sheathed sword.

"You are the Sandtiger," he declared, raising his voice. Plainly he wanted an audience.

I might have denied his opening salvo in the interests of saving time, except I'd nearly lost myself in Meteiera and would never hide from my name again. I merely stared down at him.

Expressive eyes challenged me. "Will you dance? Will you step into the circle?"

I opened my mouth to explain I couldn't dance, not the way he so clearly wanted, with a circle drawn in sand and all the honor codes. Instead I said, "Not today," and jammed heels into the stud's ribs.

Startled, he jumped forward. The young man, equally startled, lost his grip on the rein. With agile alacrity he leaped aside so as not to be ridden over, and I heard his fading curses as I struck a crisp long-trot to the end of the street.

Del waited there atop her quiet gelding. The stud took one look at him, considered spooking again, but was convinced otherwise when I cracked the long reins across his broad rump. There was no further dissent as Del fell in beside us.

"So," she said calmly, "the secret of your return is out."

"Yes and no."

She frowned. "Why do you say that?"

"He isn't a sword-dancer. Just a kid trying to make a reputation."

"How do you know?"

"He invited me to dance. A sword-dancer won't. They all know what *elaii-ali-ma* means: that there is no dance, no circle, merely a fight to the death. There's a huge difference."

"And every sword-dancer in the South will know this?"

"Everyone sworn to the honor codes, yes."

"But he recognized you."

"That," I said, "is likely more a result of the swordsmith spreading gossip."

"You think *he* recognized you?"

"Probably not. As I said, Haziz isn't a place many sword-dancers go, unless specifically hired. But as you pointed out before, we don't exactly fit in with the rest of the crowd. All it would take is a description, and anyone who'd seen or heard about us would know."

"So. It begins."

"It begins." I glanced sideways at the long equine face with its black-painted eye circles, the wine girl's dangling golden fringe—I wondered briefly if Del had told her what she intended to do with it—and mournful blue eyes. "That horse is a disgrace to his kind."

Del put up her brows. "Just because your horse is afraid of him is no cause to insult him."

"He looks ridiculous!"

"No more than yours did when he stood rooted to the ground, trembling like a leaf."

Probably not. Scowling, I said, "Let's go, bascha. It's a long ride to Julah—"

"—and we're burning daylight."

Well. We were.

Del and I stopped burning daylight when the sun went down. Then it lost itself in its own conflagration, a panoply of color so vivid as to nearly blind you. Desert orange, blazing red, yellow, vermillion, raisin purple, lavender, the faint burnished shadow of blue fading to silver-gilt. Out here twilight dies gently, shading slowly into darkness.

We were beyond the last oasis between Haziz and Julah, so there was no place in particular we wanted to bed down. We ended up settling for a series of conjoined hummocks carpeted in a fibrous, red-throated groundcover bearing tiny white blossoms, and the threadbare shelter of a thin grove of low, scrubby trees boasting a bouquet of woody limbs bearing dusty green leaves. Within weeks the leaves would dry out, curl up, and drop off, when summer seared them to death, but for now there was yet enough moisture in the mornings for the leaves to remain turgid. Mixed in with the groundcover were taller-growing desert grasses with frizzy, curled topknots.

"This'll do," I said, reining in even as Del dismounted.

Since the stud was not always trustworthy when picketed close to other horses, I led him to a tree eight paces away and had a brief discussion about staying put as I hobbled him. Del and I busied ourselves with untacking and grooming both mounts, swapping out bridles and bits for halters, pouring water into the squashable, flat-bottomed oiled canvas bags doubling as buckets, and offering them grain as a complement to the grasses. It wasn't particularly good grazing, but it would do; and the next night we'd be in Julah where they'd eat well.

Our dinner consisted of dried cumfa meat, purple-skinned tubers, and flat, tough-crusted journey-bread. Del drank water, I had a few mouthfuls of aqivi from the goatskin bota. Sated, we sprawled loose-limbed on our bedrolls and digested, blinking sleepily up into the deeping sky as the first stars kindled to life.

"That," Del observed after a moment, "was one huge sigh."

I hadn't noticed.

"Of contentment," she added.

I considered it. Maybe so. For all there were risks attendant to returning South, it was home. I'd been North with Del once, learning what real forests were, and true mountains, and even snow; had sailed to Skandi and met my grandmother on a wind-bathed, temperate island in the midst of brilliant azure seas, but it was here I was most at ease. Out in the desert beneath the open skies with nothing on the horizon but more horizon. Where a man owed nothing to no one, unless he wished to owe it.

Unless he was a slave.

Del lay very close. She set her head and one shoulder against mine, hooking ankle over ankle. And I recalled that I was man, not child; free, not slave. That'd I'd been neither child nor chula for years.

I remembered once telling Del, as we prepared to take ship out of Haziz, that there was nothing left for me in the South. In some ways, that was truth. In others, falsehood. There were things about the South I didn't care for, things I might not be cognizant of had Del not come along, but there were other things that meant more than I expected. Maybe it was merely a matter of being familiar with such things, of finding ease in dealing with what I knew rather than challenging the unexpected; or maybe it was that I'd met and overcome the challenges I'd faced and did not wish to relegate them to insignificance.

Then again, maybe it was merely relief that I was alive to return home, after nearly dying in a foreign land.

I grinned abruptly. "You know, there is one thing I really miss about Skandi."

Del sounded drowsy. "Hmmmm?"

"The metri's tiled bathing pool. And what we did in it."

"We can do that without the metri's bathing pool. In fact, I think we have."

"Not like we did there."

"Is that *all* you think about?"

I yawned. "No. Just most of the time."

After a moment she said reflectively, "It would be nice to have a bathing pool like that."

"Umm-hmm."

"Maybe you can build one at Alimat."

"I think I have to rebuild Alimat itself before building a bathing pool."

"In the meantime . . ." But her voice trailed off.

"In the meantime?"

"You'll have to make do with this." Whereupon she squirted the contents of a bota all over me.

The resultant activity was not even remotely similar to what we'd experienced mostly submerged in the metri's big, warm bathing pool. But it sufficed.

Oh, indeed.

Chapter 4

The balance of the journey to Julah was uneventful, save for the occasional uncharacteristic display of uncertainty by the stud when the white gelding looked at him. Del's mount was a quiet, stolid kind of horse, content to plod along endlessly with his head bobbing hypnotically on the end of a lowered neck—though Del claimed he didn't plod at all, but was the smoothest horse she'd ever ridden. I wasn't certain I knew what that was anymore, since the stud had forgotten every gait except a sucked-up walk that put me in mind of a man with the runs, trying to hold it in until he found a latrine. When this gait resulted in him falling behind Del's gelding, which happened frequently, he then broke into a jog to catch up and reassert his superiority. The gelding was unimpressed. So was I.

Julah was the typical desert town of flat-roofed, squared-off adobe buildings, deep-cut windows, tattered canvas awnings, and narrow, dusty streets. But there was water here in plenty, so Julah thrived. Opting to cool off before taking the risk of meeting other sword-dancers, we stopped at a well on the outskirts of town, dismounting to winch up buckets. We filled the horse troughs, permitted our mounts to drink, then quenched our own thirst and refilled botas. It was early enough in the season that the heat wasn't unbearable; but then, we hadn't reached the Punja yet. There was only one season in the Punja: *hot*.

Del dampened the hem of her burnous and wiped dust from her face. "Tonight *I* get the bath." Then, "How many sword-dancers are likely to be here?"

I backhanded water from my chin, realizing I needed to shave before we hit the Punja. "Oh, a few."

"Then we shouldn't stay longer than is necessary."

"We'll head out first thing tomorrow. In the meantime, except for a visit to Fouad's cantina, we'll keep our heads down."

"Walking into Fouad's, where at any time there may be half a dozen sword-dancers drinking his spirits, strikes me as keeping our heads *up*."

"Maybe. But we knew we'd face this coming back here."

Del said nothing. She had not argued when I said I wanted to return home—we had established that Skandi, for all my parents had come from the island, did not qualify—but she had quietly pointed out that to do so was sheer folly for a man sentenced to death by the very honor codes he'd repudiated. But the mere fact that she *hadn't* argued struck me as significant; I suspected Del was recalling that she was exiled from her own homeland and understood how much I needed to go back to mine. Unlike Del, I wasn't truly exiled. I wasn't under pain of death if I went back South. Oh, men would try to kill me, but that had nothing to do with exile. Just with broken oaths.

At my behest, we waited until sundown before entering Fouad's cantina. We had in the meantime secured lodging in an only slightly disreputable inn with a tiny stable out behind in an alley and had eaten at a street vendor's stall. The odors and flavors of spiced, if tough, mutton, sizzling peppers, and pungent goat cheese had immediately snatched me back to the days before we left for Skandi. I'm not sure Del appreciated that so much, having a more delicate palate—or so she claimed—but it felt like home to me. Then I led Del to Fouad's cantina, which was only fitfully lighted by smoking tallow candles on each small knife- and sword-hacked wooden table. I selected one back in the farthest corner from the door, a windowless nook veiled with smoke from a dying torch stuck in an iron wall sconce, dripping tallow. As we found stools to perch our rumps upon, I leaned forward and blew out our candle. Dimness descended.

"Oh, good," Del commented, brushing bread crumbs off the table. "Makes it so easy to see whom I'm to stick my sword into."

"We're not going to stick swords into anyone, bascha."

"Not even Fouad?" Del really seemed focused on the fact that my friend had betrayed us.

"Not immediately," I told her. "Maybe for the after-dinner entertainment."

Fouad, proprietor of my favorite cantina, was a small, neat, quick man of ready smile and welcome. Though he had wine-girls aplenty—Silk was working our corner, though clearly she hadn't yet recognized me—he enjoyed greeting newcomers personally. He approached the table calling out a robust greeting in Southron and offering us the best his cantina had to offer.

In bad light, wreathed in smoke, shorn of most of my hair, with double silver rings hanging in my ears and a tracery of blue tattooing along my hairline, I was no doubt a stranger to him at first glance, as I'd hoped. But Del, as always, was Del, and no man alive, having seen her even once, forgot what or who she was.

Or whom she traveled with.

Fouad stopped dead in his rush to greet new custom. He stared. He very nearly gaped.

He had, helpfully, placed himself within my reach. I rose, kicking back my stool, and leaned close, slapping one big hand down upon his shoulder in a friendly fashion. "Fouad!" I shut the hand, gripping him so firmly a wince of pain replaced his shocked expression. "Join us, won't you? It's been a long time." I shoved him toward the empty stool and pushed him down upon it. "There's much to catch up on, don't you think?"

He was trembling. Very unlike Fouad. But then, so was betrayal.

I yanked over another stool and sat down upon it. "So, what's the news? Any word out of Sabra?"

Fouad flicked a white-rimmed glance at Del, then looked back to me again. The robustness had spilled from his voice. "They say she's likely dead."

I raised a brow. " 'They say'? They're not sure?"

"She disappeared." His thin tone was a complex admixture of

emotions. "Some say a sandstorm got her, or a beast, or the Vashni. But Abbu Bensir said differently."

I grinned. "Abbu would. He's always one to tell a good tale. So, what *did* Abbu say about Sabra?"

"That you killed her."

"He did not." That from Del, who was never one to let a good story get in the way of the facts. "Sabra died of her own folly."

In truth, Sabra had died because she laid hands on a *jivatma* which was, at the time, utterly perverted by magic, full of a sorcerer wanting very badly to get out. Which he had managed. Unfortunately, the vessel he chose for freedom—Sabra—was far too weak to contain him. But I suppose "folly" fairly well summed it up.

"And just when was good old Abbu here last?" I asked idly.

Fouad had stopped trembling. Color returned to his face. We had always been friends, and I supposed he was recalling that. But wariness remained. And guilt. "Weeks ago," he said. "He's north of here now, I hear."

Well. At least I wouldn't have to grapple with Abbu Bensir immediately. "Aqivi?"

"Water for me," Del said.

It gave him something to do. Rather than calling Silk over, Fouad sprang up.

"This time," I said quietly, "leave out the drug."

His face spasmed. "I will drink first of each, if you like."

I was prepared to wave it away, knowing my point was made, but Del was less forgiving. "Do so," she said, in a tone that lowered the temperature of the room markedly. "And you will remain at this table. Let it be brought."

After a moment, Fouad bowed to her with one hand pressed over his heart and quietly bade Silk, lingering nearby and trying to catch my attention now that she *had* recognized me—Silk had always been one of my favorites and, she said, I one of hers—to bring water, aqivi, bread and cheese. Then he sank down on the stool. He looked older than he had when we first entered the cantina.

I waited.

He drew in a deep, sharp breath, then let it out in a rush of helpless sound. "She would have killed me had I not done her bidding."

"Of course she would have," I agreed.

"I begged her not to make me do it."

"Of course you did."

"I *prayed*—"

"Enough," Del snapped. She glanced at me. "Do you intend to kill him, or shall I?"

Bloodthirsty Northern bascha. I smiled, and let Fouad start sweating again. When the water and aqivi arrived—and Silk was shooed away—he poured cups of each and tasted both. Del rather pointedly turned her cup so her mouth would not touch the rim where his had touched. Me, I just picked up the aqivi and knocked back a slug.

Long practice kept me from choking. Long abstinence—from aqivi, anyway—burned a line of fire from throat, through gullet, into belly. But being the infamous Sandtiger, I did not indicate this. I merely took another big slug.

Del's brows pulled together briefly, but she blanked her face almost at once.

"So." I grinned companionably at Fouad. "At Sabra's behest, in fear for your life, you drugged our wine. I, innocent as a woolly little lamb, wandered off looking for someone and walked into a trap you helped set. Del, meanwhile—*also* drugged—was handed over to Umir the Ruthless to become a part of his collection." Umir the Ruthless had tastes that did not incline to women but to unusual objects. He was ruthless not because he was particularly murderous personally, but because he'd do anything to get what he wanted. Even if he hired others to murder for him. "Del apparently feels what you did is worthy of execution. But I'm a more generous soul. What do you suggest I do about this?"

Fouad's tone was a carefully weighed mixture of resignation, suggestion, and hope. "Forget it?"

I nearly choked on a mouthful of aqivi. Far less amused, Del stared him down.

Fouad, suddenly smaller on his stool, sighed deeply. "No, I suppose not."

"We could have been killed," Del said.

"No!" Fouad exclaimed. "Assurances were made . . ." As if realizing how ludicrously lame that sounded, he trailed off into silence. "Well," he said finally, "they were. I'm only a lowly cantina keeper, not a sword-dancer to parse between what is threat and what is honesty."

"You've parsed enough in the past," I reminded him. Fouad had always been an excellent source of information and interpretation.

He debated whether to acknowledge flattery or avoid it altogether. He shrank further inside his yellow robe.

"So," I said, "you really didn't think they'd kill us—"

"And they didn't!" Fouad, having discovered a salient point, sat upright on the stool again. "Are you not here? Are you not sitting before me, eating my bread and cheese, drinking my liquor?"

"Water," Del clarified, displaying her cup. "But yes, I will give you all of that: we are indeed alive and sitting before you. Eating and drinking. Whether you intended it or no."

"I didn't want you dead! Either of you!" He looked from Del to me, and back again. "Why would I? I have nothing to gain from your deaths. I wanted merely to prevent mine."

"What did she pay you?" I asked.

"Nothing!"

Del was clearly skeptical. "Nothing?"

"She permitted me to keep my life," Fouad explained. "I am somewhat attached to my life and considered it payment enough, under the circumstances. Though undoubtedly others might not agree." He eyed me, clearly expecting a reaction. Then a frown pinched his brows together. "You look—different."

"A full life will do that to you," I replied gravely. "Especially if you're sold off to a murderous female tanzeer intent on punishing you for killing her father, despite the fact that said father deserved to be slowly roasted to death over a nice bed of coals." As Aladar had been the one to throw me into his mines and nearly cost me my sanity, I felt justified in my stance.

Color deepened in Fouad's face. He stared hard at the surface of the table. "I am not proud of it."

"Oh, that does change matters," Del said with delicate irony.

"You would do the same!" he cried; and then abruptly recalled to whom he spoke. Two sword-dancers, who defended the lives of others—and their own—without recourse to such cowardly acts as drugging customers' wine. His breath came fast. "What do you want, then? To kill me?" He paused. "Really?"

I smiled sweetly. "Two-thirds of this place."

Del cut me a sharp glance, not being privy to my plan. Fouad missed it, being entirely taken up with the magnitude of my revenge.

I lifted a forefinger before he could sputter out a protest. "You might have told Sabra no."

"She'd have had me killed!"

"So could we," I reminded him. "Though at least we'd do you the courtesy of killing you ourselves, instead of hiring a total stranger to do the job." My gesture encompassed the cantina. "Two-thirds, Fouad. One-third for you, one-third for me, one-third for Del."

Del concentrated on drinking more water so as not to give away her bemusement. Such are the dynamics of negotiation. Even if you aren't truly negotiating but merely informing.

Fouad did not believe. His tone was incredulous. "You want to be a cantina keeper? Here? But—but you're a sword-dancer!"

"I'd have been a dead man, had Sabra succeeded," I said bluntly. "But I am very much alive, and prepared to leave *you* that way . . . should we reach an equitable agreement." I cut him off before he could speak again. "And no, I am not proposing that I play host, or tell you what kind of curtains to put in your windows, or that Del be a wine-girl." I could imagine what she'd say to that image later. "I was thinking we'd be silent partners."

"I do all the work, you take two-thirds of the profits," Fouad said glumly.

"I'm glad you grasp the pertinent details."

"For how long?" he asked.

"How long?"

"For how long do I have to put up with you?"

"What, are you already planning to hire Abbu or some such soul to knock me off?"

Fouad was stunned. "I would never do such a thing!" Whereupon he recalled that while he hadn't done precisely that, he had indeed contributed to the trap that could very well have have ended in my death.

"Two-thirds," Del said crisply. "Payable four times a year."

I nodded with grave dignity. Fouad screwed up his face.

"And *I* may just have an idea for those curtains," she added.

I suspect a knife in the gut might have proven less painful to him. But he eventually agreed, with much moroseness of expression.

"Good," I said. "As for how long, it's a lifetime arrangement. If I die, Del gets my one-third. If she dies, I get her one-third."

I'd given Fouad an opening. "And if you both die? You are sword-dancers, after all. Sword-dancers die."

I drank down the rest of my aqivi, then scratched idly at the claw marks in my face. "I plan to live forever."

Fouad looked. He saw. His lips parted. "Your finger," he said hoarsely.

I displayed both hands. *"Fingers,"* I enunciated. "As I said, I've lived a full life."

He was stunned. "Sabra did that?"

"This? No." I didn't elaborate, which left him nonplussed.

"But—can you dance?"

I felt Del's look, but I did not return it. "Try me."

Fouad was perversely fascinated by the missing fingers. I saw him turn it over in his head, applying his knowledge of my past, my reputation, to the present sitting before him and all the implications. He more closely noted the shorn hair, doubled earrings—and whatever else you might see if you looked upon me now.

"I heard—" He paused and cleared his throat. "I heard a rumor that you'd survived Sabra. That you'd declared . . ."

"Elaii-ali-ma," I supplied, when he faltered. "You've been selling drink and women to sword-dancers for years. You know very well what *elaii-ali-ma* means."

He did. "Forsworn."

"And subject to any punishment a sword-dancer—one who's still true to his oaths, mind you—cares to give me." I shrugged. "So you might get to keep my one-third of the profits, if it comes to that. One of these days."

"They'll kill you, Tiger."

"Maybe," I agreed. "Maybe not."

His gaze was on my mutilated hands, which I did not trouble to hide. "This is worse," Fouad said hollowly. "Worse than anything Sabra might have done."

"Possibly. But that does not absolve you of your responsibility." He had the grace to wince. "She intended me to die, Fouad. This way, fingers or no fingers, I have some say in the matter."

Fouad was not convinced. "They'll kill you."

I gave him my friendliest grin. "Or die trying."

"Why?" Del demanded later in the inn's tiny room high under the eaves. An equally tiny window—a lopsided square chopped into thick mudbrick—tinted the room a sallow sepia as the sun went down, glinting off the brass buckles of our belongings.

I knew better than to ask to what she referred. "Financial security." I stripped out of my burnous.

Stretched out on the rope-and-wood bed atop its thin pallet and even thinner blanket, she watched as I, dhoti-clad, began to methodically undertake the forms I found beneficial to my strength, flexibility, and endurance. For most of my life I'd depended on a natural wellspring of sheer physical strength, power, and speed, with no need to work at keeping any of them. They simply *were*. Now I needed more.

"You just didn't want to kill him."

She sounded so disgusted a brief gust of laughter was expelled as I bent from one side to the other. "Fouad's a friend."

"A friend who betrayed you."

"At Sabra's insistence." I felt the joints of my spine stretch and pop. "She was a little hard to turn down when she got a bug up her butt. Hoolies, even *I* was going to do what she wanted." Die in the circle, facing Abbu Bensir.

"But you had a choice."

I clasped hands behind my head and pushed it forward against resistance. "Sure I did. I forswore all my oaths as a seventh-level sword-dancer. I don't think cantina keepers have any oaths. Though I suppose there could be some secret society dedicated to all the arcane secrets of selling liquor and hiring wine-girls."

Del had been leaning on one elbow. Now she shoved herself upright. "Speaking of wine-girls, you made reference to *me*—"

I cut her off before we could take that route. "Certainly not."

"Certainly, yes," she said dryly. "You also mentioned something about Fouad selling wine-girls to sword-dancers."

"Well, I suppose 'rented' would be a more accurate term."

"And I assume you 'rented' your share?"

"Nah," I replied off-handedly. "None of them ever charged *me*."

After a moment of stunned silence, Del said something highly explicit in uplander.

I changed the subject hastily. "Do you really want to kill Fouad?"

"No. But I *do* want to know why you've encumbered us with a two-thirds ownership of a cantina." She paused, considering. "Unless you figure it entitles you to free aqivi."

"Well, it does. Might save me a little money." I shrugged prodigiously, repeatedly, loosening the muscles running from neck to shoulders. "It's not an encumbrance, bascha. All we have to do is drop in four times a year and pick up our share of the profits." Fortunately Fouad had been prevailed upon to give us an advance, since, having arranged for horse boarding, human lodging, and some food, we now needed money to pay for it all.

"But why, Tiger? You've never indicated any interest in owning property before. A cantina?"

"I like cantinas."

"Well, yes; you spend enough time in them . . . but why *own* one?"

"I told you. Financial security." I stopped loosening up and faced her. "I doubt I'll be taking on any jobs as a sword-dancer any time soon. I'm kind of proscribed from that."

Del was perplexed. "You told me you wanted to rebuild your shodo's place. Alimat. And take on students."

"I do. But that presupposes there will be students to teach and that they'll have money to pay me. We need to buy things, bascha.

Fouad's cantina will at least cover expenses." I gave her a quizzical look. "Isn't that the responsible thing to do?"

"Of course it's the responsible thing to do," she agreed. "It's just very unlike you to be responsible."

I scowled. "Short of killing him, and he wouldn't be around to suffer or feel remorse if I did that, it's also about the direst punishment I could think of for Fouad. He's a pinch-coin."

"Is there anyone else you want to punish? Are we likely to wind up owning a weaver's shop, a vegetable plot, or a flower cart?"

"I doubt it. None of those people has ever drugged my wine and set me up to be taken by a spoiled, bloodthirsty, murderous little bitch bent on seeing me killed in the circle." I rolled my neck, feeling tension loosen. "What color of curtains were you thinking, bascha?"

Del made a sound of derision. "As if any cantina would boast curtains in the windows. Likely some drunkard would set them on fire the first fight he got into. And we, now partners with your faithful friend Fouad, would have to bear two-thirds of the cost of damages."

I hadn't thought about that.

"I knew it," Del said in deep disgust. "Men. All they ever think about are the profits. Not about all the work that goes into such things."

Well, no. "That's why we have Fouad," I said brightly. "He'll take care of all that."

Del scowled. "I still say it was foolish to go to Fouad's. Word will be out by morning, just like in Haziz."

"It won't be Fouad who spreads it."

"Of *course* it will be Fouad—"

"No."

"Why, because you're his partner now?"

"Because we really were friends, bascha. And because he feels guilty."

"As well he should!"

"You don't know *you* wouldn't have done what he did, faced with Sabra."

After a moment, Del declared, "I find that observation incredibly offensive."

I grinned at her, continuing to work out the tension in my body; going to Fouad's had kept me on edge, regardless of what I admitted. "You didn't face Sabra." Not in the same way, at any rate. By the time Del and Sabra were in close proximity, Sabra was unconscious and tied to a saddle.

"I'd have killed her," Del said shortly.

A sudden and very intriguing image rose before my eyes: Del and Sabra. One small and dark, one tall and fair. Two dangerous, deadly women. Except Del was far more honest when she killed: she did it herself.

"Word will get out," I said, "but it won't be Fouad."

"Such a trustworthy soul," Del said dryly.

"Let me see your wrist."

Obligingly, Del extended an arm. I shut my hand upon the wrist and squeezed. Tightly. *Very* tightly.

After a moment, she asked, "Are you purposely attempting to break my wrist?" She wiggled fingers. "Let go. Tiger."

Smiling, I let go.

Del sighed. "Point taken."

"I should hope so."

"But it will still be different," she cautioned. "More difficult."

"I agree, bascha."

And it was very likely, I knew, I'd discover *how* different tomorrow. Because word was bound to get out.

The Sandtiger is back.

Yes. He was.

Chapter 5

Del and I were only just crawling out of bed in the morning when a scratching sounded at the door. I might have said vermin, except it was too repetitive. I dragged on dhoti and unsheathed my sword even as Del hastily swirled a blanket around her nudity.

The scratching came again, coupled with a woman's soft voice asking if the sword-dancer and the Northern woman were in there. No names. Interesting.

A glance across my shoulder confirmed a well wrapped Del was prepared with sword in hand. She nodded. I unlocked the door and opened it, blade at the ready. It wasn't impossible someone might use a woman as a beard. Such things as courtesy and honorable discourse were no longer required.

The woman in the narrow corridor winced away from the glint of sharp steel. She displayed the palms of her hands in a warding gesture, displaying innocent intent. I blinked. It was Silk, the wine-girl from Fouad's cantina, swathed in robes and a head covering when ordinarily she wore very little.

"I'm alone," she blurted. "I swear it."

Her nerves were strung tight as wire. I opened my mouth to ask what she was doing here when I saw her gaze go beyond me to Del. She registered that Del was nude under the thin blanket, with white-blond hair in tumbled disarray, and something flared briefly in Silk's dark eyes, something akin, I thought, to recognition and acknowledgment of another woman's beauty. Her mouth hooked briefly. Not jealousy, though. Oddly enough, regret. Resignation. Silk was attractive, in a cheap sort of way, but infinitely Southron; Del, in all her splendid Northern glory, was simply incomparable. She wasn't to every Southroner's taste—too tall, too fair-skinned, too blonde for some of them, and most definitely too independent— but no one, looking at her, could be blind to what she was.

Ah, yes. That's my bascha.

"Fouad sent me," Silk said nervously. I gestured her in, but she shook her head. "I must go back. He wanted me to tell you some- one recognized you, and word is already out of your presence here. He fears you may be challenged before you can leave."

I nodded, unsurprised, already thinking ahead to how it might occur.

"Thank you for this," Del said.

Silk resettled her headcovering, pulling it forward to shield part of her face. "I didn't do it for you."

After a moment of stillness, Del smiled faintly. "No. But we both want him to survive."

Silk cut me a glance out of wide, grieving eyes. I was startled to see tears there. I opened my mouth to speak, but she turned sharply and walked away, a small dark woman in pale, voluminous fabric.

"Door," Del said crisply.

I shut and latched it even as she shed the blanket and grabbed smallclothes and tunic. Without further conversation we donned burnouses and sandals, packed and gathered up belongings, reestablished the fit of our harnesses and that swords were prop- erly seated in their sheaths.

The horses were stabled just out back in the tiny livery. So long as no one knew we were here at this particular inn, it was possible we might get them tacked out, our gear loaded, and our butts in the saddles before we were discovered.

But maybe not.

Del's eyes met mine. Her face was expressionless. She was once again the Northern sword-singer, a woman warrior capable not only of meeting a man on equal footing but of defeating him.

Shodo-trained sword-dancers wouldn't want to fight or harm her. It was me they were after; they'd let her go. But Del would take that convention and turn it upside down.

One of us might die today. Or neither. Or both. And we each of us knew it.

She opened the door and walked out.

Del and I made an honest effort to take every back alley in the tangled skein that made up the poorer sections of Julah. For a moment I thought we might actually get out of town without me being challenged, but I should have known better. Whoever the sword-dancer was who'd recognized me, he was smart enough to know he couldn't be everywhere; he'd need to make a financial investment in order to track me down. He'd hired gods know how many boys to stake out the streets and intersections, and eventually the alleys merged with them. It didn't take long for word to be carried that the Sandtiger and his Northern bascha were crossing the Street of Weavers and heading for the Street of Potters, which in turn gave into the Street of Tinsmiths.

And it was there, in front of one of the more prosperous shops catering to the tin trade, that the sword-dancer found us.

Mounted, he'd halted his dun-colored horse in the middle of the street. Del and I had the option of turning around and going back the way we'd come, but it was one thing to attempt to avoid your enemy, and another to turn tail and run once you actually came face to face with him.

Fueled by the overexcited boys and the promise of a sword-dance, rumor had quickly spread. The Street of Tinsmiths was not the main drag through town, but the entire merchants' quarter was always thronged with people, and today was market day. The buzz of recognition and comment began as Del and I reined in, and rose in anticipation, much like startled bees, as we sat at ease atop our horses, saying nothing, letting my opponent take the lead.

"Sandtiger." He raised his voice, though our mounts stood approximately fifteen paces apart. "Do you remember me?"

The street fell silent. I was aware of staring faces, expectant eyes. The sun glinted off samples of tinware hanging on display on both sides of the narrow thoroughfare. I smelled forges, coals, the acrid tang of worked metal.

I looked at him. Southron through and through, and all sword-dancer, torso buckled into harness and the hilt of his sword riding above his left shoulder. Yes, I remembered him. Khashi. He was ten or twelve years younger than I. He'd been taken on at Alimat about the time I left to make my own way. I'd witnessed enough of his training before I departed to know he was talented and had heard rumors over the years that he was good, but we'd never crossed paths on business, and I hadn't seen him since then.

"You know why," he said.

I didn't reply. The faintest of breezes ruffled our burnouses, the robes and headcloths of spectators, and set dangling tinware clanking against one another. A child's plaintive voice rose, and was hushed.

Khashi's thin lips curled. Disdain was manifest. "What's more, I heard you played the coward in Haziz and refused to accept a challenge."

I shook my head. "He wasn't a sword-dancer. Just a stupid kid looking for glory."

Brown eyes narrowed. "And what do you say of me?"

"Nothing." I shrugged. "That's all you're worth."

We weren't close enough for me to see the color burning in his face, but I could tell I'd gotten to him. His body stiffened, hands tightening on the reins. His horse shifted nervously and joggled his head, trying to ease the pressure on his mouth. Metal bit shanks and rings clinked.

"And what are you worth?" he asked sharply. "You declared *elaii-ali-ma*."

"Oh, I am lower than the lowest of the low," I replied. "I am foulness incarnate. I am dishonor embodied. You'll soil your blade with my blood."

He grinned, showing white teeth against a dark face. "But blood washes off. Righteousness does not." Abruptly he raised his voice, addressing the crowd. "Hear me!" he shouted. "This man is the Sandtiger, who once was a seventh-level sword-dancer sworn to uphold the honor codes and sacred traditions of Alimat. But he repudiated them, his shodo, and all of his brethren. It is our right to punish him for this, and today I willingly accept the honor of this task. I call on every man here to witness the death of an oath-breaker!"

I sighed, looping one rein over the stud's neck as I extended the other to Del. "You talk too much, Khashi."

Stung, but still focused on the task, he hooked his right leg over his horse's neck, kicked his left foot clear of stirrup, and jumped down, throwing reins toward one of the boys. There were clusters of them lining the shop walls, and merchants and customers spilled out of doorways. The street was a canyon of staring faces. "Then we shall stop talking," he said, "and fight."

Unlike the stupid kid in Haziz, Khashi knew the difference between dance and fight. He stripped off burnous, sandals, and harness, wearing only the customary soft suede dhoti underneath, and set them aside. He did not pause to draw a circle, or to invite me to draw it, because there would be none. Lithely graceful, he strode forward, sword in hand.

I heard the simultaneous intake of breath from the impromptu audience as I stepped off the stud. I did not strip out of harness, burnous, or sandals. I simply unsheathed without excess dramatics and walked to meet my challenger in the middle of the street, six paces away.

He smiled, assessing his opponent. The infamous Sandtiger, but also an older, aging man who was too foolish to rid himself of such things as would impede his movements. I had given the advantage to the younger challenger.

Which is why he laughed incredulously as I halted within his reach.

I did nothing more than wait. After a moment's hesitation—perhaps unconsciously expecting the traditional command to dance that wouldn't come—Khashi flicked up his sword and obliged with the first move.

I obliged by countering the blow, and another, and a third, and a fourth, turning his blade away. I offered no offense, only defense. I conserved strength, while Khashi spent his.

Though we did not stand within a circle and thus were not required to remain within a fixed area, lest we lose by stepping out-side the boundary, we'd both spent too many years honoring the codes and rituals. There was no dramatic leaping and running and rolling. It was a sword-fighter's version of toe-to-toe battle, lacking elegance, ritual, the precision of expertise despite our training. We simply stood our ground, aware of the mental circle despite the lack of a physical one, and fought.

It was, as always, noisy. Steel slammed into steel, scraped, tore away, screamed, shrieked, chimed. Breath ran harshly through rigid throats and issued hissing from our mouths. Grunts and gasps of effort overrode the murmuring of the spectators, the low verbal thrum of excitement.

I countered yet another blow, threw the blade back at him with main strength. I felt a twinge in my right hand, and another in my left wrist. The hilt shifted slightly in my hands.

All of the things Del and I had discussed had indeed become factors: The loss of a finger on each hand did affect my grip, and that, in turn, affected wrists, forearms, elbows, clear up into the shoulders and back. I had worked ceaselessly since leaving Skandi to compensate for the loss of those fingers by retraining my body, but only a real fight would prove if I'd succeeded. Now that I was in one, I realized my body wanted to revert to postures, grips, and responses I'd learned more than twenty years before. The new mind had not yet taught the old body to surrender.

I could not afford a lengthy battle, because I could not win it. I needed to make it short.

I raised the blade high overhead, gripped in my right hand, wrist cocked so the point tipped down toward my left shoulder. Khashi saw the opening I gave him, the opportunity to win. He did not believe it. But he lunged, unable to pass up the target I'd made of my torso. The audience drew in a single startled breath.

I brought the sword down diagonally in a hard, slashing cross-body blow, rolling the edge with a twist of my wrist even as I adjusted my elbow. The inelegant but powerful maneuver swept Khashi's blade down and aside. Another flick of the wrist, the punch through flesh and muscle, and I slid steel into his belly. A quick scooping twist carved the intestines out of abdominal cavity, and then I pulled the blade free of flesh and viscera.

Khashi dropped his sword. His hands went to his belly. His mouth hung open. Then his knees folded out from under him. He knelt there in the street clutching ropy guts, weaving in shock as his gaping mouth emitted a keening wail of shock and terror.

I did him the honor of kicking his blade away, though he had no strength to pick it up, and turned my back on him. I intended to go directly to the stud. But three paces away stood the stupid kid from Haziz. His sword was unsheathed, gripped in one hand.

Blood ran from mine. I watched his startled eyes as they followed the motion along the steel, red, wet runnels sliding from hilt to tip, dripping onto hardpacked dirt.

He looked at me then. Saw me, saw something in my face, my eyes. His own face was pale. But he swallowed hard and managed to speak. "There was no honor in that."

I'd expected a second challenge, not accusation. After a moment I found my own voice. "This wasn't about honor."

His brown eyes were stunned in a tanned face formed of planes and angles gone suddenly sharp as blades. "But you need not kill a man to win. Not in the circle."

"This isn't about the circle," I said. "Not about rites, rituals, honor codes, or oaths sworn to such. It's just about dying."

"But—you're a sword-dancer."

I shook my head. "Not anymore. Now I'm only a target."

"You're the Sandtiger!"

"That, yes," I agreed. "But I swore *elaii-ali-ma*."

Color was creeping back into his face. The honey-brown eyes were steady, if no less shocked. "I don't know what that is."

A jerk of my head indicated Khashi's sprawled body, limp as soiled laundry. "Ask him."

I walked past him then, because I knew he wouldn't challenge me. Not now. Likely not ever again.

But others would.

Before mounting I wiped my blade clean of blood on my burnous, sheathed it, and took the rein back from Del. Then swung up into the saddle. "Let's go."

The mask of her face remained, giving away nothing to any who looked. But her eyes were all compassion.

I heard the chanting of my name as we headed out of Julah.

Not far out of the city, after a brief but silent ride, I abruptly turned off the road. I rode to the top of a low rise crowned with cactus and twisted trees, dismounted, let the reins go, and managed to make it several paces down the other side, sliding in shale and slate, before I bent and gave up everything in my belly in one giant heaving spasm.

I remained bent over, coughing and spitting when the residual retching stopped, and heard the chink of hoof on stone. It might be the stud. But in case it was Del, I thrust out a splayed hand that told her to stay away.

I didn't need an audience. I'd had one already, in Julah.

Finally I straightened, scraping at my mouth with the sleeve of my burnous. When I turned to hike back up to the stud, I found Del holding his reins. Silent no longer.

"Are you cut?" she asked.

"No."

"Are you sure?"

"Yes."

"Have you *looked?*"

Sighing, I inspected my arms, then ran my hands down the front of burnous and harness, checking for complaints of the flesh, though I was fairly certain Khashi had not broken my guard. I was spattered with blood, but none of it appeared to be mine. And nothing hurt beyond the edges of my palms where the fingers were missing.

"I'm fine." I climbed to the stud, took the reins from her, then pulled one of the botas free and filled my mouth with water. I rinsed, spat, scrubbed again at my mouth, then released a noisy breath from the environs of my toes. "Butchery," I muttered hoarsely, throat burned by bile.

"It was necessary."

"I've killed men, beheaded men, cut men into collops before. Borjuni. Bandits. Thieves. It never bothered me; it was survival, no more. But this—" I shook my head.

"It was necessary," she repeated. "How better to warn other sword-dancers you will not be easy prey?"

That was precisely why I had done it, knowing the tale would be told. Embellished into legend. But the aftermath was far more difficult to deal with than I had anticipated.

"Tiger," Del said quietly, "you spent many years learning all the rituals of the sword-dance. The requirements of the circle. It was your escape, your freedom, but also a way of life woven of rules, rites, codes. The formal sword-dance is not about killing but about the honor of the dance and victory. What you did today was the antithesis of everything you learned, all that you embraced, when you swore the oaths of a sword-dancer before your shodo at Alimat."

"I've been in death-dances before." They were rare, as most sword-dances were a relatively peaceful way of settling disputes for our employers, but they did occur.

"Still formalized," she observed. "It's an elegant way to die. An honorable way to die."

Killing Khashi had been neither. But necessary, yes.

"On another day, you and he would have danced a proper dance. One of you would have won. And then likely afterwards you'd have gone to a cantina together and gotten gloriously drunk. It is different, Tiger, what was done today."

"You can't know, bascha—"

"I can. I do. I killed Bron."

It took me a moment. Then I remembered. Del had killed a friend, a training partner, who otherwise would have kept her from returning to the Northern island known as Staal-Ysta, where her daughter lived.

But still.

I squirted more water into my mouth, spat again, then drank. Stared hard across the landscape, remembering the stink of severed bowels, the expression on his face as his life ran out, the weight of the blade as I opened his abdomen.

Butchery.

"Would you feel better if you had died?"

For the first time since the fight I looked directly at her. Felt the tug of a wry smile at my mouth. Trust Delilah to put it in perspective.

"You don't have to like it," she said. "If you did, if you began to, I would not share your bed. But this, too, is survival, and in its rawest, most primitive form. There *will* be others. Kill them quickly, Tiger, and ruthlessly. Show them no mercy. Because they will surely show none to you."

What she didn't say, what she didn't need to say, was that some of those others would be better than Khashi.

Chapter 6

el was initially resistent to going after my *jivatma*. She truly saw no sense in it, since very likely the sword was buried under tons of rock, and we had new blades. I still hadn't told her about the dreams of the woman commanding me to take up the sword, because I couldn't find words that didn't make me sound like a sandsick fool. Instead, I relied on Del's own respect for the Northern blades and on the loss of Boreal. As I had by declaring *elaii-ali-ma*, she had made the only choice possible in breaking the sword, but that didn't mean she was immune to regret. Eventually she gave in.

There was not a road where we wanted to go, because no one else, apparently, had ever wanted to go there. Del and I made our own way, recalling the direction from our visit to Shaka Obre's domain nearly a year before. We left behind the flat but relatively lush desert of Julah and traded it for foothills, the precursors of the mountain where we had encountered strong magic, where Chosa Dei, living in my sword, had vacated it first to fill—and kill—Sabra, then to encounter his brother. They hadn't been living beings, Chosa Dei and Shaka Obre, merely power incarnate, but that was enough. What was left of them battled fiercely within the hollowed rock formation that shaped, inside a huge chimney of stone, a circle. And Del and Chosa Dei, using my sword, my body, had danced.

Here there was rock in place of soil, intermixed with hardpan and seasonings of sand. Drifts of stone were like the bones of the earth peeping through the flesh, but there were tumbled piles of it as well as that beneath the dirt. Brownish, porous smokerock, the variegations of slate, sharply faceted shale, the milky glow of quartz, the glitter of mica coupled with glinting splashes of false gold. The Punja, with its crystalline sands, was yet miles away. This was a land of rock swelling like boils into looming stone formations crowning ragged foothills, merging slowly into mountains. Not the high, huge ranges of Del's North, shaped of wind and snow and ice, but the whimsy of Southron nature in sudden bubbles of burst rock, scattered remnants of wholeness and order, abrupt, towering up-thrustings of striated stone shoved loose from the desert floor.

Movement against the uneven horizon of foothills and rock formations caught my eye. I looked, saw, and reined in sharply. Del, not watching me as she and her gelding picked their way through, nearly allowed her gelding to walk into the back of the stud. There was a moment of tension in the body beneath me, but he, too, knew what lay before us was far more threatening than what was behind.

"What—" Del began; but then she, like me, held her silence, and waited.

I had half expected it. We were in the land of the Vashni. No one knew where the borders were, or even if there *were* borders, but there was always the awareness of risk when one traveled here.

Four warriors. Vashni are not large, nor are their horses. But size wasn't what mattered. It was the willingness to kill, and the way in which they did it.

Four warriors, kilted in leather, wearing wreaths of fingerbone pectorals against oiled chests. Black hair was also oiled, worn in single, fur-wrapped plaits. Bone-handled knives and swords decorated their persons.

Del's voice was a breath of sound. "Could these be the same four who met us when we had Sabra?"

I answered as quietly. "I don't know. Maybe. No one sees the Vashni often enough to recognize individuals." At least, no one *lived* long enough to recognize individuals.

The warriors eased their small, dark horses into motion. They rode down from the rocky hilltop and approached, marking our faces, harnesses, swords. I felt the first tickle of sweat springing up on my skin.

Is it possible to fight a Vashni? Of course. I imagine it has happened. But no one, *no one* has ever survived the battle. They are killed, then boiled. When the bones are free of flesh, the Vashni make jewelry and weapons of it. The flesh is fed to dogs.

The only reason I know this is the Vashni don't kill children. It is their "mercy" to take children into their villages, to feed them, have them watch what becomes of their parents, then deliver them to a road where they will be found by others.

If they are found. Some of them have been.

Del and I had been in a Vashni village once, when searching for her brother. They had treated us with honor; Jamail was considered a holy man, and she was his sister. Jamail, castrated, mute, had not wanted to leave the people who gave him a twisted sort of kindness after years of slavery elsewhere. Later—known by then as the Oracle—he had been killed, but it hadn't been Vashni doing. They revered his memory.

"Del," I said quietly, "come up beside me so they can see you better."

She didn't question it; possibly she also realized safety might lie in her resemblence to the Oracle, her brother. She moved the gelding out from behind the stud, guided him next to me, and reined in. Again, we waited.

That triggered a response in the Vashni. One of them stayed back, but three others rode down. One stationed himself in front of me, approximately three paces away; the other two took up positions on either side of us.

The fourth rode down then. When he was close enough, I saw his eyes were lighter than the others, the shape of his face somewhat different. I'd never heard of Vashni breeding with other tribes, but anything was possible. They had taken a Northerner into their midst. Del's brother, by the time we found him, had become one of them.

The warrior pulled up near Del. This close, we could smell them. Apparently rancid oil was considered perfume in Vashni circles.

The warrior's eyes were a dark gray. He looked hard at Del, then at me. Something moved in those eyes. He raised a hand to his face and touched one cheek, mimicking my scars.

I took it as invitation. "Sandtiger," I said.

Now he looked at Del. Now the hand rose to his hair, then indicated his eyes.

Blue-eyed, fair-haired Del said, "The Oracle's sister."

The Vashni closed in. We followed—or were made to understand it was wise to follow—the man with gray eyes.

It was a camp, not a village. A tiny clearing surrounded by boulders, a grove of twisted, many-limbed trees, a fire ring set in the middle with blankets thrown down around it. The stink of blood and entrails as well as the piles of hides told us the Vashni were a hunting party, as did the skinned carcasses hanging from the trees. Likely the village was a day's ride. Perhaps it was even the one where Jamail had been held.

Once in camp, Del and I were motioned off our horses. We dismounted, and one of the warriors led the stud and gelding away to tie them to a tree lacking the ornamentation of meat. The stud was not happy, but he didn't protest. Del's black-painted, fringe-bedecked gelding went placidly and stood where he was tied, lowering his head to forage in thatches of webby green grass spreading beneath the tree. The Vashni mounts were turned loose once their bridles were slipped; apparently even they knew better than to test a warrior's mood.

Gravely the gray-eyed man unsheathed knife and sword and set them down upon a woven blanket. The other warriors followed suit. Then it was our turn.

Unarming before anyone was not something I enjoyed. Doing it before Vashni set a knot into my guts. But a single misstep could get us killed. And they seemed to be peaceable enough—for the moment.

Del and I added our weapons to the pile. The gray-eyed man,

whom I took to be the leader, sat down, motioning us to be seated on the blanket across from him, on the other side of the fire ring. We did so. It was a comfortable spot out of the sun's glare, shaded by trees. If we'd been with anyone besides Vashni, it might have been a nice little respite.

Then, surprisingly, the grey-eyed man placed a hand on his chest and identified himself: "Oziri." Botas were brought out and passed around. We were, they made it clear, to drink first, even before Oziri.

Peaceable indeed. Courteous, even. I unstoppered the bota, smelled the pungent bite of liquor, took a surreptitous deep breath, then squirted a goodly amount into my mouth. Even as I swallowed liquid fire, clamping my mouth shut so as not to gasp aloud, I passed the bota to Del. Without hesitation she drank down a generous swallow. Then tears welled up in her eyes, and she went into a spasm of coughing.

It might have been insult. Instead, the Vashni found it amusing. Grins broke out. Heads nodded. One warrior brought out a leather bag, dug inside, then tossed out sizeable chunks of meat to his companions. I was thrown a chunk big enough for two; Del, they clearly judged, was still too incapacitated to catch her own.

"If you die," I told her, "they'll likely take your body back to the village and boil the flesh off your bones."

Her voice was thin and choked. "I'm not dying."

"Here." I divided and passed her some meat. "Maybe this will help."

She cleared her throat repeatedly, then accepted the meat even as she thrust the bota back at me. "What is it?"

"Don't ask. Just eat." I sucked down more liquor. It was unlike anything I'd had before. Already my brain tingled.

Knowing Vashni eyes were on her, Del lifted the meat to her mouth and found a promising edge. She bit into it, froze a moment, then began to gnaw at it. Eventually she pulled the bite free and began to chew. Her expression, despite her attempt to mask it, spoke of a flavor not particularly pleasing to her palate.

Now that Del was eating, it was my turn. No more excuses. I bit into my portion, tore off a chunk, tasted the sharp, gamy flavor, and began the lengthy process of chewing it into something that might be swallowed. The warriors, I noted, had no problems. But then, they likely had been given tough and mostly raw meat from the day their teeth came in.

Del's words were distorted around the bite she was clearly reluctant to swallow. "Wha' *i*' it?"

I grinned as I risked it—one big swallow to get it all down at once—and tossed the bota back. "Like I said, don't ask. Just eat. Wash it down with that."

Oziri said, "Sandtiger."

I looked at him. "Yes?"

Something very like a smile quirked the corner of his mouth. He pointed to the meat. "Sandtiger. For the Sandtiger."

Oh. *Oh.*

Hoolies—I was eating my namesake!

Del stopped chewing. She stared at the hunk of meat in her hand, plainly trying to decide if she would be forgiven for spitting out what was in her mouth, or possibly killed for it. As I expected, she took the safer road. She swallowed with effort, then squirted more liquor into her mouth. This time she didn't cough, but a hand flew to her mouth. Droplets fell from her chin.

Sandtiger meat. No wonder it was so tough. They weren't exactly known as a food source. Usually we were theirs.

I bit off another chunk and began to chew before it could chew back. It was impossible to relax, but the Vashni, eating and drinking companionably, gave every indication we were guests, not quarry bound for the cookpot.

Of course, it could just be the last meal prior to the cookpot.

I didn't say that to Del. Just watched her struggle to chew and choke down the meat, leavening it with liquor. Eventually I took the bota back and did the same.

"Sandtiger," Oziri said.

I waited politely, wondering if he were addressing me or identifying my meal.

"The Oracle's sister took you into Beit al'Shahar and freed you of Chosa Dei."

Either that had become legend in his tribe, or this man had

been one of the warriors who'd told Del where to find Shaka Obre, after she'd hit me over the head with a rock. Or perhaps he was one of the warriors who'd taken Jamail to the chimney formation where he somehow managed to learn how to speak again despite lacking a tongue.

"Yes," I confirmed.

"You are free now?"

"Yes."

He ran a forefinger along his hairline. "Chosa Dei did that?"

He meant the rim of tattoos at the top of my forehead, not yet hidden by hair. "No. This was done in Skandi. An island far away."

He didn't care about Skandi. "Did Chosa steal your mind?"

I smiled. "He tried. But no. I'm truly free of him." If I weren't, they'd likely boil me. "Thanks to the Oracle's sister."

He nodded once, glancing at Del. "We honor you, Oracle's sister."

Del was startled. But she retained enough courtesy to give him thanks for that, for his meat, for his liquor.

Oziri smiled. "You will be drunk."

Her face was rosy. "I think," she said, "I am."

He nodded once. "Good."

"Good?" she asked faintly.

"Good, yes." He glanced it me. "You, it will take longer."

"Oh, I don't know—I'm already feeling it."

"Drink more. There are tales to be told."

So I drank more, while the Vashni told us tales of the Oracle's prophecies of a man who would change the sand to grass, thus changing the future of the desert. I kept my face free of reaction, but I couldn't help wondering if that kind of future was anathema to them. Yet the warriors seemed merely to accept what their Oracle had prophesied, as if it hadn't occured to them to question what might come. Blind faith, sitting before me.

"Jhihadi," Oziri said, and the others murmured something.

I flicked a sharp glance at him.

"The Oracle said he will change the sand to grass."

I chewed thoughtfully at a final bite of meat, recalling the suggestions I had made to a young man called Mehmet about digging new wells and using cisterns linked to channels to bring the water to areas without. The suggestion had seemed quite logical to me, infinitely practical. So obvious, in fact, I found it amazing no one else had ever thought of it.

And for that suggestion, Mehmet had named me jhihadi.

A man could own a dwelling and a plot of land and call himself a king. A man could have an idea that suited a prophecy, and call himself a messiah.

And there were times when that kind of label could be valuable.

I swallowed the meat, then leaned forward, dug a shallow depression in the dirt, drew a line leading out of it, then poured liquor into the depression. After a moment, it flowed into the finger-wide channel. I reached out, plucked a sprig of grass, and set it at the end of the channel as the liquor arrived.

"Sand," I said, "is grass."

The Vashni stared at my little demonstration. Dark faces paled. Four pairs of eyes fastened themselves on my face, staring in astonishment. Clearly they were shaken.

"But don't mind me," I told them, shrugging. "I'm pretty drunk."

And indeed I was. This morning I had eaten nothing, killed a man, lost the dinner I'd had the night before, and swallowed most of the contents of an unfamiliar liquor under a warm afternoon sun.

"He *is* the jhihadi," Del declared emphatically. "My brother said so. Was he not your Oracle?" Now it was her turn to be stared at. She blinked, put a hand to her head, then said the words I never, ever expected to hear from her: "Oh, Tiger, I am so dreadfully drunk."

"Sometimes," I said, "this is a good thing." I put my arm around her shoulders, guided her close so she could slump against me without falling over, and smiled fatuously at the Vashni. "And now, if you don't mind, I think the Oracle's sister—and very probably the jhihadi—are going to pass out."

Chapter 7

I woke up to the sound of retching. Del, I realized, was no longer beside me. And she'd never been so drunk before.

Ah.

I cracked an eye and realized the sun was up, filtering down through the trees. This is not a particularly strange discovery to make unless you've gone to sleep—or passed out—in the late afternoon, and it appears to be the *morning* sun.

I opened the other eye, squinted up at arching limbs with their feathery, waving leaves, then girded my loins for battle and managed to lever myself up on an elbow. The world wobbled. So did I. I caught sight of Del several paces away, clutching a tree and looking for all the world as if she'd fall down without it.

Poor bascha.

Belatedly, I became aware of a sense of absence. A sharp glance around the camp showed me no Vashni, no Vashni horses, no skins or carcasses. Only the stud and gelding, still tied to trees but unsaddled, and our belongings piled neatly nearby. Including knives and swords.

As I moved to get up, something shifted against my chest, getting caught on the harness. I looked down, saw a handful of ivory ornaments danging against the burnous. Some kind of necklet had been put around my neck as I slept. Closer inspection showed a string of human fingerbones carefully wired together.

Ugh.

But I elected not to take the necklet off in case Vashni were watching from cover. You never know when the repudiation of a gift might get you cooked. And then *your* fingerbones would adorn someone's neck.

There is no cure for the day after a good drunk—or a bad one, depending on your point of view—but there is something that helps. I groped around, found the bota, sloshed it to test for contents, unstoppered it and drank. The bite was just as bad, the smell just as pungent. But adding new liquor to old would improve morning-after miseries.

I raised my voice. "You going to live?"

Del didn't answer except to be sick again.

I sat up all the way, shut my eyes a moment, kept my own belly down with a massive application of determination, and swallowed more liquor.

Eventually Del made her way back to the blanket, clutching a water bota. I noticed she also had been gifted with a fingerbone necklet but decided against mentioning it just yet. She was very pale—more than usual, that is—and circles had appeared beneath her eyes.

She sat down, leaned her head into her hands, and mumbled, "You must be enjoying this."

"What, seeing you get sick? Trust me, bascha, it's one of the least attractive sights in the world."

"No. That I *am* sick. After all the times I reprimanded you for getting drunk." She sighed heavily into the heels of her hands. "I don't see how you do it. I don't see *why* you do it!"

"Well, usually that isn't the point. I mean, not to get so drunk I feel that bad the next day. Unfortunately, sometimes it is the price you pay."

"I don't want to pay it."

"You didn't have much choice. It was the polite thing to do when being hosted by murdering savages."

"*You're* not sick."

"I did that yesterday, remember?" I gently slapped the bota against one arm. "Here. I know you don't want to, but I promise it'll help."

"I have water."

"It's not water."

She lifted her head and looked at me. "You can't mean more of that horrible spirit!"

"I can. I do. Just a few sips, bascha. Then lie down and go back to sleep."

"Tiger—"

"I've already had my medicine. Your turn."

She looked and sounded desperate. "I don't want any!"

"Well, I could pour it down your gullet *for* you . . ."

She knew I'd do it, too. Del gritted her teeth, took the bota, winced from the smell, then tipped the skin up to drink. Her hands shook, but she squeezed a couple of swallows into her mouth.

I thought at first she might be sick again, but she managed to keep it down. "Another swallow," I prompted.

She managed that, then thrust the bota back at me. After a moment she lay down on her side with her back to me, one hand over her face. The sun through leaves spread a lattice of dappled shadow across her body.

Smiling, I sorted out her tangled braid. "Sleep. We're in no rush."

What she replied was unintelligible. Probably just as well.

I knew better than to attempt to go back to sleep myself. Once awake after a session of too much liquor, I stayed that way for a while. I'd sleep again later. Besides, other business called me. I got up, suppressing groans, stood there a moment until the world steadied, then made my way into the brush to find a likely bush. After offering a rather prodigous libation to the gods of alcohol, I set about assessing our situation.

First I checked the horses and found them content, lipping up what remained of the grain that apparently the Vashni had given them. Our oiled canvas buckets were on the ground within reach, and each contained enough water that I knew the horses weren't thirsty. Our weapons remained on the blanket where we'd put them, though the Vashni swords and knives were gone. Our saddle-pouches were stacked next to them, and there was an extra leather bag. I loosed the thong drawstring enough to discover the contents were more meat, nearly lost my belly then, and dropped the bag instantly. Later. Maybe.

So. They had guested us in their camp, fed us, given us drink, untacked, fed, and watered our horses, left our weapons and belongings, and gifted us with meat and bone necklets. All in all, I couldn't think of a more polite visit with anyone.

Hmmm. Being the jhihadi has its advantages.

I dug through our pouches and pulled out some dried cumfa. While it's hardly a delicacy, it was somewhat more appetizing this morning than barely cooked sandtiger meat left for gods know how long in a leather bag, plus it was preserved in salt. Salt in the desert is a must. I grabbed up a water bota and went back to the blanket, settling down to a meager breakfast. Del slept on.

Lucky bascha.

When next I awoke, Del was no longer retching. Or sleeping. In fact, she was up doing what I'd already done: checking the horses, our belongings. She was moving with much less grace than usual but had rebraided her hair and changed into a cleaner burnous, since she had, as I had, used her sleeve to clean her face, and looked altogether more prepossessing than she had earlier. Though there was no question she didn't feel *good.*

"It lives," I commented.

Del peered balefully at me, shielding her eyes from the sun with a raised hand. "Barely. I had more of the spirits. What do call it?—the bark of the dog?"

I grinned. "The *hair* of the dog. Told you it works."

"Marginally." She hooked a finger under the fingerbone necklet dangling against her harness and displayed it. "What's this?"

"My guess is it's some kind of guest-gift. You're the Oracle's sister, and I'm the jhihadi. Maybe they're some kind of safe passage tokens through Vashni territory. Not a bad thing to have."

It was an understatement to mention Del was not happy. "We didn't even wake up when they put them on us. They might as easily have cut our throats."

"They could have done that while we were awake. Anyway, I think we'd better wear them for a while, just in case."

She didn't like the idea, but nodded. Then she pointed at the Vashni sack. "Can we at least get rid of that? I think we should bury it."

I grinned. "Not too fond of sandtiger, are we?"

"It doesn't taste particularly good going in either direction."

Fortunately I'd only experienced the one direction. I grabbed a bota and sucked down more water, then made the effort to climb to my feet. It was easier this time. "Better take it with us, till we're out of Vashni territory. You never know what might insult them."

"Then *you* carry it."

I glanced up at the sun. "Midday," I muttered. "We ought to get moving. Maybe we can make the chimney before nightfall."

"Or not," Del said, "considering how we feel. You said yourself there is no rush."

"That was earlier, when I took pity on you."

"And I'm not deserving of any now?"

"You're standing, aren't you? If you can stand, you can ride."

Del said glumly, "I suppose that means I must stay on my horse."

"Well, I could always throw you belly-down over the saddle and tie you on. Of course, all the blood would rush to your head, and I'm not sure that would make you feel any better. I certainly recall how I felt when you did it to *me*."

She flicked me an arch glance. "That was the Vashni who did it to you. And it was either that or let them kill you. To kill Chosa Dei."

"Well, they *were* much friendlier this time around," I agreed. Then I scratched my head and sighed, staring at the horses. "I suppose they won't saddle themselves. Guess we'd better get to work."

And work it was, with a pounding head. Took longer than usual, too, though eventually we did have both horses saddled, repacked, and ready to go. The Vashni had left us two blankets as well, which I found downright neighborly of them.

I led the stud into the center of the clearing, sorry to leave the shade. With great deliberation I stuck a foot into the left stirrup, carefully pulled myself up, and swung my right leg over. Amazingly, everything stayed attached.

"Well, bascha, I guess—" But I didn't finish, because Del arrived with the gelding in tow, thrust his reins at me urgently, and disappeared with haste behind a clump of trees.

This time I didn't tease her. I dug out some of the red silk left over from my Skandic clothing, unhooked a water bota, and handed both down to her without comment when she reappeared. Del rinsed her mouth, spat, then washed her face. She looked terrible.

I made the sacrifice. "Maybe we should stay here another night."

"No." Del took the gelding's reins back from me, flipped them over his neck, and mounted. She was clearly shaky, but determined. "I know how badly you want to get your hands on your *jivatma*. If it were mine . . ." She shook her head. "We'll go on."

The poor, pitiful bascha had reverted to cold-faced Northern sword-singer. I knew better than to attempt to jolly her out of it.

Besides, she needed to concentrate on keeping her belly where it belonged.

I realized within a couple of hours that we were not going to make the chimney before nightfall. Though I was feeling much better as the day wore on, and Del seem resigned to a generalized discomfort— at least she wasn't sick anymore—a faster pace might upset the balance. Not only that, but footing was tougher as we wound our way closer to the dramatic rock formations in the distance, beyond the foothills. Skull-sized boulders sprouted like shrubbery, abetted by drifts of bedrock peeping above the soil. The horses had to pay more attention to where they set their hooves, and we had to pay more attention to the occasional misstep, prepared to bring equine heads up to reestablish balance before they went down onto their knees.

Then a sandy area caught my eye. Like water spilled from a pitcher, it wound its way through rocks, then spread into a wider patch.

"Over here," I called to Del, riding behind me. "Footing's better."

And indeed it was. The sandy area went down a rocky hillock

and opened into something very like a shallow streambed, except there was no water. There had been once, before desert took it over. But now it was dry, with an underlayment of hard and uneven stone intermixed with sandy pockets and water-smoothed, hollowed-out boulders. Amazingly, there was a scattering of vegetation here, edging the streambed. Tough, reedy-looking shrubbery of a pallid green hue.

"Look ahead—there." Del pointed. "Are those wagon ruts?"

"Out here?" But even as I asked it, I saw what she meant. A few paces up there indeed appeared to be wheel ruts running across the streambed, visible only when they hit sand pockets. I moved the stud into a faster pace, then pulled up when I reached the ruts. "Hunh," I commented. "*Someone's* been out here in a wagon."

Del reined in beside me. "It makes no sense. There is nothing out here for settlers or caravans."

I shook my head. "Not enough tracks for a caravan. One wagon, I'd guess. Two mules. Maybe someone got lost." I marked how the ruts entered the streambed on one side and exited the other. "Let's follow the tracks," I suggested, reining left. "Maybe whoever we find will invite us to supper."

"If they haven't already been someone else's supper."

"I'm not sure we're still in Vashni territory," I said. "Which reminds me . . ." I untied the increasingly odiferous bag of sandtiger meat from the saddle and let it drop into the edge of the streambed as the stud climbed out. The gelding followed, white head swinging on the end of his long neck. Gold fringe dangled lopsidedly. "You know, you could always hang your Vashni necklet across your horse's face. He's already wearing axle grease and wine-girl fringe . . . human fingerbones might give him a little added class."

Del, not surprisingly, did not deign to reply.

We followed the tracks as they wound their way through the rocks and sand. After a while they turned in toward the mountains on our left, gaining in elevation. We wound our way up, and then almost abruptly the crude ruts gave out onto a flat area to our right, opposite the massive boulders skirting the bottom of the mountain on the left. The flat formed a plateau, the chopped off crown of a shallow bluff overlooking where we'd come from, including the streambed. A few straggly trees, low shrubbery, and modest grassy patches skirted the edge near the continuation of the ruts. I pulled up there to give the stud a blow and take a look around. Del's gelding picked its way slowly up to join us. Del was, I noticed, drinking water again.

"You all right, bascha?"

She nodded as she restoppered the bota. "Much better than this morning. Just thirsty."

"Liquor does that." I glanced around. "You know, this wouldn't be a bad place to stop for the night—" I broke off, whistling in surprise. "Hoolies—would you look at that?" I pointed. "Up there against the boulders, there. Looks like a shelter to me. And the remains of a cookfire in front of it."

"Where—? Oh, *that?*" Del rode past me, heading toward the huge tumbled boulders lining the merging of mountain with flat area. "It is a shelter, Tiger—it's a little lean-to. The wagon ruts go right past it, but they're deeper by the shelter, as if they stopped here."

I followed. Del was right. Someone had used one of the larger boulder formations for the back wall and had built a rough lean-to out of branches and canvas. The fire ring hadn't been used for a while, but clearly this was a regular camping place. No one would sacrifice canvas in the desert unless he intended to return.

"Halloo the camp!" I called. "We're coming in!"

Del reined in next to the fire ring. "No one's here."

"You never know." I dismounted and drew my sword. Del had done the same. But there was no place to hide in the lean-to; it boasted only two sides, the boulder for a back wall, and a branch-and-canvas roof. It was large enough for possibly three people, if they were very close friends. "Good enough for tonight," I said. "Let's get the horses settled, and then we can think about food."

Del recoiled. Her expression clearly announced she wanted nothing to do with food. Possibly forever.

I disagreed. "You need to eat something. You've only had water all day."

"Yes, and in fact . . ." She turned abruptly and headed toward the hillside strewn with tumbled boulders, sheathing her sword.

"Are you sick again?" I asked.

"No. But I have had a *lot* of water."

"Ah." Grinning, I strode back to the horses. I decided to be a nice, kind, thoughtful man and untack her gelding. "Hold on, old son," I told the stud. "You're next."

I untied saddlepouches and piled them beside the lean-to, tossed Del's bedding inside. The gelding gazed at me out of mournful blue eyes, peering through dangling bits of fringe.

"You look ridiculous," I told him, undoing his girth. "No offense, but you do." I lifted saddle and blankets off his damp back, set both by the lean-to. "Amazing what we let women get away with, isn't it?" His response was to thrust his head against my chest and rub. Hard. "Ah, hoolies, horse—" In disgust, I stared down at the front of my burnous. "Now I've got black gunk all over me!" Of course, the gelding also had greasepaint smeared all over his face, like an overly painted wine-girl first thing in the morning. Quite a pair, we made.

I heard the rattle of fallen pebbles high in the rocks and glanced up to see Del picking her way down from one of the piles of boulders. You'd think that since we'd been sharing a bed for several years modesty would no longer matter, but Del was fastidious. She always went off to find privacy, and I'd been ordered to do the same. I just never went as far. Men have a certain advantage when it comes to relieving the bladder.

Her arms were spread for balance as she worked her way down. She was concentrating on her path, rope of hair swinging in front of one shoulder. It's difficult to look particularly graceful when clambering down over piled rocks and boulders. Even for my Northern bascha.

I drew in a deep breath, preparing to bellow complaints about her horse. But I lost the impulse the instant I saw movement behind her.

Vashni? No—

Movement flowed down the mountainside, disappeared behind rocks.

I dropped the reins. "Del!"

Then it sprang up onto a boulder, and I saw it clearly.

"*Del*—" I was running for the rocks, yanking sword out of sheath. Her face was turned toward me.

I'd never make it, never make it—

"*—behind you—*"

Atop the rock she spun, grasping for her sword hilt, and went down hard beneath the leaping sandtiger.

Chapter 8

When in the midst of deadly danger, time slows. Fragments. It is me, the moment, the circumstances.

As it was now.

I saw Del, down. The glint of sun off her bared blade, lying against stone. The spill of white-blond braid. The sandtiger's compact, bunched body, blending into the rocky background as it squatted over her.

I bellowed at the cat as I ran. Anything to distract him, to draw his attention from his prey. Del was unmoving: probably unconscious, possibly dead.

"Try *me!*" I shouted. "*Try me*, you thrice-cursed son of a Salset goat—"

The sandtiger growled, then yowled as it saw me. I threatened his prey. For a moment he continued to hunch over Del, then came up into a crouch, flexing shoulders. Jaw dropped open. Green eyes glared.

Everything was slowed to half-time. I watched the bunching of haunches, the leap; judged momentum and direction; knew without doubt what was necessary. My nearly vertical blade, at the end of thrusting arms, met him in midair. Sank in through belly fur, hide, muscle, vessels, and viscera, spitting him to the hilt. I felt the sudden weight, heard the scream, smelled the rank breath, the musk of a mature male. Without pausing I ducked head and dropped shoulder, swung, let his momentum carry him through his leap. Over my head, and down.

I was conscious of the horses screaming, but I paid them no attention. I was focused only on the sandtiger, now sprawled on the ground, jaws agape, tongue lolling. For all I knew he was dead already, but I jerked the blade free, then swung it up, over, down, like a club, and severed his head from his body.

Then I dropped the sword. I turned, took two running strides, climbed up into the boulders. *"Bascha . . ."*

She lay mostly face-down, one arm sprawled across a cluster of rocks. Her torso was in a shallow gulley between two boulders. Legs were twisted awry.

"Del—?"

There was blood, and torn burnous. I caught the tangled rope of hair and moved it aside, baring the back of her neck to check for wounds. She had not had time to face the cat fully. His leap had been flat, then tending down. Front paws had curled over her shoulders, grasping, while back paws raked out, reaching for purchase.

He had leaped at her back, intending to take his prey down from behind. But Del had moved, had begun to turn toward him as I yelled, had begun to unsheathe her sword, and he'd missed his target. Instead of encircling her neck with his jaws, snapping it, piercing the jugular, the big canine teeth had dug a puncture and furrow into her right forearm and the top of her left shoulder at the curve of her neck. The main impetus of the bite had fouled on harness and sheath.

I planted my feet as firmly as possible in the treacherous footing, then bent, caught a limp arm, and pulled her up. I squatted, ducked, levered her over one shoulder, head hanging, braid dangling against my thigh, while her legs formed a counterweight before me. I rose carefully, balancing the slack-limbed drape of her body. Teeth clenched, I made my way slowly down the boulders, found level footing on the flat, sandy crown of the bluff, and carried her to the lean-to. I had tossed her rolled bedding there while unpacking the gelding; with care I slid her over and down, arranged her limbs, set her head against the bedroll. Then, locking my hands into the front of her burnous, I tore fabric apart along the seam, exposing her body in its sleeveless tunic.

Exposing arms and legs, and the sandtiger's handiwork.

"All right, bascha—give me a moment here . . ."

Almost without thinking I unbuckled the harness, worked the leather straps and buckles over her arms and out from under her body. Tossed it aside in a tangle of leather and brass. Yanked my knife free of its sheath, cut swathes of her burnous, and began wadding it between torn flesh and what remained of the tunic's high neck. Claws had cut through it, into the flesh beneath, baring the twin ridges of collar bones. One claw had nicked the underside of her jawbone at the angle beneath her left ear, trickling blood across her throat.

More fabric was sacrificed for her right forearm as I bound it tightly. Then I worked my left arm under her back, lifted her, tipped her forward against me. Her head lolled into my shoulder.

"Hold on, bascha—I'm taking a look at your back."

The sandtiger had attempted to set hind claws into her lower back and the tops of her buttocks, but all he'd managed to do as she turned was pierce the leather of her tunic. Very little blood showed through. So, the worst of the damage appeared to be the bite wounds at the top of her shoulder and in her right forearm, plus the deep claw lacerations reaching from the first upswelling of both breasts nearly to her throat.

Of course, that was the *visible* damage. Inside, beneath the flesh and muscle, sandtiger poison coursed through her blood.

With Del slumped against me, I untied the thongs on her bedding, unrolled it with a snap and flip of my hand, eased her onto it. Now it was time. Time I knew.

I bent over her, then slowly lowered my head. Rested my ear against her chest, petitioning all the gods I'd cursed for all of my life that she not be dead.

The beating was slow but steady.

My breath left on a rush of relief. I did not sit up immediately. I pressed dry lips against her brow and did more than petition. This time I prayed.

*   *   *

When it became clear the bite wound in the top of her shoulder did not intend to stop bleeding on its own despite my ministrations, I did the only thing I could. I built a quick, haphazard fire in the rock ring outside the shelter, arranged my knife so the blade would heat, and when steel glowed red, I wrapped a flap of leather around the handle and carried it back inside the lean-to. Del was as pale as I'd ever seen in a living woman, even to her lips. Apologizing in silence, I ground my teeth together and set the hot blade against the wound.

Blood sizzled like weeping fat over a fire. The smell of burning flesh was pungent. I felt my gorge rise and fought it back down; Del would hardly appreciate it if I threw up all over her. I was aware of a detached sort of surprise; I had cauterized various wounds in my own body more times than I could count. But never before had I done it to Del.

She stirred, twisting her head. Her mouth sprang open in a weak, breathless protest. I tossed the knife aside, caught both her hands, and hung on.

"I know, bascha. I know. I'm sorry. I'm sorry." Her eyelids flickered. "Del?"

But she was gone again, hands lying limply in my own. I set them down, noted blood had soaked through the bandage on her forearm, and turned on my knees to gather up more makeshift bandages.

The world around me wavered.

Not surprising. Reaction. I shook my head, wiped sweat out of my eyes, grabbed gauze and folded a section into a pad. After unwrapping blood-soaked bandages, I bound the pad to the seeping wound. What it needed was stitches, but I had nothing to use. The stud was gone; he'd departed in blind panic during the sandtiger attack. It meant the loss of half our food and water and other supplies, including the medicaments Del had packed. I had nothing for treating her except the crude bandages I'd already fashioned out of burnouses, cautery, and a bota of Vashni liquor, which had been put into our pouches without either of us being aware of it.

I'd considered using cautery on the forearm bite wound, but decided against it in favor of pressure and tight binding. Del would scar regardless, but using hot steel on it would twist the flesh, binding it into stiffness. She needed the flexibility to handle a sword. Nor would she thank me if I did something that harmed her ability to wield one.

I sighed when finished, let my eyes close for a moment. The day was nearly done. The sun straggled down the sky, preparing to drop below the horizon. The long desert twilight would provide light for an hour or so, and then it would be night, with only the stars, the moon, and the dying fire for illumination. I needed to find more wood, but I didn't want to leave Del that long.

Still, two swords were lying out there, hers and mine. I'd taken no time to pick them up since pulling Del out of the rocks. For the moment she was lying quietly.

I stood up, crouching beneath the low roof, and ducked out the open front. Muscles protested as I straightened. Del's gelding nickered softly as he saw me. *He* at least had remained despite the sandtiger attack. When I had time to track down the stud, who probably wouldn't go far, I intended to have words with him.

I went hunting. Del's sword lay between two of the boulders. I picked it up, climbed back down to mine beside the dead cat. I set both blades aside, grabbed the hindlegs, and dragged the sandtiger farther away from the camp. Scavengers very likely would come for his carcass; I'd just as soon they did so from a greater distance.

Something occured to me.

Smiling grimly, I unsheathed my knife. With great deliberation I cut out each of the ten curving front claws. I tied them into the remains of my burnous, then gathered up the swords and went back to the lean-to.

Del lay as I had left her, very still upon her bedding. The sun, going down in a haze of red and gold, gilded her face and lent it the healthy color it lacked. I propped both blades against one crude wall, caught up a bota, and sat down to once again dribble water into her mouth, bit by bit so she wouldn't choke.

In the final vestiges of the dying day, seated next to Delilah, I cleaned my blade of sandtiger blood—hers had never made contact—propped it once again beside hers, then untied the sandtiger claws from the rags of my burnous. Employing knife, Vashni liquor, and grim deliberation, I began to clean them of blood and tendon. When I had time, I'd drill a hole in each one, string them on a thong, and set it around Del's neck.

I glanced down at her, noting the pallor of her face. "I made it," I said. "I survived. So will you. You're tougher than I am."

Later, she was restless. A hand to her forehead told me precisely what I expected: she was fevered. Quite apart from the wounds, the poison from envenomed claws was enough to make her deathly ill, even to kill her. As a boy I'd been clawed in the face and across one thigh and had been very sick from sandtiger poison for three days despite the fact much of the venom had been expelled before I was clawed. Years later a couple of shallow scratches laid me low for hours. But Del had sustained much deeper gouges than I.

Earlier, I had hacked down some of the branches used to build the shelter, tossing them onto the fire. Now I threw the last of those I'd cut on the coals, waited for the flare of kindling flame, then knelt by her side. In the reflected firelight her cheeks were flushed, blotched red and white from the poison. Her lips and eyelids were swollen.

I dampened a cloth with water, then pressed it gently against her face. Lastly I wetted a corner, laid it on her lips, and squeezed. Her mouth moved minutely, responding to the water; I slipped a hand beneath her head, lifted it, dribbled tepid water into her mouth. Her throat spasmed in a swallow; then she began to choke.

Swearing, I dropped the bota and pulled her upright, then bent her slightly forward over my right arm. I let her head hang loose, chin hooked over my wrist. With a spread left hand, I pressed sharply against her spine several times, compressing her lungs. In a moment the choking turned to coughing. When that faded, I eased her down again, smoothing sweat-damp strands of hair away from her face.

"I'm here," I told her. "I left you in Staal-Ysta, when I thought you would die—when I thought I had killed you . . . I'll never leave you again. I'm here, bascha."

The claw stripes above her breasts were oozing blood again. I dampened more cloth, cleaned the wounds, then pressed a folded pad against them, tucking it under the shredded ruins of her tunic.

The last of the roof branches I'd cut down no longer flamed. Light was fading. Outside the lean-to, the white gelding pawed at sand and soil. In a brief break from tending Del I'd watered him, given him grain, but he wanted grazing. Though he'd proven his willingness to stay put, I couldn't risk losing him as well as the stud. He was tied to the lean-to. If the gods were merciful, he wouldn't pull it down on top of us.

My own bedding, still on the stud, was gone. But the gelding's saddle, set next to the shelter, had borne a rolled-up Vashni blanket. I tugged it over, threw it across rocky soil, set my rump upon it. I ached in every muscle, and my eyes were burning with exhaustion. I rubbed them, swore at the gritty dryness that stung unremittingly, then slumped against the boulder forming the back wall of the lean-to.

Sharp pain forced a grunt of surprise out of me. I sat forward again, reaching over the top of my right shoulder. Stung? But the boulder had no cracks, no crevices to host anything, being nothing more than a giant, rounded bulwark at the bottom of the modest mountain.

I brought my fingers around, tipped them toward firelight, rubbed my thumb against sticky residue, then sniffed fingers.

Blood.

I felt again behind my right shoulder, sliding my hand beneath the tattered remains of my burnous. Found two curving gouges there the length of palm and fingers, bleeding sluggishly.

I shut my eyes. Oh, hoolies . . . when I'd slung the spitted sandtiger over my right shoulder—

In my rage and fear, I'd felt nothing at all.

I tore the burnous off my torso, grabbed up the Vashni bota, squirted liquor down my back, aiming for claw marks I couldn't see. A burning so painful it brought tears to my eyes told me I'd found the target. I hissed a complex, unflagging string of Desert invective, breathed noisily, nearly bit my bottom lip in two.

When I could speak again, I looked at Del, whom I had liberally drenched. "Sorry, bascha—" I croaked. "—I had no idea it would burn so much!"

The world revolved again. Now I knew why. Knees drawn up,

I leaned my head into them as a stiff-fingered hand scrubbed distractedly at the back of my skull, scraping through short hair. Before, in ignorance, all my thoughts on Del, it had been a simple matter to ignore the signs. But now, knowing, feeling, they were manifest.

"Not now," I muttered. "Not *now*—"

Not yet.

We had only once been injured or sick at the same time. And then it had been on Staal-Ysta, forced into a dance that had nearly killed us both. Northerners had cared for her in one dwelling, while others cared for me. When I was healed enough to ride, knowing Del would surely die and that I could not bear to witness it, I left.

I wouldn't leave her again. I'd sworn it. But this time, now, there was no one to care for either of us.

I licked my lips. "All right," I told myself hoarsely, "you've been clawed before. Neither time killed you. You have some immunity."

Some. But enough? That I didn't know.

I traced the curve of my skull, growing less distinct as my hair lengthened. Beneath it there were elaborate designs tattooed into my skin, visible now only at the hairline above my forehead. They marked me a mage. IoSkandic. A madman of Meteiera.

I wiped sweat from my face with a trembling hand. Could magery overcome sandtiger poison? Could magery heal?

I knew it could kill.

Del made a sound, an almost inaudible release of breath coupled with the faintest of moans. I tried to move toward her, but my limbs were sluggish. Cursing my weakness, I made myself move. I nearly toppled over her, but a stiff arm jammed against the bedding kept me upright.

"Bascha?"

Nothing. Sweat ran from her flesh, giving off the stale metallic tang of sandtiger venom. I tasted the same in my own mouth.

Time was running out. Hastily, clumsily, I snagged the water bota, soaked the still-damp cloth, draped it across her forehead. Droplets rolled down into the hollows of closed eyes, filling the creases of her lids, then dribbled from the outer corners of her eyes, mimicking the tears Del never wept.

I tucked the bota under her right hand, being careful not to jar the bound forearm. I curled slack fingers loosely around the neck. I checked bandages for fresh blood. Found none. Felt a stab of relief like a knife in the belly.

"Hold on," I murmured. "Just hold on, bascha. You can make it through this."

The gelding whickered softly. I glanced out. There were, I realized, three fire rings in front of the lean-to, overlapping one another, merging, then springing apart again. I scowled, narrowing my eyes, trying to focus vision. Nothing helped.

I swore, then grabbed a corner of the Vashni blanket. Tugged it toward Del. Managed to pull it atop her, cover most of her body save head and sandaled feet.

"I know it's warm," I told her, "especially with a fever. But you need to sweat it out. Get rid of as much as you can." I stroked roughened knuckles against one fever-blotched cheek. "When I can, I'll go to Julah. Fouad can find us a healer. Then—"

I broke it off. *When. Then.* Who was I fooling?

If Del were conscious, she'd insist on the truth.

On Meteiera, near the Stone Forest where the new mage was whelped atop a rocky spire, I had conjured magic. I had dreamed and made the substance of dream real. Set scars rifted by magery back into my flesh. Formed a seaworthy boat out of little more than stormwrack and wishing.

Now I wished Del to live.

I bore tattoos under my hair and lacked two fingers, souvenirs of Meteiera, where mages and madmen lived and died. I had been then, and could be now, what I needed to be.

Del's life was at stake.

"All right, bascha, I'll try." I drew in a deep breath, sealed my eyes closed. "If I'm a mage," I said hoarsely, "if I'm truly a mage, let me find the way . . ."

I had done it in Meteiera, knowing nothing of power beyond that it existed. Blue-headed Nihko had told me those of us—*us!*—with magery in our blood had to use it, had to find a way to bleed off the power, lest it destroy us. But I had escaped the Stone Forest before learning much beyond a few simple rituals and prayers and the discipline of the priests; I was but an infant to the ways of the mages of Meteiera.

Discipline.

It claimed its own power.

I gathered myself there beside Delilah, body and soul, flesh and spirit, and tried to find the part of me that had been born atop a stone spire in far-off ioSkandi. I knew nothing of the doing but that I had done it. Once, twice, thrice. Since then I had locked the awareness away, concentrating only on the physical, the retraining of a body lacking two fingers.

A shiver wracked me. Something slammed into my body, buffeting awareness like a wind snuffing out candle-flame. Weakness swam in. I meant to move aside; I *tried* to move aside, to find and lean against the wall of stone regardless of claw gouges, needing the support. But my limbs got tangled. I could not tell what part of me were legs, which were arms, or if I even retained my head atop my shoulders.

Power eluded me. What strength was left diminished like sand running out of a glass.

Fear for Del surged up. "No—" I murmured, "—wait—" But all the strength poured out of my body. I slumped sideways, vision doubled; fought it, attempted to push myself upright; went suddenly down onto my back on hardpacked soil and sand. *"—wait—"*

An outflung arm landed against unsheathed blades propped against the sidewall. I felt one of them, in toppling, fall across my elbow. It was the flat, not the edge—but by then I didn't care.

I was dimly aware of a flicker of stunned outrage, and a voice in my head. *Not like this—*

In the circle, yes. If a man had to die. But not from the last wayward scratch of a dying sandtiger.

"Bascha—" I murmured.

But the world was gone.

Chapter 9

B ones. Bones and sand. Bones and sand and sun. And heat.

Parched lips. Burned flesh. Swollen tongue. Blood yet running, smearing her thighs. Except there are no thighs. No lips, no flesh, no tongue. All has been consumed.

From a distance, the bones are thread against sparkling silk. But closer, ever closer, pushed down from air to earth like a raptor stooping, thread takes on substance, sections itself into skull, into arms, and legs. Silk is sand. Crystalline Punja sand.

Scoured clean of flesh, ivory bone gleams. Delicate toes are scattered. Fingers are nonexistent. Ribs have collapsed into a tangled riddle. The skull lies on its side, teeth bared in a rictus, sockets empty of eyes.

I am pulled into them, lips brought to dentition, live teeth clicking on dead. Against my mouth bone moves. "Find me," she says.

I want nothing to do with her. With it. With what the bones had been.

"Find me," she says. "Take up the sword."

The hand captured my head. For a moment I feared it was sand, and sun, and death. But the hand cupped my head, lifted it, set bota against my lips. Living lips, not bone. Water trickled into my mouth.

It was enough to rouse me to something akin to panic. I lifted both arms, grasped with trembling hands, closed on leather water-skin. Squeezed.

"Not so much," he chided.

He. Not she. The dead woman was gone.

I drank. Swallow after swallow. Then he pulled it away.

"Not so much," he repeated.

I wanted all of it.

"Del," I croaked. Swollen lips split and bled. Swollen eyes wouldn't open. "Del . . ."

"She's alive." Damp cloth bathed my face. "I swear it."

"Poison," I said. "Sandtiger—"

"I know. I recognize the wounds. Here. A little more."

More water. I drank, wanting to drown. "Del?"

"Alive."

"Poison . . ."

"Yes."

Dread was a blade in the vitals. "She's dying . . ."

"Maybe," he said.

Del's bones in the sand?

"Don't let her die."

"It wants a healer," he said. "I need to go back to Julah."

Julah. "Fouad's," I told him. "Cantina."

"Later," he replied. "I'll stay awhile yet."

"I won't die," I said. "Not from a sandtiger."

I heard a breath of laughter. "I don't doubt it."

"Del?"

"Alive," he repeated.

"You swore."

"Yes. I'm not lying. She might die, but she's not dead yet."

It was something.

"Who are you?" I asked.

But before he could answer, the world winked out.

When next I roused, the weakness was less. I still lay on hardpan, itching from sand, but a light blanket was thrown over me and another, still rolled, pillowed my head. A bota lay at hand, as I had left one for Del. I shut fingers on it, brought to my mouth, drank and drank and drank.

"Del?"

No answer.

I opened my eyes. I had no idea what hour it was, or day. Merely that I was alive despite the best efforts of my body to die.

"Bascha?" My voice was hoarse.

No answer.

I collected strength. Hoarded it. Hitched myself up on an elbow. Saw the colorful Vashni blanket and the body beneath.

Shadow fell across me. I glanced up, staring blearily at the opening and the man squatting there. "You?" I croaked.

Stubble emphasized the hollows and angles of his face. He was dark as a Southroner, but with the faintest tint of copper to his tan. And those honey-brown eyes, liquid and melting, fringed in black lashes Del would claim too lush for a man, and infinitely unfair when women would kill for such.

"Me," he agreed.

I slumped back onto the ground, wanting to groan. Didn't, since we had company. "If you've come to challenge me—*again*—you picked a bad time."

"So I see. And no, I haven't. I've learned a little since you killed that sword-dancer in Julah."

When was that? I didn't remember. A day ago. A month. "Then what are you doing here?"

"I am," he said, with grave dignity entirely undermined by a glint of irony in his eyes, "looking after a man who has repudiated his honor. And the infamous Northern bascha who should be lacking in such, being merely a woman, but who appears to have it regardless. Or so some say." He crawled into the lean-to, sat down beside me. "I couldn't ask a dead man what *elaii-ali-ma* meant," he said, "but I asked another sword-dancer when he came into town."

"Oh, good." I managed my own irony despite the hoarse voice. "Then you know. You don't have to challenge me to a dance, because there can be no dance. But you can kill me if you want to." I paused. "If you can."

The faintest of smiles twitched one corner of his mouth. "Well, that would at the moment be a simple thing."

"And where's the honor in that?"

"So I asked myself." He placed a hand against my forehead.

"The worst of the fever has passed, I think, but you're far from well."

I knew that without being told. "Who are you?"

"My mother named me Nayyib."

"This isn't the road from Julah. What are you doing here?"

"It's *a* road from Julah," he clarified, "now. And I came looking for you. Fortunate thing, yes?"

"I thought you said you weren't going to challenge me."

"I'm not. At least, not in that way."

That sounded suspicious. "In *what* way, then?"

"I wish to become a sword-dancer."

I grunted. "I figured that."

"I wish you to teach me."

"What, you just decided this?"

"I decided this in Julah, after you killed that sword-dancer."

"Khashi."

"After you killed Khashi."

"Why? Didn't you originally want to kill me?"

"No. I wanted to dance against you. I didn't know anything about this *elaii-ali-ma*. You were just—you. After I saw what happened to Khashi and learned what had happened to you, I decided to follow you."

I attempted to frown, which isn't easy when you're sick. "You followed us to Julah."

"Well, yes."

"And at that point you still wanted to challenge me."

"I did. At that point I thought I was good with a sword."

"You don't anymore?"

His mouth twitched. "Not good enough."

"So *now* you want to be taught by a man who has no honor?"

"A man who once was the greatest in all the South."

Once was. Once. What in hoolies was I now?

Well, sick. That's what.

"So you figure if you look after us while we're sick, you'll earn some lessons."

His tone was exquisitely bland. "I should think saving your lives might be worth one or two."

I shut my eyes. "You're a fool."

"Undoubtedly." He placed the bota under my hand again. "I've tended her, got more water down her, wet the cloth again. And I've watered your horse. Grained him. Tied him under a tree for what little shade there is, and the few blades of grass."

"Busy boy," I muttered.

He ignored that. "But he'll need more water later. So will she. Can you manage it?"

"I'll manage it." How, I didn't know. But I wouldn't admit it to a kid. Especially not this kid, who had a mouth on him.

He seemed to know it anyway. "I'll go to Fouad's and ask him for help. I'll bring a healer, food, and more water. There isn't much left. Ration it, if you want to live. I put wood by the fire."

He had indeed been a busy boy—and it just might save us. "Wait." I levered myself up on an elbow. "You say there's a road to Julah from here?"

"Such as it is. Paired ruts, nothing more."

"We didn't come that way."

"I crossed your tracks."

But Del and I had spent the night with the Vashni, and the kid—Nayyib—had only just reached us. "There's a shorter way. Follow our tracks back to the streambed, and go from there."

Black brows drew together. "Vashni territory. Or is that your way of getting me killed?"

"Oh, I'd do that myself. No—here." With a trembling hand— hoolies, I hate being weak!—I pulled the Vashni necklet over my head, fingerbones clacking. "Wear this. It's safe passage."

He stared at the necklet, then flicked a glance back at me. "You're sure?"

"Well, I suppose they might kill you for sheer hard-headedness, but it ought to get you safely through."

He took the necklet, eyed it in distaste, then hooked it over his head. My elbow gave out and I thumped back to the ground. Shut my eyes. "Do it for Del," I said wearily, "not for me."

Against my lids his shadow shifted. Retreated. "I will try," he told me, "to make certain she doesn't die."

When I opened my eyes, the sun was down. And he was gone.

*   *   *

Wind blows. Sand shifts. It creeps upon the bones, begins to swallow them. Legs. Arms. The collapsed cage of ribs. The jewels that are spine. All that is left is skull. And the sword.

"*Find me,*" *she says.*

Could the bones belong to Del? Could she be dead?

I awoke with a start. "Auuggh," I croaked. "Stop with the dreams, already!"

Sweat drenched me. It stank of sandtiger venom. I rolled to my right side, started to use my elbow, thought better of it as the wounds in my back protested. After a moment I made the attempt to sit upright without the assistance of arms. Aching abdominal muscles warned me it wasn't such a good idea, but I managed to stay there. Eventually the world settled back into place.

The dream faded. Reality was bad enough.

I turned my head and spat, disliking the aftertaste of fever and poison. Dry-mouthed, nothing was expelled. I found the bota, rinsed my mouth, tried again. Much better. Then I drank sparingly, recalling the boy's warning regarding how much water was left.

I looked across at the blanketed form. Del did not appear to have roused. I set down the bota, took a deep breath, and made my body move.

Well, such as it could. In the end I flopped down on my belly, head near Del's pallet, and hitched myself up on a forearm.

"Bascha?" I peeled back the blanket with my free hand. Del's face remained slightly blotched, a network of red overlaying extreme pallor. Her swollen lips had cracked and bled. I rested a hand on her abdomen, waited in frozen silence, then felt the slight rising and falling. She breathed.

With effort, I pulled myself upright. Found her bota, shook it, heard the diminished sloshing. I had no idea when Nayyib had been here, when he'd left, or when he might return. For all I knew it was a week after he'd gone. I thought it more likely a matter of hours, though possibly it was the next day.

I hooked my left hand under Del's head and lifted it, placing the bota at her lips. I squeezed and dribbled water into her mouth. This time she swallowed without choking. I settled her head once more again the bedding.

The cloth across her forehead was dry. I wet it yet again, replaced it, cleared away the trickles that threatened her eyes and ears. "I'm here," I told her. "A little the worse for wear, but still here, bascha."

I did not know when Nayyib had changed her bandages. A torn burnous sat in a pile on her bedding, but I didn't recognize it. The boy's, apparently; and the fabric matched that now wrapping Del's forearm, so he had done that much. I peeled back the cloth to bare the bite wound. I bent, sniffed; did not yet smell infection or putrefaction.

So far.

I searched for and found the bota of Vashni liquor. Once again I poured it into the wound.

And for the first time in—hoolies, I didn't know how many days it was since the attack!—Del opened her eyes. They were hazy and unfocused.

"Bascha?"

But almost immediately they closed again.

"Del?"

Her lips moved, but no sound issued from her mouth. Instead of water, this time I dribbled liquor into her mouth.

Below the edge of the cloth, the faintest of frowns twitched her brows. Her left hand stirred, rose. Fingers touched her mouth. Then the hand flopped down to her neck.

I'd forgotten about the cracked lips when I'd given her the liquor.

I swore, stole the damp cloth from her forehead, and pressed it again her mouth. "Sorry, bascha. I didn't think."

I didn't think a lot.

She did not stir again. I took up Nayyib's burnous, made more bandages, wrapped her forearm again. Vashni liquor, I decided, ought to burn the poison out of anything.

I felt then at my own stripes on the back of my shoulder, cutting across the scapula. It was a bad angle, and even twisting my head until my neck complained did not bring the claw wounds into sight, but fingers told the story. The twin stripes were crusted, no longer bleeding. Leaving them alone was the best medicine.

Weariness intruded, as did dizziness. But there was the horse to tend. I drank a little of the liquor, breathed fire for a moment, then stoppered the bota and put it aside. I crawled to the opening of the lean-to, peered blearily out at the world, and wanted very badly to turn around and collapse into sleep—or unconsciousness—once more.

A few paces away, tied to a scrubby tree, Del's horse stood with a black-smeared face. With the detached, exquisite clarity of fading fever, I wondered briefly what Nayyib had thought upon first sighting the paint and fringe.

The gelding saw me and nickered, ears flicked forward.

"Fine," I muttered, "I'm coming. It might take me a day, but I'll get there."

Nayyib had left a water bota and grain pouch by the lean-to. I grabbed both, gathered my legs under me, pressed both arms against the ground, and pushed.

In grabbing the shelter roof to steady myself, I nearly brought it down. I let go, took a step away, and almost fell flat on my face. I saved myself from doing so only because most of me would have landed in the fire ring, and that was not a particularly favored destination.

The gelding nickered again.

Sun stabbed into my eyes. A lurking headache flared into existence. Everything, from bones and muscle to skin, ached unremittingly. I drew in a breath, set my teeth, and began the horrendously lengthy and perilous journey to the gelding, all of five paces away.

Upon reaching him I grabbed a hunk of mane to hold myself upright. "Hello," I said sociably, hoping he wouldn't move. "Nice weather we're having, isn't it?"

He blinked a white-lashed blue eye and nosed at the bota.

"Coming," I muttered, working at the stopper. Once free, I upended the waterskin and drained the contents into the canvas bucket. The gelding dipped his head and began to drink. I hung onto the curve of his withers, wondering if I could make it back to the lean-to. Possibly the gelding would have company tonight, right where he was.

Except Del was there. I'd make it back.

Done drinking, the gelding lifted his head. Clinging to him one-handed, I took the opportunity to relieve myself. The sharp tang of venom expelled with urine made the gelding shift uneasily.

"Not *now*," I suggested fervently, readjusting my dhoti. The gelding obliged. I thanked him with a pat, then opened the grain pouch and poured a handful into the empty water bucket. He needed good grazing, but there wasn't any. For now, this had to do.

I did not look forward to the journey back to the shelter. "One step an hour ought to get me there," I told the horse.

But he was no longer paying me any mind. He'd drawn himself up, head lifted, and pealed out a whinny of welcome. Steadying myself against his neck, I turned, expecting to see Nayyib. Relieved that I'd see Nayyib. He was bringing the healer.

And indeed, I saw Nayyib. Along with three other men on horseback. Nothing about them resembled healers. In fact, everything about them resembled sword-dancers.

Especially since I knew one of them.

He was highly amused. "Sandtiger." All his handsome white teeth were on display. "You look terrible."

I glared. It was all I could manage. "What do you want, Rafiq?"

"You."

Figured. I sighed, squinted at him, hung onto the gelding. "How about we skip the sword-fight and name you the winner," I suggested. "Right about now, as you can see, I'm not really up to a match. There'd be no challenge in it. As I recall, you like to tease an opponent for an hour or two before defeating him. Hoolies, I'd go down in the blink of an eye. No fun for you."

Rafiq was still grinning atop his palomino horse. "He said you were sick. Sandtiger, was it?" He laughed. "Appropriate."

I shot a glance at Nayyib. He sat his mount stiffly, not even looking at me. I wondered if they'd paid him to lead them back here. Or promised him a dance in a circle. Or lessons in being a sword-dancer.

"Sick," I agreed. "Probably even dying, and therefore not worth killing. So why don't you just ride on out of here and let me die in peace?"

Rafiq jumped off his horse, pulling something from the saddle. "Because," he said, approaching, "we have every intention of not letting you die. At least, not like this. If you're up and moving now, the poison's mostly out of your system."

"What's the plan?" I asked.

Rafiq had a loop of thin braided leather in his hands. "You're coming with us."

He intended to tie my hands. I debated avoiding it, even tensed to do so.

Rafiq saw it and laughed. "I can tie you standing here before me with some measure of dignity, or I can tie you with your rump planted in the dirt. Which do you prefer?"

I said nothing. He slipped the loop over my wrists and snugged it tight, preparing to knot it.

Then I moved.

Chapter 10

When I came to, my rump was not planted in the dirt. All of me was. Rafiq had one knee on my chest and was scowling into my face. I expected him to apply inventive curses to my aborted attempt to escape, but instead he asked, "What happened to your fingers?

I scowled back. "I got hungry."

Rafiq claimed a good share of Borderer blood and thus was larger than most men in the South. It wasn't an impossibility for him to jerk me to my feet, especially with me wobbly from venom residue and being knocked out. Especially with his two friends on either side of me, waiting to help. He lifted his knee, they grabbed my arms, and he yanked me up by dint of tied wrists. Which hurt. Which he knew.

His expression was odd. "What happened to your fingers?"

I blinked away dizziness, aware of how tightly the others gripped my arms. Surely they didn't believe I could offer much of a fight, after that brief travesty of a protest. "I was kidnapped by bald, blue-headed priest-mages, and they cut them off."

Rafiq accepted the truth no easier than falsehood. He studied my stumps with every evidence of fascination. "This isn't new."

Well, it wasn't that old, either, but I didn't say anything.

He thought about it. "At least I know you didn't lose them in the last couple of days."

I glared at him. "What does it matter?"

He looked at my face, searching for something. "You killed Khashi four days ago."

Actually, I'd lost count. Apparently I'd missed the night before and much of another day. Being poisoned will do that to you. "If you say so."

"You killed Khashi with two missing fingers."

"And easily," Nayyib put in.

Moral support. How nice.

Rafiq's eyes flickered. He looked again at the stumps, thoughts hidden. Then his face cleared. "Well, we'll let Umir decide. It's his business if he wants damaged goods."

"Umir?" I blurted. "Umir the Ruthless? What in hoolies does *he* want?"

"You."

"Me? Umir? What for? He never wanted me before." It was Del he'd wanted, and gotten, even if only briefly.

"He does now." Rafiq smiled. "You've apparently become a collector's item. A seventh-level sword-dancer who's declared *elaii-alima*. It's never happened before. That makes you unique. And you know how Umir is about things—and people—he considers unique."

I shook my head, slow to grasp the essentials. They were simply too preposterous. "What does he want, to put me on display?"

Rafiq's brows arched. His hair was darker than mine, but not quite black. "You haven't heard about his contest?"

"Umir's holding a contest?"

The Borderer, who knew very well how fast news traveled among the sword-dancer grapevine, stared at me. "Where in hoolies have *you* been?"

Blandly I replied, "Trying to convince bald, blue-headed priest-mages I didn't want to join them."

"Ah. The same ones who cut off your fingers?"

"The very same."

Rafiq snickered, shaking his head. "You always did have a vivid imagination."

I gifted him with a level stare. "So did Khashi. He believed he could defeat me."

That banished the humor. Rafiq nodded at his friends. I realized abruptly that while I'd been briefly unconscious they had slipped leather nooses over my head, now circling my neck. I was cross-tied like a recalcitrant horse, one man on either side of me holding a long leather leash. And currently tightening it just to demonstrate how well the system worked.

When, having made their point, they loosened the nooses, I asked, "Leashing me like a dog these days, Rafiq?"

"A cat," he answered easily. "A big, dangerous cat. Umir gets what he pays for. Fingers or no fingers, I'm not underestimating you."

"Khashi did," Nayyib said.

Very helpful, he was. And it served to bring the image back, and the knowledge, that a man lacking two fingers might still kill an Alimat-trained fifth-level sword-dancer.

Maybe even Rafiq.

Rafiq looked at me again. Assessed me. "Then Khashi was a fool. You may have broken all your oaths, but that doesn't mean you've forgotten how to kill a man. You always were good at that, Tiger."

I suppose it could be taken as a compliment. But my mind was on other things. "I'm not going anywhere without Del."

The Borderer was blank a moment. "Del?—oh, you mean the Northern bascha I've heard so much about?" Rather abruptly, tension seeped into his body. He glanced around sharply. A subtle signal had his two sword-dancer friends tightening the nooses again. "Where is she?"

Ordinarily this would be the signal for Del to sing out, offering to show them where she was, to describe what she would do to them, and how she would do it. Ordinarily it would be amusing to witness Rafiq's anxiety.

But this time it wasn't, because she wouldn't be doing any of it, and now was no time for prevarication. "In the shelter," I told him. "I'm not leaving without her."

Nayyib, still mounted, flicked a glance at me, then away. "I wanted the healer for her," he told Rafiq, "not for him."

Rafiq looked at me. Then he told his sandtiger-tamers to keep an eye on their charge and strode over to the lean-to.

If going with them got Del to help, it was worth as many leashes as they wished to put on me. It wasn't the best of situations, but some improvement in this one was worth a great deal if it helped Del.

I watched Rafiq duck down inside the shelter. In a moment he came back and glanced at his men. "Put him on his horse. We're leaving."

They shut hands on my arms again, started to turn me. "Wait," I said sharply. "We've got to make arrangements for Del. A litter—"

"We're leaving her."

"You can't do that!"

"I can." He nodded at his men. "Do it."

The gelding had been saddled. They shoved me toward him. I planted my feet, not that it did me much good. My feet weren't co-operating, and neither were Rafiq's friends. Rafiq himself turned away to his own mount, gathering reins.

"Wait," I said again. "If you want me to come peaceably—"

Rafiq cut me off. "I don't care if you come peaceably or not. The woman's too much trouble. She'll be dead by tomorrow." He swung up onto his palomino. "Get on your horse, Tiger. If you don't, you can walk all the way to Umir's place at whatever pace our horses set. Of course if you fall, we'll simply drag you."

Rafiq and I had never been friends. But cordial rivals, yes, in the brotherhood of the trade. Now, clearly, cordiality was banished, and rivalry had been transmuted to something far more deadly.

The two men made it clear I could mount Del's gelding under my own power, or they'd choke me out and sling me over the saddle. There was no way I could win this battle. It was foolish even to try. But this was Del we were discussing.

I was running out of options. Beyond Rafiq, Nayyib sat his horse wearing a curiously blank expression. I shot him a hard stare but couldn't catch his eye. Then I turned, grabbed white mane and stuck a foot in the stirrup, pulled myself up. Kicking the gelding into unexpected motion in a bid to escape would not succeed; Rafiq's leather leashes would jerk me out of the saddle and likely strangle me before I landed.

But leaving Del behind . . . that I couldn't do. I'd made a promise. If I tempted death, so be it. I wouldn't leave her alone if it cost me my life.

Without a word Nayyib abruptly turned his horse toward the shelter and rode away from us. He dismounted, looped his rein loosely around one of the roof branches, glanced back at me over a shoulder. No longer did he avoid my gaze, but seemed to be courting it. His jaw was set like stone.

Rafiq glanced back. "Aren't you coming? I thought you wanted to see some real sword-dances."

Nayyib lifted that stubborn jaw. He continued to stare at me. "I'm staying with the woman."

I released a breath I hadn't realized I was holding. Maybe he *hadn't* betrayed us. Or maybe he'd had a change of heart. I wanted no part of leaving, but at least Del would have someone with her.

The two men were mounted, one on each side of the gelding. I felt the pressure of the slip-knots on either side of my neck. A change in pace by any of our mounts, be it a side-step, a spook, a stumble, and I'd be in a world of hurt. The reins were mine to hold, but they did me no good.

Rafiq laughed, calling to Nayyib. "Well, you can catch up to us tomorrow—after you bury her."

"I don't think so," I said lightly. "In fact, I'm pretty damn certain of it. It'll be you who gets buried, and if I don't do it, she will."

Rafiq looked at me. He was neither laughing nor smiling now. "You have no idea what you're going to face. You broke every oath we hold sacred, Tiger. What Alimat was founded on. What do you expect? We were all children there, who were taught to become men. There is a cost for such betrayal, and now you will pay it."

"In blood, I suppose."

His eyes were cold as ice. "One of us will have the honor of cutting you into small pieces. I would like it, Tiger—I would like it *very much*—if that honor were mine."

I opened my mouth to answer, but Rafiq's friends suggested I not respond by employing the simple expedient of tightening their leashes. I subsided.

Bascha, I said inwardly, *please don't die on me yet. I need you to rescue me.*

If she could, she would.

If she couldn't, I wasn't sure I cared if Rafiq—or anyone else— cut me to pieces.

As the horses moved out, as mine was chivvied along, I shut my eyes. Everything in me rebelled.

But then I glanced over my shoulder. Nayyib had turned. Was ducking into the shelter. She wouldn't be alone.

I will try, he had said, *to make certain she doesn't die.*

"Do better than try," I muttered.

When Rafiq asked me what I had said, I held my silence. After a moment he shook his head and kicked his horse into a trot. Mine, and theirs, went with him.

About the time I began to doze off in the saddle for the fifth or sixth time, Rafiq woke me with a comment and a question. "Your horse looks ridiculous. What made you do that to him?"

I sighed, shifted in the saddle, swore inwardly; it is not comfortable riding with your wrists tied in front of you and leashes around your neck. Especially when your body wants to slump forward over the horse's neck, and *your* neck has nooses around it. "Bald, blue-headed priest-mages."

He had dropped back to ride near me. Now he eyed me askance. "Sticking to that story, are we?"

Well, except for the gelding's adornments, it was the truth. But I countered with a question of my own. "What exactly is this contest Umir's holding?"

"He wants to see who's the best sword-dancer."

"We already did that in Iskandar a couple of years ago." I recalled it very clearly. Del had killed the Northern borjuni Ajani there, satisfying her vow to avenge the death of her family.

"It didn't end quite the way anyone expected," Rafiq said.

That was an understatement. All hoolies had broken loose, and Del and I had left town as quickly as possible. "So Umir's decided to start putting on exhibitions? Isn't that a little odd for him?"

"He wants to find out so he can hire the best."

"The best for what?"

"Protecting his business interests. Full-time employment with one of the richest men in the South until retirement. Not bad work, if you can get it."

It was not unusual for a sword-dancer to hire on with one employer for a term of service, but it had always been situational. I'd never heard of a permanent employment. "And you want it."

"I want it, and I intend to get it."

"And these two friends of yours are just along for the ride?"

Rafiq laughed. "Oh, no. Ozmin and Mahmood will take their chances, too. But they know I'm better than they are."

"Sometimes," Ozmin said, from my left.

"Usually I just take pity on you and let you *think* you're better," said Mahmood from my right.

I ignored them and addressed my comments to Rafiq. "What does it have to do with me? I'm not a sword-dancer. I can't play with the big boys anymore."

"Oh, he's making an exception for you. Or maybe that should be we are. Not in the way you expect, maybe, but it ought to be worth it regardless."

"And what is that?"

"Dessert."

"Dessert?"

"Well, reward, really. You." He grinned. "You're not a stupid man, Tiger, and you know the South very well—as was proven by your disappearance. Everyone wants you. But it might take years for any of us to track you down in order to kill you. This way, you're right there at hand. An extra prize for the last sword-dancer standing: the chance to kill the Sandtiger in a dance to the death. Umir put out the word months ago, but you'd disappeared."

"You found me easily enough." Not that it made me happy.

Rafiq shrugged. "That was luck. I was at Fouad's waiting to meet up with Ozmin and Mahmood when your young friend came in asking about a healer. I had no idea where you were, or even that you were back from wherever it was you disappeared to." He grinned. "Probably you should have stayed there."

So, maybe Nayyib hadn't sold us out. Maybe he'd had no real choice about leading them back to us.

Or maybe he had.

Maybe, maybe, maybe.

Frowning, I guided the gelding over a rocky patch, hoping he wouldn't stumble and strangle me by accident. But he was a rather comfortable ride, despite the circumstances. Del hadn't exaggerated. If I were on the stud, I'd have been choked ten times over by now.

Which reminded me that he was still missing. And now likely to stay that way; Nayyib wouldn't know to go looking for him, and Del was too sick to suggest it.

To take my mind off that, I looked at Rafiq. "And Umir, I suppose, will reward you for bringing me in."

"Handsomely. And this way if I don't win the contest, I still benefit from it." He laughed as he saw my dubious expression. "I'm not stupid, Tiger; there's always a chance something might prevent me from winning. I could trip at the wrong time. Get a blister on my thumb. Lose a finger." He glanced pointedly at my hands. "All the other losers will just be losers. I'll walk away with Umir's coin in my purse, and the honor of bringing in the Sandtiger to face punishment."

"*We* will walk away," Ozmin clarified.

Mahmood nodded. "We're splitting it, remember? Otherwise you could have taken him on by yourself. And we all know who'd have won that contest."

Maybe not, in my current condition. I contemplated leather knots glumly. I'd known returning to the South was a risk. Being challenged by Khashi in Julah was merely the first of many I expected to face. But that was one by one. Umir's scheme likely *would* get me killed. At Alimat we'd held many such contests to test our skills against one another, because competition brought out the best. It focused the mind, honed the talent. By the time the two finalists met, regardless of cuts, bruises, and slashes, they were prepared for anything.

Whoever came out of Umir's contest the winner would be very, very good, and very, very hungry for his—dessert.

"Doesn't sound like there's much in it for me," I said lightly.

Rafiq affected surprise. "But of course there is! You'll have the honor of dying in front of men you trained with, sparred with, danced with, even drank with. Men you respect, and who respect—respected—you. Who will never forget you and will speak your name to others. How better for a sword-dancer to die? It's our kind's immortality." Then his expression hardened. "Oh, but I was forgetting. You have no honor. You aren't a sword-dancer. You're just a man whom no one will remember, whose name is never spoken. A man who never lived, and thus can have no immortality." Rafiq added with elaborate scorn, "A man such as you might just as well have been born a slave."

The verbal blade went home, as he had intended. My origins weren't a secret. They'd been part of the legend: a Salset slave had, against all odds, risen to become a seventh-level, Alimat-trained sword-dancer, favored by the shodo. When you're a legend, origins don't matter except as seasoning for the story.

Now, of course, I wasn't a legend. And Rafiq wanted a reaction. Maybe he wanted me to choke myself trying to reach him. But I merely grinned at him. "So much for honor. I don't think there is much in killing a former chula."

His face darkened. After a moment he kicked his horse into a trot and went ahead again.

While I, meanwhile, blessed the bald, blue-headed priest-mages for forcing me to rededicate myself to one of the teachings of my shodo.

Discipline.

It was its own kind of magic.

Chapter 11

By the time we reached the place Rafiq identified as Umir's somewhere near sundown, I was tired, thirsty, hungry, sunburned, and more than a little sore from a long ride with my hands tied, not to mention the residual debilitating effects of sandtiger poison. Most of it had worked its way out of my system— and this was my third encounter, so my reaction was somewhat lessened—but I wasn't exactly feeling myself. Rafiq and his friends had given me water along the way, but they didn't claim a spare burnous among them, so all I had to wear was my dhoti. Not to mention I hadn't eaten for a couple of days thanks to the sandtiger attack, and now that the worst of the sickness had passed my belly was complaining.

Last time I'd looked, Umir had concentrated his holdings farther north. It was very unlike him to take himself so far south. But he was a tanzeer who enjoyed buying all manner of items he deemed worthy of his collections, and I guess domains qualified. For all I knew he'd added five or six since I'd sailed for Skandi.

The house was, I decided as we approached, fairly modest for a man of Umir's wealth and tastes, being little more than a series of interconnected, low-roofed rooms built of adobe, the pervasive mudbrick of the South, with timber roofs. Except Umir had had his adobe smoothed into silken slickness and painted pristine white with lime, so it glowed in the sun. Tall palm trees formed clustered lines of sentinels around the house, and masses of vegetation peeped over courtyard walls, indicating there was good access to water. Which I saw proved as we rode into the front courtyard: a three-tiered fountain spilled water into a large tile basin. This was wealth incarnate. Trust Umir to find water at the edges of the Punja.

Thirst reestablished itself. I wanted nothing more than to fall into the fountain, but good old Ozmin and Mahmood still had me closely leashed. Rafiq tracked down a servant, explained his business, and within a matter of moments we were politely invited to dismount in the cobbled, shaded courtyard. The horses were taken away by grooms. Damp cloths were presented to Rafiq and his two friends to wipe off the worst of the trail dust; I was ignored. Ozmin and Mahmood still shadowed me on either side, leashes coiled in their hands. In dhoti, dust, sunburn, and sweat, I was definitely at a disadvantage when it came to presentability.

We were permitted into the house and left to wait in a reception room of airy spaciousness, with tile floors and colorful tribal rugs. Priceless items were set in nooks and adorned walls. Low tiled tables displayed other items, including thin, colored glass bowls and bottles, which I found more than a little risky with numerous careless sword-dancers trooping through the house. But maybe that was part of the appeal for Umir.

After a suitably lengthy wait intended to intimidate lesser personages, Umir's steward appeared. Said steward then led us through the reception room out into what I thought was a courtyard off the back of the house. Except I discovered it was nothing like. The back of the house was constructed of plain walls bowing out from the main house like a bubble. Thick, curved walls approximately six feet high. No exposed bricks. No adornment. No windows. No vegetation. No fountains. No nothing, except elegantly curving walls that met precisely opposite where we were standing, and imported silk-smooth Punja sand raked into perfection.

A circle.

A very large circle, more expansive than a proper sword-dance required; I suspected the sword-dancers not fighting a given match would stand against the walls to watch. There was no danger in doing so; a man who stepped out of the circle drawn in the sand forfeited the match, and we all of us had learned to dance in close quarters. That was part of the beauty, the art, and the challenge.

Umir, I realized with a start of surprise, had had the house built with his sword-dancer contest in mind. If it were true he intended to hire the winner for life—or at least for the balance of his professional career—it was no surprise sword-dancers would come from all over the South. Likely at retirement Umir would settle some land and a dwelling on him; not a bad job at all. I'd even be interested myself, if I weren't scheduled to be the post-dance entertainment.

Waiting in the sun surrounded by white-painted walls wasn't my idea of fun, especially since I was tired enough my eyes kept trying to cross. I scrubbed with bound hands at the sweat and dust filming my face and considered plopping myself down in the sand, then eyed Ozmin and Mahmood and decided against it. But as Rafiq and his friends grew impatient enough to start complaining, the master of the house appeared.

Umir the Ruthless was a tall, slender, aristocratic man with high cheekbones, arched nose, and dark skin, all classic features of a Southroner save for his eyes, which were a pale gray. I'd always assumed Umir had some Borderer in him. As was habitual, he wore robes of the finest fabrics. The toes of soft, dyed-leather slippers peeked out from under the bullioned hems.

He spoke to Rafiq, but didn't look at him. His gaze was fastened on me. "Well done."

Rafiq had never claimed any subtlety. "When do we get paid? Now, or after he's dead?"

Umir was unruffled. "Oh, now, of course. I'll have my steward tend to it." He assessed me with a faint smile. "Well, Sandtiger . . . the last time we met, I wished to acquire your woman. Does it please you to know I now wish to acquire you?"

"Depends on what you want me for," I answered. "Now, if it was me you wanted to hire for lifetime employment, we could probably work something out. But if I'm meant to be dessert, probably not."

One brow lifted delicately. "Dessert?"

"I told him what you plan," Rafiq offered. "How he's to be the reward for the winner."

"Oh, but you should have left that to me," Umir murmured. "You have deprived me of amusement." Apparently he'd made some kind of signal, because two large men appeared from the house. Umir indicated them with a negligent gesture. "Rafiq, you and your friends are free to avail yourselves of my hospitality with the other sword-dancers, in the visitor's wing. This particular guest is now the responsibility of my house."

I just love the way a cultured man finds euphemisms for everything. Guest. Hah.

Ozmin and Mahmood were happy enough to hand over the leashes to Umir's large servants. The steward presented a coin pouch to Rafiq and led them back inside. Which left me outside with Umir, and my two keepers.

The tanzeer's expansive gesture encompassed his circle. "Do you like it?"

He waited expectantly. I hitched one shoulder in a half-shrug. "Rather attractive in a spare, unassuming sort of way."

"Oh, yes. Very minimalist. No distractions that way. Merely the pure, elegant art of the sword-dance."

He had not brought me out here to discuss the attractions of his architecture but to impress upon me this was to be where I died. I thought again of sitting down, or asking if I could go back out front and fall face-first into the fountain. Did neither, under Umir's examination.

The tanzeer's nostrils flared with distaste. "Why is it whenever I see you, you are in a state of utter filth and dishabille?"

I smiled winningly. "I lead an active life."

He made a dismissive gesture. "Well, for a short time, at least, you shall enjoy the best my poor house has to offer. Scented baths, oils, the finest of food and wine, comfortable lodgings; even women, if you like. I do not stint my guests."

At this point, wobbly as I was, it all sounded wonderful—except for the women. Well, even they sounded wonderful in the abstract. (Once upon a time the women wouldn't have been abstract at all, but Del had reformed me.)

"I'm not a guest," I said. "I'm dessert."

Umir smoothed the front of his figured silk overrobe with a slender hand weighted with rings. "I would be remiss if I offered my other guests dessert lacking in piquancy. By the time you step into the circle, you will be well fed, rested, and fit."

"Hasn't anyone told you?" I asked. "I can't step into a circle anymore. That's the whole point of *elaii-ali-ma.*"

He waved that away. "Call it what you wish. A square, if you like. But you will fight for me, Sandtiger. As only you can."

I lifted brows. "What's in it for me? What possible motivation would I have for meeting the winner of your little contest?"

Umir's eyes and tone were level. "Until last year, you were a man of honor. An Alimat-trained, seventh-level sword-dancer of immense skill and repute. I saw what took place at Sabra's palace, how you stopped the dance against Abbu Bensir and declared *elaii-ali-ma.* It was for the woman, was it not? The Northern woman. Well, I understand her worth. Not for the same reason, perhaps, but that hardly matters. You made an outcast of yourself for her sake. It had nothing to do with disenchantment with the oaths you swore, the life you chose. You may deny it now, to me, but when you step into that circle—and it will be a circle—you will recall those oaths. They will once again rule your life. You will dance, Sandtiger—and yes, I do mean dance—because you will have no other choice. It is all you know. It is what you are. And you will die with whatever honor you may make of your last dance."

Umir was right. With my life at stake, I would not refuse to dance. But . . . "You know, I'm getting really, *really* tired of everyone assuming I'll lose."

The tanzeer stared at me with the faintest of puzzled frowns.

I spelled it out for him. "I might win, Umir. What happens men?"

He shook his head. "I have been given to understand that it is an impossibility you might win."

"Oh? Why? Did you ask Rafiq? Someone else? How can anyone be sure *what* will happen?" I took one step toward him, as much as I was willing to risk while on doubled leashes. "What if I win, Umir? What happens then?"

He was baffled. "But you have broken all your oaths. It was explained to me."

I laughed. "Yes, but broken oaths and loss of honor does not necessarily translate to loss of skill."

Clearly Umir had never considered I might win. Clearly none of the sword-dancers he'd consulted considered I might win. Which is just the way I liked it.

"So," I said, "does the deal apply to me? I win, and you offer me employment?"

His face was very stiff. "I find it highly unlikely you would win."

I lifted brows. "Why? Do you intend to drug me?"

Color stained his cheeks. "Of course not! I am not Sabra, who was interested only in punishing and killing you. I want a true dance. A true winner. There will be no trickery."

"Your winner won't dance with me," I said. "He'll fight me. He'll attempt to kill me. And I will do my very best to kill him. And *if* I do, I expect some reward for it. Something more than dessert."

There was only one thing worth having. And Umir knew it. "The freedom to leave my domain unchallenged."

I nodded. "That'll do."

His tone became aggressive. "But anyone may challenge you outside my domain."

"Of course. But that's not your concern. And I truly believe anyone who witnesses me killing the best of the best here in your homemade circle may think twice about challenging me anywhere."

His lips thinned. "You are overconfident."

" 'Over'? Don't think so. Confident, yes." I gifted him with a friendly smile. "I *am* the Sandtiger."

"You truly believe you can intimidate everyone?"

It wasn't false confidence or bluster. I'd done it before. Many times. It was one of my most effective weapons. I was bigger, quicker, stronger and more agile than anyone else I'd met in the South. I was simply better.

I smiled and said nothing.

"I wonder," Umir murmured, "what Abbu Bensir will say?"

Simply better—except possibly for Abbu Bensir. We hadn't settled that yet. I stopped smiling. "If Abbu's here," I said, scowling, "why have a contest at all? Offer him the job and put us in your circle."

Umir studied a ring, admiring its beauty in the sunlight. "But that would deprive me of the entry fees."

I had to laugh. No wonder Umir the Ruthless was one of the wealthiest men in the South. He charged sword-dancers to step into a circle against one another when they did it all the time for free, just to hone their skills.

A faint glint of amusement appeared in Umir's pale eyes. "I hope you do understand, Sandtiger, that my goal here is to find the best out of many. I'm not interested in death. Only in the unique. Your presence here, under the peculiar circumstances of *elaii-alima*, offers uniqueness. All of the men who lose my contest will go out and find other employment, possibly even with tanzeers as wealthy as I. But I offer something no one else can."

I knew what that was, but he detailed it anyway.

Dusky color stained his dark skin, and pale eyes glowed. "The opportunity to kill the Sandtiger in front of other sword-dancers, thus plucking the greatest of thorns from their pride and adding unassailable luster to one man's reputation. His name will be spoken forever with reverence. Tales will be told. He will go to his death one day secure in the knowledge he avenged the tarnished honor of Alimat and killed one of the greatest sword-dancers the South has ever known."

"And just when do you plan to *serve* dessert?"

Umir smiled. "In ten days."

Ten days. In ten days Del could be dead. Ten days was too long. Ten *hours* was too long. Even though Nayyib was with her. "How about now?" I asked.

Umir nearly laughed aloud. "I think not."

"I'm serious. Give me a sword, and call for the dance right now."

"You are half-dead with exhaustion; do you think I can't see it? You can barely stand up." He shook his head. "I will not present a farce. Ten days, Sandtiger. After you have rested and recovered.

Then you may prove to me if you're as good as you claim." He gestured to his servants. "Escort him to the bath chamber, then to his room. See that he is fed."

I dropped all pretenses, all facades. "Wait," I blurted sharply, as Umir began to turn away. "The Northern woman," I said, "the one you wanted so badly . . ."

He paused.

"She's ill," I told him. "Possibly dying. If you let me go to her—send any number of men with me you wish, tie me up, keep me on a leash, put *chains* on me if you like—I swear to return and take part in your contest."

Umir studied me consideringly. Then, with delicate disdain, he said, "I do not accept worthless oaths from men with no honor."

I was tired enough and dirty enough that a bath among the enemy—with the enemy's servants watching—did not unduly disturb me, especially since my wrists were finally untied and the nooses lifted from my neck. Nor did I fear drinking the watered wine servant-guards offered as I soaked in the huge hip-bath. I was too thirsty. And for all Umir had imprisoned me—and had done so before—he'd never actually tried to harm me. If he was offering the Sandtiger on a platter to his guests as a fillip to his contest, he would indeed want me fit enough to provide proper entertainment. His reputation depended on it. He was ruthless when it came to dealing for prized acquisitions—kidnapping Del was an example—but not a killer.

So, knowing I needed to be in the best physical condition possible if I wanted to survive—minor motivation—I took advantage of his hospitality and came out of the bath markedly cleaner and feeling more relaxed than I had in days. Upon being dried by female servants and anointed with scented oil, I was presented with a soft linen dhoti and a fresh house-robe of creamy raw silk and a russet-colored sash, but my leather dhoti and sandals were missing. Then the male servants escorted me barefoot down a cool, tiled corridor to a wooden door boasting a rather convoluted locking mechanism on the corridor-side latch. They gestured me in, and in I went. I knew better than to try Umir's servants. They were very

large men, and I was on the verge of turning into a boneless puddle of flesh.

The room clearly had been built to house a prisoner. The edge
of the door was beveled so it overlapped the jamb; there was no
crack into which a knife or some other implement might be in-
serted in an attempt to lift the latch. Nor was there any bolt or
latch-string in evidence. Just planks of thick wood adzed smooth,
studded with countersunk iron nailheads impossible to pry out.
The door could only be opened from the corridor, and even a concerted effort on my behalf to knock down the door with brute
strength would result only in bruised flesh and, possibly, broken
bones. No thanks.

Nor was there a window. Just four blank walls with a row of
small holes knocked through mudbrick up near the roof in the exterior wall, well over my head, and an equally blank adobe ceiling.
The floor was also adobe, lacking tiles or rugs. A large nightcrock—
in this case, daycrock, too—sat unobtrusively in one corner. The
only piece of furniture in the room was a very high, narrow bed.
Next to the bed, on the floor, was set a large silver tray containing
cubed goat cheese; mutton pie baked in flaky pastry; a sprig of fat,
blood-colored grapes; a small round loaf of steaming bread accompanied by a bowl of olive oil; and a pewter cup, plus matching
tankards of water and wine. Not to mention a folded square of
linen with which to blot my mouth upon completion of the meal.
Umir believed in manners.

Ten days. I wondered whether that included today or began tomorrow. I wondered it all through the meal, the entire water
tankard, half of the wine, and as I fell backward onto the bed. Umir
had even provided a pillow and coverlet. Then I didn't wonder
anything at all. I fell fast asleep.

In the echoes of the dream, I saw old bones. Heard a woman's voice.
And took up a sword.

Chapter 12

I woke up not long after dawn to the sound of sword blades. For a moment I was disoriented, aware of unfamiliar smells, light, and the fabric beneath my body. Then I remembered.

Swearing, I crawled out of Umir's so-called guest bed and sat hunched on the edge, scrubbing at creased face. I'd been shaved the day before during my bath, so the stubble was short instead of its usual three or four days' worth of growth.

Swords clashed outside. In the pallor of the morning, I glanced up at the line of airholes cut through mudbrick near the ceiling. Apparently the exterior wall of my room faced Umir's circle off the back of the house. But obviously I was not to be allowed sight of the matches or of the individual who might be given the honor of killing me.

The door latch rattled. The door itself was thrown open. Had I intended to move, I wouldn't have had time to get off the bed. As it was, I just sat there, scowling at my unannounced visitor.

Umir. I stopped scowling and presented him with a blandly noncommital expression of nonaggression.

Then the two large men who'd shadowed me yesterday came into the room, and even as I began to stand up they grabbed my arms and jerked me onto my feet. So much for Umir's hospitality.

"Already?" I asked.

The two men clamped grips on my wrists and extended my

hands. Umir approached. His expression was outraged. "It *is* true!" he cried, staring at my hands. "I believed Rafiq was exaggerating."

Ah. The infamous missing fingers.

"I shall have to reduce his payment," he declared grimly.

My eyebrows leaped up. "Just how much are two fingers worth compared to an entire person?"

Umir glared at me. "I expected *all* of you to be delivered. Whole in body. Those were my orders."

I wanted to laugh; the whole topic was unbelievable. "Not that Rafiq and I are friends, Umir, but he didn't do it. This happened a few months ago."

"I heard nothing of it!"

"It didn't happen here." Hoolies, what did it matter?

He swung away, took two steps, swung back. His pale gray eyes were fierce. "Can you still dance?"

I suppressed a smile. "According to the rite of *elaii-ali-ma,* I am not allowed—"

He cut me off with a shout. *"Can you still dance?"*

"What, afraid your plan for me as reward will be ruined?"

Umir took one step toward me and swung. I ducked most of the blow, but the flat of his hand still caught me across the rim of my ear. The servants tightened their grips even more as I tried to lunge at Umir, holding me back.

"Try me," I said between my teeth. "Put a sword in these hands and try me—or why not ask *Khashi* if I can hold a sword?"

Umir's expression was blank. "Khashi?"

"A sword-dancer," I told him. "We had a little contretemps in Julah. Except he's dead now, so he's not here to tell you anything about who won and who lost."

Color began to steal back into his face. "He's dead?"

"Yes."

"You killed him?"

"Yes."

"Was he any good?"

I attempted a shrug made unsuccessful by the grips of the servants. "Apparently not, since I won. But I suspect that depends on your point of view."

Umir bent down and peered closely at my hands. I found the critical examination highly offensive, but there wasn't much I could do about it. So I just gritted my teeth and waited.

"Are they still painful?" he asked curiously, the way one might ask a guest if he wants more wine.

It took effort not to bellow at him, to retain some measure of decorum. "Explain why this matters to you."

Umir seemed surprised as he straightened. "Of course it matters. Your physical well being affects the quality of the entertainment I'll be offering."

I shook my head and began to say something, but Umir abruptly grabbed both my hands and squeezed.

This did not particularly endear my host to me.

After a moment he released them. Umir debated something internally. Then he nodded. "The plans are unchanged." And he turned and strode out of the room.

When I was locked in again, I loosed a lengthy volley of curses in every language I spoke, which was significant after my sojourn at Meteiera, and wished I had numerous breakable items I could hurl at the door and walls as I paced furiously, waiting for the pain to fade.

Of course such actions would merely trigger even more pain in my Umir-abused hands, so it was just as well I didn't have that recourse. And I wasn't about to use the slops jar to vent my frustration, because then I'd have to live with the rather messy results.

Eventually I ran out of curses. The pain diminished. I threw myself onto the bed, hands resting on my chest, and contemplated the blank ceiling overhead, thinking fiercely focused thoughts of such things as sword-dances and sword-dancers, broken oaths, missing fingers, idiots like Umir, absent baschas. And the discipline I'd learned atop the Stone Forest.

Outside, in Umir's circle, sword blades rang. I heard voices raised in cheerful insults, vulgar suggestions, the occasional compliment.

I frowned. There was one voice that sounded familiar.

I heard it again. The frown dissipated. I recalled sparring matches in one of Rusali's dusty alleys. With swords and without.

Inspiration. Motivation.

I swung out of bed, pulled it away from the wall, turned it on edge, studied the legs. With care I sat on one, my own legs gathered under me. I bounced slightly, and felt the answering crack. Smiling, I stood up, smashed a foot against the leg, and was pleased to see it break off from the frame in one piece. I was left with approximately three feet of wood. One end was slightly jagged, but that didn't matter. The other end, adzed smooth at the bottom, afforded me a functional grip.

I set the bed upright again, swinging it around so the legless corner was not obvious to the eye of a visitor, and pushed it once again against the wall. Then I stripped out of house-robe to the linen dhoti. Took up the broken bed leg. Closed my hands upon it. Then, courting patience and self-control, I began the practice forms I had first learned twenty-three years before at Alimat.

I had worked up a good sweat when I heard the latch rattle. Hastily I slung the leg under the bed and donned the house-robe again, though I didn't have time to tie the sash. I thought it best not to sit on the bed with only three legs, so I stood in front of it as if I'd just risen. By the time the door opened, I wore a suitably expectant expression. Especially since I wondered if Umir was coming to inspect any other portions of my anatomy.

A woman entered with breakfast. Even as she set the tray on the floor, they locked her in. Rather than seeming startled or dismayed by her predicatment, she merely stepped aside from the tray and made a graceful gesture inviting me to eat.

She was beautiful in the way of the loveliest of Southron women, small in stature and delicately made, with huge dark eyes, expressive face and hands, and dusky skin set off by blue-black hair hanging loose to her waist. She wore luxurious silks of a brilliant blue-green, and gilded sandals. That she was here for my pleasure was obvious; she wore neither headress or veil, and did not affect the extreme modesty of other Southron women. But neither was she overt in any way. Umir's taste in all things ran to elegance and understatement. Rumor claimed the tanzeer did not like to bed women or men, but took his pleasure in acquiring and owning

those things he found intriguing and unique. Sometimes this included people. This woman was definitely unique.

Once upon a time I would not have questioned her presence in
his house or her role. I would merely have enjoyed her. Traveling
with Del had made me aware of certain Southron customs that
were not judged acceptable by other cultures. Traveling with Del
had also filled a place in my soul I hadn't known existed; I certainly
wasn't blind to other women, nor was I gelded or dead, but appreciation now found outlets other than taking attractive women to
bed, be it in my mind or in reality.

Thus I gazed upon this lovely Southron woman and asked,
"What's a nice girl like you doing in a place like this?"

Startled out of her poised serenity, she blinked. The faintest of
blushes rose in her cheeks. She gestured again, more insistently, to
the tray containing breakfast.

"Later," I said. "Umir sent you?"

She nodded, lids lowering long enough to display long dark
lashes against her cheeks.

"Were instructions given?"

She moistened her lips with the tip of her tongue. Her voice
was low and perfectly modulated. "I am to do what you wish and
be what you wish."

"Is being here in Umir's house what *you* wish?"

The dark brows arched. "But of course. How not? It is better by
far than it might be."

That was likely true. But still I heard Del's voice in my head, arguing the point. "Given a choice, would you leave?"

She was clearly baffled by my line of questioning. "My family
was well paid. They live in comfort now. But I live in even greater
comfort. Why would I wish to leave?"

"And when you are instructed to do what a man wishes, and
be what that man wishes, don't you ever ask yourself if it's worth
it?"

Unexpectedly, she laughed. "Do you?"

My turn to be baffled. "What?"

"When you hire a woman for the night, do you ever ask yourself if it's worth it?"

I hadn't hired a woman since meeting Del. But even before that, when I'd celebrated victories with women and liquor, or with women and no liquor, it had never once occured to me to ask myself if it was worth it. It was simply what I did. And there were always women who wanted me to do it.

She saw the answer in my face and smiled. "So, you see. We are not so very different."

But I was. Now. Yet there was no possible way to explain it to her. "Thank you for bringing breakfast," I said, "but I'll eat alone."

She was smiling, certain of me. "And afterwards?"

"Afterwards, I will also be alone."

That surprised her. "You don't wish my company?"

It was undoubtedly an insult, but I tried to soften it. "I choose my own companions."

A wave of color rose in her face. "Umir believed I would please you."

"What would please me, and Umir knows this, is to be given my freedom."

She studied me a moment longer, as if expecting me to change my mind. When I said nothing else, merely waited quietly, she finally accepted it for the truth. She turned at once to the door, rapped on it sharply, and slipped out without a backward glance when the guard opened it.

I listened to the latch being locked behind her. Then I walked to the nearest wall, turned, slid down with my back planted against it. Once upon a time . . .

But I regretted no part of my decision.

I sighed, thumped my head against the wall, shut my eyes. I could hear Umir's sword-dancers. But all I could think about was Del as I had last seen her, left to the ministrations of a stranger while I was here, waiting to meet a man who would do his best to kill me.

Nine days, or eight. I should have asked Umir.

Bascha, where are you? Still in the lean-to, or did Nayyib get you to Julah?

This was not how I had envisioned it. For several years I'd seen Del and me dying together, fighting any number of enemies. I had never envisioned us as old people, but as we were now. Certainly I had never considered Del might die of sandtiger wounds or poison, and me sentenced to die in a circle I was no longer allowed to enter.

Never in a thousand thousand years had I ever expected to declare *elaii-ali-ma*. Despite my time as a chula among the Salset, I considered myself truly born the day Alimat's shodo had accepted me for instruction. The day I had taken my name. The day I had defeated Abbu Bensir in an impromptu practice match with wooden swords.

That image, unexpectedly, was abruptly clear and immediate. I had been seventeen, or as close as I could reckon my age. Abbu was a good ten or more years older, the acknowledged sword-dancer of sword-dancers. He wasn't taking lessons anymore; he had made his living hiring out for years. But he had come back to Alimat to visit the shodo. Where he had heard of a tall, gangly kid who promised, with proper instruction, to be as good—or better—one day.

I smiled crookedly. Abbu had intended to laugh at me, albeit quietly, noting all of my bad habits for the benefit of others. And when he had tossed the wooden sparring blade to me, he had anticipated demonstrating to all the other wide-eyed students how my height and gangliness would hurt me in a circle.

Instead, my greater reach and speed, despite my awkwardness, had landed a blow to his throat. To this day he spoke in a husky rasp.

I had eventually grown into my gangliness, adding flesh and muscle. Strength had been trained, quickness refined. I was unlike Abbu or any other Southroner, and I could not apply all of the lessons to my particular body. Instead, the shodo had adapted to me by developing other forms. In a matter of a few years, more quickly than any prior student—including Abbu—I had attained the seventh level.

Then, and only then, had I departed Alimat to make my own way.

The way that brought me here so many years later.

I got up and stripped off the robe, tossed it on the bed, and knelt to retrieve the broken leg. Once again I opened myself to the power that wasn't magic but that might allow me to live. The rites and rituals of honing the body, controlling the reflexes, taught me by the shodo; and the discipline of honing the mind, controlling that power, trained into me by the blue-headed priest-mages of ioSkandi.

The woman was long-limbed and agile, winding her legs around mine in comfortable abandon. She wore no clothes and had teased me out of my own. The initial passion was spent; now we lay very close, almost as one. Smiling, I twined my fingers into the silk of her hair, wrapping each: thumb, forefinger, next finger, next, and eventually the little finger. I felt the binding, tested it, tugged, then let the hair side through. Fair hair, nearly white; and skin lightly gilded from the blaze of the sun. I ran hands across that skin, stroked it with fingers—

—and sat bolt upright on the pallet I'd pulled from the three-legged bed and put on the floor.

I could see nothing in the night but raised my hands regardless. I counted, tucking fingers down as I named them off in my head.

Right hand: Thumb. Four fingers.

Left: Thumb. Four fingers.

And again, and again. The woman was gone—Del was gone—but the fingers remained. I could feel them.

I stayed awake the rest of the night, arguing with myself. When dawn finally crept slowly into the room, segmented by airholes, I was able to see truth at last.

Thumb. *Three* fingers. And a stub.

I lay down again, making fists of my hands. With two thumbs and six fingers.

Thinking: No Del, either.

Dreams, I decided bitterly, conjured pain as well as pleasure.

Chapter 13

On the morning of the tenth day, I awoke not long after dawn. As always, the room I inhabited was quiet, dim, isolated, cut off from the ordinary noises of Umir's rousing household. But this time my body was poised and alert, my mind calm and prepared. Even without counting the days, I knew.

I lay on my back on the pallet and extended arms into the air. Examined hands, front and back. I had not dreamed again of having all my fingers. What I saw now was what I expected to see: that which had been left to me atop the stone spire after Sahdri had amputated two fingers in an attempt to also amputate my identity, the awareness that I was sword-dancer before anything else. Because he knew very well I would not become what he believed I should be, and could be, unless my past was extinguished.

The weeks thereafter had been a true battle as I fought an enemy such as I'd never met, to retain my sense of *self*. I had very nearly lost. But eventually I had rediscovered what and who I was and had managed to tap into ioSkandi's power. There atop the spire I'd been mage, if never priest, but also sword-dancer. And that, I knew, was all that would serve me now.

Sword-dancer.

Sandtiger.

Both—or either—would be enough.

I pressed myself up from the pallet. Used the crock. Spent time stretching myself into flexibility, cracked my joints, put my body through forms I could do in my sleep until every portion of me was loose. Took up a position in front of the door in the center of the room, composed myself, closed my eyes, and let myself go as I had in Meteiera, soaring without wings over the fertile valley at the foot of massive spires.

Far below I saw a circle made of white stones set into the ground with expert precision. I soared lower, lower, and saw there a man, dhoti-clad; a man born of Skandi, with the height, breadth, power, and quickness characteristic of the Eleven Families who claimed themselves gods-descended. Both hands grasped a sword, a full complement of eight fingers and two thumbs wrapping hilt. It was a weapon, but also an extension of the man. Steel became flesh.

He was alone and oblivious to the world at large. He danced there, he and the sword-his-partner, transforming the initial fundamental forms into a series of linked, liquid movements shaped, despite his size, of grace mixed with strength, a tapestry of motion on the frame of his will and spirit. Sweat sheened his body, slicking sun-browned flesh into a copper-bronze human sculpture of ridged sinews, tendons, and delineated muscle: the hard, ungentle beauty of a mature male trained beyond all others, fit beyond expectation, in body and mind. And then the first routines gave way to those known only by the best, known only of the best, kindling from the coals of talent into the intangible flame of rare gift.

He was alone no longer. A woman came into the circle. She too carried a sword. She too was tall, long of limb and torso, powerful but inherently graceful, manifestly and splendidly female despite her size and strength. Blonde, pale, wearing only a leather tunic, she challenged him to a dance.

When it was done, neither had lost. Neither had won. They had merely proven how perfectly matched they were, how exacting their precision, and how neither could be defeated.

Smiling, sated on self-awareness, I wheeled away on the wind, soaring back toward the spire. I descended; and cool stone lay under my feet. Power thrummed in my bones, threaded itself through muscle, tingled in my scalp. I spread my arms and gazed open-eyed but blindly into the heavens, calling on all the skills of Alimat, the courage of a slave become a man, and the fierce determination of a Northern bascha.

"Fill me," I invited.

That moment faded. I inhabited another. When I opened my eyes, I found Umir standing in the open door, staring at me oddly.

Eventually he bestirred himself and spoke. "Dress yourself. My servants will prepare you, then escort you to the circle."

The tanzeer departed. His servants held a fresh leather dhoti, a flask of oil, new sandals, and an overrobe woven of gleaming bronze samite, the finest silk in the world. Once Del had worn one similar at Umir's request, albeit white; and the interior had been lined with priceless beads, glass, and feathers. Mine, fortunately, was unadorned silk.

Mute, detached, I stripped out of linen dhoti, pulled on the soft suede. The servants poured oil into their hands and began to work it into my flesh. Once I might have wondered if the oil was tampered with in some way, but I knew Umir would not do such a thing for this match. He wanted a true dance. He wanted no one to say the Sandtiger lost because Umir had cheated.

The servants shaved me, then attempted to help me put on the rest of the clothing. I refused both overrobe and sandals. Wearing only the dhoti, I was escorted out of the room in which I had been imprisoned for ten days, and taken out to Umir's white-walled circle.

My host had, as I had expected, assembled all of his guests along the curving, white-painted wall off the back of his house. Having been present at Iskandar, I could see Umir had not been successful in luring all sword-dancers to his contest. But the number was decent. They were most of them Southroners, but there was a fair proportion of foreigners. They were taller men, heavier; brown-haired, blond, even redheads, and everything in between with eyes of every color. Skin was tanned, freckled, or burned a permanent red from exposure to the harsh Southron sun. Though Southroners all resemble one another because of similar coloring and builds, the only likeness among the foreigners was a hardness in their eyes and the swords at hips and shoulders. There is a marked difference between men who wear swords for protection or impression, and men who make a living with a blade. An ease exists among the latter, a casual confidence in carriage, in self-knowledge. A sword is more than a sword. It is a part of their souls.

Sabra, the first, if short-lived, female tanzeer, had made her exhibition garish and overly dramatic. Umir's tastes and intentions were different. He neither announced my arrival nor my name; he knew, and I knew, there was no need. The Sandtiger had been promised to the winner.

Some of these men had never seen me. Some likely hadn't been born when I first left Alimat. These men gazed at me with a quiet avidity, marking how the man matched legend and rumor.

Undoubtedly some found me larger than expected, others thought me smaller. If what Del had said of Meteiera's magic lifting a measure of harsh usage from me were true, then perhaps I looked younger than many anticipated. But there was no doubt in any of the eyes that I was who I was. It was why I could go nowhere truly disguised. Nothing can hide facial scars left by a sandtiger's claws.

Something inside me kindled abruptly into memory, and regret. Now Del would bear her share, though fortunately her face was spared.

If she had survived.

The sword-dancers, as expected, took the measure of me: noted stature, the way I moved, the length of legs and arms, the depth and spring of my ribs—and the massive scar left there by Del's *jivatma*—the architecture of bones and muscle, the fit of flesh over both. In the circle, everything counts. Particularly in a death-dance.

They also, every one of them, looked at my hands.

The pale sand was warm beneath bare feet, but Umir had selected a good time of day. Since it was Punja sand, the sun would eventually heat the intermixed crystals beyond endurance. But it was early summer and mid-morning, bright enough to see without squinting, not so warm as to burn the callused soles of a sword-dancer's feet.

I noted a few frowns, an occasional puzzled expression. After a moment's detached reflection, I realized it was likely I resembled nothing of what those who knew me by sight anticipated. Skandi had changed me. But none of them knew about Skandi. I had simply disappeared after Sabra's aborted sword-dance, after declaring *elaii-ali-ma*. All they knew was the here and now: an aging man who somehow looked younger, wearing double rings of silver in his ears, with hair cropped shorter than was his wont. The build was the same, the features the same; but the man, somehow, was not.

There were men I knew. I watched their eyes meet mine, then slide away. Faces were stiff, set in expressions designed to acknowledge the seriousness of the situation while giving nothing away of their thoughts. Some of them had been friends. Some of them had been good friends. But such things meant nothing when weighed against the shame of *elaii-ali-ma*. Here, I had no friends. No honored opponents. Only enemies.

Umir gestured me to halt. I acquiesced, marking the slant of shadows, how the sand had been raked. No clouds: Nothing would alter the intensity of the sun, thus altering the dance. I was aware of the servants just behind me. I smelled heat and sand and oil, the faint tangy musk of assembled, active males.

Then I sent myself away . . . *lost myself once more in the wind of ioSkandi, threading my way through the Stone Forest as I gazed down upon the circle, the man, the woman.*

Memory endured.

I was sword-dancer.

Sandtiger.

Legend in the flesh.

I smiled, returning. I was ready.

Umir raised his voice. "Will anyone among you draw the circle?"

No one moved. No one spoke. Everyone stared.

The tanzeer made a placatory gesture. "Yes; I do understand. There is the matter of *elaii-ali-ma*. I neither disparage it nor mean you dishonor, nor ask you to forget. What I wish is to present that which most closely resembles what this man, this outcast, threw away. He should know what he had, what he shared with you, and what he has lost. The best of you will remind him, so that he dies comprehending the worthlessness of his life." He paused. "Is there any among you who will draw the circle in which this man will die?"

I heard a murmuring among them as they discussed it. Umir was asking a lot. I had no business being in a circle of any kind, yet here I was. They could accept the tanzeer's suggestion or repudiate it even as I had repudiated the honor codes.

Then a man pushed out from behind the others, unsheathing his sword. A tall, wide-shouldered, fair-haired man, bred of Northern climes. I knew those eyes. Knew that face. Had heard the voice, intentionally raised beyond the wall of my room so I might hear and know he was present. Recognized the sword; I had met him before many times, to drink with, to spar against, to share his food. He, his wife, his two little girls—now three, if I remembered correctly. They had cared for me after injuries more than once.

Alric's eyes met mine, blue as Del's. I saw the faintest of flickers there, a tautening in his jaw. Though not born to Southron customs, he had learned them well. He lived among Southroners, danced among Southroners, was married to a Southroner. His habits were theirs. He understood them.

He walked nearly to where I stood, set his blade tip into the sand and began to pace out the circle, drawing the line.

Alric finished where he began. He turned to face me, studied me, seemed to look inside my soul. I wondered what he saw.

Abruptly he pivoted. With long strides the tall Northerner walked into the circle to the very center, bent, and set down his sword.

This time the murmuring became recognizable words of angry protest. The other sword-dancers were not pleased that one of their own spit in their faces by presenting me with his sword. Alric had just done his reputation among them irreparable harm; but then, Alric had always gone his own way.

At least one man here would mourn my death.

His message was clear: I need not worry that the sword I would use had been tampered with.

And the other message: he had not won his dance. It would not be Alric I'd meet in the circle, who would, unlike the others, make no attempt to kill me.

He inclined his head briefly, acknowledging me, then left the circle. Alric found a place to stand against the wall. He was alone, apart, as he had made himself by declaring his loyalty.

Inwardly, I laughed. Already Umir's plan had gone slightly

awry. Rafiq had brought him the sword I'd bought in Haziz, which one of the servants nearest the tanzeer held. But it would remain unused. Now I had another. One I could trust implicitly, one that suited me in weight and balance; Alric and I were very similar in build, and I had sparred with it before. It also was offered by a friend to a man who supposedly had none among those who lived in the circle.

Such intricacies of mind, such subtle subtexts, could do much for a man who meant to kill another, or to preserve his own life.

"Musa," Umir called.

After a moment bodies parted. A pathway was opened. A man came forward, walking toward the circle. I had half expected Abbu Bensir, but this man was not he. Much younger than Abbu, perhaps twenty-six or -eight; taller, though not as tall as I; heavier than Abbu, though not a big man; slightly lighter in skin, hair, and eyes. But he had the high-bridged nose and steep cheekbones present in so many of his countrymen. Not Borderer, I didn't think. But a mix of something that gave him greater size than most Southroners and, I decided, more power. He moved with the lithe, coiled grace of the snow cats I'd seen high in Northern mountains, up near Staal-Ysta.

He wore only a dhoti, as I did. No harness, no sandals. He carried his sword. His eyes were fixed on my own.

The others called out encouragement to him. He ignored them. There was a tight-wound intensity in Umir's new hired sword. His eyes did not leave mine. His expression was a predator's, fixed and unwavering. Not for him the camaraderie before a dance, the jokes and wagers exchanged. He had come to kill me. He wanted me to know it.

Musa, Umir had named him. I didn't know him. I'd never heard of him. But he was here among the others and had obviously defeated those others; I discounted nothing at all about him.

The tanzeer once again raised his voice. "As all of you have no doubt heard, the Sandtiger is no longer whole in body. But lest you believe him physically unable and thus offering no challenge, let me repeat what you may also have heard: this man killed one of you in Julah a matter of weeks ago. His name was Khashi."

There were quiet, abbreviated murmurs. Every man present knew already. Likely Rafiq had told them, bragging about how he had so easily captured the man who had so easily killed Khashi. Borrowing glory, Rafiq.

I looked at Musa. Musa looked back. He borrowed no glory. The man's carriage claimed the quiet confidence of the expert, requiring neither bragging nor flattery. The unsheathed sword dangled casually from his hand. His forearms and ribs were webbed with pale, thin, slit-like scars, unavoidable in the circle, but there were no scars of significance. Blades had gotten through his guard, had marked his flesh, but none of them had done true damage. Mere pricks and minor cuts. Either everyone he had faced had been no better than adequate, or he was truly good. Potentially great.

Based on the identities of many of the men I saw gathered in Umir's walled circle, the quality of much of the opposition, that he was good was a given.

"Umir," I said quietly, "forget the appetizer. This man wants his dessert."

The tanzeer glared at me. "Your places!"

For me, it was a matter of taking three strides to the edge of Alric's circle. I waited. Musa, opposite, crossed the circle, set his sword beside Alric's, then paced back to take up his position. There were perhaps four inches between our respective heights, and he was long-legged. The race would be of equals.

He also had hands boasting all four fingers.

I raised mine. Displayed them palm out. Let Musa and everyone else take a good look. "Surely," I said, "it will not take long to kill me. How can any man lacking two fingers hope to defeat the best of the best?"

It infuriated Umir, who clearly did not want his rebellious dessert ruining the moment. There was only one way to end it. *"Dance,"* he said.

Chapter 14

I dug the balls of my feet into sand and thrust myself forward, crossing over Alric's line into the circle. Three strides and I reached the center, snatching up Alric's sword.

I let momentum carry me forward into a somersault that took me out of immediate danger as Musa reached for his own weapon. I spun as I came up at the edge of the circle, blade at the ready, and blocked the first slashing blow. The clash of steel rang through the inner circle encompassed by Umir's wall.

Block. Block. Block and block. Musa was fast with his sword, disengaging and returning immediately to try new angles the moment I halted his blade. As with Khashi, I let him take the offense, judging foot placement, balance, strength, agility, blade speed. He had learned well, no question.

I was already at the edge of the circle because I had put myself there. One step, and I would be outside. But I knew better than to expect that would stop the dance; I was meant to die, and I was no longer honored among my peers. Musa would follow and continue the fight with no risk to his reputation, because I was, well, me. Still, I wanted this to be a true dance at least in my own mind, so that if I died, or if I won, no one could accuse me of cheating.

Well, they could. But *I'd* know better.

Musa brought more weight to bear, trying to push me beyond the line Alric had drawn. I dug in one foot and stopped the motion with a braced leg, then trapped his blade, held it, let him have a taste of my own weight as I pushed against him. Back, back, and back.

We were now once more in the very center of the circle. I yanked my blade free as Musa cursed, and slashed beneath his. Tip kissed flesh. A thin line of blood sprang up against the skin above his left knee.

My turn for offense, his to defend. And he did so admirably, blocking my blows as I had blocked his. When we broke and backed away panting, considering other methods to find a way through respective guards, we circled like wary street cats on the stalk, waiting for the most opportune moment to attack.

The first series of engagements was completed; neither of us had won. In Julah, Khashi had been dead by now. In fights too many to count, I had won by now. I suspected it had been the same for Musa.

Usually, the first moments of any match are spent testing the opponent's skill. A sword-dance is, in most cases, a *dance*, an exhibition of ability and artistry in pursuit of victory. But there were certainly dances where defeating the opponent was all that mattered, not how it looked. Musa and I had both chosen the latter, hoping to surprise the other, and neither of us had succeeded. Now the dance would shift into the testing phase as we teased one another's skills and signature movements out into the daylight, hoping to create openings we might exploit.

I saw Musa's eyes flick down to my hands wrapped around Alric's leather-strapped grip. There was no hiding the missing fingers. He was likely somewhat surprised I had matched so well against him initially in view of the disability. I wasn't, but only because I had worked like hoolies to overcome the problem, and I knew what to expect of my grip. An opponent didn't.

Musa lunged. I met his blade with my own and realized at once what he meant to do. Instead of movements aimed at my body in hopes of breaking my guard, he now went for the sword itself. Whether he drew blood didn't matter; the point was to disarm me. And that he judged a simple enough matter. I wasn't so certain he was wrong.

There was no finesse, merely strength and tenacity. Musa banged at my blade again and again, smashing steel against steel. From above, from below; from either side. The angle he applied changed with every blow, so that I constantly had to alter my grip upon leather wrappings or risk having the weapon knocked out of my hands. Then Musa could kill me at his leisure. I was at a distinct disadvantage, since not only did I have to concentrate on hanging onto my sword, but I also had to remember to block any body blow he might attempt without warning.

Which in fact he *did* attempt, and indeed without warning; I managed to turn most of the impetus aside, but the point of his blade still nicked me along the ribs. It was no more noticeable a wound than the shallow slice I'd put in the flesh of his lower thigh. The most damage either of us had managed to inflict was to our wind; both of us were panting heavily, noisily sucking air to the bottom of our lungs.

Now I went at him. Musa blocked each blow, and with each block he threw in a slight twisting of his blade. It wasn't enough to place him in danger of losing contact with or control of the steel, which would give the advantage to me, but it did continue forcing me to shift my grip each time. At some point he expected my mutilated hands to betray me. It wouldn't require much; merely a subtle change in pressure on the hilt, a weakening of my grip, that he could exploit.

The rhythm of the dance had changed. We no longer held our places in the center of the circle or kept ourselves to one specific area a step or two away from that center point; now we used the entire circle. We smashed steel against steel; hammered at one another; locked up blades and quillons; spun, ducked, or leaped away, using the time apart to recover breath. Sweat ran down my face, tickled along my ribs and spine. Musa's dark hair dripped as he shook it back, sending droplets flying. Bare feet had scuffed the neatly raked sand into an ocean of foot-formed hummocks. I didn't doubt we'd blotted out in places the line Alric had drawn, but it didn't matter. Everyone knew where the boundary lay.

Musa's strategy was sound. The stumps of my fingers ached, and the edges of my palms felt abraded from the continuous movement of flesh against leather wrappings. So far the specialized strength training of my forearms had aided me, and what I'd learned from the fight against Khashi, but Musa was clever enough to find a way around such things. All it required was time.

I was aware the sun had moved in the sky. My body told me we had been at this longer than likely anyone had expected, including Musa and me. But Umir ought to be happy.

We stood at opposite edges of the circle, facing one another. Chests heaved, throats spasmed, breath ran ragged. A half-smile twitched briefly at his mouth. I saw it, met it with raised brows. In that moment we acknowledged one another as something more than mere opponents. We were also equals. He likely had never met one since attaining this level of skill, unless he'd faced Abbu. I didn't doubt Abbu could defeat him; though acknowledging that meant admitting the possibility that Abbu was better than I. We neither of us knew, having never finished a dance.

Then Musa came at me, running, and the moment was banished. My sword met his, screeching. Teeth bared, he jerked his sword back and swung it down and under, going for my legs. I dropped to one knee, trapped his sword, pushed it up, then shoved him back with the power of my parry.

Musa staggered backward, retaining his balance with effort. He had expected to have me with that maneuver. Now he was angry. Equality no longer mattered.

"Old man," he said, "I will outlast you!"

Possibly he could. But I merely got up from the sand, laughing, and gestured him to come ahead.

He did. And in that moment I was aware of the vision I'd experienced in my room before the dance: me free of the stone spire to soar over the valley, to look down upon the man who met the woman in the circle. The vision overlay reality as Musa came on. I saw him, and I saw myself as the man in the circle in the Stone Forest, facing Del. The man with four fingers in place of three.

The priest-mages had taught me discipline was the key.

And conviction.

That the choice, the power, was mine. To make, and to use.

Something in me broke loose, answering. It—no, *I*—was swept up and up, high overhead, looking down upon the circle as I had before. Looking down upon a man, down upon myself, as I had before, and my opponent. But this time, in this circle, the opponent was not Del.

Two men, one young, one older, met within three circles: one of smooth, white-painted adobe; the second a blade-thin etching in white sand; and the third, the circle drawn in their own minds.

The younger man charged. The older met him, his smile a grimace, a rictus of effort. Muscles knotted beneath the browned flesh of both bodies, tendons stood up in ridges from neck to shoulder. Sweat bathed them, running like rivers in the hollows of straining flesh. Hands gripped hilts: four fingers, two thumbs on each.

On each.

The older welcomed the younger, challenging every fiber of his strength, every whisper of finesse, every skill and pattern he had ever learned. Challenging his belief in himself. Challenging his certainty of the older man's defeat. And the older challenged as well his own inner fear that he was unable because he was no longer whole. In the valley, in the circle, in the shadow of stone spires, he had been whole.

And was again.

"Now," *the older man roared.*

Back, and back, and back. Blow after blow after blow, the older drove the younger across the circle, forced him to stagger back, and back and back; shoved him over the line; smashed him down into the sand as the onlookers moved out of the way. The younger lay on his back, red-faced and gasping, sword blade in one hand feathered with sand. The older placed a callused foot upon the flat of the blade and stepped down. Hard.

Vision faded. Detachment dissipated. I blinked. Shook sweat away from my eyes. Was, abruptly, myself again, here in Umir's circle.

I was aware of silence. No one even breathed.

The tip of my own blade lingered at Musa's throat, pinning him with promise. I took my left hand off the grip and looked at it. Counted three fingers.

Three, and one stub.

There had been four on the hilt. I was certain of it. Four fingers and one thumb on each hand.

How in hoolies?—never mind. Time for that later.

I bent then, breathing hard, reaching down as I shifted my left foot. I pulled Musa's sword up from the sand, then flung it away hard to clang against the opposite wall. I flicked a glance out of the corner of my eye and saw what I had expected: Alric stood just behind Umir.

"Alric," I said between inhalations, "take that sword Umir's servant is holding."

The big Northerner did so and quietly moved forward to place it across Umir's throat. "Anything else?"

"Yes. Escort Umir into the house and have him give you a book."

Alric blinked. "A book?"

I smiled as I watched the color spill out of Umir's face. "It's called the *Book of Udre-Natha*. Umir places great value on it. I'm going to hold it hostage." I glanced briefly down at Musa, still lying beneath my sword. His breath was audible, chest heaving. "In the meantime, Umir will also have our horses readied—packed with food, water, grain and, of course, the book—and waiting for us in the front courtyard." Now I slid a glance over the assembled sword-dancers, swallowed, and raised my voice. "It was promised to me if I won: no one would challenge me inside Umir's domain. Right, Umir?" No answer. "Umir, if you ever expect to get your book back—"

"Yes," he said sharply. "I did agree. I will honor that agreement."

"And I think no one here will argue over the results of this dance." I glanced down. A thin line of blood trickled across Musa's neck, mingling with sweat. "Will they?"

Musa said nothing. Neither did anyone else.

I drew in a breath. "I made a choice that day when I stepped out of Sabra's circle and declared *elaii-ali-ma*. We all of us make choices. Some are good, some bad, some are right, some wrong. And we all pay the price. I accept that I am dishonored, that I have no place among you. I made the choice. And I make another now: to let this man live."

I backed away, taking my sword with me. Musa remained

sprawled in the sand a moment longer, then hitched himself up onto his elbows.

"Why?" he rasped.

I smiled. "Some day, when you meet yourself in the circle—and you will, because we all do—you'll know."

I turned away. Musa's sword lay against the opposite wall, well out of reach. Though I meant what I'd said, I wasn't entirely stupid; you don't leave a loser's weapon close at hand.

Of course, I had reckoned without the insanity of irrational pride.

I heard him move and knew, even as I spun. Musa was up on his feet again, charging at me. Time slowed as he came: I saw the ripple of a tic in his cheek, the strain of tension reforming his facial muscles.

Oh no. No.

He came on. Despite the fact that he lacked a sword, and I did not.

Stop now. Save yourself . . .

But he did not. He gathered himself. Took that fatal leap. Committed himself. So I committed as well. I ran him through with my blade.

There was no triumph. I felt hollow. Empty. "You had the world," I told him, meaning it.

Musa's world—and his legs—collapsed. He knelt in the sand, choking on blood. I withdrew the blade sheathed in his chest. Blood ran down steel and pearled in white sand.

I was aware of movement. I looked up, lifting the sword; saw men stirring. But no one spoke to protest. Musa had effectively killed himself, though I had been the man holding the blade.

Alric, escorting our friendly host, came out of the house again. "Everything's ready."

I nodded. I cast a glance at the waiting sword-dancers. I couldn't help but smile at the irony. "I expect I'll see some of you again," I said, "but not for a few days or so. Until then, why not avail yourself of Umir's hospitality? Since none of you won his offer of lifetime employment, you might as well enjoy it while you can."

I heard at my feet, from the kneeling man, an expulsion of breath. Musa seemed to fold in upon himself, upper body collapsing upon the lower. The sweat-drenched hair fell forward as his head lolled upon his neck.

A waste. A waste of pure talent, barely matched skill. Banished by pride even greater, and thus presented to death—like dessert on a plate.

The body fell.

I turned then and walked away. Alric let go of Umir. We swapped swords with practiced lateral tosses, then ducked into the shadowed coolness of Umir's house.

"Nicely done," Alric commented.

"I thought so."

"Do you think they'll wait until you're out of Umir's domain?"

I led him through the front door into the courtyard. "Not on your life." Well. Not on mine, at any rate.

"Where are we going?" he asked.

I headed for the gelding, waiting patiently with his reins in the hands of one of Umir's grooms. A harness was attached to the pommel; I shoved the sword home in the sheath. "*I* am going to Julah. Aren't you going back to Lena and the girls?"

"Eventually. Right now I thought I'd ride with a friend who's in trouble."

"Big of you, Alric." I grabbed reins and swung up.

He grinned as he mounted his own horse. "I thought so."

I sank heels into the gelding. Together, at a gallop, the Northerner and I departed Umir's courtyard.

Chapter 15

*S*ome distance from Umir's house Alric and I fell into the walk-trot-lope combination that transported us as far and as fast as possible without ruining the horses. I discovered the white gelding, for all he was a ridiculous mount for the desert, was indeed a comfortable ride in all his gaits. Too bad he needed black paint and fringe to make it practical. And just now he lacked both after his sojourn at Umir's; fortunately it was nearing sundown as we approached the big oasis a day's ride from Julah.

The oasis was a popular stopover for travelers, and thus five different routes met here. There were palm trees aplenty, plus water plants around the edges of the small artesian spring that had, over time and with human help, been widened into a pool. Desert folk honor such places by treating oases as sanctuary. Animals and humans are watered, then everyone retreats to their own patch of soil and sand to pass the night without fear of attack. Since it was early summer, more people were on the roads. The oasis was crowded.

Alric and I dismounted, led the horses to the pool, let them drink enough to cool their throats, then pulled them away and commenced the struggle of man against thirsty horse. Trouble was, they'd get sick if they drank too much too fast when they were hot. Alric and I walked them a bit as dusk approached, then led them to water again. We filled canvas horse buckets, gulped a few mouthfuls for ourselves, then made our wandering way, trailing tired horses, through the cluster of tiny campsites to find our own, settling finally for a single unclaimed palm tree on the outskirts. There we unsaddled, spent some time rubbing the horses down, then pegged them out—and carried botas back to the pool to tend our own thirst in earnest.

Kneeling at the water's edge, I sluiced my head and face, then squirted the contents of a bota down my bare torso, front and back. Once I'd refilled the waterskin, I released a gusty exhalation of relief.

Alric, squatting nearby, grinned. "He will live?"

"He will live." I used a forearm to wipe water from my brow. "But he's getting too old for this."

The Northerner grunted. "Didn't look like it to me earlier today."

I inspected the thin crusted slice along one of my ribs, dismissed it as unimportant. "Trust me, I am."

Alric stoppered his bota and rose. I splashed another handful of water through damp, spiky hair, then pressed myself up from the ground. At a more decorous pace we strolled through the oasis, exchanging nods of greeting with other travelers. I smelled sausage and spiced mutton and journey-loaf baking on a flat rock. Danjacs and oxen called to various brethren, while horses snorted disdainfully down haughty noses. I thought of the molahs of Skandi and the steep, zig-zagging trail up the caldera face.

"So," Alric said, "Just what *was* all of that about?"

"All of what?"

"All of everything."

Back at our lone palm, we grained the horses sparingly and began to unpack our gear, unrolling and spreading blankets on the warm sand. *"Elaii-ali-ma."*

"Oh, I heard about that." It didn't mean the same thing to him since he was a Northerner born and trained, but he understood what it was for me. "I mean, where have you been, what's happened to you, how'd you lose your fingers and get those tattoos, and why did you want Umir's book?"

"Oh, *that* everything." I sighed, shoved saddle pouches under one end of the blanket, stretched out with my head pillowed on wool and leather as I chewed idly at dried cumfa. I'd already told him briefly about Del's predicament and how I hoped to catch up to her in Julah, supposing Nayyib had taken her there. "We've led rather interesting lives for the past several months."

Alric flopped down on his blanket, thrusting a thick, blond-furred forearm beneath his head. "I always like an entertaining story before I go to sleep."

So I told him. Not everything. Nothing about magic, save to explain that Umir's book supposedly contained all manner of powerful spells. And nothing at all about my limited life expectancy, or my dreams of a dead woman and a sword. But I didn't need to. Even abbreviated, it was story enough for Alric.

When I finished, he lay in silence for a time. Then he grunted. "I see I'm missing a great deal, being a staid married man with four children."

"Four! Last time you had three."

"Lena's expecting again."

"Hoolies, Alric, you and Lena are worse than sandconeys. Do you plan to populate the entire South?"

"I like children."

"Good thing!"

"Lena likes children."

"Even better, since she has to bear them."

He cast me a speculative glance. "Don't you ever plan to have any?"

I cast him a look in return that informed him he was sandsick. "You and Lena can make up for my lack."

Alric laughed. "Fair enough. It gives us an excuse for more."

He *was* sandsick. "In the morning," I said abruptly, "you head back home. There are five roads out of here; they can track us this far from Umir's, but then they'll have to split up to sort out where I've gone."

It caught him off-guard. "I'd thought to go on to Julah and help you with Del."

I shook my head. "I appreciate it, Alric, but you've got three children and a fourth on the way. You don't need any part of my trouble. Go home to Lena." I might not want my own kids, but I didn't want to be responsible for depriving others of their father. "I'll be fine."

After a moment he agreed. "You certainly handled Musa easily enough."

"Hardly 'easily.' I'll feel it in the morning. Hoolies, I feel it now!"

"Musa doesn't."

I swore with feeling. "*That* was sheer waste. Talent like his doesn't come along very often."

"From what I hear, not since you did."

I made a noncommital noise. Once I might have complimented him on his insight, but Del had impressed upon me that one needn't brag to establish one's credentials.

Or something like that.

Chewing tough cumfa, Alric observed, "Musa made the choice. He might have let it be."

But Musa was—*had been*—young, supremely talented, confident, and he could not believe I had beaten him. Not a man who had dishonored himself.

After a moment, Alric asked, "Will you answer a question?"

I couldn't figure out why he felt he had to ask permission. "Sure."

"What will you do if Delilah is dead?"

Oh. Now I knew why.

"Tiger?"

"I haven't thought about it."

My tone did not dissuade him from further inquiry. "Not ever?"

"No."

"Why not?"

I hitched myself up on an elbow and scowled at him. "What kind of a conversation *is* this? How about I ask you if you've ever thought about what you'd do if Lena died?"

"I have. I do. Every time she goes into labor."

I blinked. It's not the sort of thing men speak about very often, if at all. "Well, I suppose that's a risk you have to take if you're going to have kids." Which was a pretty lame comment, but I didn't know what else to say. I flopped back down on my blanket. Since he'd brought it up— "So, what *would* you do if Lena died?"

"I have three daughters to care for. That is what I'd do."

"As a sword-dancer?"

"Oh, no. I would have to find another life. Something with no travel involved, so I would be there for my girls." He spoke so matter-of-factly about giving up the life he had always wanted. Maybe that's what happened when you got married and had kids. Gave things up. No wonder I didn't want any.

"As you have no children," Alric said, "what will you do if Del is dead?"

I really didn't want to walk this particular conversational road. Especially when I had no idea where or how she was. "Go on," I replied briefly.

"Doing what? You can't accept dances anymore."

"I own one-third of a cantina."

Alric turned to stare at me incredulously. "You'd spend the rest of your days serving liquor and wine-girls?"

"No," I replied crossly. "I mean I'd collect my share of profits. They'd be enough to live on even if I can't dance. But it doesn't really matter, because I have plans."

"What plans?"

"Alimat fell years ago. The shodo died. There hasn't been one since then—at least, not of his ability." I raised my hands into the air, inspecting them. "Even if I hadn't declared *elaii-ali-ma*, I'm a little bit hampered as a sword-dancer. So I thought I'd take a whack at being a shodo."

"You? A teacher?"

I scowled at him, lowering my hands. "Why does everyone always sound so surprised?"

Alric examined my expression. "Because you are not in general known for your patience, Tiger. And those who have a particularly rare gift for something—in your case, sword-dancing—often make the worst teachers. They can't teach what comes to them naturally and unbidden."

"How do you know I can't?"

"Tell me how you defeated Musa."

"I just—beat him."

"See?"

"Come on, Alric! Do you want me to give you a blow-by-blow description? You were there."

"How do you know precisely where a man will be in the circle, Tiger? How do you know what move he will make before *he* knows?" He grinned as I stared at him in surprise. "Yes. I have seen it in you. As I saw it on Staal-Ysta, in one of the sword-singers there. I asked him once. He couldn't tell me. He said he simply knew. He saw it in his head."

"Time just—slows." It was the first time I had ever spoken of it to anyone. It sounded ridiculous. And impossible.

Alric sighed. "You can't teach that, Tiger."

It stung. "You don't know. I might be able to."

The big Northerner snorted. Then he rolled over, displaying a broad back. Such faith he had in me.

But maybe he was right. Maybe I couldn't teach anyone anything. I just didn't know what else I might do.

I stared into the deepening sky, watching the stars emerge out of daylight into darkness. Firelight flickered at ground level, illuminating soil and sand, the dark, angular faces of Southron travelers. The aroma of mutton and sausage drifted our way. I heard quiet murmurings in several dialects, laughter, a child crying, and a faint, yearning melody sung softly by a woman.

Bascha, I said, please don't be dead.

I awoke to the sound of a baby screaming. At first I tried to block it out by pulling a corner of the blanket over my head, but it didn't help. Eventually I gave up, squinted out at the early morning sun, then pushed myself upright. Musa may have landed only one minor blow, but the dance alone had resulted in sore muscles.

I got up slowly, swearing quietly under my breath. By the time I was standing, I realized Alric was already up. In fact, he'd taken the horses off for watering. I was in the midst of stretching and attempting to lengthen my spine when he came back. He looked altogether too alert for this early.

Which reminded me. "How was it you managed to lose your dance?"

He led the horses back to the pickets. "Musa."

"You danced with Musa?"

"I was his fifth opponent, or maybe it was sixth. I lasted fractionally longer than the fourth or fifth." He tied off the horses, apportioned more grain. "It was clear from the first time he danced that he would likely win."

"So, I take it everyone lost money when I defeated him."

He grinned. "I would assume so."

"Too bad." I glanced around for something behind which I might shield my morning donation, finally settled on the palm tree just beyond the horses. "Did you?" I called.

"What, lose money? Hoolies, I didn't bother wagering."

"At all?"

"No. It would have been disloyal."

"Ah hah! Even *you* would have bet against me."

Alric was rolling up his blanket as I came back around the horses. "I didn't know where you'd been or what you'd been up to since the last time I'd seen you. I did mention to the others I thought they were giving you short shrift, but once Rafiq spouted off about the missing fingers and your bout with the sandtiger, no one wanted to listen."

I started packing up my own belongings. "You could have put coin on me for old times' sake."

"Lena expressly forbade me to wager."

I nodded sagely. "And you, of course, do everything Lena tells you. Or, in this case, *don't* do everything Lena tells you *not* to do."

"We would not be having this conversation if Del were here."

"Sure we would. She'd just be giving us the benefit of her own opinion."

"You've been together how long?"

I thought about it. "Almost four years."

"Ah. Then you're still a work in progress. Lena has had more than ten years to remake me."

"Del knows better than to try to remake me."

Whereupon Alric collapsed in paroxysms of laughter, drowning out even the screaming baby.

Eventually I noted, "I meant that as a joke."

The Northerner got up again and finished packing, but it was punctuated by occasional chuckles. After a while I ignored him and hauled pouches and saddle to the gelding, who peered at me out of watery blue eyes.

"What happened to the stud?" Alric asked.

I slipped into my harness and buckled it, reseating the sword I'd bought in Haziz. It would be another day ending in sunburn, since I still lacked a burnous. Fortunately I'm tanned enough that the burn is only mild. "He ran off when the sandtiger attacked. If I'm lucky, he wandered back after Rafiq and his friends hauled me away to Umir's. Otherwise, he might still be out there wandering around." Or more likely dead. But I didn't want to think about that any more than about the possibility of Del being dead. "He's a tough old son. He's likely bedded down in a good Julah livery about now." And Del, I hoped, was bedded down on a healer's cot.

"Are you sure you don't want company?"

"Go home to your wife, Alric. Tell bedtime stories of me to your little girls."

He grinned, reached out an arm. We clasped briefly. "Bring Del to Rusali when you have a chance. Lena and the girls would like to see her."

The gelding was saddled and packed. I mounted, settled my aching body. Whatever Meteiera may have done to me, it hadn't made life painless. "I will."

Alric's expression was serious. "Tiger—I mean it."

I nodded. "I know. I will."

His smile was of brief duration, as if something nagged at him. "May the sun shine on your head."

"And yours," I returned, then headed the gelding south, away from crying babies.

Chapter 16

I went through the cantina doorway bellowing for Fouad. It was late afternoon, and only a couple of men had yet wandered in for drinks. By sundown the place would begin to fill up. As I strode across the hard-packed floor to the plank bar, shouting for their host, they watched in mild curiosity. In Julah, in cantinas, pretty much anything was commonplace.

Fouad appeared from the hindmost regions of the cantina smoothing the front of his yellow burnous, as I dumped saddle-pouches on the bar. His eyebrows ran up into graying hair. "You're back."

"Where's Del?"

He blinked. "Isn't she with you?"

"Isn't she with *you?*"

"No."

I felt a stab of disquiet. "That kid came here, he said."

"Who, Nayyib?" Fouad nodded. "He did. He wanted the name of a good healer. He planned to take the healer to where you and the bascha were." His dark eyes widened. "Didn't he do it?"

Oh, hoolies. "He showed up," I said, "but there was no healer with him. Only three buffoons hired by Umir the Ruthless." I tapped impatiently on the plank, understanding now that Rafiq and his friends had never allowed Nayyib to find the healer, just made him lead them to me. "I figured he'd bring her here afterwards."

Fouad shook his head. "I haven't seen the bascha since she left with you, and I haven't seen the kid since he left with the sword-dancers."

I was thinking furiously. "Maybe he took her to the healer you recommended. How do I find him?"

"No, Oshet stopped by earier today for ale. He said he has no new patients." He eyed me, clearly reluctant. "Forgive me, but if she was that badly injured, it's possible—"

I cut him off. "She's not dead." Then I swore feelingly, wondering if Nayyib had brought her back to Julah but avoided Fouad's, since his last visit had ended badly. Or maybe Del was sick enough that he'd felt it best to remain at the lean-to and not risk moving her. But it made no sense that he wouldn't take her to the healer Fouad recommended. I had a hunt ahead of me.

"She might be elsewhere in town," he suggested, following my thought. "Maybe with another healer. Do you want me to ask around?"

"If Nayyib's avoiding you, you won't find him."

Fouad scoffed. "This is my town."

"He doesn't strike me as stupid."

"It's difficult to hide with a sick Northern woman."

Very true; unless she was dead, and he was on his own.

I dismissed the thought instantly, annoyed I'd succumbed to it. "Ask around," I said. "The sooner there's an answer the happier I'll be. I'll spend the night at the inn just up the street. If I don't hear anything by morning, I'll head out."

"Stay here," Fouad offered.

"In a cantina?"

He laughed. "You used to stay here all the time."

"Not in an empty bed." I hadn't stayed in a cantina since hooking up with Del. Before then, such places had been frequent lodgings.

"*That* could be remedied," Fouad asserted. But his humor died away. "One of my girls left to marry, and there is an extra room. It's small, but it claims a bed, a tiny table. You do own one-third of the place, now."

"Fine. Can you have one of your boys take my horse to the livery? I've got all my belongings off him."

Fouad looked dubious. "No one likes handling the stud."

"I don't have the stud. It's the white gelding tied outdoors." I sighed, running a hand impatiently through hair that was just beginning to regain some of its wave. "Food and drink would be welcome. And a burnous."

"I'll bring a meal out myself."

"No. To the room. I'm going to lay low."

Fouad gestured. "Back through the curtain, down the hallway, last door on the left."

As I picked up the saddlepouches I didn't remind him that I knew the layout from earlier days. I just nodded and went.

The room was indeed small. Smaller, in fact, than I remembered. But it did have the bed to recommend it, plus the tiny table next to it just inside the curtained doorway. I dumped the pouches next to the bed, then unsheathed the sword and leaned it against the bedframe. I shed the harness next. Sure enough, after two days with no burnous, I had paler stripes standing out against the copper-brown of my skin. I looked as though I were wearing the harness even when I wasn't. Leather had rubbed against the slice along my rib, but the annoyance was minimal when weighed against the rest of my body.

My smile was twisted. Nihkolara had said new scars would replace the old ones lifted from me by the mages. It looked as though I was on my way to starting a second collection.

The whisper of a step sounded beyond the privacy curtain. I caught up the sword and leveled it just as the fabric was pulled aside. Silk, Fouad's wine-girl, bearing a tray and carrying a burnous draped over one arm, stopped dead.

I gestured her in, smiling ruefully. "We're beginning to make this a habit."

This time she wasn't swathed in cloth or trying to hide her face as she bore me a warning. She wore filmy gold-dyed gauze and a sash-belt of crimson tassels riding low on her hips that accentuated her Southron coloring and lush body. She accepted my invitation, set the tray on the table, then put the burnous on the bed. Fouad is a man who likes color; the gauze was a deep bluish-purple.

Bright red in Skandi, now purple here. Whatever happened to subtlety?

Silk was gazing at me, black wings of hair hanging loosely beside her face.

"Thank you," I said feelingly, and set down the sword again. Fouad had, of course, included aqivi along with food. For just a moment, though, I thought longingly of Umir's excellent meals.

"You are alone?" Silk asked.

I nodded, realizing Fouad probably had said nothing of the circumstances. I sat down on the edge of the bed and dove into mutton stew in a bowl carved of hard brown bread.

"Will you be wanting company tonight?"

It stopped me cold. I looked at her over the spoonful of stew halfway through my mouth.

"Ah," she said, and the single word contained a multitude of emotions.

"Wait," I said as she turned to go. "Silk . . ." But I wasn't sure what I'd meant to say.

Her smile was sad. "It's the Northern bascha."

I nodded.

Her mouth twisted faintly. "All those years . . . we used to say you would never settle on one woman. But inwardly we all dreamed it might be one of us." She gestured with one square hand. "Oh, I know—it wouldn't be with a wine-girl. But even women like us have dreams, Tiger."

I felt vastly uncomfortable. "I don't know what to say."

"Then say nothing. Know only that you were—and always will be—special to me."

I groped for comforting words. I'd never been very good at them. "There will be someone for you, Silk. Didn't Fouad say one of the girls just left to get married?"

She nodded solemnly. "But she was much younger than I, and not so coarse."

The best answer was suddenly a simple matter of speaking the truth. "If you were coarse," I told her, "I would never have shared your bed."

After a moment, she said, "Thank you for that."

"I meant it."

She nodded and turned to go.

"Silk!" I stabbed the spoon back into stew and stood up. It took a single pace for me to reach the doorway, and the woman.

She wouldn't look at me. I cupped her jaw, lifted her face, brushed away the tears with my thumbs. Then I bent and kissed her gently.

No passion. No promise. She knew what it was. She knew what it meant. But still she twined arms around my neck and clung. My hands rested lightly on her hips. She smelled, as always, of wine and ale, and the faint undertang of the musky scent she wore.

Silk broke the kiss even as I did. She raised her hands to my face, fingers scraping against stubble. She traced out the sandtiger scars. "Be careful," she whispered, and the curtain billowed behind her as she left.

No message came with news of Del's whereabouts in Julah or that anyone had sighted Nayyib. Since I wasn't sitting out front watching the world go by with liquor at my elbow, for a long while I paced the tiny room, fighting back a growing feeling of impatience coupled with desperation. Finally my body explained that it was tired even if my mind was not. I sat down on the bed for a while, spine propped against the adobe wall with my legs stretched out, and tried to invent logical reasons for Del's absence.

It was entirely possible that she was still at the lean-to. Except that it had been twelve days or more since Rafiq and his friends had hauled me off to Umir's, and she ought to have recovered enough to be moved to Julah. Even if the stud hadn't returned, the kid had a horse. He could easily have fashioned a litter using the limbs and canvas from the lean-to and brought her to a healer.

They just kept going around and around in my head, all the possibilities. And the thoughts I didn't want to think. I finally scooted down to lie on the bed, staring blankly at the wood-and-mud ceiling. Alric's questions kept sifting to the forefront of my mind no matter how much I tried to ignore them. I cursed myself for it, cursed Alric, cursed Nayyib, cursed Rafiq, Umir, Musa, and the sandtiger who had attacked her.

What *would* I do if I were alone in the world again?

More than two years before when I had left Staal-Ysta, believing Del would die from the travesty I had made of her abdomen with my newly keyed *jivatma*, I had focused on the task of tracking down the hounds of hoolies and their master, to save the village of Ysaa-den. It had given me purpose. It had given me the chance to think about something other than Del, for fractions of moments.

There was, now, nothing else to think about.

I scrubbed at my stubbled face, stretching it out of shape. Then growled long and hard into my hands, needing to bleed off the tension. Finally I took the sword from beside the bed, set it *on* the bed between me and the wall, and closed my eyes. I did not expect to sleep. But my body had other ideas.

I dreamed of Del, which was much improvement over the skeleton in the desert and the sword I was supposed to "take up." I dreamed of Del in all her many guises, sparing no truths of her temperament. She could be cold and hard, faceted like Punja crystal, capable of killing at a moment's notice. She could be sharp-tongued and short-tempered, and there were times her words wounded. But she could also be a soft touch when it came to baby animals and human children, ruthlessly fierce in her tenderness; and, despite a poor beginning among borjuni, passionate in bed. She was woman enough to drive me mad on occasion, because women did that to men; but she also took my breath away with the power of her pride and strength of will.

Silk had said it *for* me as much as to me: I had never believed it likely I would settle on one woman. Unlike Alric, I wasn't made for a wife and children. I wanted no ties. Nearly two decades as a Salset chula had taught me never to be owned by anyone again; and what was a husband but a man owned by his wife?

Even Alric admitted Lena forbade him things. Who needs that?

And then Delilah arrived in my life, as driven as I to prove herself, if for different reasons, and having no more interest in putting down roots than I did. Except for an enforced stay on Skandi and then time spent on the island off Haziz to regain fitness, we had never stopped moving.

A sudden thought occurred: Now I was proposing to rebuild Alimat and take on students. Which would require me to stay put.

No wonder everyone thought I was sandsick!

I roused from sleep long enough to mutter something mostly incoherent about old men growing soft, then slid down again into the abyss.

Where the bones and the sword waited.

This time the skeleton wears flesh, and a face. It is Del, gazing at me out of empty sockets. A hand reaches, gestures. There, she seems to say, though her mouth does not move. There. Take up the sword.

It lies just out of her reach, as if flung down or lost in battle. It is more than a sword, I see, but jivatma, *fashioned in the North of Northern rites. Yet it isn't Boreal. Isn't Del's sword.*

It is mine. Samiel.

"There," she says, "take up the sword."

Sand drifts. Obscures the body. Carries flesh away. Bones remain. It isn't Del anymore but the other woman.

"Find me," she says. "Find—"

"—me," I finished, and realized I was awake.

The sword lay beside me, where I had placed it. Not Samiel, just the sword I'd bought in Haziz. It bore no runes, no Northern magic. Was nothing more than steel, with a leather-wrapped hilt.

In the darkness, I lifted the sword. Closed one hand around it. Felt again the pressure of four fingers.

Four, not three.

I closed my other hand around it, resting the pommel against my abdomen so that the blade bisected air. And again, four fingers.

After a moment I set the sword down beside me and inspected my hands. Felt two stumps where little fingers had lived.

Find me, she had said. *Take up the sword.*

Find who? What sword?

"What in hoolies do you want?" I said. "And what am I supposed to do about it? If you want me to do something, you've got to give me more to go on!"

Of course, then I felt utterly absurd for talking aloud to a dream. But I was getting more than a little tired of obscurity. I've always been a vivid dreamer, but this was new. And already old.

I considered the situation. I had fully intended to go to the fallen chimney formation to search for Samiel. Del and I were on our way there when the sandtiger had attacked. So if I was heading there anyhow, why would the dreams seem to be commanding me this way and that, like a recalcitrant child? And what did the dead woman have to do with any of it? There had been no one but Del and me in the chimney when Chosa Dei met Shaka Obre for the final time. We'd escaped. No one had been killed. What did my *jivatma* have to do with the skeleton?

I sat up, planting my feet on the floor. Out of sorts, I scrubbed at mussed hair. I was bone-tired still, since sleep had brought me no rest. Finally I lighted the candle on the table, then bent down to dig through saddlepouches. I found Umir's book and propped it on my lap as close to candlelight as possible.

It was a plain, leather-bound book. No inset gemstones, gold or silver scrollwork, no burned-in knotwork designs that might set it apart from other books. I knew it was expensive; *all* books are expensive and owned only by the wealthy. But it didn't look particularly special. The hinges and latch were made of tarnished copper, and time-darkened gut threaded the pages onto the spine. I wondered briefly if it was locked against me, but the latch opened easily enough. I turned back the cover and saw the first page: fine sheepskin vellum, scraped to a clean, level sheet. The first letter on the page was bigger than the rest, much more ornate, painted in remarkable colors. The print itself was plain black ink.

I squinted at it in poor light. Before Meteiera, I hadn't been able to read anything other than maps, since mostly those were made up of symbols denoting roads, mountains, water, rather than words. Words I'd never been able to sort out in my head, but I'd never really tried. Del could read, so I'd relied on her on the few occasions it mattered. Mostly, it didn't. Then in ioSkandi, atop the spires, something had happened. Something had changed me. Not only could I read, but I comprehended languages I'd never before learned. I'd always had a few to hand—you just learn phrases over time—but now I knew them all. Fluently.

I could read Umir's book.

Something deep in my belly fluttered. It wasn't quite fear, nor was it excitement, nor, happily, was it nausea. Then I realized it was the first blossoming of anticipation.

The *Book of Udre-Natha* was, supposedly, a grimoire containing spells, incantations, summonings, and other magical oddments. Umir had fancied himself a practitioner of the arcane arts, and indeed I'd seen him do a few tricks. But I had spent most of my life denying magic existed, so I'd paid little enough attention to such things. In time, I'd rather uneasily come to the conclusion that it did indeed exist, and some could even summon and manipulate it to almost any degree—as apparently I had managed to do once or twice. But I didn't like to think about it.

Certainly not in connection with me.

I carefully turned the pages, noting colorful first letters throughout, and diagrams, drawings, even maps. The handwriting changed frequently, which suggested more than one man had written it. Though I could read the words, they spoke of many things unknown to me. It was a comprehension of parts without understanding the whole.

Then, paging through, I came across a brief scribbled note saying something about some kinds of inborn magic coming to life late, residing unknown in the body and mind. That a man might live most of his life ignorant of his power until something kindled it. Then, suddenly beset by magic like a blind man given sight, he could react in one of several different ways. All of them seemed to entail some kind of danger to himself or to others.

One line in particular caught my eye. *Magic must be used,* it said, *as a boil must be lanced, lest it poison mind and body.*

Very familiar words. Sahdri had said something similar, as had Nihko.

I wondered, then, if my unwillingness to use whatever power I supposedly had was causing the dreams. If I had locked my magic away somehow, was it now seeping out around the edges? Would it burst free unexpectedly one day, threatening me and others?

Sahdri had said Skandic mages went mad from the magic, and that was why they exiled themselves to ioSkandi. That the discipline and devotions learned there in Meteiera could control the worst of the power when coupled with judicious use of it. But it was a finite period of control, because eventually every priest-mage merged with the gods. Of course, their idea of merging was actually self-murder, since they leaped off the spires. So I guess they really did go mad.

I'd never thought of magic as a *disease* before, but the book sure made it sound that way.

I read another line. *Magic manifests itself in uncounted ways no one may predict, depending on the individual. But it is known that overuse of the power may kill the man, and denial of it after manifestation may also kill him.*

Oh, joy. Either way I could die.

Ten years, Nihko had told me I had left. Possibly twelve. Not exactly what I call fair compensation for having magic in your blood.

Sighing, I closed the book, fastened it, set it on the table. Blew the candle out. Went back to bed.

This time I didn't dream.

Chapter 17

ouad stared at me. He wore brilliant orange this morning.
"Are you sandsick?"

My face got a little warm. "No."

"What in the names of all the gods *for?*"

"The horse," I muttered.

In his eyes I saw all manner of thought. Likely none of them had to do with the sanity of one particular sword-dancer. "You want Silk's tassels for your horse."

I stared down fixedly at the saddlepouches on the bar, picking at leather thongs. "Yes."

Amusement was replacing the incredulous note in his voice. "Are you sure this is not for yourself?"

I glared at him. "No, it's not for me!"

He cocked his head thoughtfully, examining me. "I don't know—you might look good with women's tassels hanging from your—"

"Never mind!"

"—neck," he finished, grinning.

"He has blue eyes," I explained.

Fouad reverted to surprise. "A blue-eyed horse? In the desert?"

"I know! I know! Just get the tassels, Fouad. And if you've got any charcoal and axle grease, I'll take that, too. Mixed."

"Also for your horse?"

This time I leveled my most threatening sandtiger's glare at him, and he flung his hands into the air. "All right! All right. I'll get charcoal and axle grease. Mixed."

I watched him turn away. "What about Silk's tassels?"

"Oh, you can get those yourself!"

"But—" But. He was gone.

Swearing inventive oaths having to do with Fouad's nether parts and the decreasing amount of time he would retain them, I swung the pouches over one shoulder and went back through the curtain. I didn't know which room was Silk's, which was probably intentional on Fouad's part. So at each curtained doorway I had to stop, ease the fabric aside and peer in, hoping I wouldn't awaken anyone. After a late night of entertaining various dusty and lusty males just in from the desert, Fouad's wine-girls wouldn't exactly enjoy me waking them up this early.

Fortune followed me until I found the correct room. As I eased aside the curtain, looking for a string of crimson tassels, I discovered the owner of the tassels in the midst of a morning stretch. She stood in the middle of her little room, nude, arching her back with arms outstretched. A long, luxurious, languorous stretch. When a woman does that with her back, other parts of her body shift forward.

I realized, as my face got warm, that once upon a time I wouldn't have been embarrassed. But somehow that had altered when I hooked up with Del. I guess maybe you don't have to get married for a woman to start changing your perspective about naked women who are not the woman who's doing the changing.

Not a happy thought, I reflected glumly.

Silk's eyes sprang open. I yanked my head back and shut the curtain hastily, then cursed myself for behaving like a green boy who'd never been with a woman.

"Tiger?"

She *had* seen me. My face warmed again. "Yes?"

Silk now stood at the doorway, curtain pulled around her body. The long black hair was a tangle spilling over her shoulders. Brows lifted, she waited for me to explain myself.

I floundered my way ahead. "I know this sounds strange . . . but could I buy your tassels?"

Black brows arched higher. "My tassels?"

I pointed self-consciously. "Those tassels. The red ones."

She glanced back over a naked shoulder, marked tassels, then looked at me. "For *her?*"

"Her?" It took me a moment, but I got there. "No, not for Del! For my horse." Which I realized, as soon as I said it, didn't sound particularly complimentary. At least Del was a human. I floundered on as quickly as possible. "He's white. And blue-eyed. He needs shielding from the sun."

Silk eyed me a long moment, her expression curiously blank. Then she dropped the curtain and padded naked to the table where the tassels lay. When she turned around again, swinging the tassels on one finger, there was no attempt to cover herself. In fact, she was doing her best to display everything. I cleared my throat, averted my eyes, and busied myself digging through pouches for coins.

She appeared in front of me, offering the tassels. "No charge."

I looked up, wished I hadn't. "Why no charge?"

"Because I will have my payment over and over again," she explained sweetly, "each time I imagine you telling your Northern bascha that you got these tassels from me. And what I was wearing *when* you got them."

Hoolies. Women!

I muttered thanks through gritted teeth, grabbed the tassels out of her hand, and got myself back to the front room as quickly as possible. Fouad, straight-faced, handed me a small pot of grease mixed with charcoal.

In a purple burnous, carrying a pot of black greasepaint and dangling crimson tassels, I made my way from the cantina with what dignity I could muster.

The white gelding peered at me out of sorrowful—and watery—blue eyes. He was bridled, saddled, and packed. Nothing left to do save for two final touches.

"I'm sorry," I told him, "but I have to do this."

He blinked lids edged with long white lashes. I stuck two fingers into the pot Fouad had given me, made a face denoting disgust, then began to glop on the first black circle.

"I've seen dogs like this," I said. "White dogs with black patches. But they were *born* that way. They don't have humans painting the patches on."

The gelding dipped his head briefly and snorted.

"I don't blame you," I agreed. "I'd protest, too. You look like a buffoon." I moved to the second eye. "It's not your fault. I don't mean to offend you. But you must admit this is not exactly how a self-respecting horse is supposed to look."

He extended his nose and whuffled noisily.

I filled in the last bit of white hair, stoppered the little pot, and stuck it in one of the pouches. I wiped off as much of the gunk from my fingers as I could on burlap grain sacking, then heaved a huge sigh and picked up the tassels. "It gets worse," I informed the gelding.

I had considered trading him in for a darker horse, but I decided against it for two reasons. First, he had truly smooth gaits and Del, wounded, might need them; second, he was Del's pick for a mount. I'd learned from experience not to discard any number of items she'd selected for whatever reason, even if *I* considered them worthless, because she always eventually found a use for them. (Or said she would.) Even if it meant packing them along for months at a time, taking up space. In her own way, Del was as much a collector of unique things as Umir, except she at least didn't collect humans.

Unless you count the men who lose all control of their brains at first sight of her. We'd probably have a goodly collection trailing along after us, annoying the hoolies out of me, if I didn't run them off.

So I kept the gelding. Who stood very still and obliging as I looped the string of tassels from ear to ear, tucking the ends under the browband of the headstall.

I stepped back and appraised him. Now he had two black patches around blue eyes and an ear-to-ear loop of brilliant red tassels dangling down his face. I gazed at him a long moment perched somewhat painfully between outright laughter and stoic resignation, then with great sympathy patted his nose. "Don't worry— we're leaving town the back way."

It was still early as we rode out of Julah, and I was certain that by taking the shorter route through Vashi territory I could cut a fair amount of time off the journey. If all went well, I would see Del before sundown. So I looked for and finally found the almost nonexistent wagon ruts cutting off from the main road into town, reflected I'd better make speed now while the footing was decent, and asked the gelding to once again resume the walk-trot-lope routine. Tassels swung and bobbled.

Del and I had been in no hurry before. Now I was. By asking more of the gelding when the footing was decent and letting him drop into a ground-eating long-walk at other times, in good time I located the spot where Oziri and his three warriors had appeared. Here the footing was rocky, and I couldn't in good conscience ask the gelding to do more than walk at a slower pace. I'd watered him twice already, and myself, but still felt the warmth of the sun. Within a matter of weeks it would be high summer.

I bypassed the detour to the clearing where Del and I had gotten drunk on Vashni liquor, and found the dry streambed. I dropped down into it, following the left bank. Eventually I came across the leather bag I'd dropped off the stud in an effort to evade the rank stench of spoiling sandtiger meat. The bag had been chewed and clawed open. Someone—or several someones—had enjoyed a good meal.

I exited there, trading sand for stone drifts, broken rock, and hardpan. Riding in, we hadn't concerned ourselves with marking our route. Now I depended only on my recollection of those things I'd considered landmarks, such as a tree with a twisted limb or a spill of rocks forming a shape that caught my eye. During that ride I'd been studying wagon ruts, but the land rose steadily toward the massive rock formations thrusting upward in the distance, and so long as I headed in that general direction, I knew I'd find the plateau.

I followed my inner sense of direction with a pervasive sense of increasing urgency. As Umir's prisoner, I'd been helpless; and I'd learned years before that when I could do nothing, it was best for mind and body to wait until opportunity presented itself. Now I was free, and the only thing keeping me from finding Del was the time it took me to reach her. I wanted to shorten that as much as was humanly possible.

As the route began to slope up toward the plateau, I asked the gelding's forbearance and put him into a long-trot; farther on, as the trail steepened to wind up to the tree-edged top, I gave him his head and asked for a lope. Hindquarters rounded as he dug into the incline, grunting with the effort.

I leaned toward his neck, shifting weight forward. "Not so far," I murmured. "Just a little farther." But I wasn't certain if it was the gelding I encouraged or myself.

As he topped out with one gigantic bunching leap over the lip of the plateau, I reined in, kicked free of my right stirrup and dropped off even as the gelding slowed. I released the reins and ran toward the lean-to.

"Del? Del!"

Nothing.

"Del!"

In sand and loose pebbles, I skidded to a halt by the lean-to. It was empty. No blankets, no supplies, no tack. Just the crude shelter and sandy floor.

Foreboding replaced urgency. I lifted my voice to a shout that rang in the rocks. "Hey, *Nayyib!* It's me—Tiger! Where are you?"

Nothing.

Then I heard a snort and turned, but it was only Del's gelding. He'd begun wandering over to the nearest tree, seeking grass. He found it in the shade and began to graze, tangled vegetation caught in the corners of his bitted mouth.

No one answered my calls. All I heard was the clank of bit shanks as the gelding ripped grass out of the ground and chewed noisily, the high, piercing cry of a hawk in the cloudless sky, and the faint, distant chittering of ground vermin, scolding one another.

Sweat ran down my temples. I closed my eyes, feeling the initial clench of panic in my belly. After a moment I banished it. I needed focus now, not emotion. Emotion makes you miss things.

With deliberation, I set about doing what Del had originally hired me to do years before: track someone. Only this time it was Delilah I sought, not her brother.

My examination of the campsite established there was no blood in the shelter or anywhere in the vicinity of the bluff's flat crown. There was no grave that I could find, in sand, under trees, under rocks; and the fire ring hadn't been used in days. Hoofprints criss-crossed one another, and all were old, nearly gone; likely from Nayyib's horse and the mounts Rafiq and his friends rode, not to mention Del's gelding and the stud. Breezes had scuffed the prints, and the tracks of insects and animals, but where there was soil, the impressions remained. There were piles of horse manure in several places, which could mean one of two things: two or more horses had stayed here long enough to leave deposits; or one horse had been moved from tree to tree for the grazing. The manure wasn't fresh; beyond that I couldn't tell. In the dry heat of the desert, horse droppings degraded quickly. I even found the sandtiger's skeleton, bones picked clean and scattered by scavengers. The skull was missing.

Consolation: with no grave anywhere in the area, it was un-likely Del had died here. And it made no sense for Nayyib to pack the body anywhere. In the desert, the dead were buried pretty much where they fell. This didn't mean Del was alive—she could have died along the way—but at least she wasn't dead *here.*

The campsite felt very empty. I shivered, squatted, inspected another hoofprint, then picked up a rock and bounced it in my hand, looking around yet again to see if I had missed anything ob-vious. "Bascha," I murmured, "where are you?"

The gelding shook his head, rattling bit shanks, then recom-menced grazing. I mentally kicked myself out of my reverie and went to tend him. My next plan was to see if I could find tracks leading away from the area, and though I wanted to do it as soon as possible, dealing with the gelding came first. You don't dare lose your mount to neglect in the desert. A man afoot is a dead man.

Once the gelding was haltered, unsaddled, cooled, and wa-tered, I began a careful inspection of the edges of the campsite. It did not appear that Nayyib had constructed a litter for Del, because the shelter was whole and I found no signs of poles being dragged through the dust. It was possible she had recovered enough to ride, either in the saddle with him behind, or vice versa; it was also possible the stud had returned at some point. But the only prints I found coming and going were those Del and I had made riding up the bluff, those made by Nayyib, Rafiq, and the others, and the tracks leading away as Rafiq took me to Umir's.

Which left one answer.

I stopped looking at soil and the edges of the plateau. I looked instead at the tumbled carpet of porous smokerock, quartz, and shale spreading out from the huge boulders like a river of stone. I squatted, searching for the tiniest detail that might tell a story. And there I found one: chips knocked off of rock, showing raw, unweathered stone; the hollowed bedding where rocks had been seated until hooves knocked them loose; the tiny trails left by insects and others fleeing the heat of the sun when their cover was stripped away.

It was impossible to judge how many horses, or if one was being ridden double, because the stones and their crevices held too many secrets. But *a* horse had certainly gone this way.

So I played the game. If I were Nayyib, left with an injured woman, I'd want to get her to help as soon as possible. But going back to Julah the way I'd come could be dangerous; who knew how many sword-dancers were out looking for the Sandtiger? And it was no secret he traveled with a Northern woman; they'd recognize her immediately, assume she knew where their quarry had gone, and question her regardless of her health. So I—Nayyib—would head for Julah another way, attempting to leave no tracks. I would take to the rocks and, since I now had safe passage thanks to the fingerbone necklet, cut through Vashni territory. I'd already done it once on the way to Julah, going for the healer. It was tougher footing for the horse and thus tougher on Del, but safer in the long run.

I went back to the gelding, grained him, watered him. Then collected bedding and saddlepouches. "We're staying the night," I told him. "We'll lose the light soon enough. First thing tomorrow morning, we're going hunting."

I dumped pouches at the shelter, then knelt down to spread my blanket. "Fat's going into the fire," I muttered. "My fat's going into the fire."

Because if anyone had seen Nayyib and Del on their way to Julah, likely it was Vashni. And I didn't have safe passage.

Chapter 18

I slept poorly, and awoke tired and unrefreshed. Despite circumstances that might provoke them, I hadn't dreamed at
all—at least, that I could remember. And I usually remembered
something of my dreams, even if they lacked the dramatics of dead
women lecturing me about swords. I got up with stinging eyes that
felt full of grit after a day spent squinting hard at the ground, and
even more itchy stubble clothing my jaw. I needed both shave and
bath. But I didn't suppose the Vashni would care.

The gelding, of course, also did not take note of such things, but
he did suggest from across the way that I should move him to fresh
grass, give him water, and portion out more grain. I did all of those
things, among others; then I shoved dried cumfa down my gullet,
swallowed a few gulps of water, tacked out and loaded the gelding.
But this time I put the halter on over the bridle (and tassels), tied
loose reins to saddle thongs, and paid out the lead-rope to a distance that would keep the gelding off my feet while still being close
enough to manage.

"You get the day off," I told him, slinging a bota over my shoulder. "I'm afoot, too."

I led him to the place I'd found hoof scars in the rocks, inspected it a moment in hopes of seeing some kind of route, but
there was nothing indicating such. All I could do was head out and
hope that eventually, upon trading stone river for sand and soil, I'd

locate Nayyib's tracks. They'd likely be obvious in softer ground: either a man on foot leading a horse; a horse carrying double and thus leaving much deeper prints; or two sets of hoofprints—if the stud had come back.

I sighed. "Let's go, Snowball."

The footing was worse than bad. If it wasn't me tripping over stationary rocks or having loosely seated ones roll out from under my feet, it was the gelding. Hooves were not made for balancing atop rounded rocks, be they firmly seated against one another or treacherously loose; and my sandaled feet were no more appropriate. This was a place for boots, but I'd left mine somewhere along the way. Possibly in Haziz, if I remembered right. Foolish decision, even if I had been trying to save room in saddlepouches. I could not even imagine Nayyib leading a mounted horse carrying an injured woman through here, but I didn't have to; from time to time I found additional signs of their passage, I wondered if the kid's horse would be lame by the time he got through; I wondered if the gelding would be lame by the time *we* got through.

Slowly, carefully, I picked my way, trying to find some kind of route between stones and boulders easier on the gelding. He was a game horse, coming along willingly without hesitation. At some point I noticed the rocks were decreasing in size. Footing remained a challenge, but the way was less demanding. Better yet, more sand and soil was in evidence, which not only made it easier to walk, but held prints better. I was still on Nayyib's trail.

"Almost," I murmured to the gelding. "Not much farther."

And indeed, neither of us was required to go much farther at all, because even as I turned back to encourage the gelding, I heard other horses approaching. I counted them by sound: four. They clopped down through rocks, rolling and knocking them one against the other.

Finally. I turned to face the Vashni, purposely not drawing my sword. I simply waited, easing my body into a poised awareness that wasn't obvious.

The gelding, spying other horses, pealed out an ear-splitting whinny of greeting. I winced; even the Vashni seemed somewhat startled by their mounts' answering noise. So much for the momentousness of the meeting.

In one sweeping glance I noted each man. Oziri was not among them. I didn't have the slightest grasp of Vashni politics, nor did I know if these four warriors were even of the same band, so I didn't attempt to invoke his name as safe passage. Besides, Oziri was not my goal.

What I wanted to do was immediately demand if they had seen Del and if she were alive. But haste is not the best strategy among strangers, especially dangerous ones. Instead, using the gift I'd gained in Meteiera, I told them in their own language, succinctly and without flourish, that I was the jhihadi, and the jhihadi was looking for the Oracle's sister.

No more, no less.

Vashni are not a demonstrative race on the whole, but I saw a faint ripple of response in their dark faces. They said nothing aloud, yet eloquent fingers, as they examined me from a distance, spoke a language I did not; apparently what I'd gained was limited to oral tongues. But possibly it didn't matter, because my gut was certain they knew very well who, and where, Del was.

I just needed them to *tell* me.

I waited for confirmation. The clenching of my belly tightened. It was all I could do to breathe. I applied every shred of discipline learned atop the spires to hold my silence with no indication of concern.

There was no confirmation. They simply rode down through the rocks, took up positions in front, on either side, and behind me, and gestured at the the gelding. They closed in once I had mounted, making it clear with no speech that I was to go with them.

Time turned backward. Years before, Del and I had ridden into a Vashni village. Now, as then, word had been given before we arrived, so that by the time I entered the cluster of hyorts built in the foothills, men, women, and children had turned out to witness my arrival. They formed up in parallel lines facing one another, acting as a human gate into their home. I wondered how many people had ridden the double lines to their deaths.

The lines ended in the center of the village, a common area surrounded by oilcloth hyorts. I was escorted there, still hemmed in by the four warriors, and made to wait. More conversation with hand gestures ensued, even as the double lines of villagers threaded themselves into a single circle of Vashni, a human wall between my little party and the hyorts.

Quietly, carefully, I drew in a breath, held it a moment, released it. My right hand felt naked, empty of sword. But this was not, I knew, the time to unsheathe. I sat in silence atop the gelding, ostensibly relaxed.

Then, from somewhere beyond the village, I heard the ringing call of a stallion.

My head snapped around. I knew that voice. That arrogance.

Inwardly a small knot untied. A flutter of relief blossomed briefly in my belly. I grinned like a fool.

The grin dropped away as a voice called out. At once the circle of Vashni parted, allowing a warrior to step through. He approached, flanked by two other men, both younger, both bigger, both bearing traditional Vashni swords across their backs, though he was unarmed save for a knife. Black hair was threaded with gray, and a childhood disease had left his face pocked. The seam of an old scar nicked the corner of his right eye, extending to his ear. He wore an intricate bone pectoral across his bare chest.

I know a chieftain when I see one. But I was the jhihadi. Preordained by the Oracle himself, whom Vashni had hosted for years. I did not so much as incline my head.

The chieftain halted. He eyed me briefly, then made a rapid gesture. The four warriors surrounding me absented themselves. It left me atop the gelding in the center of the human circle, facing the chieftain on foot with his two bodyguards.

Inspiration was abrupt. I eased myself out of the saddle, aware of the sudden tension in the Vashni. Without hesitation or affectation—and without offering any manner of physical threat—I moved out in front of the gelding, ran a hand down his muzzle, and knelt on one knee. I pressed two lingers into the packed soil and sand and drew a line. Shallow at one end, deeper at the other, with a slight depression made by the heel of my hand. Then I unhooked the bota from my shoulder, unstoppered it, poured water in the shallow end of the line, and watched it trickle its way to the other. I placed the blade of grass I'd pulled from the gelding's bit into the filling depression. Smiling, I looked up and met the chieftain's eyes.

After a lengthy consideration, he inclined his head very slightly. Then he turned and walked back through the ring of villagers.

For an odd suspended moment I thought I was going to be left to fend for myself in the middle of the village. But then a warrior appeared at my elbow as another took the gelding's reins and led him away. I was escorted through the silent villagers to a hyort. There the warrior pulled the doorflap aside and gestured me to enter.

I ducked in, aware the flap was dropped behind me. The light was permitted entry only through the smoke hole in the narrow, peaked top of the hyort, concentrated in the middle of the carpeted dirt floor, but it was enough. I saw the blanket-covered pallet and the woman upon it. That she slept was obvious even though her back was to me; I knew the skyward jut of shoulder, the curve of elevated hip, the doubling up of one knee intimately. Del had always stolen more than her share of the bed.

Relief was so tangible it sent a spasm through my body. I took one step, stopped, and just looked at her, letting the tension of fear, the tautness of anxiety, bleed slowly out of my body. The knot that was my spine untied itself.

I sat down then, next to the bed, close enough to touch her. I did not. I simply sat there, watching her breathe. Smiling. Happy— and whole—merely to be in her presence.

I'm here, bascha.

Del slept a long time, but I didn't care. I stretched out on my back, contemplated the peaked roof where the smoke hole opened to sky, and waited in patient contentment until she turned over onto her back, releasing a breathy sigh. I rolled onto hip and elbow and leaned upon my hand. Her eyes were still closed, but her breathing had changed. I marked the pale lashes against fair skin, the threading of bluish veins in her eyelids. She wore a burnous that hid most of her body, so I didn't know if she was still bandaged or not. She was too thin; that I could tell from the bones in her face.

Del's eyes opened. She blinked up at the smoke hole. Then, frowning, she turned her head and looked right at me.

My smile broadened. "Hey."

She gazed at me a moment. "Where in the hoolies have you been?"

I grinned. "Not a very good effort at sounding angry, bascha. Want to try again?"

An answering if drowsy smile curved her lips. She reached out a hand. "You won the dance."

I met her hand with my own. "I won the dance."

"Was it Abbu?"

"No, he wasn't there. Somebody named Musa. I didn't know him." I arched both brows. "I take it Nayyib told you what Umir planned?"

"He said Rafiq and the others were quite taken with the idea of facing you in a circle in order to execute you."

"I think *everybody* was quite taken with the idea of facing me in a circle in order to execute me. Fortunately, they forgot I wouldn't be so enamoured of it, myself."

"Are you hurt?"

"Nope."

Her eyebrows indicated subtle doubt. "Nothing?"

"One little cut along a rib." I traced it against my burnous. "Honest, bascha. You can see for yourself the next time I'm naked." I wiggled eyebrows at her suggestively, then let go of her hand to stroke a lock of hair out of her face, letting fingertips linger on the curve of her brow. "What about you?"

"I," she began, "may now rival the Sandtiger himself for the dramatic quality of my scars."

I winced. "I'm sorry, bascha."

"Why? Did you attack me?"

"No, but—"

" 'No, but' nothing," she said firmly. "The last thing I remember is going down beneath the sandtiger. That I'm alive and un-eaten likely indicates you killed him before he could kill me."

"Yes, but—"

"No 'yes, but,' either," Del declared. "Understood?"

I knew when to *appear* to surrender even if I disagreed. "Fine. Now give me details."

She caught my hand in hers again. Neither of us was the clinging sort, but we did like physical contact. "I will do very well, Tiger. The wounds are almost healed, thanks to you, Nayyib, and the Vashni healer. The poison is out of my body. Mostly I'm a little tired still, and bone-sore, but that will pass." She grimaced. "Except the healer keeps sending me to bed. I'm tired of naps."

Having years before been badly wounded and poisoned myself by a sandtiger, I knew very well *why* the healer kept sending her to bed.

"But we can go in the morning," Del said.

It caught me off-guard. "Go where?"

"After Nayyib."

"Where is he? And why do we have to go after him?"

"He's looking for you."

"He *left* you here?"

"When it became obvious I was fine, and when I insisted, yes. He did."

"You're not 'fine.' "

"Fine enough. Anyway, two days ago I sent him to look for you."

It astonished me. "You sent him to Umir's?"

"Yes."

"Why?" An idea occured, preposterous as it was. "Did you expect him to *rescue* me?"

Del contemplated my aggrieved expression in silence a moment. "Actually, *I* expected to rescue you. But I needed Neesha to scout for me first."

"Neesha?"

"Nayyib. Neesha is his call-name."

"You sent Nayyib-Neesha to scout for you, so you could come rescue me?"

"That was the plan," she confirmed gravely.

I was only half teasing. "You didn't think I could handle it on my own? A sword-dance? When I've been dancing for almost twenty-five years—which is likely longer than the kid you sent has been alive?"

"You've been dancing longer than *I've* been alive."

Which was a devastatingly effective way to remind me just how old I was, and how old she wasn't.

"Hoolies," I muttered.

Del was laughing. She carried my hand to her mouth, kissed the back of it, then rested it beneath hers against her chest.

I noted again how thin her face was, and there were shadows beneath her eyes. "Did you really think I'd lose?"

" 'Only an idiot believes he may never be defeated,' " Del quoted. "You said that, once."

"Yes, but I didn't expect *you* to believe it. You're supposed to believe I can do anything."

"And so you have."

Well, so far. Sort of.

"Anyway," Del continued, "I think we should go after Nayyib."

"Why? He should have reached Umir's by now, and he'll know what happened. I won. I left. I'm here."

Del gazed at me. "What if *he* needs rescuing?"

This whole conversation was bizarre. "Why would he need rescuing? He's not worth anything."

"That's unfair!"

"To Umir," I elucidated. "He's not worth collecting. He's just a kid."

"He's twenty-three."

"That's a kid."

"*I'm* twenty-three, Tiger."

It shut me up, as she fully intended.

Del smiled, pleased to have won. "As for not being worth anything to Umir, of course he is. Neesha can tell Umir and any other interested parties where I am. Because they know wherever I am, you will eventually be."

"He could simply *not* tell them."

"Under torture?"

I scowled. "Why doesn't he just tell them you're dead? You almost were."

"Well, perhaps he will. But that doesn't mean he won't be tortured before he says it."

"Then he should have stayed here."

"He went looking for you. Isn't that worth something?"

"I don't know," I growled. "Depends on if you think *I'm* worth something."

"*Some*times."

I closed my eyes, gritted my teeth, rubbed a hand over my face.

"He saved my life, Tiger."

"I thought *I* saved your life."

"You, and Neesha, and the Vashni healer."

I squinted at her. "This isn't another of your cockamamie female ideas, is it? I mean, he's human, a man, not a cat or dog. He's not a stray."

"You were."

"*I* was?"

"Yes. All those years ago when the shodo accepted you for training. He took in a stray human and gave him a home."

I drew myself up. "*And* I repaid him by becoming not only his best student but the South's greatest sword-dancer . . ." I thrust an illustrative finger in the air. ". . . which is, I might add, a title very recently reaffirmed."

Del's tone was elaborately innocent. "I thought you said Abbu wasn't there."

I glowered. "We're not talking about Abbu. We're talking about the kid. And now you're telling me you want me to ride back into Umir's domain, even though there will be men looking to kill me?"

"But you just reaffirmed you're the South's greatest sword-dancer. Will anyone challenge that?"

"Yes!" I cried. "Likely all of them!"

"Well," she said thoughtfully, "it shouldn't be so bad."

"No?"

"Not when *I'm* with you."

I looked for laughter in her eyes. But Del does blandly expressionless better than I do.

Of course, I knew she was overlooking one very salient detail that would give me the victory: she was still recovering from a sandtiger attack. Del could no more get up and ride out of the Vashni camp tomorrow than the kid—Nayyib, Neesha, whatever—could beat me in a circle. By the time she could, the point would be moot. Because the kid likely wouldn't even be at Umir's anymore.

"All right," I said.

The abrupt capitulation startled her. "All right?"

"Yes. We'll go tomorrow."

Del nodded. "Good."

Or he might still be at Umir's, under duress, because Umir might possibly believe he was worth something to Del and me. In fact, Umir might even expect to trade the kid to us for the book I'd liberated.

A book of magic.

"Gahhhh," I muttered. "You and your strays."

Del shifted over on her pallet. "Lie down." She tugged at one arm. "Lie down and tell me all about the sword-dance."

"I won."

"Details, Tiger."

I lay down beside her on the edge of the pallet. Hips touched. I rearranged my left arm so my shoulder cradled her head. "What do you want to know?"

"How it was you reaffirmed that you are the South's greatest sword-dancer."

So I told her. It was nice that at least two of us believed it.

Chapter 19

el and I were dinner guests of the Vashni chieftain. Apparently he'd decided I was indeed the jhihadi and wanted to pay honor. We were escorted to his big hyort, given platters full of chunks of various kinds of meat—including sandtiger, I didn't doubt—wild onions and herbs for seasoning, tubers, and bread baked from nut flour. Not to mention plenty of the fiery Vashni liquor. I drank sparingly, still felt the effects, and did my best not to make a fool of myself. Del was permitted to drink water as a nod to her recovery, and I caught her watching me out of the corner of her eye. Apparently she expected me to fall face-first into the modest fire in the center of the chieftain's hyort. I was tempted to remind her *I* hadn't gotten sick from it the last time, but decided the jhihadi wouldn't do such a thing before a Vashni chieftain.

Later, maybe.

Afterward we were allowed to wander away from the encampment without interference or company. Clearly we were not prisoners. Or else they simply knew we wouldn't get far without mounts, and the horses were closely guarded. But since I wasn't trying to escape, it didn't matter. I simply walked with Del a short distance, and sat down upon a boulder even as she did the same.

I stretched braced legs out, crossing them at ankles. Studied her face sidelong. "Tired, bascha?"

She hitched a shoulder inconclusively.

I gazed out at the deepening dusk. Vashni fires set a subdued glow over the village that would become more obvious as darkness fell. A faint breeze teased at Del's hair. I rubbed at my own, feeling added length. Maybe the tattoos along my hairline were finally hidden.

I glanced at her, noting the gauntness of her features. "You know we can't go anywhere tomorrow."

She sighed, kicking a stone away with a sandaled foot. "I know. Not together. But *you* could."

I didn't even have to think about it. "I just spent two hard days tracking you down. I'm not going anywhere without you."

Del looked at me, clearly wanting to say something. Debated it. But held her silence.

"A few more days," I told her. "We're safe here. It's probably the best place we could be, without worrying about who might come looking for us." I wanted to say she needed more time. Knew better than to do it.

Her mouth was set in a grim, unhappy line. "I have been here too long already."

I shrugged, maintaining an excessively casual tone of voice. "You'll stay here as long as you need to."

"But Nayyib . . ." She let it trail off. A frown set lines between her eyes. "I wish you would go."

I was beginning to get exasperated with all this focus on Nayyib. "We don't know that Umir has him. I mean, how can you be sure the kid actually went looking for me?"

"He said he would."

"We don't know anything about him, bascha."

Del looked at me again, comprehending the implication. "He isn't a liar."

"Maybe not, but it doesn't change anything. You can't go any-where until you're completely recovered, and I'm not going any-where until then."

Del's left hand touched her right forearm, raising the hem of her burnous sleeve. Gently she fingered the scars I knew were there.

I tried again. "If Umir has him, he'll hold onto him until we're found. He won't harm him. Not as long as he thinks the kid is worth something."

"And if he doesn't?"

"Well, that was the chance Nayyib took. It's the chance we all take, riding into a situation we don't fully understand. I've done it. You've done it. If he's done it, he'll learn from it."

"Or die."

"Maybe." I shrugged. "Like I said, that's always a chance."

Del nodded. Her head was bowed, expression pensive.

She is a woman who pays her debts, and obviously she felt she owed Nayyib one. I didn't dispute it; he'd cared for her until she could travel and then brought her to safety. I owed him, too, for that. But I wasn't about to immediately go chasing off after a kid I didn't really know now that I'd found Del again; nor was I thrilled by the idea of taking myself back to Umir's domain quite so fast. It was possible some of the sword-dancers who'd witnessed my victory over Musa would decline to track me further, but I was certain some would. Not only for the honor of killing me, but Umir undoubtedly would pay generously to get his book back.

A book that apparently knew all about me.

I slid off the boulder and stood up, reaching for her. "Let's go back to the hyort. You need to rest."

Her head snapped up. "I'm tired of resting!"

"Come on, Del." I closed a hand on her wrist, tugged gently. "A few more days, that's all."

She stood. "Will you spar with me tomorrow?"

"Tomorrow? Well, maybe the day after."

"Tomorrow."

"You're not ready for that."

"Neither were you. I did it anyway."

Nothing would be gained by arguing with her. I didn't say yes, didn't say no. Just pulled her to me, slid an arm around her shoulders, and guided her back toward the hyorts.

"Most men," Del said abruptly, "detest weakness, sickness in a woman. They ignore it, trying to convince themselves she's fine. Or tell the woman there is nothing wrong, so they don't need to trouble themselves with thinking about it. With the responsibility."

I glanced at her, wondering where the complaint came from.

"Most men want nothing at all to do with a sick woman. Some of them even leave. Forever."

I grunted. "As I said, I just spent two days looking for you. Even knowing you were sick. Hoolies, the last time I saw you there was a chance you might not even live. Did I leave then?"

Inwardly I winced. Well, yes, I had left; but that hadn't been my fault.

"You are not what you were," Del said after a moment. "Not as you were when we first met in that cantina."

I had a vivid memory of that cantina, and that meeting. "Well, no."

"You were a Southron pig."

"So you've told me. Many times."

"Tiger—" She stopped walking. Stared up into my face as I turned to her. "You are not what you were."

I had the feeling that wasn't what she meant to say. But nothing more crowded her lips, even as I waited. Finally I cradled her head in my hands, bent close, said, "Neither are you," and kissed her gently on the forehead.

For a moment she leaned into me, clearly exhausted. I considered scooping her up and carrying her to the hyort, but that would play havoc with Del's dignity. She already felt uncomfortable enough about being tired and sick, judging by her comments; I knew better than to abet that belief. I prodded her onward with a hand placed in the center of her spine, and walked with her to the hyort.

There a warrior waited, standing quietly before the door-flap. He looked at me. "Oziri will see you."

It was the first mention I'd heard of the man we'd met a couple of weeks before. I exchanged a baffled glance with Del, who seemed to know no more than I did, then saw her brief nod of acceptance. She ducked into the hyort and dropped the doorflap.

I accompanied the warrior to another hyort some distance away, the entrance righted by stave torches. There I was left, with no word spoken to the hyort's inhabitant. I paused a moment, aware of the call of nightbirds, the flickering of campfires, the low-pitched murmuring of conversations throughout the village. It was incredibly peaceful here. I turned my face up to the stars. The night skies were ablaze.

A hand pulled the doorflap aside. "Come in," Oziri said. "You have hidden long enough."

The Vashni ignored my startled demand for an explanation. He gestured me to a place on a woven rug covered by skins, fur side up, and took his own seat across from me. A small fire burned between us, dying from flames to coals. Herbs had been strewn across it; pungency stung my eyes. I squinted at him through the thin wisp of smoke. At the best of times, Vashni stank of grease, but all I could smell now was burning herbs.

Seated, I looked at Oziri. No one had mentioned him, and I hadn't asked, but here he was, and here *I* was. He wasn't chieftain or bodyguard, but obviously he was something more than warrior. A quick glance around the interior of the hyort showed me herbs hanging upside down, dried gourds, painted sticks, small clay pots stoppered with wax, a parade of tiny pottery bowls arranged in front of Oziri's crossed legs. I began to get a sick feeling in the pit of my belly. Vashni were unrelated to the Salset, the desert nomads I'd grown up among, but the accoutrements, despite differences, were eerily similar.

I looked at Oziri suspiciously. "You're a shukar."

Oziri smiled.

I drew in a breath, hoping I was wrong. "Among the Salset, the shukar doesn't hunt."

"Among the Vashni, he does. We are not a lazy people. Priests work also."

I wanted to wave away the thread of smoke drifting toward me but knew it would be rude. And I'd been trained from birth to respect, even fear, shukars. It had been years since I'd seen the old man who'd made my life a living hoolies, but I couldn't suppress a familiar apprehension.

I reminded myself I was a grown man now, no longer a helpless chula. The old shukar was dead. I cleared my throat and tried again. "You said I was hidden. Hidden from what?"

"Stillness," Oziri said simply.

I waited. When nothing more was forthcoming, I asked him what he meant.

"You are never still," Oziri replied. "Even if your body is quiet, your thoughts are not. They are tangled and sticky, like a broken spider web. Until you learn to be still, you will not find the answer."

"Answer to what?"

"Your dreams."

Apprehension increased. "What do you know about my dreams?"

Oziri took a pinch of something from one of the bowls and tossed it onto the fire with an eloquent gesture. Flames blazed briefly, then died away. Yet another scent threatened my lungs. It was all I could do not to cough.

"You must learn to be still," he told me.

"I'm kind of a busy man," I said. "You know—me being the jhihadi. There's much to think about. It's hard to find time to be still."

Another gesture, another pinch of herbs drifted onto the coals. Smoke rose. The back of my throat felt numb. This time I couldn't suppress a cough. I wanted very much to open the doorflap, or retreat outdoors altogether, but I had a feeling that among the Vashni, rudeness might be a death sentence.

Oziri smiled, handed me a bota.

I unstoppered it, smelled the sharp tang of Vashni liquor. Just what I needed. But I drank it to wash away the taste of the herbs, nodded my thanks, handed it back. Oziri drank as well, then set it aside.

"What—" I cleared my throat, swallowed down the tingle of another cough. "What exactly are the herbs for?"

"Stillness."

"So I can understand my dreams." I couldn't help it; I scowled at him. "What *is* it with you priests? Why do all of you speak so thrice-cursed obscurely? Can't you ever just say anything straight out? Don't you get sick of all this melodramatic babbling?"

"Of course," Oziri said, nodding, "but people tend not to listen to plain words. Stories, they hear. They remember. The way a war-rior learns—and remembers—a lesson by experiencing pain."

It was true I recalled sword-dancing lessons more clearly when coupled with a thump on the head or a thwack on the shin. I'd just never thought of it in terms of priests before. "So, how is you know about my dreams?"

"It is not a difficult guess." Oziri's expression was ironic. "Everyone dreams."

"But why do *my* dreams matter?"

His dark brows rose slightly. "You're the jhihadi."

I gazed at him. "You don't really believe it, do you?"

"I do."

"Because the Oracle said so?"

"Because the Oracle said so when he had no tongue."

"But—there must have been some kind of logical explanation for that."

"He had no tongue," Oziri said plainly. "He could make sounds but no words. I examined his empty mouth, the mutilation. Yet when we brought him down from Beit al'Shahar, he could speak as clearly as you or I. He told us about the jhihadi. He told us a man would change the sand to grass." His smile was faint. "Have you not shown us how?"

He meant the water-filled line in the dirt, with greenery stuck in the end of it. I'd done it twice before various Vashni. "It's just an idea," I explained lamely. "Anyone could have come up with it. You take water from where it is, and put it where's it not. Things grow." I shrugged. "Nothing magical about that. *You* could have come up with it."

"But I am just a humble priest," Oziri said with a glint of amusement in his eyes.

"And I'm just a sword-dancer," I told him. "At least, I was. There is some objection to me using the term, now."

"Among other things." Oziri took up another pinch of herb, tossed it onto the coals with a wave of supple fingers. "The jhihadi is a man of many parts. But he is not a god, and thus he is not om-niscient. Therefore he must be taught."

Be taught what? I opened my mouth to tell him I didn't understand. Couldn't. Because no more was I seated across the fire from Oziri but had somehow come to be lying flat on my back, staring up at the smoke hole. The *closed* smoke hole. No wonder it was so thick inside the hyort.

Oziri's voice. "A man must learn to be still if he is to understand."

Understand what?

But I didn't ask it. Couldn't. My eyes closed abruptly. What little control of my body I retained drained away. I was conscious of the furs beneath me, the scent of herbs, the taste of liquor in my mouth.

It would be a simple matter for the Vashni to kill me. But he merely put something into one lax hand, closed the fingers over it, and bade me hold it.

Hard. Rough. Not heavy. Not large. It fit easily into the palm of my hand.

"Be still," Oziri said, "so you may hear it."

Hear what?

"Truth," the Vashni said.

I came back to myself with a jolt. For a minute I just lay there on the rug, staring up at the hyort's smoke hole, until I felt the hand insinuating itself behind my head and lifting it up. A bota was at my mouth.

"Drink," Del said. "Oziri said you would need to."

Del. *Del.* I wasn't in Oziri's hyort anymore. I sat bolt upright, saw the hyort we now shared revolve around me, cursed weakly, and slumped back down. I took a swallow because she insisted, discovered I was incredibly thirsty, and proceeded to suck most of the water out of the skin. Then I lay there on my back and hugged the flaccid bota against my chest, scowling up at the stars visible through the smoke hole as I tried to put my world back together.

"What happened?" Del asked.

I closed my eyes. Felt the residual burning from the herbs and smoke. "I have no idea."

"Don't you remember?"

"Only that Oziri kept dumping herbs onto the fire. I thought I was going to choke." I looked at her. "They brought me back here?"

Del nodded. "A while ago."

I worked myself up onto elbows, then upright. This time the hyort did not spin so rapidly. "Did Oziri say what they did?"

"He called it 'dream-walking,' " Del replied. "I'm not sure what it is, except that Oziri said you needed to learn it." She shrugged. "He asked me questions about what happened to you on Skandi."

"And you told him?"

"I didn't see why I shouldn't."

Well, Del didn't know the whole of it, either. Some things I couldn't bring myself to talk about, even with her. I squirted the last of the water into my mouth and tossed the bota aside. "I don't remember anything. Did he say I actually did whatever it is a dream-walker does?"

"No. Just that he expects to see you again tomorrow."

"What for?"

"I don't know, Tiger. I don't speak priest."

I glared at her. Del smiled back blandly. I closed my eyes again, tried to recall what had happened in Oziri's hyort. The back of my throat felt gritty. I cleared it, hacked, then began to cough in earnest. Del dug up another bota and gave it to me. After a few more swallows, the worst of the coughing faded.

"I don't see any sense in trying it again," I said hoarsely, "whatever *it* is."

"They are our hosts. It would be rude to refuse."

"And if he asked to cut off toes to match my fingers, would it be rude to refuse?"

Del, yawning, lay down on her pallet, dragging a thin blanket up over her shoulder. "It's hardly the same."

"The point is . . ."

After a moment, Del said, "Yes?"

Nothing came out of my mouth.

"Tiger?"

I toppled backward, landing on rugs. I felt the dribble of water across my chest, the weight of bota. Limbs spasmed.

Then Del was at my side. "Tiger?"

I couldn't speak. Hearing was fading.

Hands cupped the sides of my head. *"Tiger!"*

But I was gone.

Chapter 20

Once again I came back to myself with someone pouring a drink down my throat, but this one was noxious. I choked, swallowed, choked some more. Then someone dragged me up into a sitting position, where I sputtered the dregs all over the front of my burnous. Fingers closed painfully on my jaw, holding my head still. I saw eyes peering into my own.

I wanted to ask who of the Vashni had four eyes in place of two, but then they merged, and I recognized the face. Oziri's. It was his hand clamped on my jaw, squeezing my flesh.

"Le'goo," I mumbled through the obstruction.

He let go. I worked my jaw, running my tongue around the inside of my mouth. No blood, though I felt teeth scores in flesh. "What was that for?"

Oziri ignored my question and asked one of his own. "What did you see?"

"See where?"

Del interrupted both of us. "Is he going to be all right?"

"What did you see?" Oziri repeated.

"Is he going to be all right?"

I answered both of them. "Hoolies, I don't know."

"Tiger—" Del began.

"Be silent!" Oziri commanded.

My tongue worked. So did my mouth. So, apparently, did everything. I frowned at him, because I could.

"Not you," he said more quietly. "Her."

Del's tone was the one you don't ignore, even if you don't know her. "I have a right to ask if he is well."

I put up a hand. "Stop. Wait. Both of you." I squinted a moment. "I feel all right. I think. What happened?"

Oziri's expression was solemn. "You dream-walked."

"I thought that was what you wanted me to do in your hyort."

"In my hyort, yes. This is not my hyort."

"I did it here? *Now?*"

"What did you see?" Oziri asked.

"I didn't see—oh. Wait. Maybe I did." I frowned, trying to dredge it up. "There's something, I think. A fragment. But—" I clamped my teeth together.

Oziri seemed to read my reluctance. His mouth hooked down in a brief, ironic smile. "This is why you must train yourself to be still. That way not only do you walk the dream, but you understand it. You recall it at need and allow it to guide you. Otherwise it's no different from what anyone dreams."

I glanced briefly at Del, who wore an expression of impatient self-restraint—she wasn't happy with Oziri—then looked at the Vashni. "I'm not sure I *want* it to be any different from what anyone dreams."

"Too late," he said dryly. "You are the jhihadi."

"Can I quit?" I asked hopefully.

He laughed. "But if you are no longer the jhihadi, then you are not a guest of my people. I would have to kill you."

"Ah. Well, then, never mind." I sighed. "So, I'm just supposed to remember what I dreamed?"

Oziri nodded. "No more, no less than any memory. Yes."

"And there's a message for me in it?"

"Not this one," he said. "This was merely the test, to see if you have the art. There is more, but I will explain that later." He gestured briefly. "Recall the walk."

To remember my dream did not seem a particularly dangerous

challenge. I recalled portions of my dreams the day after on a regular basis, though the immediacy faded within a matter of hours, sometimes minutes. Some stray fragments remained with me for years and occasionally bubbled up into consciousness for no reason I could fathom, but I'd never purposely tried to recall them. It seemed a waste of time. But the explanation of dream-walking, which I didn't exactly fully understand, seemed to require *enforced* recollection.

Oziri spoke of stillness. Sahdri and his fellow priest-mages had spoken of discipline. One seemed very like the other.

I closed my eyes. Focused away from the hyort, going inside myself. I waited, felt the tumult of my thoughts and apprehensions—I hate anything that stinks of magic—and purposely suppressed them. In the circle, I could be still. I had learned to relax my body. Now I relaxed my mind, and found memory.

My eyes opened even as my left hand closed. I raised it. "I saw—death." I uncurled fingers. My palm was empty. "Here, in my hand. Death."

Oziri nodded. "What else?"

"A man. From Julah. He was searching for something." I frowned. Felt weight in my hand, though it remained empty. "You killed him."

"Not I."

"Vashni killed him."

"Yes."

"Because he trespassed."

"Yes."

"You kill everyone who trespasses."

No change in inflection. "Yes."

My hand snapped closed on air and flesh. "Bone." I could feel the details of it, the small oblong circle with slight protruberances. "Backbone."

"Yes," Oziri said.

I opened my hand. Stared into it. "He strayed off the road," I said. "He heard the scream of a coney being killed and thought he might eat well, if he found it not long after it died. But he found Vashni. A hunting party. The next scream was his own." My hand was empty, but the memory was full. Fear. Pain. Ending. I looked at Oziri. "You gave me a piece of his backbone."

Oziri smiled. "Yes."

Del's voice was harsh. "What have you done to him?"

"I? Nothing. This comes of himself. Here." The Vashni put out a hand and tapped my chest. "The heart knows what he is."

"I'm glad something does," I said dryly. "Now, care to tell *me* what's going on?"

"You remembered the dream-walk. I believed the walk itself would happen in my hyort. We brought you back here when it became obvious nothing would occur." Oziri shrugged. "I should have expected it. You don't trust us."

I took a breath. Was frank. "Vashni are not known for their courtesy toward strangers. Just ask the man whose backbone you gave me."

Oziri was unoffended. "But he was neither the jhihadi nor the Oracle's sister. He was a man, and a fool, and he paid the price for it."

Del's voice verged delicately on accusation. "You kill everyone who comes into what you perceive as Vashni territory."

"We do."

"But no one knows the borders of Vashni territory."

"They learn."

"Not if they're killed."

A smile twitched his mouth. "Others learn."

"You kill them even if they trespass by mistake?"

"Yes."

She considered that. Because I knew her mind, I saw the struggle to remain courteous, nonjudgmental. "It is a harsh penalty."

"It is a harsh land," Oziri replied. "We are a part of it. We reflect it." His gesture encompassed her body. "You yourself were attacked by a sandtiger. You know how harsh the land is."

I knew it, certainly, having grown up in the desert, but I wasn't aware of another tribe quite so quick to kill as the Vashni. Certainly other tribes killed people if they perceived a threat—I'd witnessed the Salset do it—but the Vashni did it even if no threat were offered.

And yet Del and I, Oracle's sister and jhihadi, were treated honorably. And Nayyib, apparently, because he served Del and wore the fingerbone necklet.

Oziri watched me think it through. Irony put light into his eyes. But he returned to the topic of dream-walking. "Here, in this hyort, you can be still. Because you trust the woman."

I glanced at Del, whose brows arched up.

"And the smoke was still in your body," Oziri explained.

"So, it's the herbs that do it?"

"The herbs assist," he answered with precision, "when one is new to the art. In time, you will be able to do it without such things. Just find the stillness, and it will come." He paused. "If you choose."

"This is a Vashni custom," I said. "I'm not Vashni."

"But you dream," he countered, "and your dreams trouble you. If you can walk them, you'll understand what it is you're to do."

Del and I asked it simultaneously. *"Do?"*

He smiled. "Listen," he said. "Find the stillness. Walk the dreams. They will tell you."

I glared. "You're being obscure again."

Oziri rose with his bota of noxious liquid. He glanced briefly at Del, then looked down at me. "They are *your* dreams," he said. "It's for you to find the meaning in obscurity."

I waited until the doorflap fell behind him. Then I flopped down on my back, grabbed the nearest waterskin, and dragged it over my face. I growled sheer frustration into leather.

After a moment Del lifted the bota to examine my expression. "Are you sure you don't want to leave tomorrow?"

I yanked the waterskin out of her hand and let it settle its gurgling weight over my face again. "Don't interfere." My words were muffled by leather. "I'm trying to smother myself."

"With a bota?"

"Why not?"

"I can think of better ways."

"Oh?"

She peeled the bota back, tipped it off my face. She studied me a moment. Then, as she leaned over my face, her mouth came down on mine.

When she was done, I reminded her that kiss or no kiss, I could still breathe.

She kissed me again. This time she also pinched my nose closed.

I ruined the moment—and the kiss—by laughing. Del removed her fingers, removed her mouth, and stared down into my face. Loose hair tickled my neck.

"Are you *truly* all right?" she asked.

I was still grinning. "I seem to be." I threaded fingers into silken hair. "It really was like a dream. Except it didn't feel like mine. It felt like—*his*. Or, rather, it felt like his life, and I was there. Watching." I frowned, stroking the ends of her hair across my mouth. "Except it was more vivid. I could smell, and taste, and feel, too. Usually I just see and hear in my dreams."

Del nodded. "Are you going to go to Oziri tomorrow?"

"*You* were the one who said it'd be rude to refuse."

"That was before you collapsed in a heap with your eyes rolled up in your head."

The image was perversely intriguing. "They did that?"

"They did."

I felt my eyelids. "Hmmm."

"Very dramatic," Del added. "I thought you might break out into prophecy at any moment."

"You did not," I said sternly. "Besides, that doesn't really happen. Only in stories."

Del shrugged. "Jamail apparently did it. That's why the Vashni called him the Oracle."

I gazed up at her. I didn't want to think about dream-walking or oracles or stillness anymore. I tugged her hair. "Come down here."

Del followed the pressure on her hair and stretched out next to me.

"Just how tired are you?" I asked.

She suppressed a smile. "Oh, very tired. Extremely tired. Excessively tired. Far too tired for what you have in mind."

I sighed very deeply. Extremely, excessively deeply. "And here I was hoping it might be *you* I dreamed about."

Her fingers were on my belt, working at the buckle. "If you walk anywhere," she said, "I'm going with you."

The belt fell away. I arched my back so she could pull it out from under me. It took but a moment to free myself of the damp burnous. Then I performed for her the identical service, stripping away folds of cloth.

I turned her under me, taking weight onto knees and elbows. "How tired was that again?"

Del's hand moved downward from my ribs. Closed. "You tell *me*."

True to my word—well, actually it was true to Del's expectations, because I didn't feel like opening a debate—I met her for a brief match the next morning. The last time we'd sparred was aboard ship on the way to Haziz, and it had been Del's task to challenge me enough to help me regain fitness and timing as I adapted to the lack of little fingers. This time it would be me leading her through the forms trying to improve *her* fitness.

She had, of course, not bothered to don her burnous. Her cream-color leather tunic showed the aftermath of her encounter with the sandtiger, but a Vashni woman had patched it and stitched up the rents as Del recovered. The new leather didn't match, being the pale yellow hue of foothills deer, but the tunic was whole again.

Del, however, wasn't. In exploring her body the night before I'd examined with fingers and mouth the scars she bore, but I'd seen none of them. I knew better than to react as she exited the hyort, sword in hand—I was already outside—but inwardly I quailed to see the damage. Her right forearm bore a knurled purplish lump of flesh around the puncture wound and a vivid ditch left by a canine tooth as she'd wrenched her arm free. At the point of her jaw a claw tip had nicked flesh clear to bone. There were other scars, I knew—those stretching from breast tops to collar bones; and the punctures and claw wounds, not to mention the cautery scar atop her left shoulder—but the tunic covered them.

I caught her eye, then tossed her the leather thong I'd bought with a smile from a Vashni woman repairing a hyort panel. Del caught it, suspended it in midair, noted the curving black claws. Between them, acting as spacers, were the lumpy red-gold beads formed of heartwood tree resin. She'd worn them strung as a necklet as I wore my claws; I'd stolen them earlier this morning, since the Vashni had taken the necklet off to treat her wounds.

"Welcome," I said, "to the elite group of people who've survived sandtiger attacks."

Del looked at me over the necklet. "How many are there in this elite group?"

"As far as I know, two."

She nodded, half-smiling, and hooked the necklet one-handed over her head. "Too long," she murmured. "I'll shorten it later." Then she lifted her sword and placed both hands around the grip. "Shall we dance?"

"Spar," I corrected.

Her jaw tightened. "Spar."

"Until I say to stop."

That did not please her. "You'll say to stop after one engagement."

"I will not. Three, maybe." I waved fingers at her in a come-here gesture. "We're too close to the fire ring. Let's go out into the common area."

"Here, then." Del tossed me her unsheathed blade, which I managed to catch without cutting off any vital parts—I scowled at her even as she smiled sunnily—and accompanied me out to the common as she worked at the knot in the leather thong.

By the time we reached the spot I'd selected, she'd shortened the necklet and retied the knot. Then she flipped her braid behind her shoulder, gestured for the sword, and caught it deftly as I tossed it. Well, that ability she hadn't lost.

More than two weeks before, I had been clawed and sick from sandtiger poison, then unceremoniously hauled off to Umir's with both hands tied at the wrists, and imprisoned in a small room out of the sun and air. Such things should conspire to rob me of any pretense to fitness and flexibility, but I'd spent my ten days of imprisonment profitably in near-constant exercise accompanied by good food and restful sleep. I had then met an excellent sword-dancer in the circle, which had the effect of not only challenging my body but my confidence. Aside from missing two fingers—actually, *because* of missing two fingers—I was in the best condition I'd been in for years.

Del, on the other hand. . . . Inwardly I shook my head, even as I pointed to the spot where I wanted her to stand. I took up my own position, closed my hands on leather wrapping, nodded. She came at me.

It is impossible to spar in silence. Steel brought against steel has a characteristic sound; blade brought against blade is unmistakable. Before long we had gathered onlookers. I was too focused on the match to listen to what they said, but many comments were exchanged. I didn't doubt some of them had to do with a man meeting a woman; Vashni women, who look every bit as fierce as their men, do not avail themselves of the sword. No women in the South did. Oracle's sister or no, once again Del was opening eyes and minds to the concept that a woman too could fight.

Probably everyone watching expected me to "win." But, as I've said before, that's not what sparring is all about. Del and I worked until the sweat ran down her flushed face, the breath was harsh in her throat, and her forearms trembled. I let her make one more foray against me, turned it back easily, then called a halt.

"Don't fall down," I told her cheerfully as she stood there breathing hard, "or they'll think I'm punishing you unduly."

Del shot me a scowl.

"Not bad," I commented.

The scowl deepened.

"Go cool off," I ordered.

She wanted very badly to say something to me, but she hadn't the wind for it. Instead she turned, visibly collected herself, and stalked back through the ring of hyorts. Upon reaching ours, I did not doubt, she'd suck down water, then collapse. Or collapse, then suck down water. Once she could move again.

Actually, she'd gone longer than I had expected. It was sheer determination and stubbornness that carried her, but such things count, too, when it comes to survival.

After the physical exertion, the taste of Oziri's herbs was back in my throat. I hacked, leaned, spat. Heard onlookers discussing the origins of the scar carved into one set of ribs. I wanted badly to tell them Del had been the one to put it there so they'd understand she was indeed a legitimate sword-dancer, but I decided against it. Anything that demoted me from jhihadi could well end in my execution, if I believed Oziri's explanation that anyone else in Vashni territory was put to death. And I had no reason to disbelieve him. One had only to look at all the human bones hanging around the necks of men and women alike.

I turned to follow the departed Del, found a warrior standing in my path. "Oziri," he said merely.

Numerous refusals ran through my mind. All of them were discarded. Glumly, carrying a naked blade, I followed the warrior.

Chapter 21

I ducked inside Oziri's hyort. "Do you mind if I check on Del?—oh, hoolies, not *this* again!" I waved herb smoke from my face. "I thought you said this wasn't necessary."

Oziri was once again seated on furs. The hyort, as before, was closed and stuffy. "It won't be necessary, eventually. It is now."

"You going to give me another bone?"

He tossed a pinch of herb on the coals with an eloquent gesture. "No. This time I want you to walk your own dream."

I squinted against the smoke. "You want me to dream while I'm awake?"

"Not to dream but to recall your dreams. In detail. That is the walk. A man with the art may summon them at any time, may return to them, so he may understand their message."

"And what happens if he doesn't wish to understand anything? If he just wants to go on about his life like everyone else, blessedly ignorant?"

"A man with the art can't ignore such things. There is no blessing in ignorance, only danger."

I eyed him warily. "Where are you going with this?"

Oziri sighed, "You have, I'm sure, been bitten by sandflies."

I blinked, wondering what that had to do with anything. "Anyone who lives in the desert has."

"And you recall the fierce itching that accompanies such bites."

Dryly I said, "Anyone who lives in the desert does."

"And if you were bitten but could not scratch?" Oziri smiled faintly. "It would be hoolies, as you call it."

An understatement. "So?"

"Consider dreams as sandflies, and walking them, understanding them, is the scratching of the itch. One or two sandfly bites, unscratched, are bearable, if annoying, but what of an infestation? Bite upon bite upon bite, until your flesh is swollen on the bones. Without relief. No scratch for the itch."

I grimaced, wanting to scratch simply because of the image he painted. "If you say so; I'm not going to argue with my host. But we haven't established that I have any art."

There was—almost—a scowl on Oziri's face. "Last night we established that indeed you have the art, when you reacted to the bone. Now you must learn to walk the dreams, to recall them at will, so you may understand them." He paused. "And scratch the itch."

"Uh-huh. And the sandflies are supposed to give me messages." I started to laugh, but then without warning something boiled up inside me, an abrupt and painful frustration so desperate, so powerful, it overwhelmed. I wanted to wheel around, tear the doorflap open, stride away from the hyort. I wanted to get Del, throw our belongings into pouches, saddle the horses and go. Just go. Forever. Away.

I wanted to run.

To *run*.

Oziri's eyes flickered. "I know."

Stunned, ashamed, angry, I guarded neither words nor tone. "You know nothing."

"I know," he repeated.

The anger separated itself from frustration. It was an alien kind of anger, shaped not of rage and therefore comprehensible but of a cold, quiet bitterness. "Do you have any idea," I began softly, with careful clarity, "how many people have told me I have arts? Gifts? Powers? Have you any idea what it is to be told, again and again, that if that art, or that power, is ignored, it could drive me mad? Kill me on the spot? Shorten my lifespan?" I shook my head, hand tightening on my sword as every muscle in my body tensed. "I was nothing. I was a *slave*. How is it that strangers—you, Sahdri, Nihko, others—can see something I can't feel? How can you tell me I must do this thing, that thing, whatever thing it may be, or the price will be too high to pay?"

He closed his eyes a moment.

"I'm just *a man*, Oziri! Nothing more. That's all I ever wanted to be, when I was a slave. A man. And free. To go where I want, be what I want. No arts. No gifts. No powers. No end-of-life-as-I-know-it punishment if I don't—if I *can't*—measure up. Messiah?—Hah. Mage?— I want nothing to do with magic, thank you. And now dream-walker?" I shook my head vehemently. "No. Never. I don't want it. And if that means you want to kill me because I'm not what the Oracle prophesied, so be it. I'll meet anyone in the circle you like. Because *that's* what I am. Just a man with a little skill, a lot of training . . . and no need at all to contend with arts and gifts and powers, be they Southron, Northern, Skandic, Vashni, or anything else." I shook my head again as tension and anger, now vented, began to bleed away into weary resignation. "This is *your* art, Oziri, this dream-walking. Not mine."

After a moment he lowered his eyes and gazed into the coals. His fingers twitched, as if he wished to take up herbs and toss them into the fire. But he didn't. He simply sat there, expression oddly vulnerable for a Vashni warrior, and after a moment his mouth twisted as if he were in pain.

Then he met my eyes. "Will you trust me to lead you through?"

The question astounded me. "I just *told* you—"

"Yes. And I understand; your truth is a hard one, even for a priest. I have no intention of killing you; we accept what the Oracle prophesied—*wait*." He lifted a hand to belay my immediate protest. "A man is welcome to his own beliefs, yes?"

It took effort to accede, but I dipped my head in a stiff nod.

"We have hosted the woman, the Oracle's sister; and the young man who brought her here. And now we have hosted you. I ask that the jhihadi repay us by allowing me to lead him through this dream-walk."

The ice of anger was gone; its bluntness remained. "But it doesn't mean anything. Not to me."

"Then you lose nothing but a portion of time, while I . . ." Oziri smiled ruefully. "Well, it means a great deal to me. I risk losing a portion of my reputation. The Vashni hold priests to be incapable of mistakes."

I couldn't help but mock. "Will they kill you for it and boil the flesh off your bones?"

"No."

I shrugged with deliberate exaggeration. "Then it's not so much of a risk after all, is it?"

"They will boil the flesh off my bones without giving me the mercy of death beforehand."

It banished all derision, all protests, precisely as he intended. It's hard to ridicule that kind of imagery when you know it isn't falsehood.

I still wanted to walk away. But his time cost more than mine.

Finally I nodded. "Then let's get it done. What do you want me to do?"

"Be seated. Be at ease. Trust me to lead you through."

I grunted dubiously. "I can't promise either of the last two."

"Then achieve the first." Oziri paused. "And lay down your sword. It is hard for *me* to trust a man with a blade in his hand when he is the Sandtiger."

Once I would have been flattered. Now I just wanted to get it over with. I seated myself on the other side of the fire and set down the sword not far from my knee.

"Breathe," Oziri suggested. "I believe we have established you have *that* art."

I shot him a disgruntled look. He threw more herbs on the coals. I gritted my teeth and tried not to cough.

"Find your stillness."

That particular recommendation was really beginning to grate on me. I watched suspiciously as he cupped both hands and wafted smoke at me. Another pinch of herbs went on the fire. "All right," I muttered, and drew in a deep breath. "Now what?"

"What did you dream last night?"

Oddly enough, I couldn't remember. I'd slept very well after Del and I had made love, and no recollection tickled my memory. Maybe, after the dream-walking lesson, I was all dreamed out. "I'm not sure I did."

Oziri, saying nothing, took a generous amount of herbs from two bowls. He dumped them on the coals. A cloud of pungent smoke wreathed the air between us, then drifted unerringly into my face. It was nothing so much as a challenge to prove him wrong. To allow my childish obstinance to sentence him to death.

But I really couldn't remember that I'd dreamed. "Wait—" I began, then broke into a paroxysm of coughing, which succeeded in drawing even more smoke into my lungs. The world coalesced into a tiny pinpoint of existence, then burst into a vast array of fragmented awareness. I felt parts of my body, my mind breaking apart, spinning away. *"Wait—"*

Oziri laughed. "The gods are not gentle to unbelievers, especially those who repudiate their gifts."

I could barely see, could barely hang onto my senses. "You told me to trust you."

His eyes were like a dagger. His words opened my vitals. "I said I would see you safely through. I did not say it would be a painless journey."

I reached toward the sword. Then memory stirred. Stopped me.

Oziri was right: I *had* dreamed last night.

"I remember," I blurted, startled. "I—"

—remember.

And then forgot everything, including my name.

Del's face, when she dances—or even when she spars—wears one of two expressions: fierce determination or an oddly relaxed focus. The former comes from a true challenge, to prove herself and win; the latter from the knowledge that she *will* win, so the point is to refine her skill. Opponents and enemies have witnessed both. So have I.

But this time, for the first time, I saw fear.

We were yet again in the common area of the Vashni encampment, pretending a portion of it was a circle. After two more hard engagements Del stumbled back, regained her footing and balance, blocked my blow. Steel clashed. She was breathing hard. "Let's stop."

I repeated the series of maneuvers, pushing her harder. Waiting for her body to fail.

She blocked me again and again, frowning. "Stop."

I tried a new angle. Blades met, scraped, screeched.

Her teeth were bared in a brief rictus of sheer effort. The exhaustion was obvious, and oddly exhilarating, "—*stop*—"

Over the locked blades I looked into her widening eyes. I shook my head, on the verge of laughing joyously. "You can't win by quitting."

This time there was no determination. No relaxation. Not even fear. Just astonishment.

"Come on," I jeered. "We haven't even begun."

Something flickered in her eyes. Then her mouth went flat and hard.

Laughing, I expected her to renew the match. Instead, Del pushed forward briefly, released her sword entirely, threw both splayed hands into the air and took three strides backward as the blade fell. The expression now was anger.

It wasn't surrender. She didn't yield. It was—cessation. And it left me standing in the middle of a circle I'd drawn in the Vashni common, clutching my sword while hers lay at my feet.

I arched my brows. "Afraid, bascha?"

She was sucking air audibly. The single braid had loosened itself, strands straggling around her face. She was ice and sunlight, and much too tough to melt. "What," she panted, "is wrong with you?"

"You asked me to spar with you."

She managed one word. *"Spar."*

I shrugged. "You've always preferred a challenge to mere practice. Let's not waste our time."

Hands went to her hips and rested there as her breathing slowed. "That wasn't sparring. That was anger, Tiger."

I shook my head. "I'm not angry."

"Angry," she declared. "And bitter."

"You're imagining things." I bent, picked up her sword. "Let's go again."

Del shook her head with slow deliberation.

"Afraid, bascha?" I smiled, tossed the blade. "Catch."

She made no attempt to do so. She merely stepped back and let it fall into the sand. Sunlight flashed.

"That," I said severely, "is no way to treat a good blade."

Winter descended. "Nor is your behavior any way to treat me."

"Oh, come on, Del! This is how it is. You work your body, work your mind, challenge everything about yourself, until the weakness is gone. It isn't easy, no, but it's the best way. I've spent months doing it—can't you at least invest a few days?"

Del bent, retrieved her sword, turned on her heel and walked away.

"Hey. Hey!" In several long strides I reached her. Reached *for* her. "Don't turn your back on me—"

Del spun. I saw the blade flash even as my own came up. They met at neck level. My blade was against steel. Hers was against my throat.

She tilted her head slightly in an odd, slow, sideways movement almost like a cat preparing to leap. But there was no leap. She stood her ground. "Angry," she said very softly. "Bitter. And vicious."

I blurted a laugh of incredulity. "Vicious!"

"And afraid."

Laughter stopped. "I'm not—"

"What did he do to you?"

"No one has—"

Her low voice nonetheless overrode my own. "What did he do to you?"

I smiled. "You really don't like to lose, do you?"

She made no reply. Just stared. Examined. Evaluated. I saw a series of expressions in her eyes and face, but none I could name. They came and went too quickly: the faintest of ripples in her flesh, a shifting in her eyes. Nearly nonexistent.

Delilah asked, "What did he say to you to make you so afraid?"

I denied her an answer. I took a step backward, breaking contact with her blade, and lowered my own. "Go," I told her. "We're done for the day. If you aren't willing to do what it takes, I don't want to bother."

A multitude of replies crowded her eyes. She made none of them.

I watched her walk away. The anger, the bitterness drained away. I felt oddly empty.

Empty. And afraid.

"Stop it," she said. "*Stop* it, Tiger!"

I said nothing. Did nothing. The voice was very distant. I could ignore it. Did.

"Tig—oh, hoolies," she muttered, and then a hand cracked me hard across the face.

She is a strong woman, and the blow was heartfelt. I came back to awareness abruptly, catching her wrist. Realized I sat in the hyort we shared. I blinked at her, shocked. "What was that for?"

"To bring you back."

"Bring me back from where?"

"From the dream."

"I was dreaming?"

"Not now," she said. "You were awake. But—away. As if you returned to something you'd already experienced." She indicated her head. "Inside."

I felt disoriented. Detached. "I don't understand."

She knelt next to me. Desperation edged her tone. "You have to stop this. This dream-walking."

I frowned, baffled. "Why?"

Del pulled her wrist out of my hand. "Because it's changing you."

"Changing me! How?" I noticed then that it was nearing sundown. I couldn't remember where the day had gone. "I don't understand what you're saying."

"Five days ago you went to Oziri's tent after we sparred, and since then you've been—different."

I frowned. "I know you think I'm angry, but I'm not."

"I didn't say you were angry. I said you were *different.*"

"And bitter, you said. Vicious, even. Just because you can't match me in the circle."

Lines creased her brow. "What are you talking about?"

"The match earlier today. You were losing. *You* got angry. You quit on me, Del. You threw down your sword and walked away."

Astonishment was manifest. "I have never walked away from a match in my life!"

"Earlier today," I insisted. How could she have forgotten?

Del recoiled. Pale brows knit together. I saw surprise and worry. "But we didn't . . ." She changed direction. "Was that your dream?"

"It wasn't a dream, bascha."

She shook her head slowly, as if trying to work out a multitude of thoughts. "There was no match earlier." Almost absently, she added, "Something's wrong. Something inside you."

I found it preposterous. "Del—"

She overrode me. "We haven't sparred since that first time, Tiger. Five days ago. That's the *only* time we've sparred. Five days ago. Two days after you got here."

I gritted my teeth, verging on frustration. "Earlier today," I repeated. "We had an argument in the circle, as we sparred. You quit on me."

Del sat back, putting distance between us. Astonishment had faded. Now she stared. Examined me. Evaluated. Comprehension crept into her eyes. "Tiger . . . we need to leave this place. We need to go."

"Oziri says—"

"I don't care what Oziri says!" She lowered her voice with a glance at the open doorflap. "We have to leave. Tomorrow, first thing."

"You're not ready to leave, bascha. You need to rest."

"*You* need to get away from here," she countered. "And I've rested enough. Trust me."

Oziri had said that. *Trust me.* "There are still things I have to do," I explained. "Things I need to learn. Oziri says—"

Del pronounced an expletive concerning Oziri that nearly

made my ears roll up. With crisp efficiency she began to gather up her belongings. "We're going. Tomorrow."

"I'm not done learning what I need to know. I realize it's difficult for you to understand, but there are things about me that are—different. Things—"

"Yes! Different! *Wrong*. That's my whole point." Del stopped packing. She moved close, sat on her heels, reached up to trap my head in her hands. The heels cradled my temples. "Listen to me, Tiger. To *me*, not to the things Oziri has put in your head. Or to what you believe happened." Her eyes caught my own and held them. "You're right: I don't understand this dream-walking. But what I do know is that it's changing you. You spend most of each day inside your own head. You don't hear anything I say. You answer no questions. You don't even acknowledge I'm present. It's as though your body's here, but your mind is somewhere else. And what you've just told me, this conviction we sparred earlier today—you're confusing reality with what's in your mind. With the dreams. You have to stop."

"I have to learn how to control it, bascha."

Del leaned forward. Our foreheads met. Her skin was smooth, cool. "Let it go," she murmured. "Let it go, Tiger. It's Vashni magic."

"It's just another tool—"

"Magic," she repeated, "and you know how you hate magic."

"If I don't learn to control it, it will control me."

She released my head, ran one supple, callused hand through my hair, almost as if I were a muddled child in need of soothing. "It's controlling you now, Tiger. Every time you go inside yourself."

"It's just stillness," I told her. "It's like ioSkandic discipline. What happened to me atop the spire, in the Stone Forest . . ." I shrugged. "Well, you know."

Del's hands fell away. "I don't know what happened to you atop the spire," she said. "You've never told me."

My brows lifted. "You were there with me."

"No."

"Del, you were. I saw you. I dreamed you, and you came." And put the *jivatma* scar back into my abdomen, after Sahdri had lifted it.

The color ran out of her face. "No, Tiger. I was never in

Meteiera. I never saw the Stone Forest. I stayed in Skandi until Prima Rhannet's ship sailed." Something flinched in her eyes. "We all thought you were dead."

"You were *there*, Del. I remember it clearly." So very clearly. I was naked. Alone. Bereft of everything I'd known of myself, whelped again atop the rock. Until she came. "You were there."

Del shook her head.

"You're forgetting things," I told her, beginning to worry. "What happened in Meteiera a few weeks ago, and the sparring match earlier today. Maybe if you talked with Oziri—"

"No." Her tone was certainty followed by puzzlement. "Tiger, we left Skandi months ago. Not weeks. And we sparred *five days ago*. Not since. Certainly not this morning."

I opened my mouth to refute the claim, but she sealed it closed with cool fingers.

"Listen to me." Her eyes searched mine. "Trust me."

I had trusted this woman with my life more times than I could count. I was troubled that she could be so terribly confused, but I nodded. I owed her that much.

"*I* need to go," she said. "*I* need to leave. Will you come with me?"

"Why do you need to leave? You're safe here. You're the Oracle's sister. They'd never harm you."

"I need to leave," she repeated. "I promised Neesha we'd meet him."

It took me a moment to remember the kid. Then I frowned. "You don't owe him anything."

Her voice hardened. "I owe him my life, Tiger. And so do you."

"Maybe so, but—"

"It's time for me to leave," she said. "Will you come with me?"

"Del—"

"Please, Tiger. I need you."

The desire to refuse, to insist she stay with me, was strong. I felt its tug, its power. Leaned into it a moment, tempted. I owed a debt to the Vashni for tending her, and Oziri had much to teach me. But I owed a greater debt to the kid for keeping her alive so she *could* be tended.

She'd said she needed me. That was very unlike Del. Something serious was wrong with her.

With her. Not with me.

I nodded. "All right, bascha. We'll go."

Del averted her head abruptly and returned to packing. But not before I saw profound relief and the sheen of tears in her eyes.

Chapter 22

The stud, for some reason, didn't want me near him. I found it decidedly odd; he can be full of himself and recalcitrant, but not generally difficult to catch and bridle. When I finally did manage both, I noted the rolling eye and pinned ears. He quivered from tension, from something akin to fear, until Del came out to saddle the gelding. Then he quieted.

"He knows, too," she said.

I tossed blankets up on the stud's back. "Knows what?"

"That things are not right."

I had no time for oblique comments and obscure conversations. I had agreed to go, but I regretted it. "Things are what they are."

"For now," she murmured, and turned her full attention to the gelding.

Annoyed, I did the same with the stud. We finished preparations in stiff, icy silence.

It wasn't until Del and I had made our carefully courteous farewells to the chieftain and actually mounted our horses that Oziri appeared. I heard Del's hissed inhalation and murmured curse as she saw him walking toward us. I reined in the stud and waited. I could feel Del's tension. It was a tangible thing even across the distance between the two horses.

I had seen and heard him laugh. He was a man like any other, given perhaps to more dignity because of his rank but equally prone to expressing his opinion in dry commentary. But as he approached, I saw he wore no smile. His eyes, lighter than most Vashni's, were fastened on Del.

Yet when he arrived at my stirrup, the sternness vanished. "So, you have learned all there is to know about dream-walking. I am amazed; it takes most men tens of years to do so."

I tilted my head in Del's direction. "This is for her. There's an errand we must do. A matter of a debt."

Irony. "Ah. Of course. All debts must be paid."

The stud shifted restlessly, bobbing his head. He watched Oziri sidelong, pinning his ears, then flicking them at the sound of my voice.

"It's easier for me now," I told Oziri. "As you said, the herbs aren't necessary. It's just a matter of discipline and stillness." I shrugged off-handedly. "There's much left to learn—but it's a beginning."

"Beginnings," Oziri said, "may be dangerous."

I laughed. "More so than endings?"

The Vashni didn't smile. He reached to his neck, lifted a bone necklet over his head, and offered it. "This will guide you," he told me. "Wear it in honor."

On horseback I was too tall, even bending, for him to slip it over my head. So I took the necklet into my hands, noticed the meticulously patterned windings of the wire holding the necklet together, and put it over my head. Human bones rattled against sandtiger claws.

I opened my mouth to thank him but was distracted when Del's white gelding, painted and tasseled, sidestepped into me. The toe of her sandal collided with my shin bone. When I glanced at her, annoyed, she had the grace to apologize. But her eyes were not so abashed, and they were very watchful. Almost as if she'd done it purposely.

I shot her a quelling glance, then turned back to the warrior. "We'll be back this way."

Oziri smiled, looked at Del on the far side of me. "Yes." Then he dipped his head in eloquent salute. "May the sun shine on your head, Oracle's sister."

I glanced at Del, expecting her to reply. But something in her eyes said she would not return the courtesy. I was appalled. She was the one who'd been warning me about rudeness and the possible consequences.

Then something shifted in her posture. Tension departed. She inclined her head briefly, wished him the same.

As she rode away, I muttered an aside to Oziri. *"Women."*

But the Vashni didn't smile. Didn't laugh. Didn't agree. After a moment I knew he wouldn't. Somewhat nonplussed, I turned the stud, saw Del ahead, waiting, and rode up to join her.

A strange thing: her eyes were anxious. But it faded as I reined the stud in and gestured her to go ahead down the narrow thread of a trail Vashni hunters used. She murmured a Northern prayer of thanksgiving I found utterly incongruous, and took the lead.

From the Vashni encampment it was a long day's ride to Julah, and Del wasn't up to it. She said nothing, simply straightened her shoulders from time to time and kept riding, but I could tell she was exhausted. When we came across an acceptable place to spend the night, I called a halt. We had water enough in botas for ourselves and the horses, and though there was no grazing, we also packed grain. Thin pickings for the gelding and the stud, but we'd make Julah easily the next day. I figured we'd stay overnight, then head out toward Umir's.

Del is not one for asking or expecting help, so I offered her none as we unsaddled and hobbled the horses. I kept an eye on her, though, and saw how stiffly she moved, how carefully she balanced the weight of saddle, blankets, and pouches, gear she'd ordinarily swing off her horse easily. The spot I'd selected was open ground save for a huddled fringe of scrubby brush, with more sand and soil than rocks; Del dug in against an upswell like a coney, flipping her saddle upside down to form a horseman's chair. Once she'd watered the gelding and made certain he was comfortable, she flopped down on her blanket and leaned against the saddle. Her eyes drifted closed.

She wore a burnous, as I did. Save for the nick at her jawline, none of her scars were visible. But she was still too thin, and weariness hollowed her face.

I walked over, dropped a bota down next to her, and announced, "I'm cooking."

Del's eyes opened. "Cooking?"

"Yep. Here." I tossed her a cloth-wrapped packet. "Jerked meat."

She grimaced, peering down at the packet that had landed in her lap. "What kind of meat?"

"Who knows? But it's not cumfa. That's enough for me." I dug more out of the pouches, slung a bota over beside my own saddle and bedding, found the flint and steel and placed it on my blanket. "Not much wood here. I'll go scout around."

"Tiger?"

I turned back, asking a question with raised eyebrows.

She studied me a moment, as if weighing me against some inner vision. Then she relaxed. "Thank you."

Now I frowned.

"For coming."

I shrugged. "Sure. I figure we can track down the kid, make sure he's all right, then head back to the Vashni."

Her hands froze on the packet of dried meat. Tension returned tenfold. "Go *back*? Why?"

For a moment I didn't know. I was completely blank. Then awareness returned, and the answer came without volition. "Because I don't know enough yet about the dream-walking. There's much left to learn." I gestured at the ground. "If you want to start digging a hollow for the fire, that would help. And find rocks for the ring."

Del said nothing. Just stared at me. Fear was in her eyes; stiffened her body.

"*What?*" I asked.

She opened her mouth the answer, then shut it. Shook her head.

After a moment, annoyed, I waved a dismissive hand in her direction and went off in search of decent wood.

*　　*　　*

Later, after we had a bed of good coals for warmth and eaten our fill of seasoned jerked meat, Del unsheathed her sword and began to hone and oil it. I knew I should do the same with my own, but I felt just lazy enough to stay put, relaxed against my upturned saddle. I blinked sleepily as I stared into the fire ring, transfixed by the red glow of chunky coals.

Del's face bore a pensive expression. "How many days has it been since the sandtiger attack?"

I thought about it. Realized I didn't know. "A week, I think. Maybe ten days. Why?"

Muscles leaped in her jaw. But she didn't reply. Her eyes assessed the blade as she ran the stone against it. Her expression was odd.

"Being sick can make you lose track of time." I hoped to set her at ease, if she was worried she lost a few days. I watched her hand move in an even, effortless rhythm: down the blade, running the stone against steel, then carrying it back to the hilt where the motion began again. I smelled oil, tasted the metallic tang in my mouth. The sleeve of her burnous fell back; I saw the knurled scar on her forearm. "You were lucky that healed so fast."

"I haven't lost track of time," she said quietly. "But I think you have." She glanced up, then set sword and whetstone aside. For a moment her hands were pressed against her thighs as if she sought self-control. "Could I see that?"

Her eyes now were on my chest. I glanced down at the Vashni necklet. Thin wire gleamed faintly in firelight. I pulled it from around my neck, tossed it across to her.

Del caught it, held it up, turned it in the glow of coals so she might examine details more closely. "The wirework is exquisite."

I watched her handle the necklet, noting how she tested the strength of the wire, examined how it all fit together. Her face was oddly tense. Then she slipped the necklet over her own head, arranged it against her burnous. "How does it look?"

"A little long for you. But it was made for a man."

Her fingers ran down the bones. Then she arched her back in a brief stretch, yawned, pushed to her feet. "I need to find a bush," she said, "and then I'm going to bed. Could you tend the horses?"

I nodded, leaning forward to add a couple of broken branches to the coals. Del disappeared. I got up and went to refill the horse buckets, check the picket pegs, exchange a few pleasantries with the stud, who had indicated no particular joy at having me back in charge of things; I made my own pre-bedtime donation, then settled down again beside the fire.

Del was gone longer than anticipated. When she came back, it was without the necklet.

I frowned. "What happened?"

She was arranging her bedding. "I found a bush."

"Not *that*. What happened to the necklet?"

One hand flew to her chest. She looked down, then back at me. "It must have broken."

She did not sound very concerned, which annoyed me; the necklet had been a gift. "It was *wire*, Del." I sighed, shutting my mouth on a complaint; she was clearly too tired to discuss it. "I'll go look."

"Oh, Tiger, just wait until tomorrow. There's not enough light to see by."

I gathered bunched legs beneath me to push myself upright. "I'll just poke around anyway."

She uncoiled in a single sinuous motion and stepped beside the small fire, sword in hand. The tip kissed my throat, holding me in a kneeling position.

I was stunned. *"Del—"*

Tersely she said, "You won't find it, Tiger. I buried it." Coal-glow painted her face into relief, underscoring the hard set of her jaw, the jut of sharp cheekbones. "I was hoping there would be no need for this. But it's time you came to understand that something is indeed very wrong with you. And has been since you took up with Oziri."

I was frozen in place, caught between rising and sitting. It was not an appropriate position for oblique movement, which I realized was deliberate. Del knew me. Knew how I moved. Knew how to effectively put a halt to any intentions I might devise.

She wore the mask I'd seen displayed to opponents. "Do you wish to try me, Tiger?"

I eased myself down. My own sword, still sheathed in its harness, was within reach, but I knew better than to dare it with her blade at my throat. "You didn't want to see the necklet," I accused. "You wanted to get rid of it."

Del said nothing.

"What is it you think is 'wrong' with me?"

She ignored the question. "Tell me again how many days it's been since the sandtiger attack."

I held myself very still. "Six or seven. Why?"

"How many days were you at Umir's?"

"Two or three. Why?"

"How many days did we stay with the Vashni?"

I wanted to laugh, but didn't. Not with the sword at my throat. "Del, this is—"

"*How many,* Tiger?"

My teeth clicked together.

The tip bit in. "Answer me."

"Five."

"And how many since we sparred? You know—the match you say I walked away from."

"Three or four, I think." I drew in a careful breath. "You really have lost track of time."

She bit down on a sharp blurt of disbelieving laughter. "*I have—?*" But she checked it visibly. I saw something in her face, something like pain. But the sword did not waver. The tip had seated itself in the hollow of my throat. The cut stung.

I attempted sympathy. "Bascha, put it away. You're exhausted and confused. You need more rest—"

She cut me off. "What I need is for you to come to your senses. To realize what he's done to you."

"What *who's* done to me? What are you talking about?"

Her tone was bitter as winter ice. "The Vashni."

"Oziri? Hoolies, bascha, he was helping me learn how to—" I stopped. Couldn't breathe.

"How to what?" she asked, when I didn't finish.

Something built up in my chest. Something that twisted.

Something that threatened to burst. I felt as if I were on the verge of a firestorm.

Oh, hoolies. Oh, gods, no . . .

Del's tone changed. No longer was there challenge. Now there was expectation. "How to what, Tiger?"

I couldn't speak. The heat, the pressure increased. Pain filled my chest.

Her tone was almost a whisper. "Say it."

I took the step into conflagration. Denial kindled, exploded, then crisped into ash. Was blown away. Comprehension, confession, slow and painful, began to come into its place.

I couldn't say it.

"He did this," she said. "The Vashni. He did something to you. Now do you understand why I wanted to leave?"

Years of being stubbornly, selectively blind and deaf to certain impulses and speculations had created habits I found comforting. Habits that I could live with. Denial afforded me freedom. But I had stopped denying it in Oziri's presence. Had accepted it.

"Say it, Tiger. What he was teaching you. Admit it."

A spasm ran through my body. The words, slow, halting, laden with need, seem to come from someone else. "How to work magic."

Oh, hoolies . . . Memories came back then, came pouring back, tumbling one over the other like stones in a flash flood. I took what I could of them and fitted them into a whole. Hours. Days. Weeks. All had been lost to the dream-walks, the learning of the art. Now I understood Del's concern. Del's fear. Her desperation.

The Vashni had indeed done something to me: stolen sense, taken time. Turned me from my course. Set me on a new one.

Nihko had begun the process. Sahdri had explained it. Oziri had advanced it.

Oh, but it was so much easier to disbelieve, when faced with a terrible truth. A truth I could not accept, because the fear of it would overpower me. Incapacitation. I might as well be dead.

And I *would* be dead, according to the priest-mages of ioSkandi. To Umir's book.

Why would any man wish to be a mage, if the cost was so high?

Why would I?

I wished it because I'd wanted it. Needed it in the nights of my childhood, desperate to escape the Salset and the life of a chula: dreaming of a sandtiger, making it come to life; dreaming of Del atop the stone spire, who replaced a stolen scar and thus identity; dreaming of a boat to carry me to Skandi.

The intent had not been *magic*. Never. I had only ever, a very few times, wished to make a miracle to change what I could not bear.

Messiahs made miracles. Mages made magic.

Maybe one and the same.

I swore, then drew up my knees and leaned over them, elbows planted, clenching taut fingers in my short hair. I wanted to pull it out by the roots, as if that would erase the knowledge of what Oziri had done. Of what I had become.

Dreams could merely be dreams. But dreams could also be more. Now I walked them. Began to understand them. Summoned the magic within them, using the power Oziri sought, and found, and rekindled within my bones.

Nihko had told me. Sahdri had told me. I had denied them both. But somehow, with Oziri, I had not. Maybe it was because enough time had passed since my "whelping" atop the spire. Maybe it was because I was in the South again, and my walls were down. Or maybe it was because Oziri forced the issue. Whatever the reason, he had made me understand what I was. What I could do. What I *had* done.

But not what I might yet do.

My walls were down now, shattered upon the sand. Del, who realized it, released a long breath of eloquent relief and set down her sword. Knelt beside me. Put one hand on my own where they viciously gripped my hair.

I closed my eyes. I closed them very tightly. I thought my teeth might crumble.

The hand closed, offering comfort. Her tone was meditative; as a Northerner, she had never feared or denied magic. Nor refused to employ it herself. "From when I met you, I knew. There were signs of it . . . but you denied it. Refused to believe, despite evidence. Even when I showed you Northern magic. Even when you *worked* it."

I said nothing.

"I learned my magic," she said. "It's part of being a sword-singer, part of Staal-Ysta. That's what *jivatmas* are. We sing the power into being, to wield the blade."

She had told me this before. I wanted her to stop. Wanted not to listen.

"*I* have no magic," she said. "Only the sword. Only the song." Her fingers traced the back of one hand. "But you . . . you need nothing but yourself."

I shook my head.

"It's a part of you, Tiger. Just like your sword skill. Don't deny it."

Eventually I untangled fingers and looked at her. "I have to."

"No."

"If I don't . . ." But I let it go. I shook my head again, releasing pent breath. "It's too late for that, isn't it?"

"I think so, yes."

I sighed heavily, scrubbed wearily at my face. My eyes felt gritty. The beginnings of a headache throbbed at the base of my neck. "Did you really bury the necklet?"

"I cut the wire into pieces with my knife, then buried each bone in a different place."

Relief was palpable. Then comprehension followed, and amusement. No wonder it had taken her so long to find the appropriate bush. I wasn't certain anything in the necklet had controlled me or was meant to control me, but self-awareness had returned only with distance from Oziri and separation from the necklet.

"Good." I could not meet her eyes, so I stared hard at the stars for a long time. I heard the coals settling, the faintest of breezes skimming the surface of the soil, the restless shiftings of the stud and Del's gelding. "Four weeks," I said. "Give or take a day."

Del was puzzled. "What?"

"Since the sandtiger attack." I was certain of it, as much as I could be. It felt—right.

Del smiled. "Yes."

"There's something I have to tell you. Something you must understand." I swallowed heavily, aware of pain in my throat, the fear she couldn't, or wouldn't, accept it. "Bascha—you really were there. Atop the spire in the Stone Forest. With me."

Her tone frayed. "Tiger—"

"In my dreams," I told her. "And that's what saved me. That's what kept me sane. So long as I could hold onto the memory of you, could conjure you in dreams, I knew I would survive. I lost myself for a while, even lost two fingers—but I came back from ioSkandi, came back from the spires." I took a deep breath. "I'll come back from this."

It was Del's turn for silence.

"I don't—I don't remember what Oziri did. What he told me, or taught me. Enough, obviously, to find and refine whatever was born in me, what bubbled up from time to time before going dormant again, until Meteiera. Apparently he brought it back into the open." I laughed sharply. "If I couldn't remember what *day* it was, how can I be expected to remember what he did? But what I don't understand is why."

Del pondered it. "Perhaps he realized what was in you, and wanted it for himself," she said. "I think as long as you denied what you were, he could use you. Perhaps he felt your magic might augment his, make him something more than he was. But if you knew what he wanted, you would have resisted."

"Would I?"

"Oh, yes. You let no man use you, Tiger. Not Nihko, not Sahdri, not Oziri."

"But they have. Each of them." Others as well, over the long years. "For a time."

"And you have walked away from them all."

Or been dragged away by a very determined woman. I sighed. "So, you think if I admit what I am, I'll be safe from manipulation?"

"Maybe."

I scowled. "That's not much of a guarantee."

Del's brows arched. "With the kind of lives we lead, that's the best I can offer."

True enough. I ran a hand through my hair, scrubbing at the chill that crept over my scalp. "Dangerous."

"What is?"

"A man with a sword who lacks proper training." I grimaced, said what I meant: "A man with *magic* who lacks proper training."

Sahdri had said it, atop the spires. Umir's book set it into print. Oziri had proved it.

"Unless he is strong enough to find his own way."

I grunted. "Maybe."

Del smiled. "I will offer a guarantee."

I laughed, then let it spill away. "I can't believe that all dreams are bad, bascha. Everyone dreams. You dream."

"But I am not a mage."

She had said it was born in me. So had Nihkolara, and Sahdri. Oziri. Even Umir's book. Dormancy until Skandi, from birth until age forty—except for a sensitivity to magic so strong it made me ill; until ioSkandi, when Nihko took me against my will to Meteiera, to the Stone Forest; to others like him, like me. Where, atop a spire, a full-blown mage was born.

Denial bloomed again, faded. Was followed by the only logical question there could be.

What comes next?

Chapter 23

I awoke with a start, staring up into darkness lighted only by stars and the faintest sliver of moon. Sweat bathed my body. I swore under my breath and rubbed an unsympathetic hand over my face, mashing it out of shape.

"What is it?" Del's voice was shaded by only a trace of sleepiness.

We lay side-by-side in our bedrolls with the dying fire at our feet. Desert nights are cool; I yanked the blanket up to my shoulders. Muttering additional expletives, I shut my eyes and draped an elbow over my face. "I was dreaming, curse it."

After a moment, with careful neutrality, she queried, "Yes?"

"I'd just as soon not, after my recent experiences." I removed the arm and looked again at the stars, shoving both forearms under my head. "How in hoolies am I supposed to go through life without dreaming?"

"I don't think you *can* not dream," Del observed, shifting beneath her blanket. "You'll just have to get used to it."

I grunted sourly.

"Well—unless you can learn to control them. Make them stop." She was silent a moment. "And perhaps you can. Being you."

I chewed on that for a moment, then shied away from the concept. That "being you" part carried an entirely new connotation, now.

"What was this dream about?"

I scowled up at darkness. "Actually, it was a piece of one I had before. At least, I'm assuming it was a dream. Before, that is. You swore up and down it didn't happen."

"*I* did?"

"The dance," I said. "The dance where you walked away."

"Ah." She was silent a moment. "No. It didn't happen. But— are you saying you dreamed about a dream?"

"I didn't think it was a dream at the time. In which case I'd be dreaming about something that *did* happen. But it didn't, so I guess I was dreaming about a dream."

Her tone was amused. "This is getting very complicated, Tiger."

"Then there's the dream about the dead woman . . ." Oh, argh. I hadn't meant to tell her.

Del's voice sharpened. "Dead woman?"

I tried to dismiss it as inconsequential. "Just—a skeleton. Out in the Punja."

"It's a skeleton, but you know it's a woman?"

"It's a woman's voice."

"This skeleton *speaks?*"

Now she'd really think I was sandsick. "It's not the kind of dreams I had with Oziri. This is just a dream. A dream dream. You know. The kind anyone has."

"*I* don't dream of skeletons who speak with a woman's voice."

I put a smile into my voice. "Of course not. *You* dream of *me.*"

"Oh, indeed," she murmured dryly. "What else would a woman dream about but a man? It is her only goal in life, to find a man to fill her thoughts during the day and her dreams during the night."

I rolled over to face her, hitching myself up on one elbow. "So. What kind of man *did* you think you'd end up with?" It wasn't the sort of thing I'd ever asked before. Nor had I ever heard a man, even dead drunk, mention curiosity about it. But that didn't mean we *weren't* curious.

"I didn't."

"Didn't? Not at all?" I paused. "Ever?"

"When I was a girl, yes."

"A Northerner."

"Of course. I lived in the North."

"And when you got a little older?"

"I stopped thinking about what kind of man I might end up with."

"Why?"

"Ajani," she said simply.

One word. One name. Explanation. And it came rushing back to me, the knowledge. A fifteen-year-old girl, witness to the massacre of her family. The sole survivor save for her brother, and subject to the brutality so many women suffered at the hands of borjuni. No, I didn't imagine Del had ever dreamed of a man again, except perhaps of the one she'd sworn to kill.

By the time she'd done it, we'd been partners for two years. Sword-mates. Bed-mates. I'd known the minute I laid eyes on her in the dusty, drag-tail cantina that I wanted her in my bed. I don't know when the idea occured to Del.

"What?" she asked.

I raised my eyebrows at her in a silent query.

Del frowned faintly. "You're staring at me."

"You're worth staring at." I reached out, hooked two fingers into the sandtiger necklet around her neck, pulled her toward me. "I think I know of a way to turn bad dreams into good ones."

"Ah," she said as our foreheads met gently. "But will you remember my name in the morning?"

I shifted closer, sinking a hand into the hair against the back of her head. "Who needs names? 'Woman' will do."

Stiffened fingers jabbed me warningly beneath the short ribs. "What was that again?"

"Delilah," I murmured against her mouth.

The mouth curved into a smile, then parted. The tongue flicked briefly against my own with the first word. "That will do."

So would a lot of things, with this woman.

In the morning I fought the muzzy residue of too many dreams crowded together inside my skull as I grained and watered the horses. The morning promised to bleed into a typical desert day:

very bright, very warm, no moisture. Which is good for the bones, but bad for the skin. It wasn't high summer yet, nor were we in the Punja, but no part of the South lacks for heat. I could taste it on my tongue, an acrid trace of dry soil and sand; I could smell the tang of creosote and what was left of our fire, burned away to a thin scattering of coals amid the ash. Del, squatting beside it, raked the coals apart to expose all of them, then took care to blanket them in a layer of sandy soil so there was no threat of sparks that might kindle a conflagration.

I patted the stud as he nosed his morning grain, then turned back to Del. She looked tired; and it had nothing to do with our activities of the night before, which had been slow and undemanding, but satisfying nonetheless. She simply hadn't entirely recovered her strength following the sandtiger attack. "We'll make Julah in two or three hours, then spend the night before going on."

She glanced up, rising. "We'd make better time if we headed out this afternoon, after a good meal."

I hitched a shrug, turning back to gather up and pack canvas buckets away. "We'll see how we feel later today. No sense in wasting a decent bed, though, now that we own one." Or several.

"*Parts* of one," Del clarified. "Do you suppose Fouad will charge us rent on the other third?"

"Not if he wants to live."

She'd knelt and now was working on her bedroll. "Nayyib deserves better, after all he did for us."

"We'll go after him, Del. But we won't do him much good if we're both too tired to put up a decent fight. Besides, we don't even know if he *got* to Umir's place. Just because he said he'd go—"

"If he said it, he meant it." Del looped thongs around the bedding and knotted them. "I trust him."

It baffled me that she would. "We hardly know him, bascha."

"I spent nearly two weeks in his company." Her tone was clipped. "I would have died, had he not tended me. Hour after hour, day after day, at the shelter and then at the Vashni encampment. You can learn a great deal about a man in such circumstances."

"Look, I'm not saying he's a liar, just that—"

Del cut me off. "He went to look for you."

"I know that, but—"

"And likely he's risking his life for you, to walk into Umir's presence among all those sword-dancers. Look what happened with Rafiq."

"Which is precisely the point I tried to make once before: that he ran too high a risk going after me. Did he think to win Umir's little contest, then join forces with me?" I shook my head. "He's not good enough. They'd have eaten him alive in that circle."

"Which is why he came looking for you originally. To learn from you."

I placed blankets across the stud's back, then swung the saddle up. "No, originally he came looking for me to challenge me, until he saw me kill Khashi. *Then* he decided to ask me to teach him."

"We owe him, Tiger."

I wanted to growl aloud in exasperation. "We'll go, Del. I'm not saying we won't. I'm just saying we can afford a night in Julah."

"Neesha may not be able to afford—"

"*Del.*" I turned toward her. "You need the rest. End of discussion."

She stood her ground, scowling at me ferociously. "Why is it you're so opposed to helping Nayyib?"

"I'm not opposed to helping Nayyib. I just think—"

"You try to argue me out of it every time I bring it up. Despite the fact he saved your life—"

"I wasn't in any danger of dying, bascha."

Her voice rose. "—as well as saving mine; and I was in danger of dying, Tiger! Not to mention he went for help in Julah and got himself abducted by Rafiq and his friends—"

"I don't think they actually abducted him—"

"—and risked being killed by Vashni—"

"I'm not sure the Vashni—"

"—and now may have been taken prisoner by Umir. How many times has he put himself out, or put himself in danger, to help us, yet you insist on denigrating those efforts and refuse to help him when *he* may need it?"

"I'm not denigrating those efforts, Del, and I'm not refusing to help him. I'm merely saying we should spend the night in Julah before we head off for Umir's. Where he may not even be."

"See? There it is, Tiger! Denigration. Is it because he's younger than you—*my* age, in fact—and handsome? Because I spent two weeks alone with him, mostly undressed, while you were elsewhere? Because we slept in the same tent? Because I came to know him, to trust him? Are you afraid I might be taken with him?"

I stared at her, mouth open. "You're saying I'm jealous!"

"Well? Are you?"

"No!"

"Are you *sure*, Tiger?"

"Yes!"

Clearly she was dubious. "You exhibited behavior somewhat similar to this in Skandi, when we met Herakleio. Young, strong, handsome, well-set-up Herakleio."

I glared. "I wasn't jealous of Herakleio, and I'm not jealous of Nayyib."

She glared back. "You have remarked many times on the years between us. No doubt some might even whisper I'm young enough to be your daughter."

I gritted teeth. "I don't care what anybody else thinks. Or what they whisper, either." Though I'd heard it mentioned aloud a time or two.

Pale brows arched.

"I don't," I said crisply. "As for staying in Julah, it's one night. *One* night at Fouad's. That's all, bascha. Then we go."

"In one night a man could die."

"Hoolies, a man can die in one *moment*, Del! Between one breath and the next. But I find it very unlikely Umir will kill him—or that anyone else would—because there's still a price on my head, and by now they probably all know Nayyib has a better idea than they do where I might go. Plus Umir wants his book back. He won't kill Nayyib if he thinks he can trade him for the book."

Del held her bedroll in the crook of an elbow. "What book?"

In my zeal to change the subject, I'd forgotten she knew nothing about Umir's book of magic. I sighed, turning back to continue tacking out the stud. "I'll tell you on the trail."

* * *

Fouad seemed to have resigned himself to the fact that Del and I were now equal partners in his cantina. He was not in the least surprised to see us, nor that we expected to have private quarters. In fact, he led us rather dolefully down the hallway giving access to the rooms rented—along with the wine-girls—to men with coin. I fully expected Del to make some icy comment about women accepting the necessity of selling their bodies, but she held her tongue. Fouad took us to the very back of the building, then waved us inside a curtained door.

Plaster dust still lay on the floor. Raw wood and nail holes were obvious against the weathered walls. "I had a wall knocked down between two rooms," Fouad said, "and a wider bed put in." He glowered. "It's reduced the cantina by two rooms, you realize. And the income. Plus the cost of the changes will come out of your shares."

Two tiny rooms made into one slightly larger one by the deletion of a thin lath-and-plaster wall didn't leave us with much added space, but it was something. And the bed was noticeably wider. There were also two rickety tables, one battered, brass-hinged trunk, and a small, square window cut into one exterior adobe wall. I wondered inanely if Del would want to put up curtains.

"You can rent it out when we're not here," I told him, "and charge more for it because it's the best room in the house. Which reminds me—we'll need to sit down and have a good talk about how the place is run, so Del and I have an idea what to expect as partners." I caught her narrowed glance and added, "When we get back."

Perhaps he hadn't expected me to hit upon what was undoubtedly his plan. "You know where the kitchen is," Fouad said gloomily. "If you want food and drink, just ask."

I started undoing harness buckles. "I'm asking."

He sighed and nodded. "I thought so. I'll send one of the girls back with a tray."

Del stared after him as Fouad departed. I set harness, sword, and knife down on the trunk, then assigned myself the task of testing the feel of the mattress by sprawling across it, slack-limbed. I couldn't help the blooming of a lopsided smile. I was a Man of Property. I now owned one-third of a modestly successful cantina in a thriving town. But even better, I had a bed and a room to call my own for the very first time in forty years.

Well. *Our* own.

I smacked the bed lightly. "Room for two."

Del's gaze transferred itself from the curtained doorway to the bed. While I was pleased, she seemed stunned by events. Or maybe just too tired to take it all in.

"It doesn't bite," I said. "And *I* only do when invited."

Slender fingers worked at harness buckles. But she stopped before slipping out of it. "We should go after Nayyib."

I held onto my patience with effort. "Tomorrow, remember? First light. For now, we have the chance to rest under a real roof, in a real bed, and eat decent food for the first time in weeks." Well, cantina food didn't always live up to "decent," but it would be better by far than dried cumfa and flat, tough-crusted journey-bread. Especially when accompanied by something far more palatable than Vashni liquor.

Hmmm. Maybe the quality of food was something I should discuss with Fouad. After all, it was my reputation at stake now, too.

Del undid the buckles, set harness and weapons down atop mine, and sat on the edge of the bed. After a moment I wrapped a hand around the braid hanging down her back and tugged her down next to me. We lay cross-wise, feet planted on the packed-earth floor.

"Tomorrow," I said again.

Del's eyes drifted closed. She fell asleep almost at once, thereby proving my point about needing a good night's rest. I smiled, smoothing fallen strands of hair back from her face.

Then a thought occured. "I am *not* jealous," I muttered.

But I wasn't so certain I liked the idea of Del spending two weeks in a tent, mostly undressed—*mostly undressed!*— with a young, handsome, well-set-up buck like Nayyib while I was elsewhere. A young, handsome, well-set-up buck who, more to the point, was Del's age.

Now I scowled at the ceiling. What *did* she see in a man old enough to be her father?

Oh, hoolies. I got up, carefully shifted Del lengthwise on the bed, which occasioned a murmured but incoherent comment, and took myself and Umir's book into the common room. Such mean-derings of the mind called for goodly amounts of aqivi.

Chapter 24

ouad evinced extreme startlement when I'd set up my study space at a table in the back corner of the common room, on a diagonal line from the doorway. I replaced the wobbly bench with the most comfortable one available, stuffed my spine into the confluence of walls, set out the book so the light from a window fell evenly upon its pages, and proceeded to sit there for hours, a cup and jug of aqivi at one elbow. I'd eaten earlier, but there was always room for aqivi.

After I'd insistently shooed away three curious wine-girls, intrigued by what I was doing, I'd been left alone. I was aware of whispered comments going on back behind the bar, discussing the new me in tones of disbelief, but dismissed them easily as I lost myself in the words.

Well, I suppose it *was* odd to see a man reading in a cantina, ignoring attractive women.

Fouad eventually arrived. His face was troubled.

I glanced up, marking my place with a finger. "What?"

"Is this a plan I should know about?"

"Is what a plan?"

He gestured. "You sitting here all afternoon."

"I've spent many an afternoon sitting here, Fouad. Not lately, maybe, but certainly often enough before."

He leaned closer. "People wish to *kill* you."

I figured it out. "You think I'm trying to lure sword-dancers to come in here after me."

"Aren't you?" Nervously he smoothed the front of his robes. "Damages can be expensive, Tiger. Broken stools and tables, shattered crockery . . ." He trailed off, figuring that was enough imagery to get his point across.

It was. "Fouad, I'm just reading. Nothing more. Del's sleeping, so I came out here."

His expression was a fascinating amalgam of disbelief and worry. "But you can't read."

"Who told you that?"

"*You* did. Some years ago."

Well, yes, I probably had. "I learned how." I didn't bother to explain *how* I learned how; some stories are better left untold.

"So, you're reading just to read?"

"Yes, Fouad. Reading just to read." That, and to learn what I could about magery, since it seemed to concern me in very personal ways now. "I'm not attempting to lure sword-dancers to come in here after me."

"And if they do come? You're sitting out here in front of the gods and everybody."

I dropped my right hand beneath the table, closed it around the sheathed sword, and raised it to a level where he could see the hilt. "Satisfied?"

Fouad's concern bled away, replaced by a relieved smile. "Yes."

"Good." I resettled the sword against the wall, hidden behind and beneath the table. "Now, if you don't mind, I'd like to continue my reading."

"Damages should concern you, Tiger," he pointed out. "It's not all profit, you know, operating a cantina."

"I'm sure you'll provide a thorough accounting of profits *and* expenses, Fouad. I trust you." I tapped the page with an impatient finger. "Do you mind?"

Shaking his head, Fouad wandered away muttering about losing his best corner to a man who wanted to *read* and who expected all his food and drink for free.

Well, sure. Why should I pay for what I own?

*   *   *

The next interruption was Del. "What are you doing?"

I scowled up at her, annoyed as her shadow slanted across the page I was reading. Since I was losing light as the sun went down, it mattered. With no little asperity, I replied, "I should think it's obvious."

Her face was creased from the mattress, flushed from recent awakening. She looked very young. "What are you drinking?" She bent forward as if considering helping herself to what was in my cup, then wrinkled her nose as she caught a whiff. "Never mind."

Del glanced around, looking for someone to take her order, then wandered over to the bar to place it herself when all of the girls disappeared into the back; it was their way of exhibiting jealousy. Apparently Fouad hadn't yet informed them Del was their boss as much as he was.

I followed her with my eyes, as did every other man in the cantina, though as yet there weren't many. Within the hour the common room ought to begin filling up. In the meantime, Del, oblivious to the stares, served as distraction and the object of lustful thoughts, even draped in a sleep-wrinkled burnous, with a sword hilt poking above her shoulder.

I heard raised voices from behind the curtain, including Fouad's. The three girls abruptly reappeared, each wearing an outraged expression that altered to sullen resentment as they saw Del at the bar. One of them, rubbing her rump, even deigned to inquire as to Del's wishes; the other two started working the tables, suggesting more drinks. None of them looked happy.

Hmmm. Maybe *I* ought to have a word with them. Couldn't have them displaying bad tempers to the customers. No doubt Fouad would appreciate me taking a hand in the running of the business.

Del came back with a cup and flask. "Water," she declared, eyeing my aqivi. "We musn't drink up all the profits."

I poured my cup full and availed myself of a portion of the profits. Del sighed and shook her head, hooking a stool to the table.

I closed Umir's book with a thump, latched the hook and hasp, and set it down on the bench next to me so it wasn't in evidence to casual customers. "You're only half awake, bascha. Why don't you go back to bed?"

"Oh, no, I'm very awake. I doubt I'll be able to sleep again until well after dark." She drank her water, eyes guileless over the rim of the cup. "In fact, there's no need to stay the night here. We could get a start now."

"*I* haven't slept."

"But you've spent the balance of the day resting, Tiger, reading a book in a quiet corner. Unless you consider that exhausting labor."

"Well, it might be," I declared irritably. "It's written by several people in several different tongues. I have to translate all of them in my head before I can figure out what anybody's talking about, and even then I can't always sort through their meanings, since I've been a mage all of a couple of months. It's *mental* labor, bascha."

Her expression made an eloquent statement: she did not consider my explanation good enough.

"Come on, Del, we've been through this. We leave in the morning. *After* we've had a chance to sleep in a real bed."

"You could have slept in a real bed this afternoon."

"I was, in case you haven't noticed, being a considerate individual. I let you have the whole bed all to yourself."

"Considerate?" Del eyed my jug. "How much of that have you had?"

I brightened. "Enough that I wouldn't trust myself to stay ahorse."

"Hah," she retorted. "You wouldn't admit to being too drunk to sit a horse if you were lying face-down in a puddle of piss."

"I dunno," I slurred, blinking owlishly. "I might need you to help me to bed. You know, hold me up, take my sandals off, undress me . . ." I waggled suggestive eyebrows at her.

Del's face was perfectly bland, but I saw the faintest hint of a twitch at one corner of her mouth. "Dream on."

I stiffened on my bench. "That's cruel. I told you how I feel about dreams."

She was laughing at me unrepentantly even as she rose. "I will leave you to your reading, then."

"Wait—where are you going?" I started to reach for the book and my sword. "Back to bed?"

She paused. "Don't look so hopeful, Tiger. No, not to bed. I have it in mind to purchase some new clothing. Something—different."

"Why? What kind of clothing? *How* different?"

"Something suitable for serving liquor."

I stood up so fast I overset the bench. "You're not—you can't mean—tell me you don't . . ." I stopped, untangled my brain, started over from an entirely different direction, a more positive direction in view of Del's tendancy to disapprove of what she described as *my* tendancy toward possessiveness. With immense courtesy, I queried, "What is it you intend to do, pray tell?"

"Learn how to run a cantina."

Alarm reasserted itself. "By being a *wine-girl?*"

Del took note of the fact my raised voice, carrying, had stopped all other conversations throughout the common room, focusing abrupt attention on ours. With a glint in her eye she inquired, equally loudly, "What's wrong with being a wine-girl?"

I had committed a slight tactical error in the rules of war: I had taken the battle to the enemy's home. I could continue the fight valiantly if foolishly, or retire from the field with honor intact.

Not that Del ever allowed me any when she owned the ground.

"Why, nothing," I replied guilelessly. "I'm sure you'd make the very best wine-girl this cantina's ever seen."

Which, of course, did nothing at all to endear me to the wine-girls currently present, who already resented Del; yet another tactical error. Retreating with as much dignity as possible, I righted the bench and resumed my seat, whereupon I rescued the book, then promptly buried my face in a cup of aqivi.

Del said calmly, "A good proprietor understands all facets of a business."

I wanted very badly to ask if those facets included selling her favors, but I decided I'd said quite enough for the moment.

But later . . . well, later was a different issue altogether.

I gulped more aqivi as Del departed, thinking maybe it was best if I got drunk before she started serving liquor to men who were entirely too free with their hands.

Of course, Del was more likely to chop off a wandering hand than slap it playfully.

I reconsidered getting drunk, if only to bear sober witness to the justifiable murder of several men.

Then again, they were customers. It's tough to make any profits if you kill or maim the customers.

I went back to the aqivi.

Sometime later, as the girls took to setting out and lighting table candles, I gathered up book and sword and made my way back to the room that was now ours. It was kind of a nice feeling knowing we had a place to leave things as needed on a regular basis as well as to sleep. I'd bunked often enough at Fouad's in earlier days but almost never alone . . . well, come to think of it, I wouldn't be alone now, either, but back then I'd *ridden* alone, too.

I wondered as I slid aside the door curtain if this was a sign of getting soft or of advancing age, this appreciation of property. I'd never had a place of my own, nor needed one. With the Salset, as a chula, I slept on a ratty goatskin, but even that hadn't been mine; at Alimat, learning to sword-dance, I'd had a bedroll and a spot on the sand to throw it, but neither qualified as a home. A room in the cantina wasn't a home, either, but it was more than anything I'd claimed before.

I grinned wryly as I returned the book to a saddlepouch and slid them under the bed. For a while there, in Skandi, it had looked as though I might be heir to a vast trading empire, due to inherit wealth, vineyards, ships, and a chunk of property containing an immense and beautiful house. But that was when the metri had a use for a long-lost grandson; that use had changed, and so had her attitude. She had, in fact, eventually denied altogether I was her grandson, claiming her daughter had died before I was born. But Del made a surprising discovery on the way back home: I bore the keraka, the birthing mark that proved me a Stessa, one of the Eleven Families of Skandi. They claimed to be gods-descended, those families, but unless the gods they worshipped were petty and avaricious, I hadn't noted any resemblance or advantage.

Still, I couldn't help the hand that stole up to my head, fingers parting hair to feel behind my left ear. Had the priest-mages of ioSkandi not shaved my head, we'd never have known the truth. Del had once asked if I now considered the possibility of returning to Skandi and presenting my case to the ten other Families, but I wasn't interested. The metri had her heir in Herakleio, a cousin of sorts. He was Skandic-born, bred into island customs and convictions, one of *them*. I was Southron-born and -reared despite my Skandic ancestry; I belonged here.

Of course, only if I survived the current minor problems of sword-dancers out to kill me, and Umir the Ruthless.

My eyes were gritty from reading all day. For that matter, all of me was gritty; I hadn't bathed in days. It crossed my mind to ask Fouad to have the girls bring in a half-cask and fill it, but I decided not to push my luck. I was in their bad graces after my comment to Del. So I opted for the public bathhouse down the street a way. A hot bath, a filling meal, a drink or two, and a good night's sleep in a real bed. I felt my jaw: and a shave. Because come morning, we'd be back on the sand, sweating under burnouses, hunting one of Del's strays.

Of whom I was decidedly *not* jealous, thank you very much.

I donned harness, did up buckles, made sure the blade exited the sheath without catching, and took myself off to the bathhouse.

Del, who had explained that the scent of an unbathed, hot, active, liquor-imbibing male was not necessarily arousing in intimate moments, would undoubtedly appreciate it.

Me, I'd never noticed. But sometimes you just have to cater to a woman's wishes if you want her to yield to yours. It's the way of the world.

Chapter 25

Julah's public bathhouse was actually a bathtent. In a small courtyard set back from the street, not far from the main well, an enterprising soul years before had strung a cross-hatching of ropes from hooks pounded into the back walls of buildings, hung swathes of gauzy fabric over them to form tiny private "rooms," built three good-sized fires, and hired people to keep big cauldrons filled with heated water. Others filled smaller wooden buckets and hauled the water to the rough-hewn tubs in each "room." It wasn't much, but when you've been in the desert for weeks on end, it was sheer luxury. From time to time sun-baked ropes and fabric had to be replaced, but otherwise it was business as usual.

I paid the price for water and soap, which cost extra, gave the hirelings time to reheat the tepid water in a tub, waved away the attendant who offered to scrub my back, and pulled the draperies closed. There's not a lot of privacy in the bathtent, but since only men used it, it didn't really matter. I stripped down and draped the burnous over the nearest rope, bowing it slightly, then made a small pile out of sandals, dhoti, and harness next to the tub. I risked one foot in the water, hissed a bit, then worked the other one in. The introduction of netherparts required a bit more courage, but once I was down, rump planted against wood, water lapping around my navel, the contrast between cooling air and hot water faded. Sighing, I unsheathed the sword, balanced it across the width of the tub, and felt the knots in my muscles begin to loosen. Bliss.

I was about halfway through my bath when an overeager attendant pulled the curtain back, chattering to his customer, only to blush fiery red when he realized the tub already held a body. He apologized effusively and yanked the curtain closed, but not before the stranger had a good look at me hunched in the tub with one foot stuck up in the air as I scrubbed at toes.

Additional mortified apologies from the attendant were issued through the curtains. Smiling, I assured him that all was well and forgiven—even as I quietly climbed out of the tub, pulled on my dhoti (not easy over wet flesh), knotted sandal thongs together and hung them over a shoulder along with the harness. The sword was in my right hand. I bent over, sloshed my left through the water as if I was only just exiting, then waited.

Sure enough, within moments a sword blade sliced down through the back wall, severing the support rope. A body moved against falling fabric. I heard a blurt of shock, a curse—the former from an attendant, the latter from my attacker—and the clang of steel as I trapped the blade with my own and drove it down. Unweighting, twisting, I kicked out with one foot and made contact with the man's body, knocking him backward. He tripped, went down hard. Sheets of gauzy material collapsed upon him, fouling his sword. I bent, locked hands around the tub, upended it, spilling lukewarm water in my assailant's direction. Water on hardpack turns it slick; anything to slow him.

A series of quick slashes with my sword brought down every "room" in my immediate area, entangling customers and attendants alike in steam-dampened curtains and ropes. I heard angry shouting and cries of alarm. Barefoot, damp, half-naked, with harness and sandals flopping against my ribs, I light-footed into the alley, to the street, then raced toward Fouad's, hoping the sworddancer had no idea where I might be staying.

At the cantina door I paused briefly, caught my breath, examined the customers even as I entered. The first thing I saw was Del seated at a table with a man. She faced the doorway; his back was to me. Short of twisting all the way around on his stool, he wouldn't see me. Del's expression didn't change, but I did note the way she lifted a hand as if to smooth back hair, and saw the quick, subtle gesture with fingers: *go away*. Not polite, perhaps, but it got the message across: He wasn't an innocent customer making time with her but a threat, and she was making time with *him* to control his intentions. I tilted my head toward the back hallway, sending my own message, then soundlessly moved to our room.

By the time Del joined me, I had sandals and harness on and the saddlepouches packed. "We're leaving," I said. "Go back and keep him company so there's no suspicion, then meet me at the livery when you've got a chance to get away. I've got all of our things; I'll have the horses ready."

Del nodded and disappeared. I waited until I was fairly certain she owned his attention again, then made my way to the cantina's back door.

Fouad met me there. "Trouble?"

"The man with Del is a sword-dancer, likely on my trail."

"Ah. I wondered why she sat down with him." He offered me an armload of filled botas. "When Del disappears, I'll send Silk out to him with drugged wine. That'll delay him."

I opened the door. "He may have someone riding with him."

He shrugged. "We'll deal with him, too."

I grinned. "Kind of nice having another partner."

Fouad made a sour face and shut the door behind me.

It took Del a bit longer to arrive at the livery than I expected. Both the stud and the white gelding were tacked out and ready to go as we lingered in the stableyard; I tossed Del the reins to the gelding and swung up onto the stud. "What took you so long?"

"He was very curious about your habits."

She wore a fresh, pale burnous and had wound her hair up on top of her head in some kind of arcane knotwork fastened with a carved bone rod. Wisps straggled down her neck most fetchingly. "I doubt it was me he was asking about!"

Del mounted, gathering reins as she hooked her right foot in the stirrup. "Not initially, no. But we got around to you." She paused. "Where are we going?"

"North—" But I broke off as the stud sashayed sideways, snorting. I felt the tension in his body, the quivering of muscles. "What's *your* problem?"

"I think it's my gelding," Del said, amused.

"What—again?" But it was possible. Horses could be rather obtuse sometimes. I reaffirmed my control over the stud. "As I was saying, we're going north. We'll get out of town a ways, then find a place to stay the night." I shot her a glance over my shoulder. "Guess you got your wish."

"What wish?"

"To ride out after Nayyib tonight."

Del's smile was swift as she took out the hair rod, tucking it away in a saddlepouch. "Guess I did."

"And *I*, meanwhile—unlike a certain someone I could mention, who spent most of the day unconscious—did not get to sleep in a real bed."

She brought the gelding up next to the stud as we turned onto the main drag. "Take solace in the knowledge you are repaying a debt."

"Solace isn't as comfortable as a real bed."

Del nodded, tucking now-loose hair under the neckline of her burnous. "I did tell him you were a disagreeable soul. Cranky, even."

"Told who?"

"Ahmahd. The sword-dancer back at the cantina. A very courteous soul, he was—offered to buy me liquor, dinner, and a bed."

"So long as he was in the bed."

"Well, I suppose he had hopes, yes."

I shook my head, grinning; so . . . predictable. Just like me. "This way . . ." I turned the stud and led Del through one of the narrower alleys, twisting about like a tangled skein of yarn. When at last we left the last hedge of buildings behind, we were free of the town entirely, striking out northward beneath a star-pocked sky. "I suspect they won't think I'd head back *into* Umir's domain."

"I suspect Ahmahd won't, since I suggested otherwise." Del brought the gelding up next to me again. "I explained we hadn't seen one another for weeks. That you'd been hauled off to Umir's by Rafiq and his friends, and that was the last I'd seen of you. But before then you'd talked of going to Haziz to take ship back to Skandi. I was hanging around hoping you'd show up but was beginning to worry that you'd gone without me."

I grunted. "I doubt he believed you."

"There was no one left in the cantina who'd seen us together. Fouad had different girls working, and everyone else who'd seen us talking had left. Ahmahd will learn the truth, of course, at some point, but at least it will buy us a little time." A trace of dry amusement laced her tone. "Men tend to believe me, if I wish them to."

Present company included; nice of her not to mention that. "Here." I led her off the road. We rode some distance away, winding through scrubby trees and shrubbery, until I indicated a cluster of vegetation forming a leafy blockade against a rill of windblown sand and soil. It sloped into a slight hollow, good enough for a smidgen of shelter. "No one would believe anyone would camp out here, this close to Julah. This close to *real beds*." A glance southwards showed the flickering lights of the city, sparking against the dark horizon. "We should be safe. Come dawn, we can head for Umir's domain. And let's hope Nayyib's there, or this is all for nothing."

"He is." Del swung down off of her gelding even as I dismounted. "I asked Ahmahd."

Well, that was something. More than we had known. "Did he say if the kid was being held against his will?"

"That he didn't know. Just that Neesha arrived and had not yet departed when Ahmahd and his friend left."

"So it's likely the kid would have heard about any reward for me."

"It seems so."

"And how do we know Nayyib didn't tell Ahmahd about Fouad's cantina, hoping for a cut without involving himself personally?"

Del flicked me an icy glance.

"All right, fine." I was grinning as I dismounted. "We'll assume he didn't."

"He wouldn't. But if he had, don't you think Ahmahd and his friend would have arrived in Julah sooner?"

"Possibly," I conceded.

"Oh, and I did neglect to mention something Ahmahd said about you."

"About me? In between seducing you?"

"He did not seduce me. He *attempted* to seduce me."

"Ran out of time, did he?"

"He said," Del began, ignoring me, "that he had seen you dance there at Umir's and was quite impressed by your skills."

"At least he's being honest."

"He said you were better than he expected—especially for an old man."

I began untacking the stud. "He did not. *You're* saying that."

"Ahmahd said it." Del's expression was blandly serene. "Right before he asked me what a woman my age was doing with a man *your* age."

I scowled at the stud, undoing thongs and buckles, and changed the subject. "I don't suppose this friend of Ahmahd's felt in need of a bath."

"As a matter of fact, Ahmahd said he *did* go to the bathhouse. Why?"

"Because that's where I was when someone decided to interrupt my soak by taking off my head. Fortunately, I was ready. Last I saw of him, he was wrestling with curtains." I deposited the saddle on end, plus the tied-on saddle-pouches, then peeled blankets off the stud's back. They were only slightly damp; we hadn't ridden long enough for the horses to work up a true sweat. "Did your friend Ahmahd happen to mention how many others might be tracking us?"

"Oh, *I'm* not being tracked," Del said, precise as always. "At least, not as prey. For information, yes. But it's you they want to kill."

"Comforting," I muttered, kneeling to hobble the stud.

"I'm assuming a goodly number are hoping to find you," Del added. "Though they won't kill you out of hand, Ahmahd said. Apparently Umir's far less concerned that you dishonored the circle and your vows than he is in recovering the book, despite what the sword-dancers want. The orders are explicit: you are not to be killed until the book is back in his hands, in case you've hidden it somewhere. Then they can do whatever they like with you."

"Comforting," I repeated. Although it was, a little; easier for me to defend myself if they didn't want to kill me. Not that all of them would accept Umir's terms. "Well, at least we know Ahmahd and his friend won't be following us immediately—Fouad was going to take care of that." The stud was hobbled, haltered, and watered; he'd already eaten at the livery. I took myself to my pile of gear and unrolled my bedding after grooming the soil beneath it, getting rid of rocks. Aggrievedly I said, "Here I am, being hunted by the gods know how many sword-dancers . . . and *you* want us to ride right into Umir's domain, maybe even into his very house, just to make sure the kid's all right."

Del knelt as she unrolled her own bedding. "Yes."

Nothing more. I shook my head, unstoppered a bota. "I sure hope this Nayyib is worth it."

"He is."

I watched her a moment, noting the slight stiffness in her movements, the pensive frown marring her face. She was defensive about the kid, as if there were more to him than she let on.

She glanced up, caught me staring at her. "What?"

I shook my head and began to unlace my sandals.

"Tiger—"

"I'm tired." And I was. "Let's get as good a night's sleep as we can, then head out at first light."

Her bedroll overlapped my own. Del took off her own sandals, her burnous, and set both beside her bedding along with harness and sword. She crawled beneath blankets. Bathed in the light of the moon, pale hair glowed. "Are you all right?"

I started to answer her flippantly, then reconsidered. Perched on one elbow, I leaned forward and kissed her lightly on the brow. "I'm fine, bascha."

With the abrupt change of mood I'd come to recognize over the years as purely female, she said, "If you truly don't wish to go to Umir's, we don't have to. Perhaps we could find another way."

I didn't wish to go to Umir's. But Del wanted it very badly, and I didn't really have a good enough reason to refuse. I did owe the kid. "We'll go, bascha. I said so." I pulled the blanket up to my chin. "Now, let's get some sleep."

After a moment of silence, "Tiger?"

"Hmm?"

"Did *every* sword-dancer at Umir's wish to kill you? Weren't some of them your friends?"

Beneath my blanket, I shrugged. "Friends. Rivals. Enemies. That was the way of Alimat. And there's the matter of *elaii-ali-ma* . . . I was as sworn to execute an outcast as they are; that was understood from the beginning. But no—not everyone wished to kill me. One man didn't." I smiled, remembering. "Alric. In fact, he helped me escape."

Her tone was sharp as she hitched herself up on an elbow. "Alric was there? And you didn't tell me?"

"We've been a little busy, bascha."

"But if he helped you, isn't he an outcast now?"

"Alric was never an *in*cast. He's a Northerner. He didn't make any friends by helping me, and he probably lost some—or all—of those who were there, but he didn't break any Southron vows. And it's only Alimat where the codes were so binding." I shrugged. "It was the shodo's way of fashioning true men out of worthless meat."

"A very rigorous binding."

"Are the Northern vows made on Staal-Ysta any less binding?"

No, they were not. Del's silence made that clear.

She changed the subject. "Did Alric say how Lena and the girls are?"

"Fine. Lena's expecting again." I made an indeterminate sound of derision. "You know, you'd think three daughters would be enough!"

Del settled down again. "Some men insist on sons, and their poor wives keep having babies until they get one. Even if it kills them."

"*You've* met Lena. You know she loves children. She likely wants a dozen."

"Well, yes," Del conceded.

"And it's Alric who'll have to support them. See, bascha? There are always two sides. The woman has them, which, mind you, I *don't* suggest is easy or without risk, but the man pays for them. That, too, isn't easy or without risk."

"Maybe."

"Fools," I muttered, trying to get comfortable against hard ground, "both of them."

"If it's what they want, then they aren't truly foolish."

"It's one thing if you're a farmer, bascha. Or a tradesman. But a sword-dancer? If something happens to Alric—and he's not exactly in a safe line of work—Lena's stuck with raising the children on her own." I shrugged. "Though she'd probably marry again as soon as possible."

"You mean, once she found a man to provide for her and the girls?"

"Well . . . yes." I was wary of where the conversation might be heading; you never know, with Del. "I mean, it is what many women do."

"It is what *most* women do," she said curtly. "They have no other choice."

Not being up for the verbal sword-dance, I kept my mouth shut.

"Or they could do what I did, and give their child away."

After that comment, I wasn't going to sleep any time soon. I contemplated holding my silence in case that was what Del preferred, but I just couldn't let it go. "You mean Kalle."

"Of course I mean Kalle." Del sighed, staring up at the stars. "She has a good home. Better parents than *I* could ever be—or you."

The defense was automatic. "I might be a superb father, for all you know—I just don't particularly care to find out."

"You can't be a superb father if you have no children," Del declared. Then amended it almost immediately. "That is, if you *know* you have children and don't stay around to raise them. Otherwise you're not a father at all. Just the means for making them."

Did the same apply to a woman? I decided not to bring it up for fear it was a sore spot; pointed debate is one thing, but engaging in it to hurt someone is another thing altogether. I wondered how often Del's daughter crossed her mind. She never spoke about her. "You miss her, don't you?"

Del turned over, putting her back to me. "I don't even know her, Tiger."

"I mean, you miss what you might have had."

"I made my choice before Kalle was even born. There was nothing to miss."

And yet Del had once insisted on going North to see Kalle against my preferences, though I didn't know the girl existed then; she had been driven to see her daughter six years after her birth, as if it were some kind of geas. The journey had tested us both in many different ways, had taught us about strength of will, determination, the power of the binding between us; had nearly ended in both our deaths. Kalle was around eight now, I thought. Old enough to understand her mother had given her up in a quest to execute the men who'd robbed Del of a family. And Kalle as well.

"Maybe someday," I said, purposely not mentioning that Del, by breaking *her* vows, was exiled from the North and thus from her daughter.

"What?"

"Maybe someday you'll see her again."

The tone was frigid. "And how would that come to be, do you think?"

"If Kalle came looking for you."

Del's single burst of throttled laughter was bitter. "Oh yes, they would let her come searching for a woman who has no honor, a woman exiled from her homeland. And why would Kalle wish to? She has a mother and father."

"But they aren't her blood."

She was silent a moment, then turned over to face me. Her eyes, black in the glow of the moon, were steady. "Do you believe that matters? Blood? To children whose true mother and father have disavowed them?"

"You didn't disavow Kalle."

"They will have told her I did."

I scratched at the stubble I hadn't gotten the chance to shave. "I think blood matters, yes. I think a child might wish to search for her mother. Hoolies, I went all the way to Skandi, didn't I?"

"And repudiated your family."

"The metri wanted nothing to do with the son of a disobedient daughter who dishonored her exalted Family by daring to sleep with a man well below her class."

"Your mother left Skandi to be with the man she loved, below her class or no. Do you really believe she'd have disavowed you if she was willing to go that far?"

"Doesn't matter," I dismissed. "I ended up a chula with the Salset anyway. And how in hoolies did we get onto *this* subject? We were talking about Kalle."

"You say it matters to children that they know their own blood."

"I believe that, yes."

"Does it matter to men or women that they know their own children?"

"You're the one who dragged me all the way into the ice and snow so you could see Kalle again, bascha! I would say yes to that as well, based on your example."

Del did not answer. When I realized she didn't mean to, I shut my eyes and, when I could slow my thoughts, gave myself over to sleep.

Chapter 26

*B*reeze becomes wind. Wind becomes gust. Gust becomes storm:
simoom. The sky is heavy with sand, the sun eclipsed, occluded by
curtains of it, pale as water, hard as ice. At the edges of the Punja it scours
the earth of vegetation; in the Deep Desert, where the tribes take care to protect themselves, it stings but does not strip; to strangers, wholly innocent but
thus sweeter victims, it is death. Clothing is torn away. Flesh abraded.
Eventually flayed. In the end, long past death, the ivory bones are polished
white. And buried, only freed again by yet another fickle, angry simoom,
digging up the dead.

White bones in white sand. Fingerbones scattered, the vertebrae, the
toes. The skull remains, but lower jaw is lost. Teeth gleam, that once were
hidden by lips.

I walk there, find them: pearls of the desert. Out of boredom, I begin to
gather them, to arrange them against the flat sand. Not many left. The
skull, lacking half its jaw; upper arm, forearm; the ladder of ribs. The
knobby-ended thigh. I reassemble the pieces and stare at the puzzle, wondering who and what it might have been, when it wore flesh.

I sit back, studying the forgotten remnants of a living being. Then pick
up the curving, fragile short rib. Close my hand upon it.

Over the skull, as I watch, flesh grows. Hollows are filled, angles
coated, like moss on a rock. A face stares up at me, though it lacks a lower
jaw. Even without eyes, I know her.

"Time runs away," she says. "You must be faster, if you choose to catch it."

Her words are clear despite deformation. "And if I don't?" I ask.

"It is best to be the hunter, not the prey. The prey perishes."

"Unless it escapes."

"But you will not."

Sobering pronouncement, especially from a woman dead a month, a year, a decade. "If I'm to find you," I say, "how about a hint?"

"The answer is in your bones."

I hold up the rib. "Yours are more accessible."

The upper lip, lacking a lower, achieves only half a smile. "Your bones know where to find mine."

I replace the rib in the collection on the sand. "And if I am to sacrifice flesh in order to hear them? To become like you?" I hold up mutilated hands. "Why would I wish to? I have already donated two fingers."

"Count mine," the woman says, who lacks even hands.

I smile wryly. "Point taken."

"The bones know. Listen. Then come and find me."

And the flesh retreats, and the woman says no more.

"The bones know," I echoed.

"What?" Del asked.

I blinked into chilly dawn. "What?"

"What did you mean? The bones know what?"

"What bones?"

She sat up, folding back blankets. "The bones you were talking about." Del picked a stray hair out of pale eyelashes. "I hope you aren't referring to the fingerbone necklet Oziri gave you. Because if you are, it means I'm going to have to kill you."

I grunted, scrubbing at an itchy, sleep-creased face. The sun was barely up, peering over the blade of the horizon.

"Find me," she had said once. Or twice. Maybe thrice. *"And take up the sword."*

"The bones know," I declared, though mostly it was distorted by a tremendous yawn. "Mine, though, not those." Awareness coalesced. "Oh, hoolies, not that thrice-cursed dream again!"

Del crawled out of her bedroll, untangling twisted burnous from around her hips. "If we didn't have so much to do today, I'd tell you to go back to sleep. Maybe next time you woke up you'd make more sense."

I frowned. "What do we have to do today?"

Del laced up sandals. "Rescue Nayyib."

I watched her walk off, hunting privacy. I grumbled a protest, yawned widely again, contemplated going back to sleep. My bones ached.

My eyes flew open. "Bones." I sat up, threw back covers. All I wore was my dhoti, since I'd neglected to grab my burnous back at the bathhouse. That left me with an expanse of flesh tanned a deep coppery-brown, with the fine hairs bleached bronze-gold. I couldn't see any bones. Not naked ones. Just the lines and angles covered by muscle and flesh. I knocked on a kneecap, then inspected an elbow, since they were closer to the surface. "Is there anything any of you have to tell me? Like, how it is I'm supposed to find this woman?" Or whatever she was, buried in the sand.

For all they supposedly knew the answer, my bones remained stubbornly silent. Muttering, I pulled on my own sandals, crossgartered them up my calves, then got up and limped off to make my own morning donation even as Del returned from hers.

"Don't take long," she called. "I want to get started."

Not something a man wants to hear first thing in the morning when he's only barely awake. "It'll take as long as it takes," I muttered, scowling at the sunrise.

Del had everything packed and the horses loaded by the time I returned, reins in her hands; and no, I had not taken that long. She was clearly impatient to get going.

"Hold your horses," I said, wondering if she'd get the joke.

She didn't. "According to you, we could reach Umir's today if we leave early enough."

"And we will reach Umir's today, even if we leave after we eat."

"We can eat on the way." She had packed my things, leaving behind only my harness, sword, and knife. Ready to go.

I wasn't. I picked up the knife, went over to a spike-fronded plant, cut off a flat, wide, thorn-tipped leaf. "You weren't in this much of a hurry last night."

"Last night we couldn't do anything but sleep. This morning we can . . . Tiger, what are you doing?"

Methodically I trimmed the sharp tip from the leaf, then carefully slipped the knife blade into the plump edge and slit the leaf from top to bottom, peeling them apart. I now had two halves, turgid with pale green sap. I turned over one half of the leaf and began to smear the greasy sap over my shoulder. Once worked into skin, it was colorless.

"Tiger—"

"If you want to save time," I interrupted, "you might cut off some leaves and give me a hand."

"What *is* it, and why are you doing that?"

"Alla oil," I explained. "The same stuff you put on your gelding's pink skin, remember? It protects it from sunburn."

Del, who had only seen alla oil mixed with a paste in cork- or wax-stoppered pots, not in its pure form, was surprised. "Oh. But why are *you* putting it on?"

"Because I'm fresh out of burnouses, and the last time I made this trek to Umir's, I arrived with at least one layer of skin peeling off. I'd just as soon skip the experience this time." I dropped the depleted half of leaf, began to work with the other. "Gee, bascha, I can think of a lot of women who'd just love to spread oil all over me. Have you grown immune to my charms? I did bathe yesterday." I reconsidered. "Well, *half* of me got bathed. I'll let you do the clean half. And you might want to put some on your face, even with the hood."

Del shook herself out of her reverie and bent to cut off leaves. I watched her. Clearly the body was present, but the thoughts were not.

"*Have* you grown immune to my charms?"

With great concentration she slit the leaf open, frowning. "What?"

"You're not listening to a word I say, are you?"

She flicked a glance at me, then walked around behind me and slapped the leaf sap-down on my back. "I want to get going. We can talk on the way." Strong fingers began to rub oil into my skin.

She wanted to eat on the way, talk on the way. I suppose I was lucky she hadn't insisted I piss on the way. "Fine," I said tersely.

After that we worked in silence, which seemed to suit Del. Me,

I just got grumpy. It's a sad thing when a dead woman's bones are more talkative than a living woman's mouth.

I insisted we stop briefly at the big oasis at which Alric and I had spent the night. Del clearly wanted to continue, but she'd learned that in the desert one never passes up the chance to refill botas and rest the horses.

She did, however, protest as I pulled up at the outskirts of the oasis, taking time to mark the other travelers present. "What are we waiting for?"

"Oh, I don't know—maybe checking to see if any sword-dancers are here," I remarked pointedly. "We ride straight in without looking and I could end up dead in very short order, and *then* where would your precious Neesha be?"

Del was annoyed, but she shut her mouth on further protest.

"There's a spring about halfway in. Follow the main path. Keep your eyes open. I'll take the perimeter, then come in from the other side. All right?"

She nodded, giving the gelding a touch of her heels. Sighing, I reined the stud aside and began to reconnointer as I rode the perimeter of the big oasis.

I did not see anyone lying in wait for me, but that didn't mean no one who might challenge me was absent. I aimed the stud down the center path leading toward the spring and remained mounted. Being ahorse gives a man an advantage, usually. Being atop the stud gives me a huge advantage always, as he doesn't take kindly to assailants rushing up at him, even if his rider is the target.

Of course, I didn't know any sword-dancers stupid enough to do such a thing. We—they—aren't assassins, though we will take on death-dances depending on circumstances; the goal is the ritual and the challenge, not out and out murder.

Then again, there were no guarantees all sword-dancers would adhere to that unspoken custom. Me killing Musa in a dance had proven to all witnesses that out and out murder might in fact be easier. Of course, supposedly Umir wanted me alive, but I suspected there'd be a few sword-dancers willing to forgo the reward simply for the pleasure of killing me.

I rode down the path, poised for attack. There was a scattering of wagons here and there, with unhitched dray animals resting quietly in such shade as palm trees offer; half-dressed children running around, heedless of the heat—why is it we notice it more when we're adults?—and burnous-clad men and women visiting in small groups, exchanging tales of their travels, describing plans for when they arrived at their destinations. Someone was playing a reed pipe; the thin, wailing melody cut the air. No fires, as there had been the evening Alric and I stayed, merely fire rings with quiet coals hoarded against the evening meal.

As I rode up, Del was at the spring watering the gelding. He had lost his brilliant red tassels at the Vashni encampment, where someone had presented Del with a browband of dangling leather thongs, ornamented with blue beads. He still looked rather silly, especially with the black paint around his eyes, but not as ridiculous as he had wearing Silk's crimson tassels.

She had watered herself as well as her horse and had braided her hair into a single thick plait. To tie it off she'd robbed the gelding of one thong; blue beads clacked quietly against each other when she moved her head. They matched her eyes.

"All right," I said in answer to her expression, "so we didn't run into any trouble. But we *might* have." I dropped off the stud and let him nose his way in past the gelding, urging him aside with an absent nipping motion of his mouth.

Del handed me a dripping gourd ladle. "I didn't say anything."

I drank, swallowing heavily, not caring when water splashed down my bare torso to dampen my dhoti. I now wore a gritty layer of fine dust sticking to the alla oil from head to toe. So much for the half a bath in Julah.

"You didn't have to." I handed the gourd back. "I can read your expression: Hurry up; let's go; stop wasting time. And *don't* try to tell me none of those comments passed through your mind. I know better."

Del did not attempt it, though clearly she was irritated. "You said Umir's place wasn't far from here."

"We'll make it well before sundown."

"Then hand me your empty botas," she said, "and I can fill them." Because, I knew, it would speed things up.

Shaking my head, I unhooked and handed her two flaccid botas. The others I unloaded and dipped down via tie-ropes into the water, soaking the rough sacking that formed an outer casing for the leather. While wet it helped cool the water, but it wouldn't stay that way for long beneath the sun. And since I doubted Umir would be much interested in replenishing our supplies, and Nayyib might have none as we departed, we needed to conserve.

"You're filthy," Del commented, sounding somewhat conciliatory— if you want to call being told you're dirty a peace offering. "You could wash off here, cool down a little."

"It'll strip off too much of the oil." I stood, botas dripping, and began to tie them back onto the stud's saddle. "And I doubt you'd allow me the time to go bargain for a burnous."

"If the oil is working . . ." Wisely, she let it trail off.

I took the refilled botas from her, tied them on. "Let's go, basha. We're burning daylight."

I suspect she knew I was not pleased. But she didn't ask why or suggest I shouldn't be; she simply mounted the gelding and allowed me to take the lead as we rode out of the oasis.

Umir's place wasn't far, and we did arrive well before sundown. There were no gates, merely an arched opening in the white-painted walls, and I pulled up in front. "Whatever happens," I said, "you've got my back."

"What are you planning to do?"

"Ride up to his front door and ask for Nayyib." I set the stud into a walk.

"Tiger, be serious."

"I am being serious. Sometimes the only way to get what you want is to ride up to the front door and ask."

"Umir may set some sword-dancers on you!"

"Or not." I rode under the archway and into the paved courtyard with its tiled fountain. "Do you want the kid or not?"

Del kept her mouth shut. She held the gelding a few steps behind the stud, undoubtedly examining every visible nook and cranny in Umir's walled gardens. I suspected she had unsheathed and now held the sword across her saddlebow. That belief was confirmed when I caught a metallic flash of light thrown against the white-painted walls.

I halted the stud beside the fountain, marking how much room there was for him to pivot and take off if given the order. Del knew better than to crowd him, so there was no chance of a collision. I reached down to the pouch behind my right leg and undid the thong, flipping back the flap.

"Umir!" I shouted, as the stud rang a shod hoof off courtyard pavers. "Umir the Ruthless!"

As expected, it was a servant who came out to see what the ruckus was all about.

I greeted him politely. "Now, go fetch your master. Tell him we have business to transact, he and I."

The servant opened his mouth to refuse—I looked about as disreputable now as I did when Rafiq and friends had brought me in—then thought better of it. He departed.

After making us wait just long enough to notice, Umir put in an appearance. He wore a costly gold-striped robe, gem-weighted belt, soft kidskin house slippers. His expression was austere. "I do not conduct business out here in the heat and dust." His eyes assessed my condition, found it lacking. "I am a man of refinement."

Cheerfully, I told him what he could do with his refinement. "You have someone here, Umir. A young man, name of Nayyib. In fact, you're very likely guesting him in the same room I occupied. Have you replaced the bedframe, yet, or is it still missing a leg?"

"I have no guests at present," Umir retorted. "All of the sworddancers have left to look for you."

"Well, too bad for you I decided to come here on my own. Makes them all look kind of bad, doesn't it? Especially after I outdanced Musa." I flicked a glance past him, toward the depths of the house. "We've come for Nayyib. Have someone saddle his horse while someone else escorts him out here."

"Why should I do any such thing, Sandtiger?"

"Because you want your book back."

His eyes sharpened. "You have it? With you?"

I reached into the pouch, closed my hand on the cover, and dragged it out.

The tanzeer took a hungry step forward. "*Give* it to me!"

I smiled. "Nayyib first."

Umir turned and snapped out an order to an invisible servant. Then he swung back. "Let me have it."

I rested the fat book atop the saddle pommel. "Not until the kid is brought out here and is mounted on his horse."

"You don't have any idea what that book is!" Umir said. "Don't be a fool—let me have it!"

"No wonder you don't conduct business out here," I observed. "The sun boils yours brains."

"The boy is being brought!"

"Fine. Once he's mounted and on his way, you'll get your book back."

A white indentation circling Umir's mouth appeared on his face. Pale eyes were icy with anger. "Do you expect this to lift the reward I've placed on you?"

"As I understand it, the reward was for my return—alive. Well, here I am. How about you pay up?"

"Pay *you* the reward?"

"Call it a delicious irony," I suggested. I traced with two fingers the scuffs in the leather binding. "The *Book of Udre-Natha*." I turned back the cover, began to riffle pages. "Interesting."

"Don't touch it!" Umir cried. "You'll soil the pages!"

I pinned down a page with a forefinger. "What do you suppose this says?"

"Don't read it!" He glared up at me. "Not that you could. I doubt you can read your own language."

"Just a big, dumb sword-dancer, am I?" I shrugged. "Ah, well. We can't all be born tanzeers."

"Chula," he spat.

I continued turning pages. "Hmmm . . . what do you suppose *this* means?"

Umir couldn't control himself. "Stop it! Stop it!" Hands reached out. "Give it to me!"

I looked beyond him as I saw movement in the doorway. Nayyib, escorted by Umir's servant, exited the house. His near-black hair was sticking up all over his head as if he'd been rousted from a nap. In fact, his eyes looked a little bleary, too. Had Umir drugged him?

I looked at the tanzeer. "Horse."

"Coming," he retorted.

And so it was, as another servant led the bay around from the stable block. Bridled and saddled, saddlepouches and botas tied on, ready to go.

I glanced at Nayyib. He was in a sad way, blinking woozily out at the sun-washed courtyard. Umir's little joke, to drug the boy. And neither Del nor I could chance giving him a hand, or we'd endanger the entire rescue. "You," I began, "have caused me no small amount of trouble. How about you get up on your horse and head out of here? *Now.*"

Nayyib nodded vaguely, scrubbing vigorously at his stubbled face. But didn't move.

I pointed. "That horse right there."

"Neesha," Del said, still waiting behind me. The tone was a complex combination of relief, concern, and command. And something I couldn't identify.

Umir glared at me. "The book."

"When the boy is mounted and heading out of here."

Nayyib finally bestirred himself to walk haphazardly to his horse and stick a foot in the stirrup. With great effort he pulled himself up. I heard the sound of a burnous seam ripping as he fell into the saddle. I wondered if I'd have any teeth left by the time we exited the courtyard. Already my jaw ached from clenching it.

"Go," Del told him, as Nayyib lifted reins.

The stud, taking a closer look at the bay, suddenly filled the courtyard with a ringing neigh. I winced.

Del's voice again: "Neesha. Go."

Neesha went.

"You too, bascha." I heard retreating hoofs clopping agains the pavers. Then I smiled down at Umir. "Your book."

I thought he might send a servant to take it from me. But

Umir came himself, lower lip caught in white teeth as he reached up for it.

"I've locked it closed," I told him, "for safety." I handed over the book. "It may take you a few weeks or years, but eventually you'll figure out how to open it."

Eyes wide with alarm, Umir attempted to undo the latch holding the book closed. "No—*no*—"

"A little insurance," I remarked, "in case you felt like trying a spell on me when I wasn't looking."

He hugged the book to his chest, staring up at me. "But—how did you do this? It requires a spell to lock it!"

"Let's just say I picked up a few things while visiting an island paradise." I tossed him a jaunty wave as I backed the stud toward the opening in the wall. "Happy reading, Umir."

Outside the walls, I found Del and Nayyib waiting. I motioned them to ride on as I headed past them.

Del's face was white. "I can't believe you did that."

"What—give him the book? Why not? It worked, didn't it? Nayyib-Neesha is now our guest instead of Umir's." I glanced at the boy. "Are you drugged? Did Umir drug you?"

Owl-eyed, he shook his head.

Suspicion stirred. "Drunk?"

His tone was excessively grave. "I believe so, yes."

I swore deeply and decisively.

Del was still stuck on the book. "I thought you said it contains magic spells."

"It contains a number of things, including magic spells. It's a pretty amazing book, actually."

"And you gave it to *Umir?*"

"Well, I'd read it already." I grinned at her. "What did you think I was doing all day when you were asleep in bed?"

Del was stunned. "You read that whole book in an afternoon?"

"Just a little trick I picked up in Skandi." I took a hard look at Nayyib. "Are you sober enough to stay on your horse?"

"I believe so, yes."

"Do you know where the oasis is from here?"

"I believe so, yes."

"That's where we're going."

Nayyib nodded amiably. "All right." Then a hiccup emerged, attended by a modest belch.

I planted the flat of my palm against my brow. "Gods save me from a sandsick woman and a drunk boy!"

Del scowled at me. "I am not sandsick, and he's not a boy."

"But he's drunk."

Nayyib offered, "I believe so, yes."

"Oh, hoolies," I groaned. "Maybe I should take my sword to him. Or go on ahead and let him find his own way to the oasis. I only might have been killed in there getting him free, and it turns out he's drunk. Drunk!"

"Neesha," Del said gently, "I would be quiet now."

"All right." He gifted her with a luminous smile and a worshipful stare from those melting, honey-brown eyes. "You're so beautiful."

"Oh, hoolies," Del muttered.

Chapter 27

We managed to get the boy to the oasis. Or, rather, *Del* managed to get the boy to the oasis; I was so disgusted by his condition I refused to have anything to do with him. He managed to stay aboard his horse, which was all that mattered to me, and upon finding a quiet little place at the oasis that we might call our own for an hour or two, I dismounted and led the stud off to the spring. I left Del to deal with the kid.

Which maybe wasn't the wisest thing in the world to do, in view of his obvious infatuation, but I wasn't in any mood to put up with either of them. And since I knew Del had no tolerance for drunkenness, I doubted she was any more entranced with Nayyib than I was. The main thing was, he was free of Umir and my debt was repayed. Del and I could now get on about our business.

I was heading back to the trio of palm trees when I met Del leading her gelding and Nayyib's bay. "Did you get him settled all safe in his own little bed?"

Del, pausing, shot me a hard glance. "You might have a little sympathy for him."

"I just risked my life for a drunken kid! Why should I have any sympathy for him?"

"Umir could have killed him."

"Umir wanted his book back too much for that."

"Which you *gave* him."

"In exchange for the boy. The one *you* were so all-fired determined to rescue. Well, he's rescued. He can stay here and sleep it off, and you and I can get on with our lives."

She seemed startled. "I don't want to leave him here."

"Why not?"

"He's drunk."

"He can sleep it off."

"What if he gets sick?"

"*I* never died from it." I paused. "Neither did you, when you got drunk on Vashni liquor."

Color flooded her face. "We are not discussing me."

"Maybe we should."

"Why? This has nothing to do with me!"

"He's not a stray kitten, bascha, or a puppy with a broken leg, or even an orphan sandtiger cub—though you might not be so thrilled with the idea of saving baby sandtigers, now, after our last meeting with one. He's a grown man; he can take responsibility for his own binges."

Del's eyes narrowed. "You *are* jealous."

I sighed with long-suffering patience. "I think not."

"If you weren't, you'd have nothing against helping him."

"Rescuing him isn't helping?"

"He spent days nursing us both after the sandtiger attack, and weeks with me at the Vashni encampment."

"Yes, I'm aware of that."

"Yet you want to just ride off and leave him here to fend for himself when the gods know *who* might try to rob him."

"Sometimes that's what happens when you get drunk. It's called a learning experience."

"And I'm learning a little more about you just now, aren't I?" She clucked to the horses and started to move them out. "Do whatever you like, Tiger. I'm staying here with Neesha at least until morning."

I watched her disappear between two wide horse butts as she led them down the path. I found the image extremely appropriate, in view of her behavior.

Aloud, I said, "I think this was the most ridiculous argument we've ever had." I patted the stud's face. "And we've had a few."

Being a very wise horse, he did not comment.

Nayyib was sound asleep when I got back to the little encampment. Del had unloaded gear and set out his bedroll; he lay sprawled upon it on his back with one bent arm flung across his eyes. I contemplated the rest of him, which was partially hidden beneath his burnous. But the legs were free of encumbrance, and one shoulder, and a forearm. Not a big man, not like me, but not small, either. His coloring was Southron, including the big brown eyes that he used to such advantage, curse him. A good-looking kid, no doubt, if still a tad soft around the edges; and certainly closer to Del in age than I was. Maybe that's why she wanted to mother him. She couldn't do it to me.

Not that she'd ever indicated she wanted to.

Scowling, I turned my attention to the stud, pulling off pouches, saddle, and blankets. I had thought to ride on after a rest, believing the oasis too obvious if Umir sent anyone after us or if there happened to be sword-dancers in the vicinity, but there was not much time before sundown. This place offered water, a little shade, safety in numbers.

Or maybe just more witnesses than usual.

I hobbled the stud, grained him, draped the halter-rope over one of the spiky bark segments sheathing the bole of the nearest palm tree. Someone else had built a modest fire ring not far from Nayyib's unconscious body, but we lacked kindling for it, and I didn't feel like going on a lengthy hunt for wood. Over the years pickings had become very slim near the oasis, so that most people on wagons carried wood with them if they wanted a fire, and a pot of embers they kept alive by feeding it twigs regularly. Del and I didn't pack that heavy; if there was no wood for a fire, or circumstances warranted it was safer to go without, we didn't bother.

I didn't bother now. I just set up my own little area with upside down saddle, drying blankets spread next to it, and bedding unrolled. I shed the harness and sword and set the blade within reach.

Then I lay down in a posture very similar to the kid's, if without the accompaniment of liquor fumes, and let myself drift.

Del came back a little later. Eyes closed, I listened as she finished untacking her gelding and Nayyib's, hobbled them, told them to behave themselves, then crunched over to where the kid lay.

"He's alive," I remarked.

She didn't answer. She just arranged her own bedding—closer to him than to me—and settled down.

"We'll spend the night, all right? Make sure he's alive in the morning. Then we'll go."

There was no reply. Swearing under my breath, I rolled over onto one hip and pulled the corner of a blanket over my face. With one hand draped across the hilt of my sword, I went to sleep. If she was so concerned about the kid, Del could keep watch for any stray sword-dancers looking to get some of Umir's reward money.

I woke up to morning when I heard the sound of a body moving nearby. My hand locked around the sword hilt, lifted the blade even as I sat upright—and discovered Nayyib staggering off from our little camp with the frenzied focus of a man in dire need of relief. Since it was very likely his head, bladder, *and* belly were ready to burst, I hoped he found it in time.

Dropping the sword back onto my bedroll, I arched backward to stretch my spine and shoulders. Del, coming out of the cocoon of blankets between me and the kid's bedding, squinted at the early sunlight. Not far from our camp a danjac brayed and was answered by another, which began a whole chain of ear-shattering morning greetings from one end of the oasis to the other. No one could have slept through that.

Del finger-combed hair off her face as I crawled out of bed and stood. Across the oasis other bodies were doing the same, murmuring to one another as the day began.

I bent and picked up the sword. "I think the kid's got the right idea—" I yawned. "—though I don't believe I'm in quite the same distress. Be back in a bit."

Nodding, Del gathered up horse buckets and headed for the spring. Everyone carried water to their animals first thing in the morning, since to take livestock to the spring would form a milling mass of thirsty, impatient animals all insisting they deserved to drink first. Much safer to do it this way.

When I got back to the camp, I found Nayyib standing near his bedroll, staring at mine and Del's as if he had no idea who they belonged to. He heard me coming and turned sharply. Momentary alarm faded.

"Oh," he said.

"Yes, oh. It's us. Or did you forget what happened yesterday afternoon?"

"I think I have forgotten *all* of yesterday, not just the afternoon." He scooped up a bota, unstoppered it and took a long pull. The last mouthful he turned and spat out. "Yeilkth," he remarked— or something like it. He backhanded excess moisture from his jaw and looked at me. "What happened?"

"We rescued you."

"Oh." He nodded vaguely. "Good."

Near-black hair stood up in clumps all over his head. Stubble darkened the hollows beneath his cheeks, enhancing the steep, oblique angles of the bones above them. He had the look of a slightly disreputable but appealing young man coupled with boyish innocence down to perfection. But the honey-brown eyes, I saw with a stab of satisfaction, were bloodshot, and his color was slightly off.

"Bright day," I commented cheerfully.

Nayyib squinted.

"Feels like it'll be a warm one." I set down the sword, then gathered up my bedding and began to shake it out.

Nayyib very carefully sat down on his own and squirted more water into his mouth, then soaked his hair and let droplets run down his face.

I spread my blankets, began rolling them up. "You probably won't feel much like riding today, huh?" He scrunched up his face thoughtfully as he slicked hair back into the merest shadow of obedience.

"Probably better if you stayed here, waited another day." I tied thongs around my bedroll. "No reason to get in a rush. Del and I'll make our goodbyes and head on out."

That got his attention. "Head out?"

"We've got business to attend to." I set the bedroll by my saddle, checked the condition of the saddle blankets. Dry. "Del and I." Just to make it clear who the "we" meant. "I imagine you've got things to do, too."

"Not really."

Figures. "Well, I imagine something will come up."

Del was back with the buckets. Nayyib immediately stood up, took a somewhat wobbly sideways step to regain his balance, then gallantly offered to assist her.

She took one look at his face and smiled. "No, but thank you. Tiger can help me. Why don't you sit back down—or *lie* down—and rest?"

Recognizing an order disguised as casual comment, I took one of the buckets from her. "He's a little worse for the wear this morning," I remarked cheerfully as she and I hiked over to the horses. "But he'll get over it by tomorrow, and then he can be on his way."

Del set the bucket down in front of her gelding. "Why don't we have him come with us?"

Startled, I nearly tripped over my bucket as I put it down in front of the stud. "What for?"

"He said he wanted to take lessons from you."

"Yes, but I never said I wanted to give them."

"But that's what you're going to do. Give lessons. Remember?" She patted the gelding's neck. "The plan is for you to resurrect Alimat and take on students. At least, that's what you told me. Has that changed?"

"No." Though I wasn't certain when it might come to be, since we were a bit busy trying to keep me alive.

"Then you've got your first student in Neesha." She grabbed the bucket, shoving the gelding's nose away, and lugged it over to Nayyib's horse.

"That sounds like a very tidy arrangement—from your point of view—but maybe I'm not ready to start lessons yet."

"Why not? Aren't we heading to what's left of Alimat? Couldn't he help us rebuild it?"

I glanced over my shoulder at Nayyib and saw him lying on his bedroll with an arm draped over his eyes once again. I lowered my voice. "What *is* it with you, Del? Why do you care so much about someone who's practically a stranger?"

Her face was set, though her tone was pitched as quiet as mine. "I told you, he helped me when I was ill. I would have died without his help."

"Does this mean we have to adopt him?"

She cut her eyes in Nayyib's direction, then stepped close to me. Since Del is six feet tall, you tend to notice when she gets that close. "Why don't you just say what's on your mind, Tiger? That you'd rather he didn't ride with us because you don't want a good-looking man my own age spending time with me."

I ground it out between my teeth. "That's not it."

"Then what *is* it?"

"I like it the way things are. You and me. *Just* you and me. It has nothing to do with the fact he's a good-looking kid with eyes that can likely get any woman to spread her legs for him with the first puppy-dog glance and who just happens to be your own age."

A wry male tone intruded. "Really?"

Del and I both turned as one. Nayyib stood three strides away, legs spread, arms folded against his chest. "I wasn't asleep—*or* unconscious—and I'm not deaf. I don't particularly care to eavesdrop, either, but when one hears his name mentioned, one tends to pay attention." His brows arched up as he met my gaze. "Do you think I really can get *any* woman to spread her legs for me?" He touched a finger to skin below one eye. "With these?"

I said, "Not the way they look today."

His rueful grin was swift, exposing white teeth; at least he could laugh at himself.

"Maybe by tonight," Del said thoughtfully.

Outraged, I glared at her.

"Really?" Nayyib repeated, sounding more than a little hopeful.

"Really," Del confirmed.

"This is ridiculous," I announced. "We're standing here talking about how this kid can get women to sleep with him when there are any number of people who want to kill me?"

Del seized the opening. "Which is *another* good reason for him to come along."

"Why, bascha? He's not a sword-dancer. I don't think he'd be much of a challenge." I glanced at Nayyib. "Hey, I'm telling it the way I see it."

He nodded. "Fair enough. But if you taught me, maybe I *could* be good enough to provide something of a challenge. I do have some skill, you see . . . though actually you never have, have you? Seen my sword skill." He shrugged. "So I believe you're making assumptions with no evidence to shore them up."

"Stay out of this," I suggested.

"Why? It's *about* me."

"Because you've already proven you're unreliable," I retorted.

"How has he proven that?" Del demanded.

"Hoolies, bascha, he got drunk while he was a prisoner!"

Del's disdain was manifest. "*That's* your evidence?"

"I got drunk," Nayyib said, "because Umir felt I might know some things about you that *he* wanted to know. Something to do with a book. But I didn't know anything about any book, nor do I know anything about you—except what everyone in the South knows, and Umir already knows all that, too."

"What does that have to do with you getting drunk?" I asked, failing to see any point.

"Because after it became evident that beating me wouldn't gain him his information, he tried another tactic. He had a supposedly sympathetic servant slip me a jug of—something. I don't know what it was, but it was certainly more powerful than anything *I've* tasted before. And while I lack your vast experience with liquor—you are old enough to be my father, after all, and thus you have the advantage of *significant* additional years—I have made the aquaintance of it in various forms." He shrugged. "It made me very, very drunk."

Del was furious. "Umir had you beaten?"

I was beginning to be intrigued in spite of myself. "Did you tell him anything?"

"No, because you arrived before he could ask me anything. But it would have gained him nothing anyway. I *don't* know anything more about you, or whatever this book is."

"The *Book of Udre-Natha*," I said, "is a grimoire. It contains all manner of Things Magical: spells, incantations, conjurations, recipes for summoning demons, notes made by men who studied it for years, and so on and so forth. Pretty much anything you want to know about magic is in that book."

The kid had the grace to look stunned. "And you *gave* it to him?"

"Gave it *back* to him," I clarified, "and yes, because it was the only way to get you free."

Nayyib looked somewhat diminished, losing the cocky stance as he stared at me in surprise. "You gave it to him for me?"

"I did."

But confidence reasserted itself. "Why didn't you just ride in there and take me? Without the book. I mean, you are *you*. Umir couldn't have stopped you."

"He might have."

"Stopped the Sandtiger?"

"I'm eminently stoppable," I told him. "Permanently, even. What, did you think I was immortal?"

His chin rose and assumed a stubborn tilt. "You've never yet been killed."

"Well, no, since I wouldn't be standing here involved in this ludicrous conversation if I had been. But 'not yet' doesn't mean 'never.'"

Del said, "Which is another reason Neesha should come with us. So 'not yet' doesn't become 'now.'"

I stared at her. "You really want him to come along."

"I've said that several times, I believe. Yes."

"Fine." I stalked past the kid. "Get your sword."

He turned. "What?"

"Get your sword." I bent and picked up my own. "Let's see just what kind of skill you have that I haven't seen. And then maybe my assumptions will be proven by evidence."

Nayyib was aghast. *"Now?"*

I smiled. "Why not?"

His mouth opened, then closed. Opened again. "Because . . . now is not a good time."

"You don't always get to choose your times, Nayyib-Neesha. Let that be your first lesson." I indicated his bedroll and pouches. "Your sword."

"I can't," he said faintly.

"I thought you wanted me to teach you."

His color was fading. "I do."

"Well then?"

"Because now . . . because now—" He swallowed heavily, looking pained. "—I'm going to be sick." He turned, staggered two steps, bent over—and promptly suited action to words.

"Gee," I marveled, "I've never had quite *that* effect on anyone before."

Del scowled. "Are you happy now?"

I grinned. "Yep." Particularly since it's hard for anyone, even a pretty kid like Nayyib, to look particularly attractive to a woman while he's bringing up the inside of his belly.

She picked up an empty bucket and slung it at me. "Go fill this up. The horses need more water."

I caught it, laughing, and took it and my sword with me to the spring, whistling all the way.

Chapter 28

Some while later, Nayyib presented himself to me. He had washed, dusted himself off, neatened his hair. His eyes looked better, and his color was also improved. I had readied the stud and now occupied myself with splitting alla leaves and applying a new coating of oil, waiting for Del to finish tacking out and loading the gelding. It was taking a suspiciously long time, and when Nayyib stopped in front of me and drew himself up, I knew why.

I sighed and assumed a patient expression.

He didn't beat around the bush. "I would like to come with you."

I smoothed oil across the back of my neck. "We've had this conversation before."

"And you have never given me a definitive answer."

"*No* isn't definitive?"

"You haven't said 'no.' You have made objections. There's a difference."

Well, yes, there was. "You're absolutely certain you want me to teach you to be a sword-dancer."

"Yes."

"Why?"

Something in his eyes flickered briefly. It was neither doubt that he could answer nor fear that he'd answer wrong. Maybe it was merely a question he'd never expected of *me*.

The stud nosed my shoulder. I patted his muzzle, then eased his head away. "Well?"

"It's what I've wanted to be since I was very young."

I wiped alla oil across my abdomen between harness straps and began working it in. "Why?"

"My sister and I . . ." A quick smile curved his lips as he thought of her. "We made swords out of sticks. Drew circles in the sand. Eventually my mother made her spend more time in the house, so I had to dance alone. But my sister knew, and I knew, that some-day it would come to this."

"What made you choose me?"

A muscle jumped in his jaw. "I didn't, at first. There was a sword-dancer in the village, on his way to Iskandar. For the dances there two years ago." His eyes flickered again. "Do you recall?"

Did I recall? Oh, yes. With infinite clarity. Del did too; it was where she'd killed Ajani.

I tossed used leaves aside, worked at splitting a new one. "So this sword-dancer rode through your village, and you asked him for lessons?"

"Yes."

"Did he give them to you?"

"Yes. He needed money, and I offered to pay him."

I nodded, bending to work oil into thighs. "And you decided by the time he left that you wanted to challenge me."

Once again color warmed the dusky tan of his face. "I didn't mean it as a challenge. I just wanted to step into the circle with you. I knew I would lose."

I grinned lopsidedly. "Not necessarily."

"Against you? Of course."

"Nayyib, the first time I stepped into a circle against a legendary sword-dancer, I won."

"But you're you."

I straightened up. "I wasn't me *then*," I said in exasperation. "I was just a gangly seventeen-year-old kid with hands and feet too big for his body, who was underestimated by a man who should have known better. Complacence in the circle is dangerous—it nearly got him killed, and I had only a wooden sparring blade, not live steel." I shook my head, remembering Abbu's shock. I waved a depleted leaf at him. "And there, Neesha, is another lesson."

His mouth twitched in a half-smile. "Will you give me more? It would be my honor—and I have the money to pay *you*, too."

I laughed, tossing aside the leaf. I was aware of Del moving even more slowly as she prepared the gelding. Nayyib's horse was already tacked out and loaded, ground-tied some distance away. "Look . . ." I paused, thought about it briefly, gave it up. "I have every intention of reopening the school at Alimat, but not quite yet. There are a few things to settle first. If you truly want to learn—if you haven't lost interest or gotten distracted by something else by then, like a woman—come find me then."

His jaw tightened. There was nothing puppy-doggish about his eyes now; he was angry, but he was suppressing it with unexpected self-control. Some of the boyishness faded behind a harder veneer. Suddenly he wasn't a kid at all, but a man.

His voice was very quiet. "What would it take?"

"Time." And then I heard my shodo's words come out of my mouth. "There are seven levels. But there is no prescribed length of time required to reach any of those levels. It may take two years to reach the first level. You may leave after you reach it, if that is your choice—but to leave before you can walk means you'll be killed before you can even dream of running."

"And to achieve seven levels?"

I shrugged. "Few men last that long. They leave to make a living."

"You are a seventh-level sword-dancer."

"I was. I'm not anything now, other than outcast."

"*Elaii-ali-ma,*" he said. "Rafiq told me, when I asked."

"Time and oaths," I told him. "It's a demanding service, the circle. Too many believe it's about glory. Rafiq does, and it's why he'll never survive. In truth, it's mostly about honor, and oaths, and service. The elegance of the dance, the beauty of live steel. Glory comes, if you win enough, *well* enough—but that's not the point. It only *seems* like it to young men who don't want to stay in the village, get married, and father babies on the first village girl they bed."

He had controlled the anger. His voice was steady. "And if I choose to achieve the seventh level, as you did?"

"Can you afford ten years?"

He blinked. "It took you ten years?"

I bent to apply oil to my calves and shins. "No, it took me seven. But I was the first to do it that fast."

Nayyib nodded once. "Seven levels. If it requires *twelve* years, then I will give you twelve."

Del led the gelding around in front of the stud. Waited, saying nothing.

"Don't swear any oaths just yet, Nayyib," I suggested. "Not until you know what they are. Because at Alimat, the oaths you swear are for life."

He didn't shy from it, was not afraid of me. "You broke yours."

"And every sword-dancer in the South is trying to kill me."

His glance slid to Del. Quietly, he said, "There are times when certain oaths must be broken, if to keep them breaks oaths you have made to others."

So. She'd told him. It seemed the Northern bascha had been doing quite a bit of talking to the Southron boy.

Who wasn't really a boy. Just considerably younger than I.

Like Del.

He was still gazing at her. She didn't avoid it. I saw a look pass between them, though I couldn't interpret it.

Something pinched deep in my gut. Jealousy? No, not really. But an awareness that things were changing; that they would continue to change.

And Del knew nothing about my limited time. *Her* life would change, too.

I looked back at Nayyib. He said he'd give me twelve years. In twelve years, or possibly ten, I would be dead.

Abruptly I tossed away the rest of the leaf. Turned and mounted the stud. I reined him in and looked down at Nayyib, waiting for my answer. "You can come with us as far as Julah. We'll spar there, and then I'll decide."

*   *   *

The stud has a very comfortable long-walk, once he consents to settle into the gait. Too often he has a burr under his blanket, or a bee up his butt—figuratively speaking, of course—and takes it out on me. But for now he was content to just walk on, head bobbing lazily at the end of his neck. I very nearly fell asleep, until Del's voice woke me up.

"Tiger!"

I let the stud go on, twisting in the saddle to look back. Del and Nayyib had stopped some distance away and were staring at me. "What?"

"Where are you going?" Del called.

"Julah!"

"Julah's *this* way."

I reined in. "No, it's not." I pointed. "This way. South."

"That's east," she declared.

Was she sandsick? "No, it's not. This is south. Julah's this way."

Del stabbed a finger in front of her horse. "There's the road."

"That's *a* road," I told her. "Five of them meet at the oasis. This is the road to Julah."

Nayyib shook his head and said something to Del I couldn't hear.

"What?" I asked, irritated.

"It's east," he answered.

"How would *you* know? You're not from around here."

"No, but I do know my directions."

"That's not a road at all, Tiger," Del called. "Take a look."

This was ridiculous, having this pointless discussion in the middle of the desert. I looked. Blinked. Saw that indeed the stud and I were striking out across the desert with no road, trail, or track in sight.

I scowled. It *felt* right, this direction. It felt south. Or else I really had fallen asleep, and the stud had chosen his own route.

I turned him around and headed back. Felt an abrupt sense of wrongness so powerful I reined in sharply. "No," I insisted, "it's this way."

Del pointed down the road. "South. Julah. I'm not from around here, either, but I know that much."

But it was wrong. *Wrong.* I knew it. Felt it in my bones.

And abruptly I swore, remembering the dream. My bones would know, she'd said.

Del's voice, "Tiger?"

I closed my eyes tightly. Tried to reorient myself. Tried to let my lifelong sense of direction tell me which way was the correct one. Yet when I opened them again, I still felt that they were wrong and I was right, despite the evidence of the road.

Or maybe we were both right. Julah lay south, but where I was *supposed* to go lay east.

"*Find me,*" she had said. "*And take up the sword.*"

I looked at Del. "Which way is the chimney from here?"

"The chimney?"

"The rock formation we brought down when you broke your sword. When Chosa Dei fought Shaka Obre." Oziri had called it Beit al'Shahar.

Del pointed. "That way."

"West."

She nodded. So did Nayyib.

The stud and I were facing west. Del's gelding and Nayyib's bay faced south, toward Julah, with the oasis not terribly far behind them. East lay behind me, and that was the way I—or my bones—wanted to go.

Well, we don't always get what we want. I clucked to the stud and headed him toward the road. Once there, I stopped. Shuddered from head to toe.

Del's expression was concerned. "What is it?"

"I don't know. Something . . ." I shook my head, knowing how it sounded. "Something keeps telling me we need to go east. Or I do, at least."

"What's east?" she asked.

A dead woman, apparently. A scattering of bones: pearls of the desert.

"The Punja," I said.

A line appeared between her brows. "It makes no sense."

"And I agree with you wholeheartedly," I said. "All I know is, something in me wants to go east."

Nayyib, wisely keeping out of the conversation, looked past me and changed the subject. "Someone's coming."

I turned in the saddle, looking in the direction of the oasis. A cloud of dust accompanied the ride, obscuring the horizon. I noticed then that one arm was waving. A man's voice was raised over the hoofbeats of his horse.

"Wait!" he cried. "Wait!"

"Someone from the oasis?" Nayyib wondered.

"Wait!" He sounded frantic; had something happened at the oasis that required help?

"Guess we'll find out," I said. At least the distraction kept me from heading east.

The stud snorted, pawed, shifted sideways restlessly, not happy to be standing in one spot. I reined him in, had a brief discussion with him when he protested, and glanced up as the rider grew closer. I could make out his features, but I recognized none of them.

"Wait!" he called.

Then I saw the flash of steel.

I twisted, gesturing at Del and Nayyib with a sweeping left arm. "Move! Out of the way!"

As I swung back, yanking blade free of sheath, everything around me slowed. Swearing, I reined the stud back sharply, off the road, but by then it was too late. The rider neither reined in nor reined aside. With sword raised above his head, he crashed his dun horse into the stud.

Perception fragmented into shards of images, impressions. I felt the impact rock the stud, knocking him sideways. Was aware of the dun's head smashing into my left elbow, of rolling eyes and hot breath. The stud staggered, nearly went down. A flash of steel blinded me even as I tried to yank the stud's head up into the air, trying to keep him on his feet, to pivot left so I would have a clean line for my own blade. But we were too cursed close, my assailant and I, with our horses jammed together.

I dropped the reins and, cursing, hammered a fist into the dun's nose, trying to get him off me, off the stud. I saw the flash of a blade, brought up my own. In the mass of tangled horseflesh it was impossible to parry properly, but I did block the worst of the blow's impetus. Then the stud was trying to fight the dun, mouth agape, neck snaking, head swinging sideways, teeth snapping.

The dun reared, screaming. My stirrups were gone anyway; I pushed off, diving sideways, and lost my sword on the way down. I landed hard, tasted sand and blood, saw stars; I tried to scramble up, to get out of the way, but my momentum was off, and I tripped over my sword and fell. Escape was now impossible in the midst of the equine battle; I couldn't tell which way was up or down, in or out. I just rolled myself up in a tight ball, arms hooked over my head, and prayed no hoof would land on any part of my anatomy.

Dimly I was aware of shouting. Del's voice. Nayyib's. And a stranger's. The screaming was terrible, the frenzied trumpeting of an enraged stallion. I focused on it, sorted out which direction it came from, and decided to take the chance. I lunched upward from the ground, ran two steps, fell again, rolled, came up into a crouch. In the midst of the battle I saw Nayyib dart in on foot and bend, sword bared. He sliced at something, and nearly got his head smashed for his trouble. But I saw the dun go down as Nayyib leaped back out of the way, and realized what he'd done.

The rider flung himself off as his mount, hamstrung and pressured by the stud, crashed to the ground. He rolled away, scrambling even as I had, and lunged upward—only to come face to face with Del. He had lost his sword in the melee, but grabbed for his knife. Del, who still claimed her blade, used it with fierce efficiency, driving it through his belly.

The stud reared, trumpeted again, came down with both front hooves striking. I heard the sickening crunch as he smashed the dun's skull. He spun then, took two leaps away, whirled back and stood trembling, front legs twitching, tail slashing. Ribbons of sweat rolled down his flanks.

And blood.

Nayyib was there immediately. Not everyone will approach a horse in the stud's condition; probably no one should. He could easily strike again, or bite. But Nayyib caught the cheekstrap of his bridle, quickly looped the rein around his nose, then through bit shanks, and pulled it taut. He was done so quickly the stud had no chance to react. Nayyib held him there, soothing him with his voice, using the looped rein as a makeshift stud-chain.

Del was with me. "Are you all right?"

I spat blood and sand, felt grit in my teeth. Wiped a hand across my mouth and managed only to smear things around. "Fine." I tried to get up. My left leg protested vociferously. I sat back down. "Well, maybe not so fine." I inspected the sore leg. The side of my knee was scraped and sore. But what—? Oh. Yes. I recalled the dun's shoulder slamming into the stud, with my leg trapped between.

Del knelt, putting one hand on the reddened, abraded area. "Is it broken?"

"I don't think so. But I'm betting it'll color up nicely by morning." I tried again, arrived on my feet. The leg was very sore but whole. I was lucky it hadn't been crushed. "I've got to see the stud."

"Nayyib has him. He'll be fine."

I limped over anyway, talking to the stud as I approached so I wouldn't startle him. "He's cut," I said sharply.

Nayyib, still holding the stud's head, nodded. "Sword blade. Just a slash, I think, but painful."

It was in the fleshy part of the stud's left haunch, about six inches long. It wasn't deep enough to sever muscle, but it had laid the flesh back. Blood bathed his left hind.

"Oh, son," I murmured, "the bastard got you."

"It'll need stitches." Nayyib stroked the stud's nose gently even as he worked the rein. "I have silk thread in my pouches, and a needle."

The stud, bothered by dripping blood and sweat, kicked out sideways with his left hind. I shook my head. "He's not about to put up with that right now."

Nayyib nodded. "We'll need to get him down, have someone sit on his head. And tie his legs—and probably his tail—so he can't kick or blind me."

I looked at him sharply. "You?"

"I've done it before." He smiled crookedly. "When I was no longer a child playing with sticks, I dreamed of being a sworddancer in my head. What I did outside of it was work with stock; my father has a small horse farm near Iskandar."

"Then why aren't you there?" I asked. "Or do you have so many brothers he doesn't need you?"

"Oh, no, there is only me and my sister. But we had a disagreement, he and I."

"Don't tell me. You told him you wanted to be a sworddancer."

Nayyib soothed the stud with his hands and voice. "He did not approve."

I sighed, winced as I put too much weight on my aching leg. "I think about all I'm good for is sitting on his head. But he'll go down if I give him the signal; I trained him to that for sandstorms."

Nayyib looked doubtful. "After a fight?"

I considered it. Possibly not. "Let me try," I said.

Nayyib nodded.

I went to the stud's head, looked him in the eye, told him I needed him to go down, then gave him the signal: a slap on the left shoulder. He wrung his tail and made no move.

"Oh, come now," I said. "You've done this before."

Another slap, plus a prodding thumb.

Nothing. Except for a very stubborn look in his eye.

"All right, we'll do it my way," Nayyib said. "Del can mind the rope snubbing up his one leg, while I stitch." He glanced over his shoulder at Del, who had caught her gelding and Nayyib's and waited out of the way. "Can you get into my saddlepouches? There is a leather pouch in there, dyed blue. It contains medicaments. And I need you to bring me every halter rope and my spare burnous."

She nodded and turned to his horse.

Nayyib eyed me sidelong. "I've stitched men, too."

I shook my head. "Bruised, not bloodied. I'll wrap my knee later for support." And maybe my elbow as well.

His tone was coldly angry. "I have never seen anyone purposely run a horse into another. To purposely risk a mount with such brutality, just to kill another man."

I wasn't sure if he was angrier about the risk to horseflesh or human. "If you live long enough, I guess you see everything."

And then Del was back, bringing ropes, burnous, and pouch, and we forgot about dead men, dead horses, and tended a live one.

Chapter 29

*B*y Del's tense silence, I knew she was worried. It's not often you attempt to drop a stallion to the ground when he has no interest in going there. But Nayyib was right: the only way we could get the slash stitched up was to put the stud out of commission temporarily. He wasn't a man; you couldn't explain to him what needed to be done and why and expect him to agree. Nor could you get him drunk, and none of us was strong enough to knock him unconscious. So while Del and I got him unsaddled, with blankets and pouches pulled off and deposited on the ground, Nayyib calmly rigged a lip-twitch and a rope harness, winding wide strips of his spare burnous around the hemp to pad it.

"Hobble his back legs." He handed me a pair of sheepskin-padded hobbles he'd conjured from his saddle-pouches. "And bind up his tail."

Very dictatorial, Nayyib, when it came to horses. But I deferred, impressed by his confidence and quick thinking. Carefully I did as he asked, snugging the padded cuffs around both back legs. They were shorter than usual, also, meant to keep the legs closer together. A long leather thong controlled the tail, which was long enough—and strong enough—to blind a man if it slashed tough horsehair across his eyes.

"Hold him a moment," Nayyib told Del quietly, and as she took the bridle the kid efficiently set about looping padded ropes around various parts of the stud's body. "All right," he said. "Tiger, come hold his head. Del, take this rope. When I say to, pull as hard as you can."

It sound risky to me. "What will *you* be doing?"

Nayyib's smile was brief. "I'll be on the other leg. If all works well, he'll go over onto that right shoulder. Once he does, sit on his head. *Hold* him there. Use the twitch to take his mind off everything else." He glanced at Del. "Keep that rope snubbed tight. I'll stitch as fast as I can. If I'm lucky, the rear hobbles will keep him from kicking my head off."

"Then what?" I asked.

"Once I'm done, I'll clear out. Del, you'll loosen your rope. Tiger, you get off his head. He'll come up lunging, but the hobbles will hold him in place. All right?"

"Yes," Del said. I nodded.

Nayyib drew in a deep breath, moved to the stud's left fore. "Pull, Del!"

She pulled. Nayyib grabbed the left leg and folded it up. The stud flung his head, which nearly decapitated me, then went down hard on the ground, rolling onto his right shoulder as the kid had hoped. I was aware of Del working swiftly to snub and hold taut her rope. Then I plopped myself down on the stud's head up behind his ears, where the neck began, and caught hold of the rope twitch in my left hand. He was breathing hard, muscles twitching, nostrils fluttering with explosive snorts that raised puffs of dust. The visible eye rolled, displaying reddened membranes.

"Hurry up!" I gritted, gripping the twitch and bridle.

My back was to the stud's body, so I couldn't view anything Nayyib did. If I glanced to my right, I could see Del leaning against the rope crossing over the stud's neck. But mostly I watched his visible eye, balancing my weight evenly. With a knee on either side of him, one hand locked into the headstall of his bridle and the other tightening the rope twisted around his bottom lip, I realized my gehetties were in a rather perilous position. If he flung his head up, I'd likely be unmanned.

I swore again, spitting a faint sifting of dust from my mouth.

"How is your leg?" Del asked tightly.

"Ask me when we're done."

Stitching seemed to take forever. But eventually Nayyib warned us to be ready. "Del, loosen the rope just a little. When Tiger gets off his head, give the stud as much slack as you can. He'll come up hard and fast, but clumsy." He paused. "Tiger?"

"I'm ready."

"Del?"

"It's loose."

"All right, Tiger."

I let go of twitch and bridle and pushed up and away with planted legs, propelling myself forward. I rolled, crouched, stood, hopped briefly as my left leg complained. Saw Del feeding more rope, then jumping back. Nayyib was near the stud's head, freeing the twist of rope around his bottom lip. And indeed the stud came up hard and fast, lunging frenziedly. The padded rope slid from his neck and chest, pooled on the ground around his right leg. He wobbled a little, discovering his rear legs were still hobbled, then found his balance. He stuck his big head high in the air, eyeing me, then released a pent-up snort of severe annoyance that sprayed slime in all directions.

I wiped muck from my chest. "Thank you."

Nayyib held his bridle again, soothing him. Quietly he told me, "You can take those hobbles now."

Ah, and let *me* get my head kicked off. Smart kid. Smiling crookedly, I limped toward the stud's rear quarters, sliding my left hand over his spine and rump so he'd know I was there. I carefully avoided the wound, marked by a curving row of neat silk-thread stitches, then bent and quickly untied the padded hobbles and tail thong. And skipped back out of the way with alacrity as the stud took to slashing his tail in indignation.

"There now," Nayyib crooned, and led him forward. "See? Not so bad. An affront to your dignity, I do know, all this abuse, but you will survive it. You are the best of all horses, a stallion among stallions—even if you are a jug-headed ugly son of a goat."

"Hey," I protested.

"Not so bad, not so bad," Nayyib continued, leading the stud in a wide circle. "You'll have a fierce scar, you will, much like your rider. But you are *much* more handsome."

Del wandered over to my side. "He's like a horse-speaker."

I remembered the fair-haired kid we'd met years before at the kymri, a gathering of peoples in the North. "I don't think Nayyib can read their minds."

"He doesn't have to. He knows what they need. See? The stud's calming."

She was smiling. I watched her watching Nayyib.

Horses weren't the only thing the kid could handle.

Nayyib brought the stud up to me. "I would recommend we go on," he said. "The cut hasn't interfered with his muscles, so he can be ridden. But if we stay the night here, or even if we go back to the oasis, which isn't that far, he'll stiffen. Best to keep him moving."

Del glanced at me warily. "To Julah?"

I shrugged, taking the stud's reins. "Let's see what happens when I'm in the saddle again."

As Nayyib packed away his supplies again, I set about readying the stud. He was unusually subdued, as if he'd spent all of his temper and strength. Once he was saddled and loaded, I filled a canvas bucket with water from a bota and let him drink. He sucked it up greedily, lifted his dripping muzzle out of the bucket, then shoved it against my chest as if asking me to commiserate.

I smiled, scratching his jaw. "I'm sorry, old son. You didn't deserve that. It's me they want to kill, not you."

I packed away the bucket, turned to mount him, and discovered how much a half-crushed leg doesn't like being asked to bear all my weight. Swearing, I managed to make it up into the saddle, left knee throbbing. So much for the healing I'd encountered at Meteiera. I'd been told any new injuries would be mine to keep; seems like I was repeating old habits.

I turned the stud. "This way. To Julah, right?"

In concert, Del and Nayyib shook their heads.

"East?" I asked reluctantly.

"East," Del confirmed.

"What's east?" asked Nayyib.

I ran a hand over my face, trying to rein in anger and frustration. "Who in hoolies knows? Something that seems to think I need to be there." A dead woman who spoke to me in dreams. "Look, it doesn't feel *far*, whatever it is. If you two want to go on to Julah, go ahead. Maybe I'm supposed to do this alone anyway.

Del shook her head. "If you go east, I go east."

I looked at Nayyib.

He hitched one shoulder in a dismissive half-shrug. "You said I could ride with you to Julah. We're not there yet."

I sighed deeply. "Fine. Let's go east, shall we?"

East. Toward the sunrise—and whatever else might be lurking out there.

I became dimly aware of voices. Del and Nayyib were talking quietly, as if I weren't present. I felt rather as if I were waking up from a dream, except I hadn't been sleeping. I was working like a human lodestone, following the compulsion that pulled me east. For the moment that compulsion had slackened, and I glanced up at the sun. By its position, I knew we'd been riding about two hours.

Then I became aware of the surroundings. A vast ocean of cream-pale sand, sparkling with crystals afire from the sun. The Punja, the deadliest of the South's deserts.

I pulled up, stopping the stud. Del and Nayyib, reining in also, were staring at me warily. I frowned, scratched idly at facial scars, then reached to pull up a bota hanging from the saddle and slake increasing thirst.

"We need to water the horses," Del said.

I nodded as I unstoppered the bota. "Apparently I'm being allowed time to do just that. Or else whatever it is insisting I come has decided we're far enough." I knew how it sounded, but it was the only way I could think to describe it. I sucked down water, climbed down out of the saddle, easing onto my left leg, and unhooked another bota. This I emptied into the canvas bucket and let the stud drink.

"You said it wasn't far," Del remarked.

"I said it *felt* like it wasn't far. I can't say for sure." I shook my head, grimacing. "I sound sandsick. Hoolies, maybe I am."

"No." Del's voice was quiet. "You have instincts I have always trusted—and now more than instincts."

Ah yes, more. Magic. Magery. I'd used a little on Umir's book, spelling the lock, and then shied away from the idea like a spooked horse.

As the stud drank, I squinted across the expanse of sand, sheilding my eyes with the flat of one hand. The Punja had killed more people than would ever be counted, sucking the life from their bodies, scouring flesh from their bones. Whole villages had been swallowed by sand carried miles in dangerous simooms, burying all signs of life. Caravans, crossing from oasis to oasis, paying huge amounts of money to guides who knew the Punja, often disappeared despite their best efforts to anticipate the dangers. Sometimes you just can't anticipate everything.

I certainly hadn't, when Del had hired me to guide her across the Punja. I'd have never guessed a few years later we'd still be together as sword-mates, bed-mates, life-mates.

I smiled, recalling those first days. The ice-maiden from the North, summoning frigid, killing banshee storms with her magical sword. Boreal was long dead, broken and buried in the chimney formation in the mountains by Julah. Beit al'Shahar. My Northern *jivatma*, Samiel, was there as well, whole and unblemished, left behind as the chimney collapsed.

"Find me," the woman had said, *"and take up the sword."*

If the sword she meant was Samiel, why were we out here in the Punja, at least two day's ride from Beit al'Shahar? I had intitally wanted to go get the *jivatma*, if possible; it was why we'd headed for the mountains in the first place, once out of Haziz. It hadn't felt like a compulsion then, merely a plan. Something I wanted to do.

Now, here, I *needed* to do it. Yet there was no *jivatma* anywhere nearby. That I knew. So maybe I was meant to find another sword, a different sword.

Unless only the woman was here for me to find. Or what was left of her.

Shaking my head, I packed the squashable bucket away, hung empty botas back on my saddle, made to remount. Then stopped. Stood there, clinging to the stud.

"What?" Del asked.

I flung up a hand, stopping her from saying more.

Silence, save for the familiar sounds of horses. They shifted position, pawed at sand, shook manes, rattled bit shanks, snorted, chewed at the metal in their mouths. I heard nothing else.

But I *felt* it.

Abruptly I stuck my foot in the stirrup and swung aboard, ignoring the complaints of my leg. "Turn back," I said urgently. "Simoom!"

I reined the stud around. Del and Nayyib mounted quickly and turned as well.

But that was where the storm came from. Behind us before; now ahead. The first faint haze was visible along the horizon, like a wisp of ruffled silk.

"The other way!" I shouted, sinking heels into the stud. Maybe my sense of direction was forever skewed, thanks to—whatever.

We ran, but the wind and sand ran faster. The storm spilled across the land like a vast, rolling wave, filling the sky from horizon to sun. The day grew dark.

"There's no shelter!" Nayyib's voice, pitched to cut through the first whining of the wind.

No. None. In such circumstances the best bet was to put the horses down and use *them* as shelter. I suspected Nayyib's horse was trained for it, if the kid had grown up on a horse farm in the South; but then Iskandar was up near the border, more soil than sand, and he might not know much about simooms. He probably knew even less about the Punja, though he had made it to Haziz. Probably paid a guide.

No guide could help us now. The leading edge of the storm was very close, collecting gouts of sand as it howled across the land. Del's gelding probably wasn't trained to lie down—I couldn't see anyone taking a blue-eyed white horse into the Punja—and the stud, after his experience earlier in the day, would likely refuse all inducements. We didn't have time to try Nayyib's trick of cross-tying and hobbling legs.

Knowledge flickered deep in my mind. Fear followed swiftly, churning in my belly.

Not me, I said. *Don't expect* me *to do this*.

But of course something did. Something inside. Something that had been teased back into awareness with the writings in Umir's book, full of spells, incantations, conjurations. Despite what I'd said, I hadn't quite read it all, but enough. More than enough.

I could build us shelter, the way I had conjured a boat on ioSkandi, to search for Del.

If I didn't do so, we'd likely all die.

Swearing, I reined the stud in. Del and Nayyib hadn't seen me and kept riding. But I had more to think about than when or if they'd realize where I was. I turned the stud loose and swung to face the storm.

It was magnificent and malevolent. Even the sun was shrouded, hazed by the towering storm. By the time I counted to ten on my hands—well, to eight—it would have us.

I went into my head, thinking. Wind was air. It was air that carried sand. Air was the impetus. If the air itself could be used, could be manipulated, I could make us shelter.

I wore no burnous, only dhoti, sandals, harness, and a sword across my back. It was not a *jivatma*. Was just a sword. But I was a *sword-dancer*, and in my hands a sword, any sword, could be made to conquer anything.

I unsheathed. Slitted my eyes against wind and sand. Shut the hilt in both hands as firmly as I could and raised the sword. Set the blade into the air over my head. Felt the wind buffet it, sand grains hissing against steel. I closed my eyes, bit into my lip. Even as I stood there, my flesh was abrading. Chest and legs stung.

I heard someone call. Del, then Nayyib. I shut them out. Wished them away. Made myself alone. Just me—and the simoom.

I saw the spell in my head. Unraveled the words I'd read but days before, comprehending only half of them. I *knew* the words but not their meanings. I was but a first-level mage, as sword-dancer skill was measured. Full of potential but raw, wild, dangerous.

Abbu Bensir learned that.

We stood no chance unless I surrendered denial and accepted truth. As I had to Del, saying the word. Naming myself.

Mage. Whelped upon a spire in the Stone Forest, weeks away from here.

I gripped the sword, felt two thumbs and four fingers. *Four.* Slowly brought the blade down, sundering the sky.

The fabric of the storm, the heavy curtain of sand, split apart. Poured around me, roaring. Sand whirled by, carried on wind. But wind was merely air, and I could command it.

Mage I might be, but I was also the Sandtiger, and *that* I valued more than magic. The greatest sword-dancer legendary Alimat had ever produced. No one, and nothing, could defeat me. Not even a simoom.

Paltry, petty storm. Insignificant.

I grinned into it, knowing no sand would touch my scarred, stubbled face, scour out fragile, gelid eyes. I had parted the simoom, cut through its gritty fabric, shattered gemstones made of crystal, and gave us room to live.

In a matter of moments, the storm, like torn silk, flapped itself into shreds. The curtain of sand fell to the earth. Crystals dulled, then flared anew into dusty sunlight. Haze dissipated. The air began to warm.

The sword was still in my hands, tip set against sand. Slowly, aware of trembling in my arms, I raised it, re-sheathed it, then turned to see if I was alone.

No. Three horses and two humans. A man and a woman. The latter two knelt on the sand, hands shielding their heads. But slowly the heads raised. The faces opened. Del, whose smile was as odd as it was faint, spat grit out of her mouth. Then she stood up.

"Nicely done," she observed. "That one will come in handy."

Nayyib still knelt, looking dazed as well as windblown. "That was magery?"

Del laughed. "That was Tiger."

I bent, ruffled my hair vigorously to free it of the worst of the sand. Nothing had gotten through once I'd applied myself to cutting open the storm to divert it around us, but we'd gotten a faceful before then. The horses, being horses, not foolish humans, had promptly turned their rumps to the wind. Now they shook violently, banging stirrups and botas against sandy sides. A cloud of fine dust rose from each of them.

I staggered, laughed, cut it off sharply, lest I lose the last shreds of self-control. "Ah, yes, the wonderul sensation of bones turned to water. And one hoolies of a headache." I shut my eyes, pressed the heels of my hands to either side of my head. "Why don't they warn you about this part of it? The book didn't say a word."

Del came to me, put one hand on my arm. "Are you all right?"

"No, but I'll likely survive it." I opened my eyes and looked at her. "Maybe you can put cool cloths on my brow and croon to me, the way Nayyib crooned to the stud. Lay me down, cradle my poor, aching head in your lap, stroke my tender temples, and tell me repeatedly I am a man among men."

Del brushed a rime of sand from my forehead. "I rather think not."

"A mage among mages?"

"No more that than the other."

"Why not?" I asked plaintively. "Didn't I just save your life?"

Del opened her mouth to answer, but Nayyib's voice intruded. "Come look at this!"

Del turned. I took my hands away from my temples. "What?"

He stood several paces away, staring at something. At several somethings, actually: odd, lumpy shapes uncovered by the storm. Simooms swallowed, but they also uncovered.

Del and I walked over. It was a scattered graveyard of wood boards, scoured smooth like gray satin over years of burial and disinterrment. The Punja, goaded by storm, had tossed back one of its victims.

Nayyib knelt, fingering a section of wood. An edge showed, and inches of a flat surface. He locked fingers around it, pulled up with effort. The board broke free, showering sand. Nayyib sat down hastily, then held up the section of wood. "What is it from, do you think?"

I took it from him, studying it. "Looks like part of a wagon." I gestured to the other remnants poking above the sand, like tilted grave markers. "Likely the rest of it is still buried."

"Would it be whole?" Del asked. "If we dug it up?"

Aside from the fact that we couldn't do that, lacking shovels, I doubted it. "It's probably been here for years, bascha. The weight of the sand has broken it apart. We'd only find pieces."

Nayyib feigned deep disappointment "No treasure?"

"Well, likely borjuni on a raid took everything of value and left the wagon—along with the people in it, I'd assume—or a simoom got them. Either way, there'd be nothing left worth digging for." I tossed the board aside. "For all we know, there could be a whole caravan buried under the sand."

Del had wandered to the far side of the wagon remnants. I saw her stop, roll something over with the toe of her sandal, then drop to her knees. She picked up something, examined it, blew a feathering of sand from it, then set it aside. Hastily she began brushing sand away with her hands, but carefully, as if whatever she'd found was fragile.

Curious, I went to see what had caught her attention. Nayyib was still playing with the exposed wood, digging up fragments and sections of boards, stacking them like cordwood.

I stopped next to Del, "What did you find?"

She set it into my hand. Said nothing.

It lay in my palm. Grains of sand remained caught against my flesh, flecks of mineral, a tracery of Punja crystal. The wind- and sand-polished fragment lay atop it, with a faint oily sheen of pearl. It had three worn protrustions, and a hole through the middle.

My hand clamped shut.

"Bone," Del said.

Human bone.

Find me, the woman had begged.

I looked down at Del's excavations. I didn't recognize the hoarse timbre of my voice. "What else is there?"

She bent close to the sand, blew it away from the suggestion of a shape. She picked it out of the sand, smoothed and blew it free of dust and crystal, then offered it to me.

Time-weathered, sand-polished bone. A slender piece perhaps five inches long. Curved.

In one hand: vertebra. In the other: rib.

I fell down to my knees. "She's here. She's *here*. We've found her."

Del asked, "Who?" Then she stilled. "You think—the woman you dreamed about? The skeleton?"

I displayed both palms. "Bone."

Del's eyes were full of wonder as she lightly touched the rib in my right hand. "This is what brought you here?"

"I think so."

Her eyes lifted to mine. "Who do you think she was? A mage?"

"I don't know," I said. I locked eyes with Del. "But I can find out."

"How can you—?" She broke it off. "Oh, Tiger. No."

"I did it back at the Vashni encampment."

Her face was pale. "It's dangerous. Remember what Oziri did to you?"

I closed my hands. The bones were warm. "This is the woman in my dreams. The one who told me to find her. Now I have, and I have to know who—and what—she was."

"Tiger," she begged, "don't do it. You worked magic only a matter of moments ago. You're weak—you said so yourself. You have a 'hoolies of a headache.' "

I sat down on the sand. Opened my hands. Gazed at the pearls of the desert. "I have to do this."

So I shut my eyes, and did it.

Chapter 30

The voice was the voice of a stranger, yet also mine. I heard it inside my head; heard it in my ears. In fits and starts, stumbling to find its way, it told the story the bone had guarded for years.

"The caravan was small, short-handed, traveling too late in the season. Its master was not well respected, and those with enough experience or money hired others to get them across the deadly Punja. But those who lacked both, those unaccustomed to the South, to the desert, and certainly to the Punja, knew nothing more than that the man promised to take them where they wished to go: from Haziz through Julah and then across the Punja to where South met North and formed the borderlands, cooler than the desert, warmer than the mountains. The most temperate of all locales but dangerous because of its raiders, both Southron and Northern."

I sat on sand; cross-legged, left hand hanging limply in my lap, right hand holding bone. My eyes were open, but blind.

"The caravan, being small, short-handed, traveling too late in the season, and led by a man who prized coin over lives, was caught by a storm. The simoom was but an immature version of its larger relatives, but it was enough. The beasts were made to lie down, and the people took shelter in their wagons, trying to save the canvas that formed their roofs. Eventually the simoom blew itself out, and it was discovered by the folk, as they dug themselves free, that no lives were lost.

"The road, however, was."

I choked, coughed, drew in breath. I felt shivers course my body, but I could not stop. It needed to be told.

"The caravan master and his guide, trusting to their questionable instincts to find the right way, led the caravan on, and into disaster. A party of borjuni, taking advantage of the storm and its aftereffects, swept down upon the wagons. Men and children, being worth nothing, were killed outright. The women were taken to be sold as slaves or kept as camp whores. The horses, mules, and danjacs were rounded up. Everything of value easily carried was taken; everything requiring too much effort, or beasts to haul it, was left."

I was dimly aware of being wet with sweat, but cold. Shivers coursed my flesh. Someone's hand was on my knee, urging me to stop. But I could not.

"And also left was the foreign woman big with child, deemed too much trouble to take with them but worth some sport. That sport left her half-dead and in labor. The borjuni, finding it amusing, deserted her as she bled into the sand, deserting also the body of her husband, who had brought her out of Skandi to find a new life where a man and a woman, despite differences in birth, might settle and be content. Alone, beaten, raped, the woman who had been raised the privileged daughter of the Stessoi, one of Skandi's Eleven Families, found her dead husband, wept for him, then crawled under their wagon and, in a river of blood, bore him a son. She managed to take that son to her breast, to suckle him, to cover him with the scraps of her torn clothing. And died before she could name him aloud to the gods that had surely forsaken him.

"The child lived. He grew hungry, emitting wailing cries, and grew weak when the cries were not answered. But there was strength in him yet, and when the desert tribe that named itself Salset came across the caravan, he cried again. Was found. Was taken."

I swallowed, aware of pain in my throat, of exhaustion, of fever.

"The child, when judged old enough, was made a slave. His name was chula."

"Tiger . . . Tiger, stop now. Please. Please stop."

I stopped, because I could. Because the tale was told. The truth was known.

I opened eyes that had, at some point, closed. No longer did I sit on the sand, cross-legged. Now I lay on the sand with my head in a woman's lap. Her hands were on my forehead, fingers stroking.

"Tiger, come back. It's done. It's over. It happened a long time ago."

"Forty years," I rasped.

Del took the rib bone from my hand. "Enough. Enough."

"She didn't abandon me." A hollow, hoarse voice. "Neither did he."

"No one abandoned you," she said. "Never. They wanted you. You would have brought them great joy."

"The Salset told me I was abandoned."

"They would never say, even had they known, that you were the grandson of the Stessa metri, of one of the most powerful of Skandi's Eleven Families."

"I was a chula."

"But not anymore. Not for many years." Del's fingers stroked. "You should be happy, Tiger. I have crooned to you, soothed your tender temples. After I said I would not."

I grinned weakly. "You never could keep your hands off me."

She smiled. Laughed. Her eyes were the blue of Northern lakes, glistening with unshed tears, her hair pale as Punja sand.

I shivered. Realized the sun was down. Someone had thrown a blanket over me as I lay with my head in Del's lap. I turned my head, saw a fire. "Where'd *that* come from?" We were in the Punja, in a sea of sand; there were no trees.

"Neesha made a fire with the wood from the wagon."

It felt odd to think that the wagon might even be the one my mother and father had bought in Haziz. Now set on fire to warm the son neither had ever known.

Nayyib came close, squatted down next to me. His color seemed pale, though it was difficult to tell in shadows and firelight. "What you saw—what you *said* you saw . . . your mother?"

"Mother. Father."

"Did the bone take you there?"

A smile twitched my lips, but I was too weary to hold it. "Memories, Neesha. The bones know what happened. I can conjure up the memories if I hold a bone. I can walk my dreams to find out what they mean."

I had said too much. Nayyib's gaze slid away, avoiding mine; talk of magic bothered him. Then his eyes returned. "Was she a mage, then? Your mother?"

"No. Well, not that I know of. There is magery in some of the Eleven Families of Skandi, and apparently in the Stessoi, if I'm any indication . . . but in males, not females." And it drove them mad. But that I wouldn't say. Not to him. Not to Del.

"Then it could have come through your father."

"No. He wasn't one of the Eleven Families. It had to have come through my mother." I remembered the metri, my grandmother, dismissing me out of hand when she was done with me, swearing her daughter had died before I was born. I swallowed heavily against the dryness in my throat. "Is there water?"

"Here." Del picked up the bota by her knee. "Don't drink too much at once."

I drank as much as I could, until she took it away. I sighed, closed my eyes. ". . . tired."

"Sleep," she said. "You went far away, and came back the long road."

I let go a trembling breath. Felt her take the bone from my slack hand. "I still have to find the sword."

"But not tonight."

Ah. Good.

I faded then, slipping bit by bit out of reality, out of consciousness, as Del, with gentle fingers, smoothed the lines from my forehead.

"Will he die?" Nayyib asked.

"Oh, no." Her voice seemed to smile. "Not for a long, long time."

Ten years. Twelve.

Then darkness took me.

I awoke sometime later, feeling limp as shredded rags, still covered by the blanket. I lay on bedding; wondered if Nayyib and Del had simply rolled me onto it. I had no memory of waking to put myself there. Not good for a sword-dancer. But obviously something in my mind believed I was safe in their care, not to stir at all when they moved me.

I stared up at the sky. Still night, still dark, wreathed in brilliant stars. The fire had died to embers. It was very quiet; even the horses slept.

Del was close beside me. I sensed her there even without looking, as if every part of my awareness was attuned to her presence. She slept as she often did, coiled on her left side with a fold of blanket pulled over her ear. Loosened hair fell across her face and strayed onto bedding.

I wanted to reach out and touch it, to feel the silk. But it felt good just to lie here unmoving, letting the night bathe me.

Oh bascha, I don't want to die in ten or twelve years. I don't want to lose you. I want to be with you, to see you grow old even as I do.

Nayyib slept on the other side of the foe. I knew he was attracted to Del; I wondered if he thought he might win her from me. If maybe he considered me too old for her, wondering what she saw in a forty-year-old man. He was her age: young, strong, athletic, undeniably attractive. He had a gentleness about him coupled with strength of mind, a quiet confidence that set him apart from other young men. Maybe it came from working with horses, from understanding their needs and fears, their moments of inexplicable recalcitrance. Or maybe it was just him.

What *would* Del do when I was gone? Find another?

Find Neesha?

I had no way of knowing what to expect when my time approached. Nihko and Sahdri had said nothing of that, merely that a Skandi-born mage went mad if he didn't learn to control his magic, and that the magic would eventually burn him out merely by its presence. If I refused to use it, I might die that much sooner.

Well, I had used it. With Oziri, learning to dream-walk; spelling Umir's book; dividing the sandstorm; reading the bones of the woman who was my mother.

Had used it even in childhood, conjuring the living sandtiger out of a carved one, in order to find freedom.

I wanted none of it.

It appeared to want me.

I sat up, suppressing a groan. Everything ached, even my skin. I didn't feel forty; I felt sixty. An age I would never reach.

Slowly I pushed myself to my feet, wavered a moment, steadied, then picked my way across the sand to the dozing horses. The stud roused as I touched him, whickering softly. I felt his warm breath against my hand. Then I turned, went a few steps away and attended to my business, aware of a clenching deep in my kidneys. Maybe mages died early because they used themselves up, aging their organs ahead of time.

I turned, took three steps, found Del waiting at the stud's head. Maybe she'd heard my joints grinding as I walked across the sand.

I saw the question in her eyes. Smiling faintly, I hooked an arm around her neck and stood next to her. "I'm fine."

I heard the pent breath expelled. For a moment we just stood there side by side, staring across the Punja glowing faintly in moon- and starlight.

She spoke very quietly. "I don't want to lose you."

I kept my voice as low, not wanting to wake Nayyib. "What? You mean Neesha hasn't won you from me with a glance of those eloquent eyes?"

"Neesha's eyes may indeed work wonders on other women, but not on me."

"Are you immune?"

"Oh, no. He is a beautiful young man."

"Beautiful?"

"As a man may be," she clarified. "Not like a woman. He isn't *pretty*. But the bones of his face are well suited to one another, and he moves very well. He understands his body."

I hadn't really asked for that much explanation. But I'd never thought about how women view men, other than appreciating that many of them seemed to view me with favor. "What do you look at in a man? Women, I mean. Not just you."

Del's breath of laughter was a quiet expulsion of air. "We don't all necessarily see or want the same thing. There are pretty men, and handsome men, and men who lack the features that most would name attractive but claim a sense of *presence* that makes looks unimportant. There is no describing that. It simply is. Tall, short, heavy, thin . . . it doesn't matter."

I thought of brutal Ajani, long dead. Handsome, huge, filled with undeniable presence. Yet he had used the power to rape and kill, to alter forever the life of the woman next to me. "But there are handsome men who have it."

"Yes. And those are the men that turn a woman's knees to water and her brain to mush."

"I, of course, exude it."

"There are also men who are *too* confident, too certain of themselves and their appeal, and who believe they may blind women to their faults."

"Thanks very much for that."

"But I, however, am not so easily blinded."

"I sort of figured that."

"Some men may begin that way but are trainable when in the hands of the right woman. Other men are hopeless."

I wasn't certain either of those attributes was something I aspired to.

"And age doesn't matter," Del said. "Not when a woman meets the right man."

"Even if she's young enough to be his daughter?"

"Lo, even then."

I had been curious a long time. Now I asked her. "When did you know you wanted to sleep with me?"

"Oh, within days. But you were such a pig-headed, insufferably *male* Southroner that I was appalled by my response."

"Thank you very much!"

"I argued with myself for weeks."

"As I recall, it was months before we finally did the deed." Months and months, in fact; it had been very hard on me.

"I intended it to be never. But one day I realized that ignorance could be changed, even in a Southroner. Besides, by then you knew I would never be the kind of woman Southron men prefer: soft, quiet, deferential little mice who keep their houses and bear their children."

"We don't have a house to keep and you can't, well . . ." I realized belatedly that blurting out her inability to have children was not perhaps the most tactful thing. Del loved children. Enough to give her daughter to good people who could care for her when Del, consumed with vengeance, couldn't. "Sorry, bascha."

She shied away from it, not even acknowledging my apology. "I am not like most Southron women," she went on, "but more of them could be like me if they let themselves be free."

"Maybe they're happy the way they are."

"Or maybe they don't know any better because they are trained from birth to be blind to their own ambitions."

"Maybe their ambitions are to keep house and raise children. Lena seems to be happy."

"Lena *is* happy. But then, Alric is a Northerner; he expects her to be free to express herself. I have no objection to women keeping house and bearing children, Tiger, if that is what they truly wish in their hearts, and not because their men demand it of them. I only object when men won't allow the women who wish to be more to acheive it. To even imagine it."

I thought of Del, Northern born and raised, allowed to learn the sword even before she went to Staal-Ysta to become a swordsinger. I thought of my grandmother, the matriarch of a powerful family, conducting business with ruthless brilliance. I thought of my mother, who willingly left behind that wealth and power to go with the man she loved to a distant land known for its harshness and died because of it.

I sighed. "Maybe I was trainable because I'm actually Skandic, not a Southroner."

"Or maybe you have more flexibility of mind."

"Is that a good thing? If one's mind is *too* flexible, one never has an opinion of one's own."

"Tiger, you would never let anyone change your opinion until you were certain they were right."

"So, am I inflexibly flexible, or flexibly inflexible?"

She elbowed me in the ribs. "What you are is incorrigible."

"Is *that* a good thing?"

"Only when I'm in the mood."

I turned to her, wrapped her up in my arms. Lightly rested my chin on her head. "I'm a little too tired, bascha."

"Not that kind of mood."

I smiled into the darkness. "I know."

"He is attractive, Tiger, and not without charm and that sense of presence I mentioned before. But he is not you."

"Next best thing?"

"Well, I suppose if you got yourself killed in a sword-dance tomorrow, I might consider it."

"So as long as I'm alive, you're satisfied?"

"Unless you decided to revert to the Tiger I met in that dusty cantina four years ago. Then I'd have to kill you myself."

Considering she'd nearly done it once, I knew she was capable. "Then I'll be on my best behavior."

"Oh, no, be on your worst. Because then I can train *that* out of you."

I sighed deeply, rubbing my cheek against her hair. Stubble caught on it. "I want to live to be an old man, with you there beside me."

"So you will, and so I will be."

The truth was, either of us could die tomorrow. But we knew it. Accepted it. Were unafraid.

For ourselves, that is. I know we feared for one another.

Chapter 31

At dawn, as the others lay sleeping, I carried the vertebra and rib bone out to where Del had found them. Nayyib had dug up all the visible pieces of wood; hollows and indentations were left to show where he had worked, but the first whisper of wind would cover those up, leaving no trace of the wagon. A few paces away Del had found the bones. I knelt, set the two fragments aside, used the edge of my right hand to ease away more fine sand. After some time I gave up the search; the rest of the bones could be anywhere, carried away in countless simooms over forty years. That any had been left for our discovery was miraculous.

I smiled wryly, remembering that supposedly I was the jhihadi. It was a ludicrous idea—and utterly untrue. I was just a man who seemed to fit pieces of the prophecy certain religious zealots had adopted, and I'd come up with a good idea in channeling water to the desert. But *anyone* could have come up with that idea. It just happened to be me.

I sat there on the sand, vertebra in one hand, rib in the other. It was very difficult to believe they were from my mother; that with flesh over them, and muscle, tendon, ligament, not to mention the vessels carrying blood, they had been part of a living woman.

A living woman who had somehow sent a message to me in my dreams.

But I wished I could have seen her as she had been, before the borjuni raid killed her. When she had been woman, not a scattering of bones across the sand, or a speaking skull telling me to find her, to take up the sword.

I leaned forward, dug a pocket in the sand, pressed the bones into it. Feathered sand over the top. The next storm would bury them more deeply, or strip away the covering so that the wind, in its exuberance, might carry them on a journey.

It crossed my mind that perhaps I should have them sent back to the metri on Skandi, so she might have a little something of her daughter to bury or burn, according to Skandic rites, and to mourn. But my grandmother didn't strike me as the type of woman who would do that. Or appreciate the thought.

Love for my father had brought my mother here. Best they remained together.

I pressed three sword-callused fingers over the slight up-swell of sand, bid her goodbye, then left her.

Some time later we rode out of the Punja, onto the road—this time I had no problem heading south—and into Julah. I suggested we put up the horses at a different livery, which we did, then went to Fouad's by way of alleys and entered via the back door. It startled Fouad half to death as we snuck in, but when he saw who it was, he settled. His look at me was oddly assessing; I wondered what he saw. I was still tired from the magery I'd used first on the storm, then to read my mother's bones, and was looking forward to a night's sleep in a real bed. Especially since I'd missed it the *last* time we were here.

Then Fouad looked at Nayyib, narrowed his eyes as he sought to figure out who he was; his face cleared, and he nodded. He recalled the kid from when he'd come looking for a healer. Del shut and latched the door behind us.

"Food, no doubt, and drink," Fouad said. "Yes?"

"Yes to both," I agreed. "Del and the kid will eat in the front room; how about you send something back to me? I'd rather keep my head down, after what happened the last time."

Fouad's eyes flicked to Nayyib again, clearly questioning his presence. The kid had been taught his manners: He bowed slightly, smiling. "Neesha," he said. "I am privileged to be the Sandtiger's student."

Fouad's eyebrows ran up into his hair as he looked at me. "Student?"

I shrugged, deciding now was as good a time as any to announce my intentions. "I plan to restore Alimat and take up my shodo's role."

"Alimat! But it was destroyed years ago!" Fouad shook his head. "And I doubt the other sword-dancers will let you. Particularly Abbu Bensir."

"If they want to take it up with me, they're welcome to. That in itself would provide a valuable lesson for the students."

"Watching you die? I would say so!" He glanced at Del. "You're amenable?"

Del mimicked my shrug. "Why not? There will be two teachers: a Southron sword-dancer and a Northern sword-singer. What other school may claim that?"

"And one student already," Neesha added.

Fouad wagged his head back and forth thoughtfully. "Well, you will most certainly draw students—until someone kills you."

I scowled. "I appreciate the confidence. Now, how about that food and drink?"

"I'll eat with you," Del offered, turning toward the back hallway.

Neesha grinned wickedly. "While *I* eat out front and attempt to charm Fouad's wine-girls."

Fouad grunted. "I suspect you'll have any number of offers before the food's on the table. But come along; I'll introduce you as a friend of the new owners. That ought to be good enough for a discount." His tone went dry as dust. "That is, if they don't decide to offer themselves for free, as has been known to happen with certain regular customers I won't mention in present company."

Neesha, still grinning, threw a conspiratorial look over his shoulder at Del and me as if to make sure we understood what he was doing.

"Well, at least he's not *entirely* oblivious." I turned Del and propelled her toward the back bedroom. "I guess if he's got enough sense to know when we need some privacy, it won't be so bad having him ride with us."

Del, allowing herself to be propelled, merely laughed. "I don't think he's doing that so much for *our* privacy as he is for his own! Fouad's right: The girls will be fighting over him the moment he sits down. I rather think our new student will be most busy tonight."

I pulled back our door curtain. "I rather think *we* will be most busy tonight."

"And tomorrow?"

"Tomorrow we load the horses and head out again for the chimney at Beit al'Shahar. There's a sword I need to have a discussion with."

Del sat down on the bed and began to unlace her sandals. "If you can find it. The whole formation collapsed, Tiger. Your *jivatma* may be completely buried."

"Worth a look anyhow." I stripped off the harness, unsheathed the sword, set it point down against one of the bedside tables. "If I can't get to it, no one can; but my mother seemed fairly certain it could be found. I mean, who would have thought I could find her bones out there in the Punja? On the basis of dreams? It may be possible I can find Samiel, too."

"And if—" She corrected herself, "*when*—you do?"

"Dunno." I sat down, yawned, rolled my head against my shoulders, stretching tendons.

"He's still a *jivatma*, Tiger. You used Northern magic to make him—and now you have your own magic as well."

"A magical sword, wielded by a mage who is also the long-lost grandson of one of the Eleven gods-descended Families of Skandi—and who also happens to be the jhihadi." I flopped down against the bed. "Something for people to write sagas and sing songs about, don't you think?"

Del, barefoot now, undid the buckles of her harness. " 'The Sword-Dancer's Tale.' Well, perhaps."

"Maybe *'The Tale of Tiger.'* "

" *'And Del.'* "

My eyes drifted closed. "As long as my name goes first."

"Not when it's sung or told in the North, it doesn't."

I smiled. "Depends on the audience, I guess. Hmm—what about *'The Tiger's Tale'*?"

"Or *'The Tiger's Tail'*?"

I stuck my tongue out at her.

"If you're asleep when the food and drink arrives, do you want me to wake you up?"

"I'm not going to sleep. I'm resting my eyes."

"Do you want me to wake you up from resting your eyes?"

"Sure," I mumbled, "a man's got to keep up his strength to satisfy his woman." And slid into the abyss before she could respond.

Del did indeed wake me up when the food and drink arrived. She slapped a cupped hand across my abdomen, making odd, hollowed, clapping sounds against my skin. Not entirely the most subtle way to awaken a sleeper.

"Up," she said. "Food's here."

I scrunched up against the wall at the head of the bed, inspecting the skin of my abdomen. Then I helped myself to the platter bearing bread-bowls of mutton stew, cheese, grapes, and a small jug of what turned out to be ale.

"Tiger, we need a door on this room."

I slugged down about half the ale, then licked the foam from my upper lip. "We have a door."

"That's a doorway. I mean a door. I'd like some privacy, if we're to stay here now and again."

"There's a curtain."

"I would like a *wooden* door. With a latch."

I plucked grapes from their stems with my teeth and spoke around them. "Why so formal?"

"Because unless you don't mind everyone else knowing our business, with all manner of false conclusions drawn about the fair-haired Northern bascha—for example, how much does Fouad charge for me?—I think we need a door. A wooden door. With a latch."

"You have a point." I dropped the denuded grape stems back on the platter. "I'll have a word with Fouad. Anything else you'd like, while we're at it?"

"Well, *I'd* recommend he dismiss all the wine-girls who double as whores, but I'm quite sure he would not agree to that."

"I think that's a safe conclusion. We'd probably lose all kinds of business and thus all kinds of profit. We'd have to close down."

"The gods forfend," Del said dryly, reaching for the other jug; water, no doubt.

I paused before putting a chunk of cheese in my mouth. "You don't sound particularly enamored of being a partner in a thriving cantina. Just think of the benefits!"

"What benefits? Other than free drinks for you?"

"We'll be the first to hear all rumors and reports of whatever may be going on in the world. At least, our little corner of it."

"That's a benefit?"

"It is when you know anywhere from ten to twenty men are bent on executing you."

"And you'll run back here to hide any time one of them comes into the cantina?"

"Oh, no. We'll clear all the furniture out of the common room, cut a circle into the hardpack, then charge admission for the dance. Plus take a percentage of the side bets." I grinned wickedly. "Rather like *we* used to do, when we needed money."

Del used her knife to carve curling strips of cheese from the hunk Fouad had sent along. "Those were not actual dances."

"Which means we can charge even more money for a real one."

Her eyes were on the cheese, but her idle tone was nonetheless underscored by solemnity. "What will it take to make them stop?"

"Once I kill enough of them, the rest will find other things to do."

"I'm serious, Tiger."

"So am I. It's true. I killed Khashi quickly and brutally in front of many witnesses. Then I won a difficult sword-dance against a very, very good young man, in front of a whole slug of sword-dancers. Once I kill a few more, most of them will stop coming."

"And will it be like Fouad suggested, that they'll want to stop you from resurrecting Alimat?"

"Very likely." I took up horn spoon and bread-bowl of stew and began scooping the contents into my mouth. Seeing Del's concern, I paused between bites. "I have to see it settled, bascha. We can't go North, and I have no desire to return to Skandi, where I'd likely be hauled off to ioSkandi again and stuck back atop the spires in Meteiera. I also have no desire to go haring off to foreign lands. The South, despite all its problems, is my home. Coming back made me realize that. I won't run away again."

She nodded, clearly troubled. "I know."

I sighed, set down the bowl and spoon. "Del, something happened to me. I became aware of it when I was Umir's 'guest.' I don't know how it happened, and I can't even be sure it will happen again, but when I danced, when I took up my sword—I felt as if I had all four fingers on each hand."

Blue eyes widened.

"I know it sounds impossible. But it's true. I mean, I *know* the fingers are gone—hoolies, I saw Sahdri throw them off the spire!— but when I dance, it feels as if I still have them."

Del was staring at my hands. One thumb, three fingers on each.

"I don't know, maybe I'm just imagining them there. But when I danced against Musa, I could have sworn I had all my fingers again."

She met my eyes. "Is it possible that it's—"

"—wishful thinking? Sure. And it could be. But it might also be something in me now, something that's a part of the magic. I conjured a living sandtiger out of carved bone once. Who's to say I can't conjure two fingers when I need them?"

"Does it—does it feel the same?"

"Not exactly. And when I look at them, I see the stumps, not the fingers. But when I take up the sword, I feel whole again. That my *hands* are whole again." I hitched one shoulder in a half-shrug. "I'm not saying I can't be defeated or that no one could use it against me. My grip is different. I'm not the same as I was before. Anyone looking at my hands would see only three fingers. But if I can dance as though I have four on each hand—"

"But you don't." Gently insistent, afraid I'd become complacent in something that didn't truly exist.

I heaved a sigh, ran one hand through my hair, scrubbing

against my tattooed scalp. "I've heard men who've lost a limb talk about ghost pain. That they feel as if the missing limb is still attached, still functional. Maybe that's all it is. I sense the ghosts of my fingers somehow, and it helps." I tapped. "Up here, in my head."

Del nodded. "And if the ghosts ever go away?"

I laughed a little. "Bascha, I'm forty years old. I don't have many more good years left to me as a sword-dancer; and I'm *not* a sword-dancer, according to the oaths of Alimat. But I think I can teach."

The smile broke free from the tension in her face. "I still can't believe it. The Sandtiger, opening a school . . . and *teaching!*"

"Oh? What about you? You seem willing enough to stick in one place and take on students. Is that what you envisioned for yourself when you left Staal-Ysta?"

"I envisioned killing Ajani. Beyond that—?" She shook her head. "Nothing. My song ended that day in Iskandar. The South is not my home, but I can't go to the North. And it doesn't matter. I chose to be with you. If you want to restore Alimat and reopen a school, then I will be a part of it."

I was only half-joking. "Until Neesha steals you away from me."

Nothing in Del's expression suggested there was anything that supported what I'd suggested, even in the back of her mind. "Well, then we have a few weeks, at least."

Relief. I grinned, handed her the other bread-bowl, stuck the second horn spoon into it so it stood up in the center. "Here. Just don't eat up all our profits."

Chapter 32

el and I were packed and eating our morning meal by the time Neesha came dragging out of one of the smaller rooms to knock at the doorframe, since, as Del had noted, we had no actual door.

My mouth was full, so Del, tying saddlepouches closed, waved him in; he sidled through the curtain split. "Is everyone decent?"

Del and I assessed him silently. His face was stubbled, his eyes faintly bloodshot, his hair an unruly tangle. I swallowed and said, "Aparently more decent than you."

His smile blossomed, lighting honey-brown eyes. "Oh, no. I am far better than decent. Or so Silk tells me."

I nearly choked on my next bite, swallowed hastily. "Silk? You ended up with Silk last night?"

"Silk was the *last* one I ended up with last night, yes."

I glowered at him. "And I suppose she didn't charge you."

Neesha's grin was a superior smirk. "As a matter of fact, she said she ought to pay *me*."

Del looked from me to him and back again. "Is this for my benefit, this ridiculous male posturing?"

Neesha started laughing even as I grinned. Hey, in front of a beautiful woman you like it to be known that you have alternatives.

"But you do look, um, used up," I noted.

He attempted to tame his hair. "Ridden hard and put away wet," he agreed in horse parlance; then he glanced at Del solemnly. "And that *isn't* posturing."

She made a sound of absolute scorn and waved a dismissive hand. "You men."

Indictment in two words. Neesha and I exchanged grins. *"Women,"* we said simultaneously.

Del scowled, buckling on her harness. "Are we ready to go?"

"My things are packed and by the back door," Neesha told her.

My mouth full again, I gestured illustratively at waiting saddle-pouches.

"Good," she said. "Why don't you two *men* go saddle the horses? I'll be along in a few moments."

I washed breakfast down with ale. "What's keeping you?"

"Something *men* wouldn't understand." She gestured again. "Run along, boys."

I already wore my harness and sword; I hooked my set of saddlepouches over my shoulder, tossed Del's to Neesha. "By all means, let's allow the *woman* to do *woman* things."

Del scowled at us both as we departed the room.

The kid and I went to the livery housing the horses and set about getting them ready to go. It was companionable as we worked, exchanging a sentence now and again, but mostly just tending the horses. Neesha did indeed have a way with them that I envied. I wondered if I should have him ride the stud . . . nah, better not. I really didn't want to get the kid hurt.

Nor, for that matter, did I want to witness the stud's defection.

He had finished tacking up his horse and worked on Del's white gelding, smearing black paint around his eyes and stringing the Vashni browband across his face. When done, he looked over at me. "When do you want to try this sparring match?"

I was inspecting the line of stitches in the stud's left haunch. "Oh, let's wait till we get to Alimat. I figure what you did for the stud bought you a lesson or two, no audition necessary." I patted the stud's rump well away from the stitched wound. "It looks good."

"My father taught me well."

I shook my head, leading the stud into daylight. "If you are the only son, you stand to inherit."

Neesha followed with his bay and Del's gelding. "Yes."

"Owning a horse farm is not a bad way to live."

"It's a good way to live."

"Then—"

He replied over the beginnings of my question, knowing what it would be. "Because it's not what I dreamed about. Not what I wanted to do since—" He broke off, glanced away from me. "Since I first understood what sword-dancing was. My father followed *his* father's footsteps, and his before his, but I want to follow . . . well, I wanted to go elsewhere. To make my own way." Now we stood in the alley not far from the cantina. "It may be a good life—I don't suggest it isn't—but it isn't the one I want. Not yet. Maybe someday when I'm your age and want to retire, I'll use my winnings to buy my *own* horse farm."

I nodded inwardly; I could admire a kid who wanted to make his own way in the world despite having advantages. If he had any true talent for the sword, I'd find out; if not, I'd send him back to the horses. Most didn't have that choice.

"Sword-dancing is a very hard life, Neesha. The work isn't steady, it's often painful, and now and again there's a very real chance you could be killed, even if it isn't a death-dance. Accidents happen. And outside of the circle, there are any number of jobs that could get you hurt or killed."

He nodded. "Abbu told me so."

I went very still. "Abbu Bensir?"

"He was the sword-dancer who came through my village."

"Hunh." That put a different light on things. "How many lessons did he give you?"

"Four." A self-deprecating grin kindled quickly. "Enough to have him humiliate me but not enough to dissuade me."

"You took lessons from Abbu, then decided to find *me?*"

"I decided to find you before then." His gaze on me was level. "I heard stories about you."

Ah, yes. The legendary Sandtiger. Abbu would certainly appreciate that. "Did you tell him that was your plan?"

"No. It was my business, not his."

I released a low whistle of appreciation. "Had Abbu known, he might have offered to teach you some tricks."

Neesha's smile was slight. "I knew that. But I didn't want to learn tricks. I wanted to learn the *art*. I think Abbu believed I would change my mind."

I saw Del approaching. "You'll do," I said, patting the stud's neck. "At least, for a while."

He grinned. "Ten years? Or maybe seven, to match the shodo?"

"Or maybe six, to better him?"

Neesha didn't hesitate. He simply shook his head. "Who could?"

I laughed. "Abbu would say otherwise."

"Possibly. But I didn't come all this way to be Abbu's student."

Del came up and took the gelding's rein from Neesha's hand. "So, we are bound at last—again—to the fallen chimney."

"Beit al'Shahar." I gave it the Vashni name. "Yes. And if I manage to accomplish my task, then we'll head for Alimat. It's a good five or six days' ride from here, depending on the mood of the Punja. In the meantime, we can start beating up on Neesha so he understands what schooling is *really* all about."

Del cast him a glance, expression questioning.

He nodded. "I am duly forewarned."

I mounted the stud. "Then let's ride."

Not far out of Julah we found and followed the faint trail of wheel ruts Del and I had come to recognize, noting familiar landmarks. Somewhere along it we'd camped out on the way back from the Vashni settlement, where Del had scattered the pieces of the necklet Ozrri had given me. I was aware that I no longer had any inclination to return to the Vashni encampment or to learn more about dream-walking. I had used a form of it to read my mother's bones, but there was no desire in me to sort out what my dreams meant. I *knew* what those involving the dead woman meant; by finding her bones, I'd fulfilled half of her repeated commandment. Now all that was left was to take up my *jivatma* and forget all about magery.

If I could.

Not long before sundown we rode up the familiar twisting trail to the top of the tree-hedged plateau. The lean-to against the boulders still stood. I shook my head in bemusement, recalling how Del and I had spent days there sick from sandtiger venom, and how Neesha had helped us both.

Apparently so did he, and so did Del. I saw them exchange long, intent glances. It was more than mere memory, more than a friendly recollection worth reciting to others over food and drink, but something strangely intimate. And indecipherable. It left me with an odd feeling in my belly. There was nothing in Del's behavior suggesting she was attracted to Neesha, and she had even come right out and *said* there was no interest on her part. When drunk on Umir's liquor the kid had divulged his attraction to her, but that didn't surprise me. Most men fell under Del's unintended spell merely by being in her presence. I was used to that. But I had seen looks exchanged between them before, glances I couldn't translate. Not the silent communication of lovers, but something else. Something—more.

But what more is there? You are lovers, friends, acquaintances, strangers, or enemies. I could attach none of those descriptions to what I saw passing between Del and Nayyib.

Could she be lying? I didn't think so. She had explained once in Skandi that if she ever intended to leave, she'd tell me. That, I believed. It wasn't Del's way to hide behind lies and subterfuge. She had also demonstrated her affection for me in physical ways, ways that were no different than had been employed before. Could a woman hide her attraction to a new man while sleeping with the old?

Well, yes. But not Del. Not with her honesty. She had never learned to dissemble.

And when Neesha had quietly bragged about his conquests of Silk and other wine-girls, it hadn't been done in a way to kindle jealousy or to make a point, the way a man might if he wanted a woman who refused him.

Which left—what?

I didn't know. Before Del, I'd kept myself to wine-girls and other women who wanted nothing more than a night or two together. I'd never sworn myself to any kind of bond. Del and I were not oath-bound, not vowed to one another save by what lived in our spirits. But I knew that could change. That it had, for others.

Hoolies, it was too complex to think about right now, after most of a day spent on horseback.

I dismounted over by scraggly trees rimming the edge of the flat-topped bluff and set about unloading and tying out the stud. The grass grazed down earlier by our horses had recovered some-what, which suggested no one had been here since I'd come look-ing for Del. She and the kid found separate places for their mounts and began to unload as well. When the stud had cooled, I'd water and grain him; for now he was content to nose and lip at grass. I humped my tack and pouches over to the lean-to and dropped them outside.

"Wood," I announced tersely. "I'll be back."

"I'll go, too, when I'm done here," Nayyib offered.

"Not necessary." I stalked off, aware both were staring at me in startled bafflement.

Well, fine, so I'm prone to occasional bouts of jealousy. I'm human.

Maybe *that* proved I wasn't the jhihadi. Did messiahs get jeal-ous? For that matter, did messiahs sleep with women?

Feeling somewhat better, I began looking in earnest for appro-priate deadfall.

I made two trips to gather firewood. Nayyib made one; he piled it next to the fire ring, then lingered to talk with Del. From some dis-tance away, it seemed an odd conversation. The kid stood with his head lowered, shoulders poised stiffly. Not deferential exactly, but not precisely happy, either. Del stood very close to him, and *her* body language suggested she was doing most of the talking.

It was interesting to see them together from a distance. Nayyib was an inch taller than Del, and certainly broader and thicker of limb, but, though larger in general than most Southroners, he was not truly a significantly big man. Still, he was young yet; I didn't truly fill out until halfway through my twenties, though I had my height. Del is no delicate flower, but a tall, strong woman who moves unencumbered by the perceived requirements of femininity. They matched well together, Nayyib and Delilah.

His head came up sharply. Posture stiffened even more. He said something to Del, something definitive, because *her* posture abruptly tensed. Then he turned and walked away, looking for all the world like a house cat offended by the taint of splashed water.

Del watched him go—perhaps he was after more wood—then shook her head slightly. She knelt, began building a fire.

All in all, it did not put me in mind of a lovers' quarrel. Or a woman withstanding the blandishments of a man who wanted her. In fact, I couldn't put a name to it at all, save to say that he wasn't pleased by what she had told him, and she was no more pleased by his response.

But how much of that was wishful thinking?

I went over with my second supply of wood, piled it by the fire, and looked at her questioningly. "Something wrong?"

Del denied it crossly, then ducked into the lean-to to begin arranging her bedding.

Which left me even more confused than before. Wood delivered, I went off to check on the horses and to water and grain them. When Nayyib came back, he dumped his wood on the pile and came over to tend to his bay, though I had things under control.

The day was dying quickly, the way it does in the desert, but I could still see the stubbled planes of his face and the hollows of his eyes. He was unhappy about something. It struck me as odd, since Neesha seemed a mostly equable sort.

In view of my own sharp temper earlier, I didn't think it would help to inquire if he had a problem. So I lingered as I tended the stud and Del's gelding, and eventually he sighed, let the tension go, and spoke.

"Why is it we're going to this chimney place?"

"Beit al'Shahar. It's a rock formation."

"But what's there?"

"Something I left behind." I collected emptied canvas buckets and set them out of reach, so inquisitive equine teeth wouldn't chew them to bits. "Del and I were out this way about a year ago, give or take."

"She said something about a sword."

"*Jivatma,*" I clarified. "A Northern sword. Blooding-blade. Named blade." I smiled when I saw his frown of incomprehension. "Northern ritual. Mostly, it's just a sword."

"You have a sword. Why go looking for this Northern one?"

"Something I need to do."

"Like find the bones in the Punja?"

"Something like that." I smoothed a hand down the stud's neck. "Kind of hard to explain. There are swords—and there are swords. If you own one long enough—if you form a partnership, odd as it may sound—it becomes more than just a weapon or a means of making a living."

"Singlestroke."

"Ah, the infamous blade of the Sandtiger!" I dropped the melodramatic tone. "A good sword. Kept me out of serious trouble many times."

"But you don't carry it any more."

So, he didn't know everything about the legend. "Singlestroke was broken a number of years ago."

His head came up. "So you want the Northern blade in its place?"

I remembered Samniel's begetting at Staal-Ysta, the days and nights I spent in Kem's smithy. "It too is a good sword. A special sword." I shrugged. "It's hard to explain."

"Much about you is hard to explain."

"I'm a complicated guy, Neesha." True dark had fallen; there was nothing more to be read in expressions, which couldn't be seen. Only in voices.

"Del told me some stories when we were with the Vashni."

Finished with the horses, we fell in together as we drifted back toward the fire. "It's been an interesting life."

"And a dangerous one."

"I warned you about that."

"Yes." He sounded pensive.

"Thinking the horse farm sounds a bit better?"

His head came up sharply. "No."

"Then what's bothering you?"

He did not answer immediately. When he did, his tone was stiff. "You have your secrets. I have mine."

By then we were at the fire. Del sat next to it, drinking from a bota and gnawing on dried cumfa. She did not look at Neesha. She looked at me as if her eyes were knives. Seems we were *all* being complicated tonight.

And it hurt.

Ignoring the thought, I squatted beside the fire. "First thing tomorrow morning I'd like to head out for the chimney. You two can wait here if you'd rather—it's not that far—or come along and wait for me there at the formation."

Del stopped chewing. "Why would we not come?"

I hooked my head in Neesha's general direction. "You and he appear to have some things to discuss."

Their eyes met. Locked. Del seemed to wait. Nayyib's jaw and raised brows suggested *she* had something to say.

"Fine." I pulled my pouches over, dug through until I found my share of burlap-wrapped cumfa. "The kid said it best, I guess—we all have our secrets. I don't know if each of you has a different one, or if you share the same one. What I *do* know is I'm left out of it. Which is probably for the best; I'm really not in the mood to deal with childish nonsense."

Del's brow creased, but she didn't reply. Nayyib sat down and pointedly turned his attention to the contents of *his* saddlepouches.

My jaws worked to soften the preserved meat. It's almost impossible to talk with a mouth full of cumfa, so I didn't even try. We all just ground our jaws and thought thoughts none of us wished to share.

I've got to admit it: I've spent more companionable nights in the desert. But it didn't interfere when I decided to go to bed.

Del and Nayyib, not talking, were still sitting by the fire as I unrolled my bedding in the lean-to and crawled into it.

I sighed, turned over, tried to go to sleep. It took me a while, but I got there.

I awakened in the middle of the night, heart pounding against my chest. A residue of fear still sizzled through my body. A dream . . .

Not one like the others. Nothing like the others. This was a normal dream in all respects, except for its content.

I've always dreamed vividly. Maybe it was because of the magic in my bones, incipient dream-walking, bone-reading, or some such thing. Sometimes the dreams were fragments, sometimes connected scenes that told some kind of story. Often they entertained me; usually they confused me, in that I could see no cause for them.

I saw no cause for this one, either.

I lay wide awake beneath a blanket, staring up at the haphazard roof of the lean-to. Del and Nayyib were deeply asleep. I let my breathing still, my heartbeat slow, and considered what I'd dreamed.

Me, in the desert. Older, but not old. I wore dhoti and sandals, held a sword in my hand. All around me were people I knew: Del, Alric, Fouad, Abbu, also Nayyib, and my shodo; even people from the Salset, including Sula and the old shukar who had made my life a misery. My grandmother. A younger woman whose features were obscured, but whom I knew was my mother. And any number of other people I'd known in my life.

One by one they turned their backs on me and walked away. I was left alone in the desert with only my sword.

Remembering it helped. Tension eased. Fear abated. I banished the images, relaxed against my bedding, and let myself drift back into sleep.

Chapter 33

*I*n the morning the air remained chilly, but it had nothing to do with the temperature. Del and Nayyib both seemed out of sorts. Feeling left out but not sorry for it, I went about my morning routine. Eventually I had the stud fed, watered, saddled, and packed, and I led him over to the lean-to. Del and the kid were still repacking bedrolls. I suspected there had been a verbal exchange held too quietly for me to hear; they seemed tense with one another, and they were behind on preparations.

"All right, children, how long are you going to carry on with this?"

My tone and implication annoyed Del, who'd heard it before. It always annoyed Del. She gathered up her belongings and stalked past me on her way to the white gelding. It left Nayyib with compressed mouth, set jaw, and sharp physical movements at odds with his normal economical grace.

So I came right out and asked it. "Does this have anything to do with Del?"

He didn't look at me. "Yes."

"And you?"

He stood up, hooking saddle pouches over one shoulder. Paused long enough to look me in the eyes. "Ask *her*." And marched himself across the flat to his horse.

Oh, hoolies. And other various imprecations.

*   *   *

We wound our way along the wagon ruts, going deeper into the low, boulder-clad mountains. I led, Del followed, and Nayyib brought up the rear. We were strung out, allowing the horses to pick the best footing, since the boulders began to impinge on the tracks. Some things looked familiar, some did not; but it was years since Del and I had been here, and we'd certainly been in a hurry to leave once the chimney collapsed. Other than a slight delay as I was declared a messiah by Mehmet, part of a Deep Desert nomadic tribe dedicated to worshiping the jhihadi, nothing had prevented us from leaving. Del had purposely broken her *jivatma* after drawing Chosa Dei out of my body, freeing him to fight it out with his brother sorcerer, Shaka Obre. We hadn't been certain how violent that fight would be since both had been refined to essences of power, not physical bodies, so we'd departed the area as soon as we could.

More memories came back. I recalled Umir's incredible feathered and beaded robe, which he'd put on Del when she was his prisoner. The whirlwind in the chimney had been been so powerful that it stripped all the ornamentation from the white samite fabric. We had picked feathers out of our hair for days.

I tried to stretch my senses, to get a feel for my own *jivatma*, buried in the ruins of the rock formation somewhere ahead. Nothing answered. There was no compulsion to continue as there had been to find my mother's bones; perhaps she trusted to me to complete the task without resorting to walking my dreams. I wasn't aware of anything except heat, the smell of stone and dust, the stillness of the air, the unceasing brilliance of the sun, and the sound of horses chipping rocks as the walked.

The wagon ruts were more difficult to follow as they passed over ribbons of stone extruding from the earth. Someone not intentionally looking for them might miss them altogether. But it struck me as odd that anyone would travel out here. There was no known road from Julah heading this way, the area skirted Vashni territory, and there was no known destination. Or if there were, it was a Vashni place; they had named the chimney decades before. In fact, I recalled being told they'd brought Del's brother to Beit al'Shahar, and when he'd returned he could speak again despite missing a tongue. Some kind of holy place, maybe. Except Vashni didn't use wagons, so the tracks didn't belong to them. We rode on a little farther, and then the trail made a wide sweeping turn to the left around an elbow of mountain flank. The stud abruptly pricked up his ears, head lifting. I reined in. He stood at attention, almost vibrating with focus. He nickered deep in his throat, then let it burst free as a high, piercing whinny.

In the distance, echoing oddly, a horse answered him.

Del, halted behind me, voiced it. "There is someone ahead."

"A horse, at least," I agreed. "Possibly two, or maybe a team of four; the wagon ruts got here somehow."

"Who would be out here?" Del asked. "There's nothing."

I shook my head. "It's a bit more than a day's ride from here to Julah on horseback; it would take longer with a wagon and team. Someone built that lean-to as a stop-over, a place to spend the night."

Nayyib brought his horse in closer. "So you're saying someone *did* settle out here."

"It's a guess," I said. "But we can find out." I brushed heels to the stud's sides and went on, more attentive now than I had been.

The trail took us down and around another tight turn, then leveled out. We were hemmed in by mountain walls. Then those walls fell away as if bowing us into a palace. And palace it was; I pulled up abruptly. Del fell in beside me, while Nayyib ended up on her far side.

"But—it wasn't like this . . ." Del said, astonished.

"Nothing like this," I agreed. Something had happened. Something that had riven the mountains apart, shaping out of existing stone and soil a long, narrow canyon. It wasn't terribly deep, nor was it huge. A compact slot cut between mountains and rock formations, opening up into a flat valley floor.

"Water," Nayyib said, pointing.

There hadn't been before. Now, bubbling up from a pile of tumbled boulders and fallen mountain, was a natural spring. It flowed outward into the canyon, finding its way through scattered rocks, then carved a fairly substantial streambed through the canyon floor.

I looked left, following the line of fallen hillside. And found the chimney.

Beit al'Shahar.

It had collapsed, breaking apart into sections. You could still see the suggestion of the columnar formation here and there, but it no longer existed as a true chimney. Del and I had not left it that way. Something more had happened.

Something powerful enough to open the way for an underground spring.

I tapped the stud back into motion and rode on. We passed the tumbled pile of slab-sided rock sections that gave birth to the stream, still following wagon ruts. Here we traded stony ground for soil, the first sparse scatterings of grass. Ahead, vegetation sprang up along the stream's meandering sides: reeds, shrubbery, thick mossy growths. Grass increased. The canyon widened. Thin, infant trees stood no higher than my knees. Oasis. Sheltered by canyon walls, with access to water, it was cooler here, shaded, with grazing and fertile soil.

"It was *nothing* like this," Del murmured.

Nayyib raised his voice. "Someone's farming here."

Indeed, someone was. The spring fed narrow, manmade ditches dug to water patches of fields and gardens, set apart from one another by low walls built of stones no doubt hacked out of the soil. We left behind wilderness and entered a private paradise.

"There," Nayyib said.

There, indeed. A scattering of flimsy pens held sheep and goats. A small pole corral contained a handful of horses. They had already smelled our mounts; now that we were in sight, all came trotting over to the fence rails to offer interested greetings. The stud stuck his head high in the air and commenced snorts of elaborate superiority, stiffened tail swishing viciously.

Behind me, Del's gelding pealed out a whinny.

"Look," she called. "They've built houses against the walls."

Low, squared, small houses built of adobe brick, surfaces hand-smoothed, with poles laid side-by-side and lashed together for roofs, chinked with mud to keep the rain and wind out. Unpainted, the dwellings were the color of the clay mud from which they were built: rich tan with an undertone of red. They blended into the canyon walls.

Faces appeared in wide-silled windows. Then the bodies took residence in the open doorways. Wagon ruts continued along the stream, fronting the dooryards of mudbrick homes standing cheek-by-jowl. Chickens had free run of the place, pecking in the dirt around the houses, pens, and corral.

"Sandtiger! *Sandtiger!*" A man emerged from one of the little houses. He came pelting down the ruts, brown burnous flapping, turban bouncing on his head.

"Mehmet!" Del exclaimed.

I grinned. "And his aketni."

"Sandtiger! May the sun shine on your head!" Mehmet arrived, dark eyes alight. At once he dropped to his knees, bowed his head, slapped the earth with the flat of his hand, then drew a smudged stripe across his Desert-dark forehead.

"Oh, stop that," I said. "You know how I hate it."

He sat back on his heels, enthusiasm undimmed. "Jhihadi," he breathed. And then he sprang up and began shouting in a dialect spilling so quickly from his mouth that I could only catch a third of what he said.

"Jhihadi?" Nayyib asked dubiously.

I arched supercilious brows. "Didn't you know? I've been declared a messiah. I'm even worshiped by—" I paused. "—however many people remain in Mehmet's aketni."

"Aketni?"

"His little tribe. An offshoot of his original tribe. Apparently not everyone wants to worship me."

"And the Vashni," Del put in. "Remember?"

Nayyib's expression was odd. "This is a joke."

I sighed. "No, actually, it's not. Though it certainly feels like one to me."

"You're a messiah?"

"I'm not a messiah. They just *think* I'm a messiah."

"My brother said you were," Del remarked.

Nayyib was totally lost. "Your brother said Tiger was a messiah?"

"It's complicated," I explained.

"A *messiah?*" he repeated.

I made a dismissive gesture. "Don't worry, it's not true."

"You're a legendary sword-dancer, the grandson of a wealthy Skandic matriarch, a mage—*and* a messiah?"

"A man of many parts," Del told him. "That's what the prophecy says."

I knew she was taking great joy in this, despite her bland expression. I shot her a quelling look. "Look, I have no control over what people say or think. Or that my grandmother is wealthy and powerful, or that I'm stuck with whatever this magic is inside me. What *I* know is that I'm a sword-dancer. That's good enough for me."

Neesha's expression was indescribable. Del took pity on him.

"We rescued them," she explained. "They'd been led into nowhere by unscrupulous guides, robbed, and left to die. Tiger and I found them, helped them."

Neesha's brows rode high on his forehead. "So they declared Tiger a messiah?"

"Not exactly." Del seemed to realize no explanation could sound reasonable. "But they worship the jhihadi, and they think Tiger fits."

"Why are they *here?*" Neesha asked.

"Because this is Beit al'Shahar," I answered crossly, knowing the whole thing sounded ludicrous, "and this is where I led them." I paused. "Supposedly."

Mehmet was waving his people out of their little homes. I saw the old women swathed in veils and robes, gray braids dangling from beneath head coverings, but also a few younger men and women and even a handful of children. Mehmet's aketni had increased in size since we'd last come across the tiny caravan.

Everyone gathered around, falling into a semicircle. All eyes were fastened on me, staring avidly. Mehmet stood in front of them, eyes alight with pride.

"We have done as you wished," he announced.

Since I didn't know what he was talking about, I prevaricated. "And you've done it well, Mehmet."

An outflung hand encompassed stream, ditches, grass, pens,

corral, fields and gardens, and the small, square adobe houses huddled against the canyon walls. "We have turned the sand to grass!"

Ah, yes. The infamous prophecy.

And then I realized it was true.

Del, behind me, began to laugh.

Nayyib muttered, "I don't believe *any* of this."

Mehmet was exceedingly proud to know the jhihadi personally. After everyone had offered deep obeisances, he sent them all away to begin preparations for an evening feast. In the meantime, he offered us the hospitality of his own "unworthy house." He and his wife would sleep in the front room, while Del and I were gifted with the tiny bedroom.

He tripped a little over what to do with Nayyib, until the kid said he'd be perfectly happy sleeping outside near the water, if that was all right. He even added he was unworthy to be under the same roof as a messiah, which earned him a scowl from me and a snicker from Del.

"When did you get married?" I asked Mehmet. "And where did you find a wife?" The first time we'd met, Mehmet had been the only young male left in his aketni, which was comprised of old women and one old man, who'd later died. There was no one to marry in his own small tribe.

"I found my wife in Julah," he said proudly. "A caravan came through and stayed a few days. I went out to their encampment to welcome them, and I preached the prophecy of the jhihadi. A few of them decided to stay on and serve. Yasmah was one." His joy was infectious. "Now, come—these men will take your horses and make them comfortable."

I decided against protesting the preaching part for the moment. Certainly the sand *had* been changed to grass, at least right here; when we'd left it was desert, if not the sere harshness of the Punja and its immediate vicinity. But I rather had my own idea about what had caused the change.

Mehmet bowed us into his house, whereupon he presented us to his wife. She was a small, slight, black-eyed woman wrapped in robes and veils, quite shy, unwilling to meet my eyes at all. The gods only knew what Mehmet had been telling her about his jhihadi.

We were served food and drink at the low table surrounded by lumpy cushions rather than stools or benches, while Mehmet explained that they grew most of their own food, raised goats and sheep for wool, milk, and meat, chickens for eggs, and only infrequently went into Julah for additional supplies.

"And no one knows you're out here?" Del asked. "No one knows this canyon exists, or the water?"

Mehmet shook his head. "No one."

"Someday people will come," I warned. "We came. We found your ruts and followed them here."

Mehmet spread his hands. "Were you not already coming here?"

Well, yes. Come to think of it.

He nodded even though I'd said nothing. "No one has cause to come here, except for the jhihadi."

"I didn't come here as the jhihadi," I explained. "I have business in the chimney, and then we'll be on our way."

His eyes widened. "But—are you not staying?"

I felt bad about disappointing him. "No. We're headed for Alimat, across the Punja."

"But—but we did this for you." He spread his hands. "All of this. You told me, remember? Find water where none exists. We have made a home here."

"You and your people have done very well, Mehmet—but I didn't mean *I* wanted to live here. I'm sorry."

He leaped to his feet, gesturing sharply. "Come, then. All of you. Hurry."

The meal apparently was over, even if we weren't quite done eating it. Mehmet's little wife collected the dishes from the low table and took them swiftly away even as her husband ushered us out of doors.

Two young children were playing down by the stream; Mehmet called to them to find some of the men and have them bring our horses.

I looked up at the chimney formation, or what remained of it, on the other side of the canyon across the stream. No horse could make it up there through the tumbled rocks and scree. I'd have to go on foot.

The horses were brought. The stud had a wisp of lush grass hanging out of the corner of his mouth. Apparently they'd been enjoying a meal, too.

"Go on, go on," Mehmet insisted. "Get on your horses. Hurry!"

We did as we were told. Our host nodded. "Now, ride into the canyon. You see that elbow of hill up ahead? Go around that. The canyon curves to the right. Follow the stream. You will see."

"See what?" I asked.

"Go, go. Go and see."

"And do what?"

"Go and *see*."

I gave it up. Until we went and saw whatever it was he wanted us to go and see, we'd make no progress toward actual communication.

"You're not coming?" Del asked Mehmet.

He shook his head vigorously. "It's for you. We kept it that way. Now, go and see."

"Let's go," I said to Del and Nayyib, and led the way.

As Mehmet instructed, we followed the stream around the designated elbow. Here the canyon narrowed until there was very little good footing on either side of the stream, mostly the steep sides of canyon walls. Huge sections of stone had broken off the walls, falling to the floor where they blocked most of the way. The stream, undaunted, had found a new way through. But I noticed the fallen rocks were all sharply angled and faceted, not yet worn smooth and round by water. Whatever brought them crashing down was but a few years in the past.

The horses picked their way over dribbles of fallen stone. There was no actual trail through here, and clearly none of Mehmet's people had ever attempted to bring in a wagon. The only tracks I saw belonged to animals.

And then the walls reared back. A passageway lay open, and the stream purled through. Beneath hooves, grass sprang up, thick, lush grass. Rocks in the water were mossy, wearing streamers of vegetation. Canyon walls became crumbled hillsides, cloaked in a tangle of shrubbery and trees.

Old trees. Mature trees. Mehmet's little canyon was new. This one was not.

The path we made took us out of shadow into sunlight. Out of canyon into valley. Out of paradise into perfection.

We stopped, because we had to. We gazed upon it, marking how the stream cut through the middle of meadow. Here was the true heart of the canyon with high walls surrounding us except for the throat we'd passed through.

Nayyib released a blissfully appreciative sigh. "Good grazing."

Del climbed down off her gelding and knelt on one knee, digging into the soil. She brought up a handful, rolled it through her fingers, then smelled it. "It should be," she agreed. "This is fine, fertile soil." She shook her hand free of damp dirt, then led the gelding by me, intent on something. After a moment Nayyib and I followed.

Del paralleled the stream. All around her lay the meadow, stretching from canyon wall to canyon wall. We were nearly to the far end when she stopped and shielded her eyes against the sun's glare as she looked up and up, studying the rim of the canyon and the blue sky beyond.

I saw her smile, and then she pointed. "Eagle."

Nayyib and I looked. Sure enough, an eagle spiraled lazily over the canyon.

Del's smile didn't fade, but grew. She stood in one spot and turned in a full circle, taking it all in. Her expression was rapturous. "It's almost like the North, this place. Not exactly, but very close."

I frowned. "In the borderlands, maybe."

"There are high valleys in the mountains very like this. You just never saw any of them." She began unbuckling her harness.

"What are you doing, bascha?"

"I'm going wading."

"Wading?"

"Maybe even swimming." She gestured up the way. "There's a pool, Tiger. See where the stream is partially dammed by rocks? On the other side there's a natural pool."

I hadn't paid any attention to it. But she was right. Nayyib rode up a little way, seeing for himself.

I recalled the big tiled bathing pool in the metri's house, heated by some means I didn't understand. Del had splashed around quite happily in it. I'd never learned how to swim and thus wasn't as enamored, though it did feel good, but the pool was shallow enough that I could stand in the middle with water up to my shoulders and not worry about going beneath the surface.

Mehmet had said this place was for us. That he'd kept it for us. His people had settled just inside the mouth of the new canyon. This one had remained untouched. This one, much older, had been untouched forever.

Del, who had tied up the reins so the gelding wouldn't trip over them, stripped out of harness, sandals, and burnous. She wore only the patched leather tunic a Vashni woman had repaired for her. Long-limbed, fair of skin, she strode to the water's edge as she unplaited her braid and shook it free. She was magnificence incarnate.

I realized it was the first time in months I'd seen her looking so relaxed. The tension had fled her face, leaving an incandescent joy. Every fiber of her body was reacting to this place.

I smiled, enjoying the sight. *Ah, bascha, if you only knew what I see when I look at you.*

Then I noticed Nayyib but a couple of paces upstream, staring at her. Del glanced at him and laughed. "Come in, Neesha. Lift the dust from your skin."

She had invited *him*. Not me.

Pleasure was extinguished. A chill washed through my body. It left me sick, angry, and afraid.

"I'm going back," I told her abruptly. "I'll leave the stud with Mehmet, hike up to the chimney and try to find the sword."

Del, picking her way carefully into the water, was startled. She halted, bare feet perched on round, slick stones. Sunlight gilded her skin. *"Now?"*

"I need to do it." And as she made as if to turn back, I waved her away. "No, no—you stay here. I'd rather do this alone." Which wasn't true, but I couldn't face taking her away from the canyon. I swung the stud. "I'll look for you when I'm done."

"And if you can't find it today?"

"I'll look again tomorrow morning." I turned my back on them both and headed out the way we'd come in.

Chapter 34

Mehmet, who knew nothing about *jivatmas* or that I'd left one behind, was perplexed when I said I wanted to climb up to the chimney. He reminded me that its collapse might have killed me. I reminded him that it hadn't and that I had business up there. Whereupon he, recalling I was the jhihadi, offered to guide me there.

I shot him a strange look. "Mehmet, I've *been* there."

"Things have changed," he explained. "After you and Del left, the earth trembled. Rocks fell. Mountains shook. This part of the canyon came into being. You don't know what's up there."

"Do you?"

He was forced to admit he didn't.

"Fine. You stay here. I'll be back before nightfall."

"But, Tiger—"

"I'm going. Look after my horse." I unsheathed my sword and offered it to him. "And look after this."

He was startled. "Why not take your sword?"

"Because I hope to find another one." I clapped him on the shoulder. "I'll be back in time for the feast. I promise."

Mehmet was unhappy, but he nodded. I left him carefully cradling my sword to his chest.

The climb up to the chimney was more demanding than I remembered or expected. But Mehmet had confirmed my suspicions:

Something indeed had happened after Del and I left to collapse the remains of the chimney and crack open the earth to form the newer canyon Mehmet's aketi had made their home. Probably it had opened the entrance into the older canyon, which looked as though no humans had ever been there. I groped my way up, clutching rocks for handholds, trying not to stub my toes. Sandals are not approriate footgear for climbing, but they were all I had.

Originally the chimney had been the hollow core of a mountain. Del and I had found a tunnel and made our way into the heart of the mountain. There we'd discovered the ribbed, rounded chamber open to the sky far overhead. It was purportedly the home of what was left of Shaka Obre, the so-called *good* sorcerer; his brother, Chosa Dei, who had taken up residence in my *jivatma* and later in me, was considered the bad one.

I'd go along with that.

I found no trace of any tunnel or passageway. What remained of the chimney lay in pieces, broken up as if a capricious god with a giant ax had chopped it into sections. Parts of it were indistinguishable from the shattered mountain. But something drove me on.

"Take up the sword," she had said. I would do my best. But it was possible I couldn't. That I might not even find it.

In which case, what?

Portions of mountain towered over my head. I picked my way carefully, gripping boulders as I pulled myself up. I remembered our flight from the collapsing chimney, knowing we might be crushed at any moment. I remembered how Del had shoved me out into the passageway when I wanted to turn back for the *jivatma*. She had no doubt saved my life.

Up and up. Eventually I found the bottom portion of the chimney surrounded by fallen segments of rock. Sections had broken off and collapsed all of a piece, like a stone cairn purposely kicked over. I prowled around, trying to sort out one part from another. If there was no actual chimney left, where might my *jivatma* be? How could I find it?

I stopped, looked around at the remains of the mountain. I wondered if Shaka Obre and Chosa Dei had brought about the additional change in topography.

Had they died? Had their essences faded away? Or had they merely taken their battle to another part of the world?

I went on, rounding a bulge of stone. And found the opening.

Here. *Right* here. The last section of tunnel. It was mostly blocked by fallen rock, and beyond the jagged mouth the interior was dark. I lingered on the cusp a moment—I hate closed-in places—then decided that jhihadis and mages had no reason to fear anything at all.

Or so one might think.

I took a breath, ducked my head, began to make my way in.

"Tiger!" It echoed oddly in all the rocks. "Sandtiger!"

Startled, I stood up and whacked my head on the tunnel roof. Cursing, I backed out. "Here!" Rubbing my head, I made my way around the nearest boulder. "I'm up here."

Nayyib was picking his way through rockfalls and boulders, head bowed as he watched his footing. He had taken off his burnous and now wore only a dhoti, as I did, and sandals. He was brown all over, darker than I, with no scars of significance and none at all from a blade.

If he was serious about becoming a sword-dancer, that would change.

When he reached me, there was no sign of shortness of breath. Very annoying. "What?" I asked testily.

His gaze went past me to the tunnel mouth. "Is that where the sword is?"

"Maybe. I can't be sure. Everything's changed. But this is a portion of the tunnel that existed, so it's possible I can get to the chimney floor."

He nodded vaguely, looking everywhere but at me. Something was on his mind.

Having seen how he stared at Del in the stream, I had a good idea what it was. "Why are you here, Nayyib?"

His eyes flicked to my face, then swiftly away. He turned and stared down the way we had come. "You can see part of the valley from here."

I waited. His posture was stiff even as he ran a hand over his head, smoothing springy hair.

And I knew. Even though I asked. "Neesha, why are you here?"

His back was to me. It nearly vibrated with tension. "Del sent me. She said I should come."

I closed my eyes a moment, then made myself cold and hard. "Not now."

"She said—"

"I don't care what she said." Because I knew. "I don't want to hear it." Because I *knew.* "I have business to attend to."

I bent and began to make my way into the tunnel section, leaving the kid behind. In the darkness I took care not to bash my head once again on some unseen protrusion. Hands followed the line of the walls, testing solidity. There was air aplenty but no light. I should have brought a torch.

I heard Nayyib's sandals crunching on grit. He was right behind me.

"Cool in here," he remarked.

I wasn't happy that he'd followed, but I felt a little better knowing someone, even he, was with me in a confined space. "There was ice in here originally. Not much, but a little." I peered ahead. "I think there's light up there."

So there was. The tunnel ended against two large boulders, but sunlight crept down through the cracks. It wasn't much, but it allowed me to see.

There was a slot to the left. The tunnel ended against the boulders straight ahead, but the narrow opening gave into something else. I pressed myself up against it and peered through. "I think that's it."

"The chimney?"

"What's left of it." I thought about it a moment, trying not to shiver in front of the kid; then reconciled myself with the memory that I'd been in here before and survived. I turned sideways and tried to edge my way through. Abdomen and spine scraped against rock. "There's a little light in there . . . it sure looks like it's a portion of the chimney. There's sand."

"Why does sand matter?"

"The floor of the chimney was sand. Just big enough for a circle." I grunted, sucking in my belly. Left a little more skin on the rock behind me.

"You're too big," Nayyib said. "Let me try."

I didn't want to let him do anything. "If I can just get through this one narrow spot—"

"Don't," he said sharply. "You'll get stuck."

He had a point. It was tough enough being in and under all this rock. The idea of being *stuck* here did not appeal.

"Let me try," he repeated.

I couldn't help the snap in my voice. "Why would you want to?"

For a fleeting moment there was pain in his eyes. Then it passed. "Because I'd like to."

No way could I get in there. It was Nayyib or no one. "All right." I slid back out, gritting my teeth. "It's tight, though. I'm not sure you'll have any more luck."

"I'm not as big as you." Nayyib poked his head through the slot, saw what appeared to be part of a chamber, sand floor and all, then sucked in his belly, straightened his shoulders, and started the slow, careful journey.

"Don't breathe," I suggested.

He released a brief hissing puff of air that served as laughter.

"If you find a sword in there, don't touch it."

His face was turned toward the chamber. All I could see was a body attempting to work its way through the slot. He seemed to be making progress.

And then he scraped through to the other side, disappearing from my range of vision. I heard cursing, though I couldn't see anything. "You all right?"

His voice echoed weirdly. "I think I left fourteen layers of skin on that rock."

"Well, having less meat on your bones will make it easier to get back out." I couldn't contain the frisson of dread that scoured my flesh. I wanted to go back out into the sun. Hurry up, kid. "See anything?"

"Anything like a sword? No. But there's not much light in here."

"I left it lying on the sand. It wasn't under anything."

His voice sounded hollow, deformed by rock. "Well, it probably is now." A pause. "Maybe I should get down on my hands and knees and feel around for it."

"Don't touch it! If you find anything at all like a sword, don't touch it."

"Then how am I supposed to bring it out to you?"

"Strip out of your dhoti and use that."

I heard the ghost of laughter. "I don't much favor coming back through that slot naked, thank you. There are parts of my body I don't want to scrape off against stone!"

"Then push the sword through first. You can cover up your precious parts afterwards."

He was silent. I waited impatiently.

Finally I gave up holding my silence. "Anything?"

After a moment his voice came back. "Lots of cracks and crevices. I'm checking them all."

"It wasn't *in* a crack or crevice."

"Then," he agreed, sounding irritated. "It may be now."

Well, that was true. I subsided again into silence, wishing I could pace. Wishing I could leave.

Then I heard a choked-off expletive make its way through the slot.

"What? What happened?"

"Is your sword broken?"

"No. It's whole. Why? Did you find a broken sword?" Hoolies, he'd found Del's broken *jivatma*. "Don't touch it!"

"I didn't intend to!" he called back. "But when you're barefoot and you stumble over it, it's hard not to."

"Why are you barefoot?"

"I took my sandals off."

"What for?"

"So I could feel the sand with my feet."

"You *stepped* on the sword?"

No answer.

"Nayyib?"

Nothing.

"Neesha?"

His voice sounded muffled. I couldn't understand.

"What are you doing?" I called.

Now he sounded cross. "Taking off my dhoti."

Was he bringing Del's *jivatma* out? Was that what Del had asked him to tell me, that he bring Boreal out if we found her?

"Neesha?"

"Here." His voice sounded closer, but pinched off. "Here, take the sword . . ." The hilt appeared through the slot.

Not Del's. Mine.

Samiel.

Mine.

I closed one hand around the hilt. Felt the familiar warmth, the welcome of Northern named-blade to wielder.

Mine. *Mine.*

Samiel.

Something deep in my soul surged up. I had forgotten what it felt like to hold a keyed *jivatma* bound to me. I couldn't restrain the fatuous smile that split my face.

Mine.

I heard grunts and mutters. Nayyib, dressed again, was working his way back through the slot. I saw a hand and arm reaching, a sandaled foot sliding through; heard the hiss of indrawn breath. In a moment he was free, pressing a hand against his abdomen. "There went a few more layers."

"Let's get out of here." I turned, stepped back into the darkness of the tunnel.

"Wait," Nayyib said. "Tiger—wait."

I didn't want to wait. "I don't want to wait."

"Please."

"It's dark in here."

"That's why I want you to wait. It might be easier."

The pleasure in finding the sword spilled away. For a moment I had been able to forget. "*What* might be easier?"

"To tell you."

I said nothing. I couldn't. There was only pain and acknowledgment. An understanding that had everything to do with practicality and none whatsoever with the feelings of the heart.

Oh, bascha.

But I could be alone. I'd been alone all of my life, until she had come.

And now she wanted to go.

"Del said I shouldn't put it off any any longer. That if I didn't tell you, she would."

Suddenly I was grateful we were in darkness. I didn't want him to see my face; didn't want to see his.

More silence.

Then, "I don't know how to say it."

I wasn't about to be patient as he tried to find the right words to tell me what I didn't want to hear. "I'm done in here." I turned, took a step.

"Tiger, *wait—*"

I swung back, filled to bursting with dread and anger. "Spit it out!" I bellowed. "Get it over with! Tell me what you've come to say!"

"All right!" he bellowed back. "You're my father!"

Chapter 35

No.

No.

Of course not!

Of course not.

Not possible.

He had come to tell me something else entirely. Something to do with Del.

Hadn't he?

Not possible.

"It's true," he said, when I did not respond.

Because I couldn't. I could not make a sound. I wasn't even certain I was breathing. I had prepared myself to hear something entirely different. This was . . . this was wholly alien, like an unknown language that sounds familiar but you can't make out the words.

"It's true," he repeated.

I was numb all over. The hairs stirred on the back of my neck. It took everything I had to force halting words past a throat tight with shock. "You said your father has a horse farm."

"He does. That is, the man who raised me does. He married my mother when I was a boy. He *is* my father in all ways—except blood and bone. He raised me. *You* made me."

My chest constricted. I felt the banging of my heart against ribcage. I didn't know how much of that had to do with his words and how much with my hatred of small, enclosed places. Breath rasped noisily through my throat.

"It's true," Nayyib said.

Couldn't be.

Wasn't.

Couldn't be.

My voice came out sounding very hoarse. "I don't have any children."

"That you *know* of. Del said."

Del had said a great deal.

My bones felt oddly hollow. "Why should I believe you?"

He released a long, resigned breath, as if I had finally said something he'd anticipated. "You were seventeen. Newly freed from the Salset. You wanted to be a sword-dancer. You stopped at a tiny village on the way to Alimat and spent the night with the headman's daughter."

I went on the offensive. "Not to brag, but I've spent the night with a lot of women over the years."

"She was, you told her, your first as a free man. And you intended to take a name—a *true* name—to mark that freedom."

"So? A lot of women know my name."

"You told her Sula had named you, when you lay sick from the sandtiger poison."

Only Del knew that. And Sula, who was dead.

Seventeen then, barely. Forty now.

Twenty-three years.

Del was twenty-three. So was Nayyib. He'd said so; she had. Not a kid, she'd said. Not a boy.

I had said I was old enough to be her father. And thus his.

"And you told Del this?"

"Del and I talked about many things when she was ill."

My voice sounded rusty. "There's one way to find out if this is the truth."

Startlement edged his voice. "You still don't believe me?"

I wanted to ask, Why should I? "Go out into the light."

"But—"

"Go out into the light."

Nayyib went out into the light. I followed him. Both of us blinked against the sun. Samiel, forgotten in my hand, flashed blindingly brilliant.

The kid eyed the sword. He marked the runes edging the blood channel, the satiny steel. Then he looked at me. Lifted his head with a slight aggressive tilt. Anger was in his eyes.

I stared right into them. "Is there a mark on you? A birthing mark?"

A muscle leaped in his jaw.

"Show me."

He stood very still before me, clad in only a dhoti and sandals. Stubble was turning into beard, just as my own was. I saw nothing of me in his face, nor anything of the woman he claimed was his mother. But it had been twenty-three years. It was true I had slept with many over the years, and most of them I couldn't remember.

That woman, I did. Sula had been my first, followed by others in the Salset; I was a slave; I did what I was told. But only one woman had been my first as a free man. A headman's daughter in a tiny village on my way to Alimat.

"Show me."

Abruptly he hooked thumbs into the top of his dhoti and jerked it down, displaying his lower abdomen, the thin line of dark hair vertically bisecting paler flesh. And the small, purplish mark the Stessoi called keraka, the god's caress. I'd seen it on Herakleio; Del had seen it on me.

I nodded once.

Nayyib pulled his dhoti back up. The anger simmered.

He wanted something. Acknowledgment. Confirmation. But I was empty of all emotions save overpowering disbelief, despite the presence of the keraka. Nothing in my life had ever prepared me for this. I had never even *imagined* it.

He stood waiting, every fiber in his body tensed with increasing anger. I had not responded to his announcement, had given him no clue to what I was thinking.

Inane, incongruous laughter bubbled up. I blurted the first thing that came into my head. "What did you expect?" I asked. "That I would fall at your feet and praise the gods?"

His eyes flickered. Those liquid, melting, honey-brown eyes, set beneath mobile eyebrows. "I don't know what I expected."

"Oh, I think maybe you do."

He met the challenge. "All right. I dared to hope, once or twice, that you might be pleased."

I was completely, tactlessly honest with him. "I'm not certain that's possible at this particular moment."

It shocked him. Shook him. Then he put on a mask, hiding his feelings. "Now what?"

"Now you go back to Mehmet's little village."

"What about you?"

"Oh, I'm going to go sit in the dark for a while and think about things."

He opened his mouth. Then shut it. No doubt there were all manner of things he wish to say, of questions he wished to ask, but he had the sense to realize now was not after all the best of times to say or ask any of them.

He turned to go.

Went.

I walked unsteadily back into darkness, gripping my *jivatma*.

When I came down from what remained of Beit al'Shahar, Del was waiting. She sat beside the stream on the far side, watching idly as I made my way across the stepping stones. By the time I got there, arms outstretched for balance, she was standing.

She smiled, lifting her voice over the rushing of the water. "You look as if someone hit you over the head with a cantina stool."

Since she had seen me be the victim of that very occurence, she knew what she was talking about. "Someone did."

She looked more closely. "Are you all right?"

"For someone who's been hit over the head with a cantina stool." I was still trying to reconcile emotions. "I just can't make my brain understand it. It heard the words, even understands them, but refuses to acknowledge that they apply to me. I mean, I know he told me the truth—"

"Do you?"

I looked at her. "Yes."

"*Do* you?"

I released a long breath. "Yes."

"But you didn't feel inclined to fall at his feet and praise the gods."

I winced. "He told you."

"I believe he got hit with the same cantina stool."

"Hoolies, Del, I didn't mean it to come out like that. But he wanted me to say I was pleased, and how could I? I'm too confused to be pleased!"

"Are you *dis*pleased?"

"No! I'm too confused to be anything." I stared at her pleadingly. "Don't you understand? It's not something I ever contemplated. Not once."

Her chin lifted. "Nor ever wanted?"

I flung out a hand. "Look at what happened to me! I was born as my mother lay dying in the middle of the Punja. I survived only because the Salset came along—and they made me a slave! Salset slaves don't have children. They may sire some, or bear some, but they aren't allowed to keep them. Then for twenty-three years I've been a sword-dancer, never sticking anywhere. It's no kind of life for a woman—" I saw the flicker in her eyes but didn't retreat. "—who wants to have her man nearby, and a family. I can't be that kind of a man for that kind of a woman. So I never thought about it, until that foolish foreign kid with the axes went around telling everyone he was mine, knowing full well he wasn't."

"Neesha isn't that foolish foreign kid. He *is* your son."

"I know. I know." I shook my head. "I just can't think, bascha. There's too much in my head. I need time to work through all of it."

"Why? You don't have to *raise* him. He's a grown man. All you have to do is acknowledge him."

That stung. "I didn't say he wasn't my son!"

"But you told him you weren't pleased."

"Because I wasn't! I wasn't anything. Hoolies, I was lucky I could find the words to say anything at all."

Del smiled faintly. "The Sandtiger—speechless. Truly a miracle."

I had to make her understand. "There is nothing, *nothing* in this world that could have stunned me more than what that kid told me. I don't know how else I could have reacted under the circumstances. I did the best I could. Maybe it wasn't enough, maybe it wasn't what he wanted, but it was all I had in me right then." I shook my head, still lacking words. "I've never claimed to be a perfect man, and I sure as hoolies wouldn't claim to be a perfect father. Especially when I didn't know I was a father at all."

I must have made some headway; her tone was kinder. "I did warn him not to have expectations."

"Well, I think he did!"

"Hopes, perhaps. How could he not? He has known since childhood you were his father. He's heard all the stories of the legendary Sandtiger. He has wanted to find you for all of those years. But he was afraid."

"Afraid?"

"That you would disbelieve."

"I did *not* tell him I disbelieved him."

"Nor did you welcome him." She put up a hand to halt more protestations. "It took him a very long time to find the courage to search for you. And even more to look into your eyes and tell you."

"He didn't 'tell' me. He yelled it at me."

"Sometimes yelling at you is the only way to get anything through your head. But that's not the point." Her eyes were sad. "He swore me to secrecy. I was not to say anything to you at all. It was *his* task."

"But you did threaten to tell me if he didn't get to it today."

Del nodded. "Because I knew what you were thinking."

"You did?"

"You were becoming more and more certain something was growing between Neesha and me."

"Ah, Del . . ." I planted my rump on the cool earth of the stream bank, rubbing hands through my hair. "He's twenty-three. He's a good-looking, smart kid with a head on his shoulders who's got his whole life ahead of him. What woman wouldn't be attracted?"

Del sat down next to me, left leg touching mine. "A woman who is content with what she has."

I didn't prevaricate. *"Why?"*

She leaned against me, put her head on my shoulder. "I can't define it. I just know it. Better than I know anything in this world."

I stared hard at the rushing stream, trying not to weep. "I don't deserve you."

"Probably not."

After a moment I smiled. "That time we talked about children wanting to know who they are, who their blood parents are—that was because of Neesha."

"That was part of it, yes."

"And as it turned out, I was searching for my mother. I just didn't know it at the time."

"But you knew how important it was that you find her."

"Yes."

Del nodded against my shoulder. "It was the same for Neesha."

I watched the water run. "You were so protective of him, so obsessed with his welfare. Always claiming we owed him a debt, insisting we rescue him from Umir. Because he was my son."

"And I *like* him, Tiger. There is that as well."

I sighed, nodded. "He's a good kid. I like him, too."

She lifted her head from my shoulder and leaned in to kiss my cheek. "Go tell him that."

I stared into water for a moment longer. Then pressed myself up from the earth, reaching down for Del. She rose as I pulled, and I wrapped her up in my arms. "Thank you, bascha."

After a moment she leaned away. Her smile was luminous. "He's out with the horses. They're picketed near the corral."

Chapter 36

I did not immediately go to find Neesha. I watched Del walk away, heading back toward Mehmet's house. Then I turned, stared pensively up at the broken chimney for a time, then into the rushing water.

I have a son.

Alien words. Alien concept.

I have a *son.*

I had believed it impossible. Not because I was incapable or infertile, but because at the core of my being a small, cold, piece of me remembered all too well how the Salset treated the get of chulas, if the women were unlucky enough to carry to full term when herbs didn't loosen the child. They were made slaves themselves, or sold to slave-dealers, or exposed out in the desert.

When you have lived among the Salset for sixteen years, you do not easily forge a new identity, a new view of yourself. I had spent far more years as a sword-dancer, but slavery had shaped me. A part of me would always be a chula in mind if not body.

I have a son.

Born into freedom, not slavery. Not sold. Not exposed.

Despite what I had told others, I had never *not* wanted children. I had simply never allowed myself to consider that I could.

I have a son.

I felt the kindling of a new emotion. Felt tears on my face.
Praise the gods.

As Del had said, I found Neesha near the corral, grooming and talking quietly to the horses. It struck me yet again how good he was
with them. Firm but not heavy-handed; calm, soft-spoken, yet
clear on who was in charge. He had already groomed his horse and
Del's gelding; now he worked on the stud. More than a little surprised by the stud's quietude, I watched without indicating I was
nearby.

But he knew. Whether it was the stud's pricked ears or just an
extra sense because of his background, he glanced over a shoulder
as he smoothed the brush around the healing wound on the brown
haunch.

It was too difficult to say what I wished to say. So I opened with
a compliment that was also the truth. "You are very good with
horses."

He looked away. "Is that your way of suggesting I should go
back to the farm?"

Oh, he was indeed in a mood. "It was my way of saying you're
very good with horses."

He ran the brush down to the stud's hock. "But you *think* I
should go back to the farm."

I told myself to be patient, that I had set up this scene by my
own reaction to his news. "If that was a question, I'll answer it: If
you want to. If it was an accusation, then I'm denying it."

"Maybe you don't care enough to have an opinion one way or
the other."

Anger flared; of course I cared. But how could he know if I
didn't tell him? Even if I had no idea how to begin.

I let the anger die. "Maybe I have an opinion but don't care for
people trying to put words in my mouth."

"I thought about leaving." He eased around the stud's rump,
moved to his head to brush the far side. "I thought about saddling
up and just going, with no word to anyone. But I decided that
would be childish."

I smiled. "Well, yes."

"And besides, I really *did* come to ask you for lessons, and I really *do* want to be a sword-dancer."

Finally I had to ask it. "And when did you plan to tell me you were my son?"

He moved to the stud's withers and looked at me across his back. "When I felt I was good enough that you'd be proud of me."

That was a kick in the gut, if not a stool over the head. "So, you had not planned to tell me at any point during the ride here."

"No."

That hurt. "Then why did you? I know what Del told me; but she wouldn't have given you away. You could have kept your mouth shut."

He hitched a single shoulder in a self-conscious shrug. "When I got up there in the rocks and came face to face with you, I thought I couldn't. Decided not to. But then I brought your sword out, and I thought that would please you—"

"It did please me."

"—so I decided to take a chance. And then—I couldn't. I couldn't say it. And you got angry."

Dryly, I explained, "I hate it when people won't say what's on their mind. I tend to yell sometimes, or so Del tells me."

"And then it just came out. And you—didn't care. Didn't believe me, until I showed you the mark."

"And then you decided I wasn't pleased."

"Because you said—"

Hoolies, couldn't he see? "What I said was that it wasn't a good time to expect anything out of me. I had just had the shock of my life. There were too many thoughts in my head for me to make any sense at all of *any* of them, let alone to say anything worthwhile! Think of it as being so drunk you can barely remember your name . . . the gods only know what will come out of your mouth." I twisted mine. "For what it's worth, seeing the mark was only confirmation. I did believe you. But I wasn't remotely prepared for that kind of announcement. Hoolies, I was expecting you to say something entirely different! Had expected it for some time."

He had stopped brushing and stared at me, brows knit. "What were you expecting me to say?"

I drew in a breath. "That you wanted Del. And she wanted you."

His mouth dropped open. *"What?"*

"That's what I was expecting."

"I—but . . . but what—I mean . . ."

I laughed. "See? Sometimes you can't make your brain form a real sentence."

He got the point. Closed his mouth. Tried again. "Why would you think anything of the sort?"

"I saw how you looked at her. Today in the other canyon. And at other times."

He stared at me as if I had two heads. "Gods, she's breathtaking! She's what we all dream of. How could *any* man not stare at her?"

I could not keep the curtness from my tone. "Or not wonder what she'd be like in his bed?"

Color bloomed in his face. "You tell *me*, Sandtiger! You're the one who took my mother to his bed when she was barely sixteen!"

After a moment, I said, "You know how to pick your weapons."

"But it's true."

"Yes." I nodded, aware of a trace of shame. "Yes, I did take her to my bed. I was a scared, foolish kid drunk on freedom, dreaming of making himself someone of significance in the circles at Alimat. She was very pretty, and I couldn't understand how she might be attracted to me. But she made me feel special." I had to look away from him; couldn't face his eyes. "She made me feel like a *man* instead of a chula."

He too looked away for a long moment. Then met my eyes again. "She said you were kind."

My reply was heartfelt. "I hope I was. She deserved kindness."

"She said—" Abruptly his mouth jerked into a crooked smile. "She said I take after her father, the headman. That I have a little of your height but not your eyes. Or hers."

I smiled, remembering. "She had very dark eyes."

"My grandfather has Borderer blood in him. It shows in me."

"There's Skandic in you, too. But your grandfather, if he had those eyes, probably could have taken his pick of any woman on the border."

Neesha grinned. "Ah, that's right. You said I could make every woman spread her legs for me."

"A not inconsiderable feat."

"Except for Del." He shook his head. "Would I want to?—hoolies, I'm a man, not a fool! But she sees no one but you. That was quite clear when I tended her in the lean-to."

Unable to speak openly about something this important, I resorted to off-handedness. "Nah, she just wants me for all my vast riches." Then I grinned. "And now, let me say this: You are a good-looking, smart kid with a head on his shoulders. And I like you. But I have never been a father, nor ever expected to be. I don't know how."

With wide, melting eyes, Neesha told me, "It's not as if you'll need to change my diapers."

"And you've got a smart mouth on you, too."

He affected innocence. "My mother doesn't, nor the man she married. I must have gotten it from someone else."

I scowled. Pointed to the stud's immaculate left leg. "You missed a spot." Then I stalked away.

Later that night as we lay in Mehmet's bed feeling the effects of a large feast, Del asked, "Did you tell him?"

I had been just at the edge of sleep. "Tell him what?"

"That you like him."

I yawned widely. "Yes, I told him that I like him. I told him everything you told me to tell him, that I had told you."

I heard a breath of laughter. "What did *he* say?"

"That he must have inherited his smart mouth from me."

After a moment of startled silence, Del began to giggle against my chest. I went back to sleep.

When I awoke not long after dawn, I discovered Del was missing. No wonder the bed felt so empty. I dragged myself out of it, slipped into harness and sword, wandered through the front room to the dooryard and saw Neesha lying belly-down at the edge of the stream, staring into the water with one arm submerged beyond his elbow. He didn't move. Finally I went over and asked what he was doing.

"I'm hoping to catch some fish."

"There are fish in there?"

"Del and I saw them yesterday, after you'd gone back. Quite a few up in the pool in the other canyon."

I decided to mention it. "You don't have a hook or line."

"No, I'm planning to tickle them."

"*Tickle* them? Fish?" I'd always considered tickling for women and children, not fish.

"If you tickle their bellies, they get a little sleepy. Or whatever fish do; I'm not sure. Maybe they just stop paying attention. But you can grab them and throw them on the bank."

I grunted skeptically. "I wasn't born yesterday, and you're not fooling me with such nonsense."

"It's not nonsense. I've done it many times."

"Where?"

"In the borderlands, close to the North. Lots of streams and creeks up there."

It still sounded unlikely to me, but I didn't know him well enough to be certain when he was joking. "Huh. I'll bet Mehmet has a hook and line."

"Probably, but I didn't want to disturb him. And I like doing it this way. Sometimes you need to know you're smarter than the fish."

Dryly, I observed, "I wouldn't think that'd be too hard."

Equally dry, he told me I'd be surprised.

I observed him a moment longer, marveling. *This is my son.* Then I reached over with a foot and bumped his leg. "Come on. It's time for your first lesson."

He was startled. "Now?"

"Why not? I like to believe I'm better company than the fish."

Neesha shot me an elaborately assessive glance.

I smiled, baring teeth, and unsheathed my *jivatma*. After that he didn't look at anything else. "Come on, Nayyib-Neesha. This is just the beginning of a long and painful process."

He stood up from the bank. Eyed me again, this time seriously. And sighed. "Yes, I suspect it will be."

Chapter 37

I broke through Neesha's guard six times in a row. By then he was frustrated and humiliated. He'd wanted very badly to show me he had some grasp of the essentials, when what he felt he'd shown me were weaknesses. Of course, that's what I'd expected; but I'd also anticipated that maybe, just maybe he could do to me what I'd done to Abbu so many years before, if I wasn't careful. And while that no doubt would have pleased Neesha, it might also have gotten me hurt.

So I was careful.

And I am, after all, the legendary Sandtiger, seventh-level sword-dancer out of Alimat . . . besides, if I was to shape a new legend, he needed to understand he had to be better than good.

Sweat ran down his face, bathed his chest. He was quick, graceful, focused. He was also angry with himself. So I told him we were done.

He lowered his sword. "Already?"

"Already."

"We've barely begun!"

"And we're finished. For now. We'll go again tomorrow."

I jerked a thumb over my shoulder. "Go wash off in the stream. Cool down."

He wanted to say more. But he shut his mouth on it, put his sword back in his harness, and stalked past me.

"And kid . . ." I waited until he turned around. "It will be a long ten years—or seven, or six—if you get this frustrated every time."

His mouth was a grim line. "I wanted to be *good.*"

I grinned. "Good doesn't happen overnight—or even after four lessons with Abbu Bensir." I bent, grabbed up my own harness, sheathed the *jivatma.* "Tomorrow. In the meantime, I'm going to track down Del."

"She told me she was going up to the other canyon."

I shook my head in resignation. "Seems like Del tells you more than she tells me."

An odd look passed across Neesha's face. Then abruptly he turned on his heel and headed for the stream.

By the time I hiked up around the elbow and through the passageway, the morning chill had faded. The sun now stood above the rim of the canyon walls, slanting blankets of light down the tree-clad mountain slopes. I heard birds calling and the chittering of something in the bushes, probably warning of my coming. The rush and gurgle of water underscored everything.

Del was where I expected her to be, up near the natural pool. At first I almost missed her as she lay on her back in thick meadowgrass. High overhead the eagle circled again against brilliant skies, accompanied by his mate.

I paused long enough to strip my sandals off, tie them together and sling them over a shoulder, then took pleasure in feeling the grass and cool soil under my feet. Remarkably different from Punja sand. My callused feet liked it very much.

I strode along the stream bank. "Catch any fish?"

I saw Del's hands go to her cheeks, wiping them hastily. Then she sat up. Her hair, worn loose, tumbled down her back. She smiled as she saw sandals dangling from my shoulder. Hers were lying near the water, along with her harness and sword.

Good idea. I dropped my sandals, got out of the harness, set it and *jivatma* in the grass. "All right," I said, "I may be male, but I'm not completely heartless. Tell me why you were crying."

Her eyes widened slightly, and then she laughed self-consciously. "Because it's so beautiful here."

This explanation seemed incongruous. "*That's* why you're crying?"

"Tiger—" She stood up abruptly, grabbed my hand, tugged me along the bank. Her free hand gestured broadly. "*Look* at it, Tiger! The trees are leafing out, the bushes are setting fruit, there are flowers in the grass, sweet water in plenty—"

"And fish that apparently like to be tickled."

In full spate, she disregarded the comment. "—and eagles in the sky, game on the slopes, a far more benevolent sun than anywhere else in the South—*no* searing heat, *no* Punja, *no* sword-dancers hunting you . . ." She released my hand and dropped to her knees, plunging fingers into the ground and bringing up clods. "Look at this soil! So much would grow here . . ." She tossed the clumps aside and rose, grabbing my hand again. "Come here." She led me away from the water. "Do you see? There against the canyon walls? We could build a good house. Smaller houses—just rooms, really—could go across the stream against *that* canyon wall. And here, *here* there is room for multiple circles." Her gesture was all encompassing. "As many circles as you need in a school. And Julah isn't far for when we need supplies. Or if you and the students wanted to go in to the cantina for wine-girls and aqivi."

Ah. Now I knew where she was heading. And it apparently wasn't Alimat, if she had anything to do with it. "This is why you're crying?"

Color stained her face. "Because it's beautiful, yes. Because it offers us everything we could want. Because it gives us a future different from anything we've known, something we can build together, starting over again."

Carefully I noted, "That's what I'd planned to do at Alimat."

"In the *sun*. In the *heat*. In the *sand*. Where, if there's water, it's always warm. Where I have to paint my horse's eyes and hang tassels off his browband so he doesn't go blind."

"Hey, that was your idea! I told you to get another horse, remember?"

"He's got the softest walk I've ever ridden. Probably softer than any *you've* ridden, you with that stubborn, nasty-tempered, jug-headed demon—"

"Now, let's not get personal about my horse!"

"—who'd just as soon throw you as carry you a yard—"

"All right!" My hand was in the air, silencing her. "We've established that your gelding has a better walk than my horse. Go on."

Del glared. "Because for the first time in more years than I can remember, I can let down all my walls. I thought I had forgotten how. My song is sung, Tiger. I found my brother and lost him again. I avenged my family by killing Ajani. I've proven to you I can dance with all the skill and honor of male sword-dancers—"

"With *more* skill and honor."

"—and defeat them as well." She was as fierce in her focus as I had ever heard her. "I have accomplished all that I set out to do, that day along the border when Ajani and his men killed my family, abducted my brother, and raped me. And I have given up a daughter, killed my *an-kaidin*, blooded—and broken—my *jivatma*, and have been exiled forever from my homeland." Her tone was sere as desert sand. "You asked me once what kind of man I dreamed of finding, and I told you I had stopped thinking of that the day Ajani came. I gave up all my dreams, all my hopes, all my *humanity* to become the weapon needed to kill Ajani. I even made a pact with the gods to keep me from conceiving again, so another child would not delay my plans as Kalle did." Her face was stark with pain. "So I would not have to give yet another child up."

"Del—"

"Two things, two things only, existed in my life: finding my brother and finding Ajani. I did both. My song is ended."

"Del—"

"And I was crying because this place is so beautiful it hurts my heart and because I know you won't want to stay here because there's Alimat, always Alimat—" She broke it off, drew a tight, rasping breath, began again. "And I even understand that because it's *your* song, *your* goal, *your* need, the way making myself into a weapon was mine. I understand it, and I hate it. I hate the sun and the sand and the heat, and the men who refuse to see a woman's true worth is in being something other than a vessel to bear babies and keep houses—" Now the tone was angry. "—and I hate it that you made yourself an outcast for my sake, breaking all your oaths and sentencing yourself to death by declaring *elaii-ali-ma* in front of all the others *and* Abbu Bensir—"

I raised a hand. "Del—"

Her voice tightened, "—and I hate it that you don't want children, because I'm going to have one and you'll want to leave."

Standing there suspended in disbelief, I discovered that once again I lacked the ability to find words, any words at all that began to address the situation in a calm, rational, sensible manner. Or, for that matter, that even approached coherency.

"And I hate it because I want this one to have a mother and a father of its blood—" She was running out of breath and intensity. "—and to keep it, to *keep* it, instead of giving it away as I gave away Kalle, to be a mother, a true mother, even though I know you'll want no part of this child or this life."

Empty of everything save sluggish shock and a wish to end a pain I could not begin to comprehend—and thus would lessen by any attempt—I walked away from her on unsteady legs and stood at the stream's edge, staring into rushing water. Lost myself in the sound, the tumult, the motion that required no words, no decisions, no compromises.

The cantina stool was getting harder all the time.

I squatted, leaned, scooped up and drank water. Sluiced it over my face and through my hair. Considered falling face-first into the stream and drowning myself, just so I never had to find myself yet again so utterly, completely, incoherently stunned.

Too much. All of it, too much. And Del knew it. Expected my reaction. Because I had told her what I'd told everyone: no children for me.

Go? Oh no. I had sworn oaths to Del, though she was unaware. And these I would not break.

And then I thought, *I'll be dead in twelve years.*

I would never see the child as an adult, like Neesha. Another good-looking, smart kid with a head on his shoulders—or a girl with all the glorious beauty and strength of her mother.

But twelve years, ten years, were better than none.

It seemed, after all, there was no decision to make. No reluc-

tance to forcibly sublimate. There was merely comprehension—
and a little fear.

Then I remembered the dream. Me, alone, as everyone I
knew—and some I didn't—walked away from me. That is what my
life could be like. Me, refusing to accept responsibility for my own
actions. Even for my children. And deserted because of it.

I'd survived hoolies all alone among the Salset. I wouldn't—
couldn't—do it again.

I pressed myself up from the ground and went to Del. I cradled
her jaw, smoothed back her hair, kissed her on the forehead, then
took her into my arms.

Her body was stiff, her voice tight and bitter. "And here I was
prodding Neesha to tell you *his* secret, when I've been keeping my
own."

Into her ear I said, "I think I'd have figured it out one of these
days even if you never said anything."

She pulled back. Walked away from me. Stood staring at something I couldn't see and probably never would. Her tone was oddly
detached. "Don't worry, I don't expect you to stay."

It hurt. Badly. But I had done it to her. Had done it to myself.

She turned. The angles of her cheekbones were sharp as glass.
Her eyes were ice. "I will not force a man to stay who has no wish
to. I have been alone in much of what I've done since my family
died; I can be alone in this."

I drew in a shaking breath that filled my head with light. "Well,
it's not an entirely new idea, this being a father. I've had all of, oh,
about a day to adjust to the idea of Neesha being mine."

Her tone was scathing. "Neesha is not a *child*."

"But it's a start. I mean, you're not going to drop this kid
tonight or tomorrow." I paused. "When *is* it due?"

"Around six months from now."

I shrugged off-handedly, keeping it light. It was what she was
accustomed to. "I figure if I can get used to having Neesha around,
I can get used to a baby."

Del was not in the mood to be amused. "Babies are considerably more trouble than a twenty-three-year-old man."

"Bascha . . ." I wanted to go to her, to take her into my arms once again. But I had learned to read her over the years, and that was not what she wished me to do. So I stayed where I was and told her the truth. "I knew when I stepped out of Sabra's circle and declared *elaii-ali-ma* that the life I'd known was over. I knew when Sahdri chopped off my fingers that the life I'd known was over. There on that island, with you lying next to me in the sand, I decided to build a school and become a shodo. Whether it's here or at Alimat isn't important; what matters is that I'd *already* made the decision to stick in one spot. Knowing there's to be a baby doesn't alter that." I paused. "Though I confess I'm not exactly sure how this has happened, since you made that pact with the gods. But then, I don't have much to do with gods—except when I curse—so what do *I* know?"

Her mouth compressed. "It happened because my song is over. Being gods, they knew it."

"Your song isn't over."

"That part of it is. I vowed to find my brother and kill Ajani." Her tone chilled. "Apparently they decided the pact no longer applied."

"Then make a new song. You're a sword-singer, after all."

Pain warped her words. "A sword-singer without a *jivatma*."

"Well, I've got one of those. And a terrible voice, as you've pointed out—you can sing *for* me."

It did not set her at ease. "This is not a casual decision, Tiger. This is a song that lasts a lifetime. Kalle I gave up. At the time it was all I could see, were I to achieve the goal I set myself, the goal that allowed me to survive. It wasn't a wrong choice; it was the *only* choice. But I am older now. I am different now. I have killed and will undoubtedly kill again; I know I will dance again. That is what I am; no child changes that."

"No," I agreed.

"But this time, I wish to preserve life. I have no goals beyond that, no song to sing, save I wish to make a new beginning with a new life." She said her walls had come down. I could hear in her voice the attempt to rebuild them, should it be necessary. "I will ask no man to do what he cannot do."

"Then don't ask me. Just tell me what you need. Now—or after the baby's born. If Alric can do it, I can."

One pale brow arched. "Do you really believe so?"

I needed badly to knock down the nascent walls. "Well, maybe only until the first time it spits up on me."

Her mouth twitched in a faint smile. "You missed all that with Neesha."

I feigned wide-eyed hope. "I don't suppose you could arrange for it to be born as a twenty-three-year-old?"

"Twenty-three-year-olds spit up. *You* spit up. That's what happens when you drink too much."

"As you found out."

Del sighed. The tension began to seep out of her shoulders. "As I found out."

"Look, bascha, what I said yesterday was the truth. I've never claimed to be a perfect man, and I won't ever claim to be a perfect father. And getting hit over the head with a cantina stool two days in a row is more than a little tough to take in! But if you'll give me the chance to do it—*and* forgive my lapses—I'll never say anything rude about how big you look when you're about ready to drop the kid."

"You don't drop a baby, Tiger; it isn't a foal. You *have* a baby. And you will too make rude comments."

"Well, all right, yes, I probably will. Some things I just can't change." I glanced around. "But I guess I can change where I'd planned to start a sword-dancing school. This place *is* beautiful. Alimat had its shodo and became a legend. This is Beit al'Shahar, and we can found a new one."

She hadn't yet relaxed. "A child is not a stray kitten, or a puppy with a broken leg, or even an orphan sandtiger cub. A child is for life. Make no promises you cannot keep."

"As I made to my shodo?"

From that, she flinched. "I didn't mean it so."

"Then let me make this promise: I will try."

She lifted her chin. "Are you certain?"

"Hoolies, no! But I don't know that I'd be any more certain if we were at Alimat just now." I smiled crookedly. "I never really planned to become a teacher. I never thought beyond dancing. I expected to die in the circle, to meet an honorable death. But that song for me is ended just as yours is for you. It's time I began another."

Her eyes searched my own. "Can you do that?"

I lifted my hands. Displayed them. "I knew I would have to that day atop the spire in ioSkandi. A child played no role in that decision."

"It does now."

Softly I said, "Give me a chance, bascha."

She closed her eyes a moment, as if praying. Then she opened them. "No wine-girls for you when you go into town."

I sucked in a dramatically stricken breath. Then, "Aqivi? At the very least?"

She considered it. "If you'll have Neesha tie you on the stud when you're too drunk to ride, and bring you home safely."

"If we're tying me on horses when I'm too drunk to ride, can I borrow your gelding?"

"Hah. I *knew* you liked his walk."

"And I'm thinking I'll invite Alric to pack up Lena and the girls—and maybe a boy, now—and come down here to live. I'll send Neesha to Rusali to ask. Lena could tend the baby while you're tending sword-dancers."

She didn't say anything for several moments. Then she took the steps necessary to put herself into my arms.

I cradled her head against my shoulder. "Are you crying again?"

"No."

"You are, too."

"Maybe a little."

"What's your excuse this time?"

She drew her head back and looked me in the eyes. "Not excuse. Truth: I may have stopped dreaming about the kind of man I wanted long ago, but I found him anyway."

I grinned. "You're just trying to sweet-talk me into your bed."

She took my hand, drew it down to her belly. "I think this baby proves you've already been there."

I laughed. "Well, yes."

Her hand, without excess fanfare, shifted from her belly to mine. And slipped lower, sliding suggestively between dhoti and skin. Which quivered.

"Uh, bascha . . ."

Her other hand was working at the tie-strings. "Hmmm?"

"What if Neesha comes?"

"Neesha knows better."

"What if Mehmet comes, or some of his people?"

"Then they'll all simply discover that their beloved jhihadi is also a man."

Self-control was on the verge of departing. "What about the baby?"

Del laughed. "The baby won't mind. The baby won't even notice."

I caught the hem of her tunic, slipped it up above her hips. "Are you sure?"

Her smile was glorious. "I'm sure."

"Well, if you're *sure* you're sure . . ."

Her mouth was against mine. "*Shut up*, Tiger."

Tiger shut up.

Epilogue

Alric dragged me out of the house. "Come on, Tiger."

"I'm not going—Alric, let go . . ." I tried to free my arm. "This is my own house, you know!"

He didn't give up. "Yes, I know that. I helped you build it. Now, come on."

Another harsh, half-throttled cry came from the bedroom where Del was in labor. Lena was there and one of Mehmet's aketni, an old woman who'd borne many children herself. Alric's children were off being tended by another of Mehmet's aketni, to get them out from under our feet.

I planted mine. "Alric—"

"We're going." He practically jerked me off my feet. "Trust me, there is nothing we can do except get in the way. Lena told me that with the birth of every baby. Now that it's you in my sandals, I understand why."

He'd gotten me as far as the dooryard. The panoply of the canyon opened before us, a spectacular fall day with trees ablaze, but I was in no mood for scenery. "How can you expect me to wait out here? She's been in labor since last night. She could die from this!"

He shoved me toward the stream. "Yes, she could, but I doubt it. Del is strong, and she's had a baby. Now, go sit down with your feet in the water."

"She had that baby nine years ago!"

"Tiger, she's young enough to have ten or twelve more after this one."

Hoolies, what an image! I stomped down to the stream, swearing all the way. Alric followed me, likely making sure I didn't try to go back to the low-roofed house built of mudbrick hauled in from elsewhere, since the soil here was better fit for crops. It's what Mehmet and his aketni had done.

I stood on the streambank and listened for Del's cries over the sound of the water. I didn't hear anything, which was probably Alric's intent.

Something occurred to me: absence. "Where's Neesha?"

Alric sat down in the grass, then leaned back on elbows. "He and Ahriman climbed up to the chimney earlier. Your new student is very eager to learn everything he can about his shodo."

I grimaced. "Ahriman won't make it past the second level."

"No, probably not. But he's a paying student for the time being."

One student in six months. Two if you counted Neesha, but I didn't expect him to pay; I figured a father owes his son that much, especially when he's been absent for almost twenty-four years of his life.

I smiled. "Neesha will make it past the second level."

Alric laughed. "*Oh* yes."

"He wants very badly to achieve seven levels faster than I did."

"Of course. He's your son. But he's hungrier than you were."

I glared at Alric. "You weren't there. How do you know he's hungrier than I was? He's certainly had an easier life than I did!"

"It's a different kind of hunger, Tiger. Your ambitions were to escape slavery in body and mind. Neesha wants to live up to the legend he's held in his mind since childhood *and* to make you proud of him."

"I *am* proud of him!"

Alric shrugged. "He has to discover it in his own way."

But my mind turned from Neesha and back to Del. Unable to stand still or sit, I began to pace. "Hoolies, I'd rather be in the midst of a death-dance than this. How can you stand the waiting, Alric?"

"Well, I've done it four times, so I have experience. And will likely do it again a few more times." His smile was content. "Four healthy daughters."

I stopped pacing. "Del says men make their wives keep having babies until they get a son, even if their wives don't want to."

"That may be true of some men," Alric agreed equably, "but I'll have sons enough when my daughters marry."

If I had a daughter . . . if I had a daughter, men would think of her as they did of all women. Even as *I* had, before Del trained me out of it.

Well, mostly.

"I'll kill them," I said.

Alric's brows ran up beneath the fair hair hanging over his forehead. "Kill who?"

"The men who try to get my daughter into bed."

The big Northerner laughed. "She's not even born yet, Tiger—and she may be a *he!*"

"I need to think about it, though. What I might face. Because, you know, if it is a girl, and she looks like Del . . ."

"Let's hope so. I'd rather a daughter look like Del than a big, slow danjac such as her father."

"I can't do this," I said abruptly. "I can't just wait out here. What if Del wants me with her?"

"Trust me, Tiger, Del doesn't want you with her. Best you stay out here—unless you *like* having her curse you."

"I'm going." I started toward the house, taking huge, long strides to get me there the faster. Then Lena appeared in the doorway and I began to run. "Is she all right? Is she all right?"

Lena was smiling as I arrived. "She's well, Tiger. So is the baby."

I stopped dead. "The baby? It's here?"

"Yes, the baby is here. Go in, Tiger. You've been waiting long enough."

But suddenly I couldn't make myself move. "Maybe I shouldn't. Del will be tired. She'll want to rest."

Lena laughed. "Go on, Tiger."

I felt a hand come down on my shoulder. Alric's. "She won't curse you now. They never do once the baby's born."

I took a deep, steadying breath, then a second one. And I went in to see what the Northern bascha and I had wrought.

The old woman of Mehmet's aketni was helping Del drink a cup of something that smelled slightly astringent. When she saw me come into the bedroom, she smiled, set the cup down, and waved me in. Staring at Del, I didn't notice her departure.

I couldn't see any baby. Just Del, lying beneath the covers. She was propped up against pillows. Lines of exhaustion were in her face, but there was also a contentment that outshone everything else.

I lingered in the doorway until she saw me. Her hair, wet with perspiration, was pulled back, braided out of the way. Her smile was weary, but happy.

"Where is it?" I asked.

"Where is *she*, Tiger. A baby is not an it."

Ah, good. She sounded normal.

Then it struck me. "It's a girl?"

"That's what 'she' usually means. And she's right here."

I saw then that they had wrapped the baby in so many layers that she looked more like a lump of bedclothes than a person. Del lifted that lump from beside her. I heard a muffled noise that sounded suspiciously like a sandconey warning of predators.

"Come see your daughter."

I didn't move. "You don't want to do this again, do you? Ten or twelve more times?"

Del looked horrified. "No! Why do you ask me such a thing?"

"Alric said you could have ten or twelve more . . . and he and Lena are already headed in that direction."

She laughed. "Tiger, stop putting it off and come and see your daughter."

When I reached the bed, Del put up a hand and urged me to sit. I did, very carefully. And then she peeled back the wrappings and I saw the face.

I was aghast. "What's wrong with her?"

"There's nothing wrong with her."

"She's all red and wrinkled! And she has no hair!"

Del's smile bloomed. "The red will fade, the wrinkles will go, and the hair will grow. But she does have *some* hair, Tiger. It's baby fuzz. See?"

To please Del, I said that yes, I could see the wisps of something that approximated hair. But if that's all she was going to have the rest of her life, I wouldn't have to worry about what men might think.

"Hold her, Tiger. She's yours, too."

I recoiled. "I'd drop her!"

"You won't drop her. Have you ever dropped a sword?"

I refused. "You can hold her. I'll just look at her."

"I'm very tired," Del said. "I'm very weak. I need you to hold her."

I cocked an eyebrow at her. "You aren't any better at lying now than you were before she was born."

Del was aggrieved. "I *am* tired, Tiger."

She was. Some of the animation in her face had faded. "Are you all right? I mean, *will* you be all right?"

"I will be fine just as soon as you hold your daughter."

I scowled. She always did drive a hard bargain. "All right. What do I do?"

"Just take her in your arms and cradle her. Put her head in the crook of your elbow."

"What if she cries?"

"Just hold her."

"What if she's hungry?"

"Then give her back to me."

I leaned forward, grasped the lump, lifted. Discovered she weighed nearly nothing.

Del's tone was appalled. "Don't just clutch her in midair, Tiger! Hold her against your chest."

Apparently I got it sorted out, because Del quit giving me advice. She lay there smiling at us both.

I ventured, "Does she have any arms and legs, or is she just a lump with a head attached?"

Del sighed. "I should have known you wouldn't appreciate the moment."

I grinned. "It's not a moment, bascha. Its a *baby*."

She reached out a hand and stroked the wrappings. "I thought maybe we could call her Sula."

It shocked me. I could think of nothing to say.

"That woman gave you your freedom," Del said. "As much as there was to be found in the Salset. Not enough, I know—but more than you might have had otherwise."

After a moment, when I had my emotions under control, I nodded. "Take her," I said. "Bascha—take her."

She heard the tone in my voice. "What is it? What's wrong?"

"Nothing's wrong. Nothing, bascha." I leaned forward, steadied the little bundle as she was taken from me, then bent down and kissed Del's forehead. "Rest. I'll come back later."

I waited until she had settled the baby beside her. As her eyes drifted closed, I left the room.

Alric saw my face as I came out of the house. "What's wrong?"

"Nothing's wrong."

"You look—odd."

"I'm fine."

"Then why are you in harness?"

"There's something I need to do."

"Tiger—something's wrong."

"Nothing's wrong," I repeated. "There's just something I need to do." I paused. "Alone."

Alric was troubled. He and Lena were sitting outside the house on the wooden bench I'd built. The chickens Mehmet had given us darted around the dooryard, and the half-grown gray tabby cat was chasing an insect. We had, in six months, accumulated all the trappings of a regular family: a house, chickens, mouser, two goats.

And now a daughter.

"I have to, Alric. I'll be back later."

He nodded and let me go.

I met up with Neesha and Ahriman at the passageway into the upper canyon. Ahriman was a short, compact Southroner with black hair and eyes. He was several years younger than Neesha and rather shy in my presence. Which made it difficult to get him to actually attack me in the schooling circle. He did better with Neesha, whom he did not hold in awe.

"How's Del?" Neesha asked at once.

"She's fine. So's the baby."

"She had it?"

"Her. She had 'her.' " I nodded. "A little while ago."

Neesha was studying me. "What's wrong?"

"Nothing's wrong."

"Tiger—"

I stopped him with a raised hand. "Nothing is wrong. Go on up and see Del and the baby—she's your half-sister, after all. I'll be back."

Neesha didn't look any less concerned than Alric. But I had no time for them.

No time for much of anything.

The climb up to the broken chimney was easier now than when I'd made it six months before. Not only did I know where I was going, but I was utterly focused on my goal. When I reached the tunnel, I didn't think twice about the darkness. I ducked my head, went inside, followed it back to the slot near the boulders blocking the rest of the passageway. There I took off the harness, dropped it to the dirt floor, and pulled the stopper from the little pot I'd collected on the way out of the house. I smeared grease on my abdomen and spine, tossed the empty pot away, unsheathed the *jivatma*. I left the harness where it lay.

It wasn't easy getting through the slot. Neesha had been right about leaving layers of skin on the rock. But the grease served me well, and at last I scraped myself into the chimney.

The chamber was small, about one-quarter the size of the original circle. Sunlight worked its way down through cracks, illuminating the area, but the chimney wasn't a chimney anymore. Mostly it was a pile of rocks and sections of ribbed wall. But the floor was still the pale Punja sand Del and I had discovered before.

I glanced around. Found what I expected: Del's *jivatma*. Boreal lay in two pieces. I didn't touch them. I set down my sword and bent to unlace my sandals. When that was done, I stripped out of my dhoti. I collected my sword, moved to the center of what remained of the chimney chamber, and sat down cross-legged with the *jivatma* across my thighs.

In fractured light, I looked at my hands. Two thumbs, three fingers on each. The stubs were no less obvious than before, but I hadn't really noticed them for a while. The training I'd done on the island near Haziz still served me. Since settling in the canyon, I had spent every day working through the forms, keeping myself fit. Sparring matches with Neesha and Alric—I had refused to fight Del once I knew she was pregnant, which irritated her to no end— maintained my speed, strength, and technique. In fact, Alric said I was better than before.

If that were true, it was because something inside me, some facet of the magic, lent me an edge. When I danced, I felt four fingers on the hilt. Not three. My grip was the grip it had been before losing them. And I had no explanation. Only gratitude.

I closed my hands lightly over the sword. Went into my head. Dug into my soul. Peeled the flesh off the bones, shed muscle and viscera, until I found the magic buried so deep inside.

It wasn't a flame, but a coal. It burned steadily, unceasingly, using me as the fuel. It would kill me one day, merely because it existed. Because my mother was of the Stessoi, one of the gods-descended Eleven Families of Skandi, and those gods had been capricious enough to set their mark on me even as my mother, and I, lay dying in the Punja near my father's body. Because I was ioSkandic, a mage of Meteiera, meant to leap from the spire to merge with the gods when the madness overcame me.

In ten years. Twelve.

I had a son. A daughter. I had Delilah.

I wanted to live forever.

Or at least as long as I possibly could as man, not mage, without the interference of a magic I never wanted. Even though I'd used it.

"Find me," she had said, *"and take up the sword."*

My mother had died giving birth to me. But she had served me nonetheless by setting me on the road to this place. To this moment. To this decision.

No other was possible.

I found the coal inside. Took it up. Blew gently upon it. Felt the heat rise; saw the flame leap. I coddled it. Cradled it. Nursed it into being. Kept it alive. Bade it serve me.

Made it serve me.

Once I had had a sorcerer inside me. And in my *jivatma*. It was time to put the mage that was me in the *jivatma*. The power, if not the man.

For the first time since I'd been reborn atop the spire in Meteiera, I thanked the priest-mages who had altered mind and body. Because in doing so they had given me the key.

Discipline.

"Mother," I said aloud; and discovered how odd it was to use the word as an address. A title. "Mother, you bred me for this. Bred it *in* me, bequeathing me something else of your people besides height, coloring, even keraka. Magic, magery, is not a gift I desire, or require. I wanted freedom—and won it because of Stessor magic. I wanted to be a sword-dancer—and became one because of Skandic strength, the heritage of you, my father, and everyone before us. But now comes the time for me to look forward instead of backward. To, as Del would say, make a new song. To do that, I must make a new man. One who wishes to live for the children *he* has made, children who are of Stessoi flesh and bone even as I am. But also of the North, and of the South. If to do that I must cut away a part of me that you gifted me, so be it. I have made the choice."

There was no answer. I had no bone to fuel the dream-walk. But I had clarity of purpose, and the certainty to fuel that.

It took time. It nearly took me. But I felt the flame of the power become conflagration, feasting on my flesh. I poured it into and through my arms, down into the sword. Into Samiel, whose song I sang in a broken, shaking voice.

Discipline.

And when it was done, when the magic that had, at age sixteen, won me my freedom, resided in the sword, I stood up from the sand. Walked to the chimney wall. Found a crevice. I thrust the *jivatma* blade into the stone as deeply as I could.

And then I broke it.

I was a sword-dancer. It was all the magic I needed.

I smiled even as I wept. Even as I placed the two halves of the broken *jivatma* with Del's. Even as I shakily put on dhoti and sandals and went back through the slot, leaving layers of grease and skin.

In the tunnel, I collected my empty harness.

When I walked up the canyon I was thinking about Del. Not about circles, or sword-dancers, or *elaii-ali-ma*. Not about challenges. Not about dancing. Not about the price for breaking lifelong oaths.

Certainly not about Abbu Bensir. But he was there. And I understood why. On this day of all days, we had finally arrived at the moment we both had known would come: the dance that woud define us both.

He stepped out of the doorway of my house as I approached. He wore only a dhoti and held a sword. "You were hard to find," he told me, "but then I heard about Alric and his family heading down here with a kid who'd been seen with you and Del, and I knew."

I said nothing. I waited.

His tone changed. "Sandtiger," he said, "by the rite of *elaii-ali-ma* I am not required to challenge you or to meet you in the circle. I am required only to kill you. But I have not forgotten the ignorant boy who, all unknowing, taught me a lesson before others at Alimat, even before the shodo. For that, I will offer you the honor of meeting me in the circle."

Very slowly, I unbuckled my harness. Dropped it to the ground. Spread my hands. I had no sword; I could not accept.

Abbu Bensir smiled. "The boy has said he will lend you his."

The boy. My son. Who had once been taught by the man before me.

"Where are they?" I asked.

Abbu stepped out of the doorway into the yard. Neesha came out. And Alric.

The big Northerner said, "Lena's with Del. She's fine."

"Does she know?"

Something spasmed briefly in Alric's face. "She's asleep."

Ah. Well, probably for the best.

Abbu nodded. "I have asked the boy to start the dance for us. Shall we waste no more time?"

"The boy," I said, "has a name."

"Nayyib. I know. I met him some years ago, apparently, though I confess I don't recall." He flicked a glance at Neesha, standing white-faced in the dooryard. "Give him your sword."

We had met several times, Abbu and I. That first time at Alimat, when I nearly crushed his throat. His voice still bore the scars. Once or twice after that, merely to spar because we ran into each other in a distant desert town with no other entertainment. Then for years, nothing. The South is a large place, and we ranged it freely. We were to meet again at Iskandar during the contest, but I'd been kicked in the head by the stud and was in no shape to dance. More recently, we had met at Sabra's palace, where I had aborted the dance by declaring *elaii-ali-ma*.

To this day neither of us knew which was the better man.

I walked over to Neesha and looked him in the eye. "I thank you for the honor of the use of your sword."

He wanted to speak. Didn't. Just unsheathed and gave me his sword.

I led Abbu to one of the sparring circles and waited. He studied it, walking the perimeter, noting how the turf was incised and marked with small pegs denoting the circle, so the grass wouldn't cover it. Inside, the meadowgrass was beaten down, crushed by feet. He walked there, too, to learn the footing. In a strange place, we would not have done so; but this was my home, and Abbu was due the chance to learn what its circle was like. He set his sword in the center, then walked away. I did the same. We faced one another from opposite sides.

He was older than I, smaller, lighter. But he'd always been fleet of foot. Age lay on him more heavily than the last time we'd met, but he was as fit as ever.

"I hear you danced against Musa."

So, he knew him. Or knew *of* him. "Umir's idea. But yes. I did."

"I hear you killed him."

"He insisted."

"Ah." Abbu nodded. "Musa was a proud boy. I did warn him it would get him killed one day, if he didn't quench it. I didn't believe it would be this soon."

"How well did you know him?"

"I taught him. Oh, not as the shodo taught us. He didn't stay with me for years, learning the forms. He came to me with a natural skill honed by other instructors: the sword-dancers he'd already defeated. He wished to defeat them all and desired my help. When I saw how he danced, I gave it to him." His creased face tautened briefly. "I did not believe you could defeat him."

I nodded. "Neither did Musa."

Dark eyes flicked to Neesha. "Now."

Neesha stood two paces away. Alric had moved to stand behind me, well out of the way.

I looked at my son and nodded.

His jaw clenched. "Dance."

It was a fast-moving, vicious fight, unlike anything Abbu and I had engaged in before. But then, though not friends, we had been friendly rivals, more interested in the challenge. We had never fought to the death. Even before Sabra, he had retained the honor I'd always seen in him, doing his best to respect the honor codes despite Sabra's desire for me to die.

He respected those codes now. But this time he wanted me dead.

Within four engagements each of us had drawn blood. I had a slash across one thigh and a cut along my ribs, matching the one Musa had given me on the other side. Blood dripped from the inside of Abbu's right arm, but it wasn't a mortal wound. We were a long way from dying.

And I had discovered that the ritual I performed to rid myself of the magic had also tired me. I felt as if a part of me were missing; and maybe it was. The fingers were. No more was there the odd conviction that they were still attached. My hands were as Sahdri had made them: a thumb and three fingers, no more. The stumps were sore. My grip was weakened. As Abbu engaged my blade again, the sword twisted in my hands.

Abbu Bensir was not as young as Musa, but he was far wiser. He would not make the mistake Musa had.

And I could die for it.

My world closed down. My mind registered all of the factors that affected a dance, such as footing, footwork; how the light lay; the reach of blades and arms; the rhythm of my breathing and his; even the blood running down my flesh. The canyon was filled with the belling of blades, the screech of steel on steel.

Yet again his blade touched me, slashing high across one hip. I broke away, stumbled, felt more blood running, saw the light in Abbu's eyes. He came in, blade raised and moving. I blocked it, held it, spun away. Felt the pain in my hip. Felt the sudden tilt of the world.

I took a step forward. Went down. Caught myself with both hands splayed against the ground. The hilt of Neesha's sword remained beneath my right hand, but I couldn't grasp it properly. The stump banged against leather grip, sending fire through my arm.

Abbu came on. I grabbed the fallen blade, stayed on my knees, brought the hilt up. I planted the pommel in his belly even as his sword sang down on the diagonal, slicing straight into the meat up my upper arm. I felt the steel grate on bone.

But Abbu had lost the impetus of his blow when I jabbed the sword hilt into his abdomen. He fell back, gasping, slightly hunched. I got to my feet, aware that the wound was a bad one. The arm didn't want to work. I wavered, nearly fell down, caught my balance with effort. Blinked as sweat ran into my eyes.

Abbu went to one knee. He cradled his lower belly with his left arm. His face was gray.

I was one-armed now. I stayed on my feet with effort, aware of the roaring in my ears. And then, as it so often did, time slowed for me. I had no magic, but I had skill and the odd accuity that always served me.

Abbu got up. He winced as he straightened, then wrapped both hands around his sword hilt. He came across the circle.

Slowly. So slowly.

I saw the blade rise. Saw my blood on it.

As he came on, I let go of the sword—Neesha's sword—in

midair and caught it upside down as it hung there at the apex. I held it overhand now, the pommel exiting above my thumb. I pulled it and my arm back across my body, elbow bent; as Abbu closed, I snapped my arm toward him in a backhanded, punching thrust, keeping the power close to my body. The desperate maneuver allowed Abbu inside, to make contact with my body, but by then my blade had been shoved straight through his body. I heard his outcry, felt the warmth of his breath on my face, took his weight on my right shoulder as he fell forward.

With the last bit of my strength, I thrust him away from me with my right arm, letting him take Neesha's sword. He fell hard, full-length, his head smacking dully against the ground. The sword stood up from his body.

They were with me then, Neesha and Alric. I felt hands on me, holding me upright, supporting my left arm. Someone tied something around my upper arm to try to slow the bleeding. But I pushed them away, staggered to Abbu. Saw the blood on his lips. Before I could say a word, before I could speak the ritual blessing for a seventh-level sword-dancer at the edge of death, he was gone.

Over.

Ended.

The first of the shodo's greatest lay dead in the circle.

This time I didn't fight them as Alric and Neesha gathered me up, kept me on my feet, aimed me toward the house. We were nearly there when I saw Del in the doorway. Hollows lay like bruises under her eyes, and her lips were pale. One hand clutched the doorjamb; the other lay across her mouth, as if to physically restrain the fear that she would not confess.

But a smile of relief began behind the hand, and she lifted her fingers away. She reached out, closed that hand on the back of my neck, shakily pulled me close. Her robes were immediately soaked with my blood. "Come inside."

Alric and Neesha got me there. Del directed them to the bed in the other room. I protested weakly. "What about the baby?"

"She's in the cradle," Del told me. "She missed her father proving once and for all that he *is* the greatest sword-dancer in the South."

"Well," I gasped, "she'll probably see it again."

Alric and Neesha helped me to sit on the bed. Unconsciousness crowded in. I was aware of people moving around, bandaging me, of words exchanged about a heating knife; but none of it made any sense. Everything felt distant.

"What about you?" I asked Del, even as they made me lie down.

She had moved around to the other side of the bed. She sat down, caught her breath, then took my right hand. "I'm here."

I wanted to tell her she had no business sitting up in bed hanging onto me so I could hang onto her, but then Alric thrust a twist of cloth between my teeth, told Neesha to hold my arm, and pressed the red-hot knife blade against the wound in my upper arm.

I woke the baby up. Dei said something about having *two* screaming infants in her house, and then she very suddenly lay down next to me.

Ridding my mouth of cloth, I croaked, "You all right?"

Her head moved against mine in a weak nod.

I glanced at Alric, who was dropping the knife into a wooden bowl. "You enjoyed that. Making me yell."

He grinned. "So I did."

Now I looked at Neesha. "Still want to be a sword-dancer, after seeing that?"

He drew in a breath. "After seeing that, I want to be nothing else."

Guess it was in the kid's blood after all. I smiled faintly to tell him I approved, then rolled my head toward Del. I heard the sounds of Neesha and Alric leaving. The baby had gone back to sleep. I thought her mother was on the verge herself. "You awake?"

Her voice was a breath of sound. "Barely."

"I have a question."

She was fading fast. So was I. "What?"

"Who's really the best? You or me?"

Del lifted her head enough to stare at me in wide-eyed, rigid disbelief. Then dropped it back down again. "I guess we'll just have to have a dance to find out."

"All right. Tomorrow?"

"Fine," she murmured.

I turned my head enough to feel her hair against my face. Opened my mouth to tell her we'd have to be vigilant about the men who lusted after our daughter—and then exhaustion hit me over the head with a cantina stool.

A woman. A son. A daughter.

Was this what I had expected?

No.

But it was what I had dared to dream, at night among the Salset.

Author's Note

What Comes Next?

I have, in my professional life, written books that were "easy," and books that were difficult—though of course "easy" is a matter of degree and context. Though at eight volumes the Cheysuli series was a lengthy task, it also offered escape from college classes (I was an adult student), and part-time work. I lost myself in an "alternate universe," if you will, and, being an organic writer, discovered much of the tales as I went along, just as readers did. Every free moment I had was spent creating the worlds, the characters, and stories of the Cheysuli. But in the midst of writing the series, *Sword-Dancer* appeared in my head. It arrived completely out of the blue one summer evening and more or less wrote itself in a burst of white-hot creative energy; it was what many authors call an "attack book." *Sword-Dancer* came pouring out of my typewriter over two weeks of twelve- to fifteen-hour days. Tiger had a story to tell, and I was his chosen scribe. I had so much fun I went on to write five more novels featuring Tiger and Del.

Then there was *The Golden Key*, a collaboration with Melanie Rawn and Kate Elliott. I said from the beginning that no one of us could have written that massive, complex novel. All of our brainstorming on world, customs, characters and plotlines was interconnected, and we critiqued one another's work along the way. We each of us was responsible for writing our specific sections (me,

Part I; Melanie, Part II; and Kate, Part III), but they were born out of many three-party discussions via phone, e-mail, and fax machine. *The Golden Key* was a huge undertaking and an immensely challenging task, but it was also a creative "high" and made all of us better writers. To this day I am extremely proud of that novel.

Authors always have ideas bubbling away on the back-burners of the brain, and eventually there came a day when I told my agent I had an idea for an entirely new fantasy universe unrelated to the Cheysuli and *Sword-Dancer* series. By saying it, I made it real. Now I had to write it. And so in fits and starts and bumps along the way, I embarked on a new fantasy journey.

It was the first brand-new universe and cast of characters that I, as a solo author, had created since 1983, when I wrote *Sword-Dancer*. *Karavans* wasn't another volume in an existing series with people, places, and plots already in place, but a wholly new undertaking. And I knew I wasn't the same person, much less the same writer, that I was in the early to mid-'80s when the Cheysuli and *Sword-Dancer* series debuted. *Karavans* became, in fact, the most challenging fantasy novel I'd ever written. Afterall, in keeping with traditions of the time, the first several Cheysuli novels and *Sword-Dancer* arrived on the bookshelves without fanfare. I was a completely unknown author. But *Karavans* would be published *with* fanfare. I knew readers would have expectations. And I had expectations about those expectations. (Never let it be said that authors don't speculate about what their fans will think!)

I've been most fortunate to have two fantasy series, both markedly different from one another (and both published by the same publishing house), become very successful. It allowed me the luxury, with DAW's blessing, of alternating between worlds, writing styles, and plots and characters instead of living in the same universe day in and day out, something that can make an author— and her work—go quite stale.

Now, with *Karavans,* I begin all over again once more, some twenty-eight years after I began writing about a race of shapechangers and their magical animals, and twenty-six since Del walked through the door of a Southron cantina and into Tiger's heart. With those experiences behind me, I have high hopes for the new world and an eclectic slew of characters.

In the aftermath of a bitter, brutal war waged by ruthless neighboring warlord, many residents of Sancorra Province have turned refugee, fleeing the destruction of farmsteads and settlements to begin new lives in another province. But it is very late in the karavan season with the rains due any day, and the roads are made even more dangerous by opportunistic bandits and the warlord's vicious armies and patrols. Also threatening the safety of the refugees is the land called Alisanos, a living hell-on-earth that changes location at will, swallowing everything—and every*one*—in its path. Infamous as the dwelling place of demons, devils, gods and demi-gods and countless other horrors, Alisanos wreaks tragedy on entire villages or single individuals. Few humans, once taken into Alisanos, ever escape—and those who do have been terribly altered in mind and body by the poisonous magic of Alisanos, fated to be shunned by the human race they were once a part of.

I invite readers to join karavan guide Rhuan and his cousin, Brodhi, a courier, both born of a legendary race called the Shoia; Ilona, the karavan diviner who reads in the hands of others the dangers and griefs facing them, but cannot read her own; demons Darmuth and Ferize, hiding true forms and secrets; and a farmstead family desperate to reach Atalanda Province before the new baby is born, each on a perilous journey along dangerous roads much too close to the living evil threatening them all as Alisanos prepares to go active.

Karavans *will be published in hardcover by DAW Books in April 2006.*

Watch out for

KARAVANS

Jennifer Roberson's first all-new fantasy universe in twenty years

New in hardcover in April 2006

Read on for a special introduction to the series: the short story that debuted the world of *Karavans*

Ending and Beginning

Four had died. Killed ruthlessly. Uselessly. Three, because they were intended as examples to the others. The fourth, merely because he was alone, and Sancorran. The people of Sancorra province had become fair game for the brutal patrols of Hecari soldiers, men dispatched to ensure the Sancorran insurrection was thoroughly put down.

Insurrection. Ilona wished to spit. She believed it a word of far less weight than war, an insufficiency in describing the bitter realities now reshaping the province. *War* was a hard, harsh word, carrying a multiplicity of meanings. Such as death.

Four people, dead. Any one of them might have been her, had fate proved frivolous. She was a hand-reader, a diviner, a woman others sought to give them their fortunes, to tell their futures; and yet even she, remarkably gifted, had learned that fate was inseparably intertwined with caprice. She could read a hand with that hand in front of her, seeing futures, interpreting the fragments for such folk as lacked the gift. But it was also possible fate might alter its path, the track she had parsed as leading to a specific future. Ilona had not seen any such thing as her death at the hands of a Hecari patrol, but it had been possible.

Instead, she had lived. Three strangers, leaving behind a bitter past to begin a sweeter future, had not. And a man with whom she had shared a bed in warmth and affection, if not wild passion, now rode blanket-wrapped in the back of the karavan-master's wagon, cold in place of warm.

The karavan, last of the season under Jorda, her employer, straggled to the edges of the nameless settlement just after sundown. Exhausted from the lengthy journey as well as its tragedies, Ilona climbed down from her wagon, staggered forward, and began to unhitch the team. The horses, too, were tired; the karavan had withstood harrying attacks by Sancorran refugees turned bandits, had given up coin and needed supplies as "road tax" to three different sets of Hecari patrols until the fourth, the final, took payment in blood when told there was no money left with which to pay. When the third patrol had exacted the "tax," Ilona wondered if the karavan-master would suggest to the Hecari soldiers that they might do better to go after the bandits rather than harassing innocent Sancorrans fleeing the aftermath of war. But Jorda had merely clamped his red-bearded jaw closed and paid up. It did not do to suggest anything to the victorious enemy; Ilona had heard tales that they killed anyone who complained, were they not paid the "tax."

Ilona saw it for herself when the fourth patrol arrived.

Her hands went through the motions of unhitching without direction from her mind, still picturing the journey. Poor Sancorra, overrun by the foreigners called Hecari, led by a fearsome warlord, was being steadily stripped of her wealth just as the citizens were being stripped of their holdings. Women were widowed, children left fatherless, farmsteads burned, livestock rounded up and driven to Hecari encampments to feed the enemy soldiers. Karavans that did not originate in Sancorra were allowed passage through the province so long as their masters could prove they came from other provinces—and paid tribute—but that passage was nonetheless a true challenge. Jorda's two scouts early on came across the remains of several karavans that the master knew to be led by foreigners like himself; the Hecari apparently were more than capable of killing anyone they deemed Sancorran refugees, even if they manifestly were not. It was a simple matter to declare anyone an enemy of their warlord.

Ilona was not Sancorran. Neither was Jorda, nor one of the scouts. But the other guide, Tansit, was. And now his body lay in the back of a wagon, waiting for the rites that would send his spirit to the Land of the Dead.

Wearily Ilona finished unhitching the team, pulling harness from the sweat-slicked horses. Pungent, foamy lather dripped from flanks and shoulders. She swapped out headstalls for halters, then led the team along the line of wagons to Janqueril, the horse-master. The aging, balding man and his apprentices would tend the teams while everyone else made their way into the tent-city settlement, looking for release from the tension of the trip.

And, she knew, to find other diviners who might tell a different tale of the future they faced tomorrow, on the edge of unknown lands.

Ilona delivered the horses, thanked Janqueril, then pushed a fractious mass of curling dark hair out of her face. Jorda kept three diviners in his employ, to make sure his karavans got safely to their destinations and to serve any of his clients, but Tansit had always come to her. He said he trusted her to be truthful with him. Hand-readers, though not uncommon, were not native to Sancorra, and Tansit, like others, viewed her readings as more positive than those given by Jorda's other two diviners. Ilona didn't know if that were true; only that she always told her clients the good and the bad, rather than shifting the emphasis wholly to good.

She had seen danger in Tansit's callused hand. That, she had told him. And he had laughed, said the only danger facing him were the vermin holes in the prairie, waiting to trap his horse and take him down as well.

And so a vermin hole *had* trapped his horse, snapping a leg, and Tansit, walking back to the karavan well behind him, was found by the Hecari patrol that paused long enough to kill him, then continue on to richer pickings. By the time the karavan reached the scout, his features were unrecognizable; Ilona knew him by his clothing and the color of his blood-matted hair.

So Tansit had told his own fortune without her assistance, and Ilona lost a man whom she had not truly loved, but liked. Well enough to share his bed when the loneliness of her life sent her to it. Men were attracted to her, but wary of her gift. Few were willing to sleep with a woman who could tell a lover the day of his death.

At the end of journeys, Ilona's habit was to build a fire, lay a rug, set up a table, cushions, and candles, then wait quietly for custom. At the end of a journey clients wished to consult diviners for advice concerning the future in a new place. But this night, at the end of this journey, Ilona forbore. She stood at the back of her wagon, clutching one of the blue-painted spoke wheels, and stared sightlessly into the sunset.

Some little while later, a hand came down upon her shoulder. Large, wide, callused, with spatulate fingers and oft-bruised or broken nails. She smelled the musky astringency of a hard-working man in need of a bath; heard the inhaled, heavy breath; sensed, even without reading that hand, his sorrow and compassion.

"He was a good man," Jorda said.

Ilona nodded jerkily.

"We will hold the rites at dawn."

She nodded again.

"Will you wish to speak?"

She turned. Looked into his face, the broad, bearded, seamed face of the man who employed her, who was himself employed several times a season to lead karavans across the wide plains of Sancorra to the edge of other provinces, where other karavans and their masters took up the task. Jorda could be a hard man, but he was also a good man. In his green eyes she saw grief that he had lost an employee, a valued guide, but also a friend. Tansit had scouted for Jorda more years than she could count. More, certainly, than she had known either of them.

"Yes, of course," she told him.

Jorda nodded, seeking something in her eyes. But Ilona was expert at hiding her feelings. Such things, if uncontrolled, could color the readings, and she had learned long before to mask emotions. "I thank you," the master said. "It would please Tansit."

She thought a brace of tall tankards of foamy ale would please Tansit more. But words would have to do. Words for the dead.

Abruptly she said, "I have to go."

Jorda's ruddy brows ran together. "Alone? Into this place? It's but a scattering of tents, Ilona, not a true settlement. You would do better to come with me, and a few of the others. After what happened on the road, it would be safer."

Safety was not what she craved. Neither was danger, and certainly not death, but she yearned to be elsewhere than with Jorda and the others this night. How better to pay tribute to Tansit than to drink a brace of tall tankards of foamy ale in his place?

Ilona forced a smile. "I'm going to Mikal's wine-tent. He knows me. I'll be safe enough there."

Jorda's face cleared. "So you will. But ask someone to walk you back to your wagon later."

Ilona arched her brows. "It's not so often I must *ask* such a thing, Jorda! Usually they beg to do that duty."

He understood the tone, and the intent. He relaxed fractionally, then presented her with a brief flash of teeth mostly obscured by his curling beard. "Forgive me! I do know better." The grin faded. "I think many of us will buy Tansit ale tonight."

She nodded as the big man turned and faded back into the twilight, returning to such duties as were his at the end of a journey. Which left her duty to Tansit.

Ilona leaned inside her wagon and caught up a deep-dyed, blue-black shawl, swung it around her shoulders, and walked through the ankle-deep dust into the tiny tent-city.

She had seen, in her life, many deaths. It rode the hands of all humans, though few could read it, and fewer still could interpret the conflicting information. Ilona had never *not* been able to see, to read, to interpret; when her family had come to comprehend that such a gift would rule her life and thus their own, they had turned her out. She had been all of twelve summers, shocked by their actions because she had not seen it in her own hand; had she read theirs, she might have understood earlier what lay in store. In the fifteen years since they had turned out their oldest daughter, Ilona had learned to trust no one but herself—though she was given to understand that some people, such as Jorda, were less likely to send a diviner on her way if she could serve their interests. All karavans required diviners if they were to be truly successful; clients undertaking journeys went nowhere without consulting any number of diviners of all persuasions, and a karavan offering readings along the way, rather than depending on itinerant diviners drifting from settlement to settlement, stood to attract more custom. Jorda was no fool; he hired Branca and Melior, and in time he hired her.

The night was cool. Ilona tightened her shawl and ducked her head against the errant breeze teasing at her face. Mikal's wine-tent stood nearly in the center of the cluster of tents that spread like vermin across the plain near the river. A year before there had been half as many; next year, she did not doubt, the population would increase yet again. Sancorra province was in utter disarray, thanks to the depredations of the Hecari; few would wish to stay, who had the means to depart. It would provide Jorda with work as well as his hired diviners. But she wished war were not the reason.

Mikal's wine-tent was one of many, but he had arrived early when the settlement had first sprung up, a place near sweet water and good grazing, and not far from the border of the neighboring province. It was a good place for karavans to halt overnight, and within weeks it had become more than merely that. Now merchants put up tents, set down roots, and served a populace that shifted shape nightly, trading familiar faces for those of strangers. Mikal's face was one of the most familiar, and his tent a welcome distraction from the duties of the road.

Ilona took the path she knew best through the winding skeins of tracks and paused only briefly in the spill of light from the tied-back door flap of Mikal's wine-tent. She smelled the familiar odors of ale and wine, the tang of urine from men who sought relief rather too close to the tent, the thick fug of male bodies far more interested in liquor than wash water. Only rarely did women frequent Mikal's wine-tent; the female couriers, who were toughened by experience on the province roads and thus able to deal with anything, and such women as herself: unavailable for hire, but seeking the solace found in liquor-laced camaraderie. Ilona had learned early on to appreciate ale and wine, and the value of the company of others no more rooted than she was. Tansit had always spent his coin at Mikal's. Tonight, she would spend hers in Tansit's name.

Ilona entered, pushing the shawl back from her head and

shoulders. As always, conversation paused as her presence was noted; then Mikal called out a cheery welcome, as did two or three others who knew her. It was enough to warn off any man who might wish to proposition her, establishing her right to remain un-molested. This night, she appreciated it more than usual.

She sought and found a small table near a back corner, arrang-ing skirts deftly as she settled upon a stool. Within a matter of mo-ments Mikal arrived, bearing a guttering candle in a pierced-tin lantern. He set it down upon the table, then waited.

Ilona drew in a breath. "Ale," she said, relieved when her voice didn't waver. "Two tankards, if it please you. Your best."

"Tansit?" he asked in his deep, slow voice.

It was not a question regarding a man's death, but his antici-pated arrival. Ilona discovered she could not, as yet, speak of the former, and thus relied upon the latter. She nodded confirmation, meeting his dark blue eyes without hesitation. Mikal nodded also, then took his bulk away to tend the order.

She found herself plaiting the fringes of her shawl, over and over again. Irritated, Ilona forcibly stopped herself from continuing the nervous habit. When Mikal brought the tankards, she lifted her own in both hands, downed several generous swallows, then care-fully fingered away the foam left to linger upon her upper lip. Two tankards upon the table. One: her own. The other was Tansit's. When done with her ale, she would leave coin enough for two tankards, but one would remain untouched. And then the truth would be known. The tale spread. But she would be required to say nothing, to no one.

Ah, but he had been a good man. She had not wished to wed him, though he had asked; she had not expected to bury him either.

At dawn, she would attend the rites. Would speak of his life, and of his death.

Tansit had never been one known for his attention to time. But he was not a man given to passing up ale when it was waiting. Ilona drank down her tankard slowly and deliberately, avoiding the glances, the stares, and knew well enough when whispers began of Tansit's tardiness in joining her.

There were two explanations: they had quarreled, or one of them was dead. But their quarrels never accompanied them into a wine-tent.

She drank her ale, clearly not dead, while Tansit's tankard remained undrunk. Those who were not strangers understood. At tables other than hers, in the sudden, sharp silence of comprehension, fresh tankards were ordered. Were left untouched. Tribute to the man so many of them had known.

Tansit would have appreciated how many tankards were ordered. Though he also would have claimed it a waste of good ale that no one drank.

Ilona smiled, imagining his words. Seeing his expression.

She swallowed the last of her ale and rose, thinking ahead to the bed in her wagon. But then a body blocked her way, altering the fall of smoky light, and she looked into the face of a stranger.

In the ocherous illumination of Mikal's lantern, his face was ruddy-gold. "I'm told the guide is dead."

A stranger indeed, to speak so plainly to the woman who had shared the dead man's bed.

He seemed to realize it. To regret it. A grimace briefly twisted his mouth. "Forgive me. But I am badly in need of work."

Ilona gathered the folds of her shawl even as she gathered patience. "The season is ended. And I am not the one to whom you should apply. Jorda is the karavan-master."

"I'm told he is the best."

"Jorda is—Jorda." She settled the shawl over the crown of her head, shrouding untamed ringlets. "Excuse me."

He turned only slightly, giving way. "Will you speak to him for me?"

Ilona paused, then swung back. "Why? I know nothing of you."

His smile was charming, his gesture self-deprecating. "Of course. But I could acquaint you."

A foreigner, she saw. Not Sancorran, but neither was he Hercari. In candlelight his hair was a dark, oiled copper, bound back in a multiplicity of braids. She saw the glint of beads in those braids, gold and silver; heard the faint chime and clatter of ornamentation.

He wore leather tunic and breeches, and from the outer seams of sleeves and leggings dangled shell- and bead-weighted fringe. Indeed, a stranger, to wear what others, in time of war, might construe as wealth.

"No need to waste your voice," she said. "Let me see your hand."

It startled him. Arched brows rose. "My hand?"

She matched his expression. "Did they not also tell you what I am?"

"The dead guide's woman."

The pain was abrupt and sharp, then faded as quickly as it had come. *The dead guide's woman.* True, that. But much more. And it might be enough to buy her release from a stranger. "Diviner," she said. "There is no need to tell me anything of yourself, when I can read it in your hand."

She sensed startlement and withdrawal, despite that the stranger remained before her, very still. His eyes were dark in the frenzied play of guttering shadows. The hand she could see, loose at his side, abruptly closed. Sealed itself against her. Refusal. Denial. Self-preservation.

"It is a requirement," she told him, "of anyone who wishes to hire on with Jorda."

His face tightened. Something flickered deep in his eyes. She thought she saw a hint of red.

"You'll understand," Ilona hid amusement behind a businesslike tone, "that Jorda must be careful. He can't afford to hire just anyone. His clients trust him to guard their safety. How is he to know what a stranger intends?"

"Rhuan," he said abruptly.

She heard it otherwise: *Ruin.* "Oh?"

"A stranger who gives his name is no longer a stranger."

"A stranger who brings ruination is an enemy."

"Ah." His grin was swift. He repeated his name more slowly, making clear what it was, and she heard the faint undertone of an accent.

She echoed it. "Rhuan."

"I need the work."

Ilona eyed him. Tall, but not a giant. Much of his strength, she thought, resided beneath his clothing, coiled quietly away. Not old, not young, but somewhere in the middle, indistinguishable. Oddly alien in the light of a dozen lanterns, for all his smooth features were arranged in a manner women undoubtedly found pleasing. On another night, *she* might; but Tansit was newly dead, and this stranger—Rhuan—kept her from her wagon, where she might grieve in private.

"Have you guided before?"

"Not here. Elsewhere."

"It is a requirement that you know the land."

"I do know it."

"Here?"

"Sancorra. I know it." He lifted one shoulder in an eloquent shrug. "On a known road, guiding is less a requirement than protection. That, I can do very well."

Something about him suggested it was less a boast than the simple truth.

"And does anyone know *you?*"

He turned slightly, glancing toward the plank set upon barrels where Mikal held sovereignty, and she saw Mikal watching them.

She saw also the slight lifting of big shoulders, a smoothing of his features into a noncommittal expression. Mikal told her silently there was nothing of the stranger he knew that meant danger, but nothing much else either.

"The season is ended," Ilona repeated. "Speak to Jorda of the next one, if you wish, but there is no work for you now."

"In the midst of war," Rhuan said, "I believe there is. Others will wish to leave. Your master would do better to extend the season."

Jorda had considered it, she knew. Tansit had spoken of it. And if the master did extend the season, he would require a second guide. Less for guiding than for protection, with Hecari patrols harrying the roads.

Four people, dead.

Ilona glanced briefly at the undrunk tankard. "Apply to Jorda," she said. "It's not for me to say." Something perverse within her flared into life, wanting to wound the man before her who was so vital and alive, when another was not. "But he *will* require you to be read. It needn't be me."

His voice chilled. "Most diviners are charlatans."

Indeed, he was a stranger; no true-born Sancorran would speak so baldly. "Some," she agreed. "There are always those who prey upon the weak of mind. But there are also those who practice an honest art."

"You?"

Ilona affected a shrug every bit as casual as his had been. "Allow me your hand, and then you'll know, won't you?"

Once again he clenched it. "No."

"Then you had best look elsewhere for employment." She had learned to use her body and used it now, sliding past him before he might block her way again. She sensed the stirring in his limbs, the desire to reach out to her, to stop her; sensed also when he decided to let her go.

It began not far from Mikal's wine-tent. Ilona had heard its like before and recognized at once what was happening. The grunt of a man taken unawares, the bitten-off inhalation, the repressed blurt of pain and shock; and the hard, tense breathing of the assailants. Such attacks were not unknown in settlements such as this, composed of strangers desperate to escape the depredations of the Hecari. Desperate enough, some of them, to don the brutality of the enemy and wield its weapon.

Ilona stepped more deeply into shadow. She was a woman, and alone. If she interfered, she invited retribution. Jorda had told her to ask for escort on the way to the wagons. In her haste to escape the stranger in Mikal's tent, she had dismissed it from her mind.

Safety lay in secrecy. But Tansit was dead, and at dawn she would attend his rites and say the words. If she did nothing, would another woman grieve? Would another woman speak the words of the rite meant to carry the spirit to the Land of the Dead?

Then she was running toward the noise. "Stop! *Stop!*"

Movement. Men. Bodies. Ilona saw shapes break apart; saw a body fall. Heard the curses meant for her. But she was there, telling them to stop, and for a wonder they did.

And then she realized, as they faded into darkness, that she had thought too long and arrived too late. His wealth was untouched, the beading in the braids and fringe, but his life was taken. She saw the blood staining his throat, the knife standing up from his ribs. Garotte to make him helpless, knife to kill him.

He lay sprawled beneath the stars, limbs awry, eyes open and empty, the comely features slack.

She had seen death before. She recognized his.

Too late. Too late.

She should go fetch Mikal. There had been some talk of establishing a Watch, a group of men to walk the paths and keep what peace there was. Ilona didn't know if a Watch yet existed; but Mikal would come, would help her tend the dead.

A stranger in Sancorra. What rites were his?

Shaking, Ilona knelt. She did not go to fetch Mikal. Instead she sat beside a man whose name she barely knew, whose hand she hadn't read, and grieved for them both. For them all. For the men, young and old, dead in the war.

In the *insurrection.*

But there was yet a way. She had the gift. Beside him, Ilona gathered up one slack hand. His future had ended, but there was yet a past. It faded already, she knew, as the warmth of the body cooled, but if she practiced the art before he was cold, she would learn what she needed to know. And then he also would have the proper rites. She would make certain of it.

Indeed, the hand cooled. Before morning the fingers would stiffen, even as Tansit's had. The spirit, denied a living body, would attenuate, then fade.

There was little light, save for the muddy glow of lanterns within a hundred tents. Ilona would be able to see nothing of the flesh, but she had no need. Instead, she lay her fingers gently upon his palm and closed her eyes, tracing the pathways there, the lines of his life.

Maelstrom.

Gasping, Ilona fell back. His hand slid from hers. Beneath it, beneath the touch of his flesh, the fabric of her skirt took flame.

She beat it with her own hands, then clutched at and heaped

powdery earth upon it. The flame quenched itself, the thread of smoke dissipated. But even as it did so, as she realized the fabric was whole, movement startled her.

The stranger's hand, that she had grasped to read, closed around the knife standing up from his ribs. She heard a sharply indrawn breath, and something like a curse, and the faint clattered chime of the beads in his braids. He raised himself up on one elbow and stared at her.

This time, she heard the curse clearly. Recognized the grimace. Knew what he would say: *I wasn't truly dead.*

But he was. Had been.

He pulled the knife from his ribs, inspected the blade a moment, then tossed it aside with an expression of distaste. Ilona's hands, no longer occupied with putting out the flame that had come from his flesh, folded themselves against her skirts. She waited.

He saw her watching him. Assessed her expression. Tried the explanation she anticipated. "I wasn't—"

"You were."

He opened his mouth to try again. Thought better of it. Looked at her hands folded into fabric. "Are you hurt?"

"No. Are *you?*"

His smile was faint. "No."

She touched her own throat. "You're bleeding."

He sat up. Ignored both the slice encircling his neck and the wound in his ribs. His eyes on her were calm, too calm. She saw an odd serenity there, and rueful acceptance that she had seen what, obviously, he wished she hadn't seen.

"I'm Shoia," he said.

No more than that. No more was necessary.

"Those are stories," Ilona told him. "Legends."

He seemed equally amused as he was resigned. "Rooted in truth."

Skepticism showed. "A living Shoia?"

"Now," he agreed, irony in his tone. "A moment ago, dead. But you know that."

"I touched your hand, and it took fire."

His face closed up. Sealed itself against her. His mouth was a grim, unrelenting line.

"Is that a Shoia trait, to burn the flesh a diviner might otherwise read?"

The mouth parted. "It's not for you to do."

Ilona let her own measure of irony seep into her tone. "And well warded, apparently."

"They wanted my bones," he said. "It's happened before."

She understood at once. "Practitioners of the Kantica." Who burned bones for the auguries found in ash and grit. Legend held Shoia bones told truer, clearer futures than anything else. But no one she knew of used *actual* Shoia bones.

He knew what she was thinking. "There are a few of us left," he told her. "But we keep it to ourselves. We would prefer to keep our bones clothed in flesh."

"But I have heard no one murders a Shoia. That anyone foolish enough to do so inherits damnation."

"No one *knowingly* murders a Shoia," he clarified. "But as we apparently are creatures of legend, who would believe I am?"

Nor did it matter. Dead was dead, damnation or no. "These men intended to haul you out to the anthills," Ilona said. Where the flesh would be stripped away, and the bones collected for sale to Kantic diviners. "They couldn't know you are Shoia, could they?"

He gathered braids fallen forward and swept them back. "I doubt it. But it doesn't matter. A charlatan would buy the bones and *claim* them Shoia, thus charging even more for the divinations. Clearer visions, you see."

She did see. There were indeed charlatans, false diviners who victimized the vulnerable and gullible. How better to attract trade than to boast of Shoia bones?

"Are you?" she asked. "Truly?"

Something flickered in his eyes. Flickered red. His voice hardened. "You looked into my hand."

And had seen nothing of his past nor his future save *maelstrom*.

"Madness," she said, not knowing she spoke aloud.

His smile was bitter.

Ilona looked into his eyes as she had looked into his hand. "Are you truly a guide?"

The bitterness faded. "I can be many things. Guide is one of them."

Oddly, it amused her to say it. "Dead man?"

He matched her irony. "That, too. But I would prefer not." He stood up then; somehow, he brought her up with him. She faced him there in the shadows beneath the stars. "It isn't infinite, the resurrection."

"No?"

"Seven times," he said. "The seventh is the true death."

"And how many times was this?"

The stranger showed all his fine white teeth in a wide smile. "That, we never tell."

"Ah." She understood. "Mystery is your salvation."

"Well, yes. Until the seventh time. And then we are as dead as anyone else. Bury us, burn us . . ." He shrugged. "It doesn't matter. Dead is dead. It simply comes more slowly."

Ilona shook out her skirts, shedding dust. "I know what I saw when I looked into your hand. But that was a shield, was it not? A ward against me."

"Against a true diviner, yes."

It startled her; she was accustomed to others accepting her word. "You didn't believe me?"

He said merely, "Charlatans abound."

"But you are safe from charlatans."

He stood still in the darkness and let her arrive at the conclusion.

"But not from me," she said.

"Shoia bones are worth coin to charlatans," he said. "A Kantic diviner could make his fortune by burning my bones. But a *true* Kantic diviner—"

"—could truly read your bones."

He smiled, wryly amused. "And therefore I am priceless."

Ilona considered it. "One would think you'd be more careful. Less easy to kill."

"I was distracted."

"By—?"

"You," he finished. "I came out to persuade you to take me to your master. To make the introduction."

"Ah, then *I* am being blamed for your death."

He grinned. "For this one, yes."

"And I suppose the only reparation I may pay is to introduce you to Jorda."

The grin flashed again. Were it not for the slice upon his neck and the blood staining his leather tunic, no one would suspect this man had been dead only moments before.

Ilona sighed, recalling Tansit. And his absence. "I suppose Jorda might have some use for a guide who can survive death multiple times."

"At least until the seventh," he observed dryly.

"If I read your hand, would I know how many you have left?"

He abruptly thrust both hands behind his back, looking mutinous, reminding her for all the world of a child hiding booty. Ilona laughed.

But she *had* read his hand, if only briefly. And seen in it conflagration.

Rhuan, he had said.

Ruin, she had echoed.

She wondered if she were right.